WOLF

Rachael Ball

First published in English in 2018
by SelfMadeHero
139–141 Pancras Road
London NW1 1UN
www.selfmadehero.com

Publishing Director: Emma Hayley
Sales & Marketing Manager: Sam Humphrey
Editorial & Production Manager: Guillaume Rater
Designer: Txabi Jones
UK Publicist: Paul Smith
US Publicist: Maya Bradford
With thanks to: Dan Lockwood

A CIP record for this book is available from the British Library

ISBN: 978-1-910593-54-7

10 9 8 7 6 5 4 3 2 1

Printed and bound in Slovenia

WOLF

Rachael Ball

SELF
MADE
HERO

For my Dad

Chapter One

Summer 1976

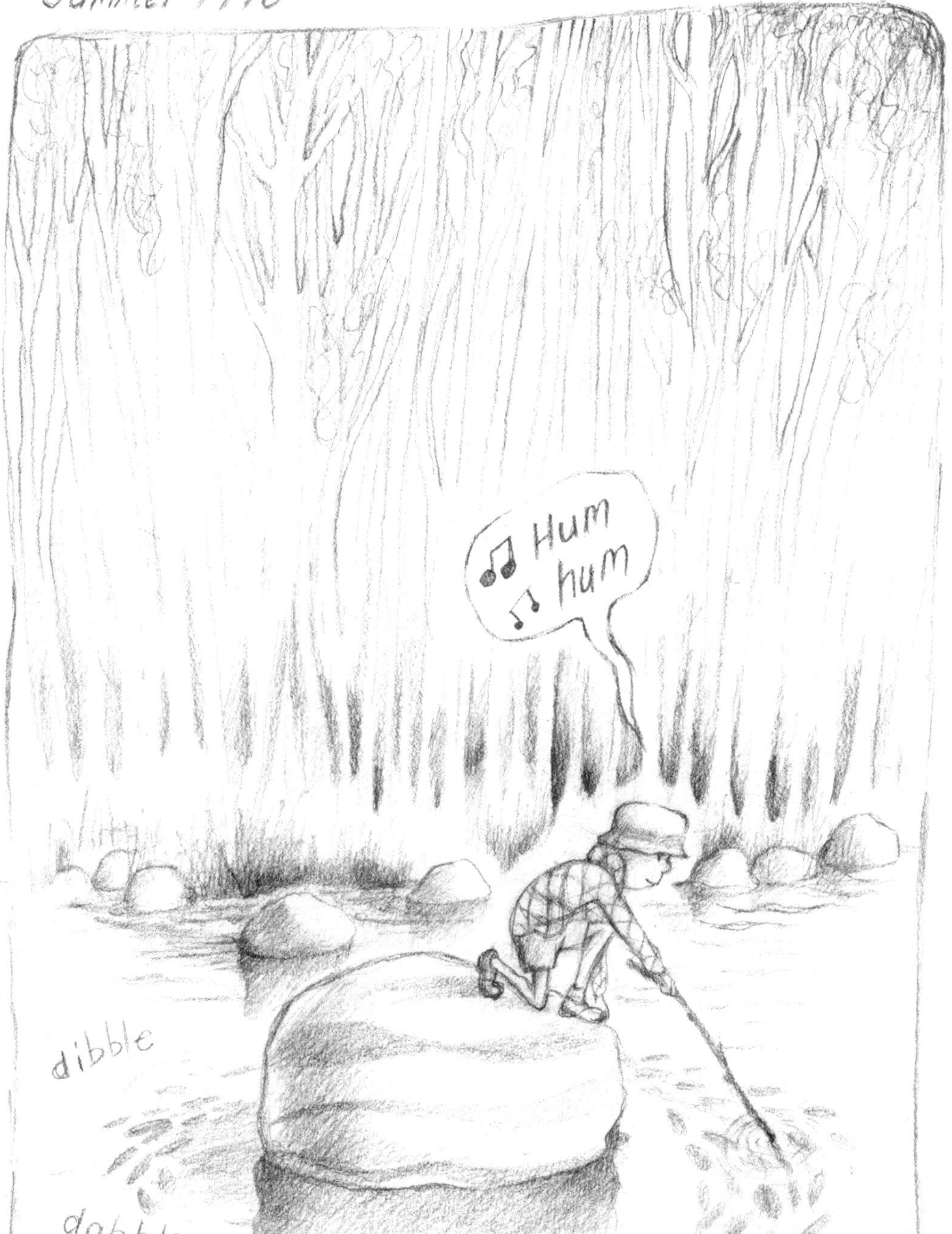
Hum hum
dibble
dabble

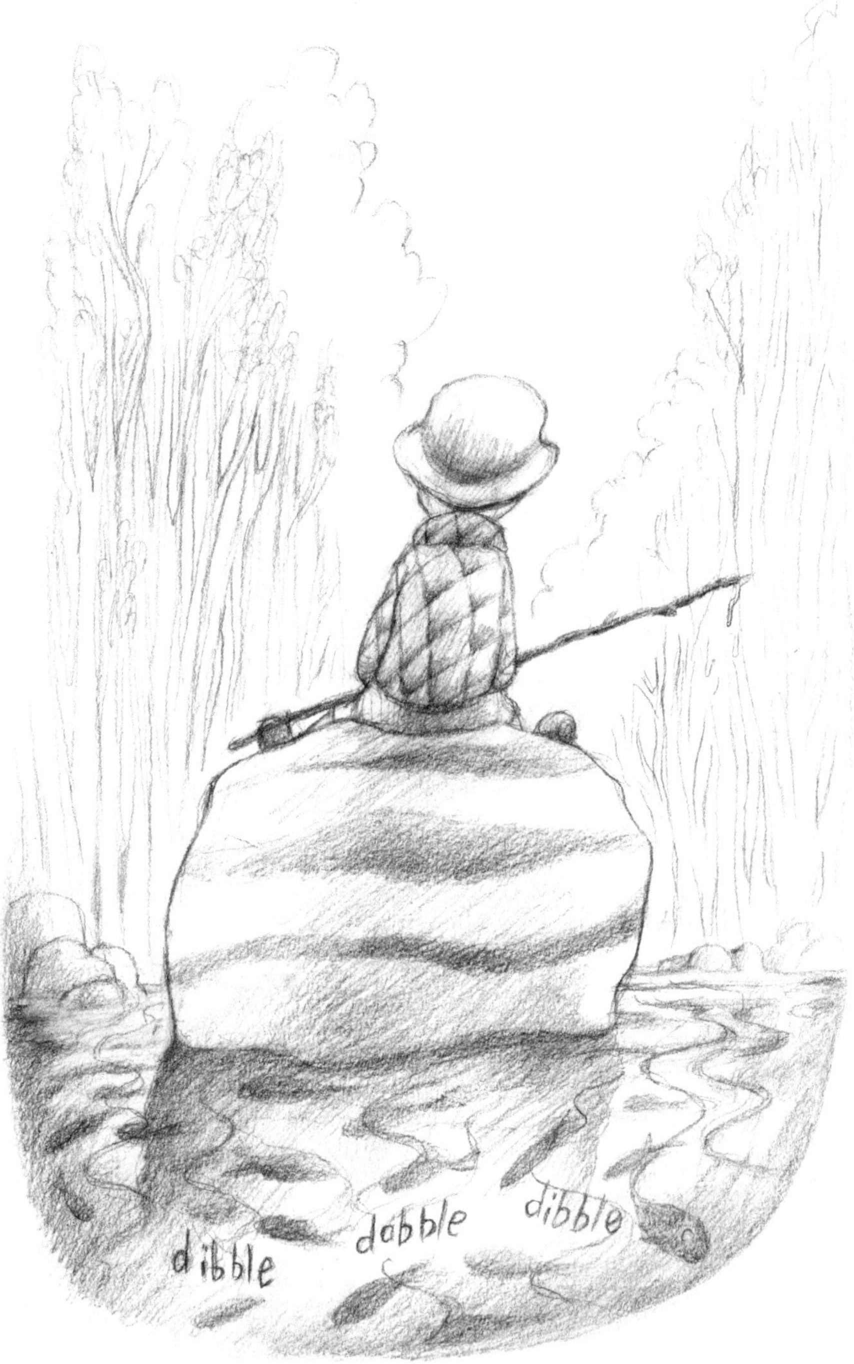
dibble
dabble
dibble

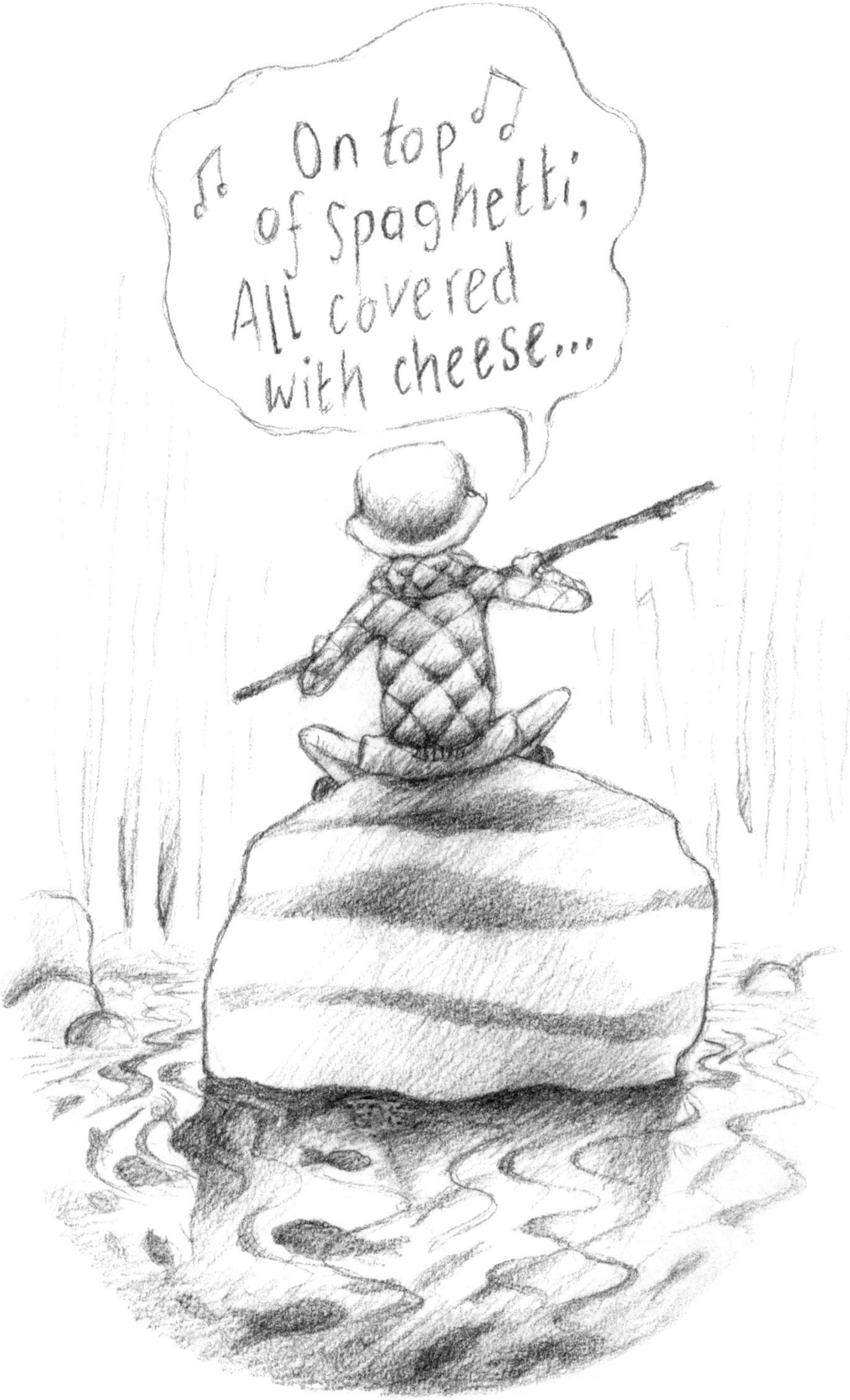
On top of Spaghetti, All covered with cheese...

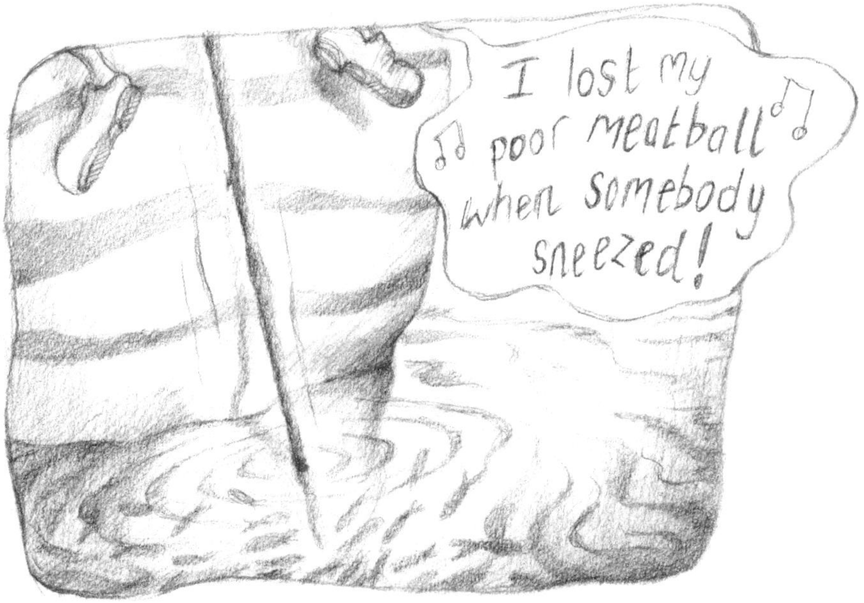
I lost my poor meatball when somebody sneezed!

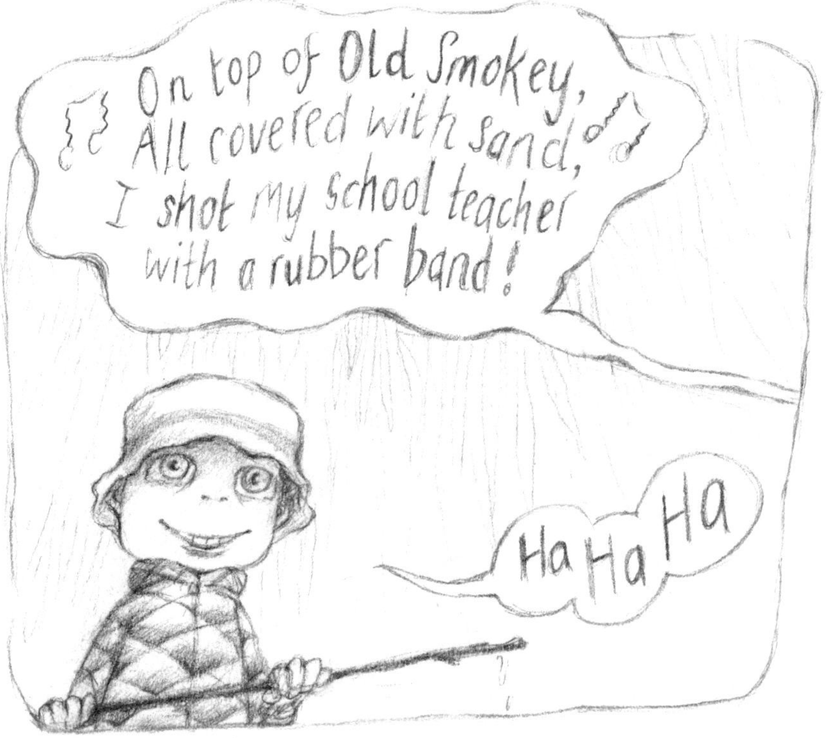
On top of Old Smokey, All covered with sand, I shot my school teacher with a rubber band!
Ha Ha Ha

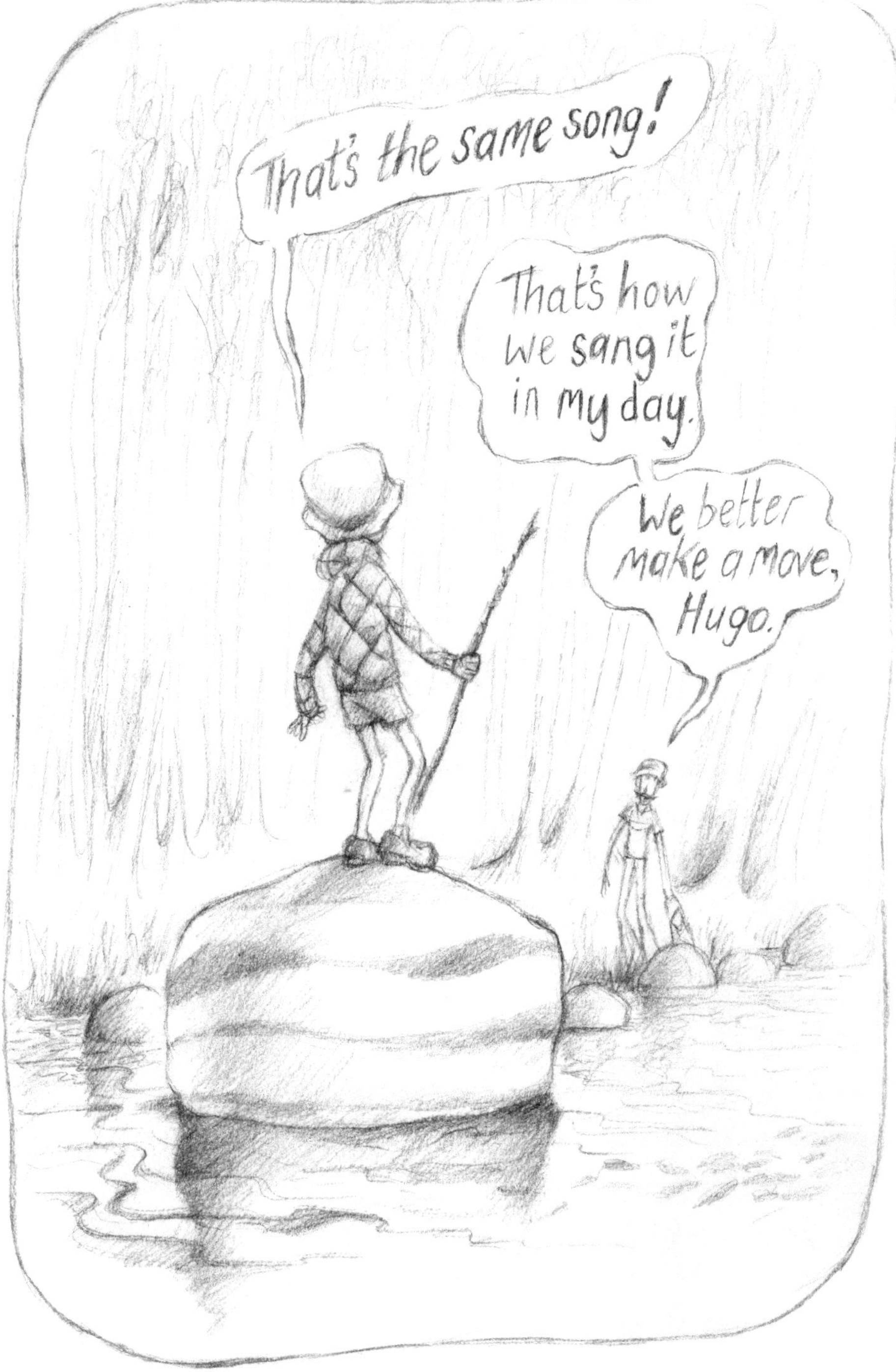
That's the same song!
That's how we sang it in my day.
We better make a move, Hugo.

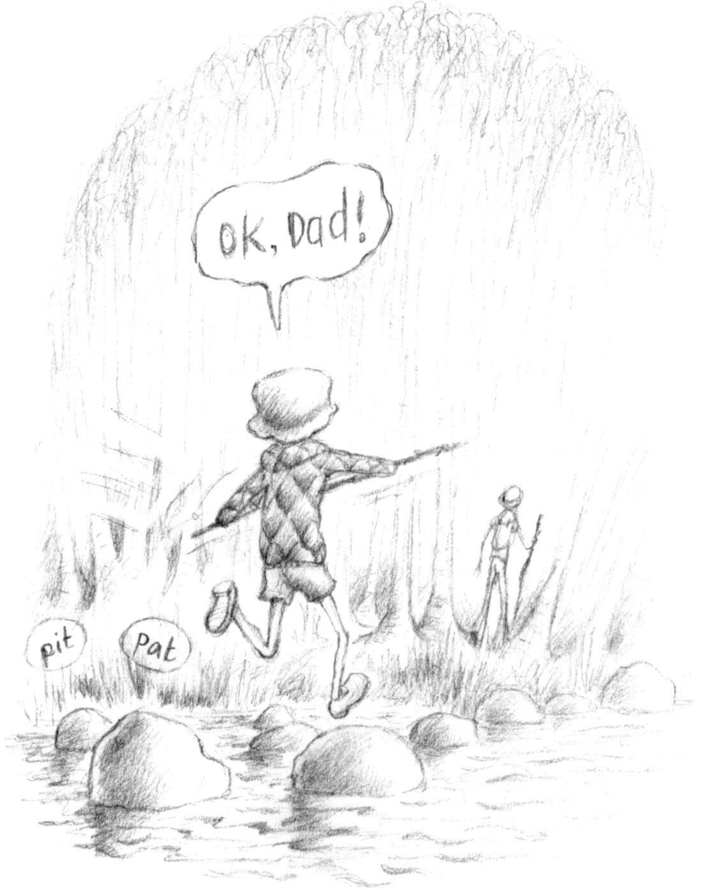
OK, Dad!
pit
pat

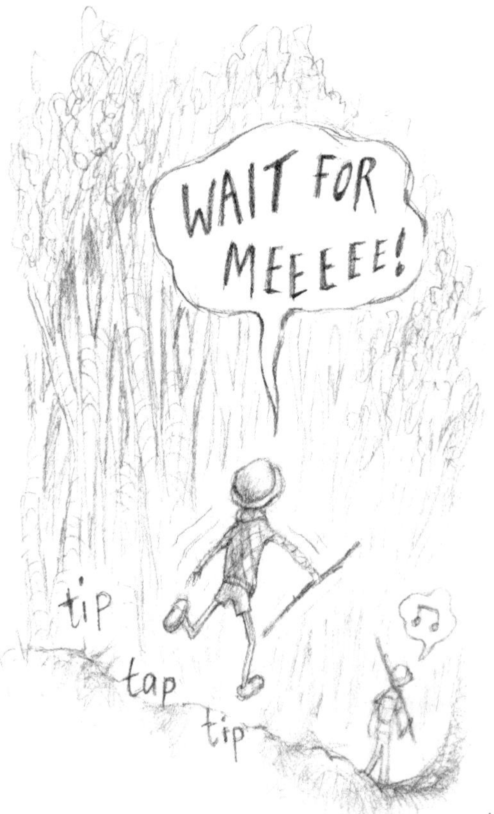
WAIT FOR MEEEEE!
tip
tap
tip

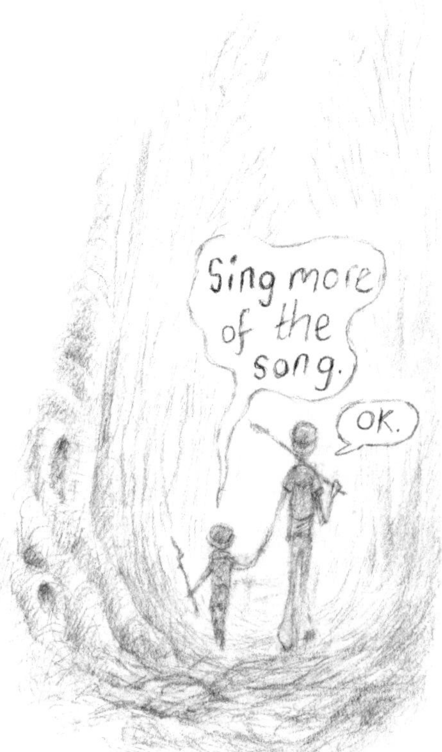
Sing more of the song.
OK.

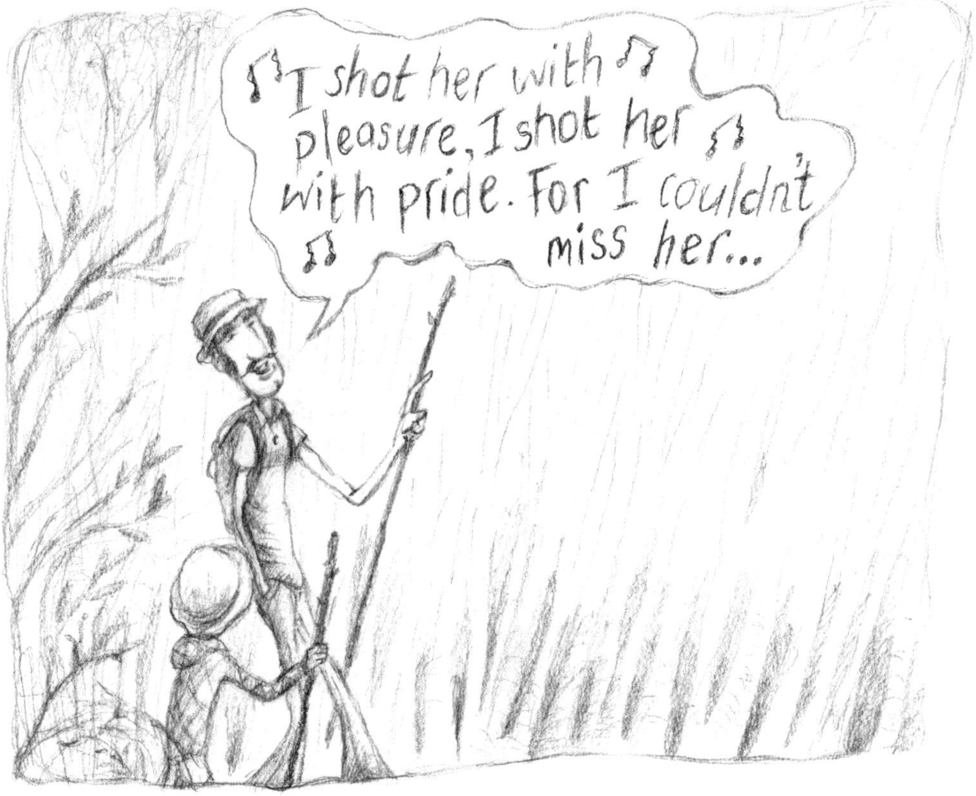
I shot her with pleasure, I shot her with pride. For I couldn't miss her...

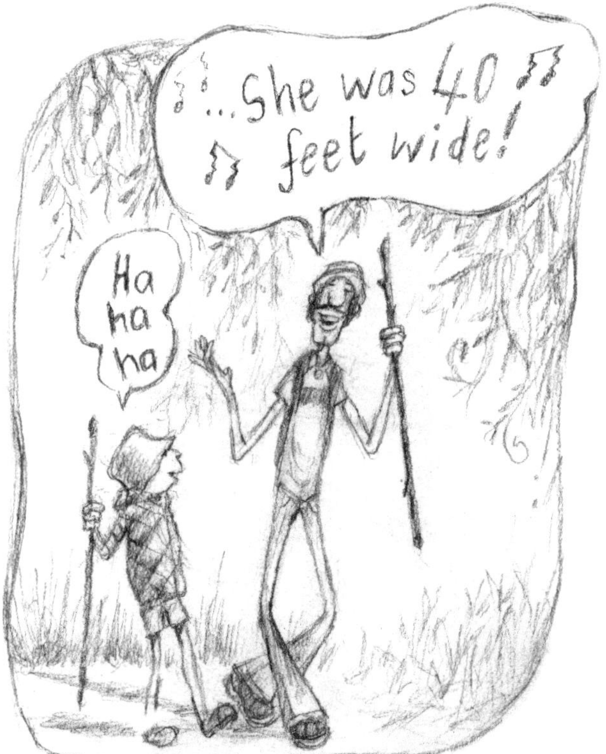
...She was 40 feet wide!
Ha ha ha

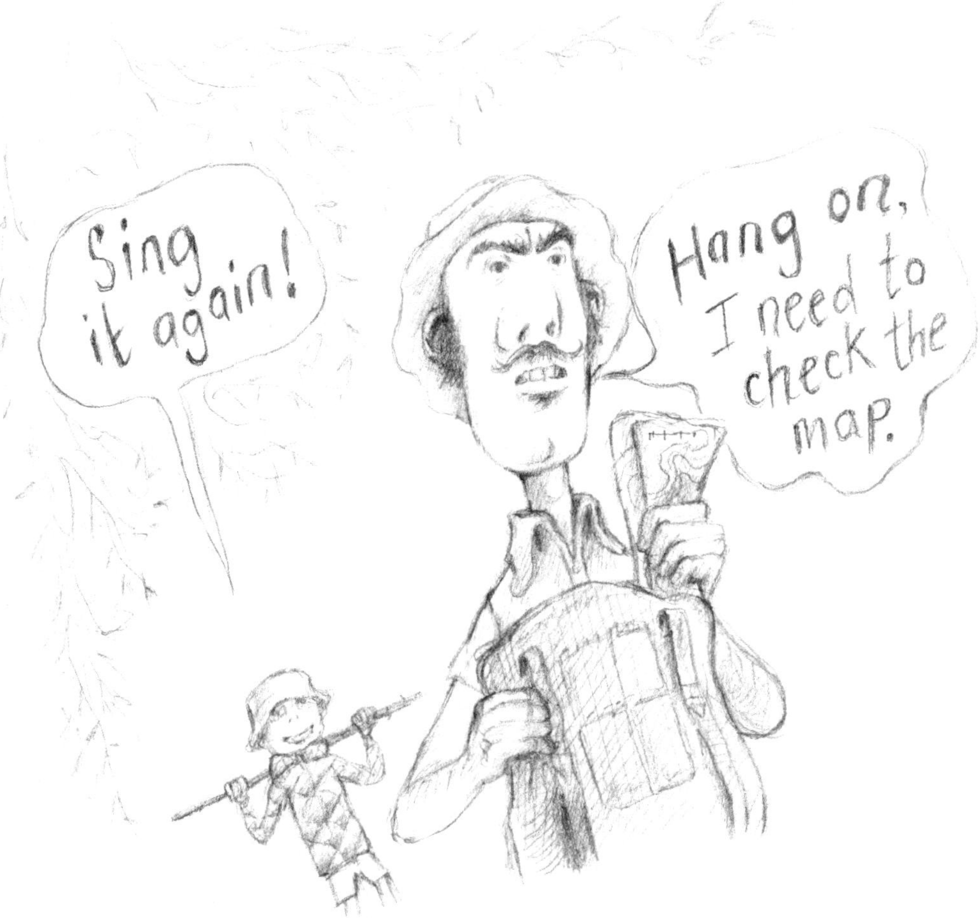
Sing it again!
Hang on, I need to check the map.

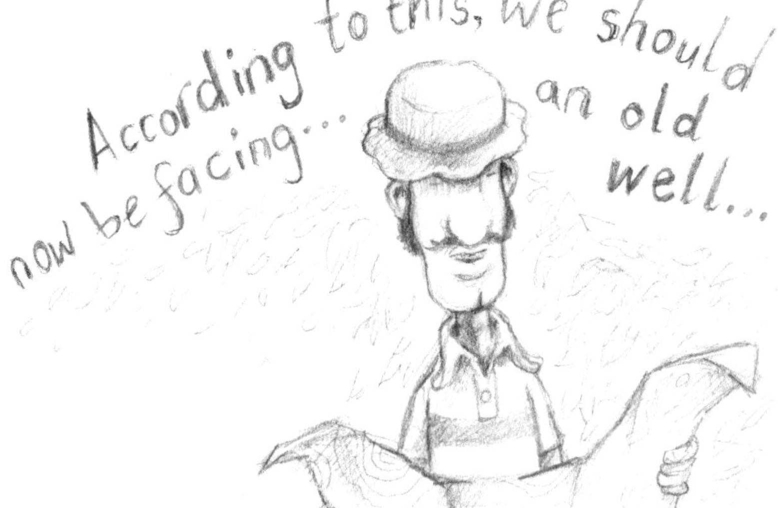
According to this, we should now be facing... an old well...

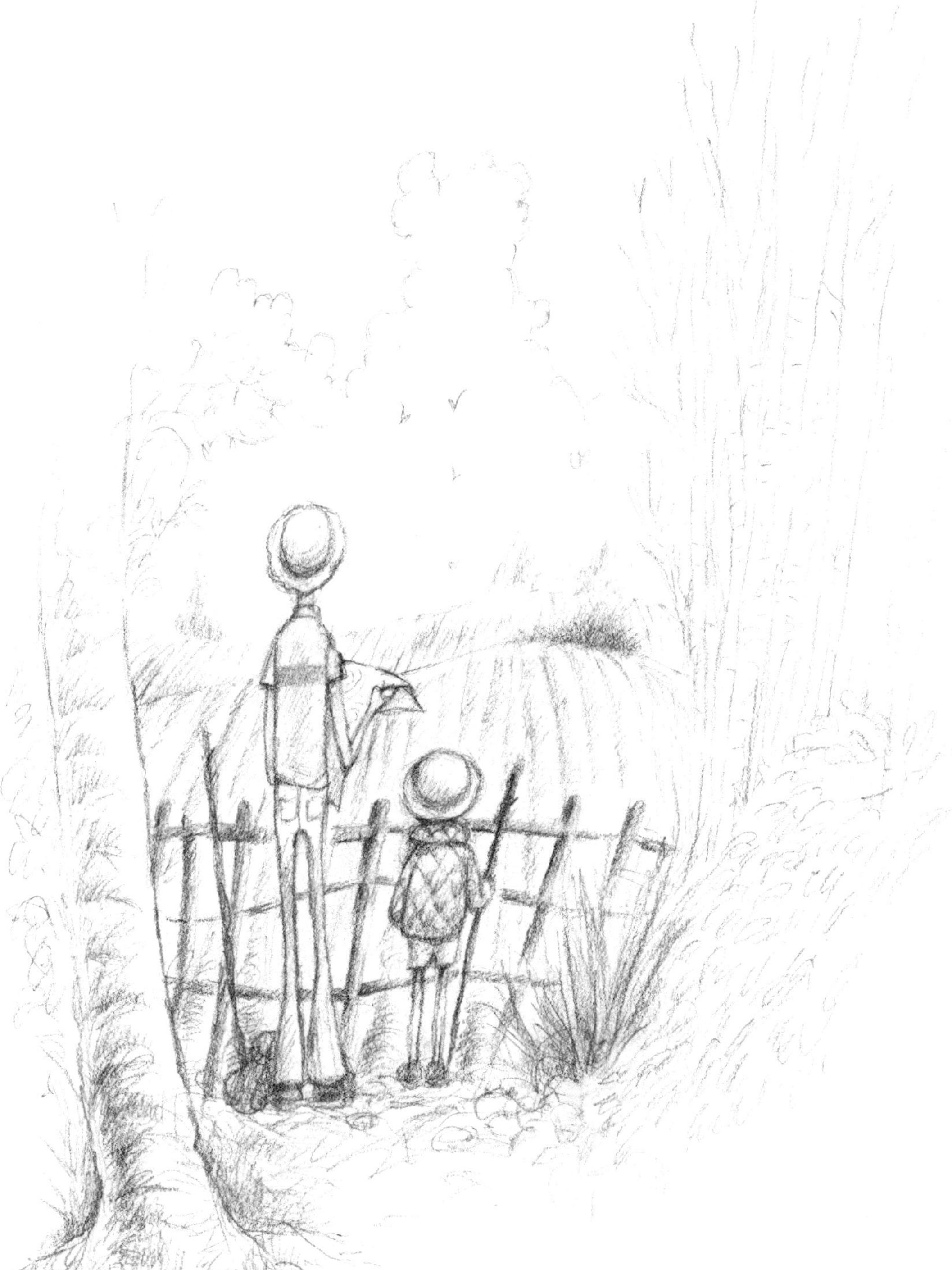

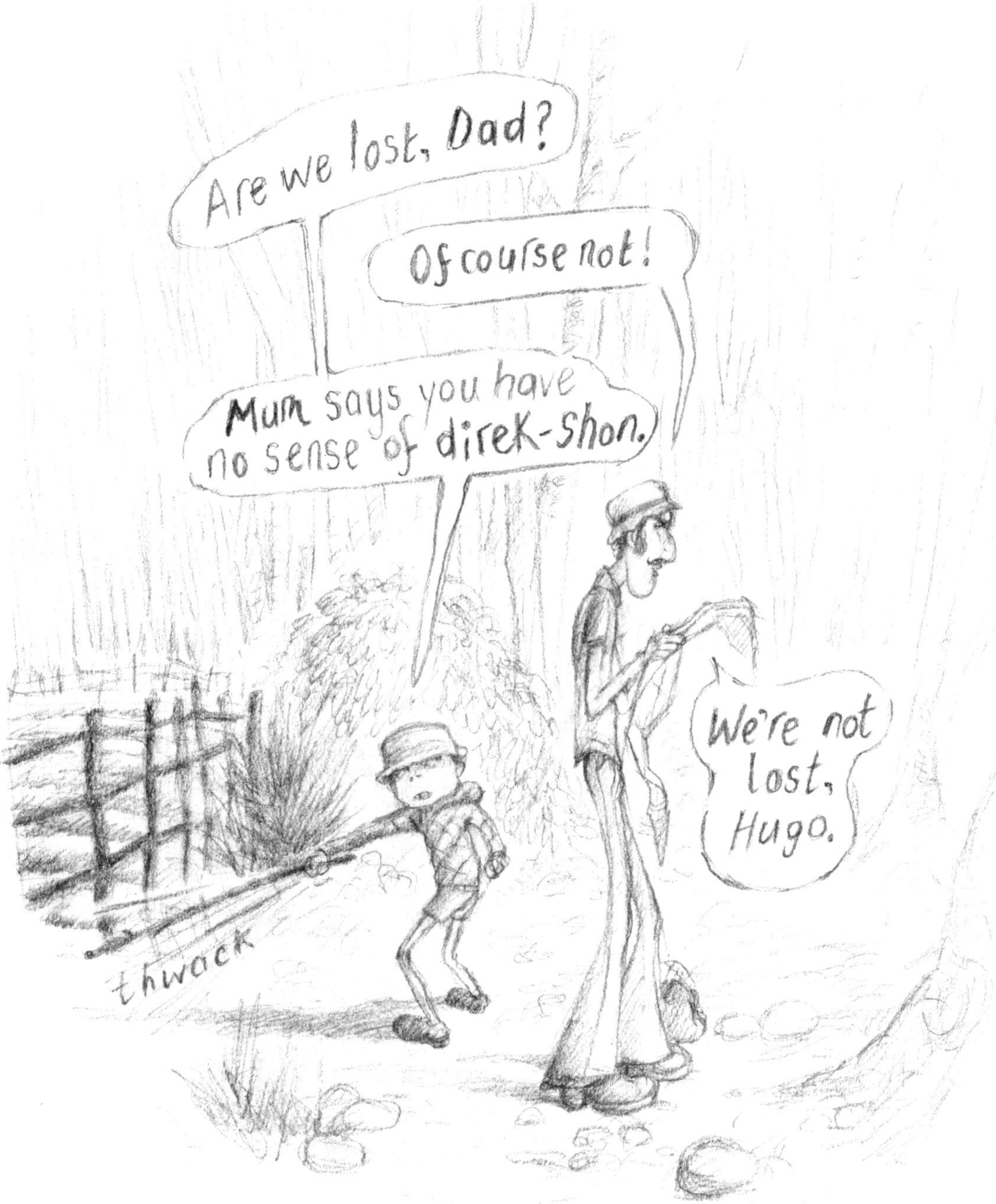
Are we lost, Dad?
Of course not!
Mum says you have no sense of direk-shon.
We're not lost, Hugo.
thwack

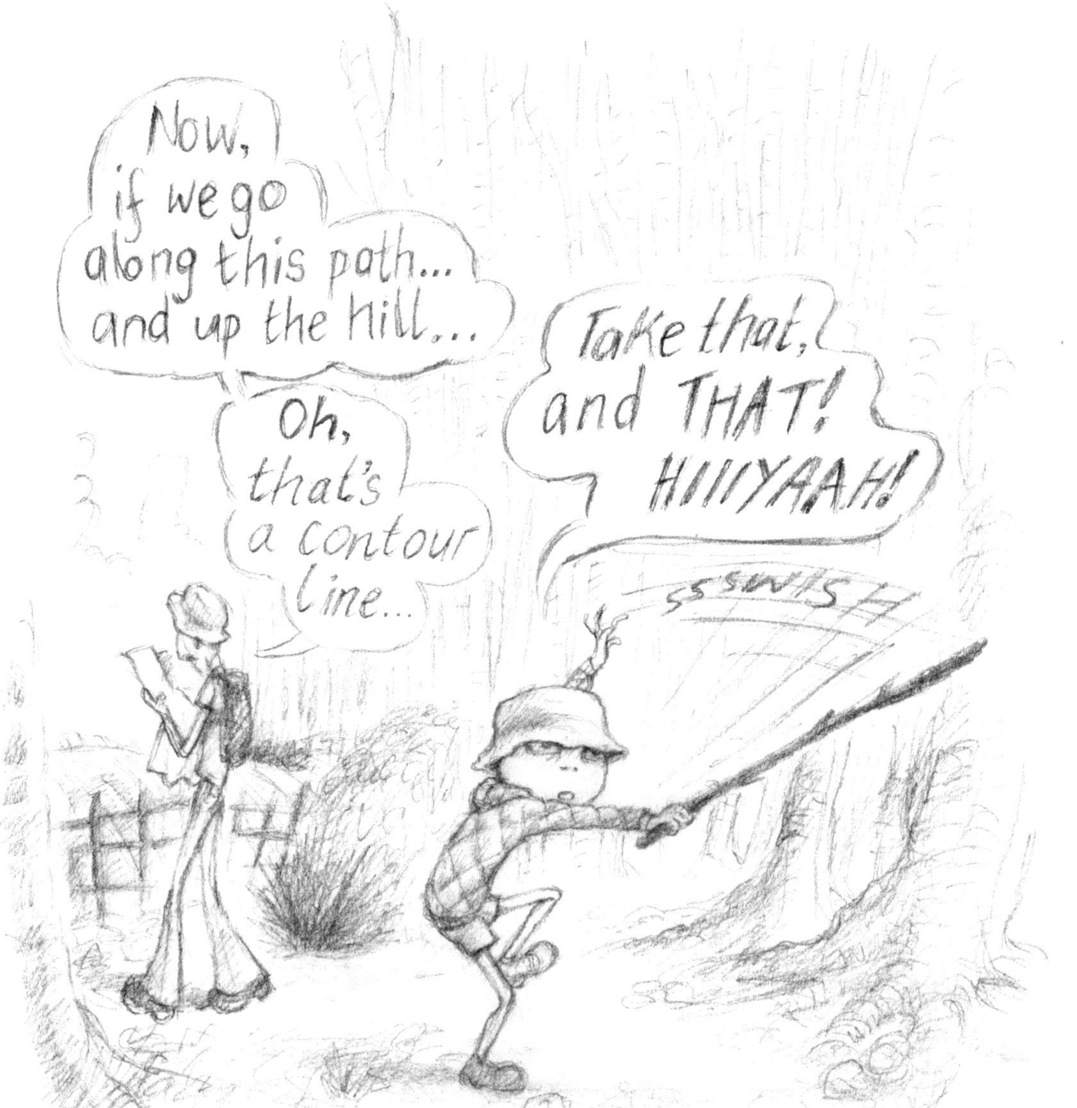
Now, if we go along this path... and up the hill...
Oh, that's a contour line...
Take that, and THAT! HIIIYAAH!
SSSWISH

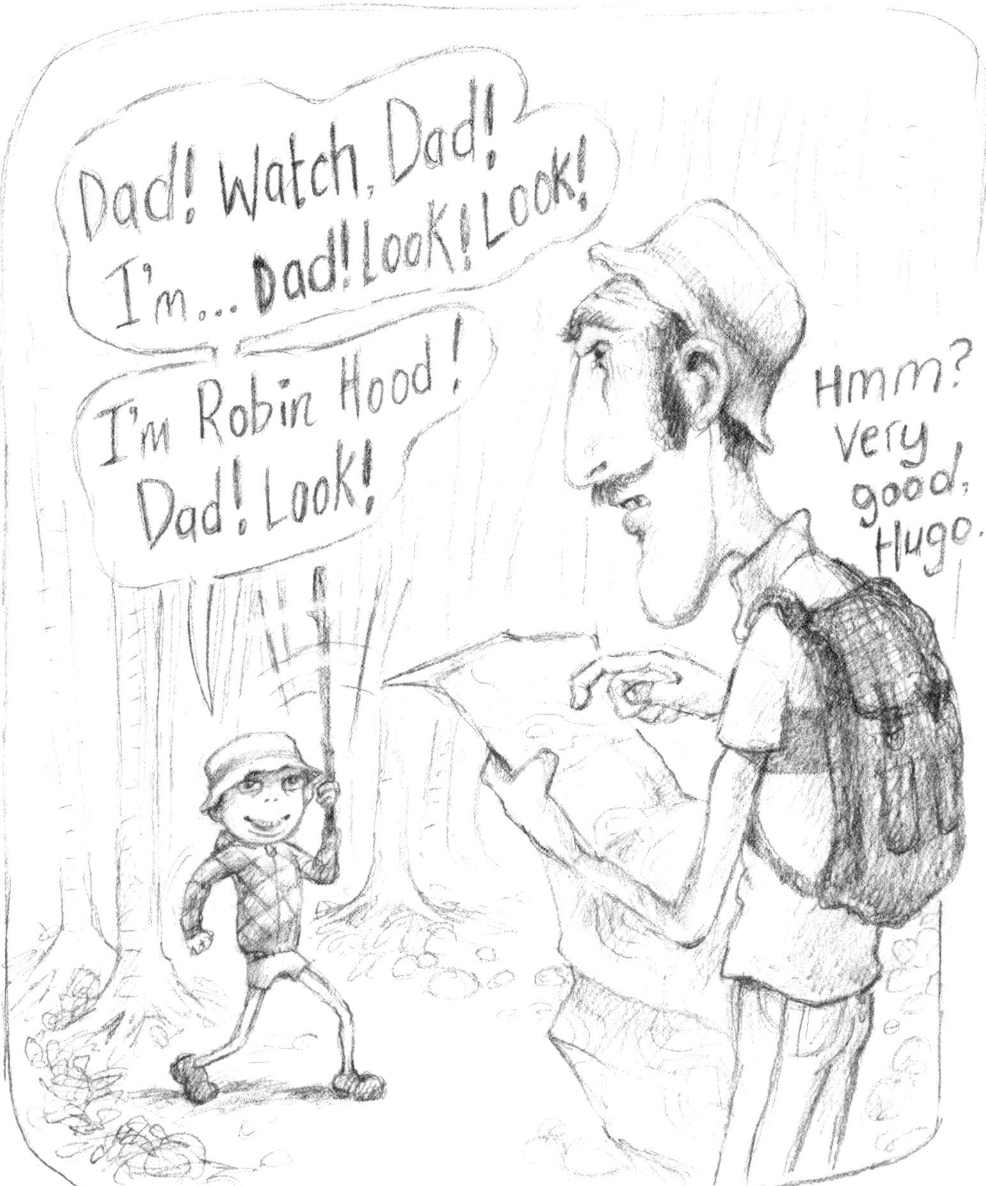
Dad! Watch, Dad! I'm... Dad! Look! Look!
I'm Robin Hood! Dad! Look!
Hmm? Very good, Hugo.

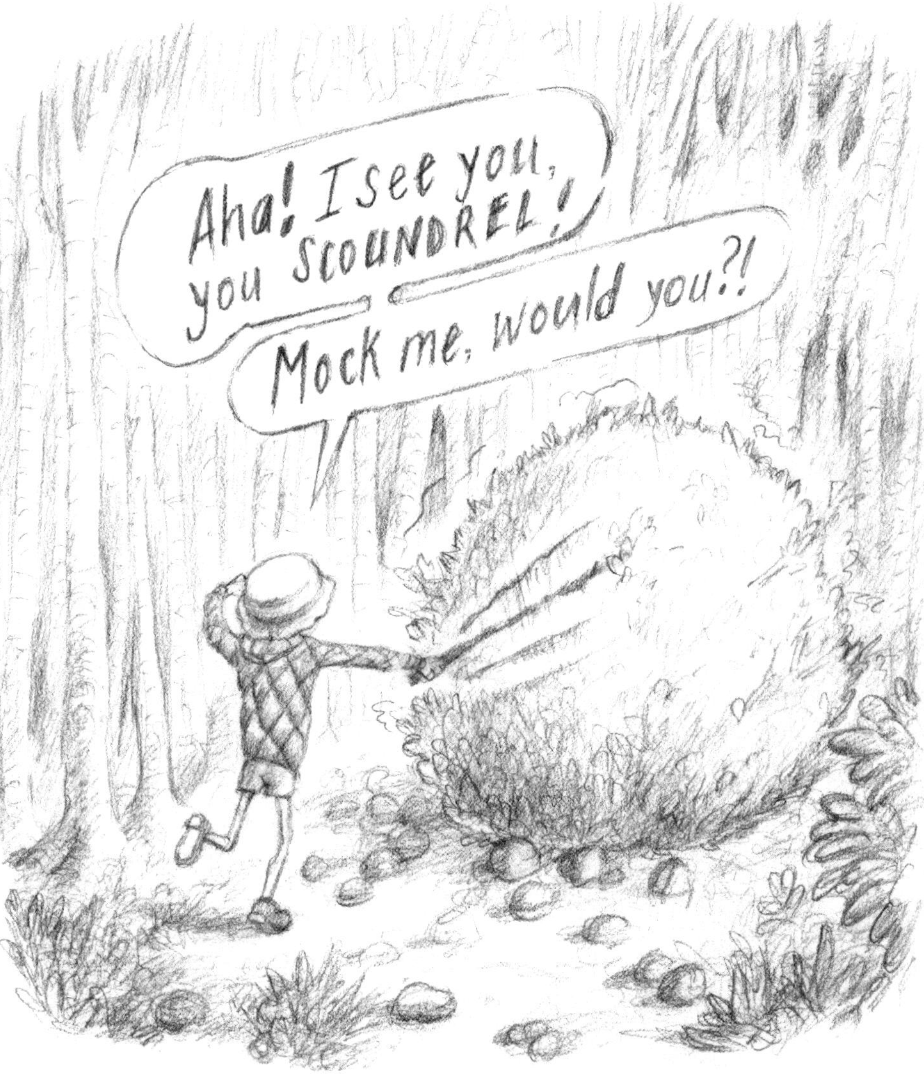
Aha! I see you, you SCOUNDREL!
Mock me, would you?!

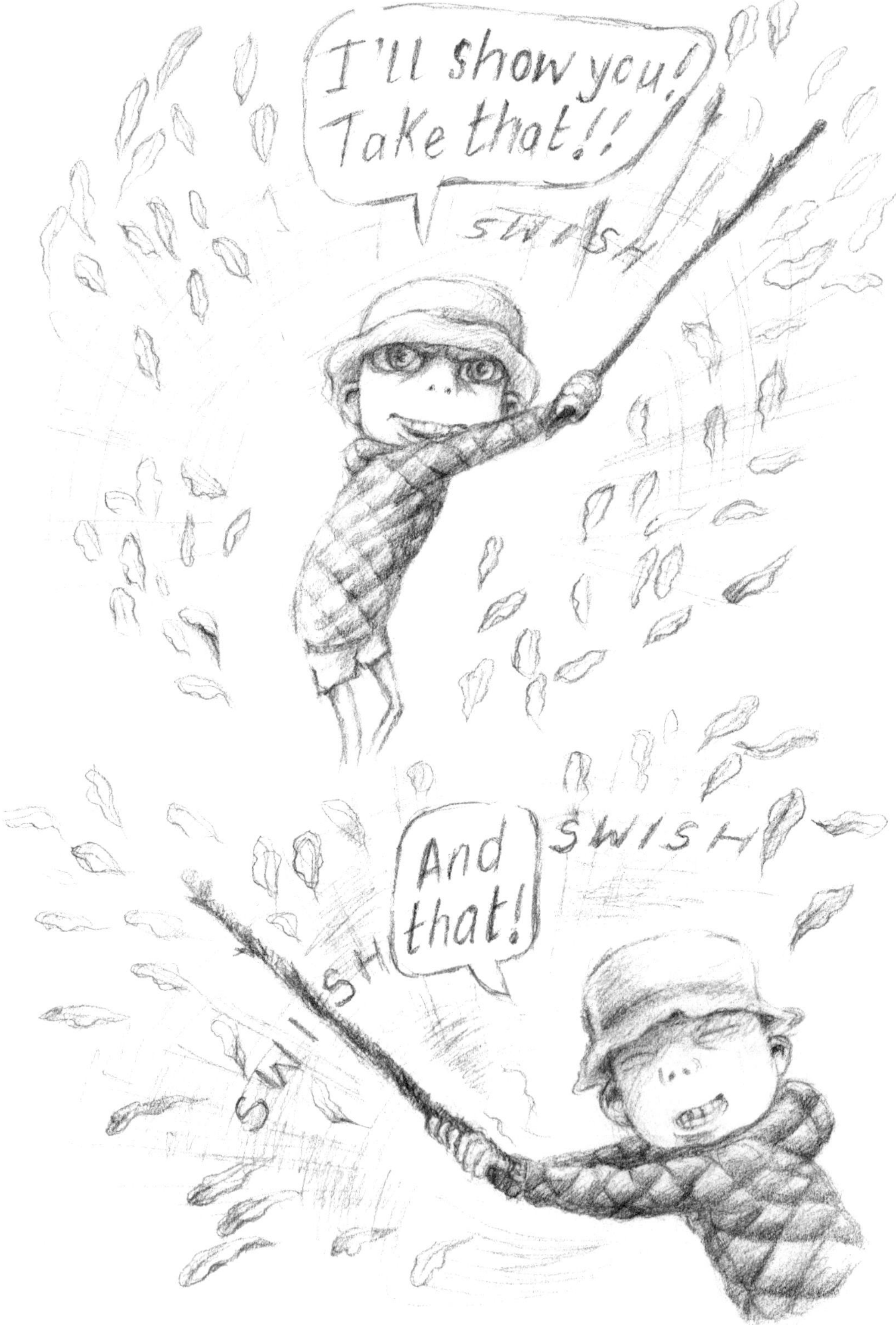
I'll show you! Take that!!
SWISH
SWISH
And that!
SWISH

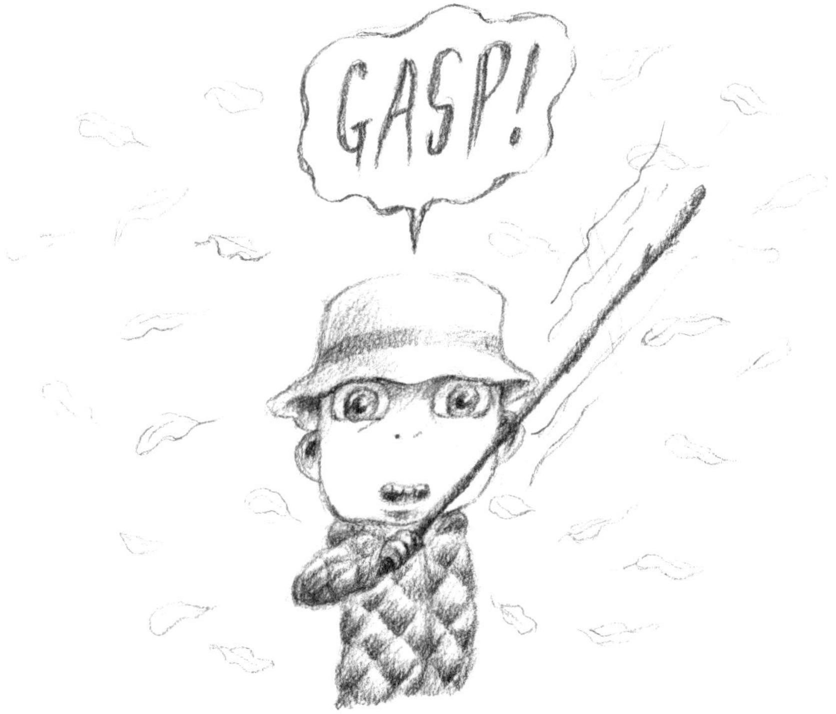
GASP!

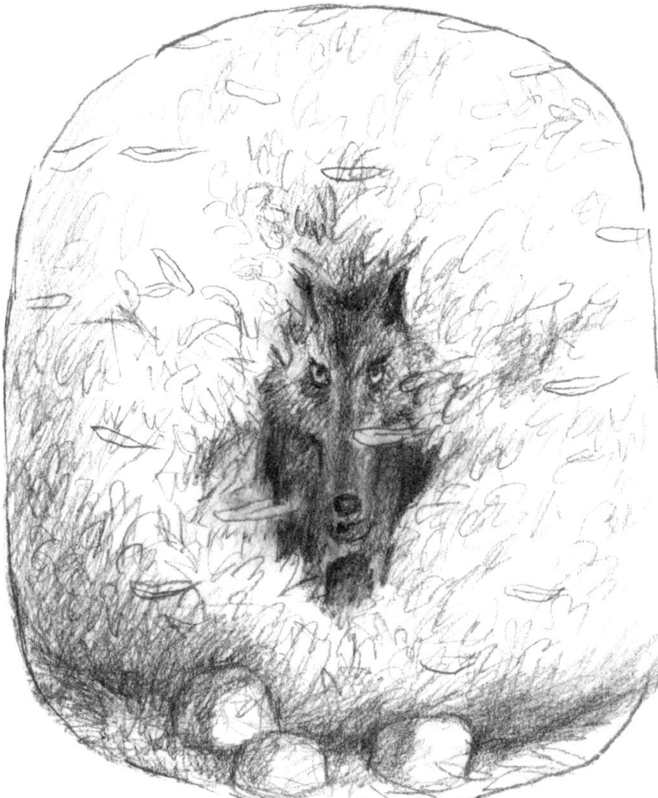

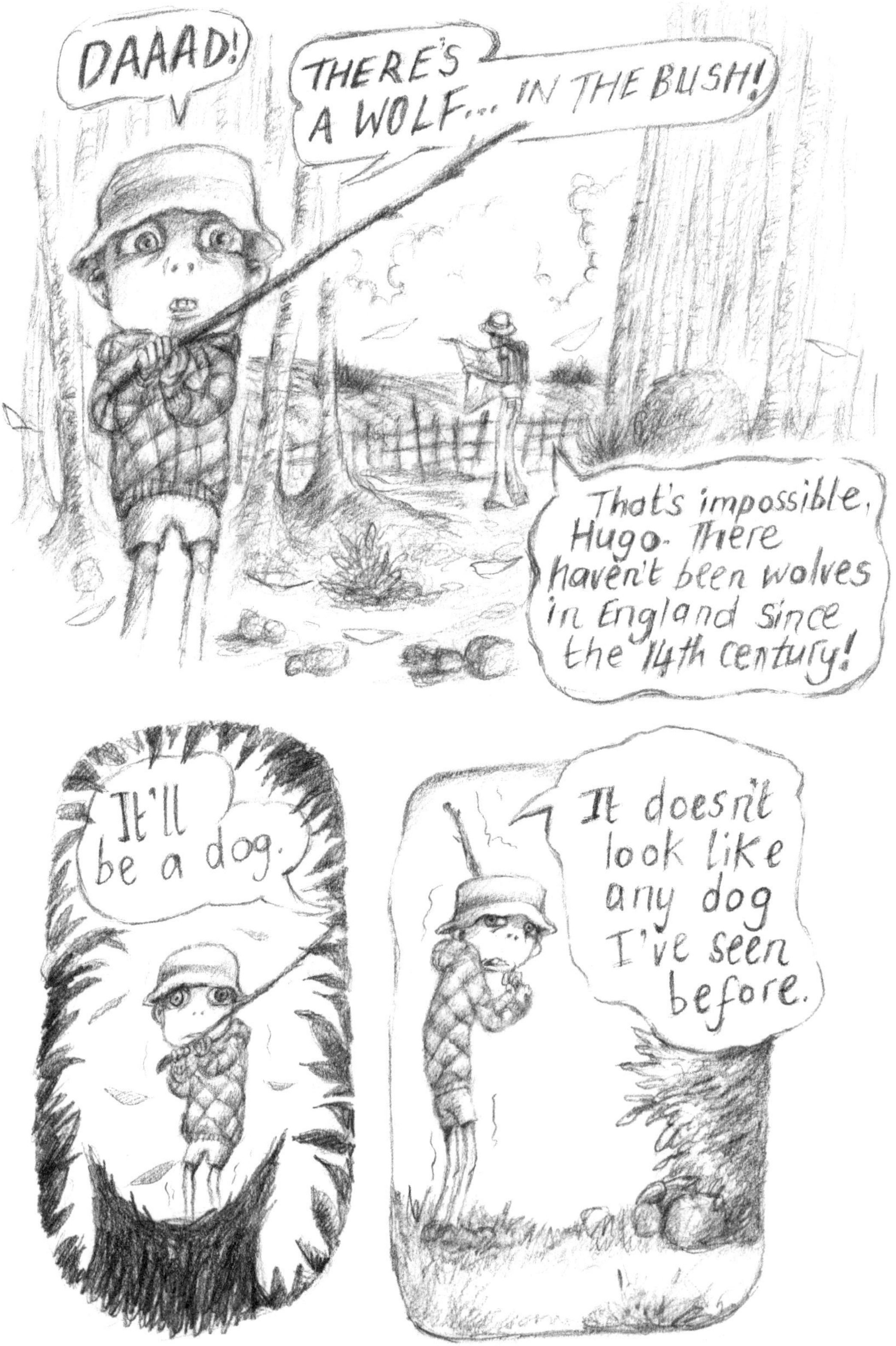
DAAAD!
THERE'S A WOLF... IN THE BUSH!
That's impossible, Hugo. There haven't been wolves in England since the 14th century!
It'll be a dog.
It doesn't look like any dog I've seen before.

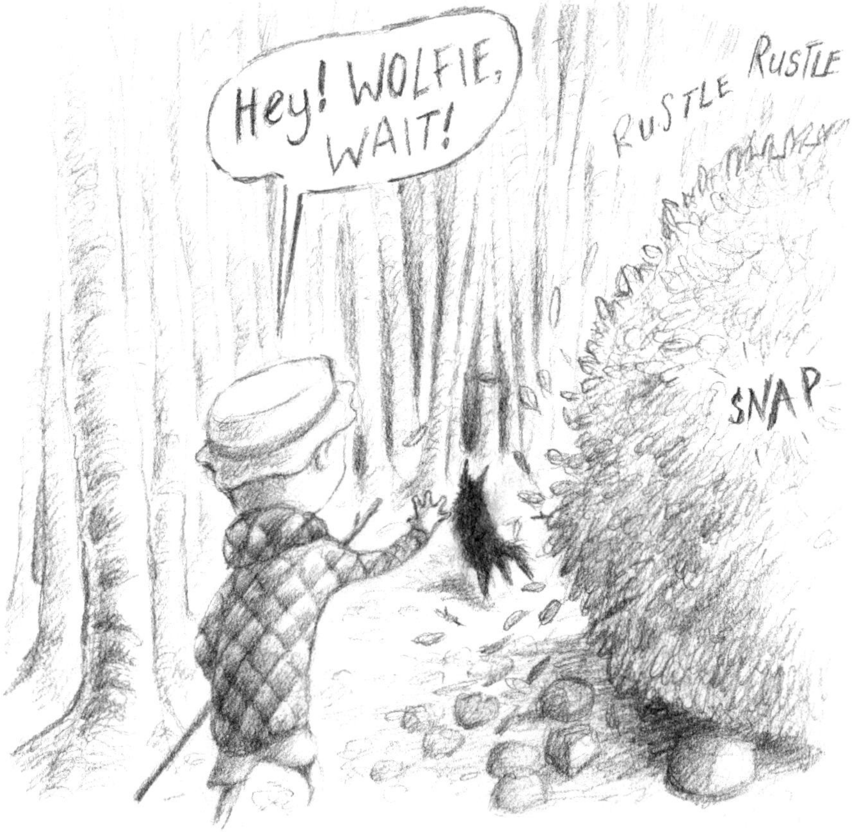
Hey! WOLFIE, WAIT!
RUSTLE RUSTLE
SNAP

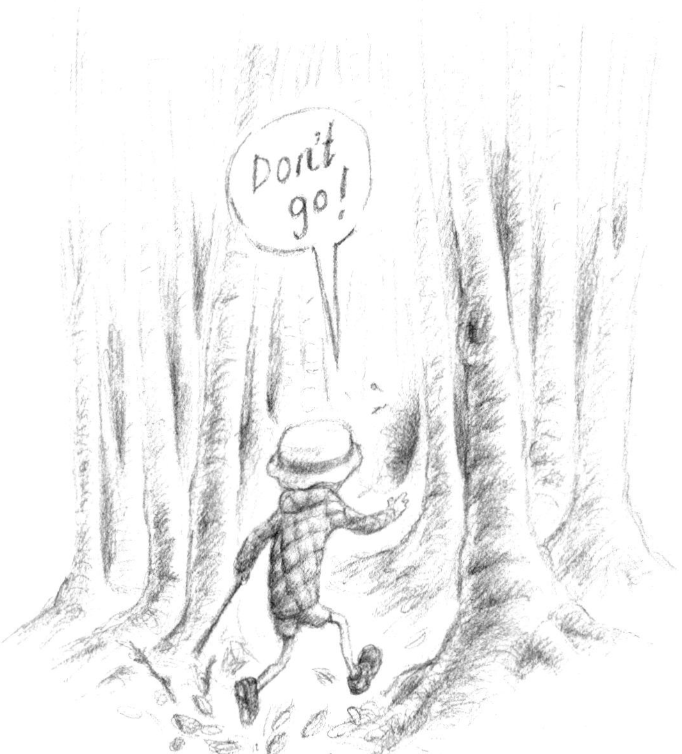
Don't go!

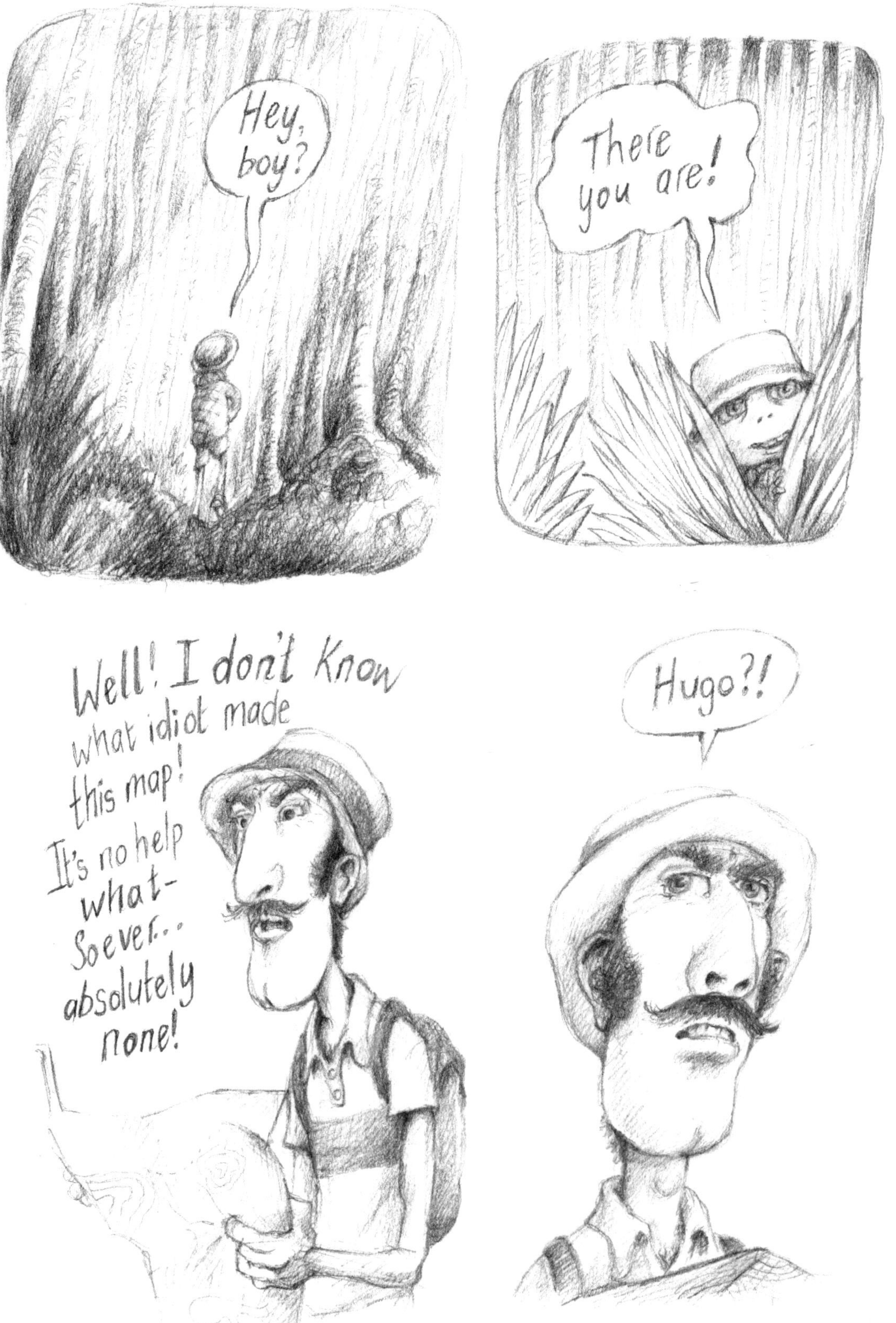
Hey, boy?
There you are!
Well! I don't know what idiot made this map! It's no help what-soever... absolutely none!
Hugo?!

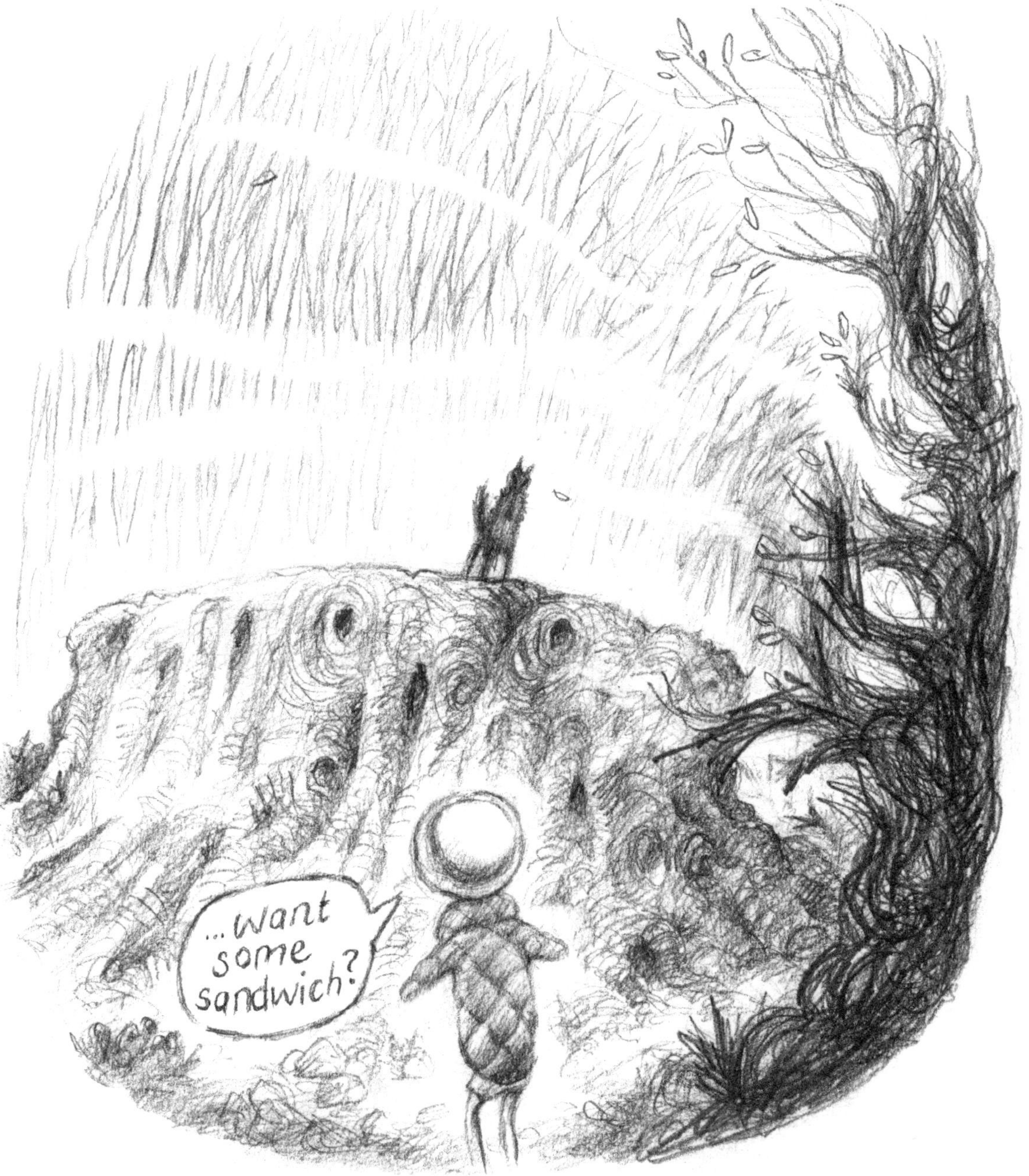
...want some sandwich?

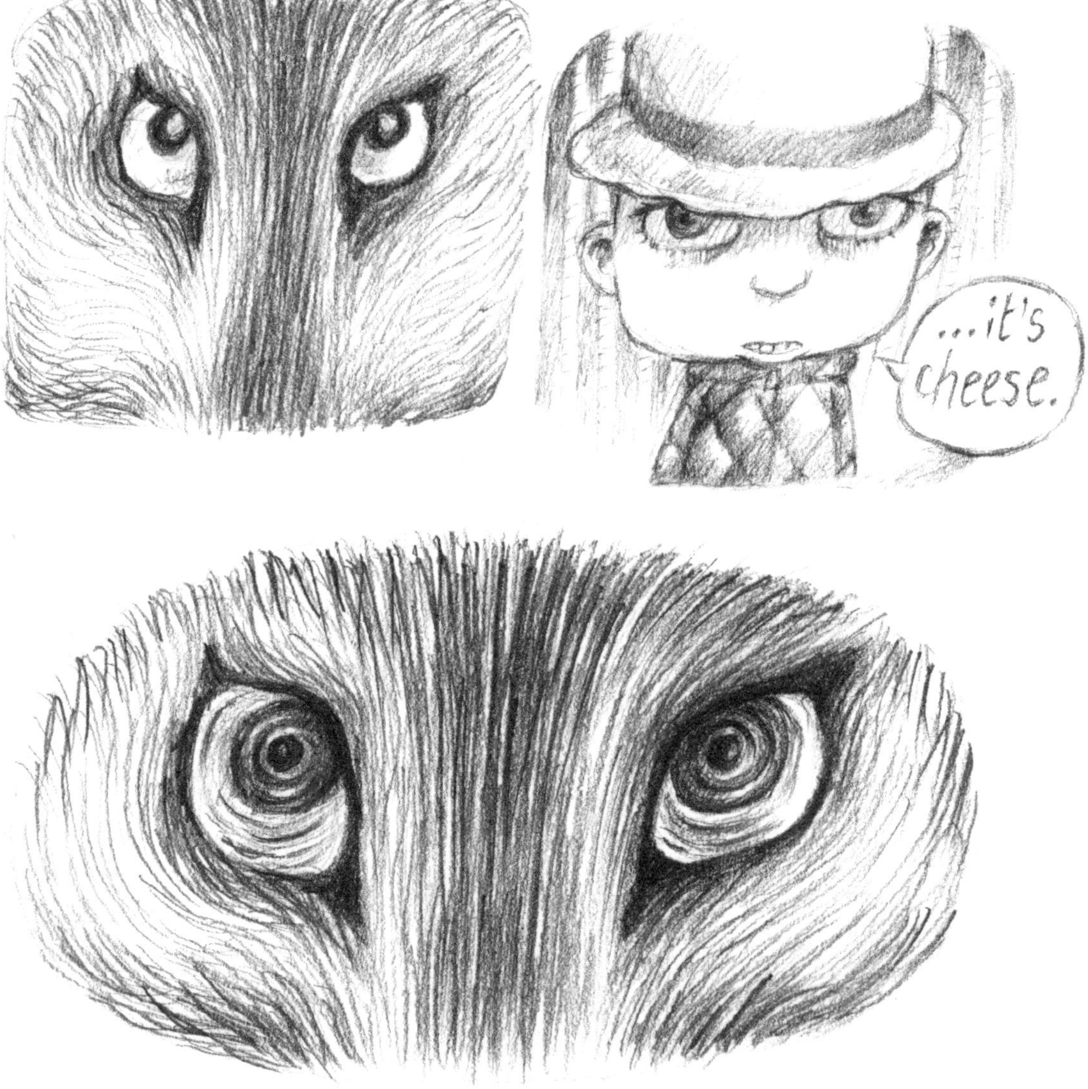
...it's cheese.

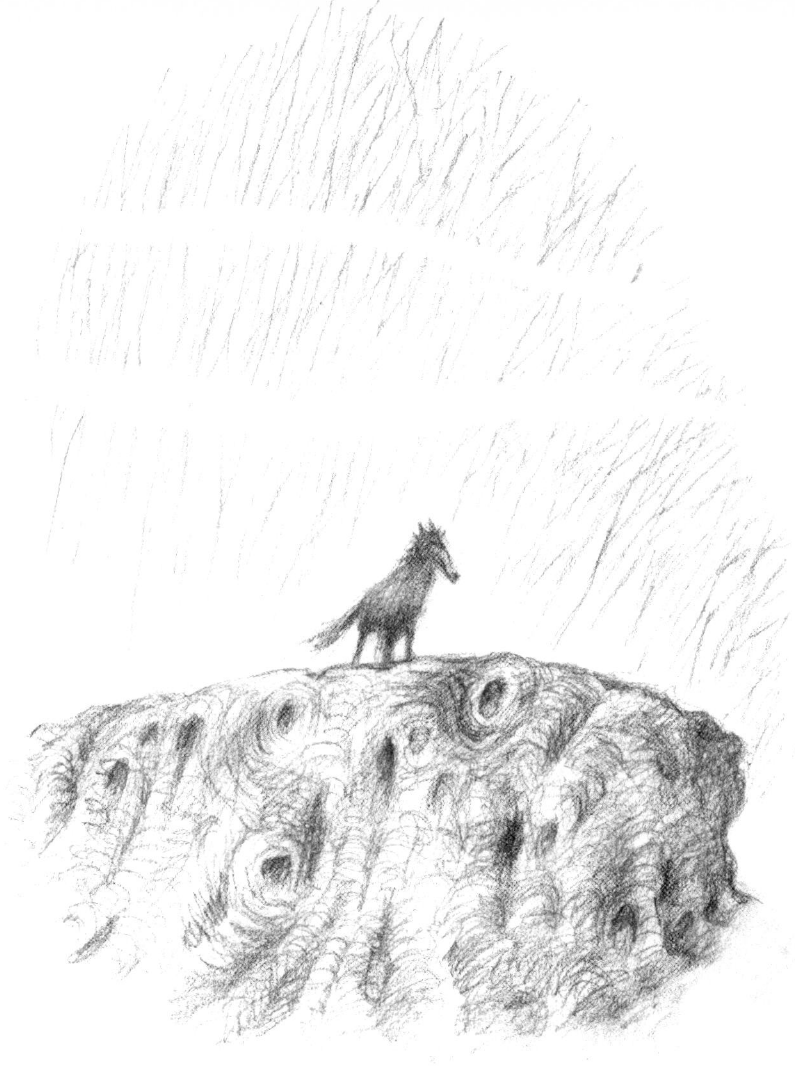

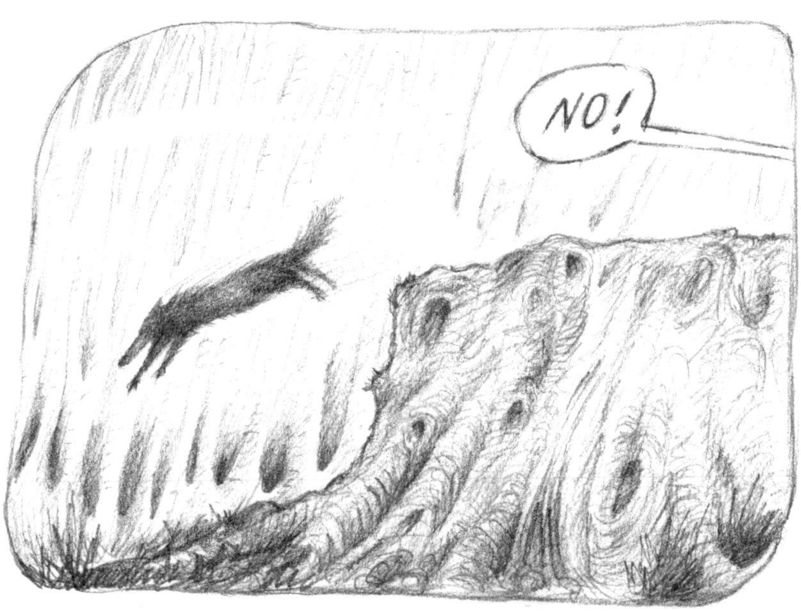
NO!

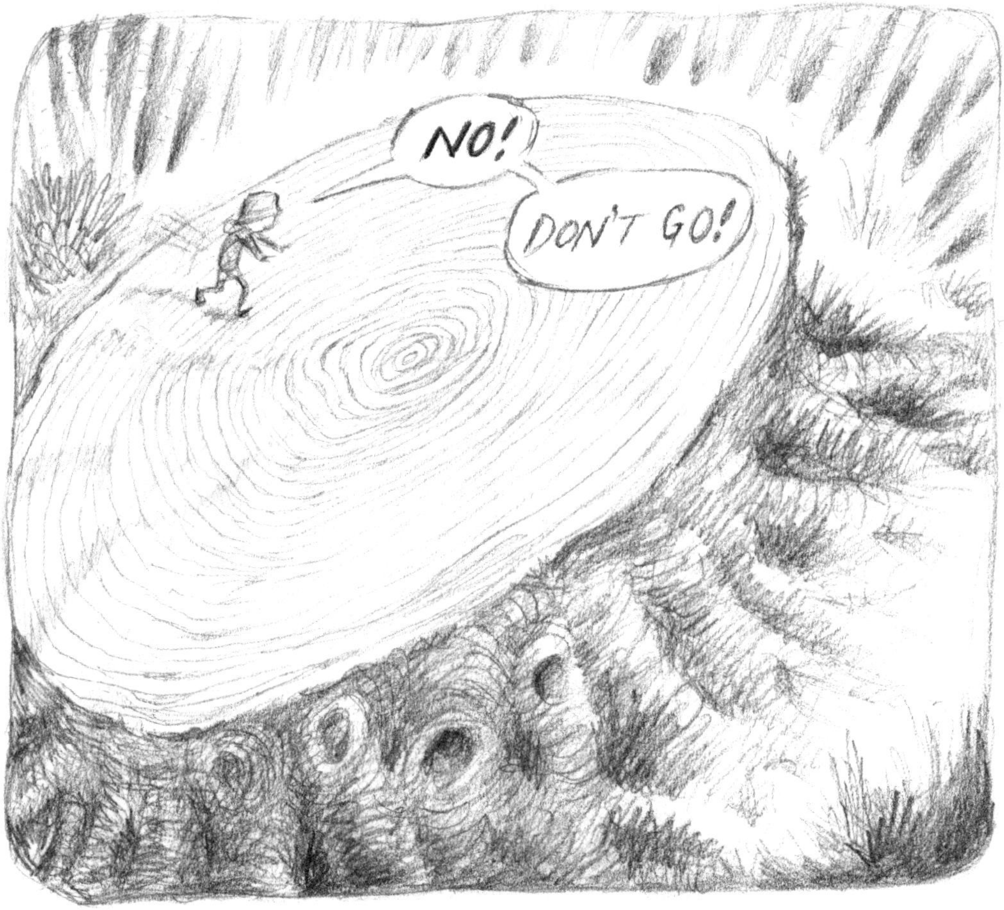
NO!
DON'T GO!

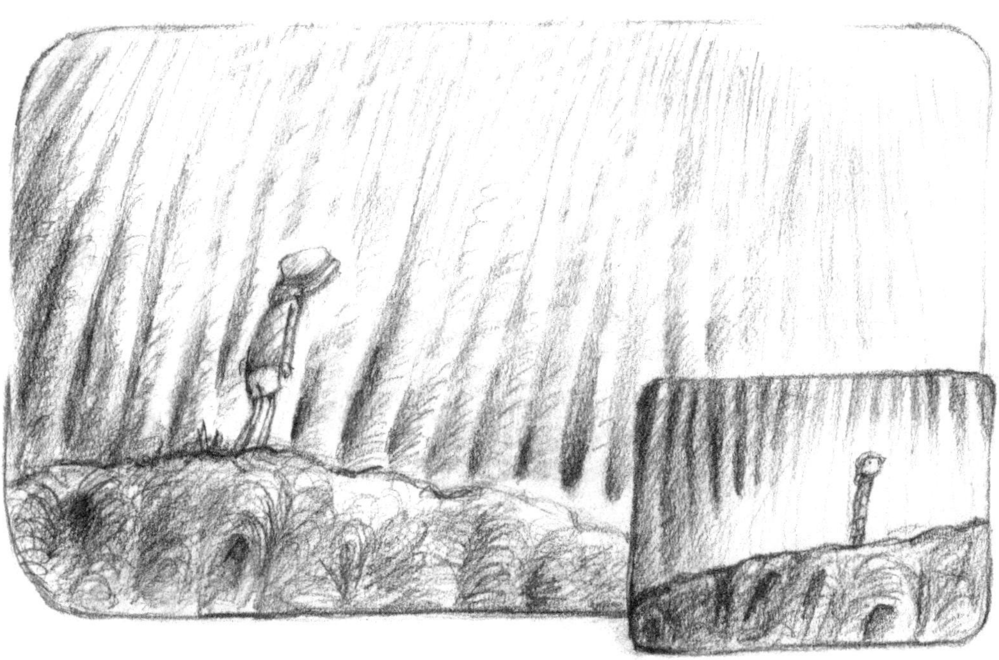

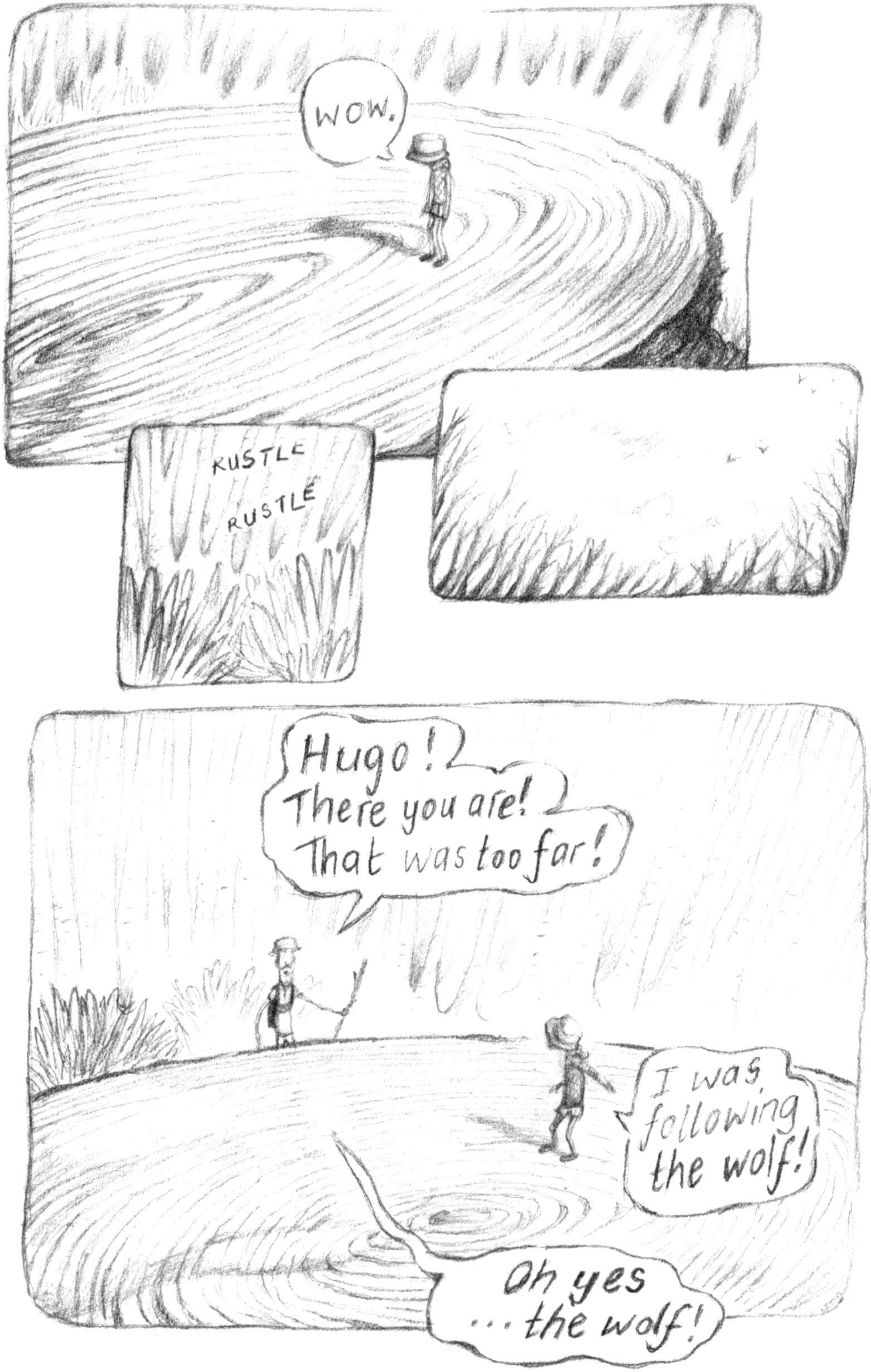
WOW.
RUSTLE
RUSTLE
Hugo! There you are! That was too far!
I was following the wolf!
Oh yes ... the wolf!

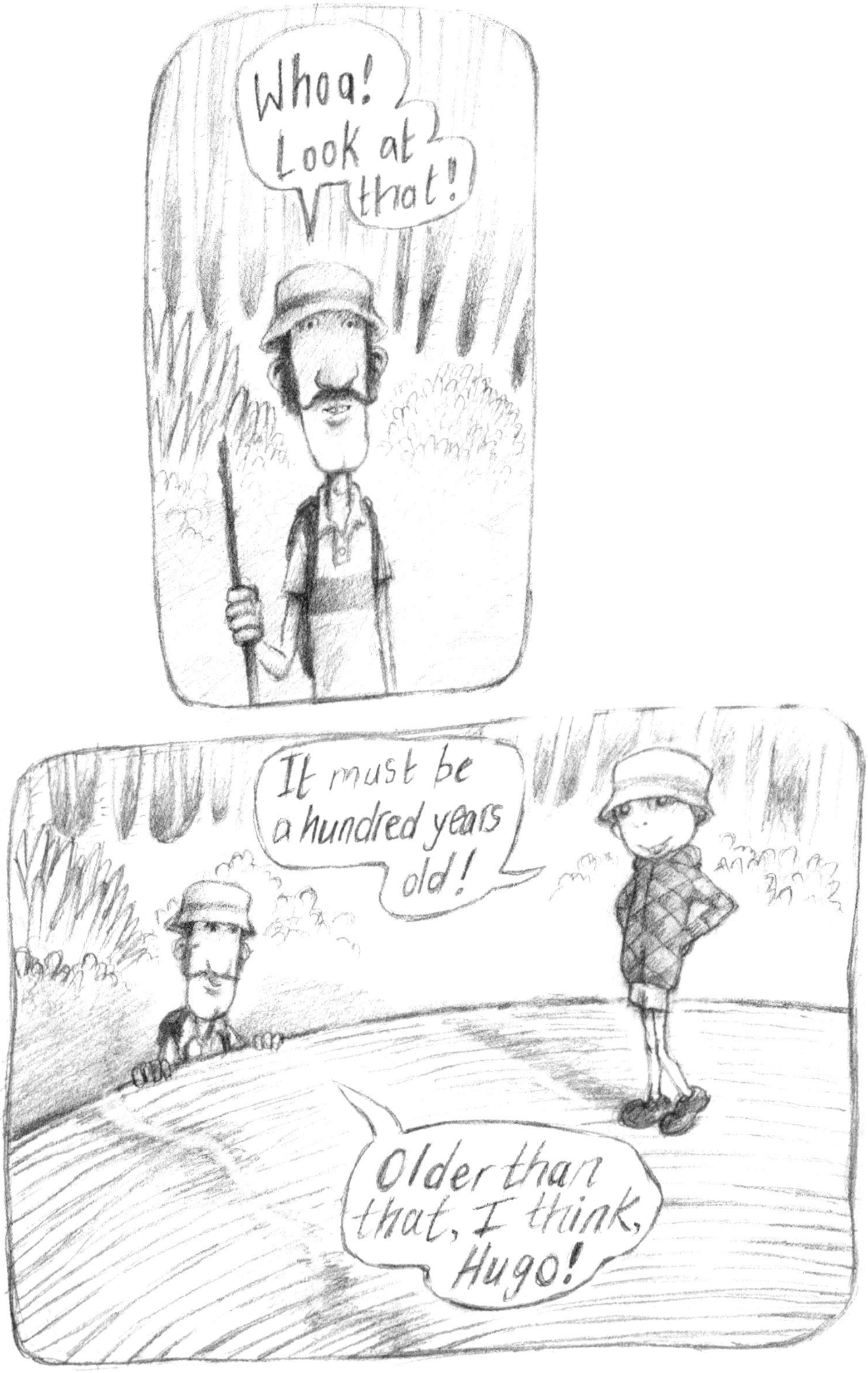
Whoa! Look at that!
It must be a hundred years old!
Older than that, I think, Hugo!

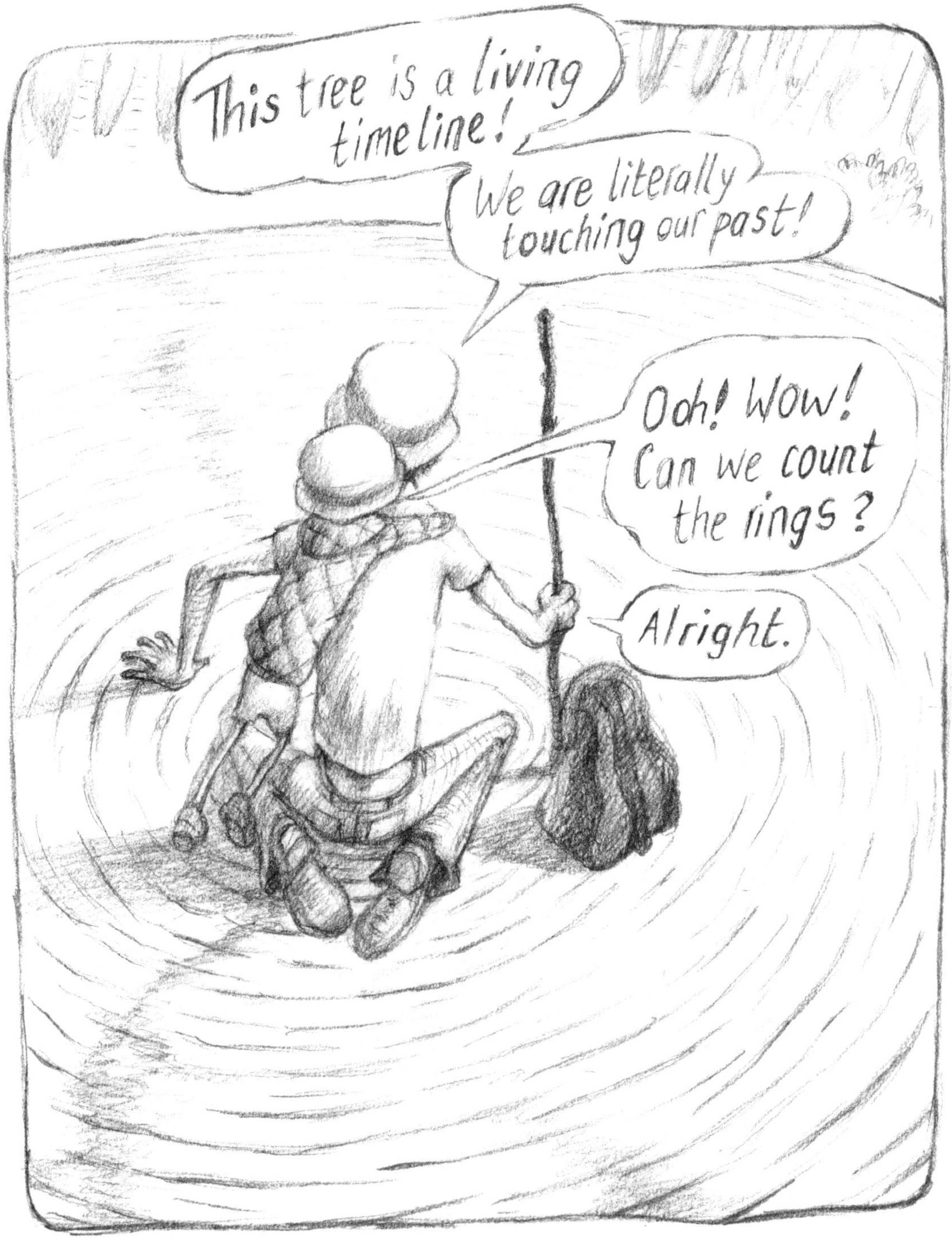
This tree is a living timeline!
We are literally touching our past!
Ooh! Wow! Can we count the rings?
Alright.

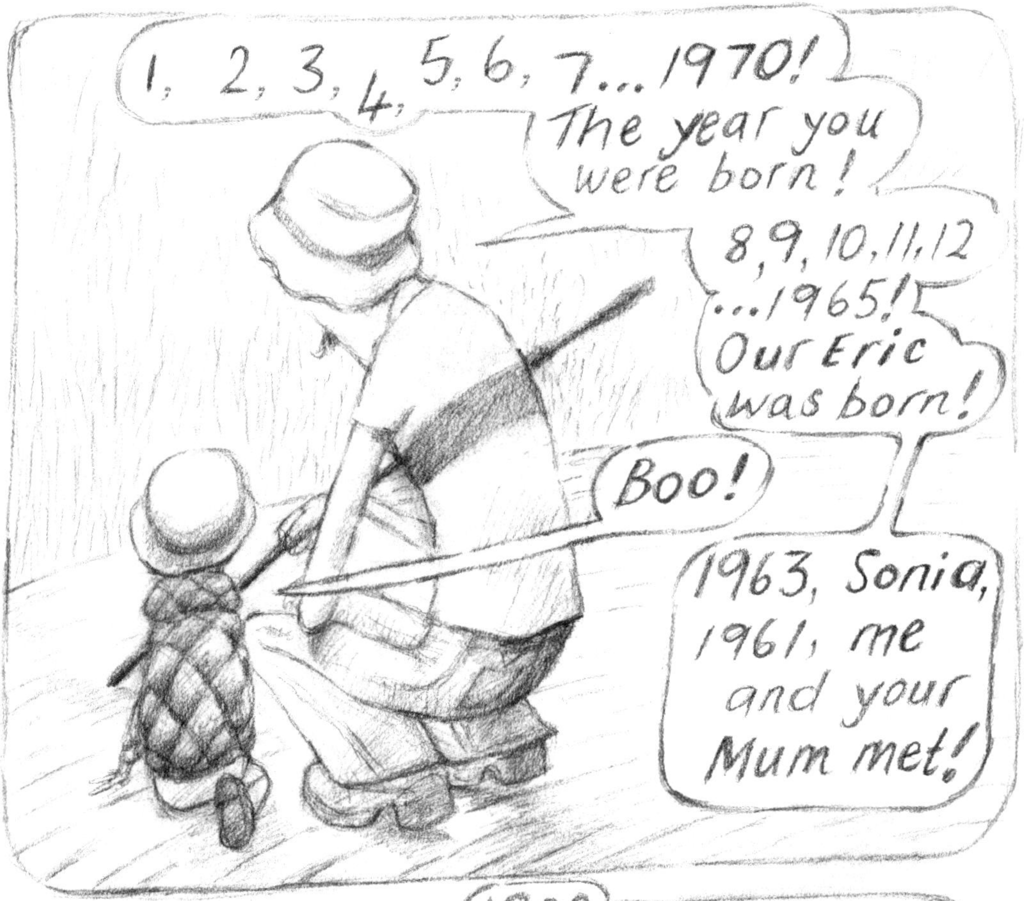
1, 2, 3, 4, 5, 6, 7... 1970! The year you were born!
8, 9, 10, 11, 12 ...1965! Our Eric was born!
Boo!
1963, Sonia, 1961, me and your Mum met!

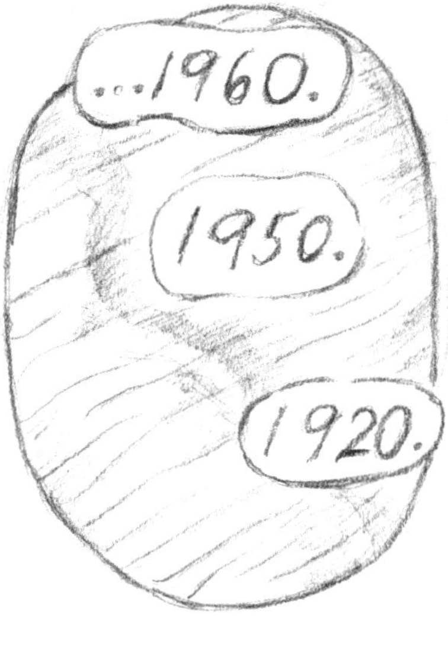
...1960.
1950.
1920.

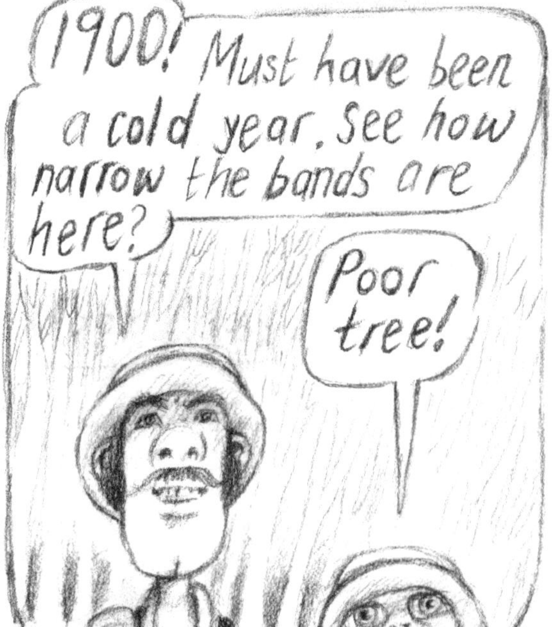
1900! Must have been a cold year. See how narrow the bands are here?
Poor tree!

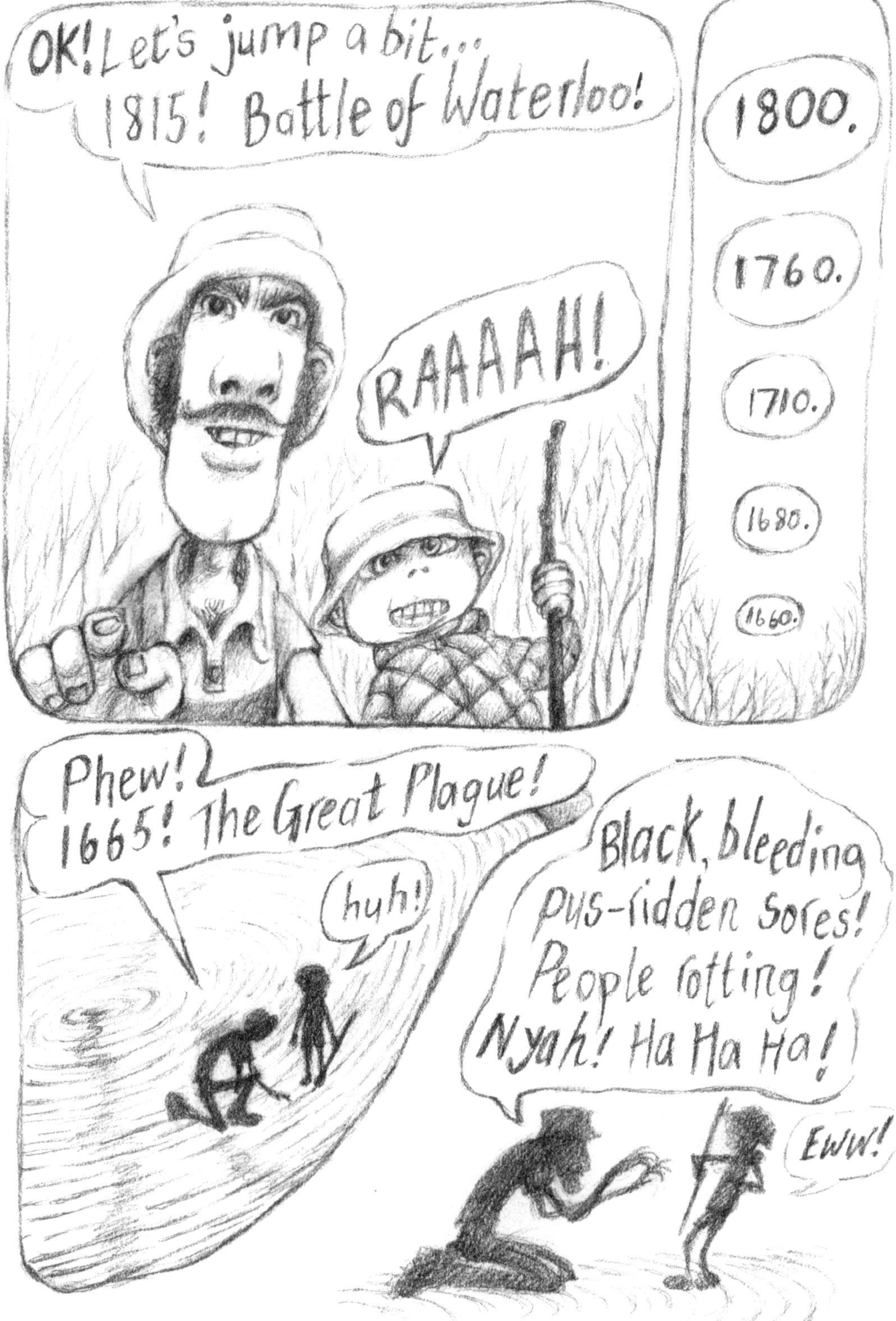
OK! Let's jump a bit...
1815! Battle of Waterloo!
RAAAAH!
1800.
1760.
1710.
1680.
1660.
Phew!
1665! The Great Plague!
huh!
Black, bleeding
pus-ridden sores!
People rotting!
Nyah! Ha Ha Ha!
Eww!

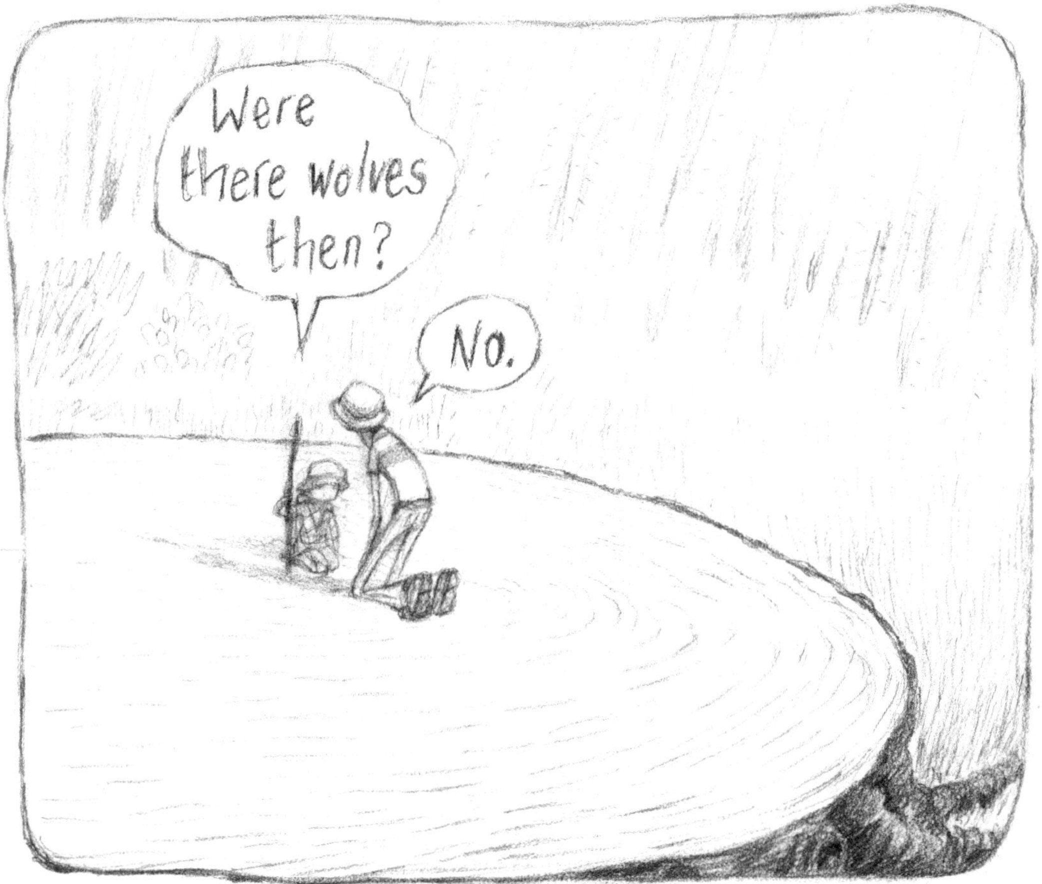

Were there wolves then?
No.

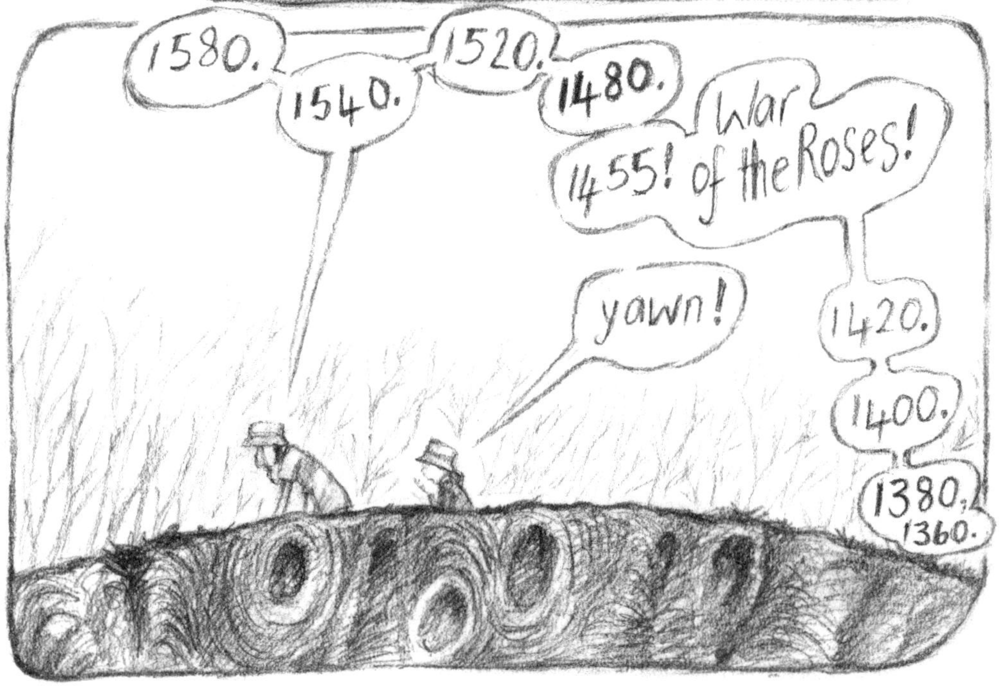

1580.
1540.
1520.
1480.
1455! War of the Roses!
yawn!
1420.
1400.
1380.
1360.

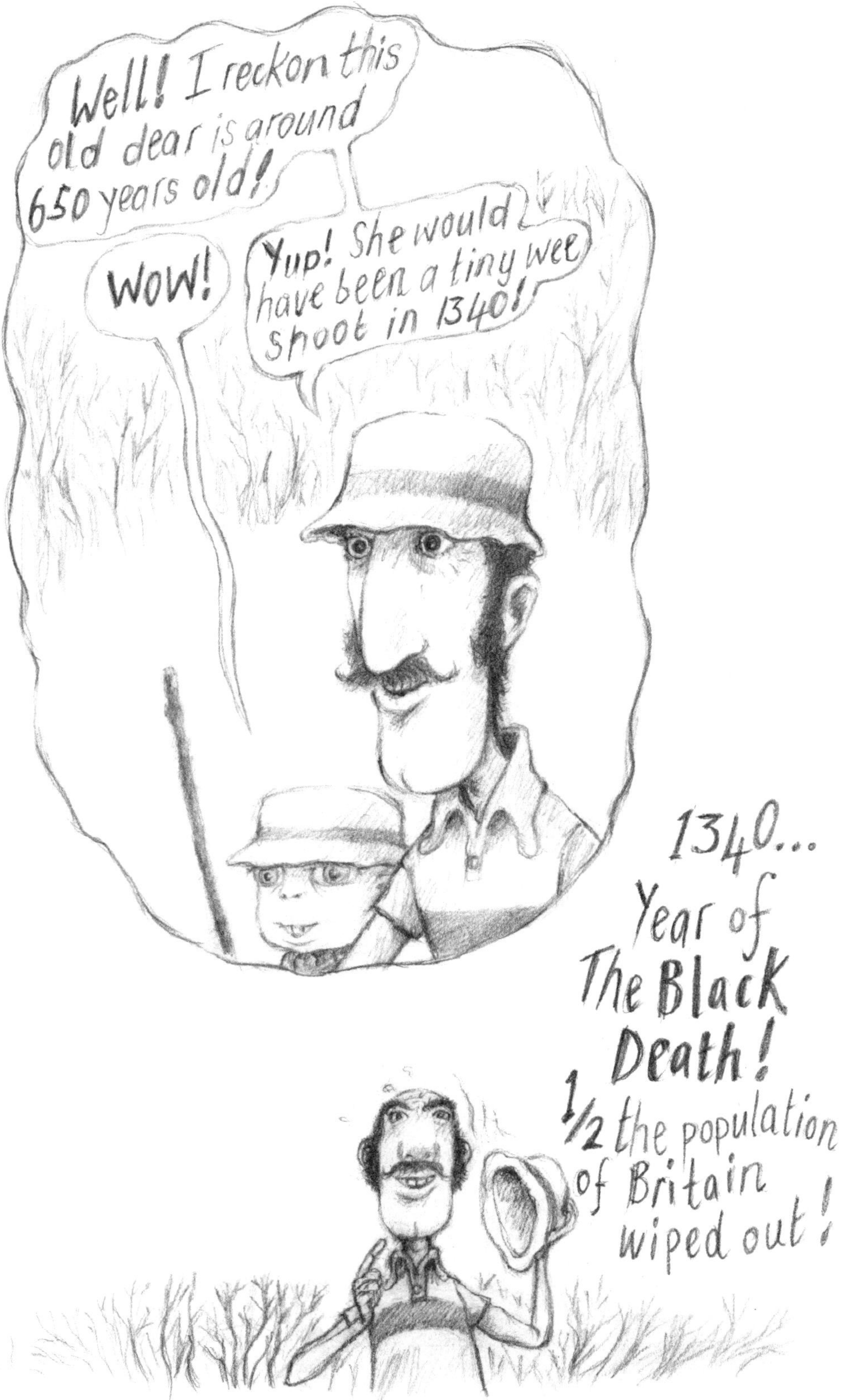
Well! I reckon this old dear is around 650 years old!
WOW!
Yup! She would have been a tiny wee shoot in 1340!
1340... Year of The Black Death! 1/2 the population of Britain wiped out!

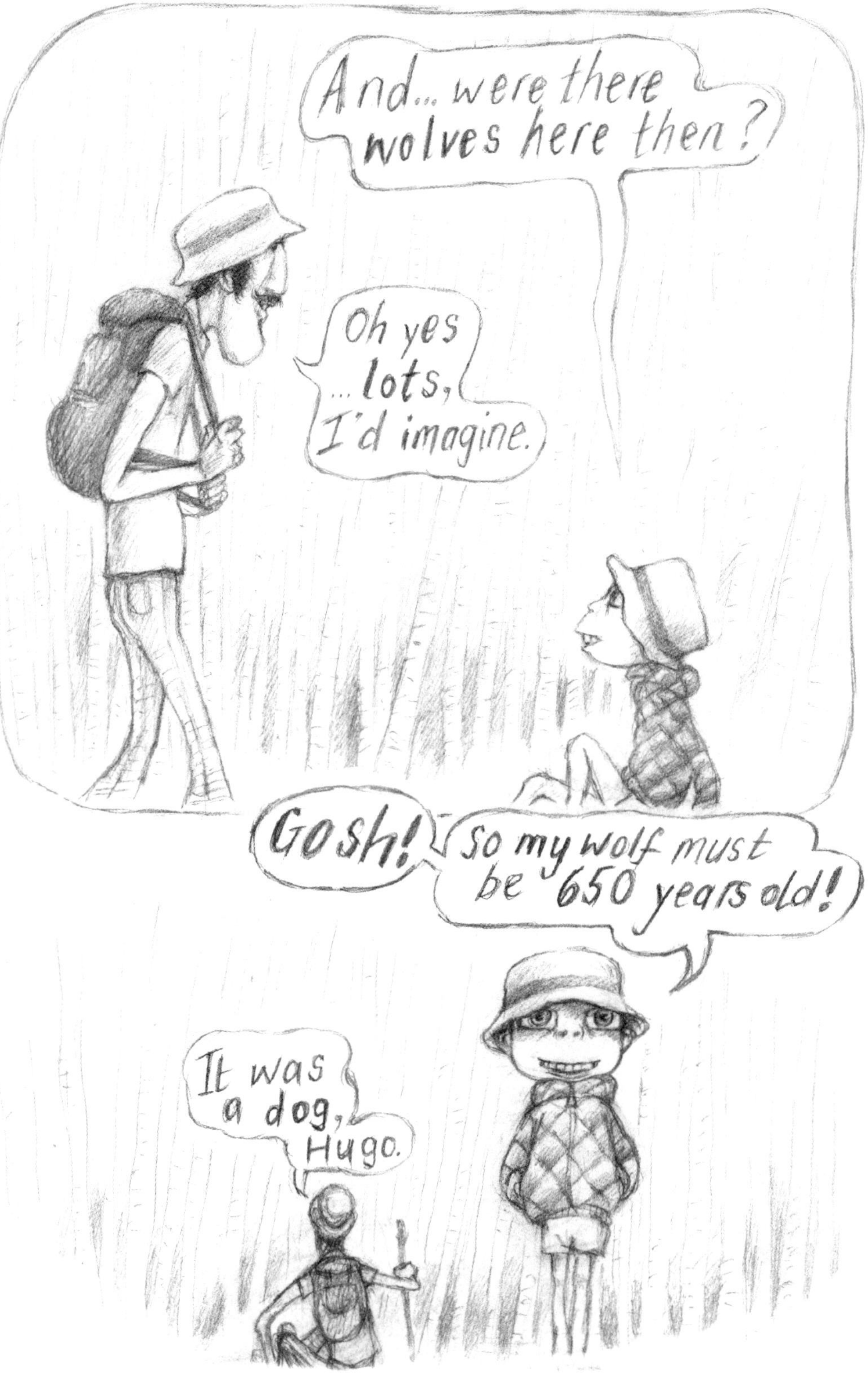
And... were there wolves here then?
Oh yes ...lots, I'd imagine.
Gosh!
So my wolf must be 650 years old!
It was a dog, Hugo.

Come on! We'll be late for lunch. The others will be at the river by now.
Coming!
snap!
Hugo?
uh-huh.

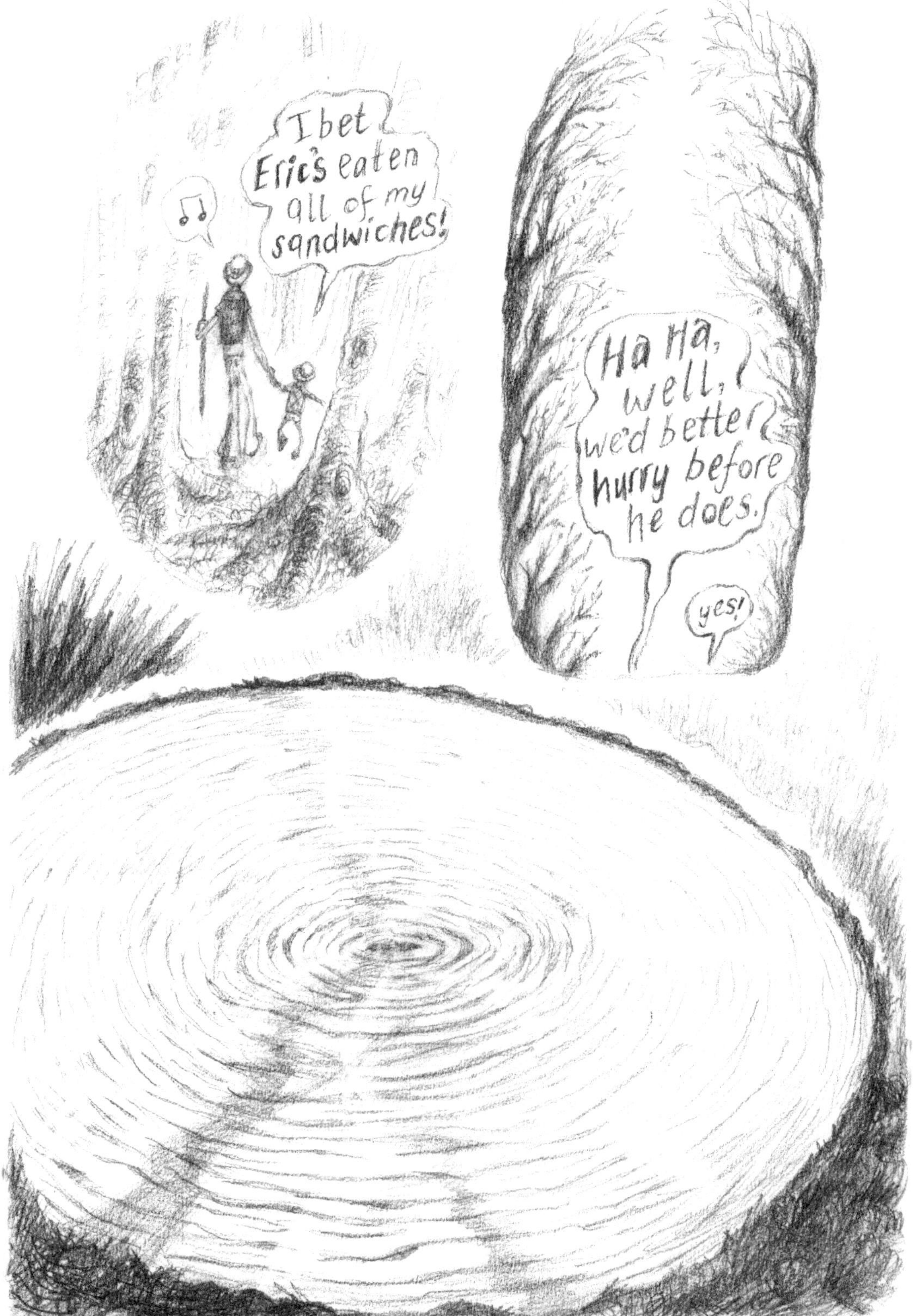
I bet Eric's eaten all of my sandwiches!
Ha Ha, well, we'd better hurry before he does.
yes!

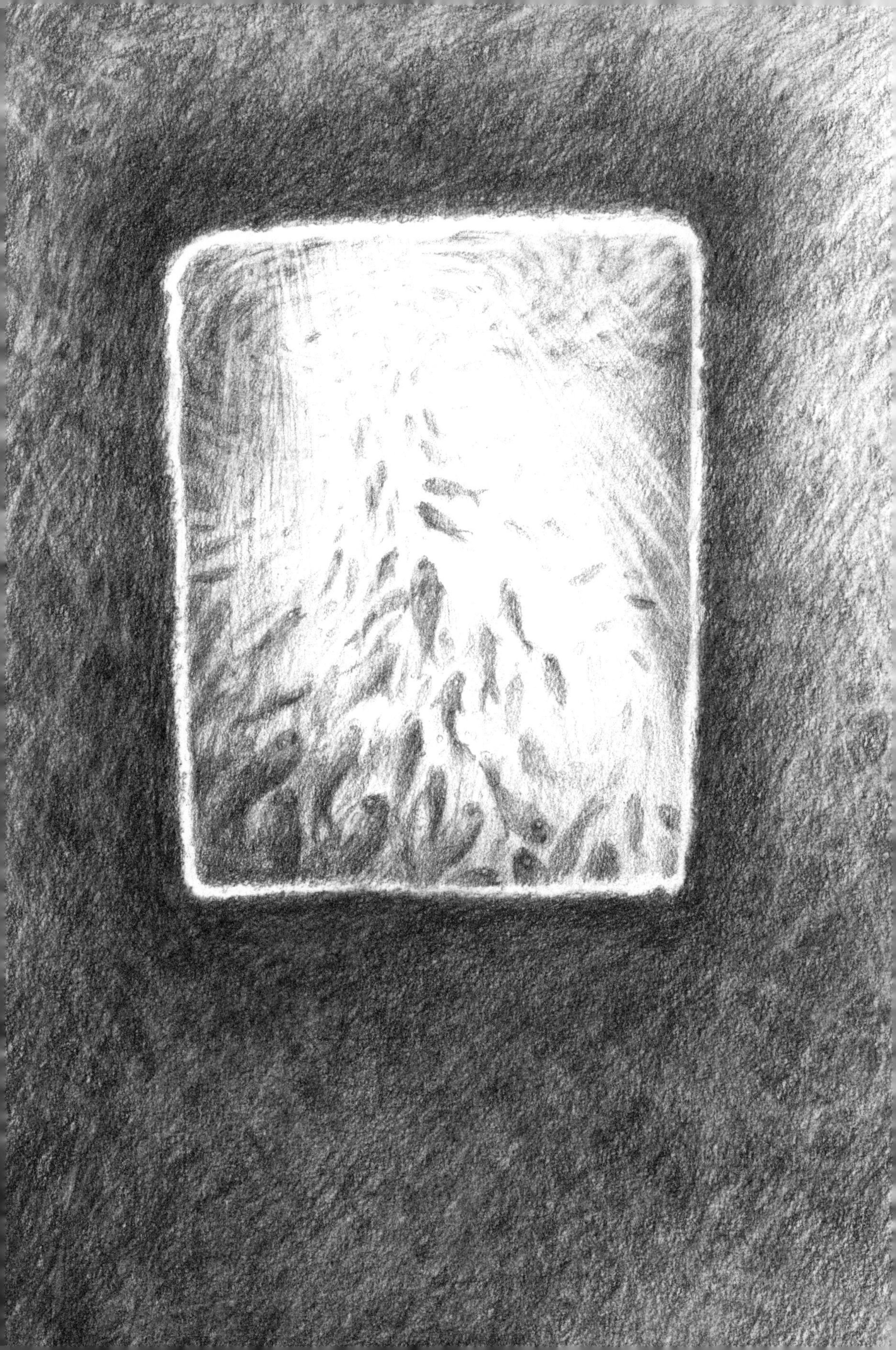

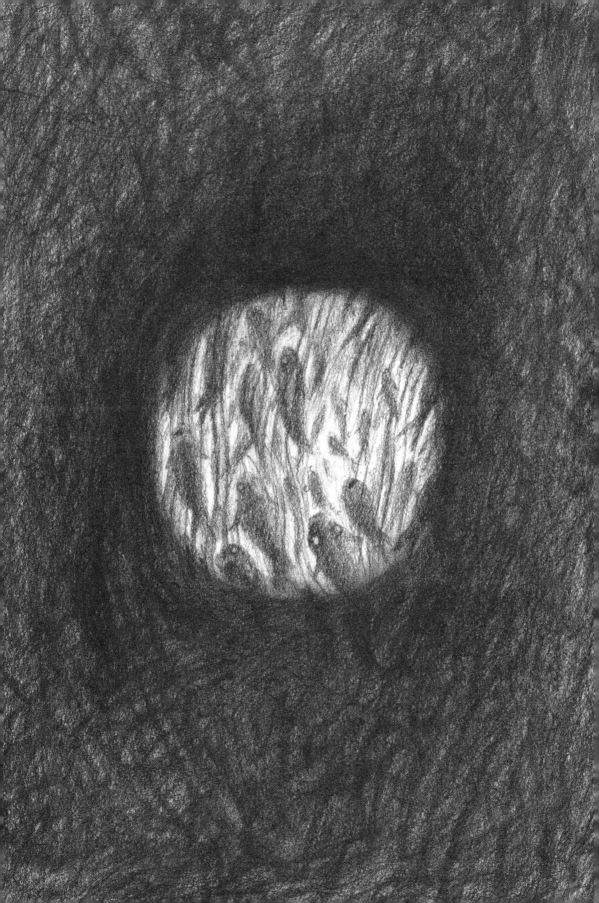

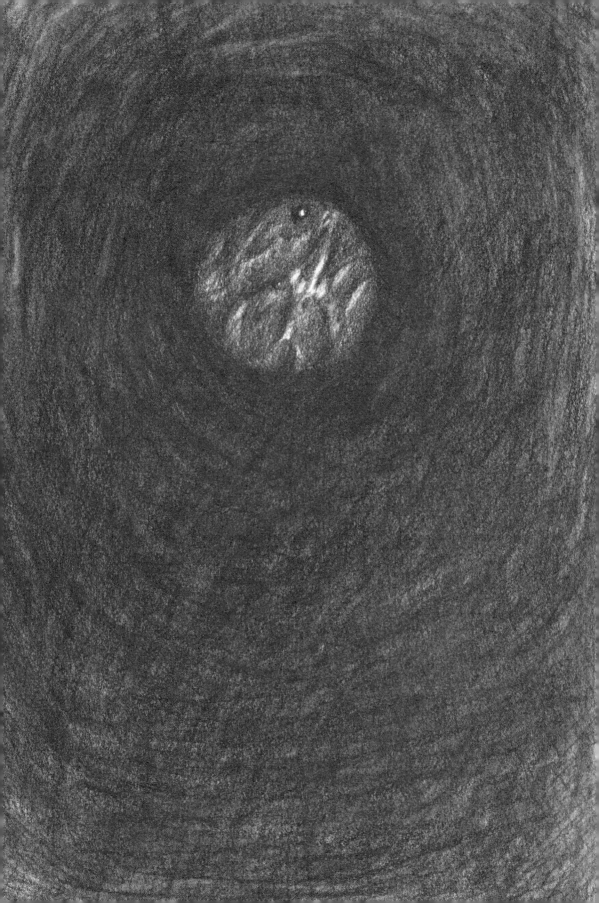

Chapter Two

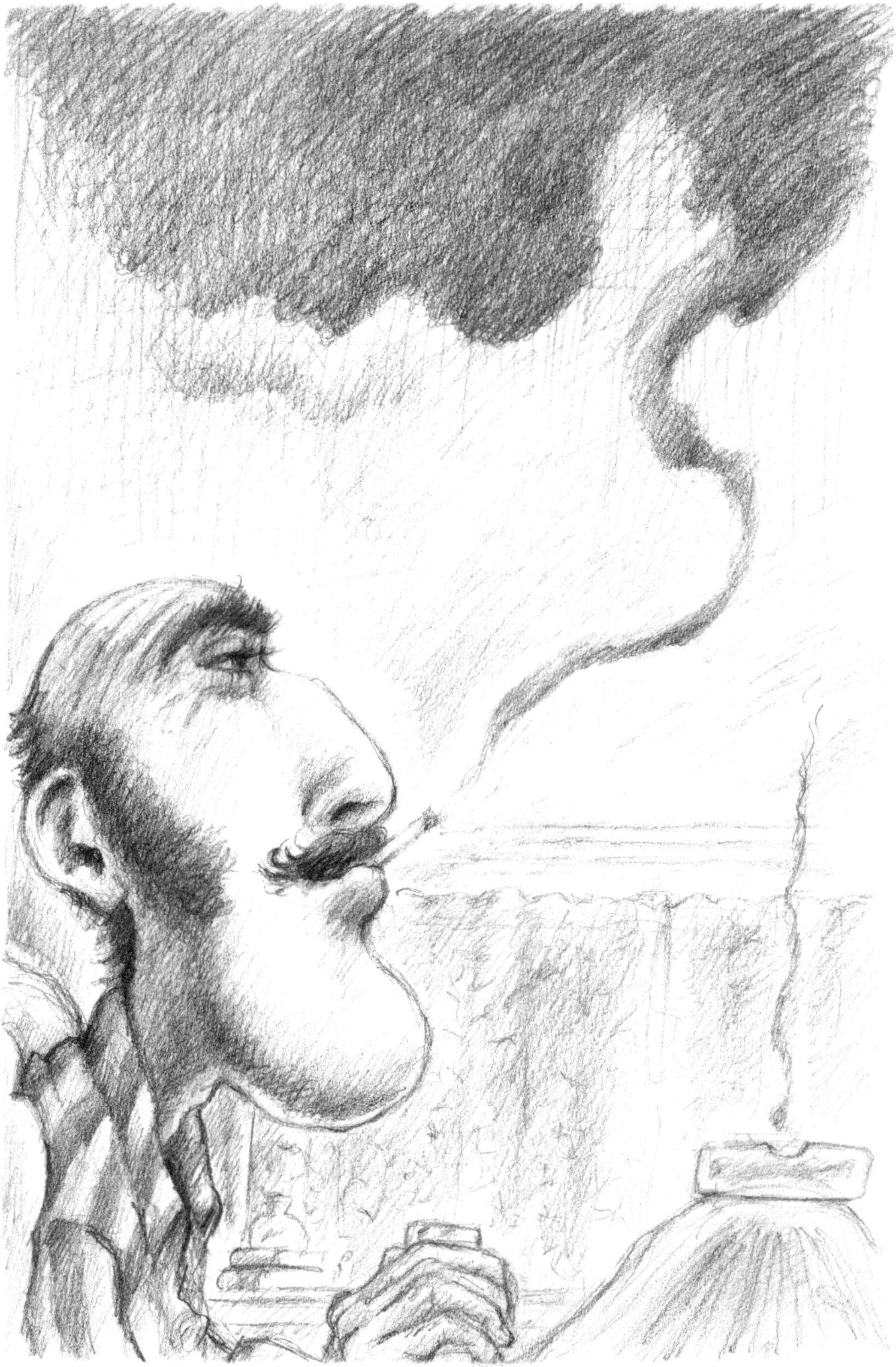

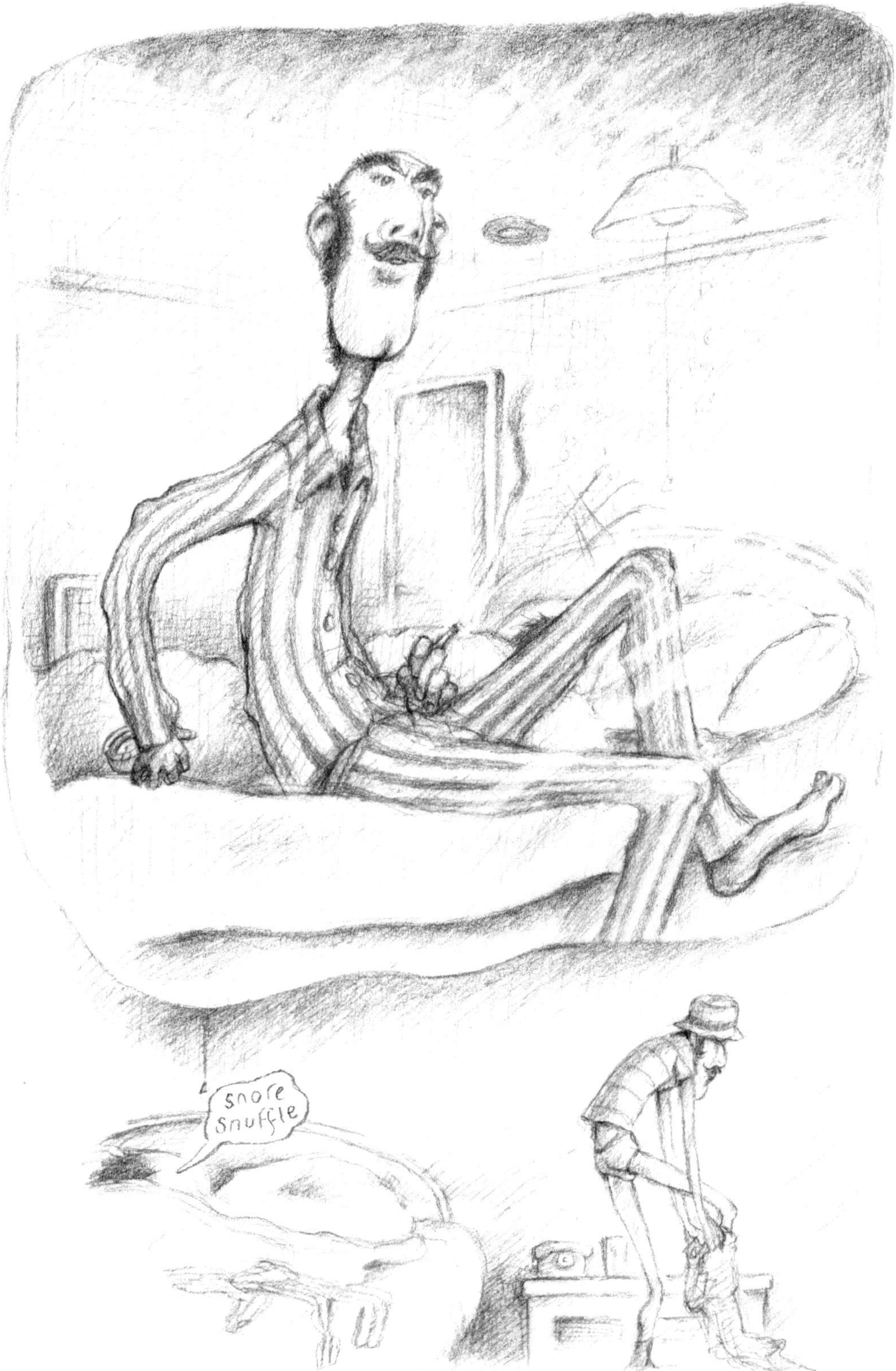
snore snuffle

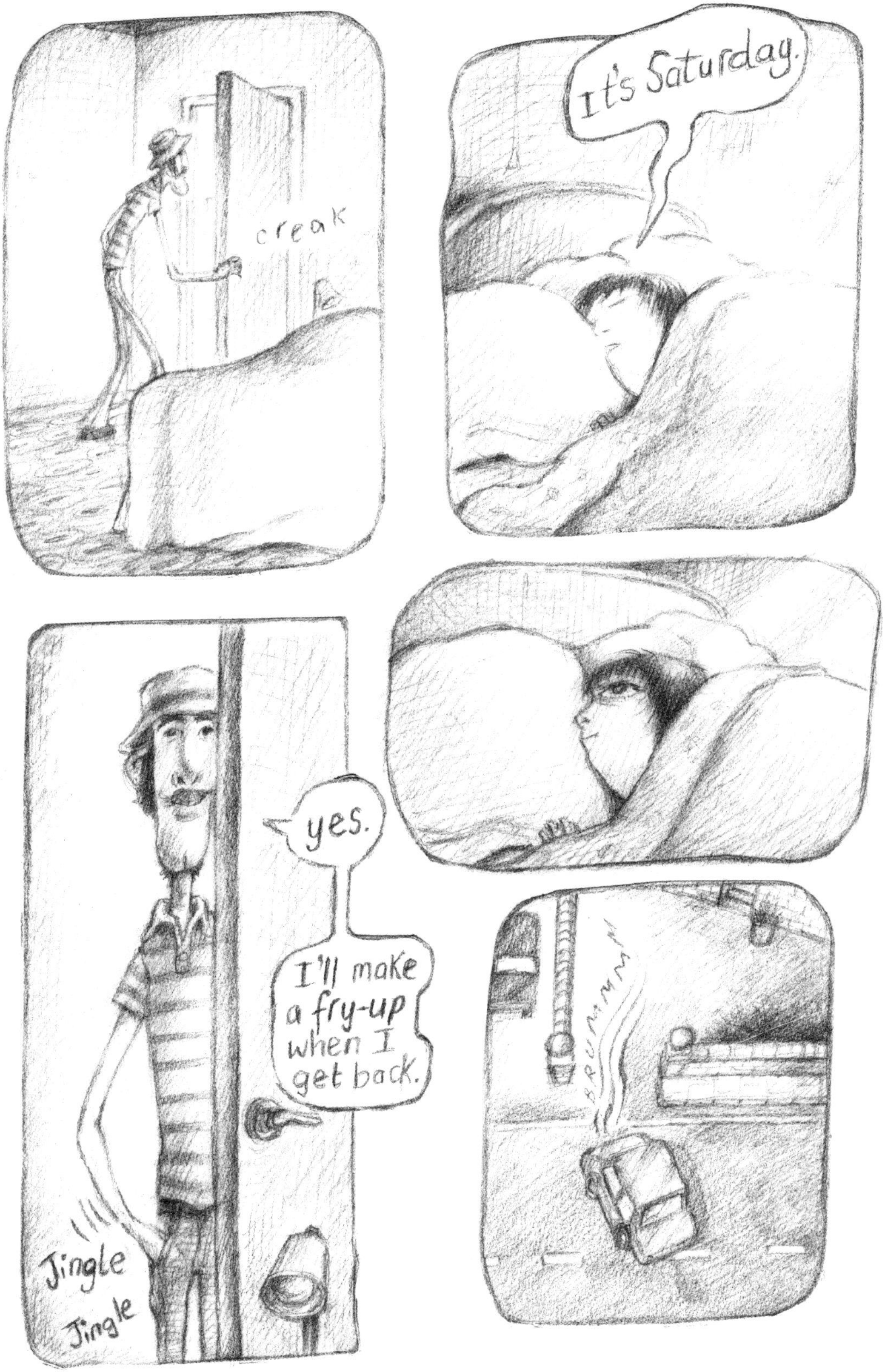
creak
It's Saturday.
yes.
I'll make a fry-up when I get back.
Jingle
Jingle
BRUMMM

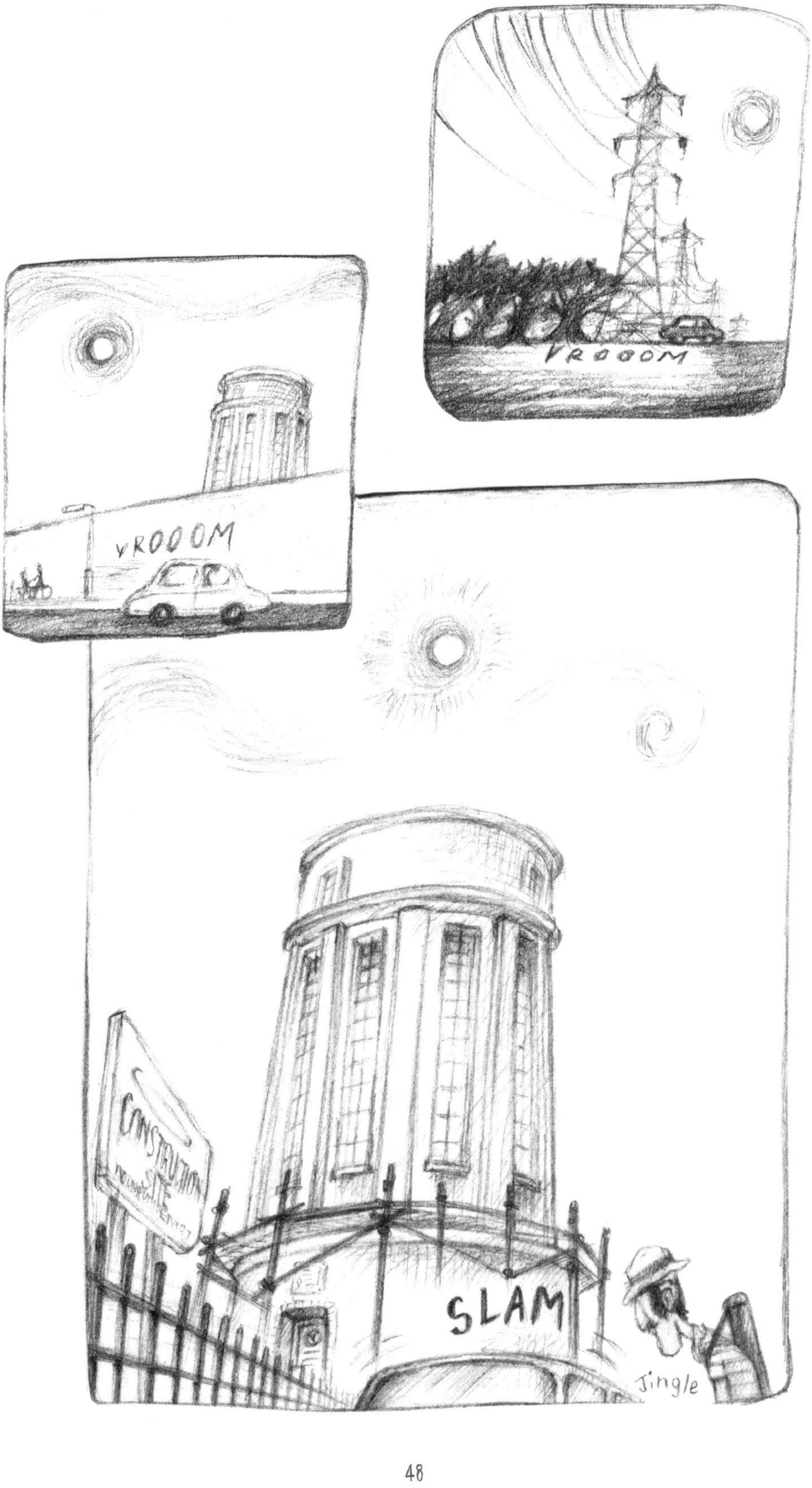
VROOOM
VROOOM
CONSTRUCTION
SITE
SLAM
Jingle

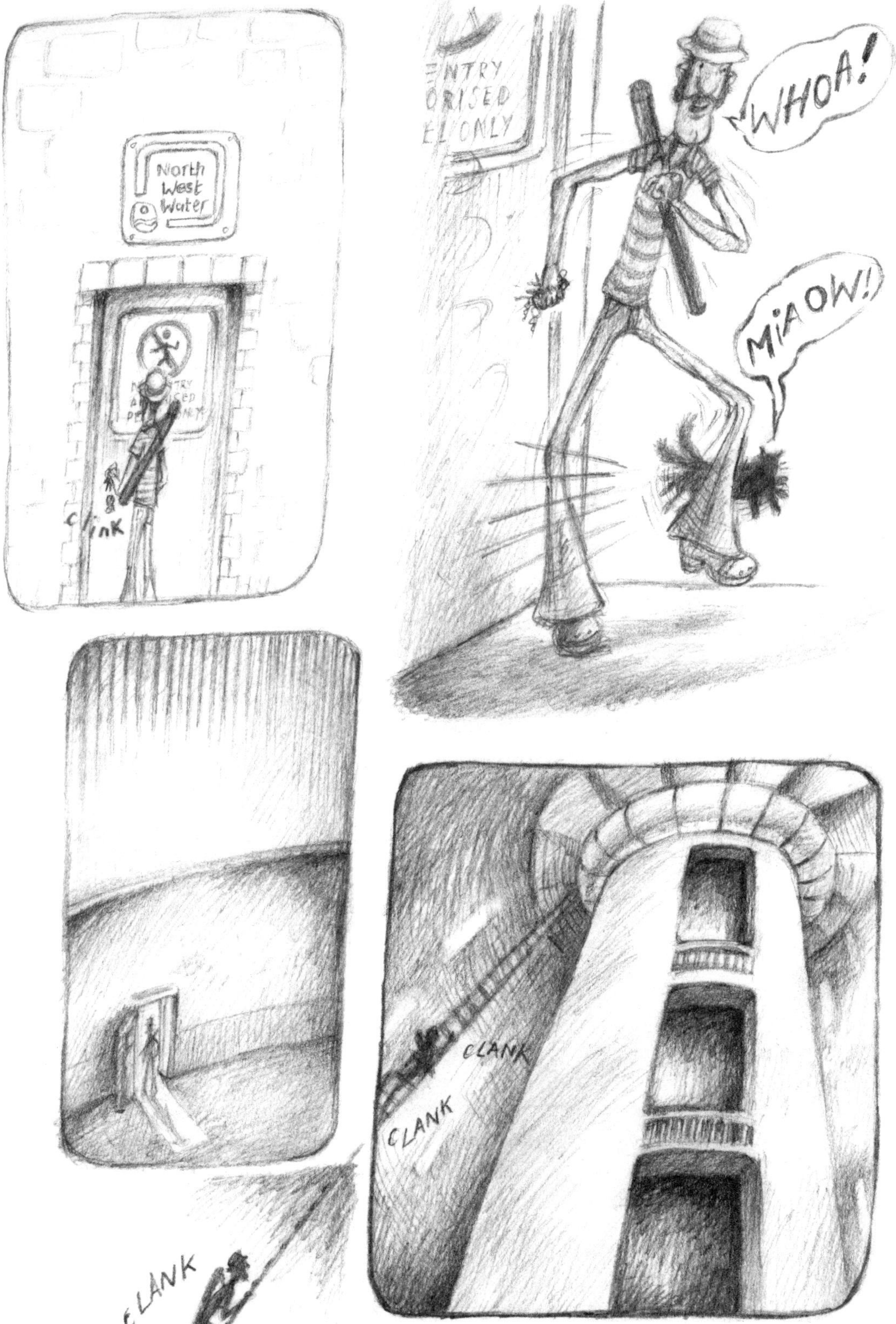
North West Water
CLINK
WHOA!
MIAOW!
CLANK
CLANK
CLANK

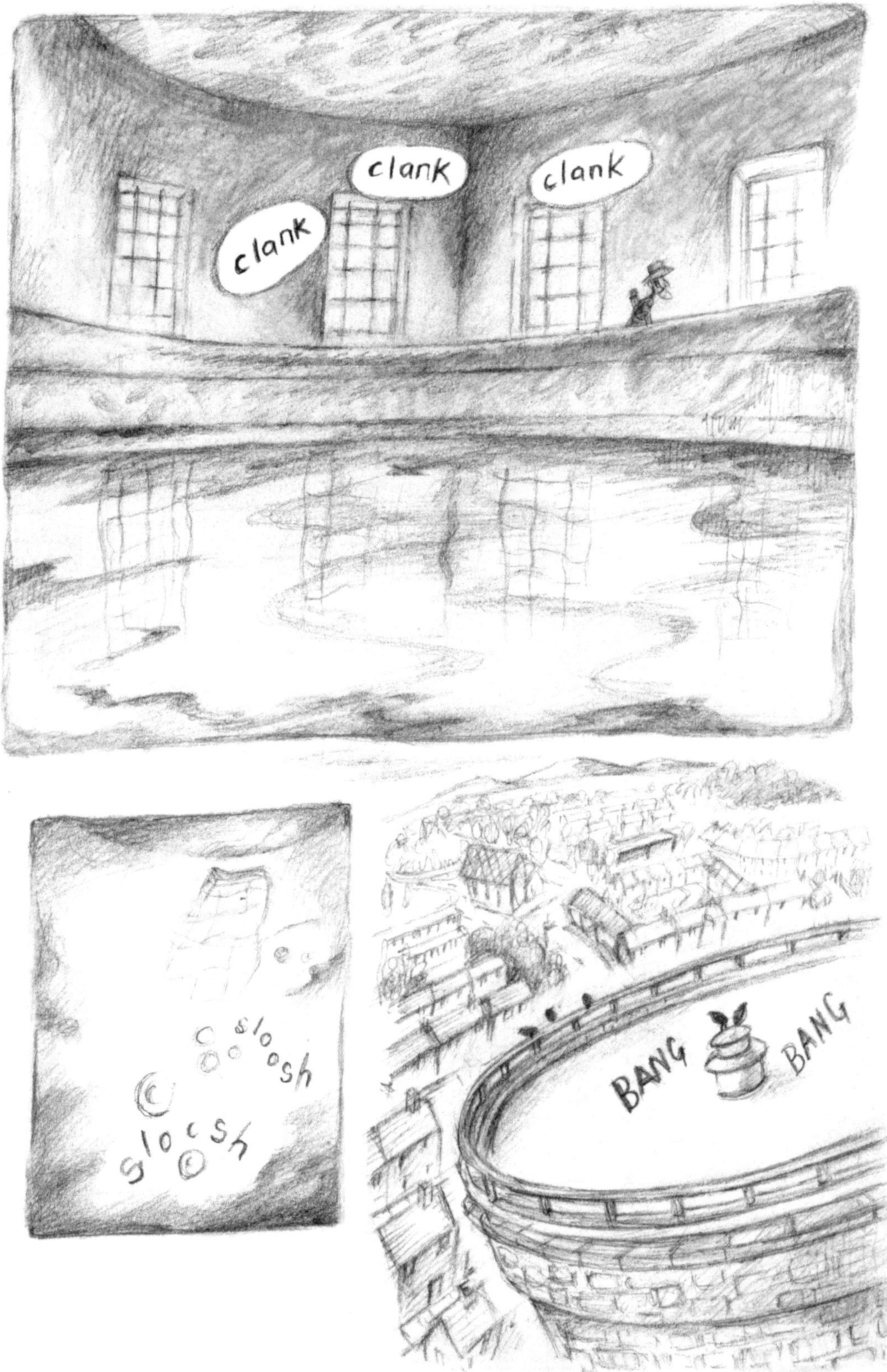
clank
clank
clank
sloosh
sloosh
BANG
BANG

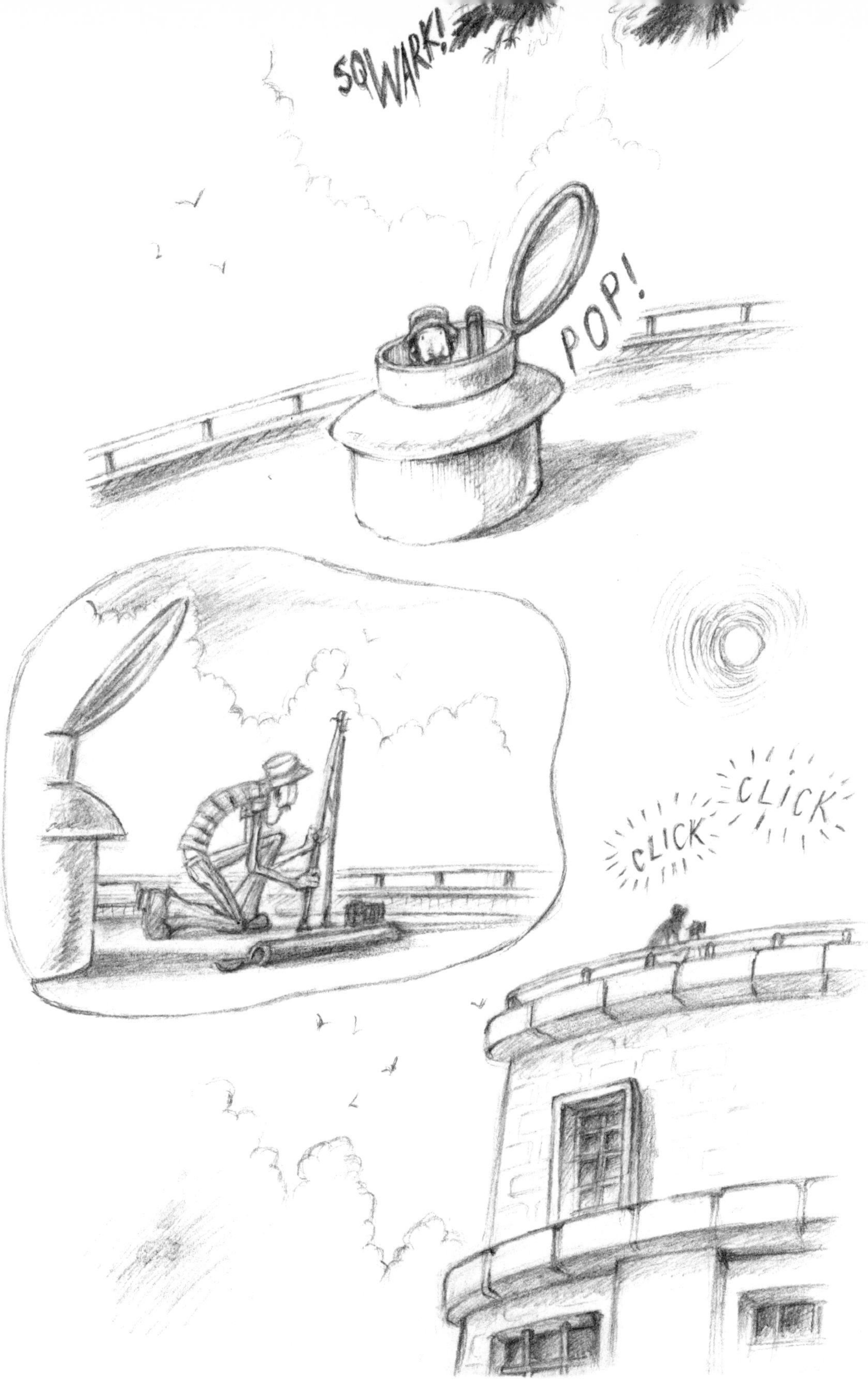
SQWARK!
POP!
CLICK
CLICK

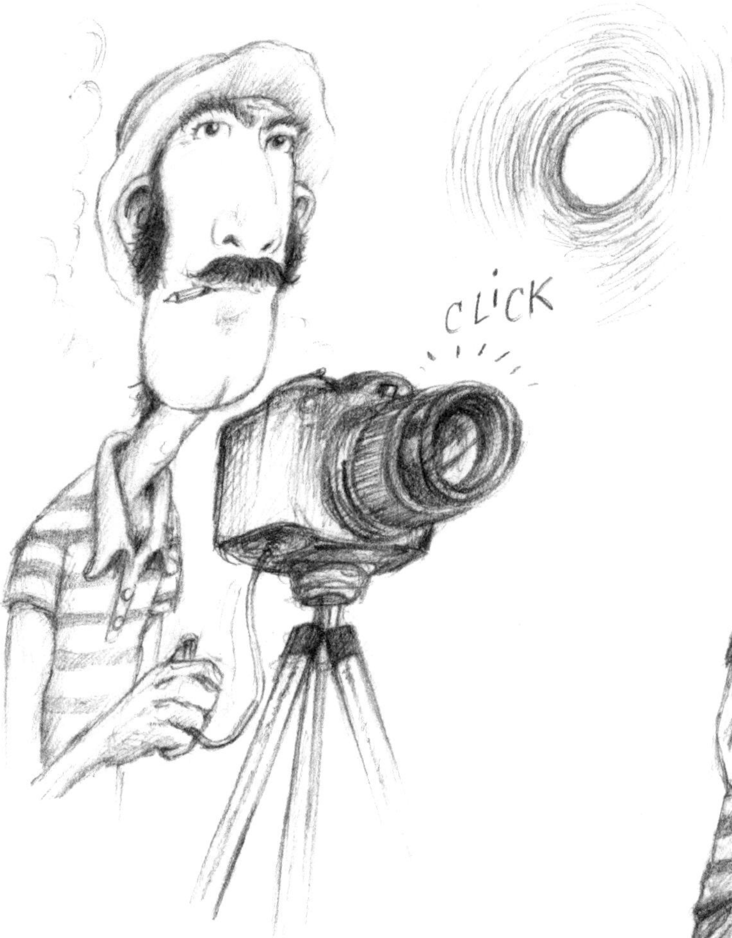
CLICK

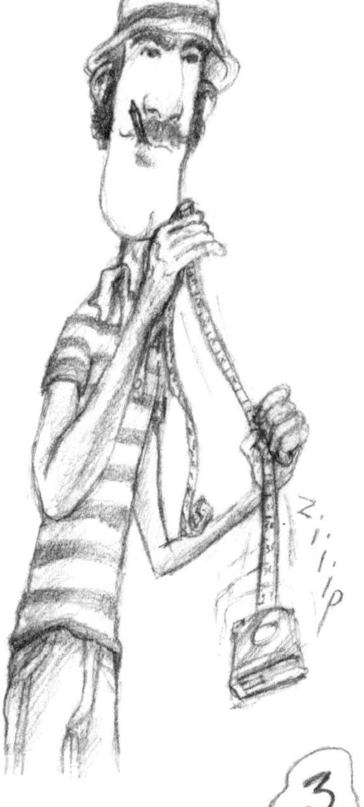
Ziiip

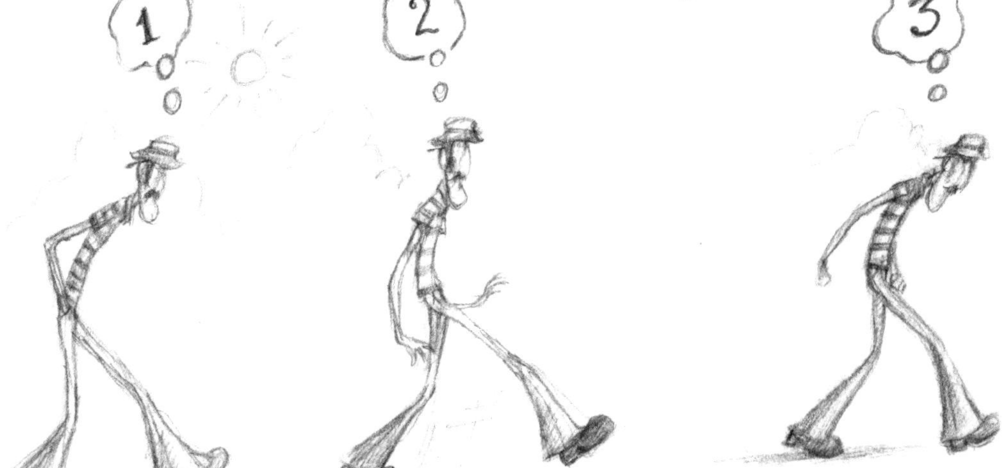
1
2
3

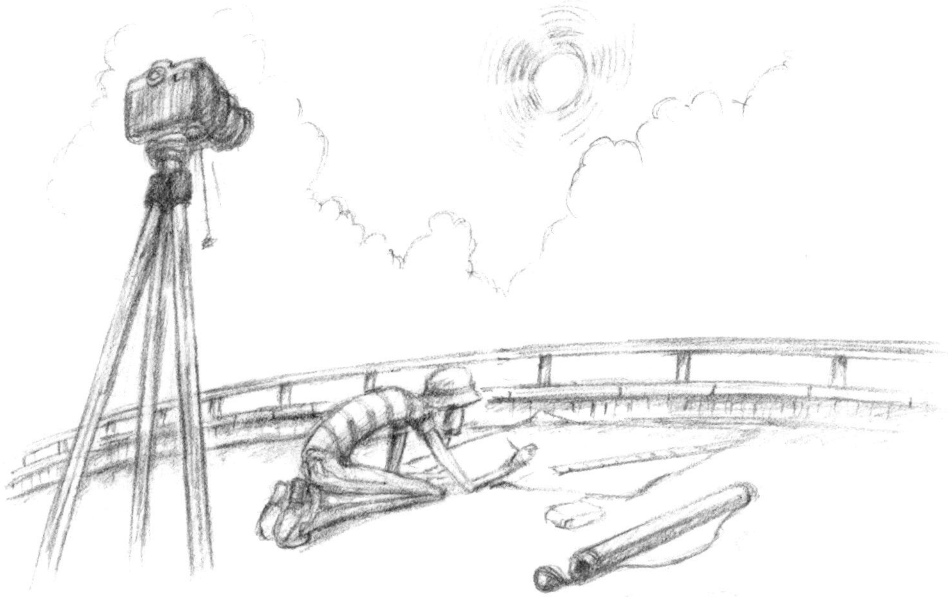

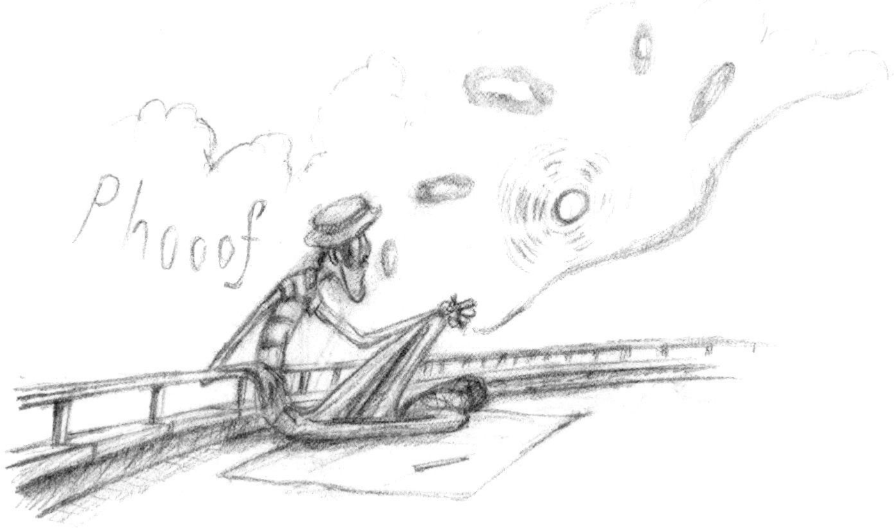
Phooof

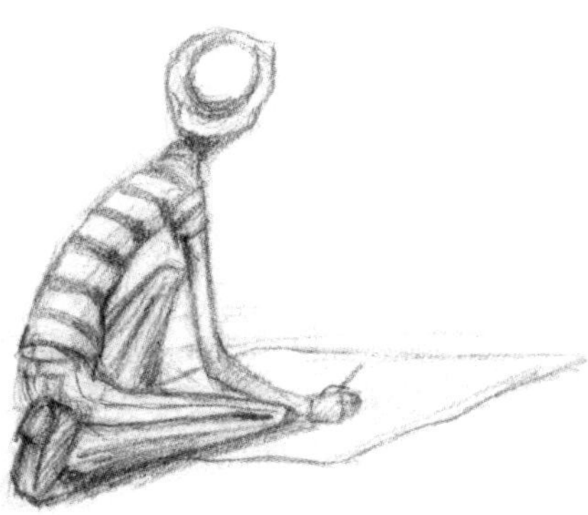

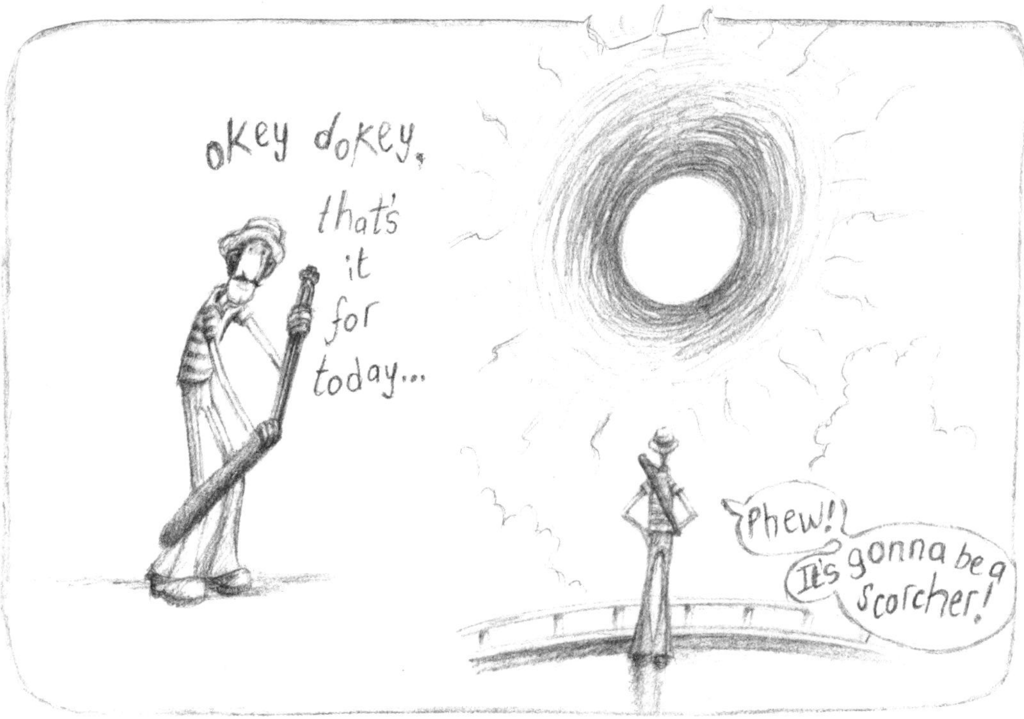
okey dokey.
that's it for today...
Phew!
It's gonna be a scorcher!

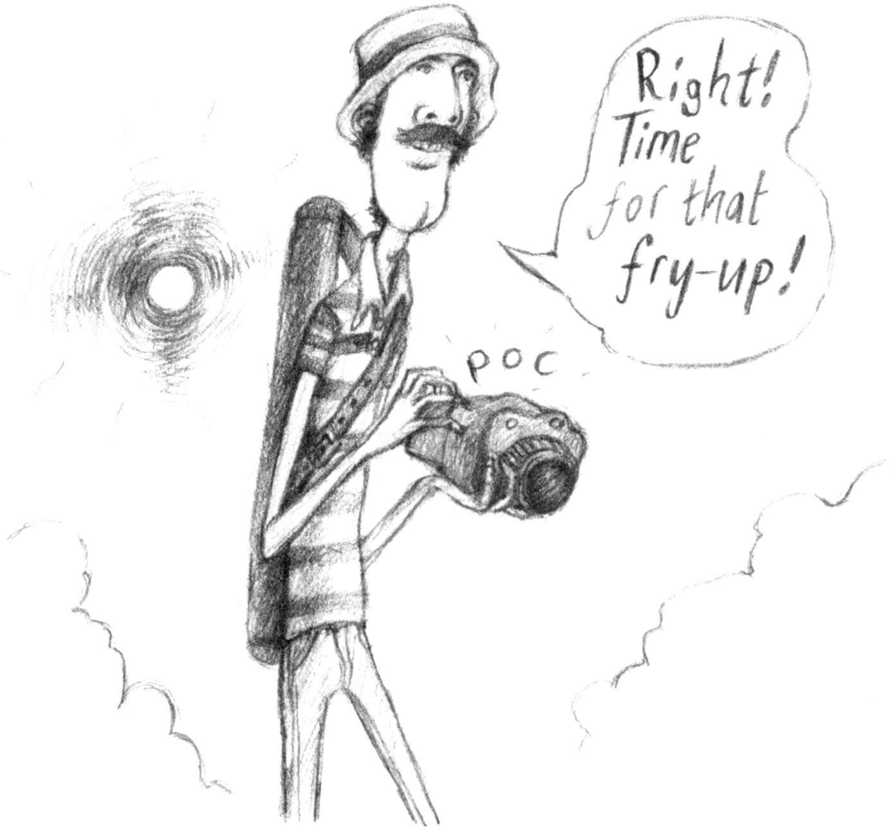
Right! Time for that fry-up!
POC

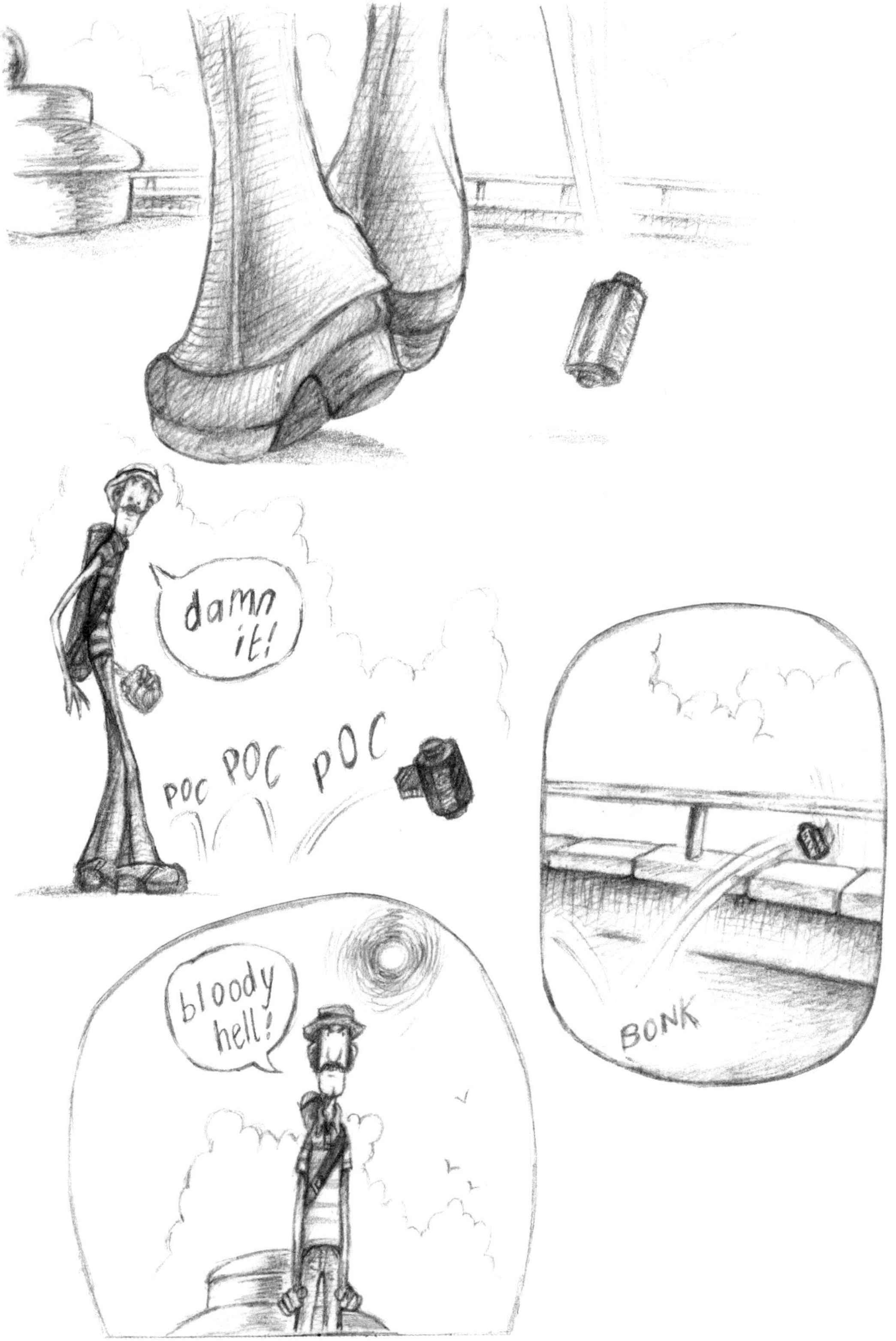
damn it!
POC POC POC
BONK
bloody hell!

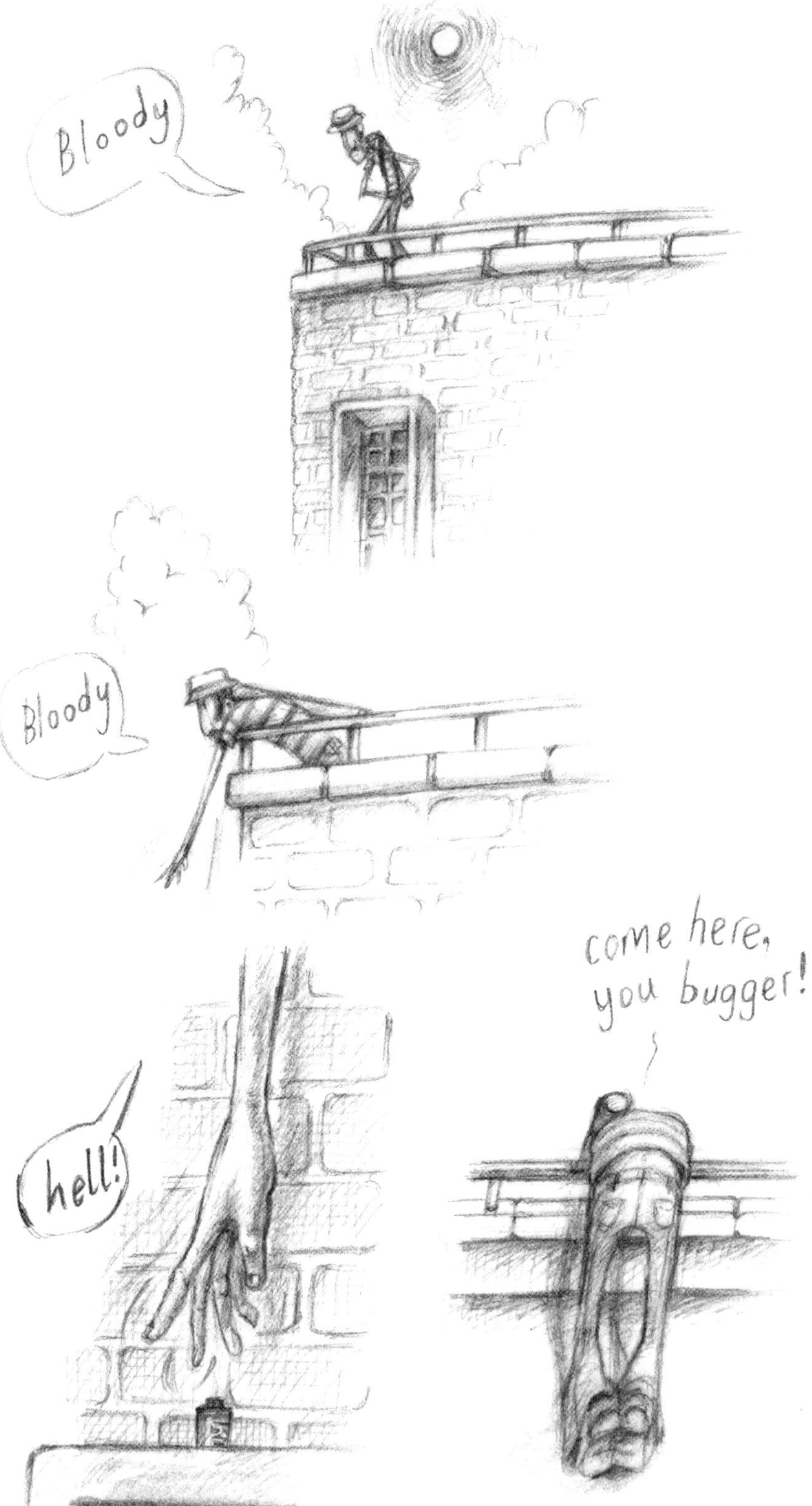
Bloody
Bloody
hell!
come here, you bugger!

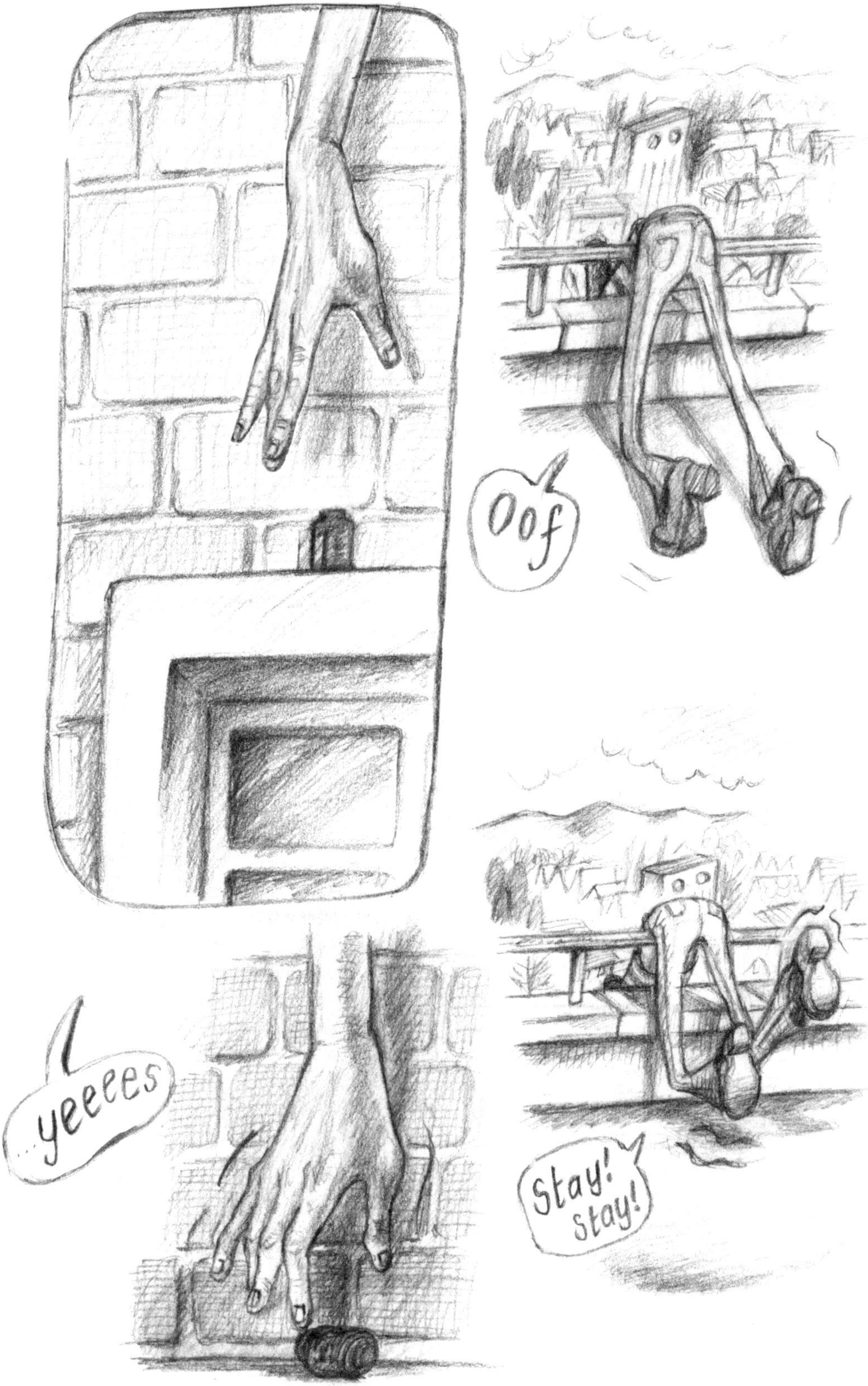
Oof
...yeeees
Stay! stay!

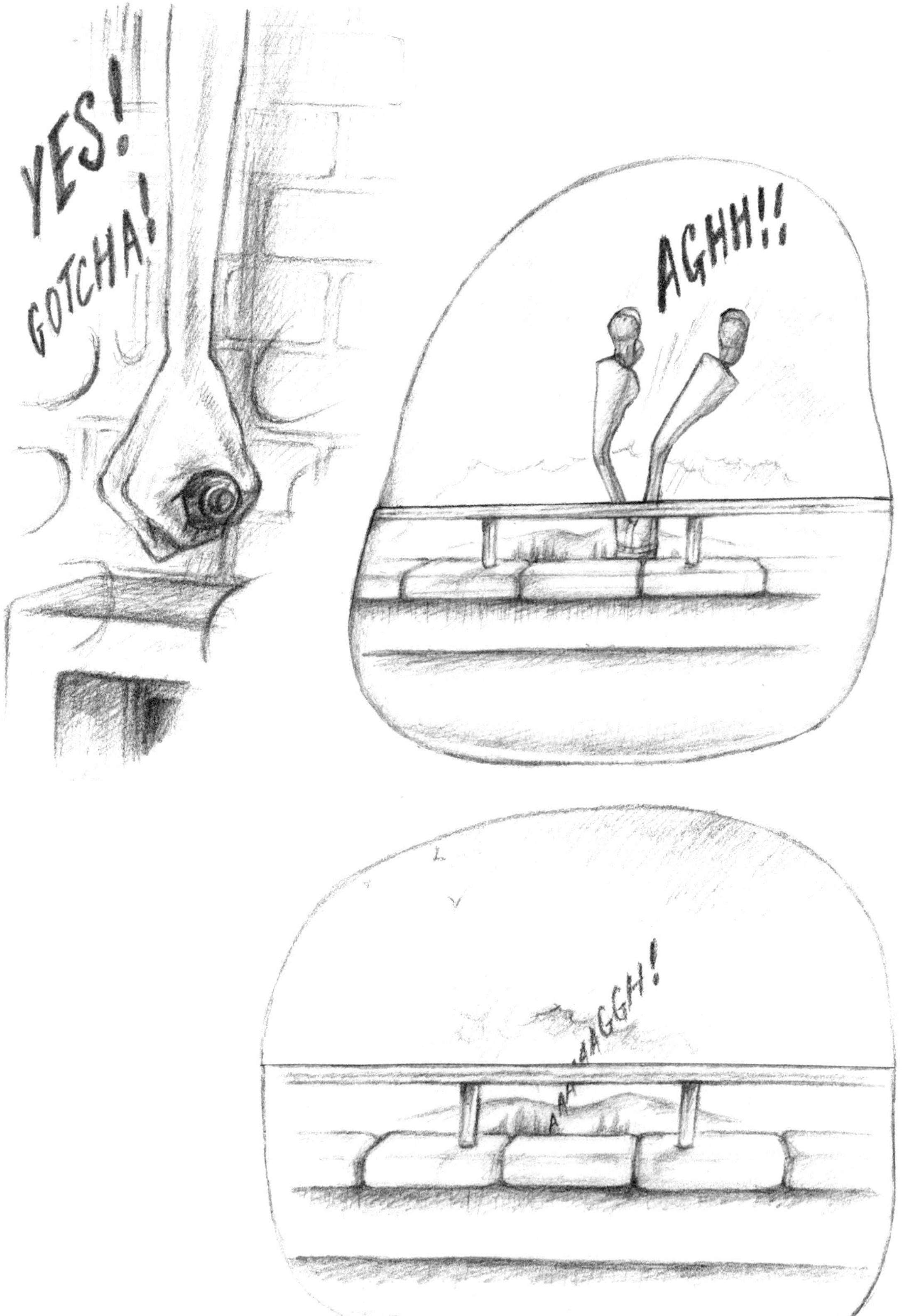
YES! GOTCHA!
AGHH!!
AAAAAGGH!

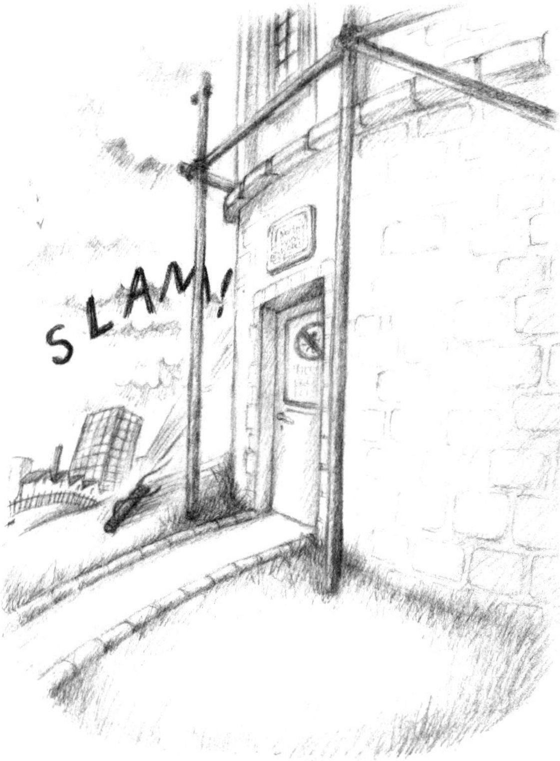
SLAM!

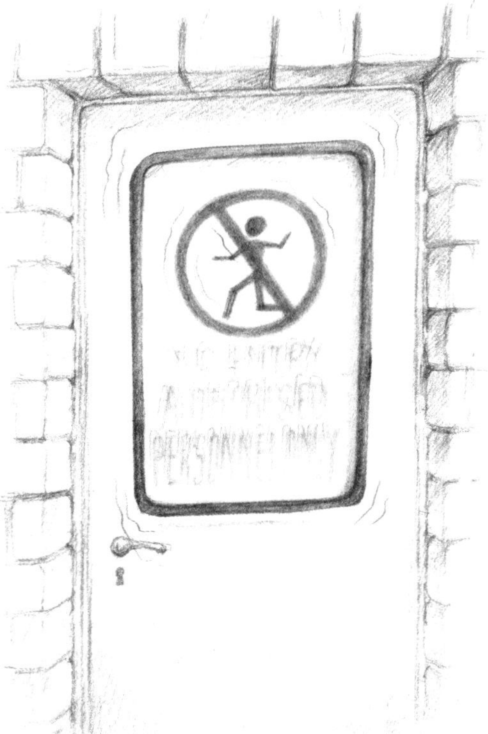

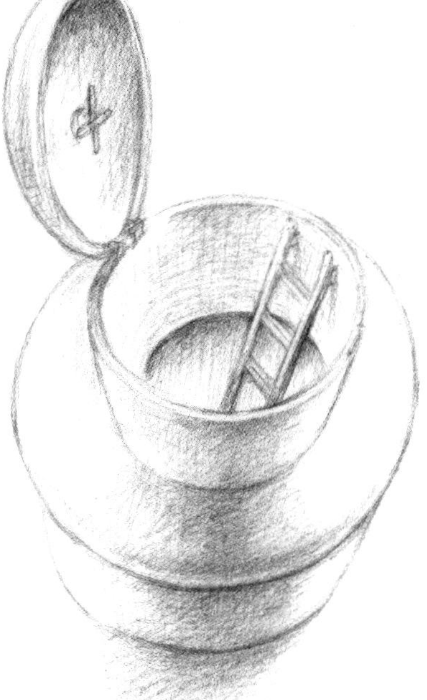

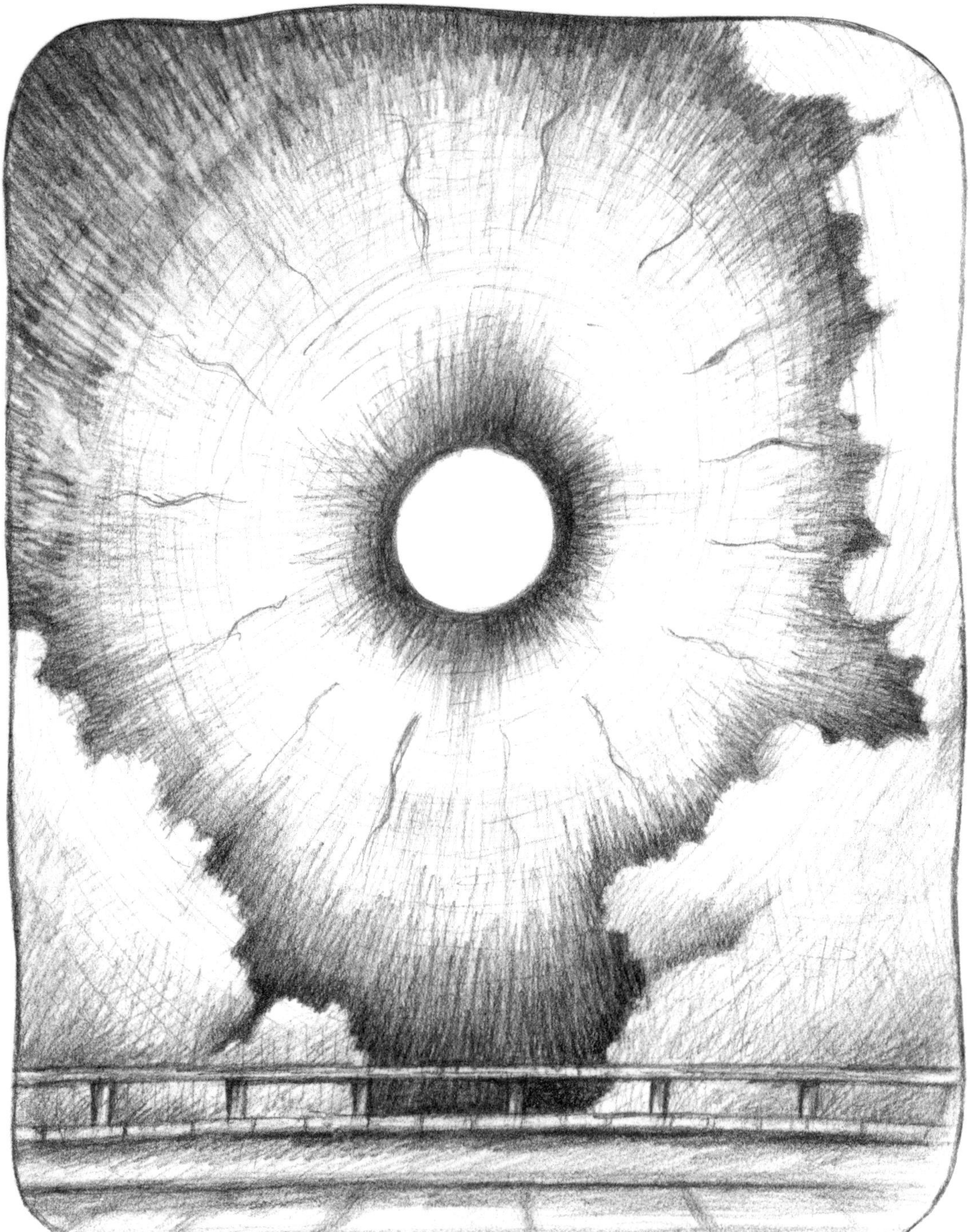

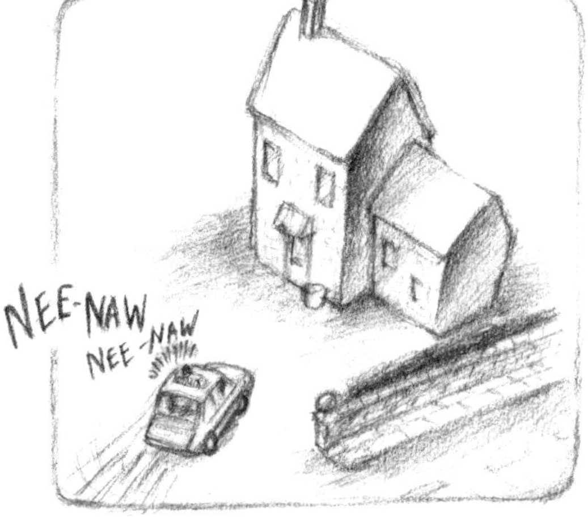
NEE-NAW
NEE-NAW

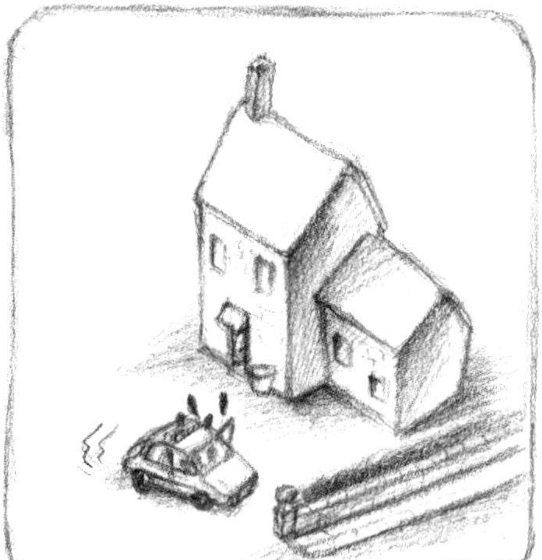

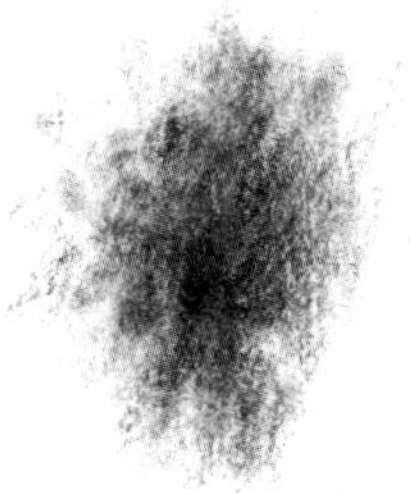

Chapter Three

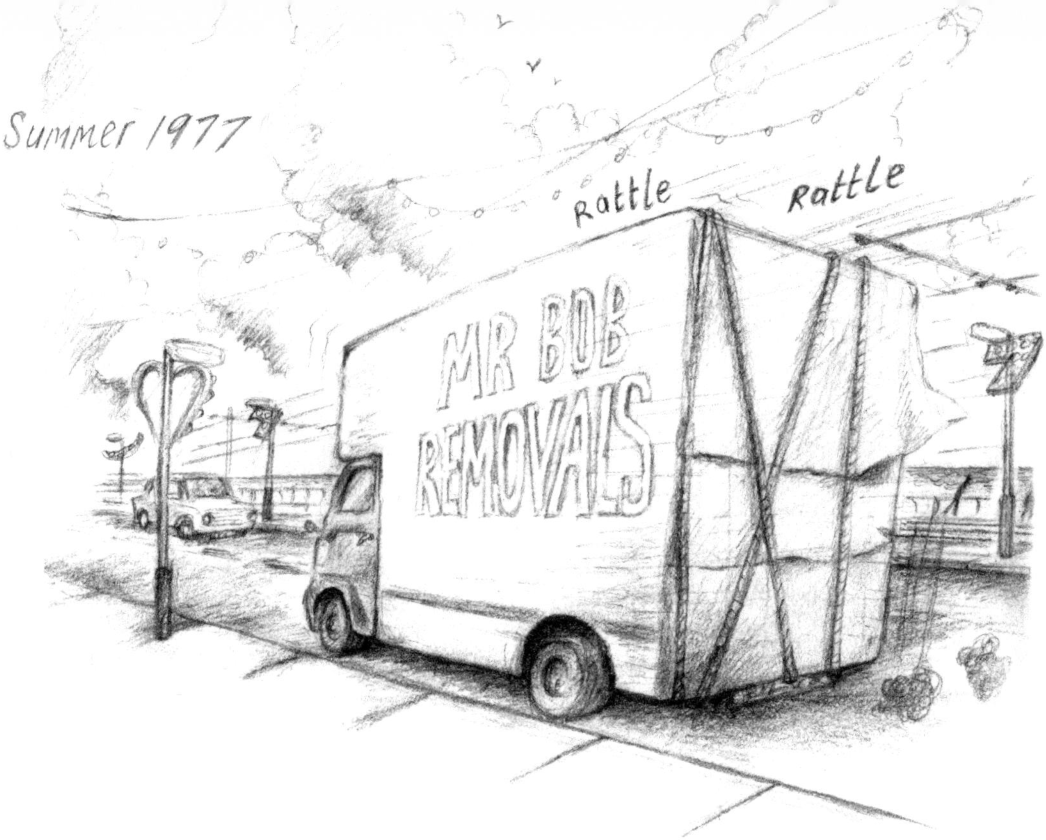
Summer 1977
Rattle
Rattle
MR BOB
REMOVALS

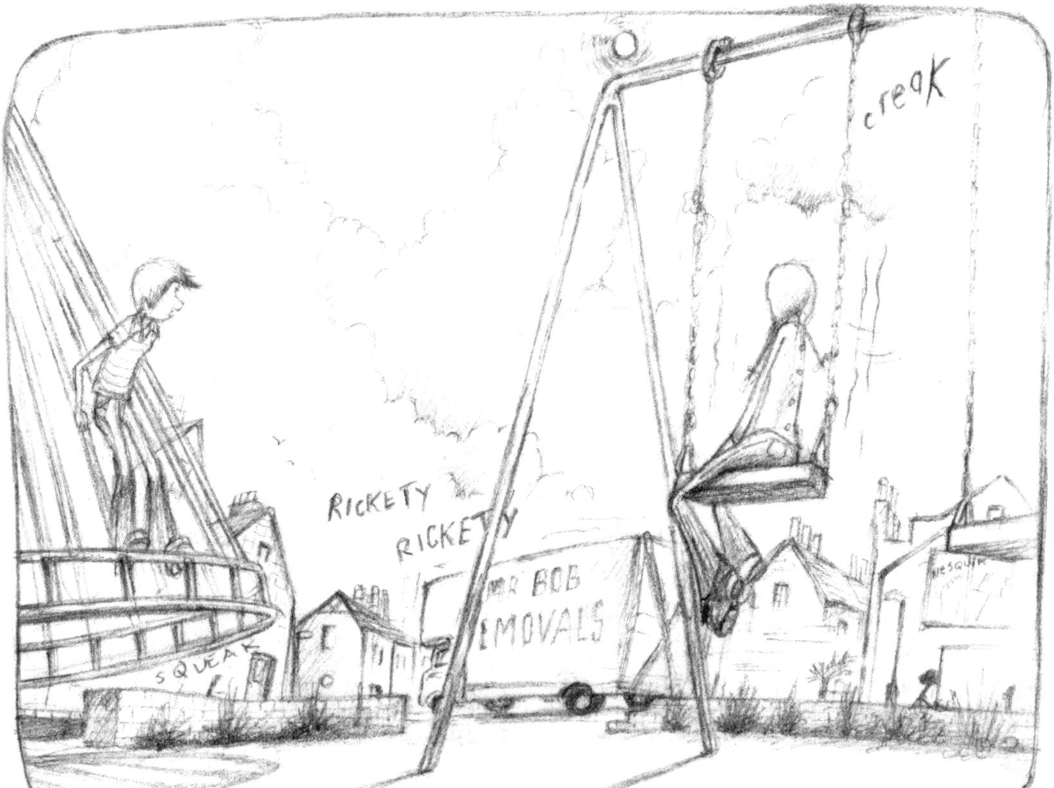
creak
RICKETY
RICKETY
MR BOB
EMOVALS
SQUEAK
NESQUIK

VROOOM

SHUDDER
16
SKREECH

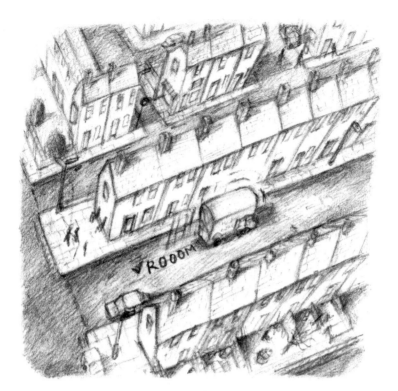

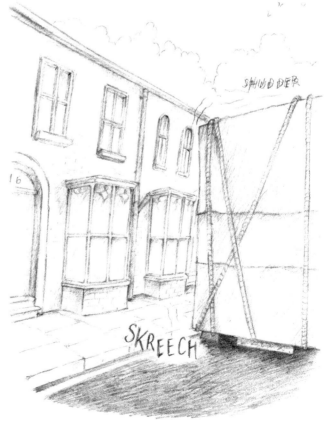

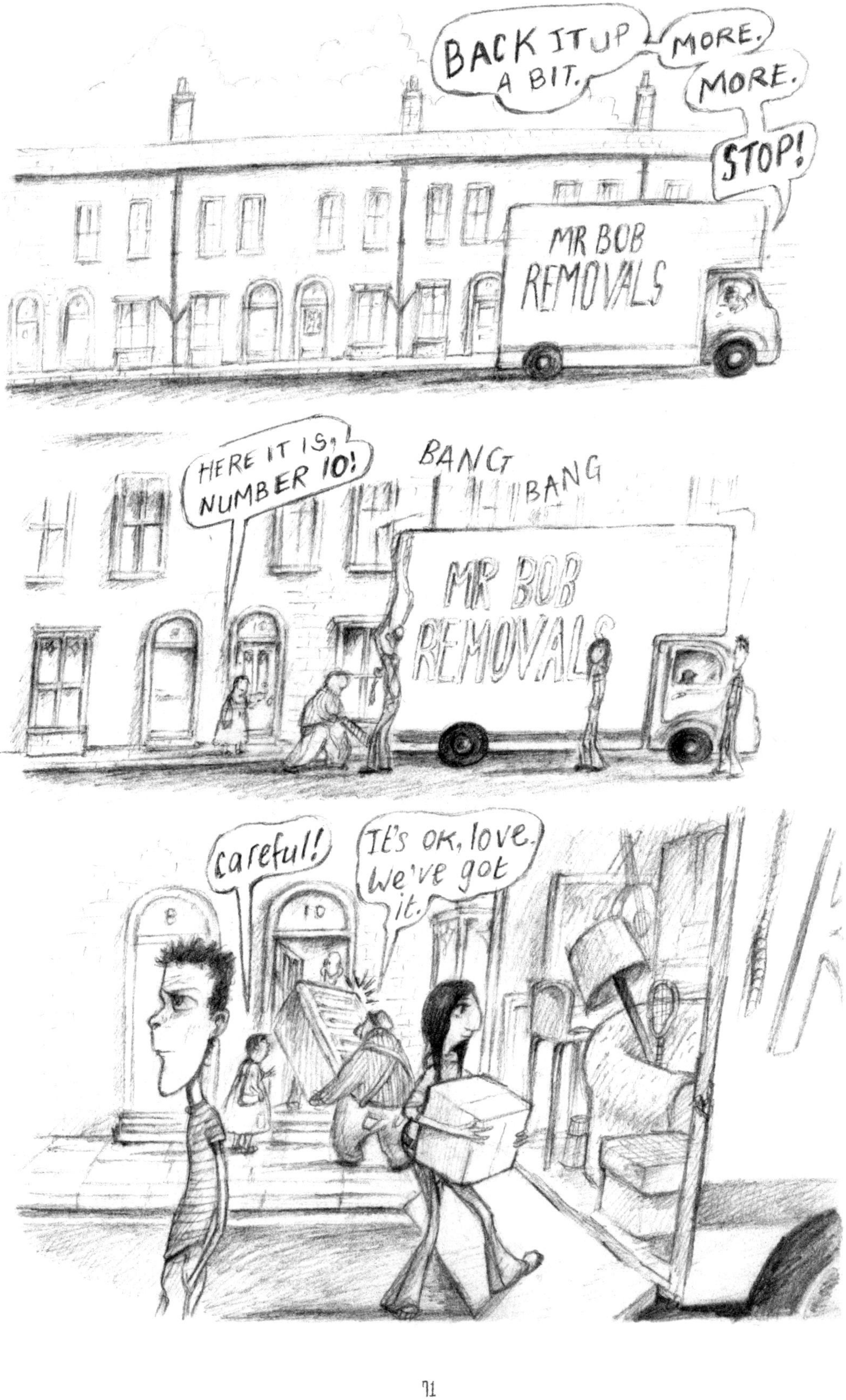
BACK IT UP A BIT.
MORE.
MORE.
STOP!
MR BOB REMOVALS
HERE IT IS, NUMBER 10!
BANG
BANG
MR BOB REMOVALS
careful!
It's OK, love. We've got it.

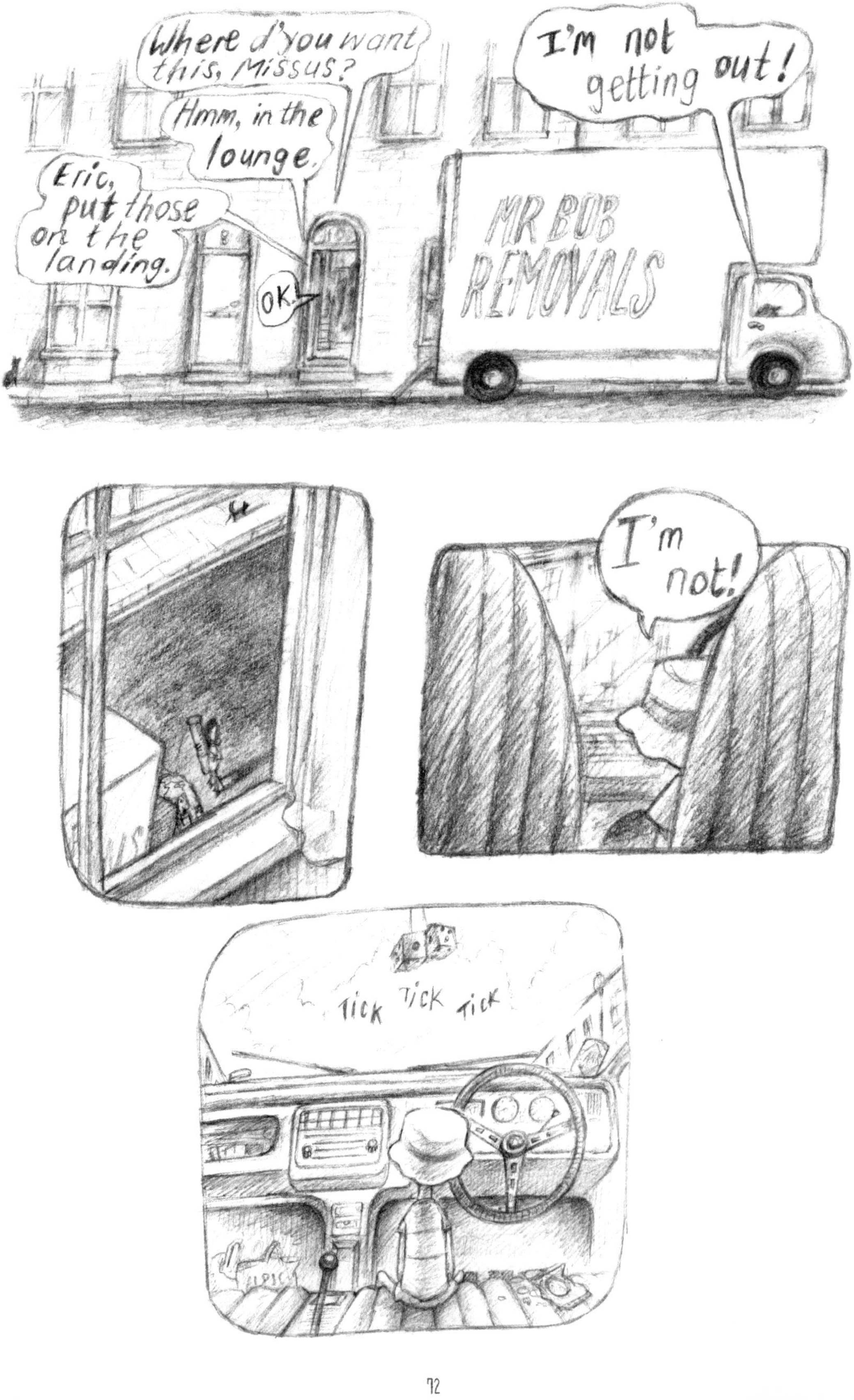
Where d'you want this, Missus?
Hmm, in the lounge.
Eric, put those on the landing.
OK!
MR BOB REMOVALS
I'm not getting out!
I'm not!
TICK TICK TICK

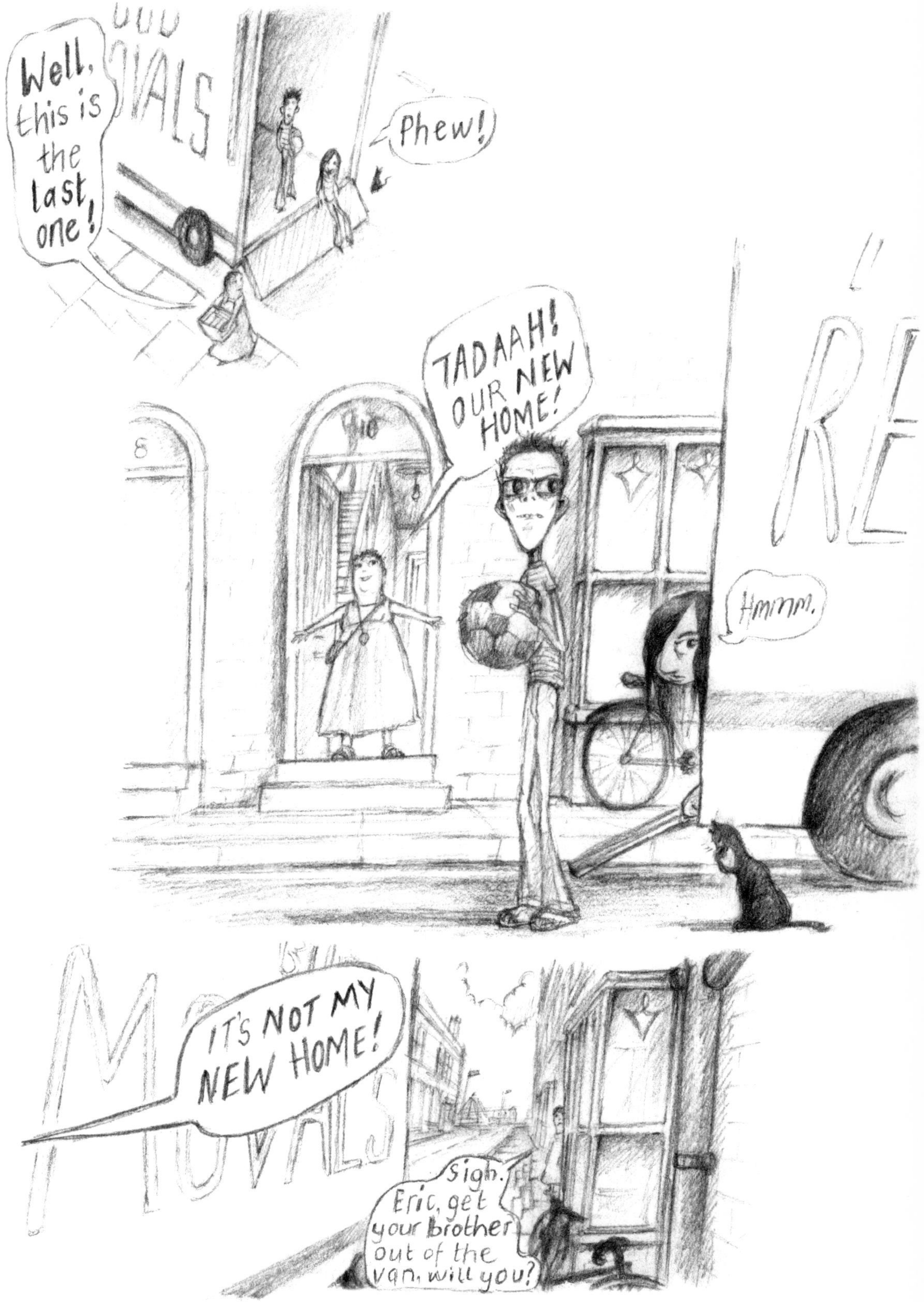
Well, this is the last one!
Phew!
TADAAH! OUR NEW HOME!
Hmmm.
IT'S NOT MY NEW HOME!
Sigh. Eric, get your brother out of the van, will you?

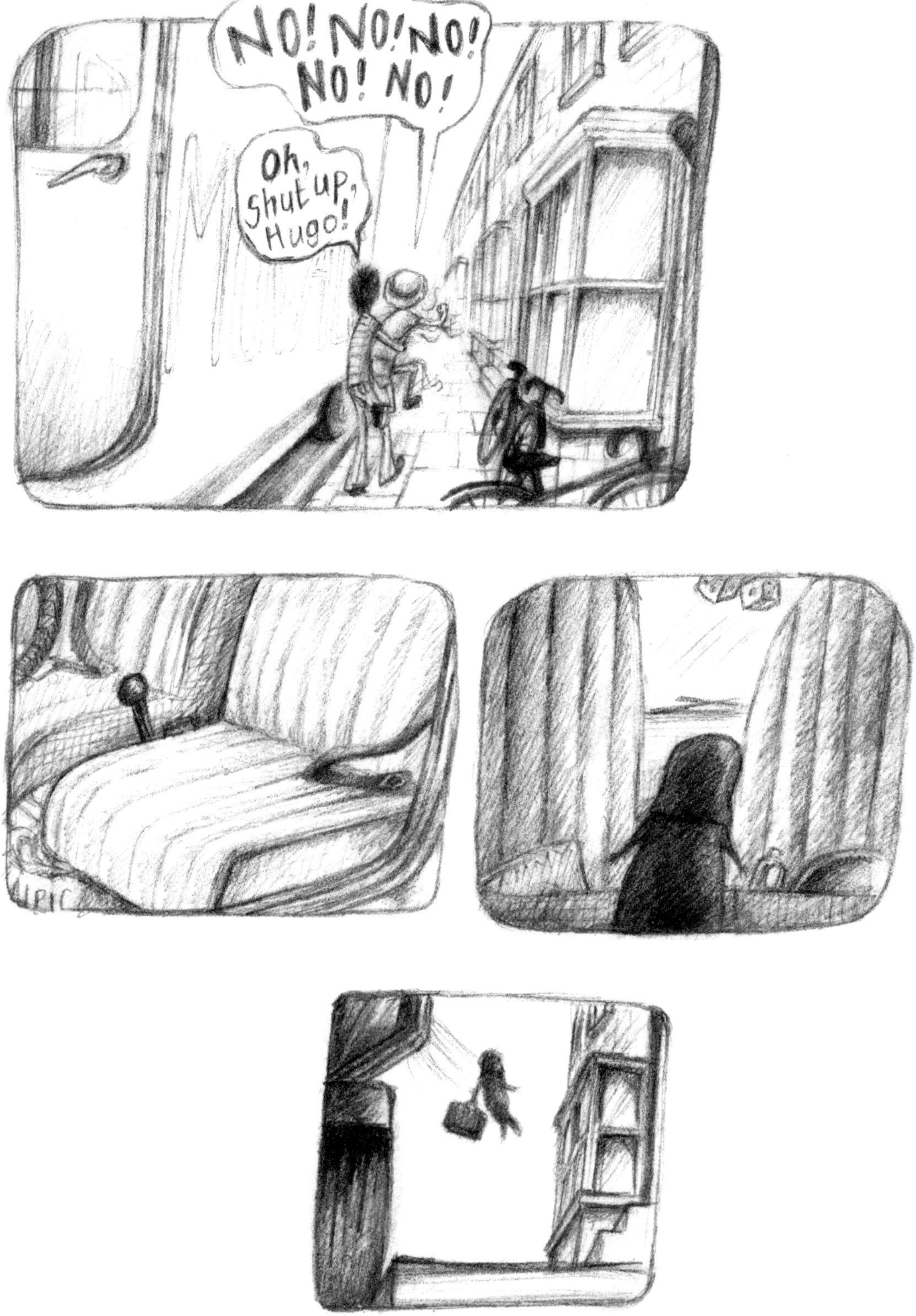
NO! NO! NO! NO! NO!
Oh, shut up, Hugo!

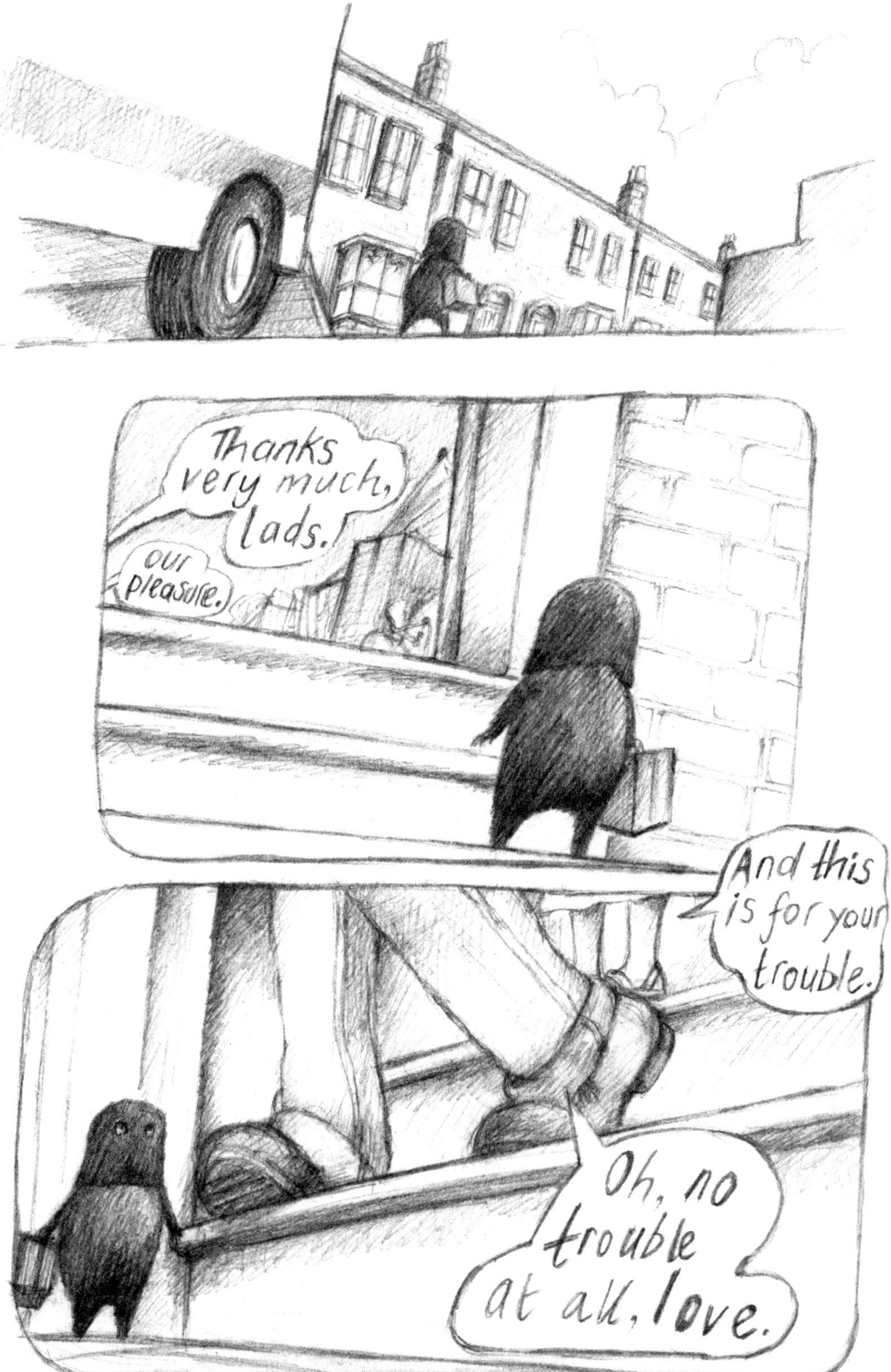
Thanks very much, lads.
Our pleasure.
And this is for your trouble.
Oh, no trouble at all, love.

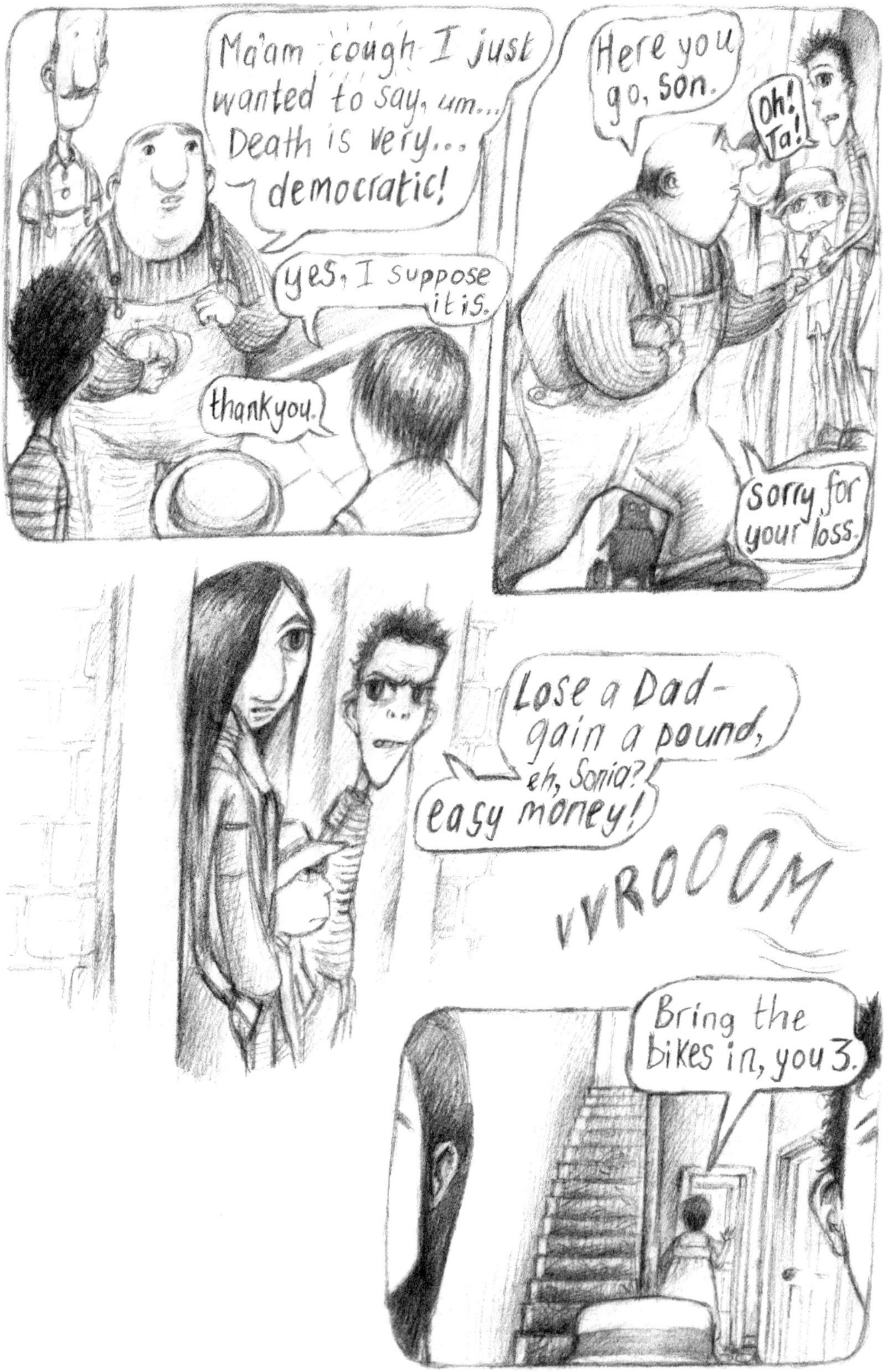

Ma'am cough I just wanted to say, um... Death is very... democratic!
yes, I suppose it is.
thankyou.
Here you go, son.
Oh! Ta!
Sorry for your loss.
Lose a Dad- gain a pound, eh, Sonia?
easy money!
VVROOOOM
Bring the bikes in, you 3.

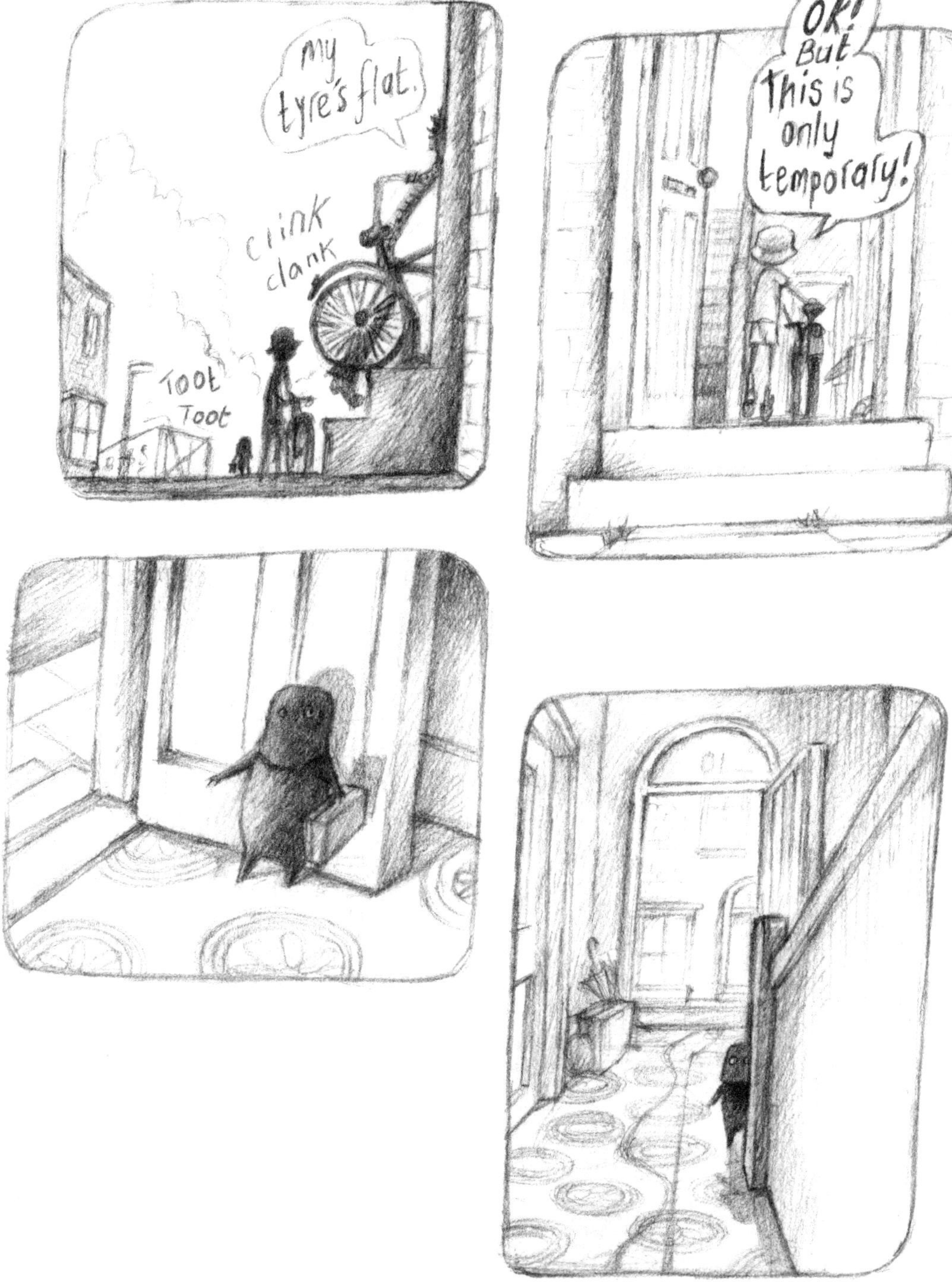
My tyre's flat.
clink clank
Toot Toot
OK! But This is only temporary!

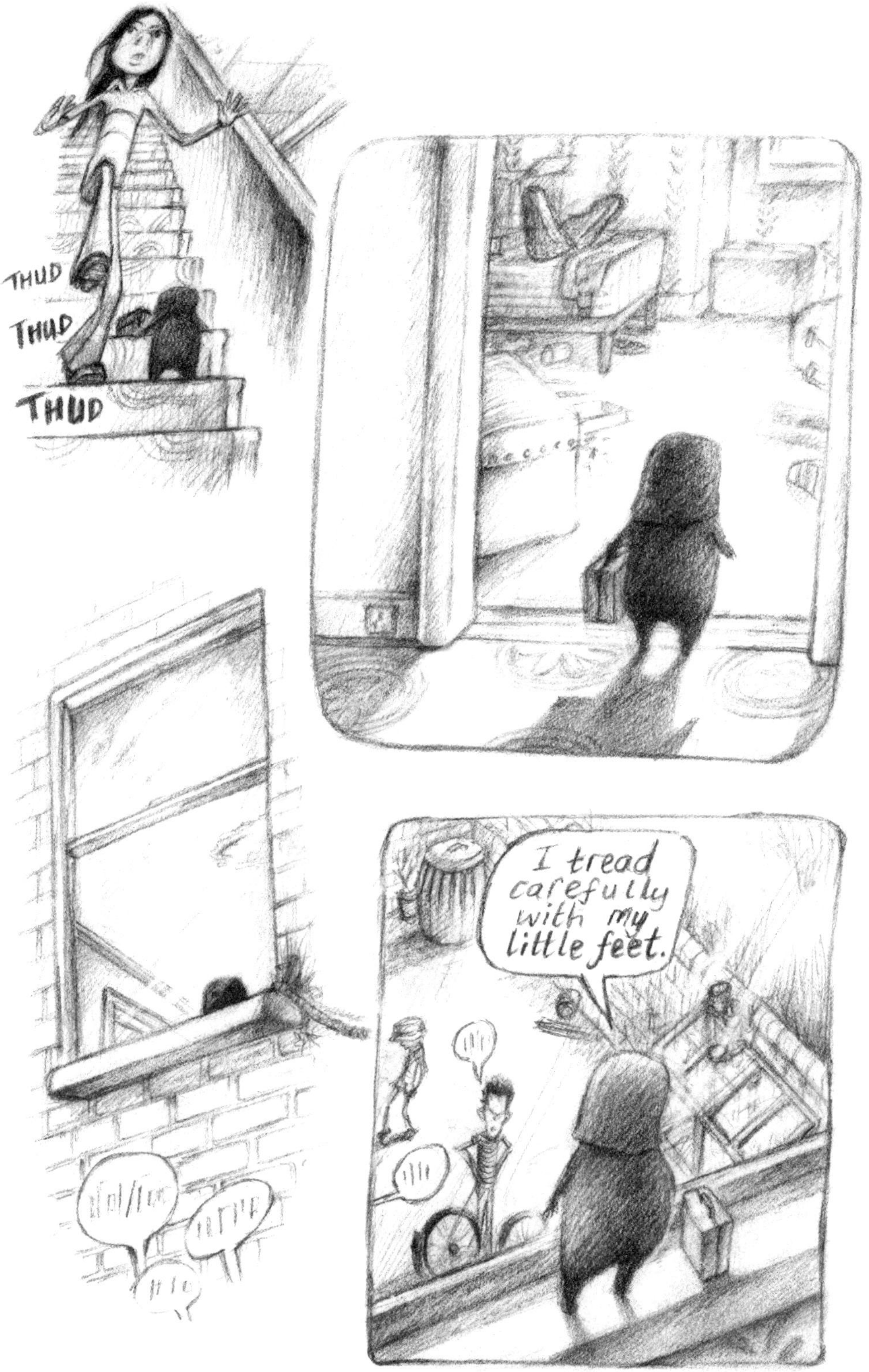
THUD
THUD
THUD
I tread carefully with my little feet.

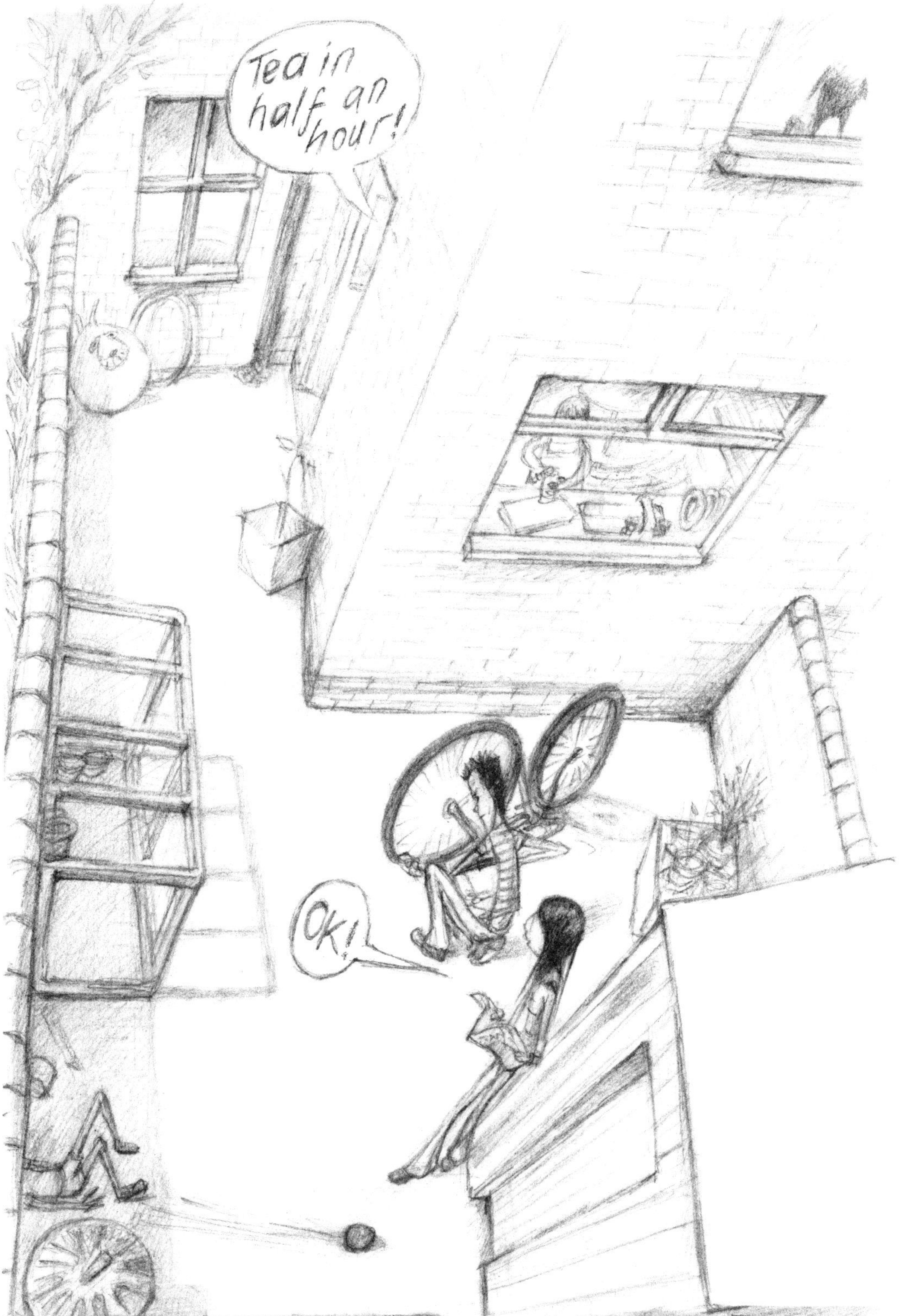
Tea in half an hour!
OK!

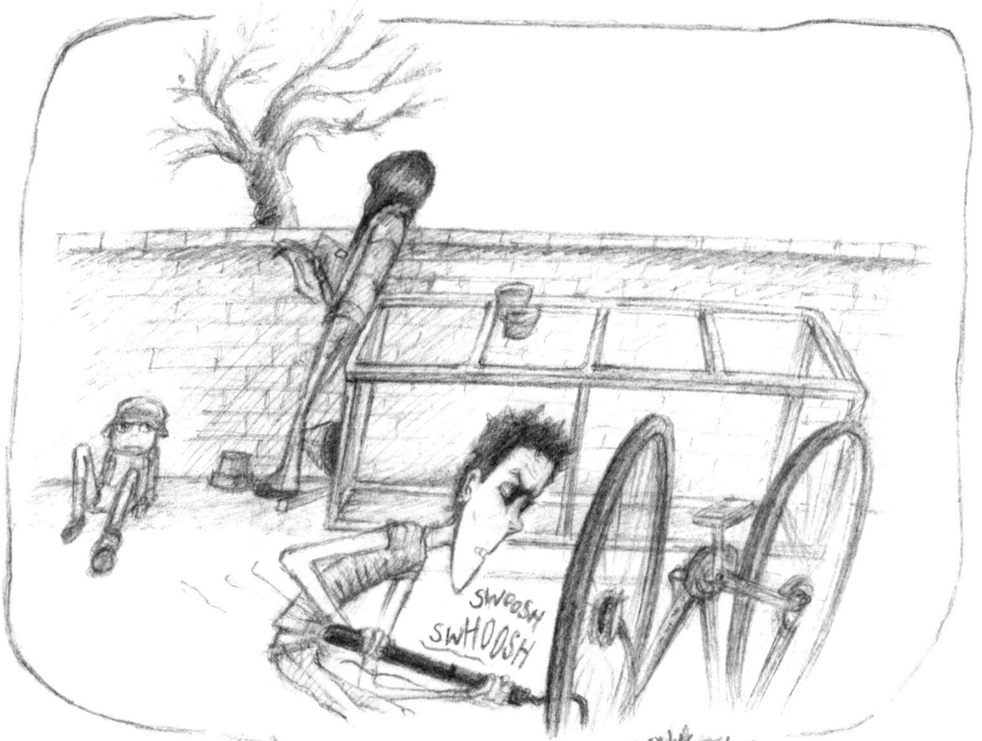
SWOOSH
SWHOOSH

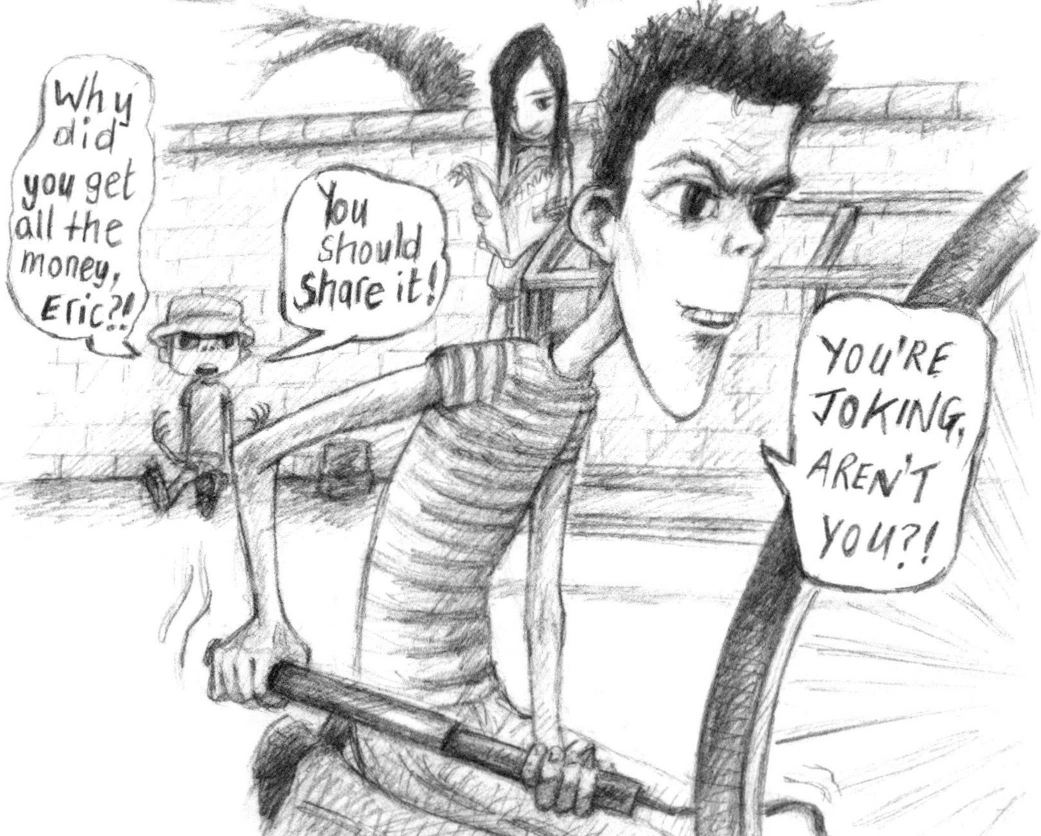
Why did you get all the money, Eric?!
You should share it!
YOU'RE JOKING, AREN'T YOU?!

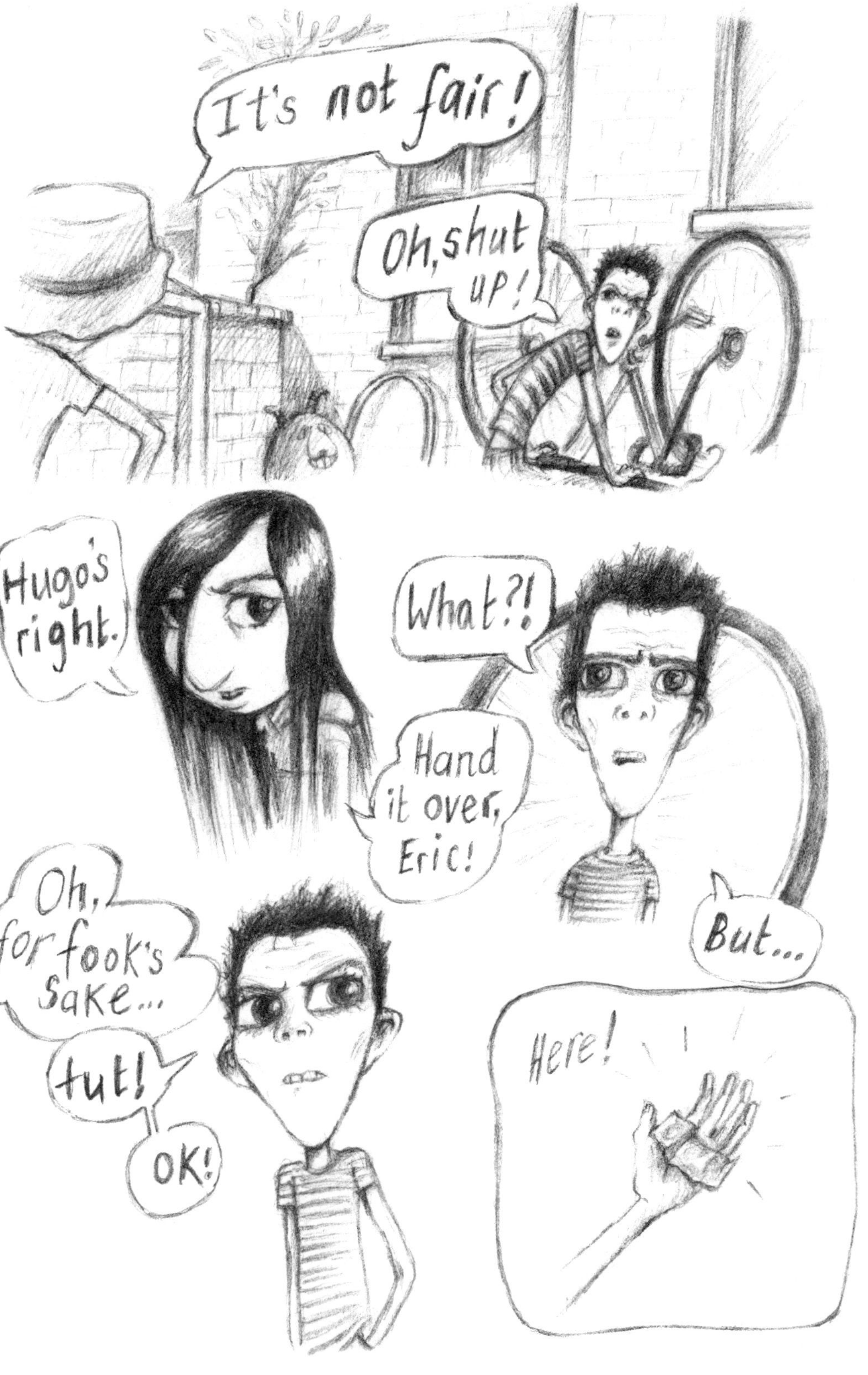

It's not fair!
Oh, shut up!
Hugo's right.
What?!
Hand it over, Eric!
But...
Oh, for fook's sake...
tut!
OK!
Here!

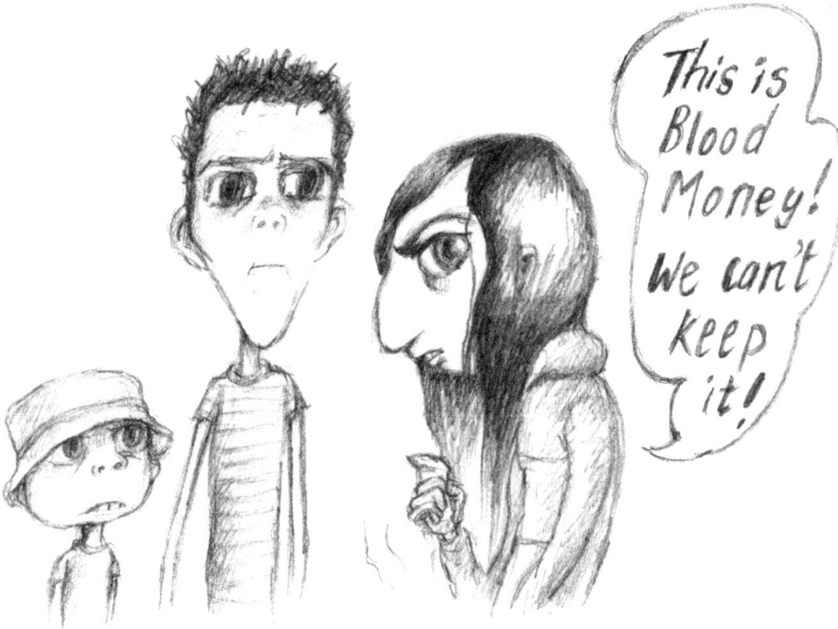
This is Blood Money! We can't keep it!

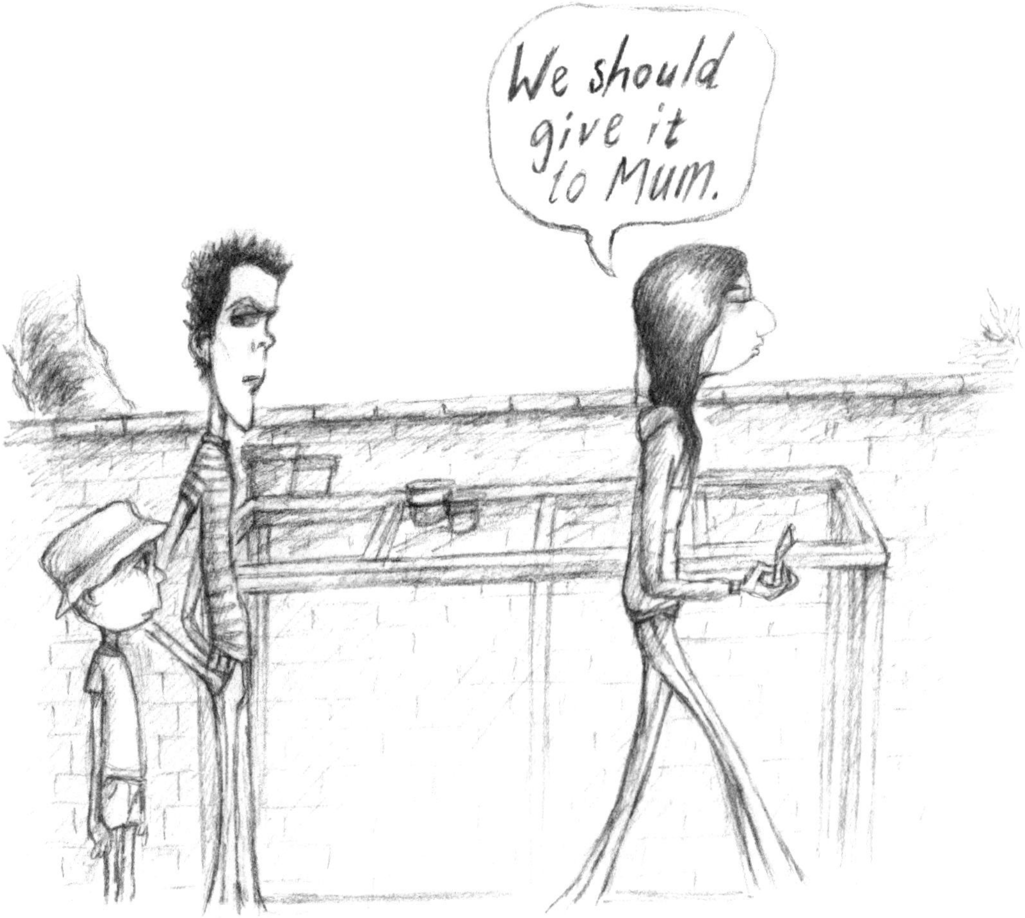
We should give it to Mum.

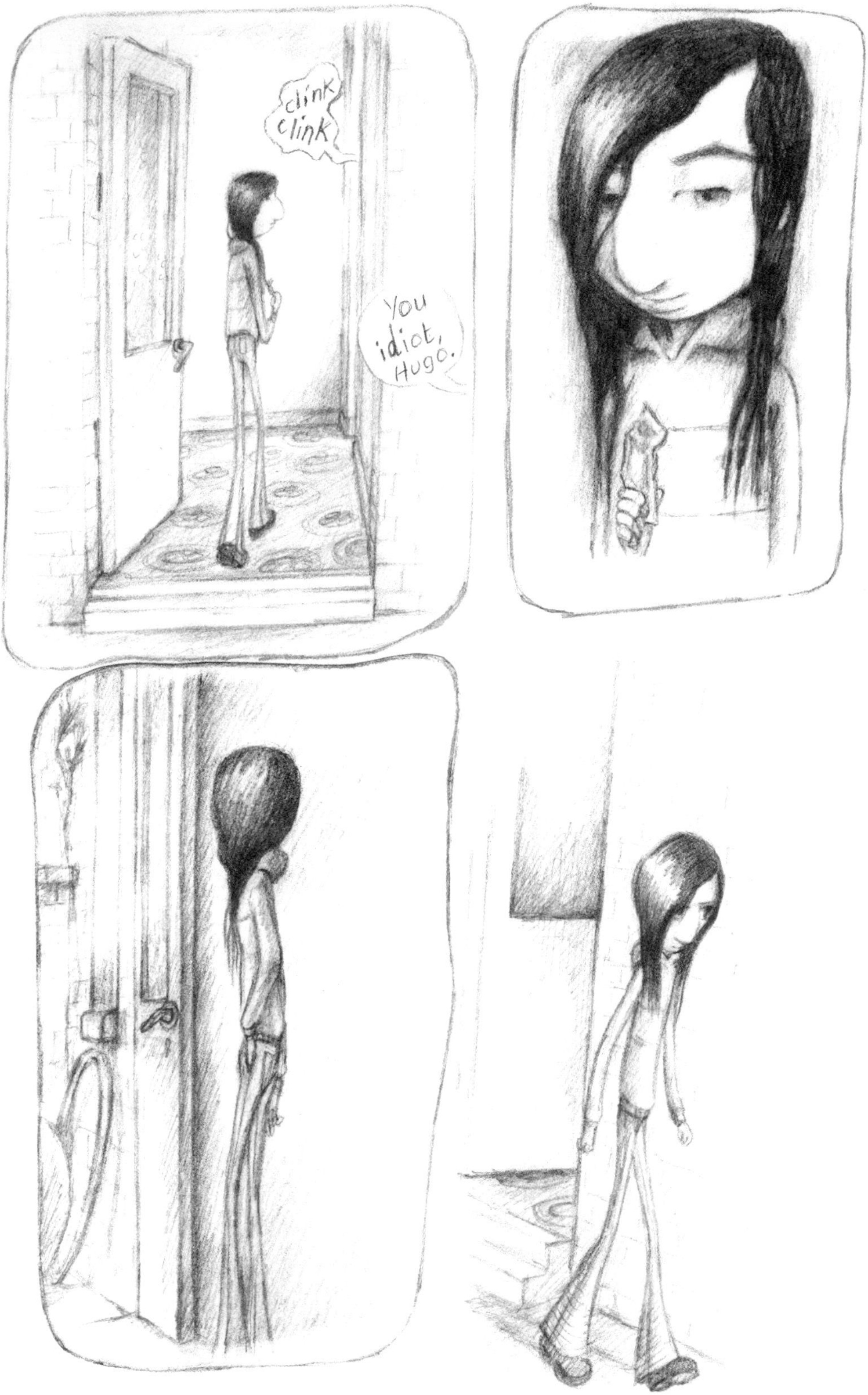
clink clink
You idiot, Hugo.

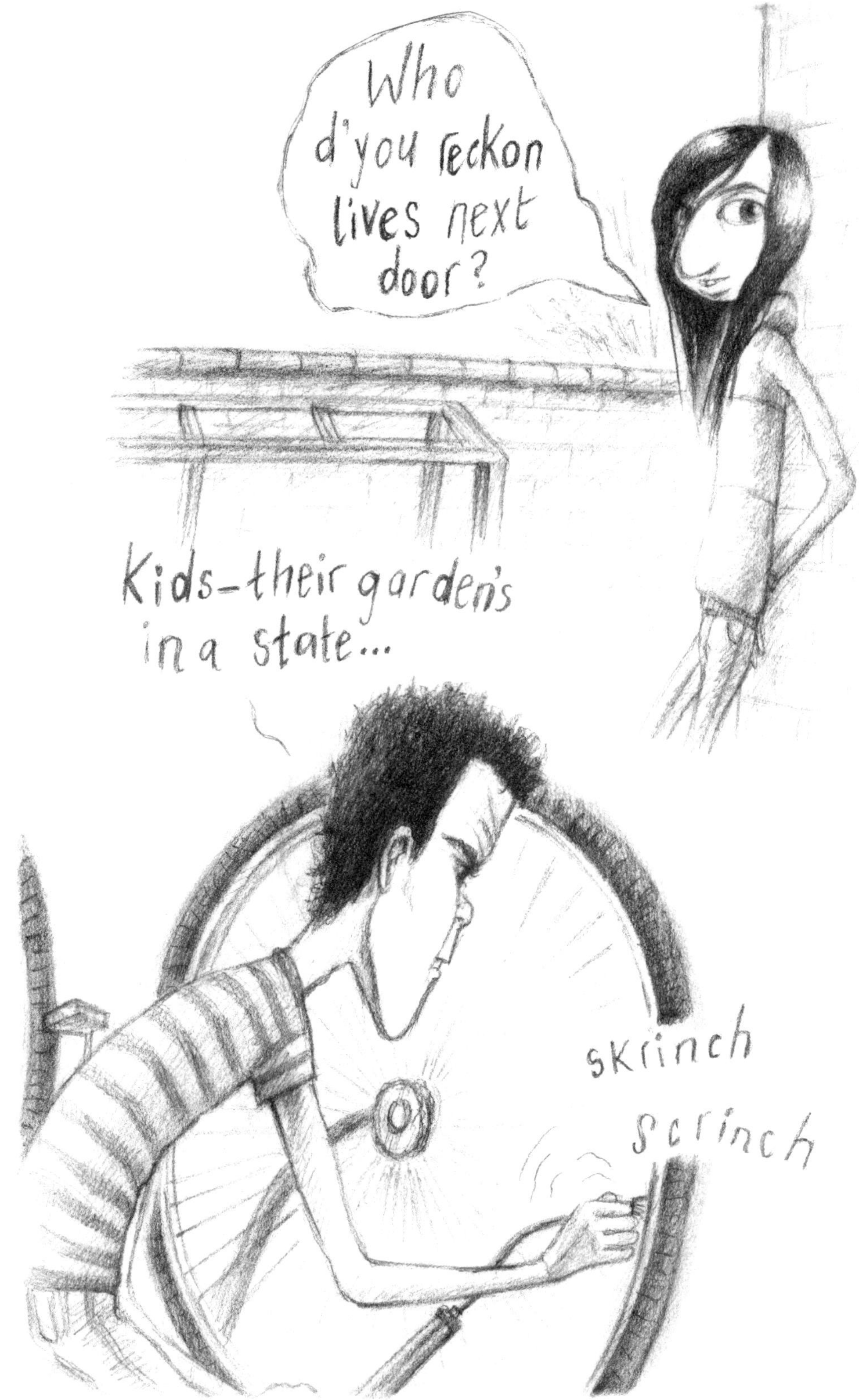
Who d'you reckon lives next door?
Kids–their garden's in a state...
skrinch
scrinch

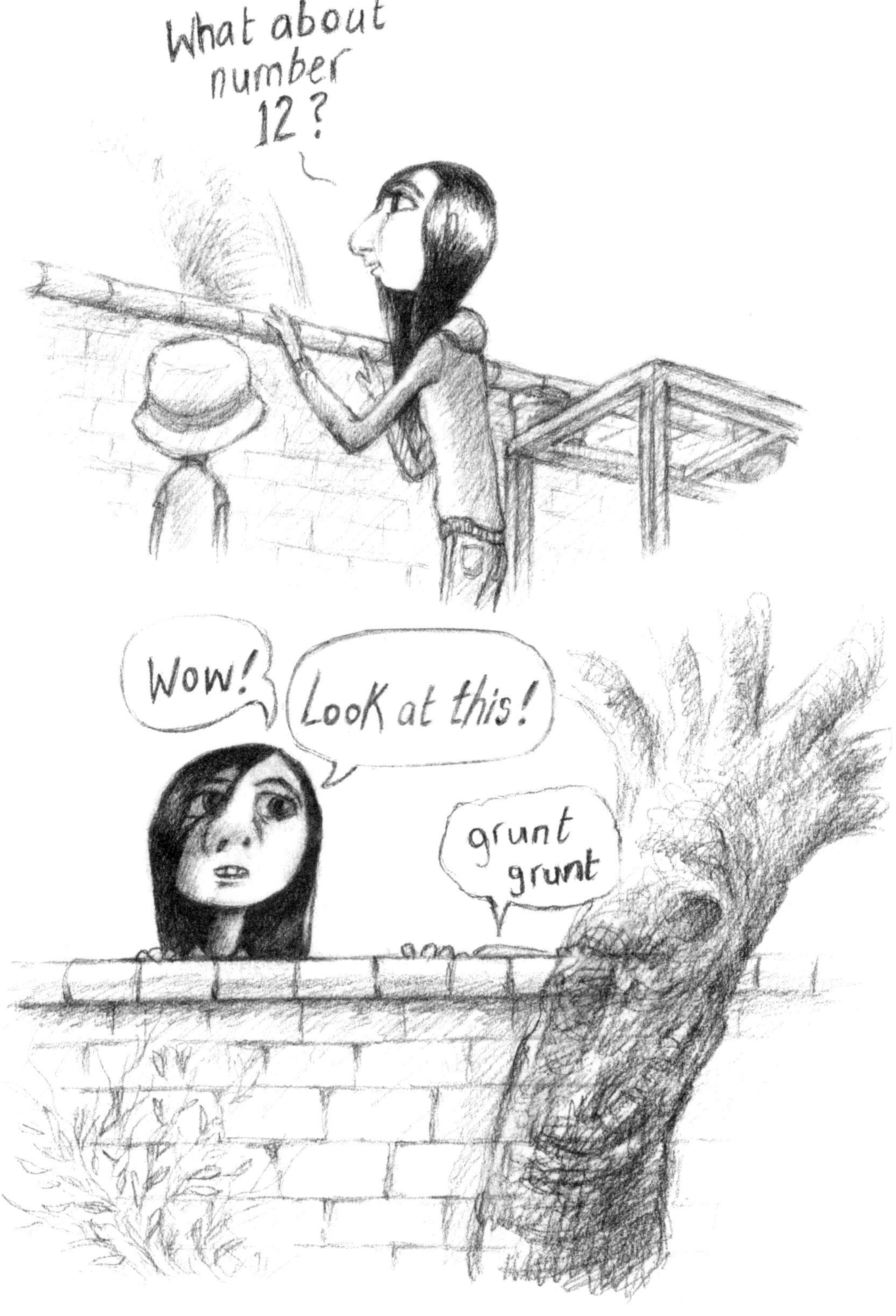
What about number 12?
Wow!
Look at this!
grunt grunt

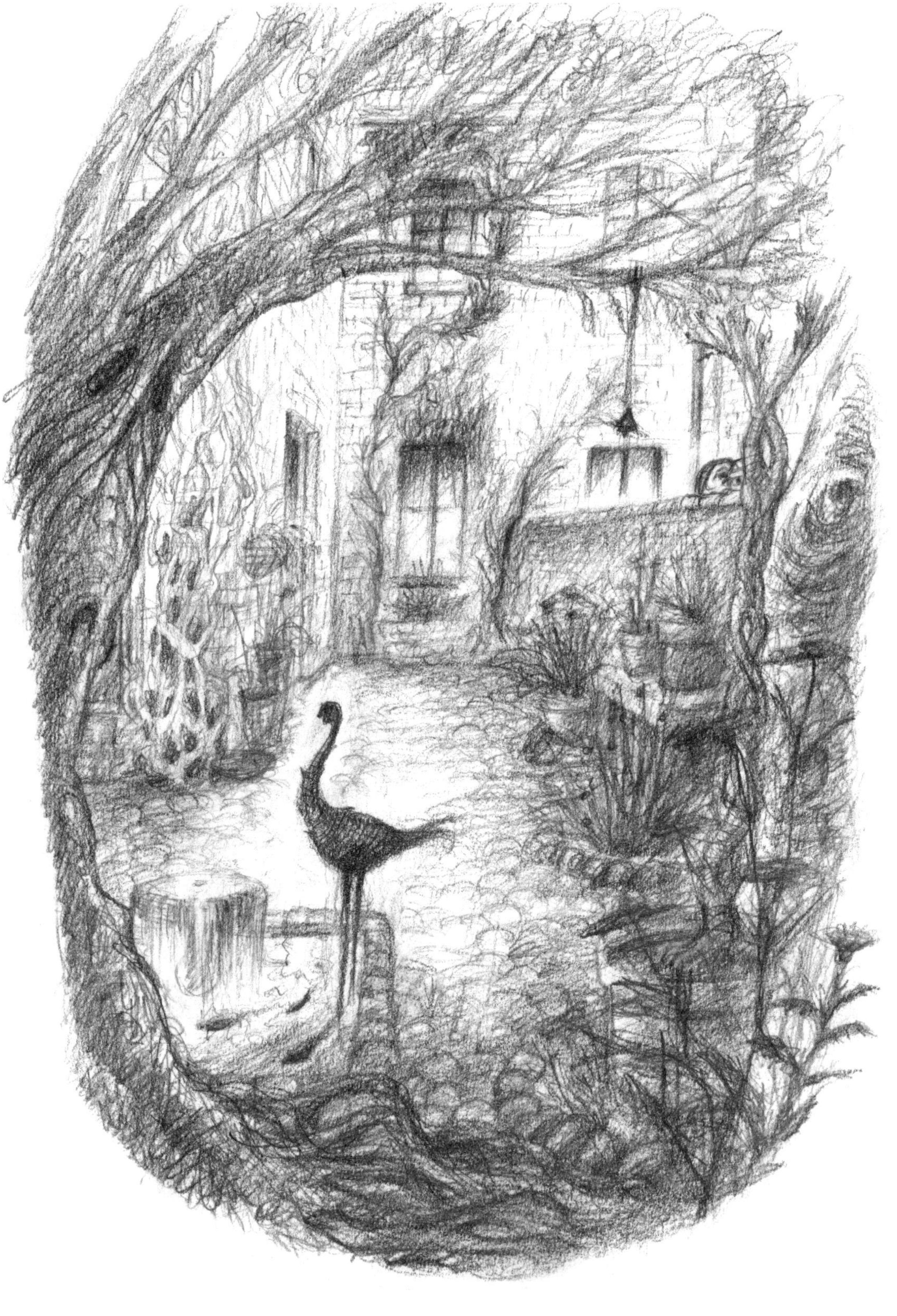

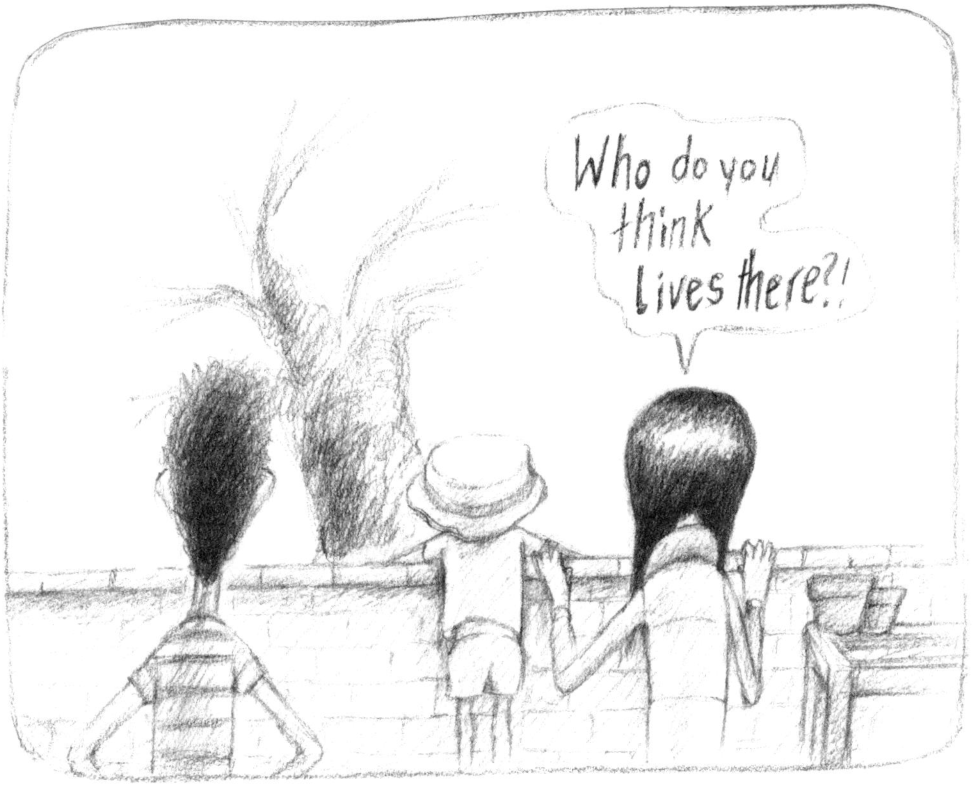
Who do you think Lives there?!

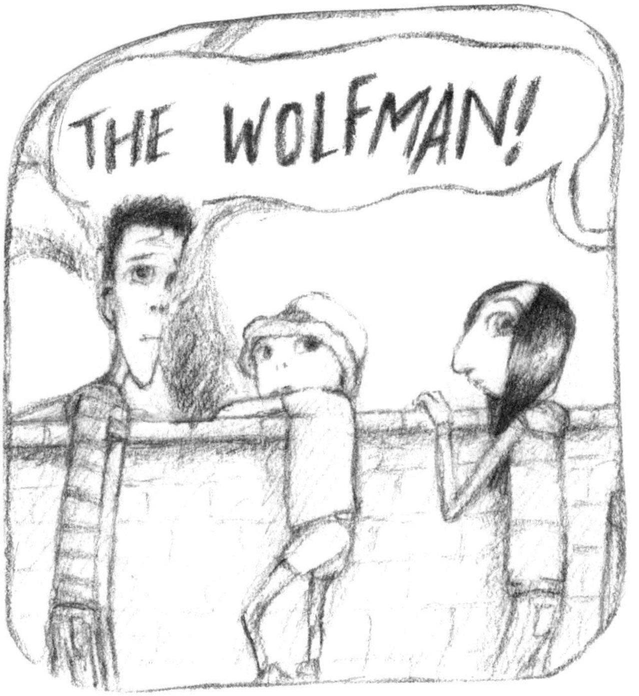
THE WOLFMAN!

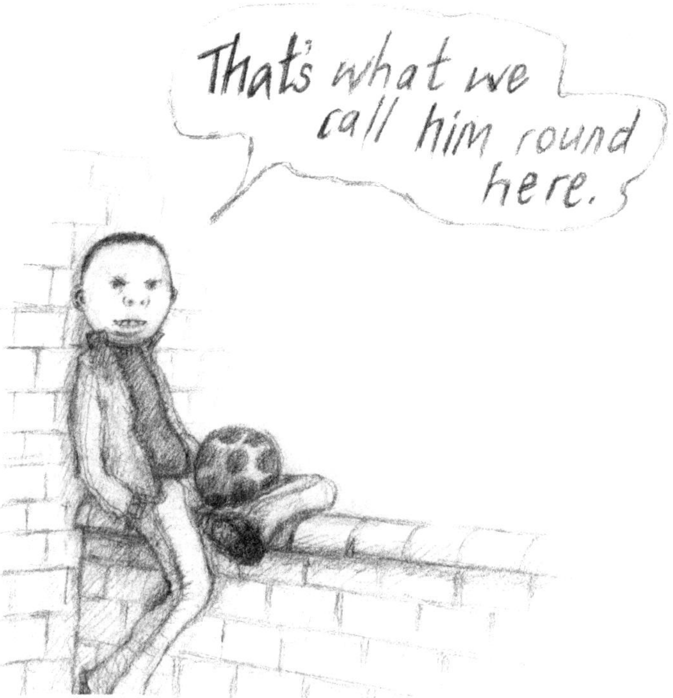
That's what we call him round here.

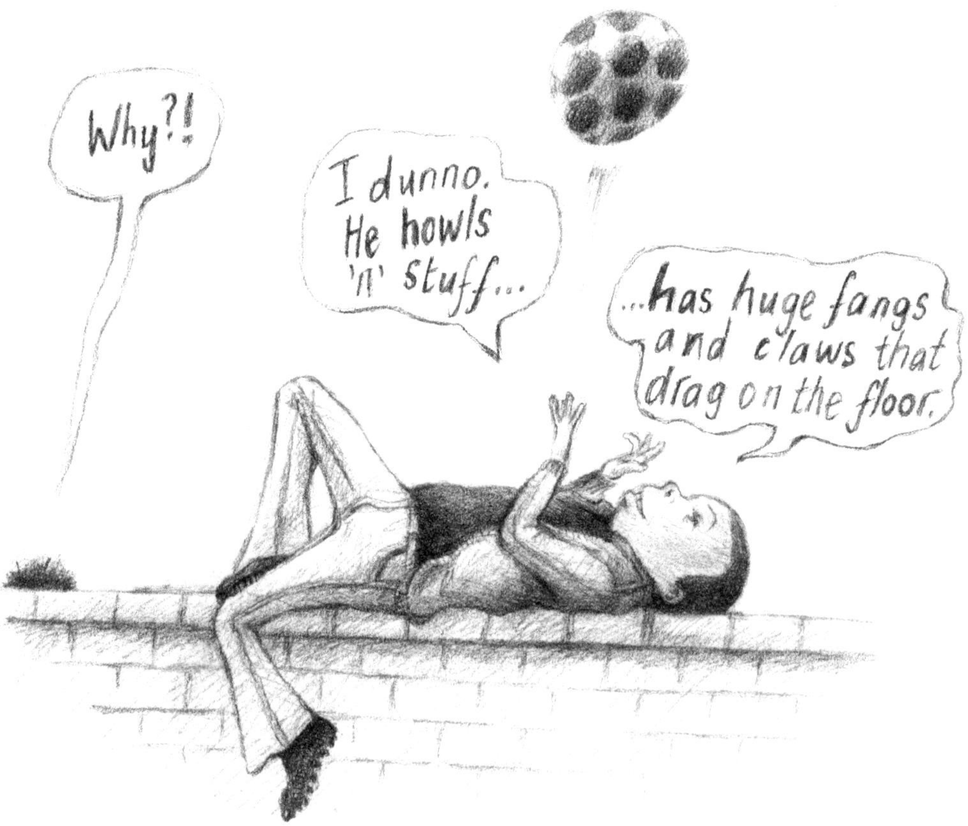
Why?!
I dunno. He howls 'n' stuff...
...has huge fangs and claws that drag on the floor.

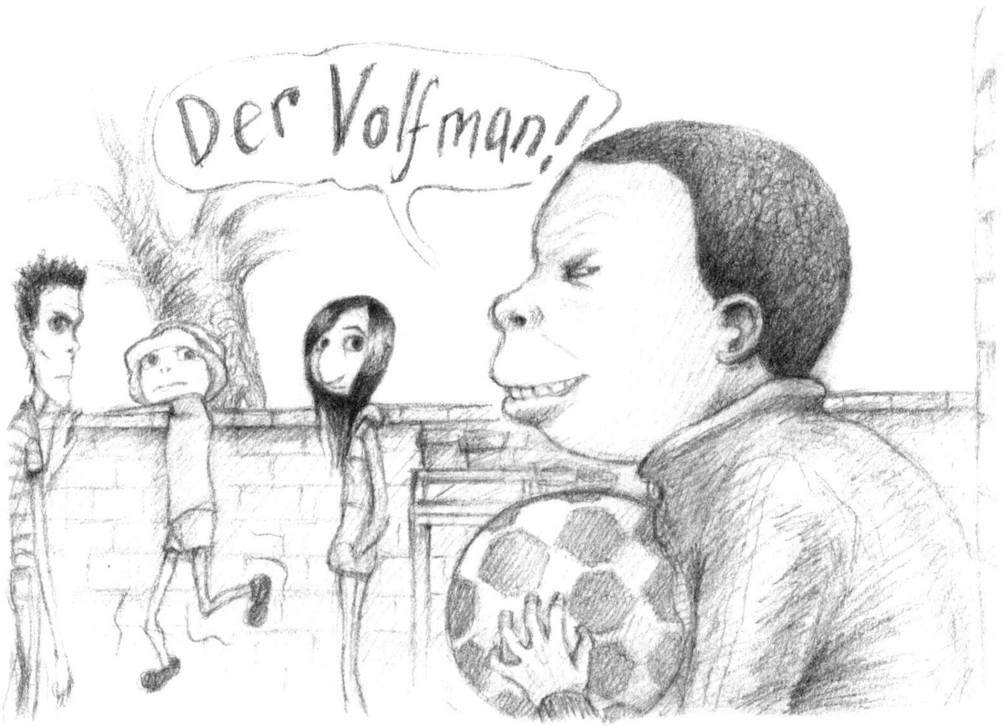
Der Volfman!

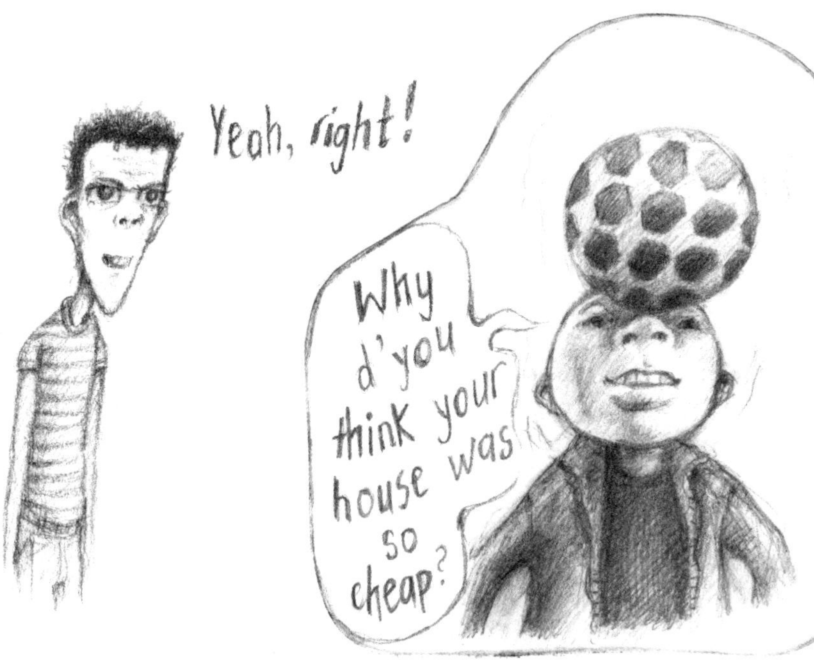
Yeah, right!
Why d'you think your house was so cheap?

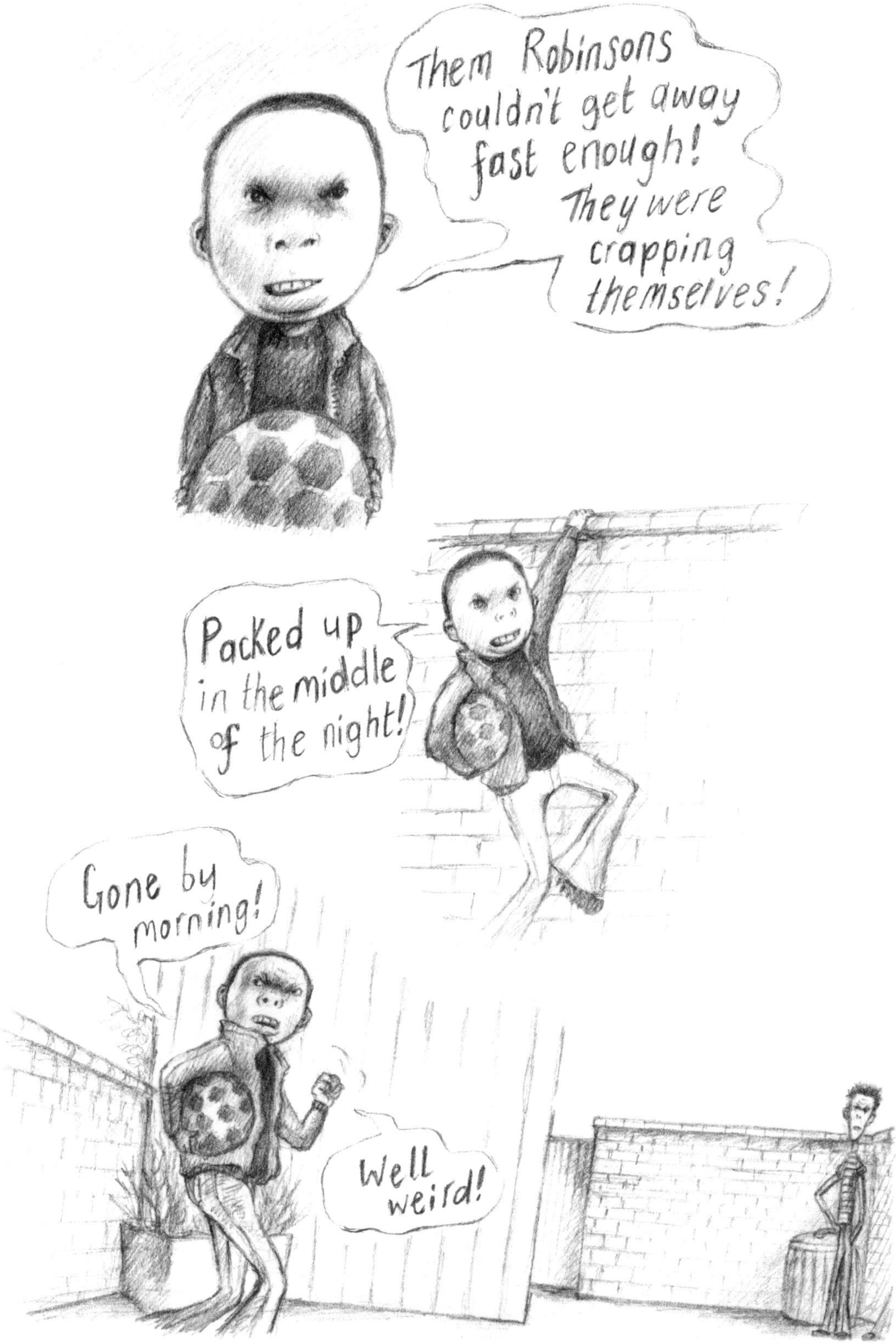
Them Robinsons couldn't get away fast enough! They were crapping themselves!
Packed up in the middle of the night!
Gone by morning!
Well weird!

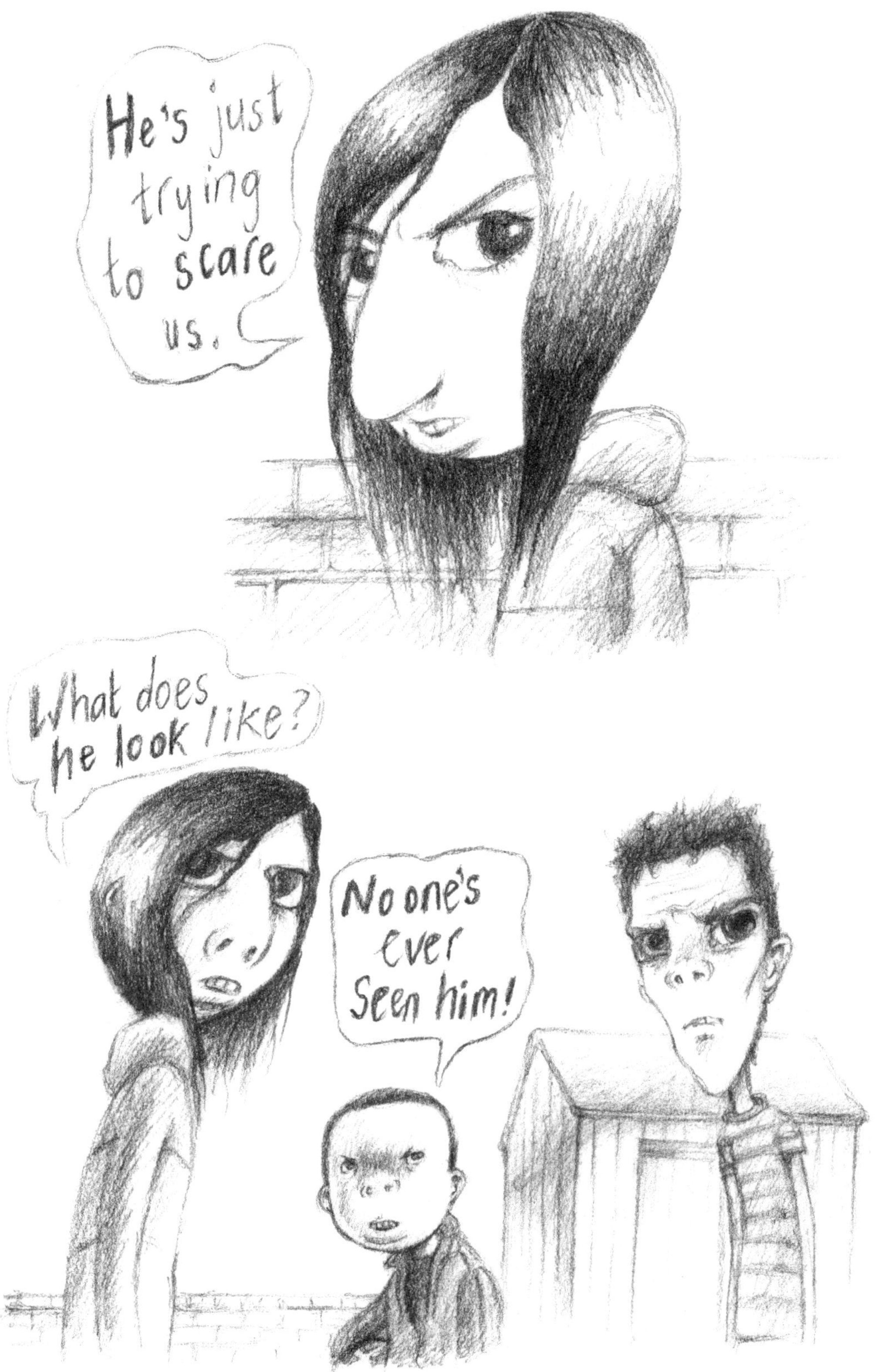
He's just trying to scare us.
What does he look like?
No one's ever seen him!

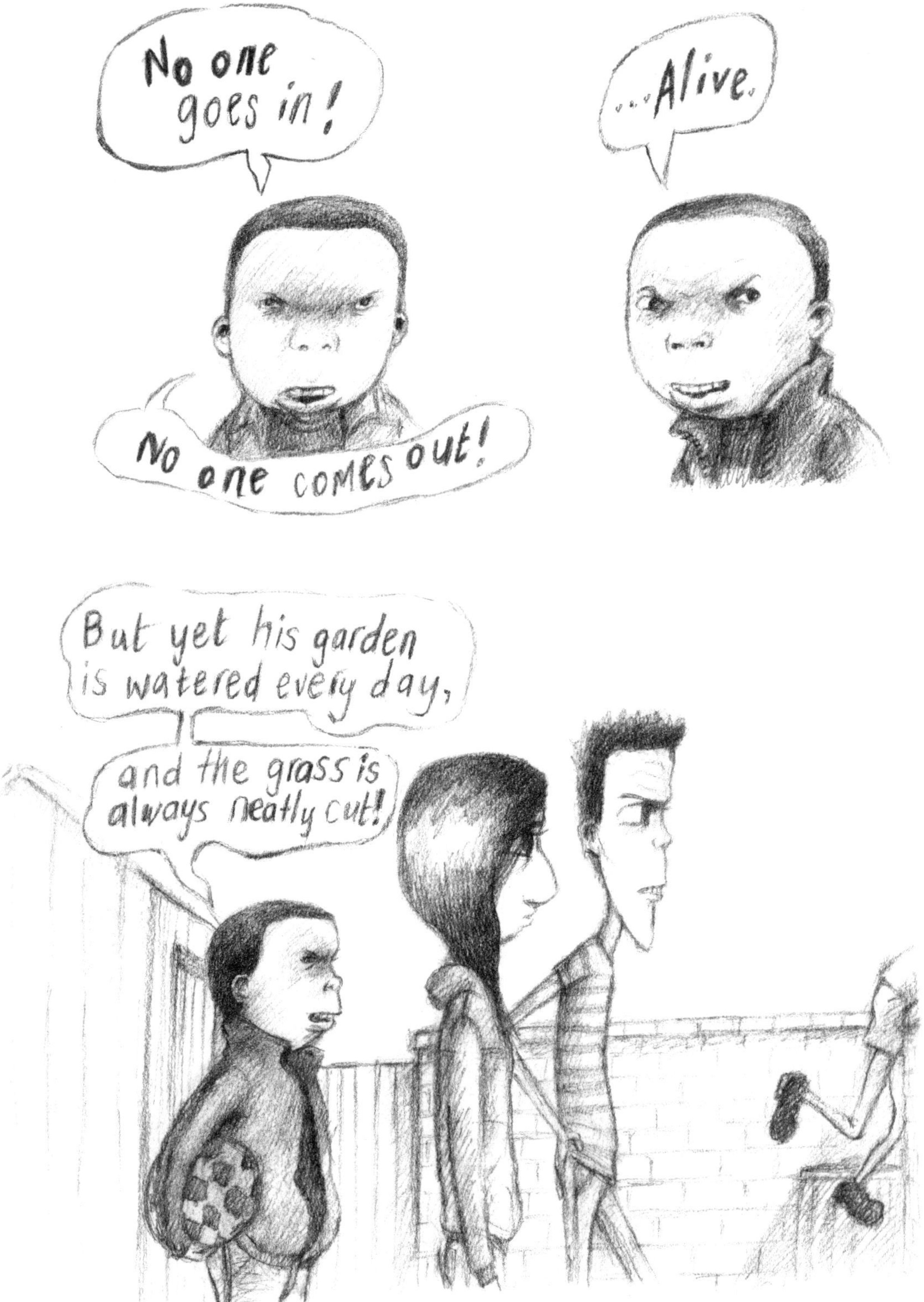
No one goes in!
No one comes out!
...Alive.
But yet his garden is watered every day,
and the grass is always neatly cut!

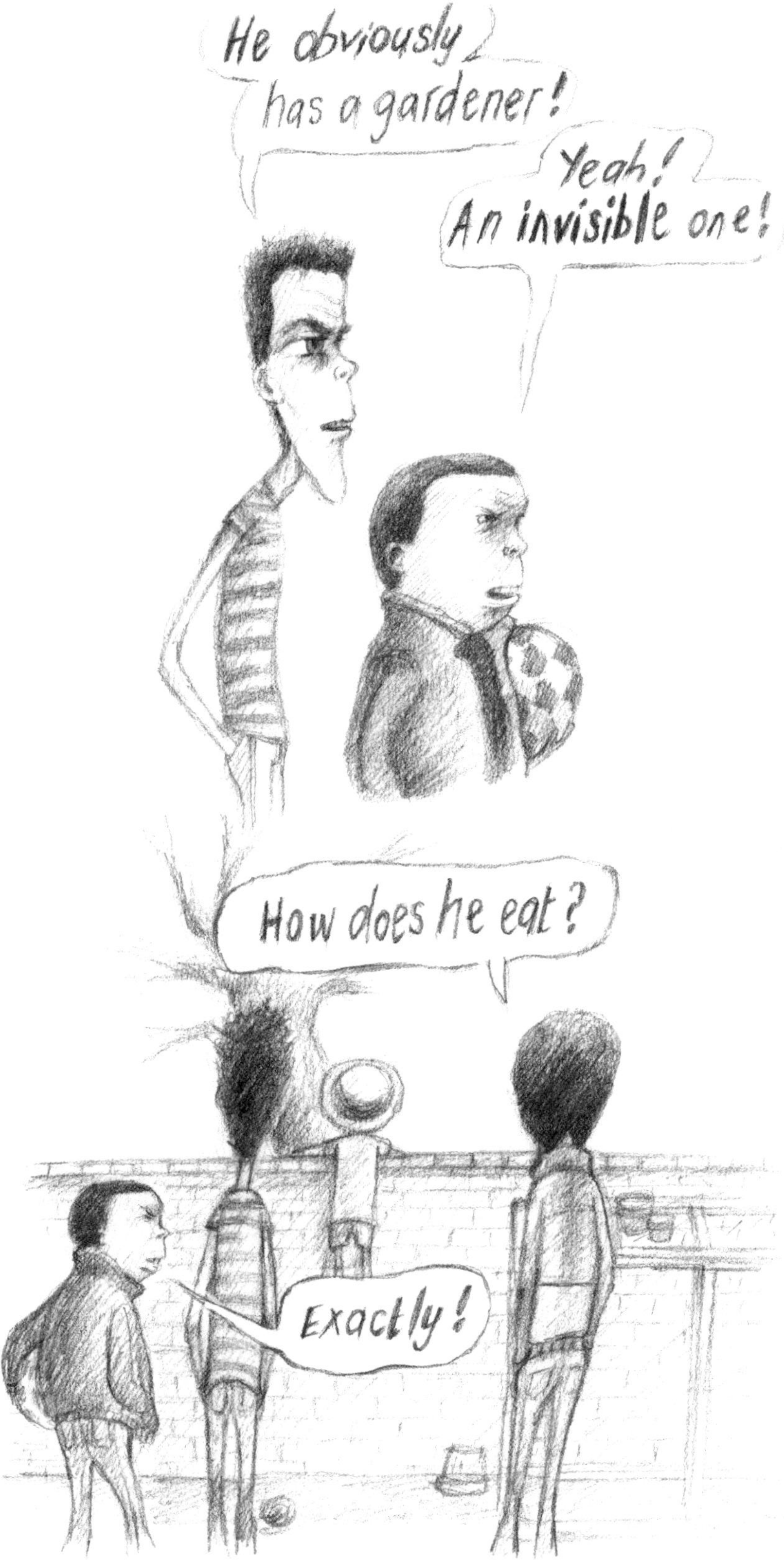
He obviously has a gardener!
Yeah! An invisible one!
How does he eat?
Exactly!

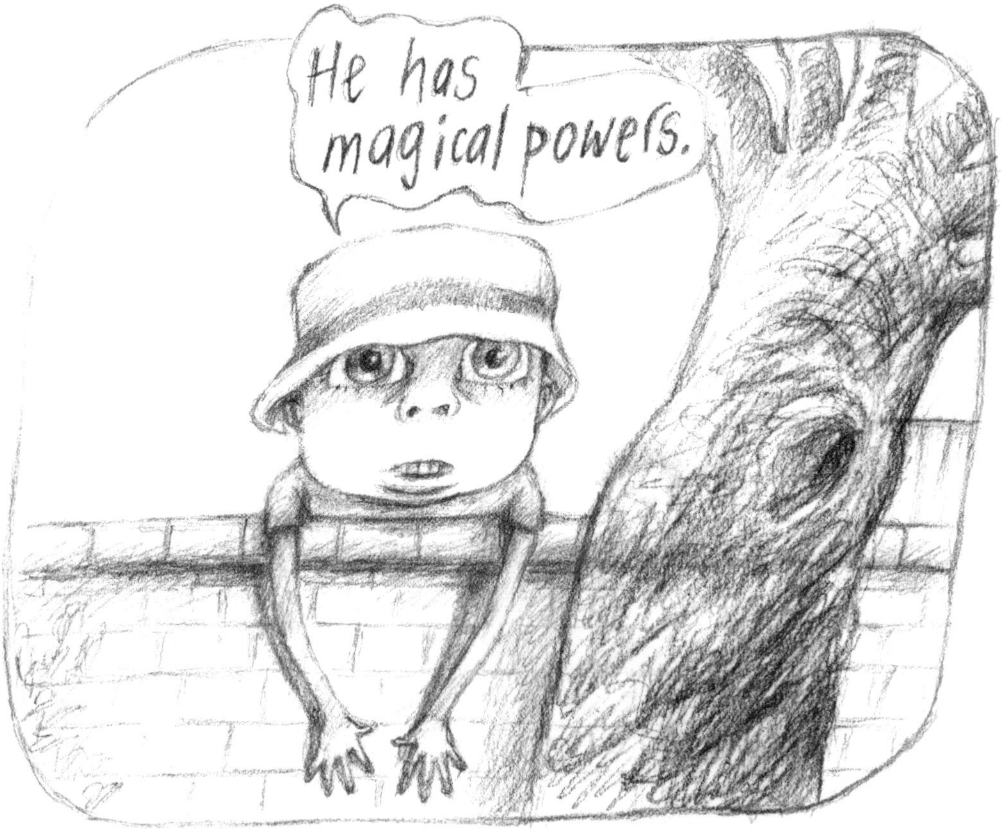
He has magical powers.

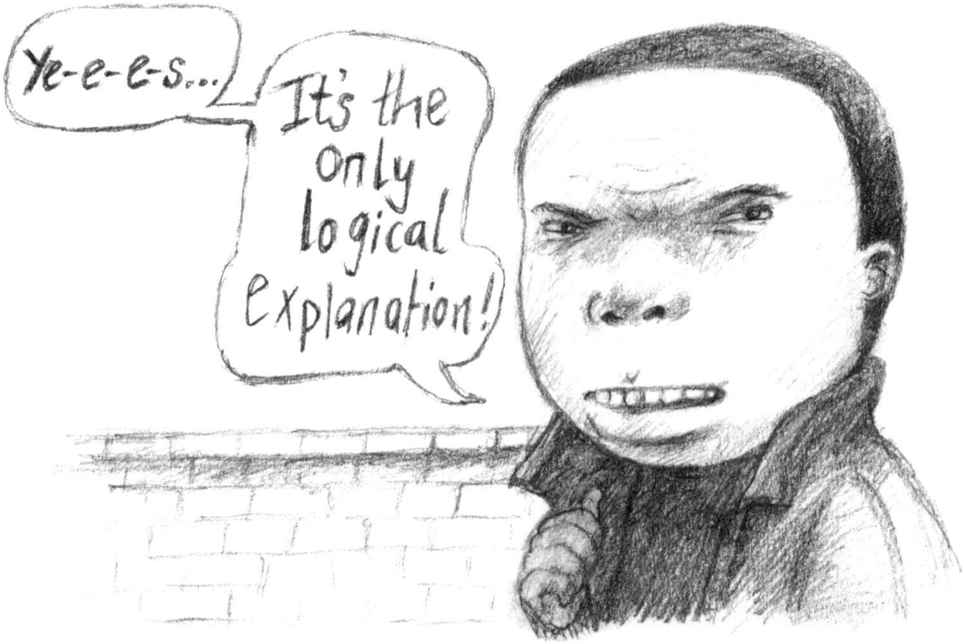
Ye-e-e-s...
It's the only logical explanation!

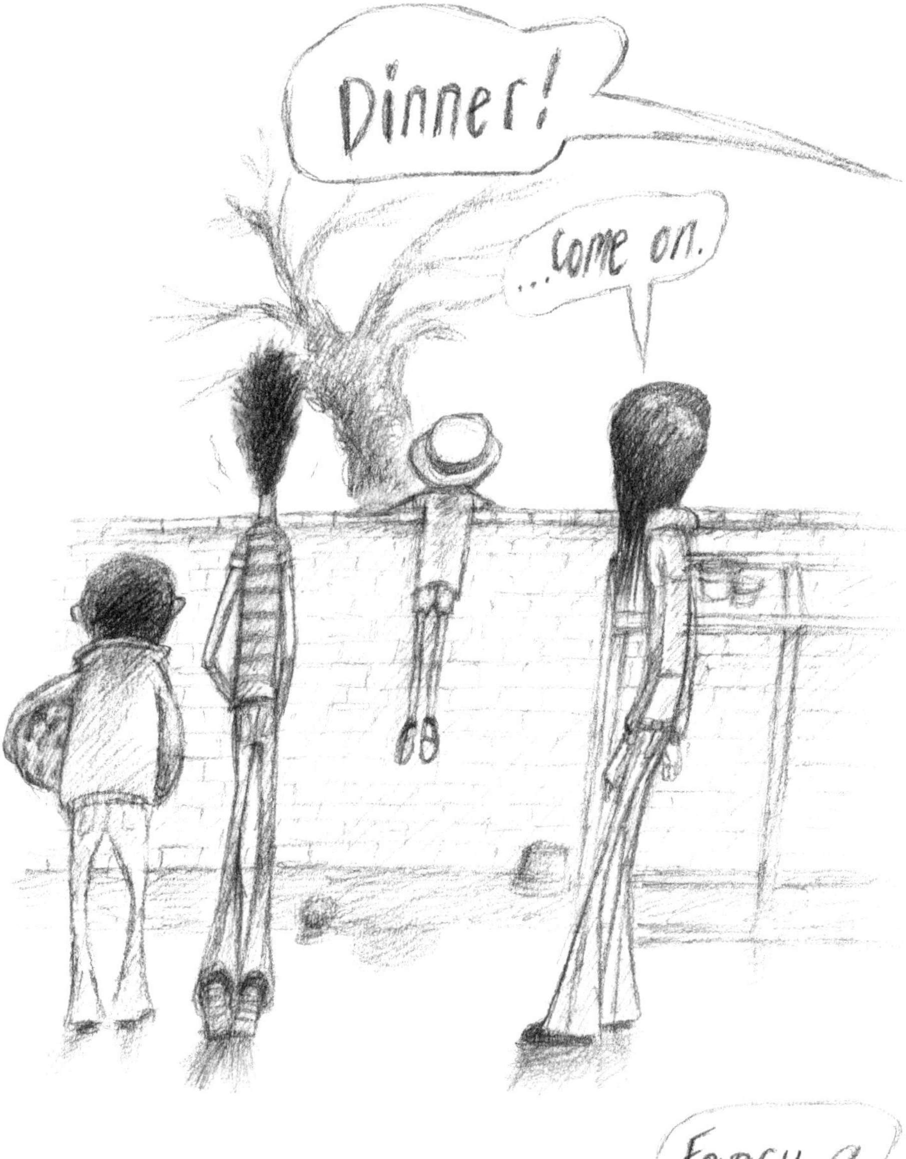

Dinner!
...come on.

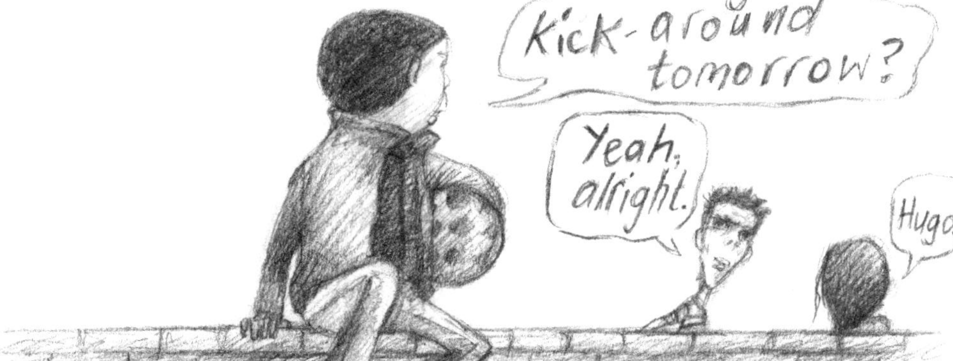

Fancy a kick-around tomorrow?
Yeah, alright.
Hugo.

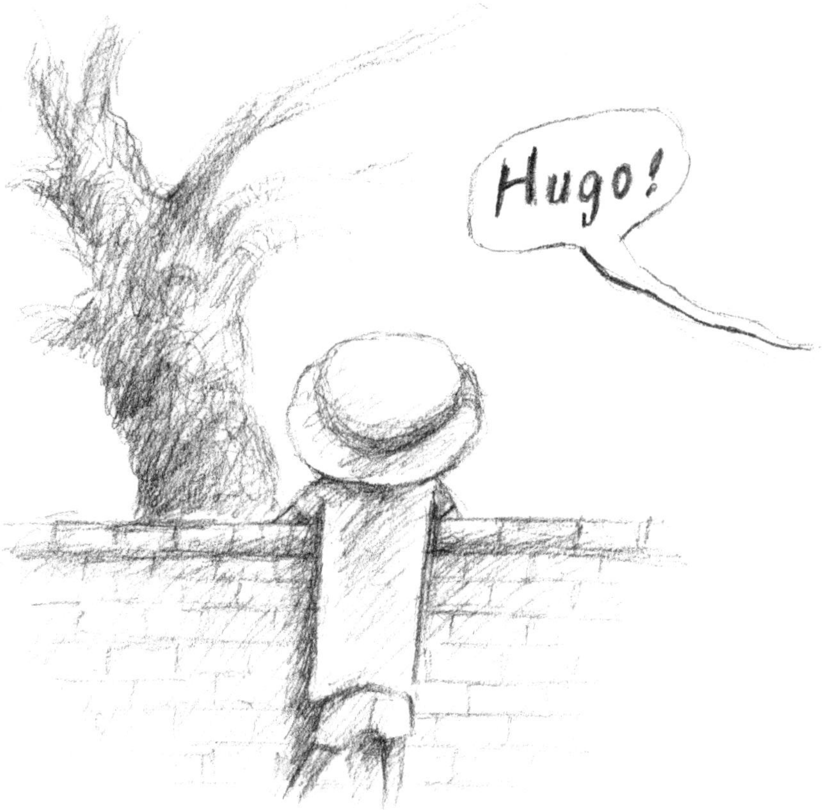
Hugo!

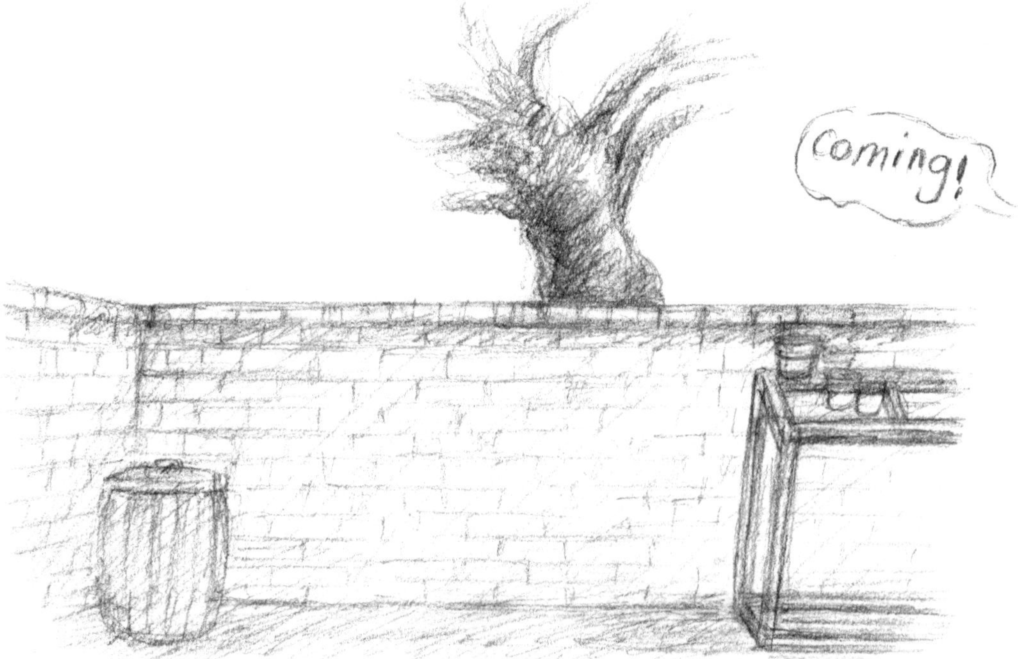
Coming!

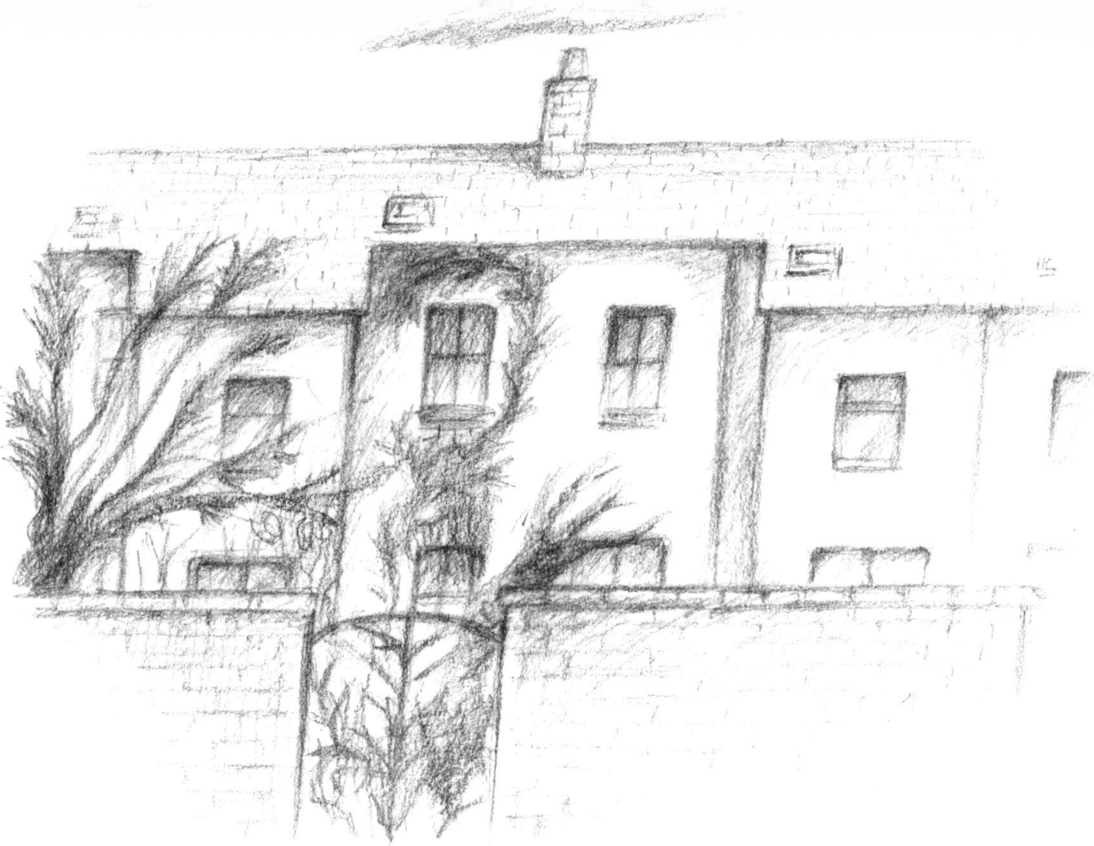

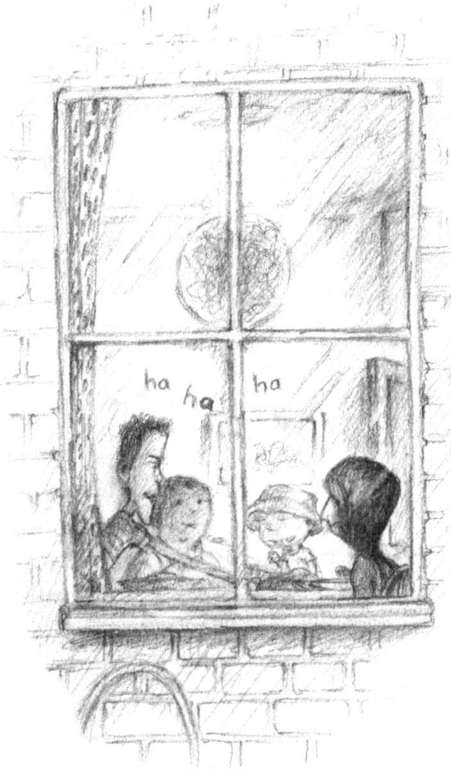
ha ha ha

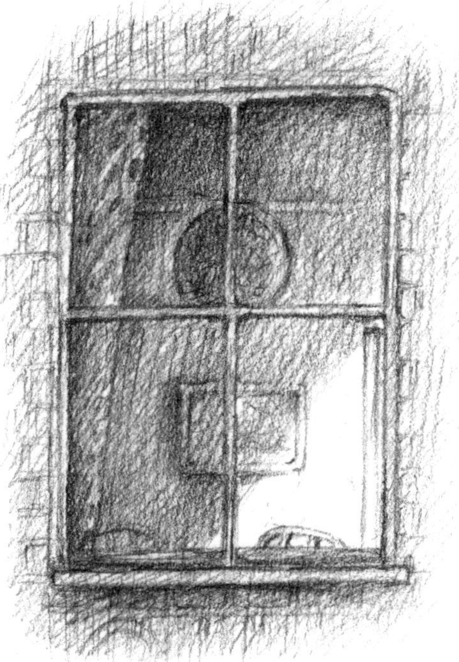

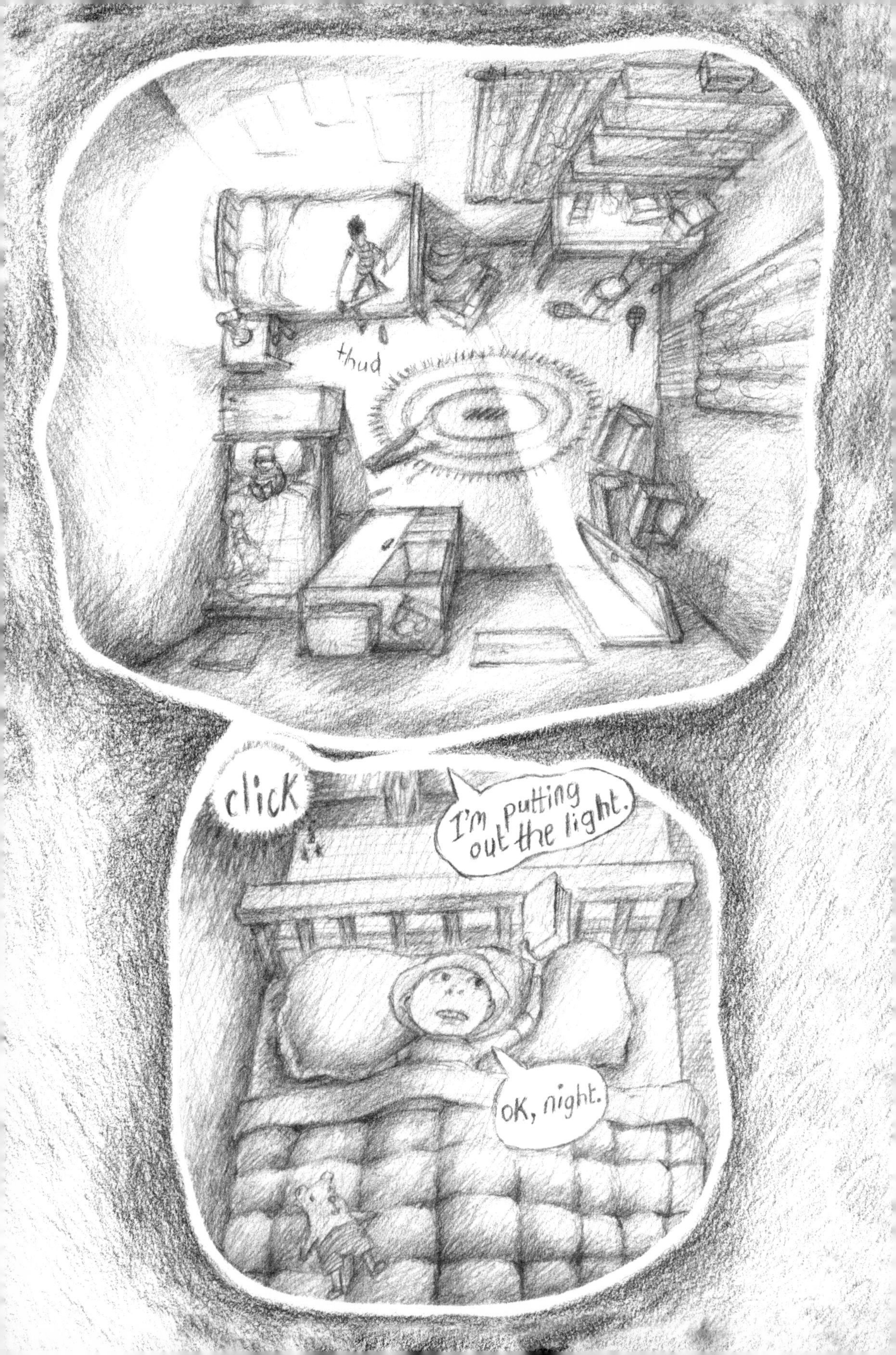
thud
click
I'm putting out the light.
OK, night.

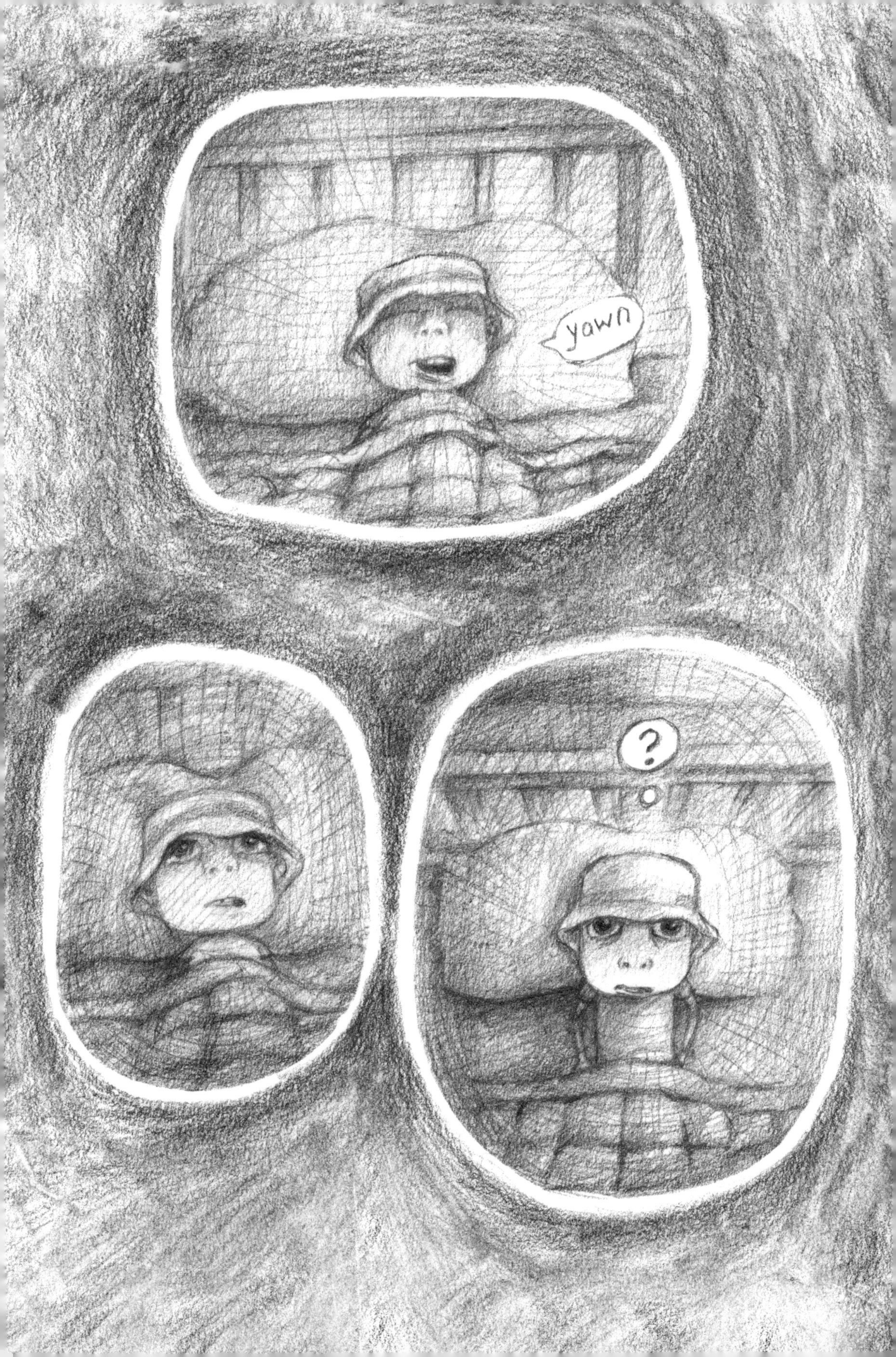
yawn
?

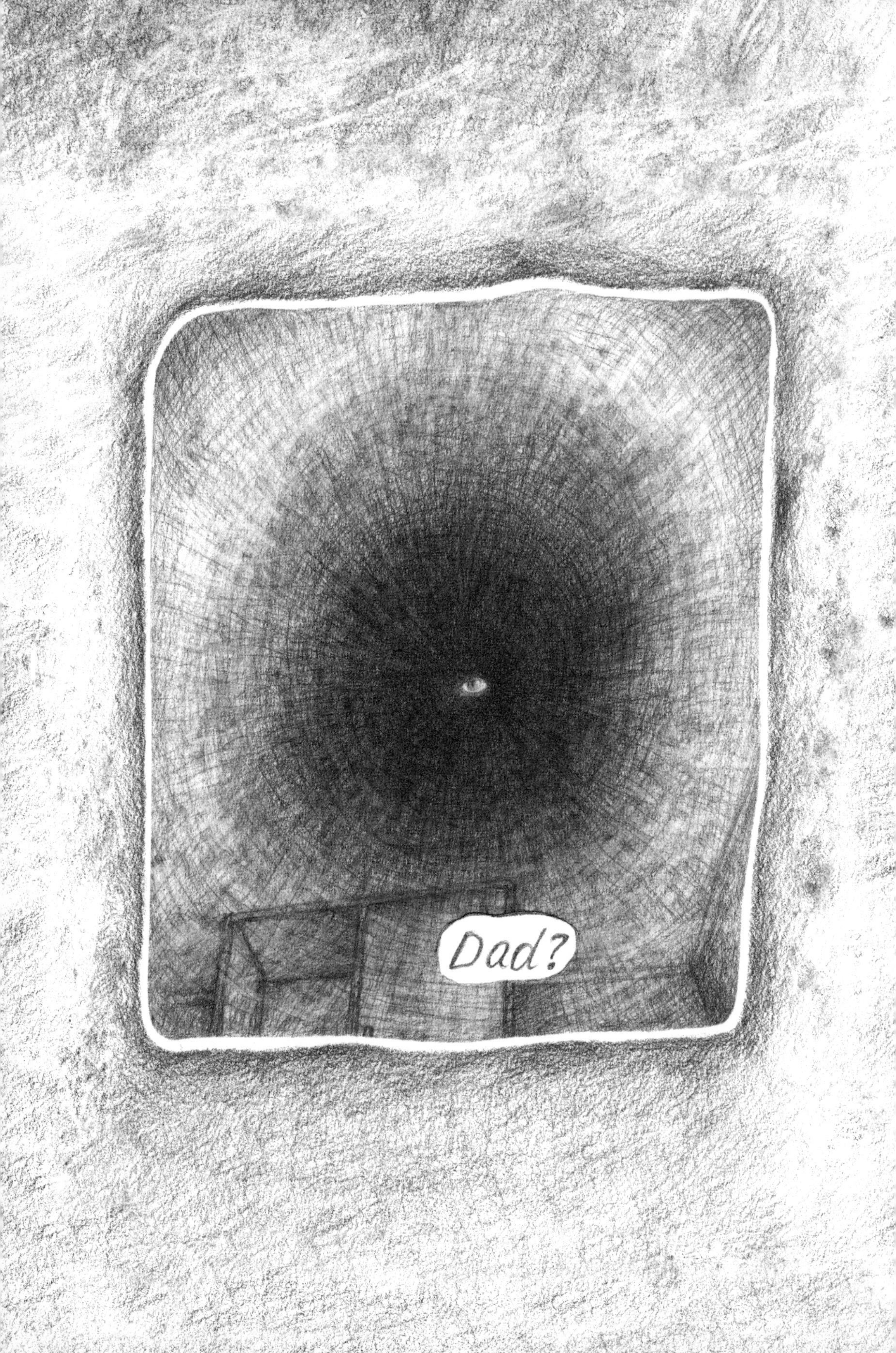
Dad?

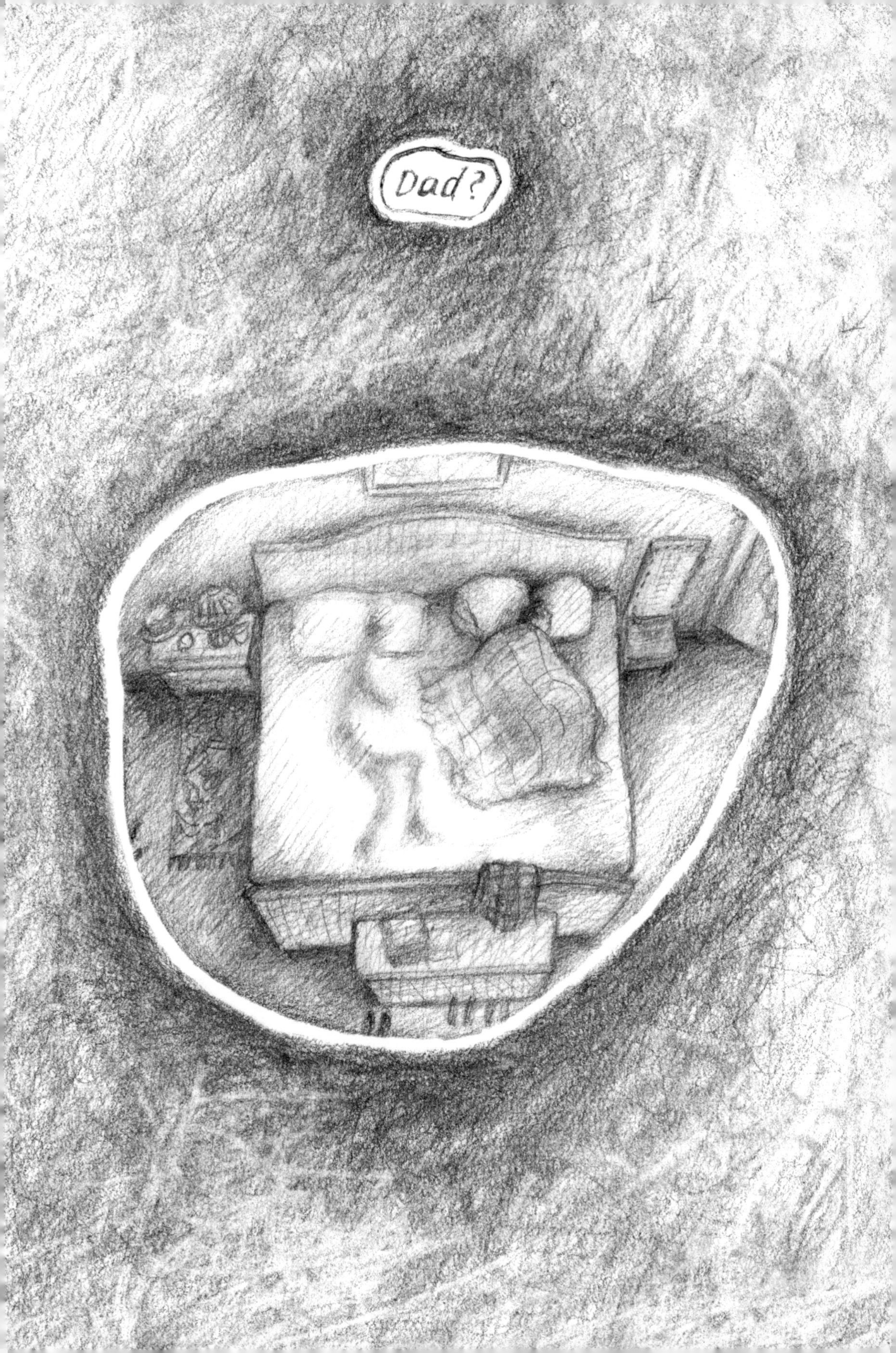
Dad?

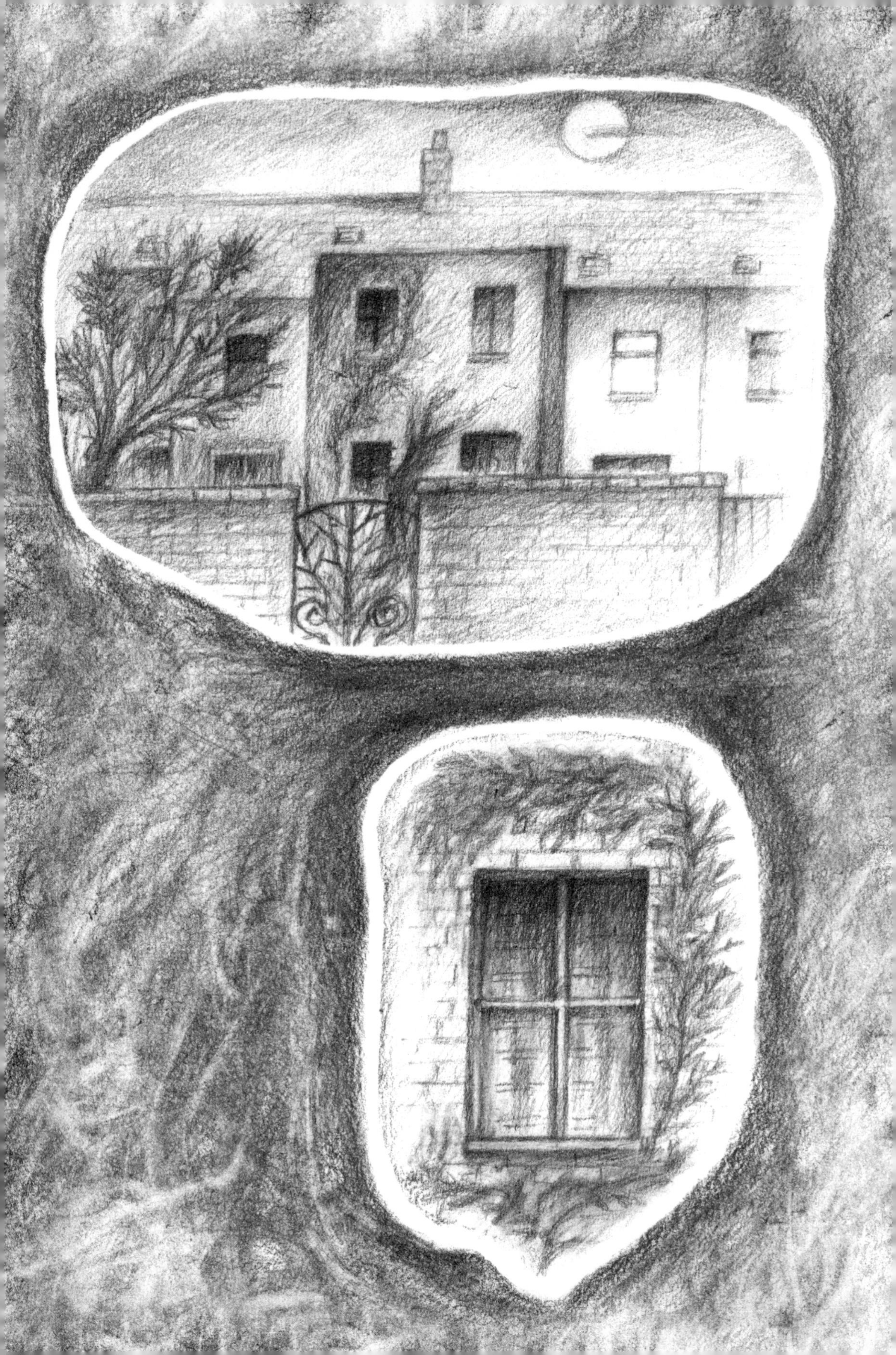

Chapter Four

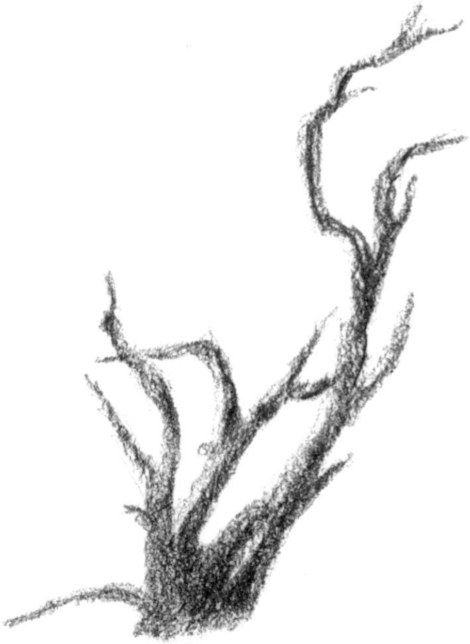

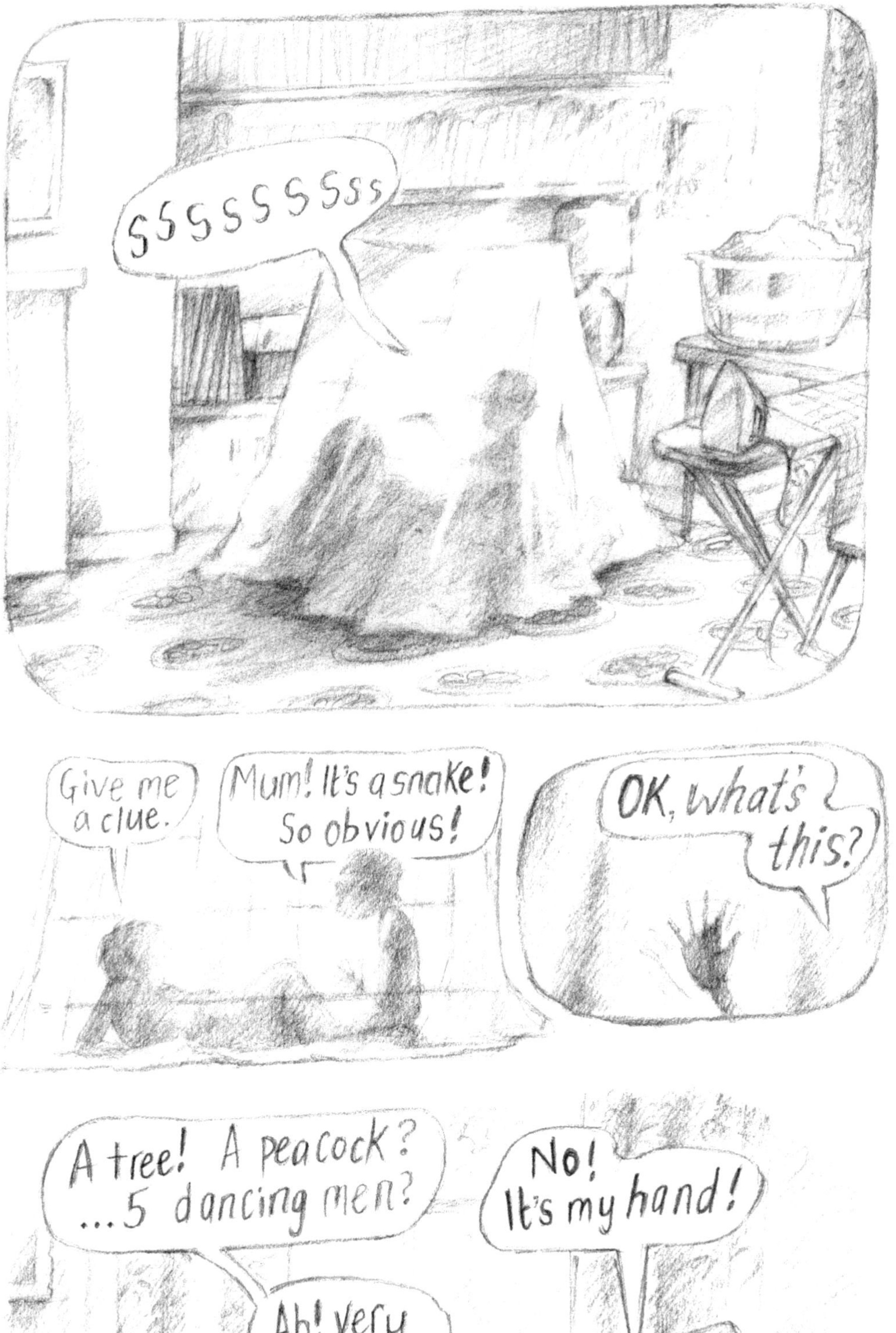
SSSSSSSSss
Give me a clue.
Mum! It's a snake! So obvious!
OK, what's this?
A tree! A peacock? ...5 dancing men?
Ah! very funny!
No! It's my hand!

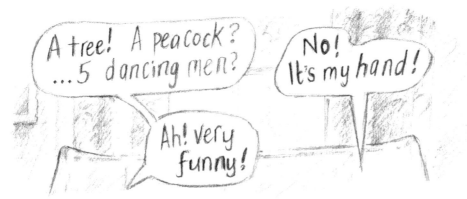

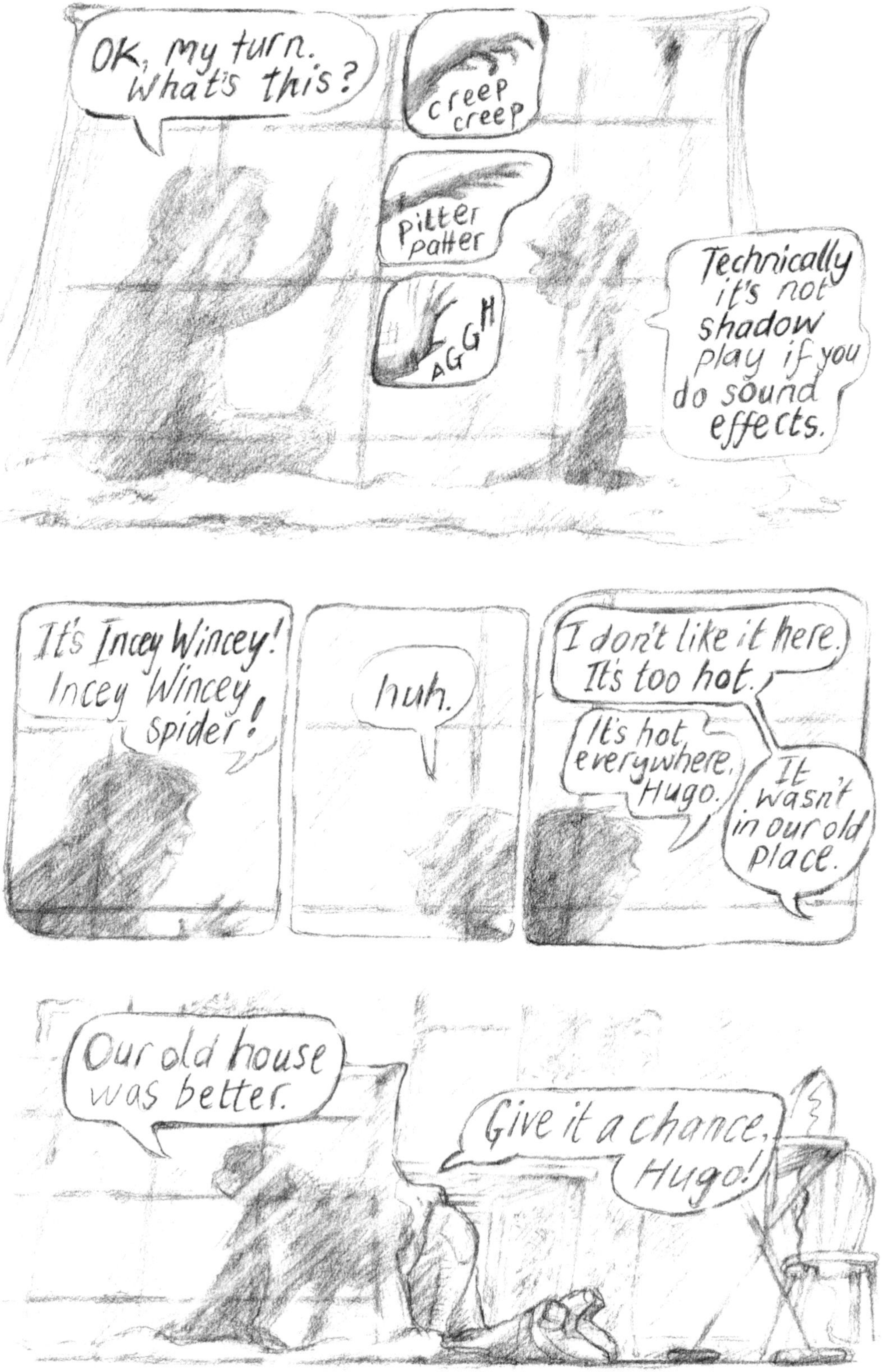
OK, my turn. What's this?
creep creep
pitter patter
AGGH
Technically it's not shadow play if you do sound effects.
It's Incey Wincey! Incey Wincey spider!
huh.
I don't like it here. It's too hot.
It's hot everywhere, Hugo.
It wasn't in our old place.
Our old house was better.
Give it a chance, Hugo!

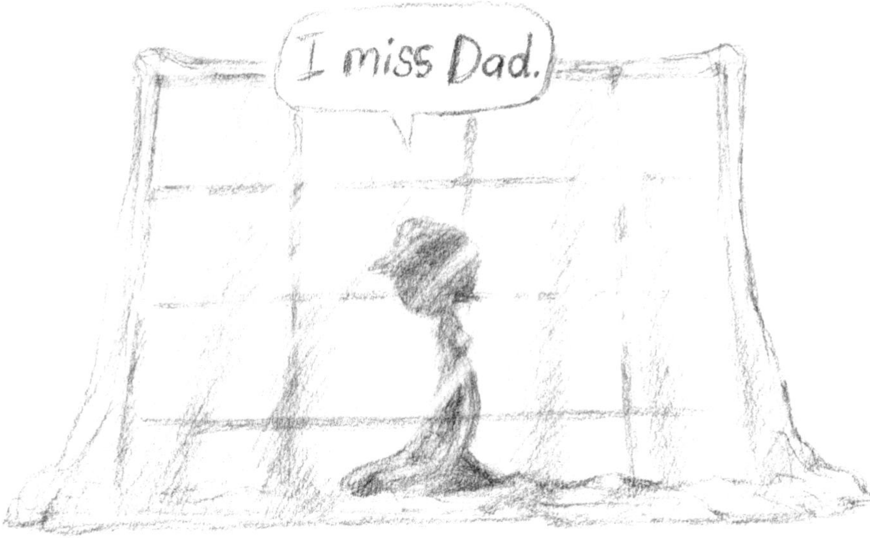
I miss Dad.

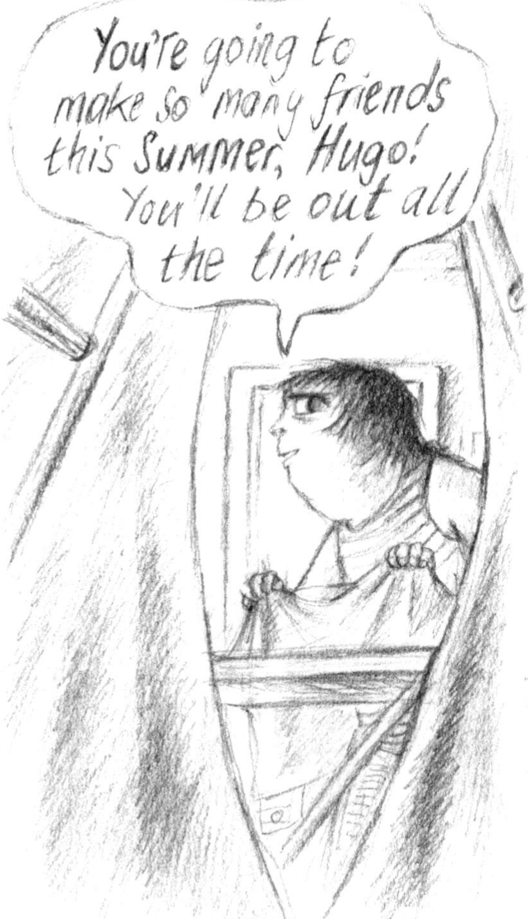
You're going to make so many friends this Summer, Hugo! You'll be out all the time!

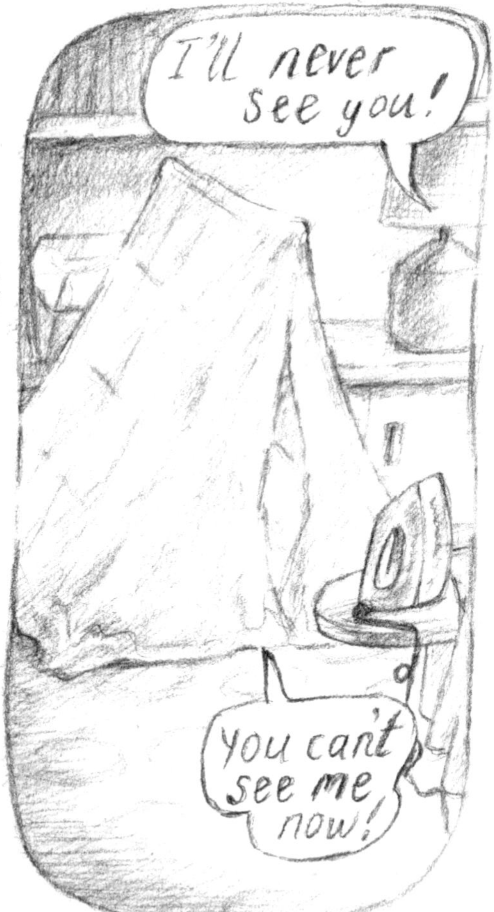
I'll never see you!
You can't see me now!

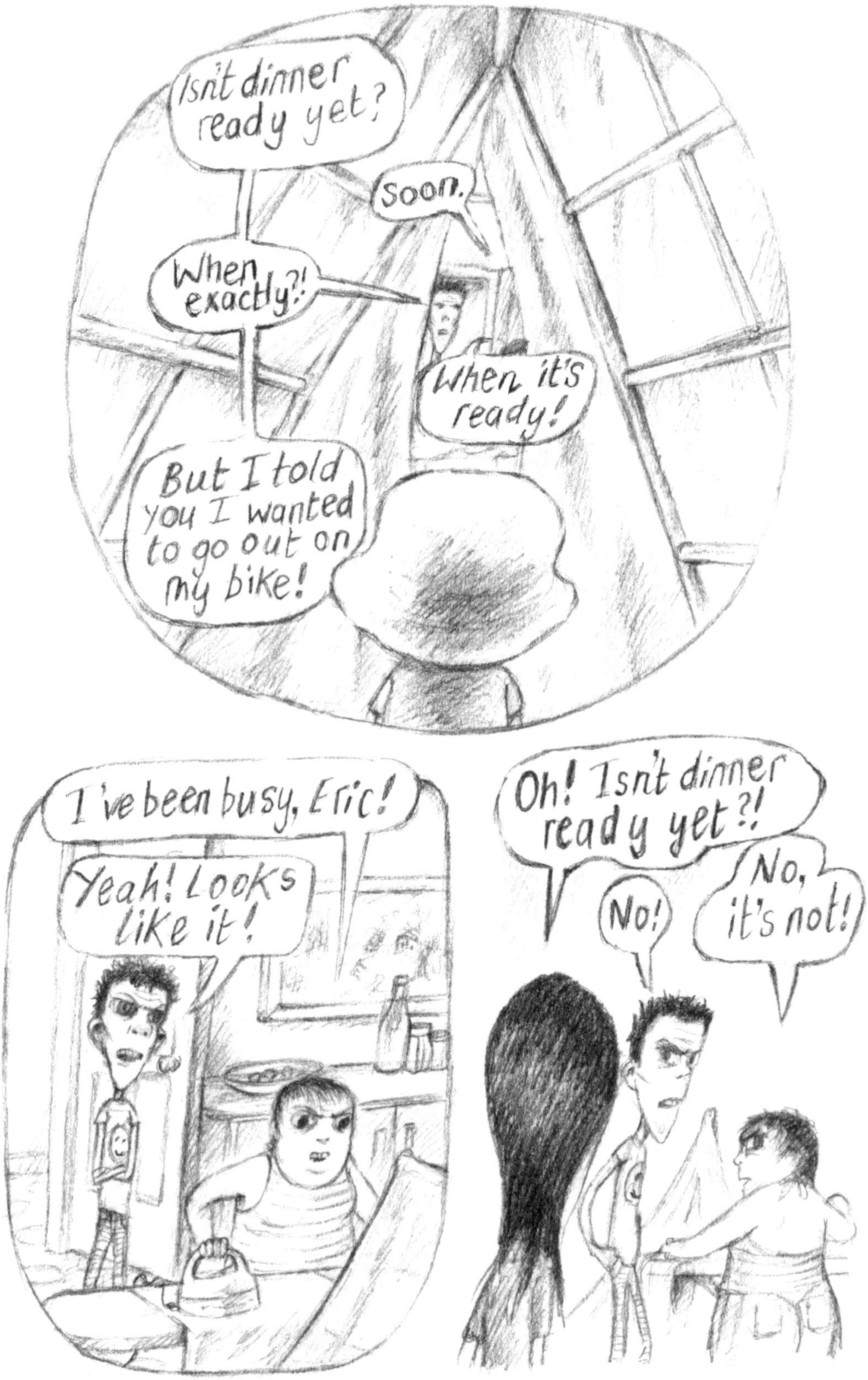
Isn't dinner ready yet?
Soon.
When exactly?!
When it's ready!
But I told you I wanted to go out on my bike!
I've been busy, Eric!
Yeah! Looks like it!
Oh! Isn't dinner ready yet?!
No!
No, it's not!

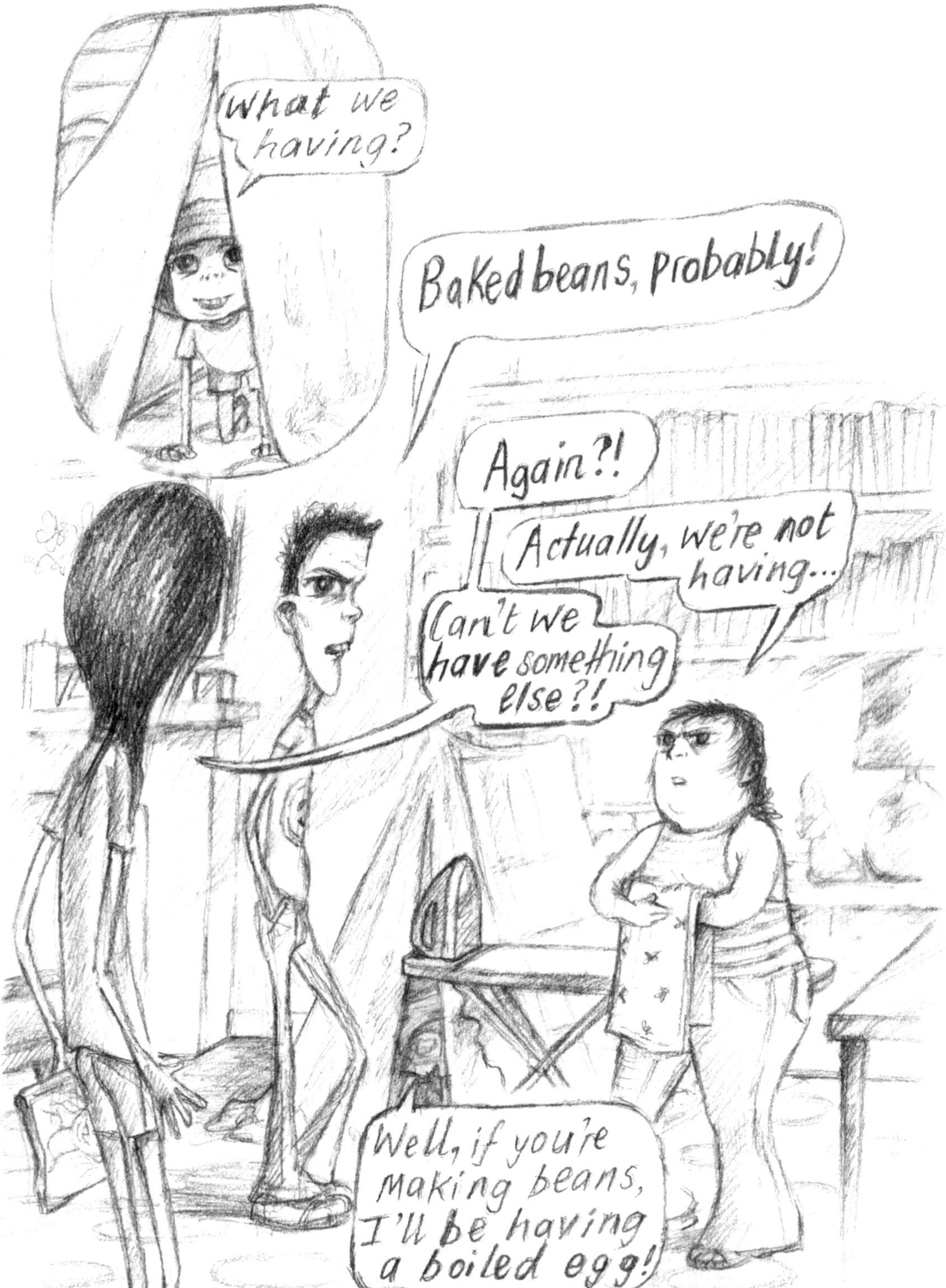
What we having?
Baked beans, probably!
Again?!
Actually, we're not having...
Can't we have something else?!
Well, if you're making beans, I'll be having a boiled egg!

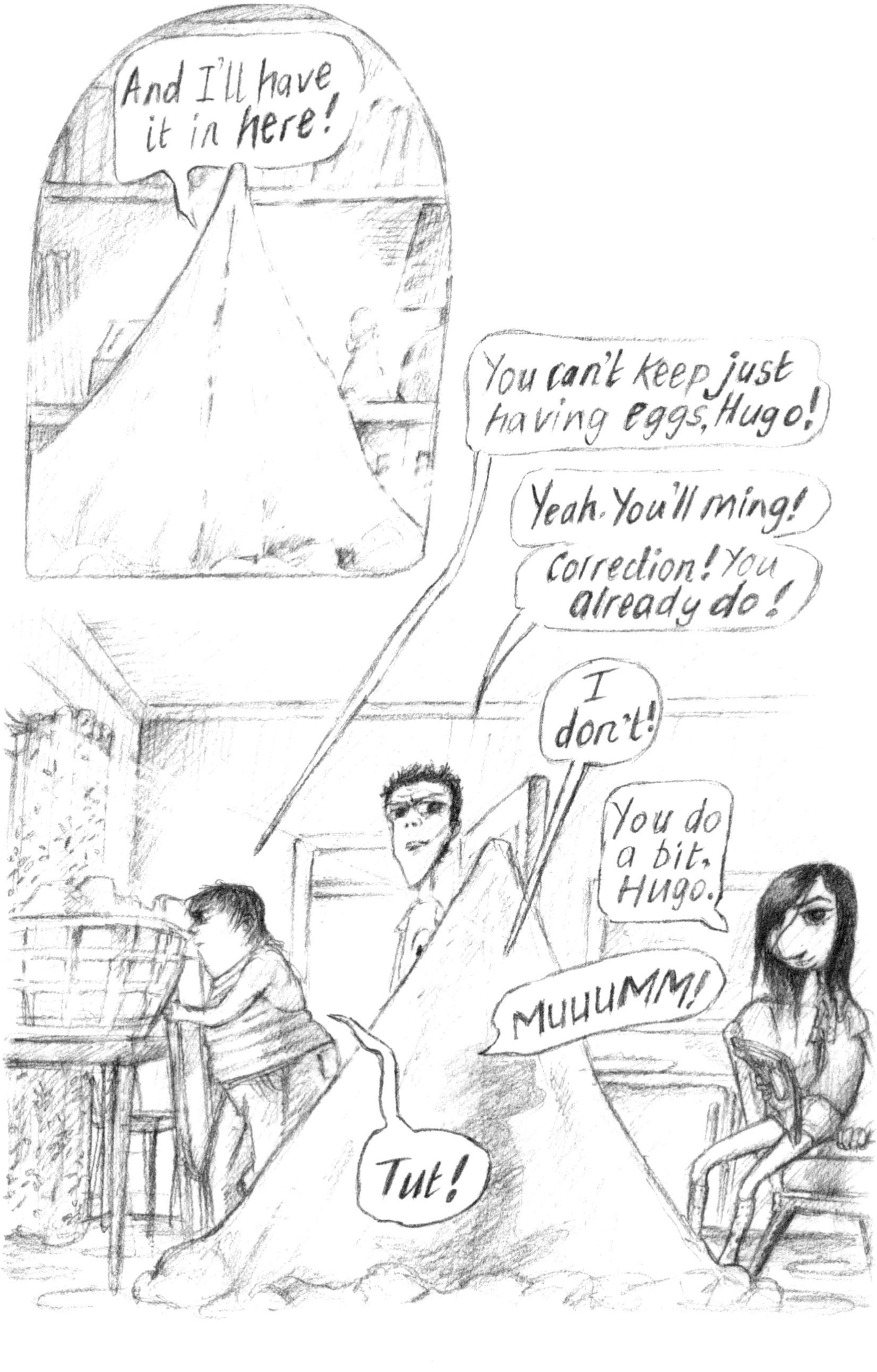
And I'll have it in here!
You can't keep just having eggs, Hugo!
Yeah. You'll ming!
Correction! You already do!
I don't!
You do a bit, Hugo.
MUUUMM!
Tut!

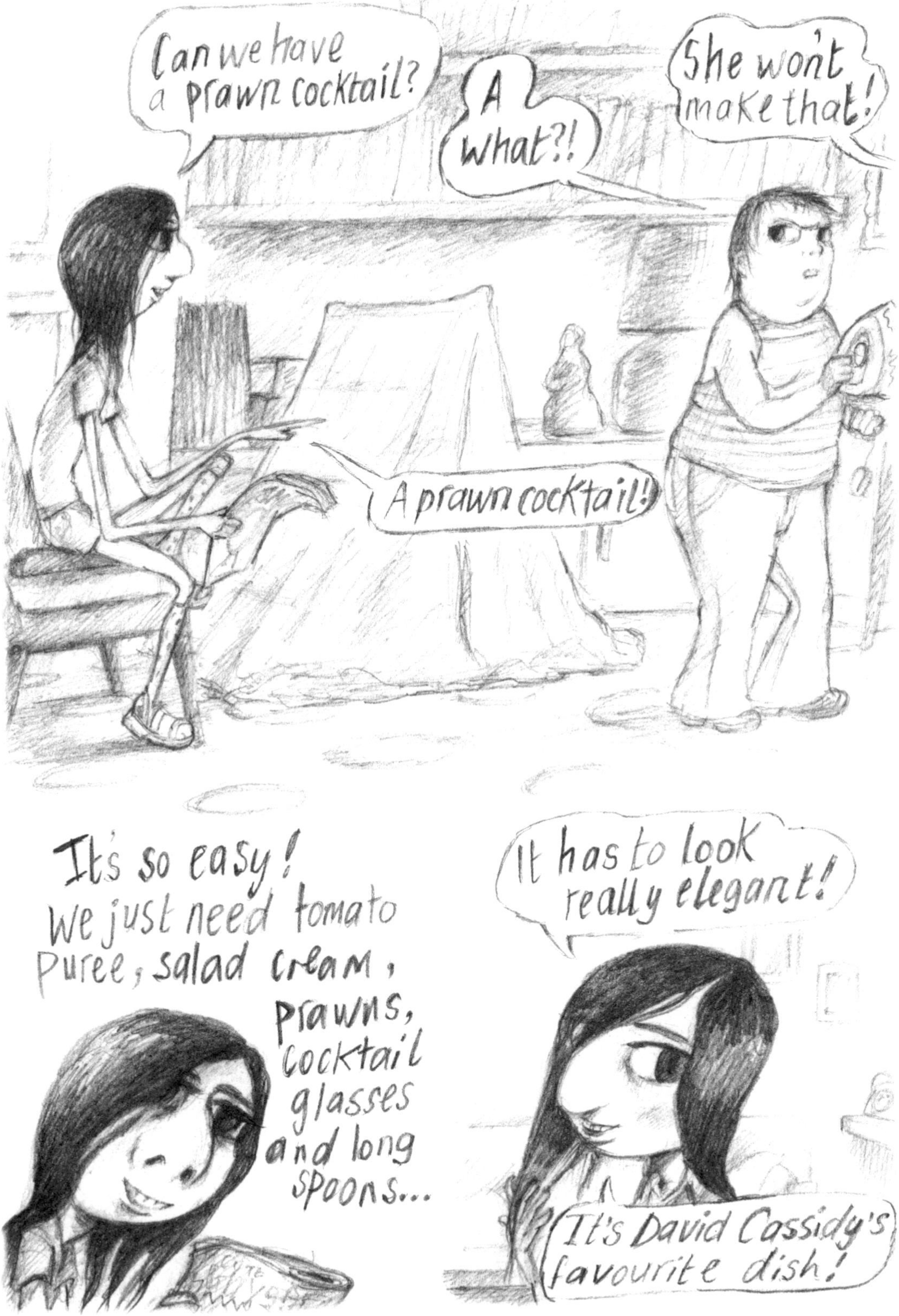
Can we have a prawn cocktail?
A what?!
She won't make that!
A prawn cocktail!
It's so easy! We just need tomato puree, salad cream, prawns, cocktail glasses and long spoons...
It has to look really elegant!
It's David Cassidy's favourite dish!

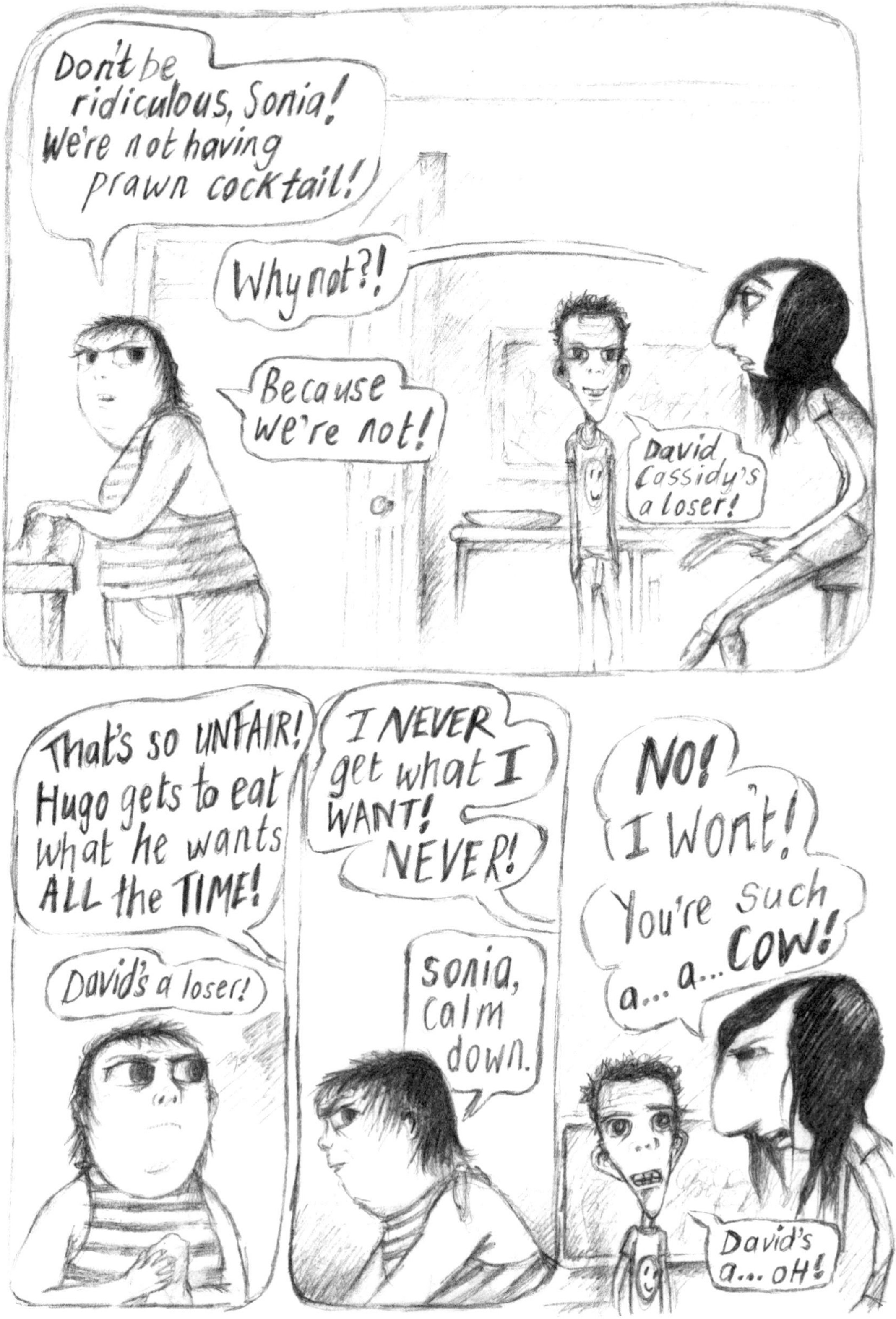

Don't be ridiculous, Sonia! We're not having prawn cocktail!
Why not?!
Because we're not!
David Cassidy's a loser!
That's so UNFAIR! Hugo gets to eat what he wants ALL the TIME!
David's a loser!
I NEVER get what I WANT! NEVER!
Sonia, calm down.
NO! I won't!
You're such a... a... COW!
David's a... OH!

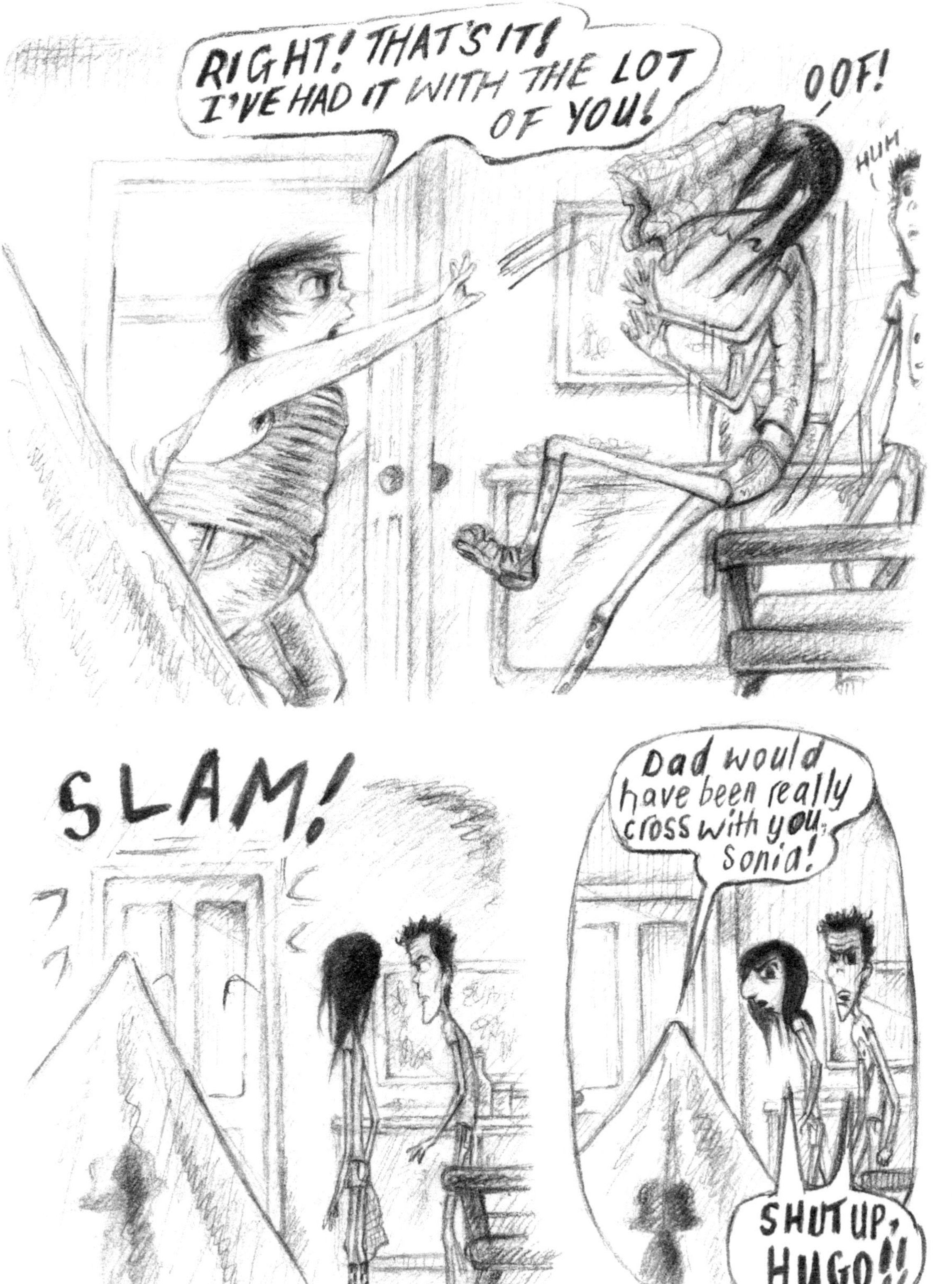
RIGHT! THAT'S IT! I'VE HAD IT WITH THE LOT OF YOU!
OOF!
HUH
SLAM!
Dad would have been really cross with you, Sonia!
SHUT UP, HUGO!!

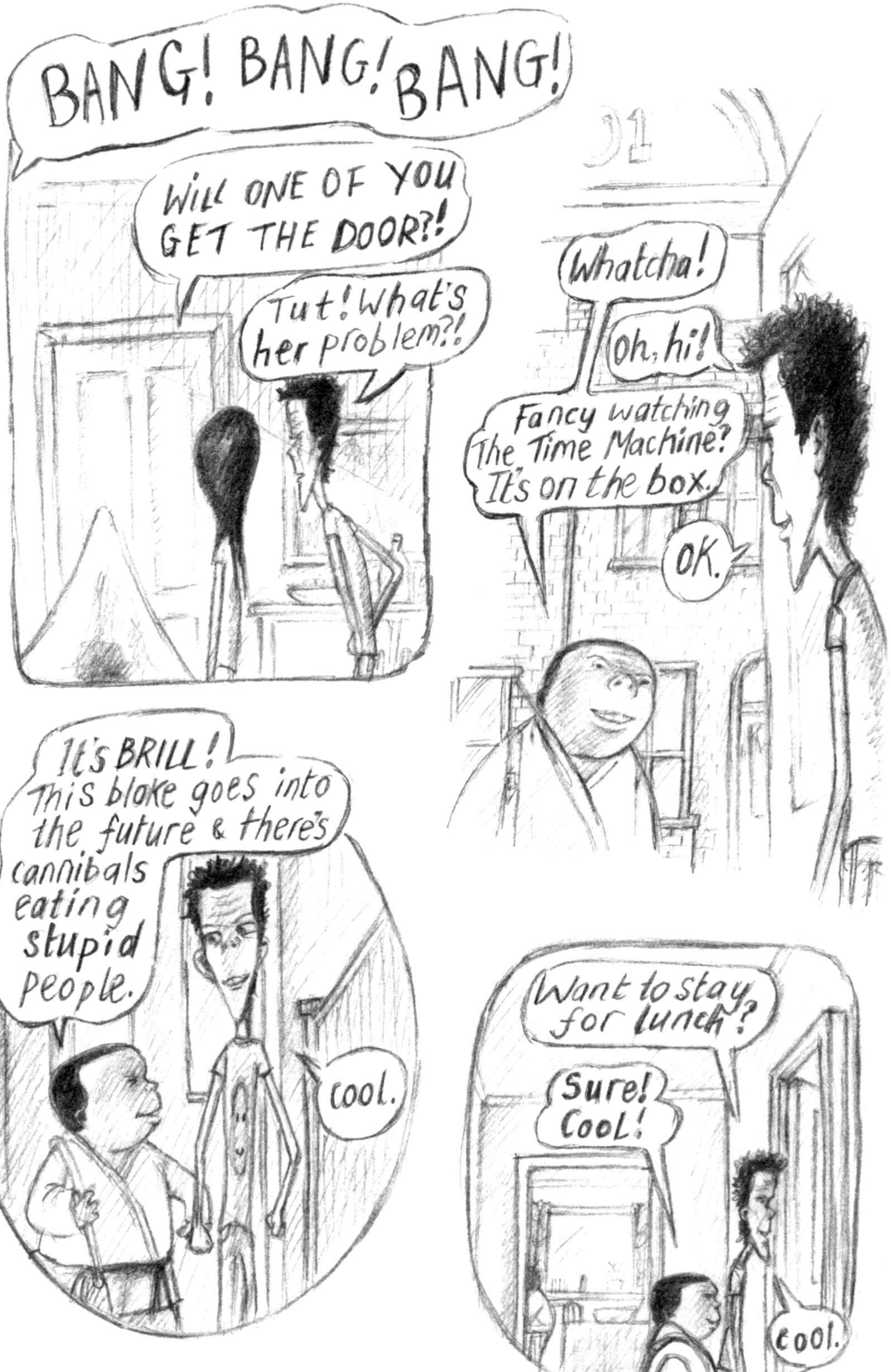
BANG! BANG! BANG!
WILL ONE OF YOU GET THE DOOR?!
Tut! What's her problem?!
Whatcha!
Oh, hi!
Fancy watching The Time Machine? It's on the box.
OK.
It's BRILL! This bloke goes into the future & there's cannibals eating stupid people.
cool.
Want to stay for lunch?
Sure! Cool!
cool.

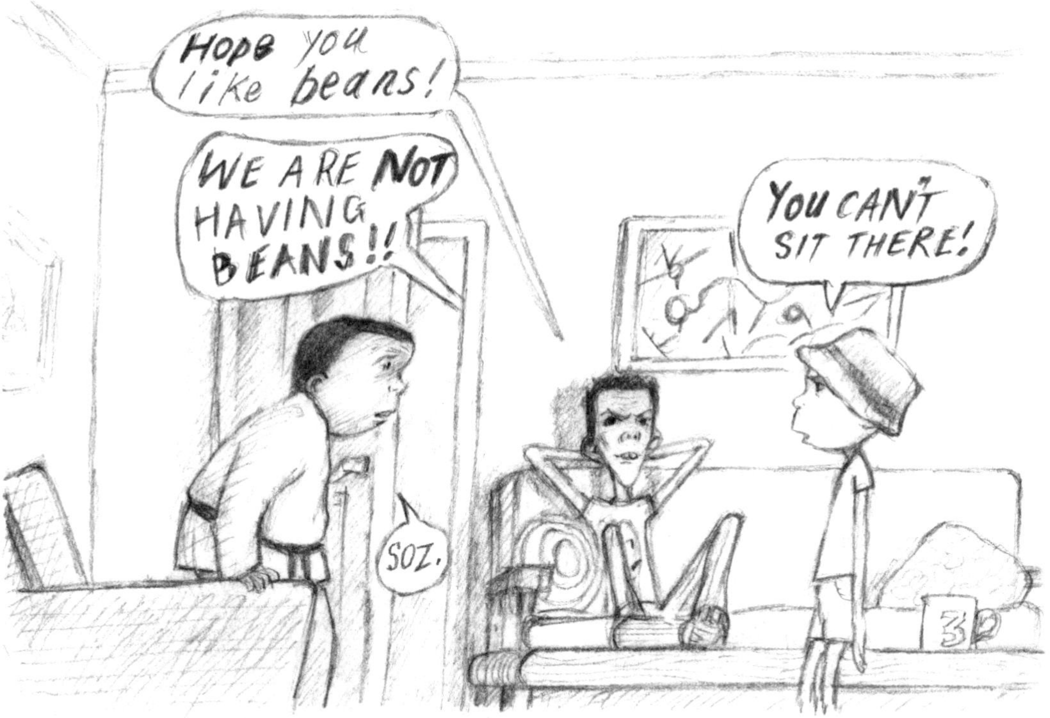
Hope you like beans!
WE ARE NOT HAVING BEANS!!
YOU CAN'T SIT THERE!
SOZ.

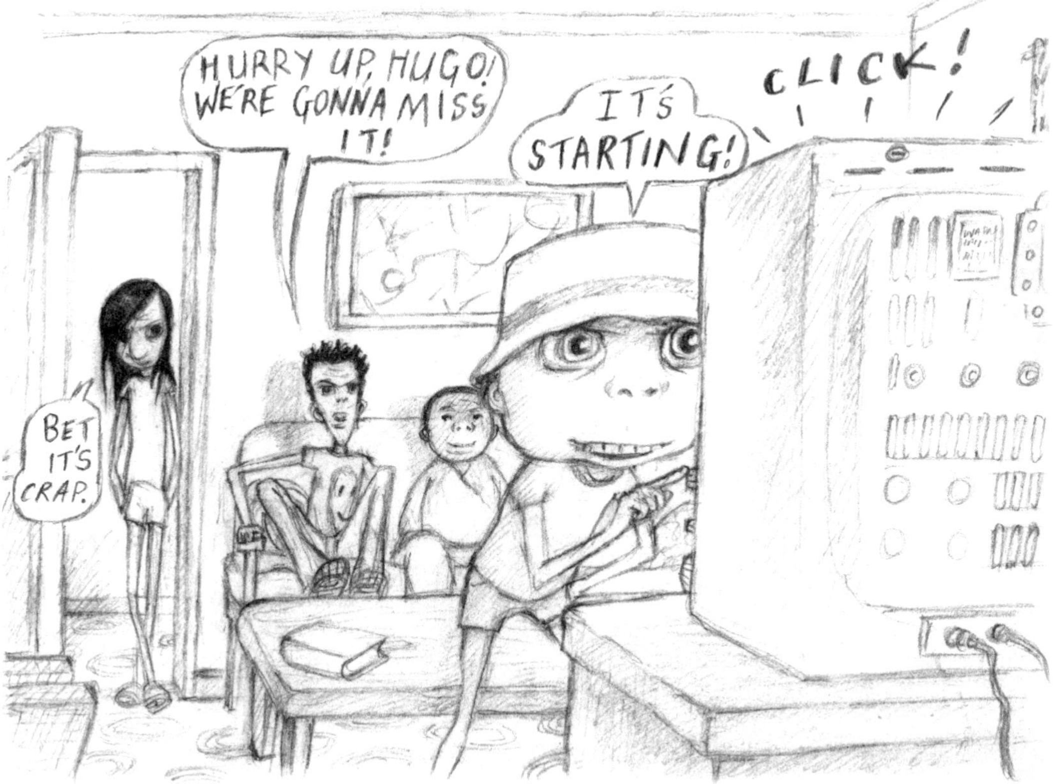
HURRY UP, HUGO! WE'RE GONNA MISS IT!
IT'S STARTING!
CLICK!
BET IT'S CRAP.

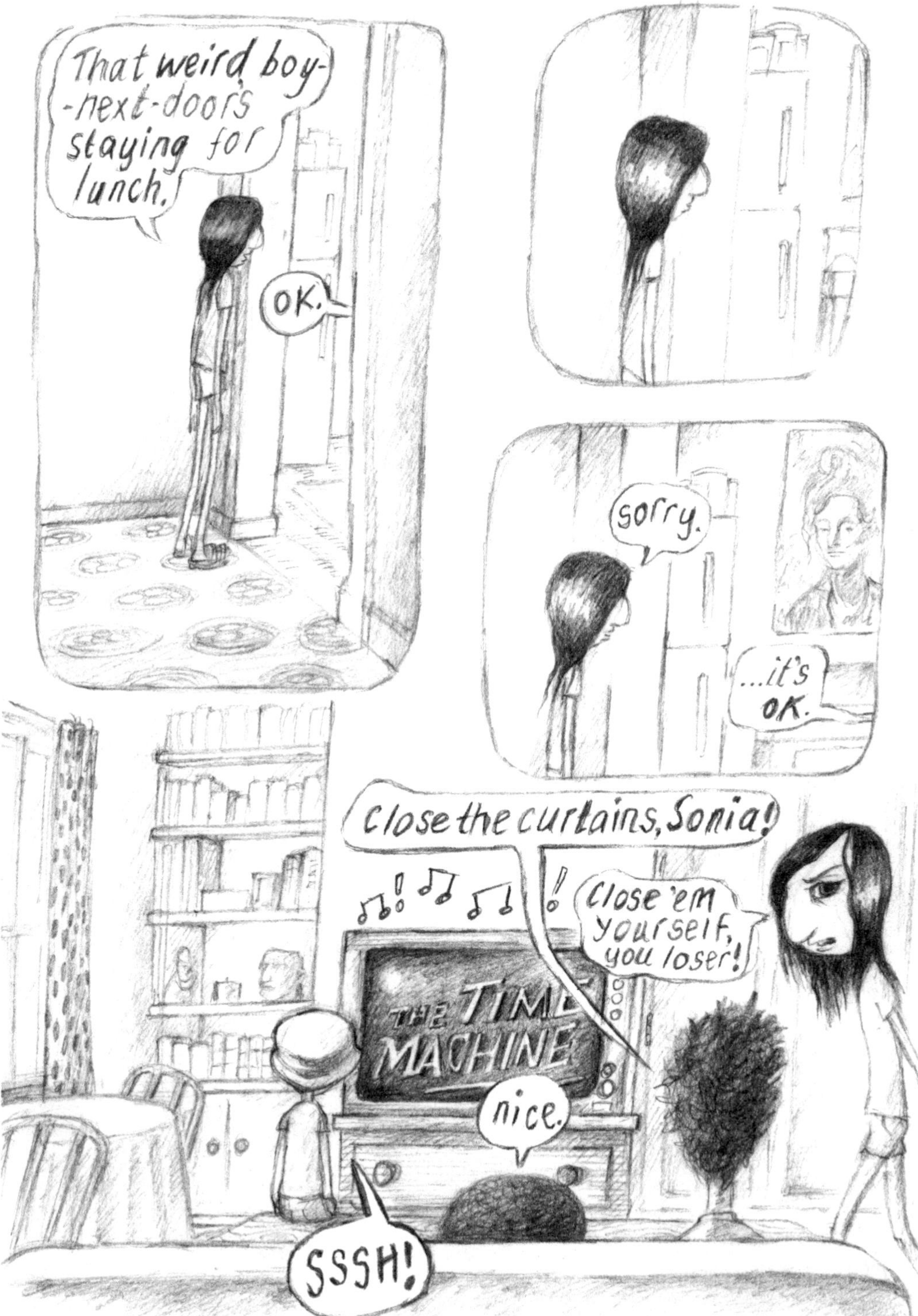
That weird boy-next-door's staying for lunch.
OK.
sorry.
...it's OK.
Close the curtains, Sonia!
Close 'em yourself, you loser!
THE TIME MACHINE
nice.
SSSH!

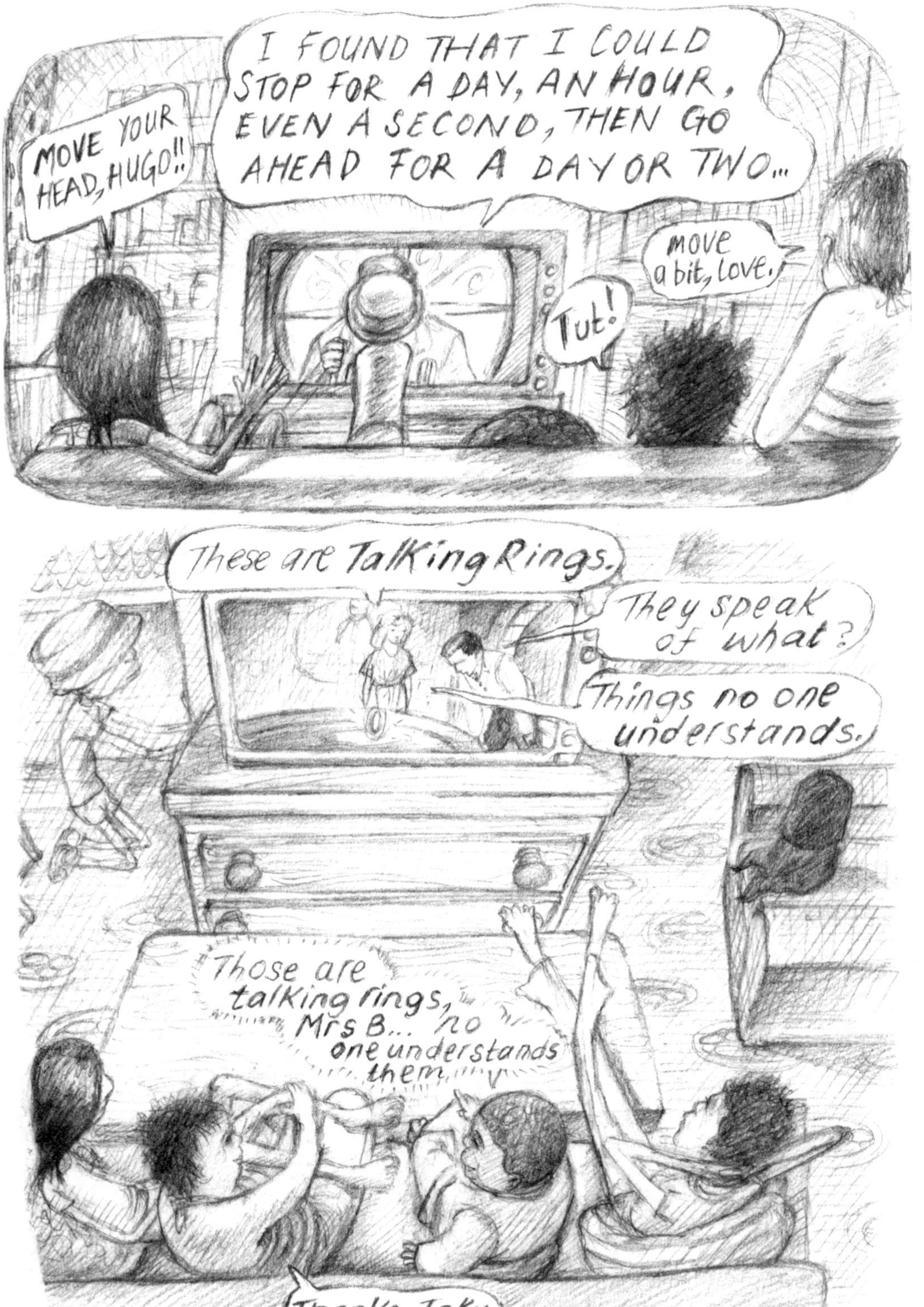
MOVE YOUR HEAD, HUGO!!
I FOUND THAT I COULD STOP FOR A DAY, AN HOUR, EVEN A SECOND, THEN GO AHEAD FOR A DAY OR TWO...
Tut!
move a bit, love.
These are TalKing Rings.
They speak of what?
Things no one understands.
Those are talking rings, Mrs B... no one understands them.
Thanks, Icky.

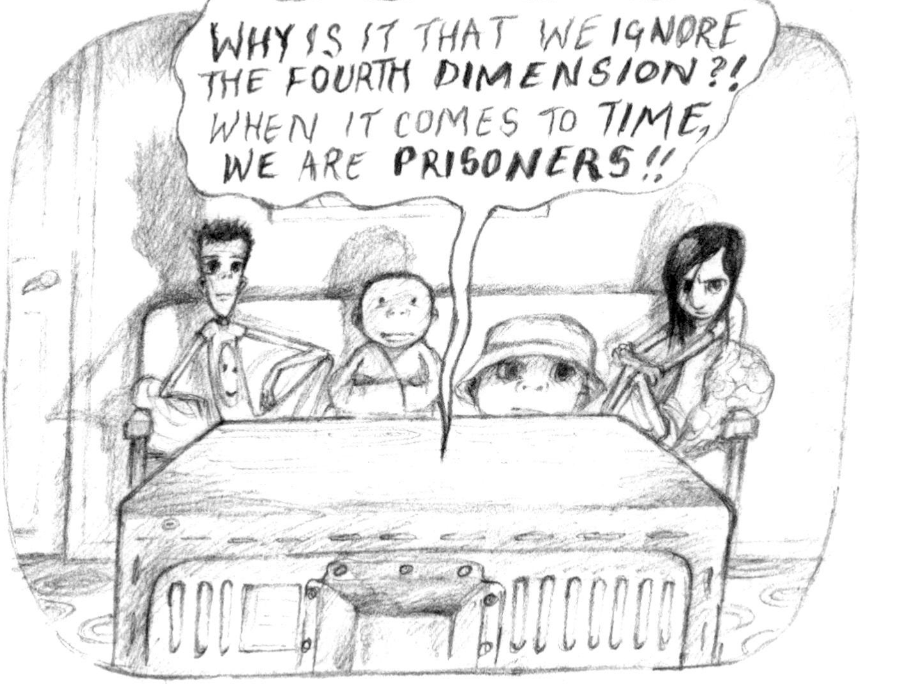
WHY IS IT THAT WE IGNORE THE FOURTH DIMENSION?! WHEN IT COMES TO TIME, WE ARE PRISONERS!!

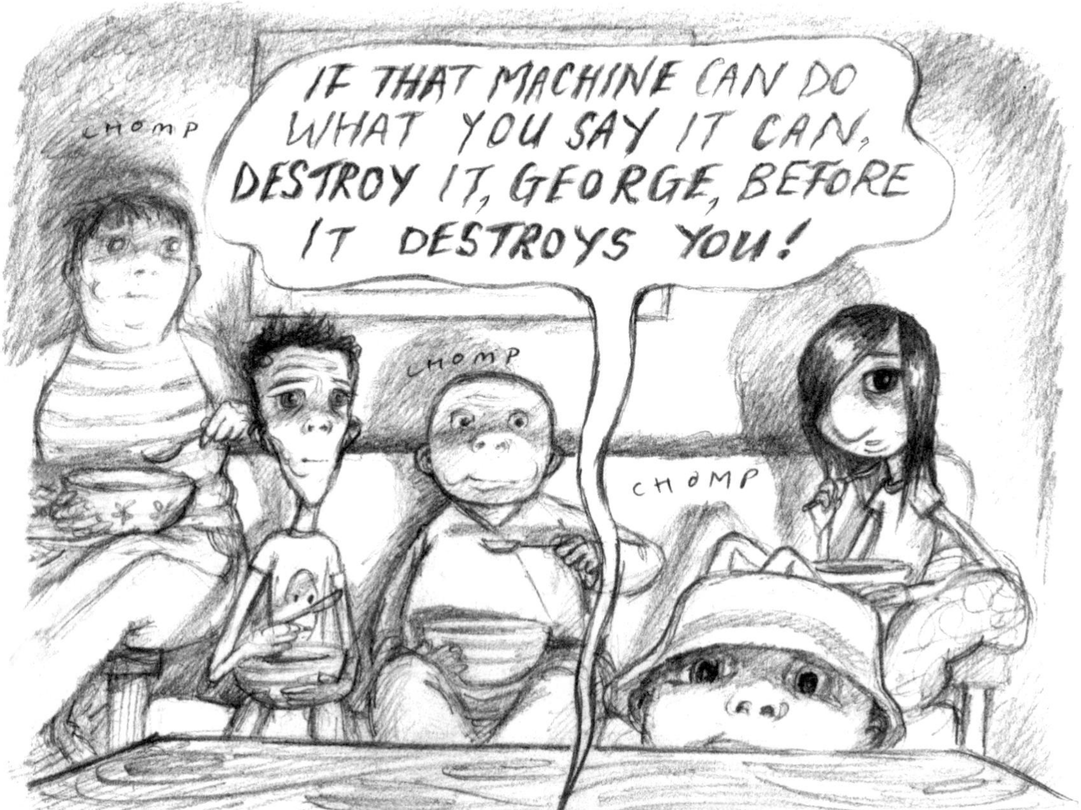
CHOMP
IF THAT MACHINE CAN DO WHAT YOU SAY IT CAN, DESTROY IT, GEORGE, BEFORE IT DESTROYS YOU!
CHOMP
CHOMP

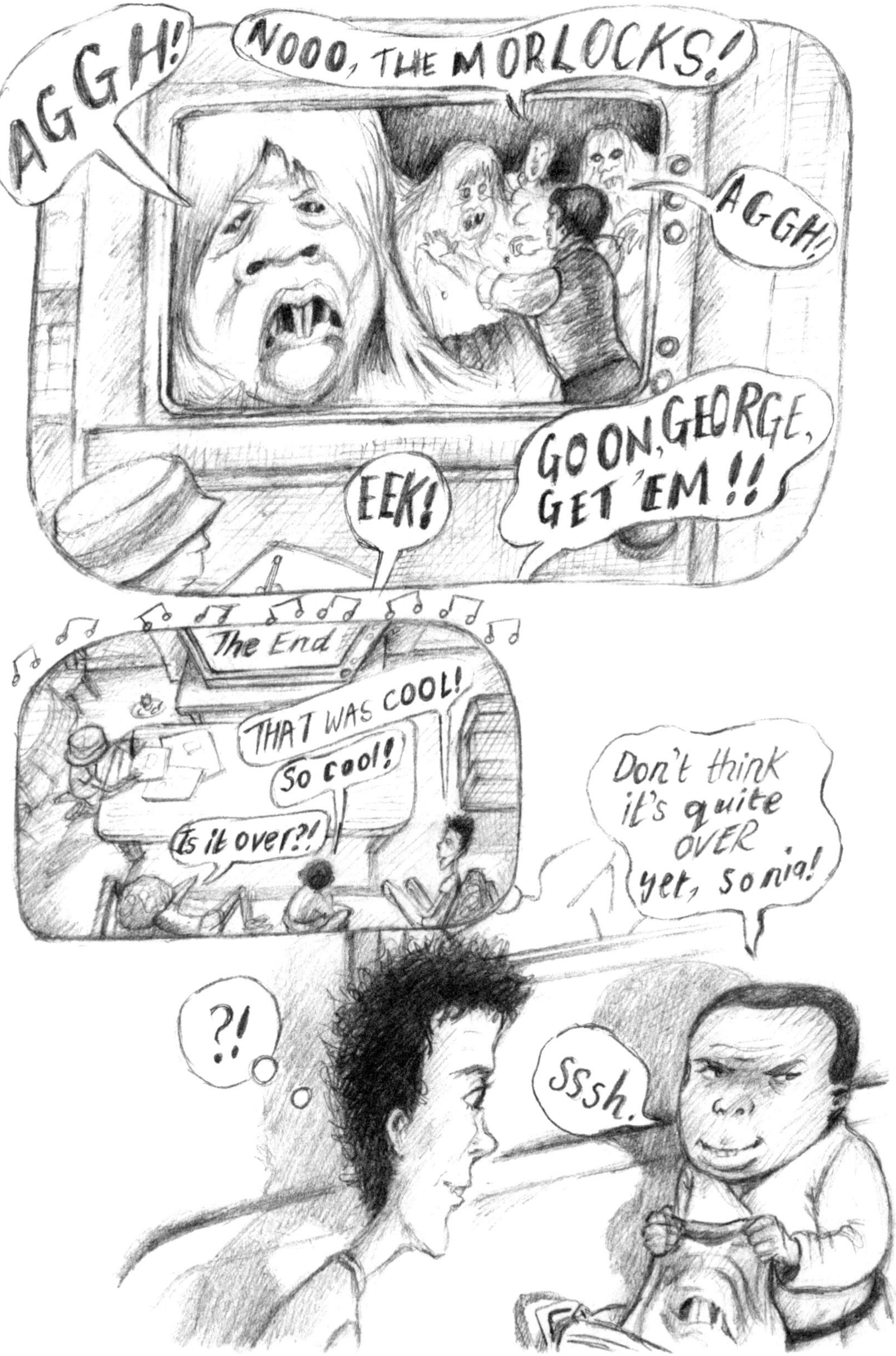
AGGH!
NOOO, THE MORLOCKS!
AGGH!
GO ON, GEORGE, GET 'EM!!
EEK!
The End
THAT WAS COOL!
So cool!
Is it over?!
Don't think it's quite OVER yet, Sonia!
?!
Sssh.

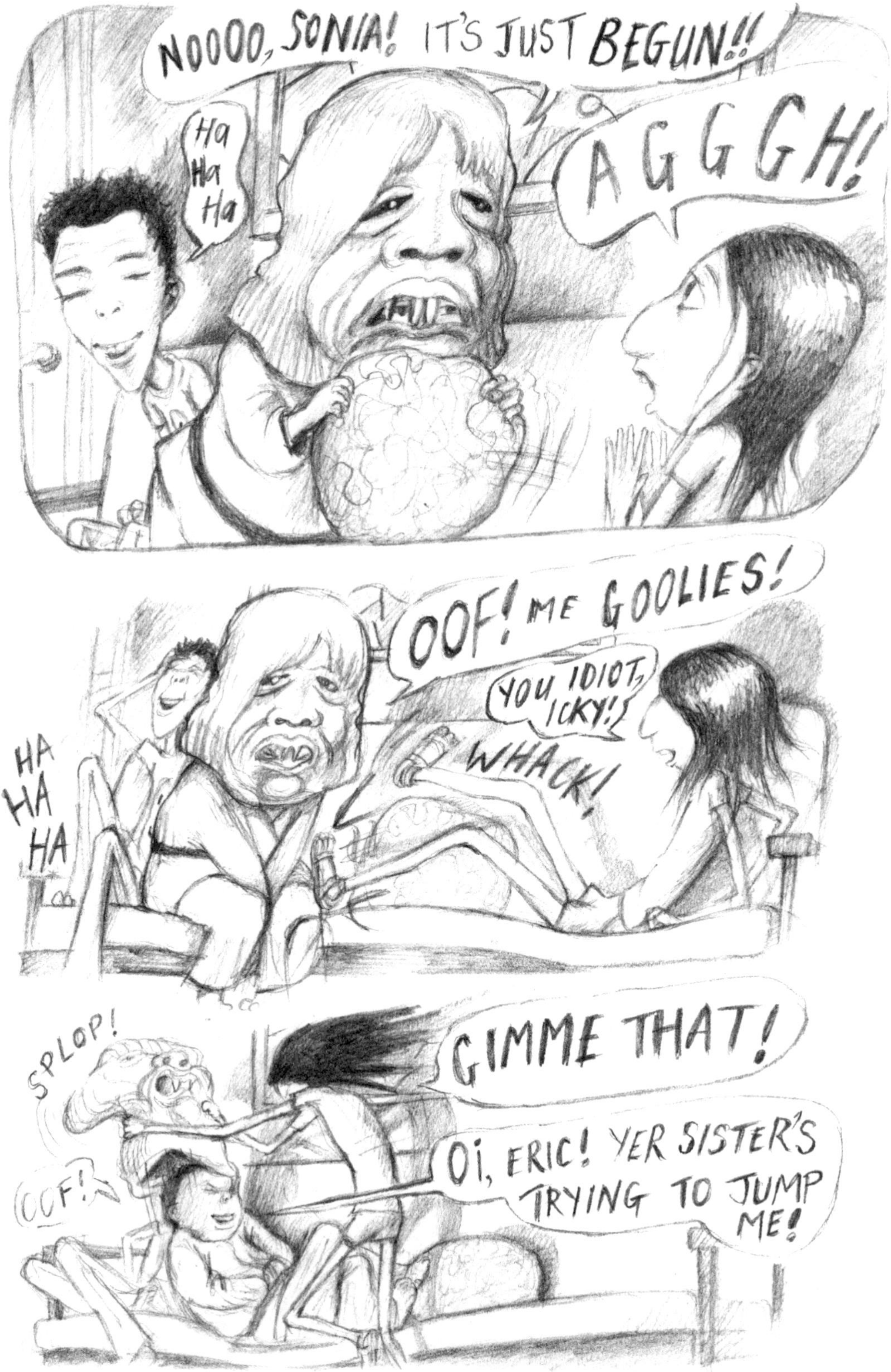
NOOOO, SONIA! IT'S JUST BEGUN!!
Ha Ha Ha
AGGGH!
OOF! ME GOOLIES!
YOU IDIOT, ICKY!
HA HA HA
WHACK!
GIMME THAT!
SPLOP!
OOF!
Oi, ERIC! YER SISTER'S TRYING TO JUMP ME!

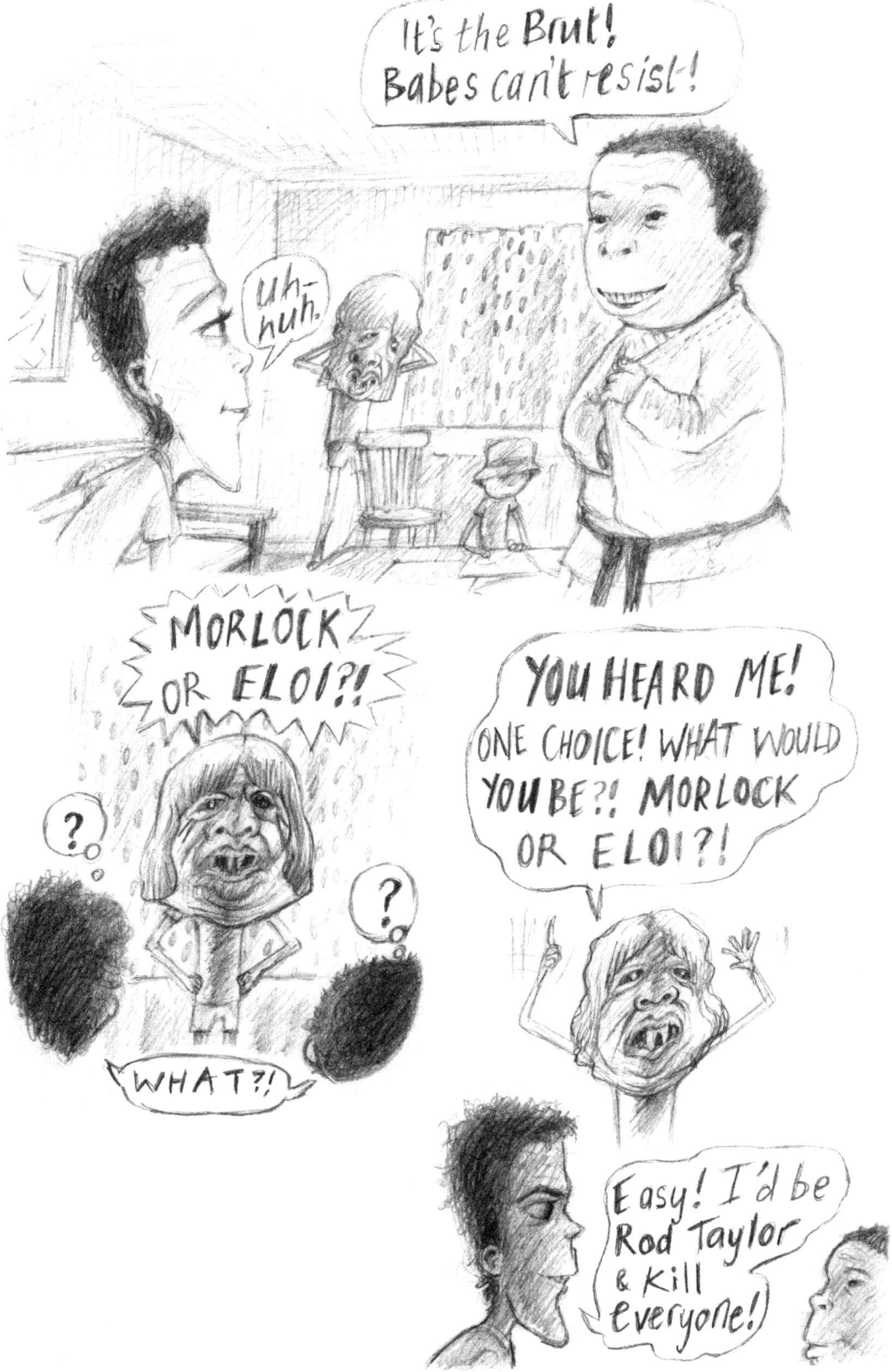
It's the Brut! Babes can't resist!
uh-huh.
MORLOCK OR ELOI?!
?
?
WHAT?!
YOU HEARD ME! ONE CHOICE! WHAT WOULD YOU BE?! MORLOCK OR ELOI?!
Easy! I'd be Rod Taylor & kill everyone!

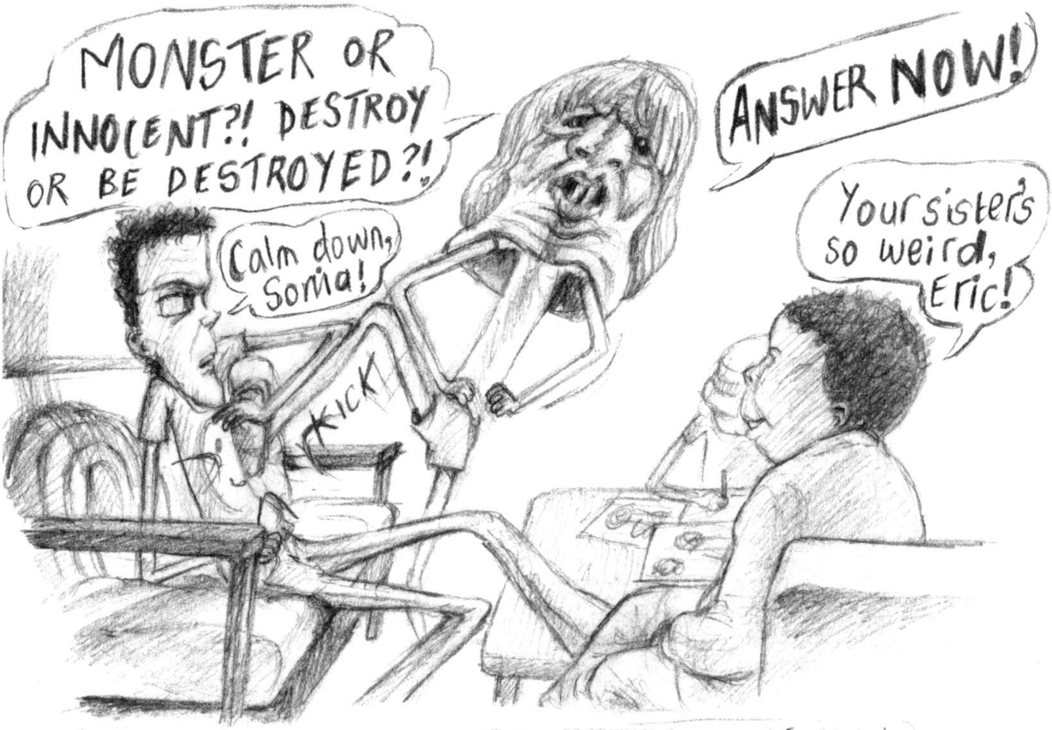
MONSTER OR INNOCENT?! DESTROY OR BE DESTROYED?!
ANSWER NOW!
Calm down, Sonia!
KICK
Your sister's so weird, Eric!

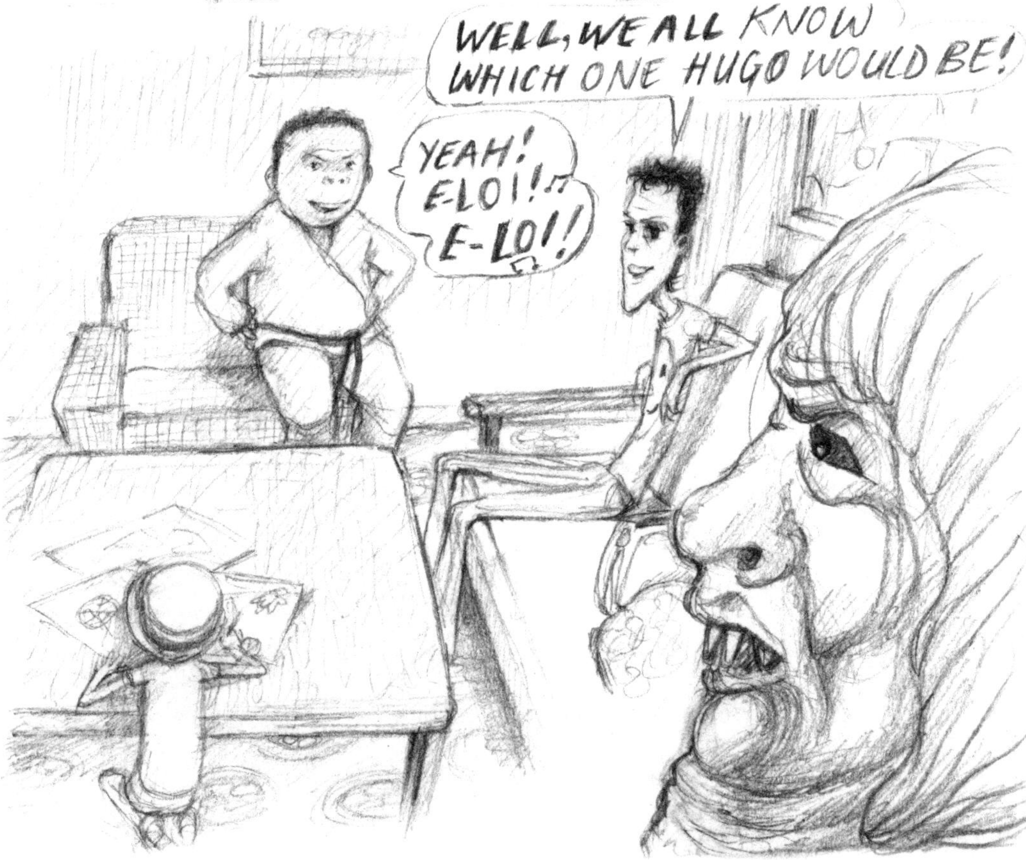
WELL, WE ALL KNOW WHICH ONE HUGO WOULD BE!
YEAH! E-LOI! E-LOI!

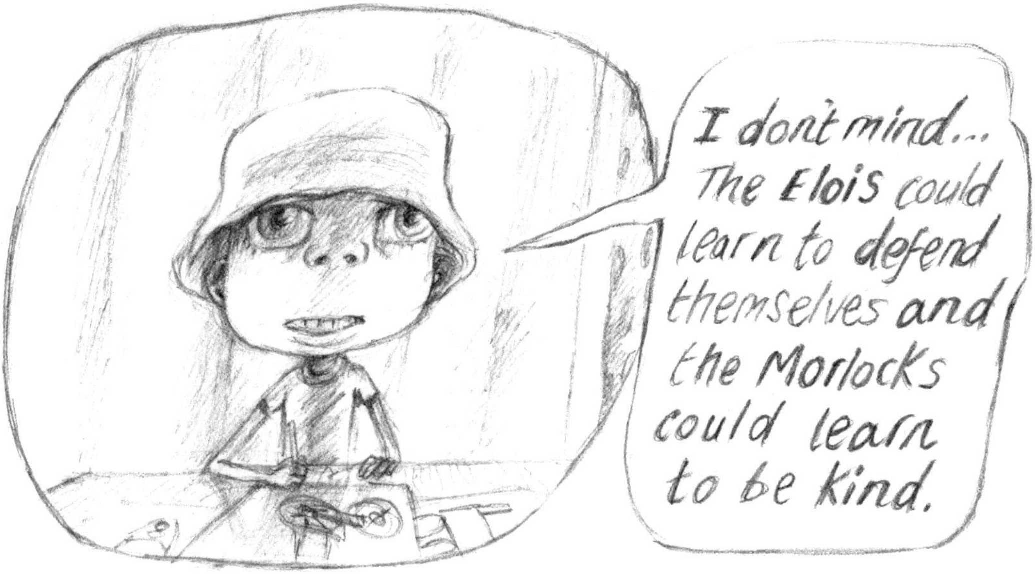
I don't mind... The Elois could learn to defend themselves and the Morlocks could learn to be kind.

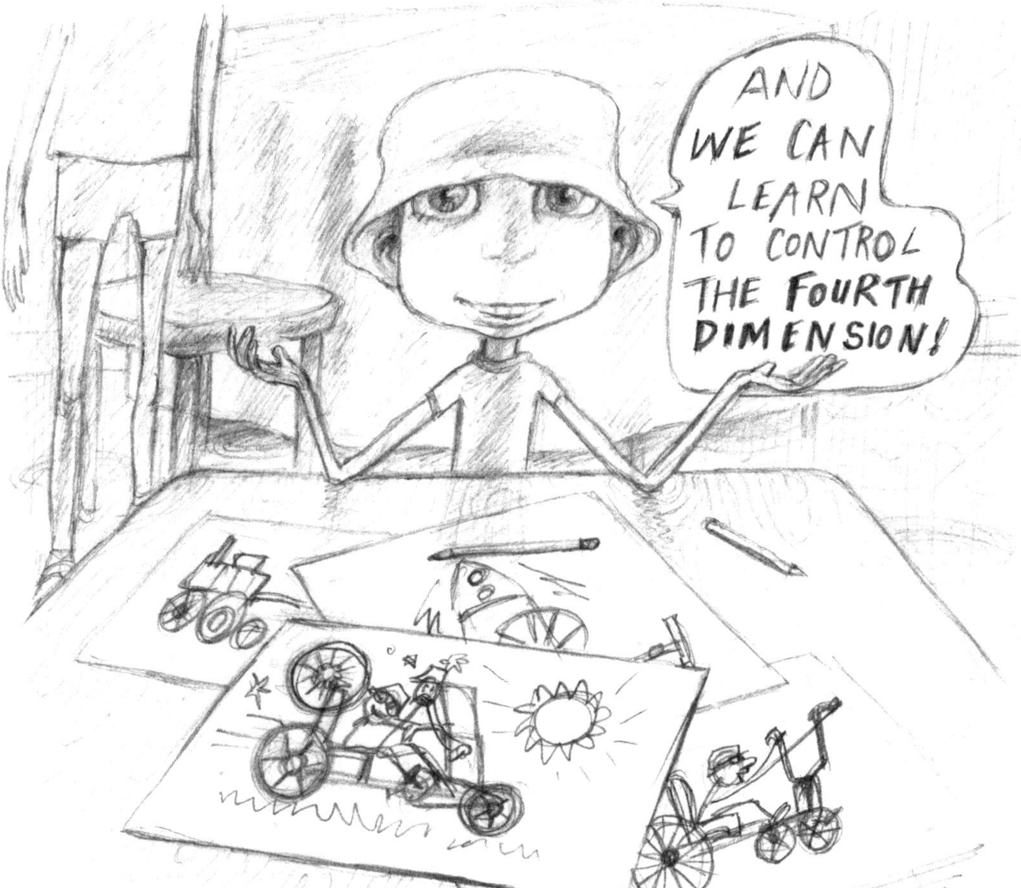
AND WE CAN LEARN TO CONTROL THE FOURTH DIMENSION!

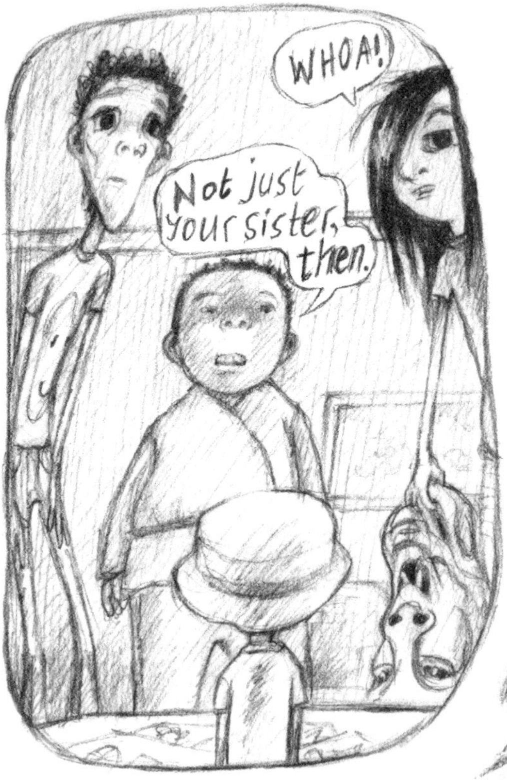
WHOA!
Not just your sister, then.

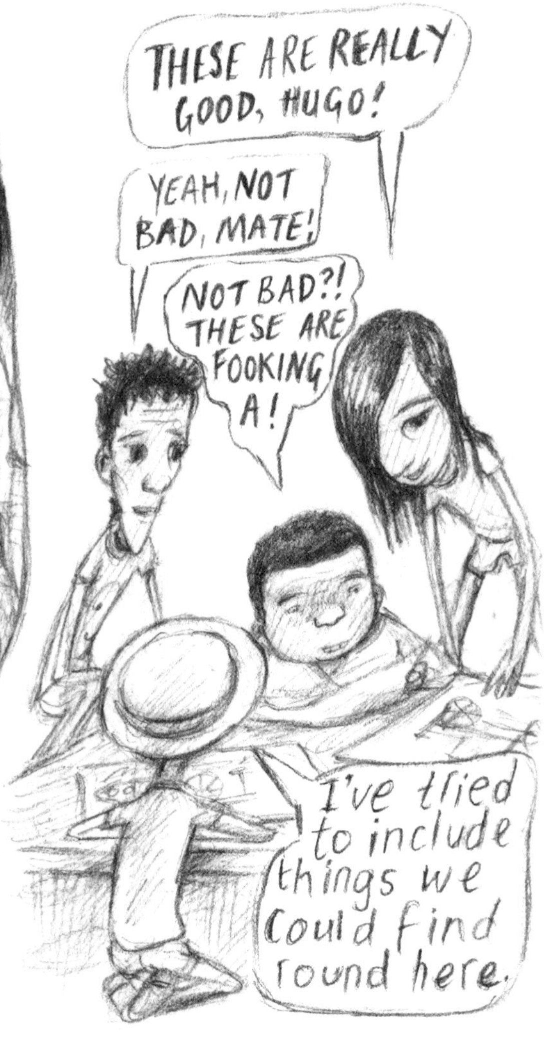
THESE ARE REALLY GOOD, HUGO!
YEAH, NOT BAD, MATE!
NOT BAD?! THESE ARE FOOKING A!
I've tried to include things we could find round here.

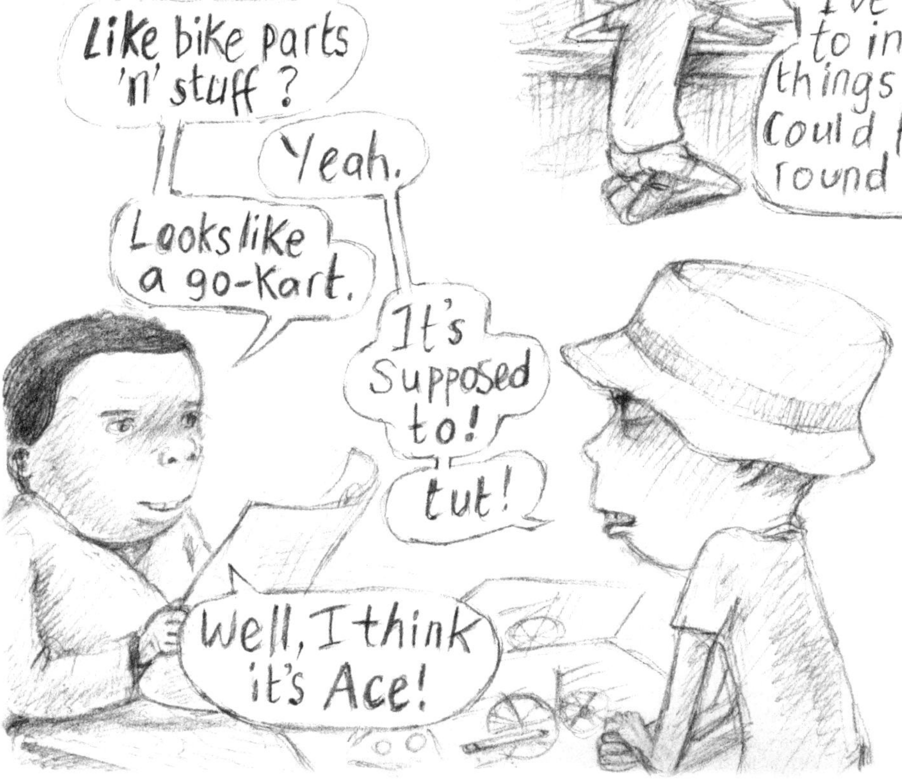
Like bike parts 'n' stuff?
Yeah.
Looks like a go-Kart.
It's Supposed to!
tut!
Well, I think it's Ace!

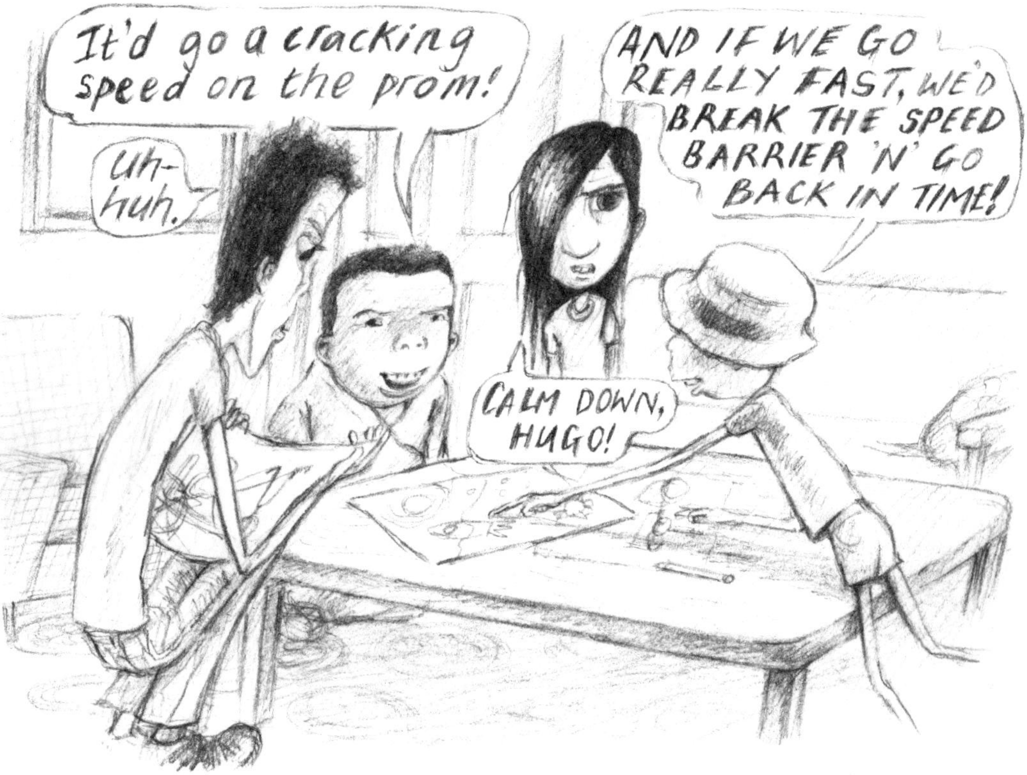
It'd go a cracking speed on the prom!
Uh-huh.
AND IF WE GO REALLY FAST, WE'D BREAK THE SPEED BARRIER 'N' GO BACK IN TIME!
CALM DOWN, HUGO!

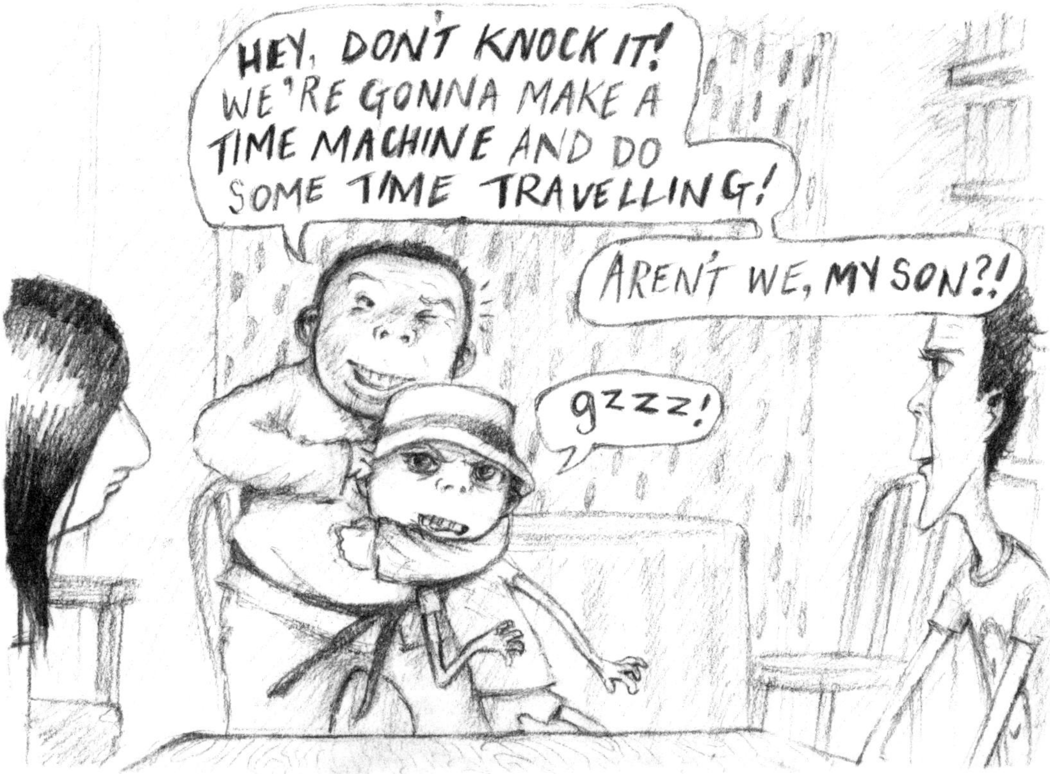
HEY, DON'T KNOCK IT! WE'RE GONNA MAKE A TIME MACHINE AND DO SOME TIME TRAVELLING!
AREN'T WE, MY SON?!
gzzz!

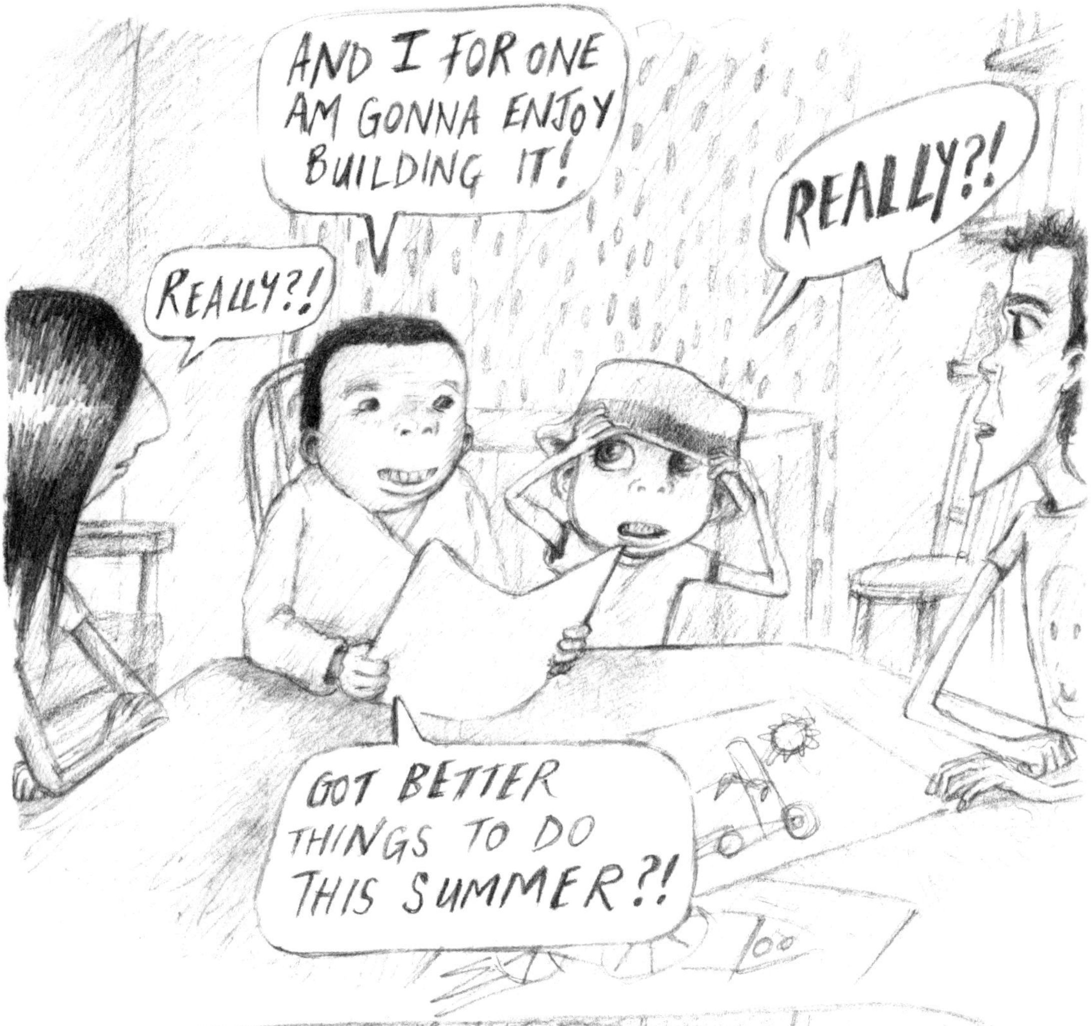
AND I FOR ONE AM GONNA ENJOY BUILDING IT!
REALLY?!
REALLY?!
GOT BETTER THINGS TO DO THIS SUMMER?!

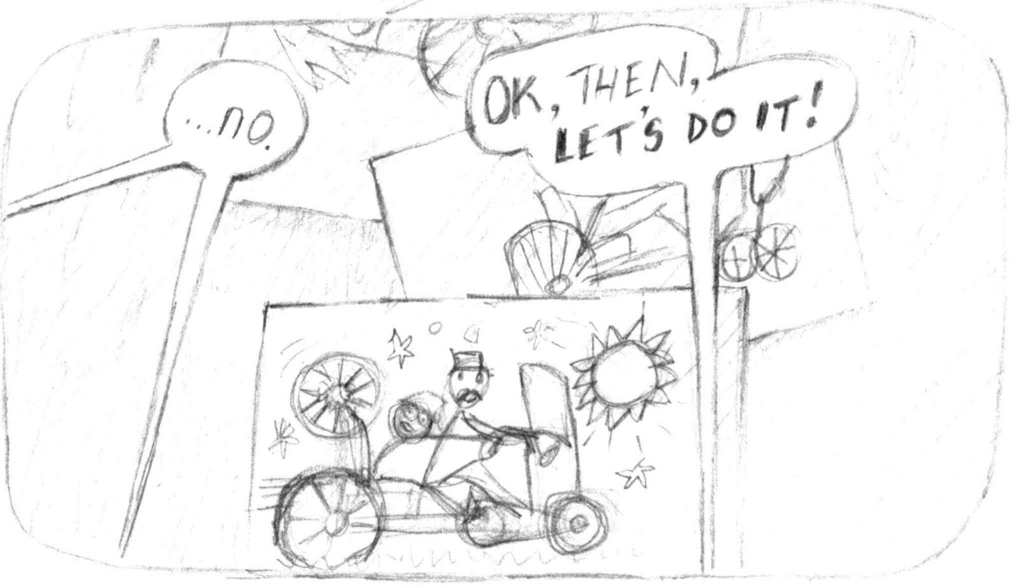
...no.
OK, THEN, LET'S DO IT!

Chapter Five

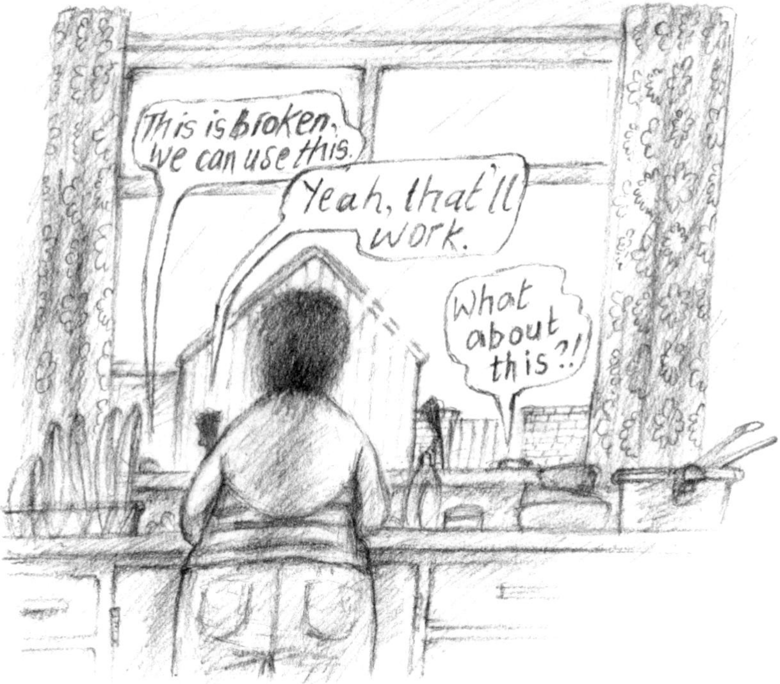
This is broken, we can use this.
Yeah, that'll work.
What about this?!

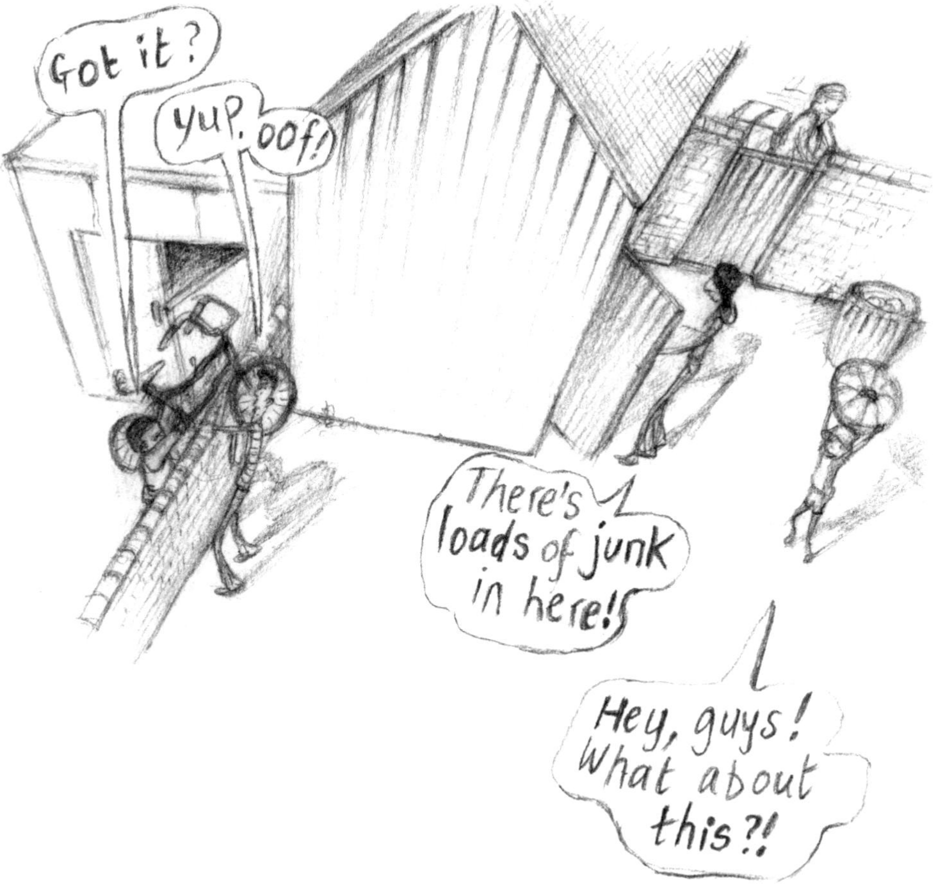
Got it?
yup.
oof!
There's loads of junk in here!
Hey, guys! What about this?!

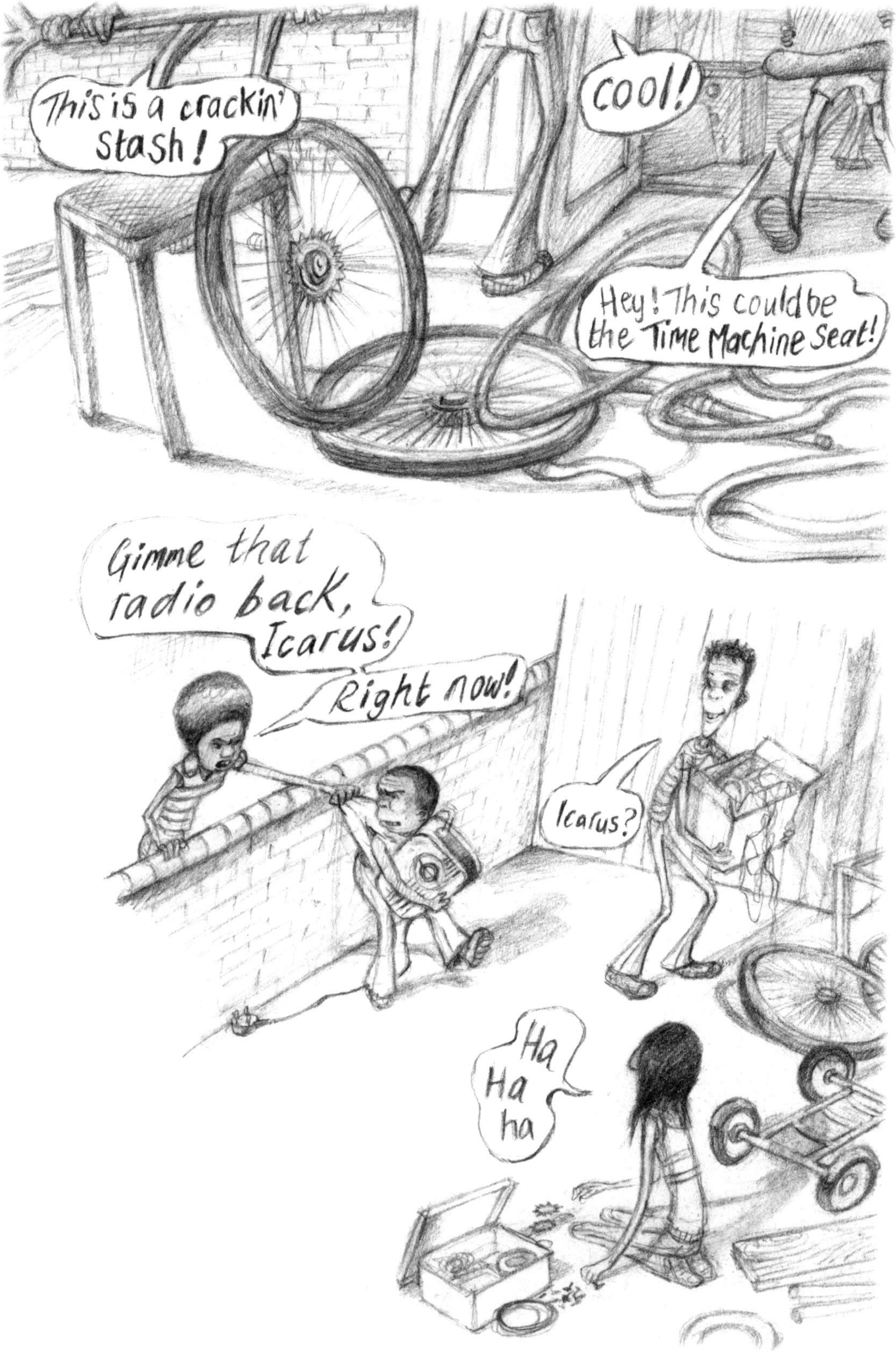
This is a crackin' stash!
cool!
Hey! This could be the Time Machine Seat!
Gimme that radio back, Icarus!
Right now!
Icarus?
Ha Ha ha

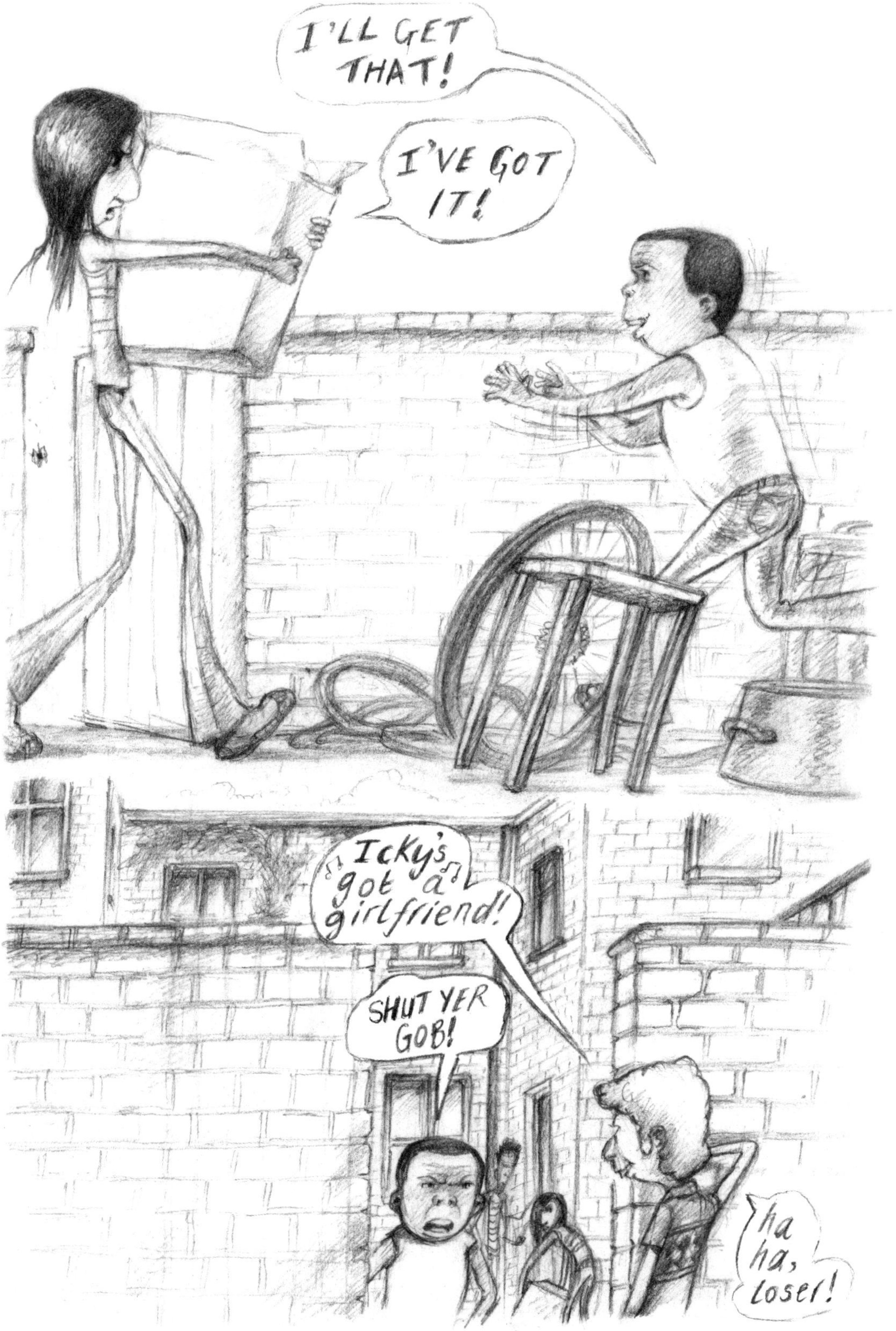
I'LL GET THAT!
I'VE GOT IT!
Icky's got a girlfriend!
SHUT YER GOB!
ha ha, loser!

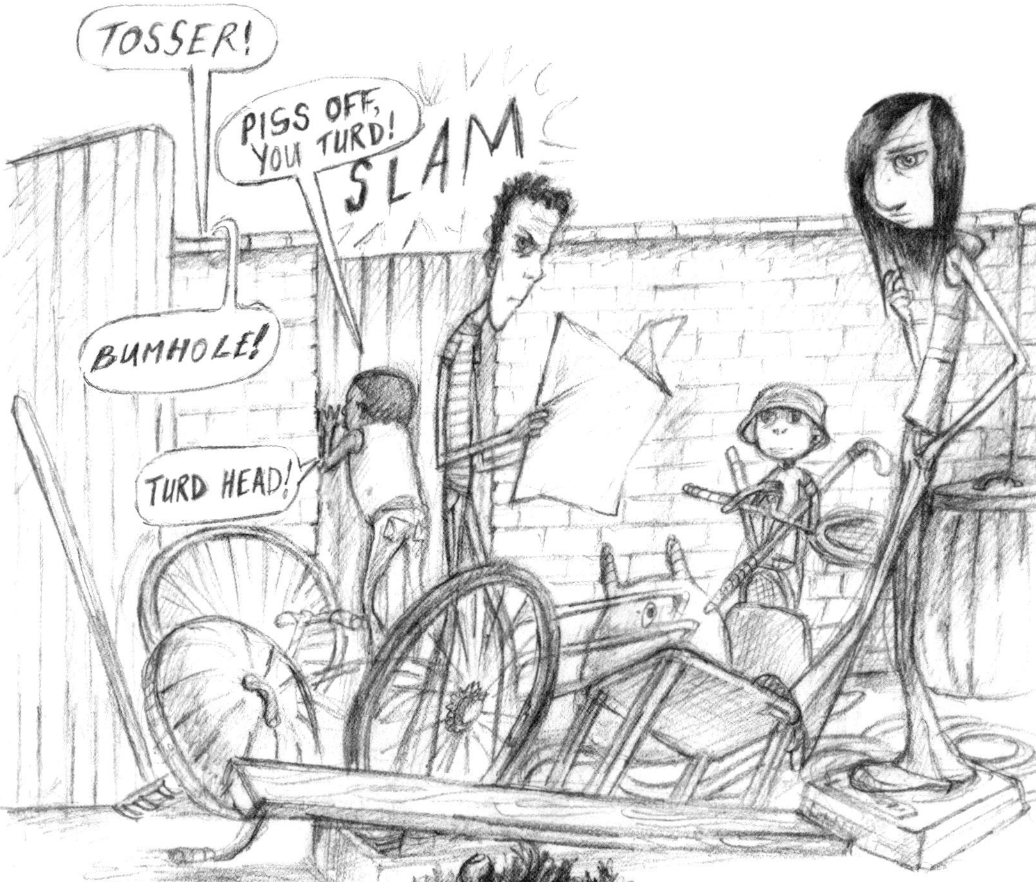
TOSSER!
PISS OFF, YOU TURD!
SLAM
BUMHOLE!
TURD HEAD!

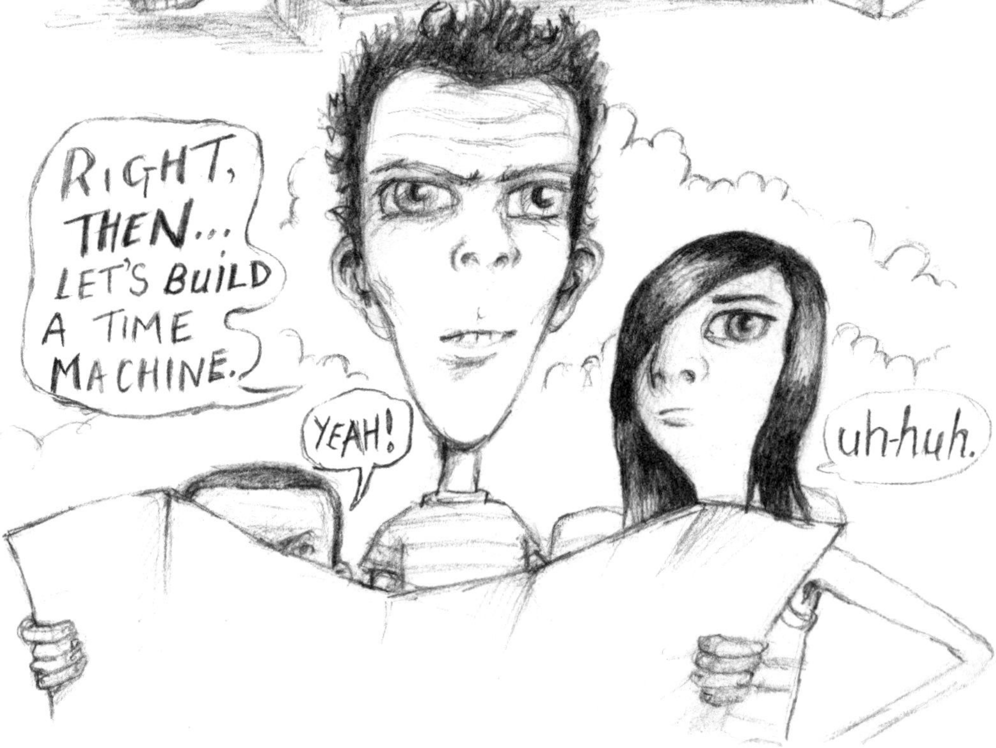
RIGHT, THEN... LET'S BUILD A TIME MACHINE.
YEAH!
uh-huh.

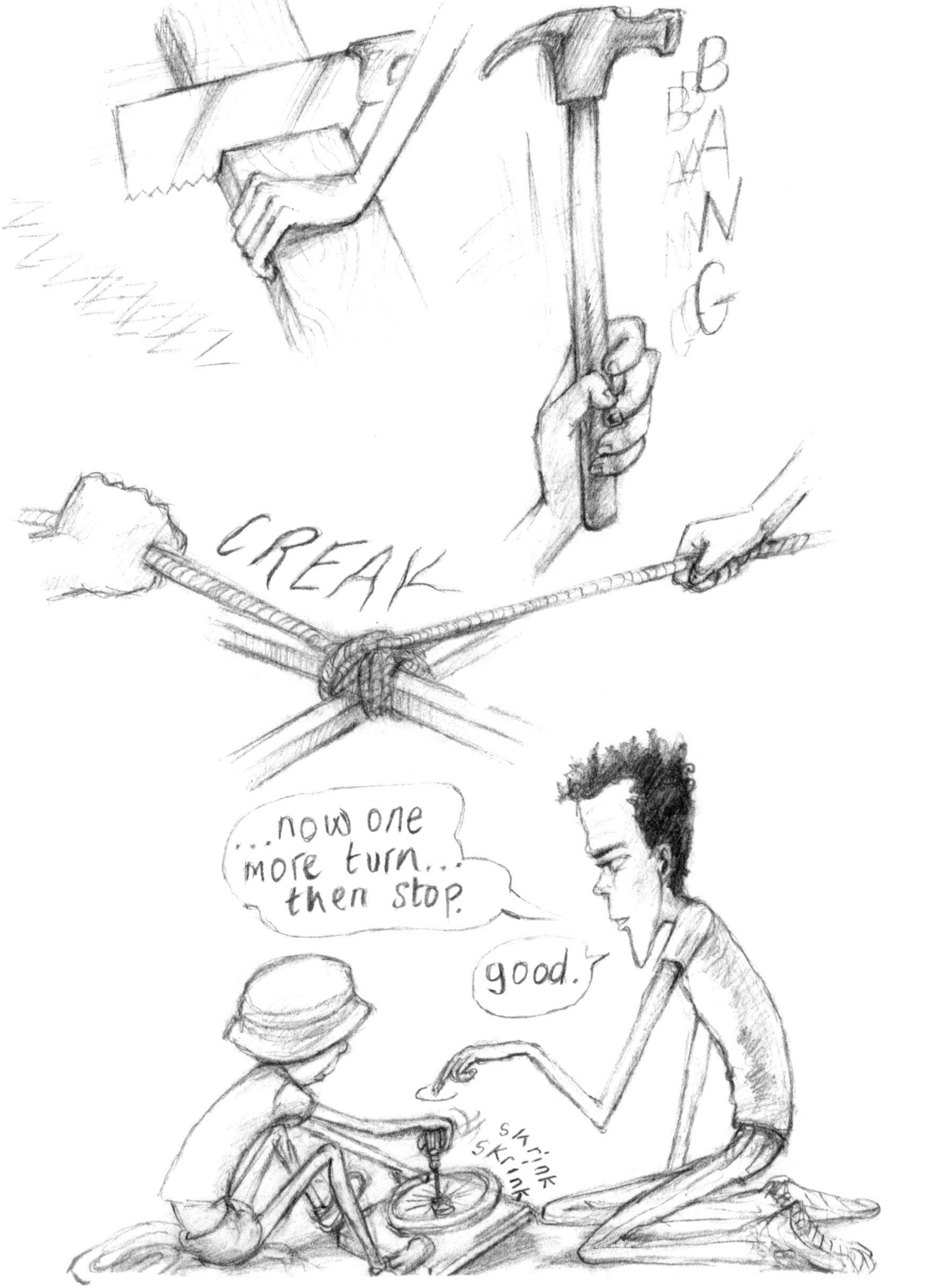
BANG
CREAK
...now one more turn... then stop.
good.
skrink
skrink

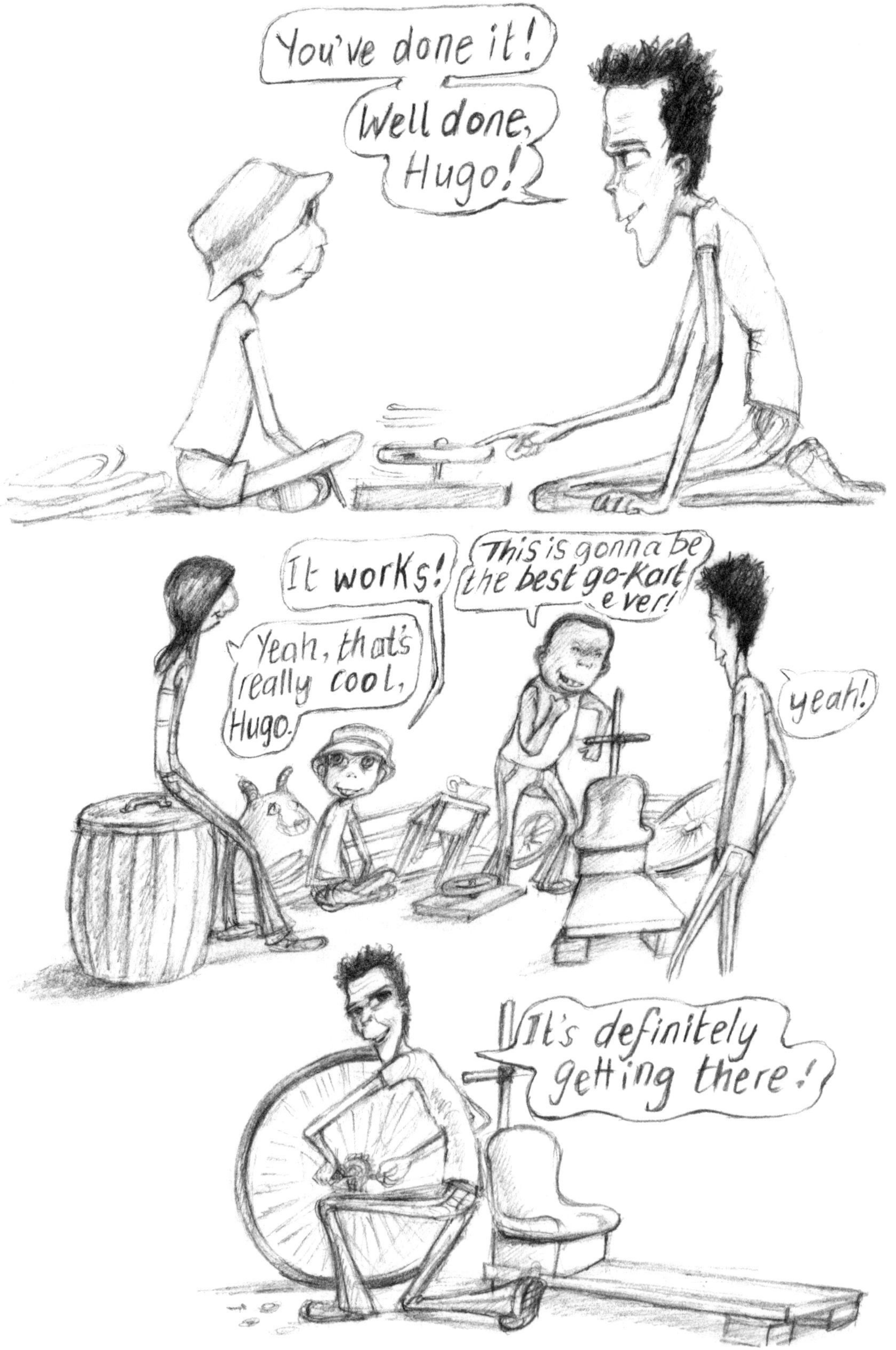
You've done it!
Well done, Hugo!
It works!
Yeah, that's really cool, Hugo.
This is gonna be the best go-kart ever!
yeah!
It's definitely getting there!

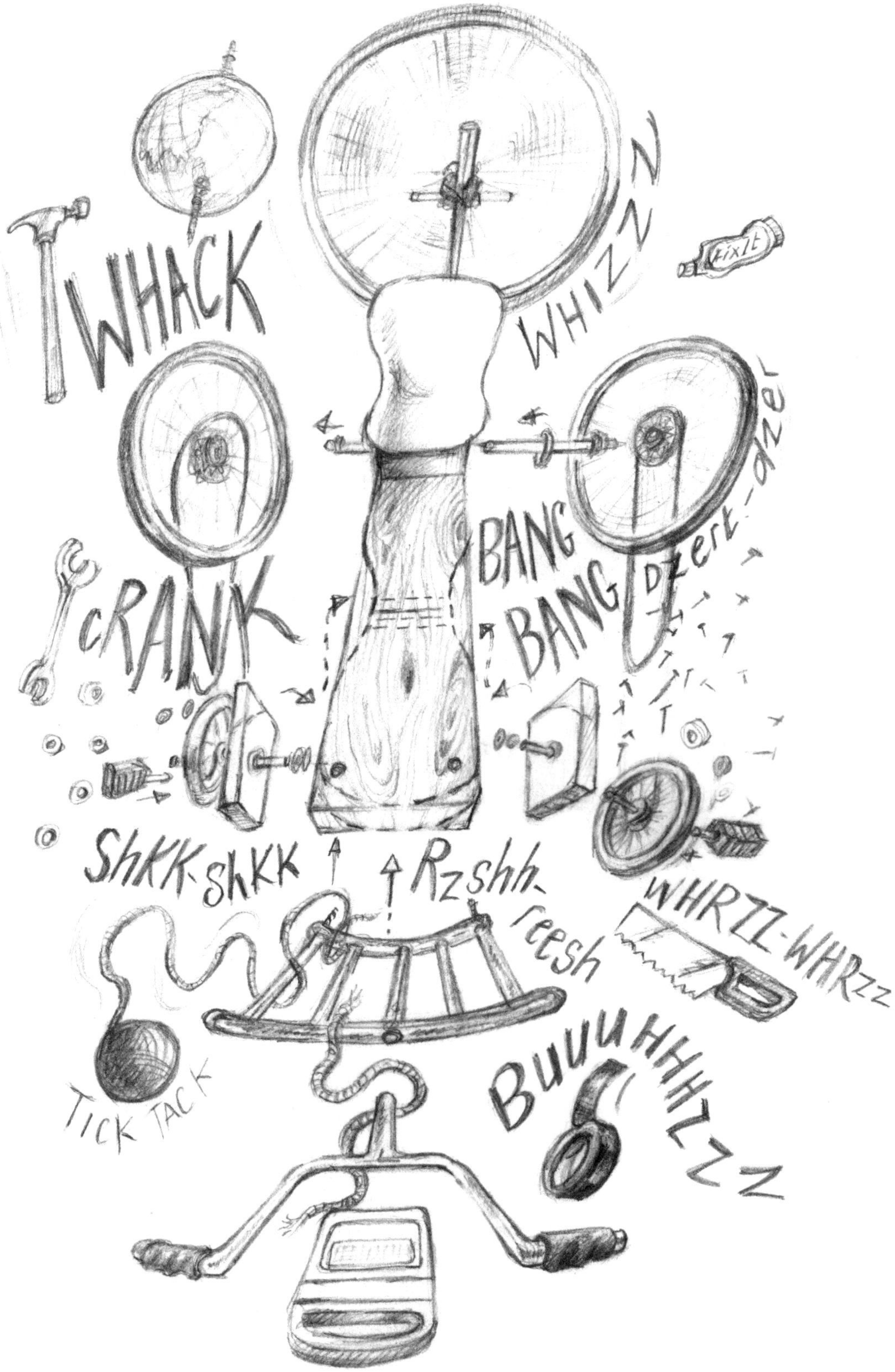

WHACK
WHIZZZZ
fixit
cRANK
BANG
BANG
dzert-dzer
ShKK-ShKK
Rzshh-reesh
WHRZZ-WHRzz
TICK TACK
BuuuHHHZZZZ

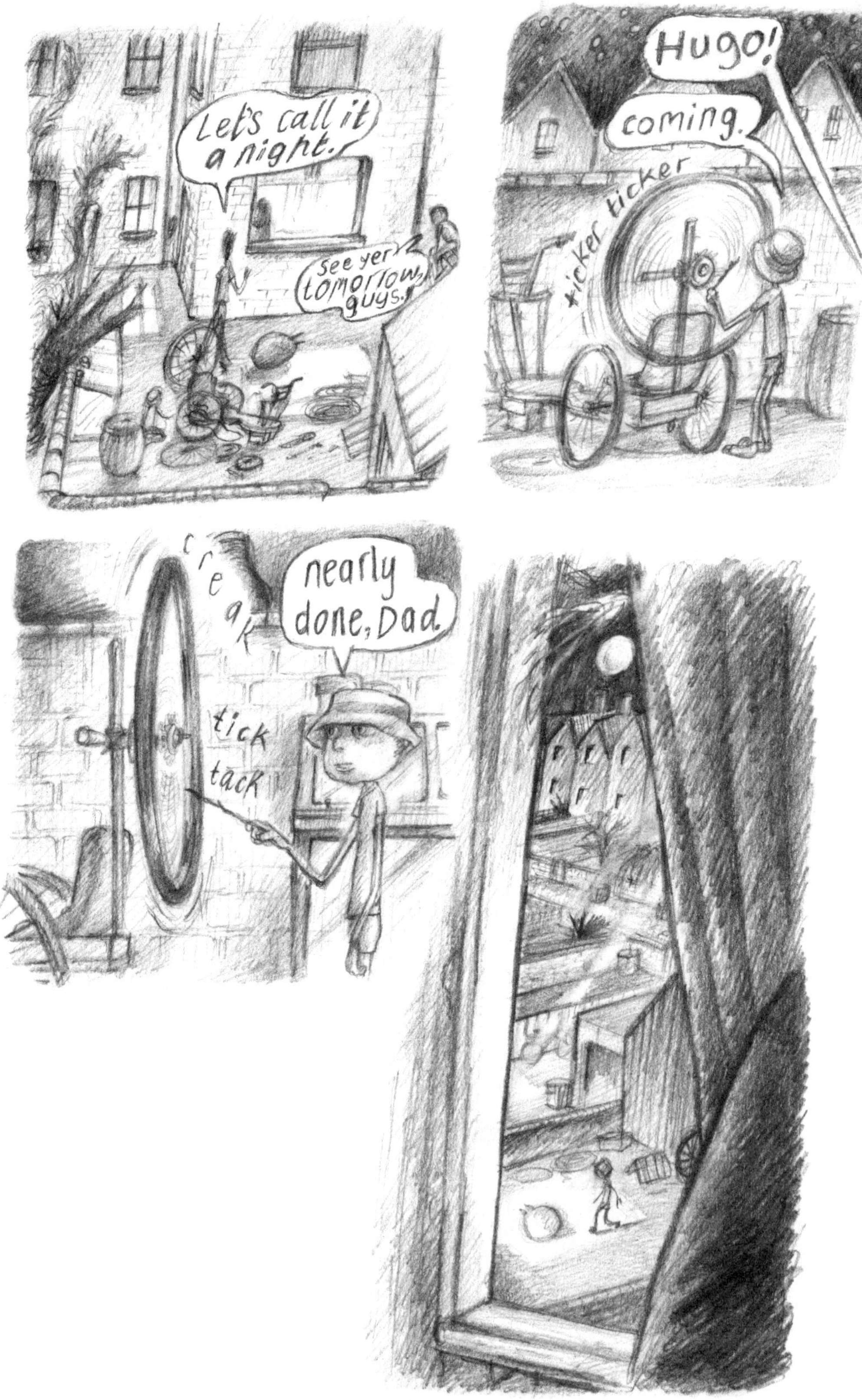
Let's call it a night.
See yer tomorrow, guys.
Hugo!
coming.
ticker ticker
creak
nearly done, Dad.
tick
tack

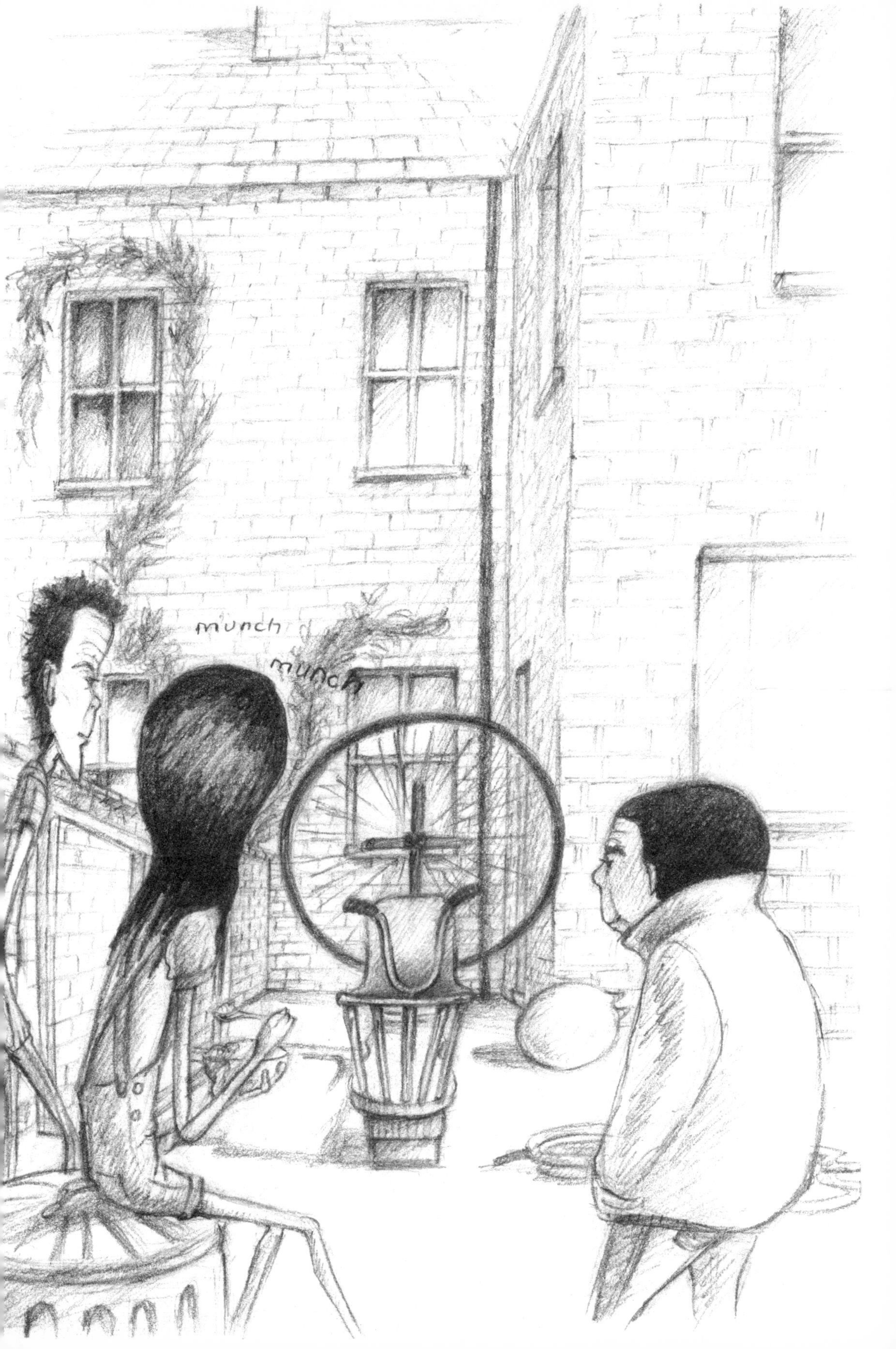
munch
munch

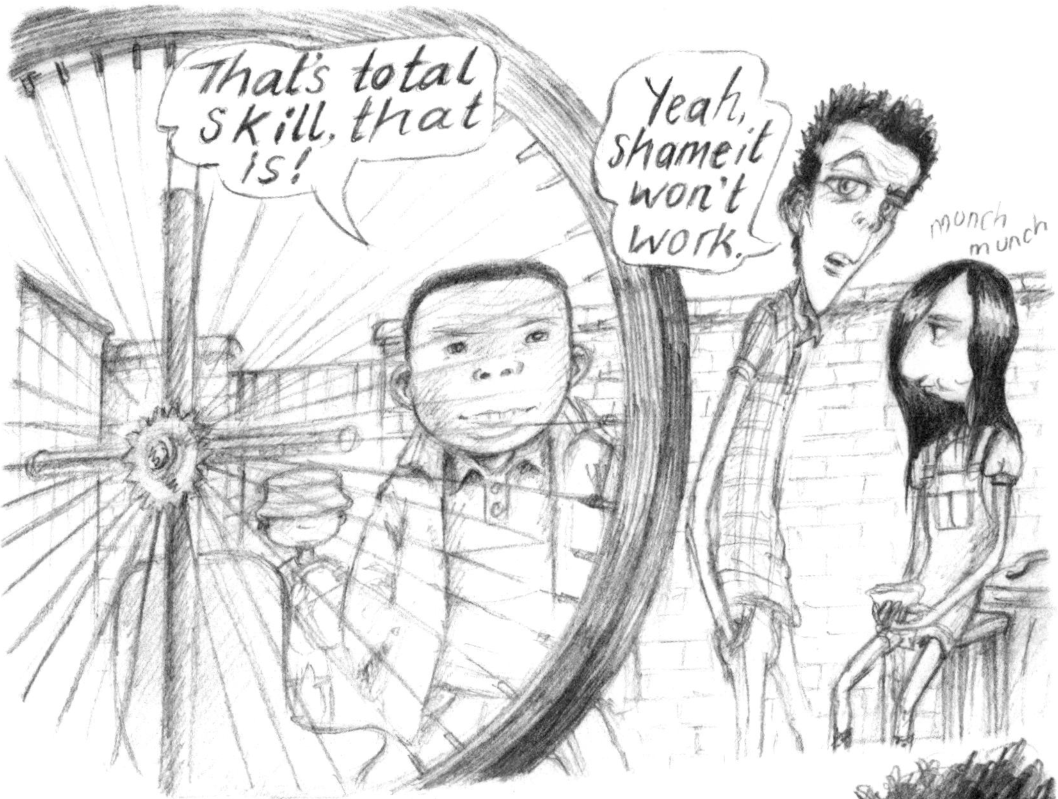
That's total skill, that is!
Yeah, shame it won't work.
munch munch

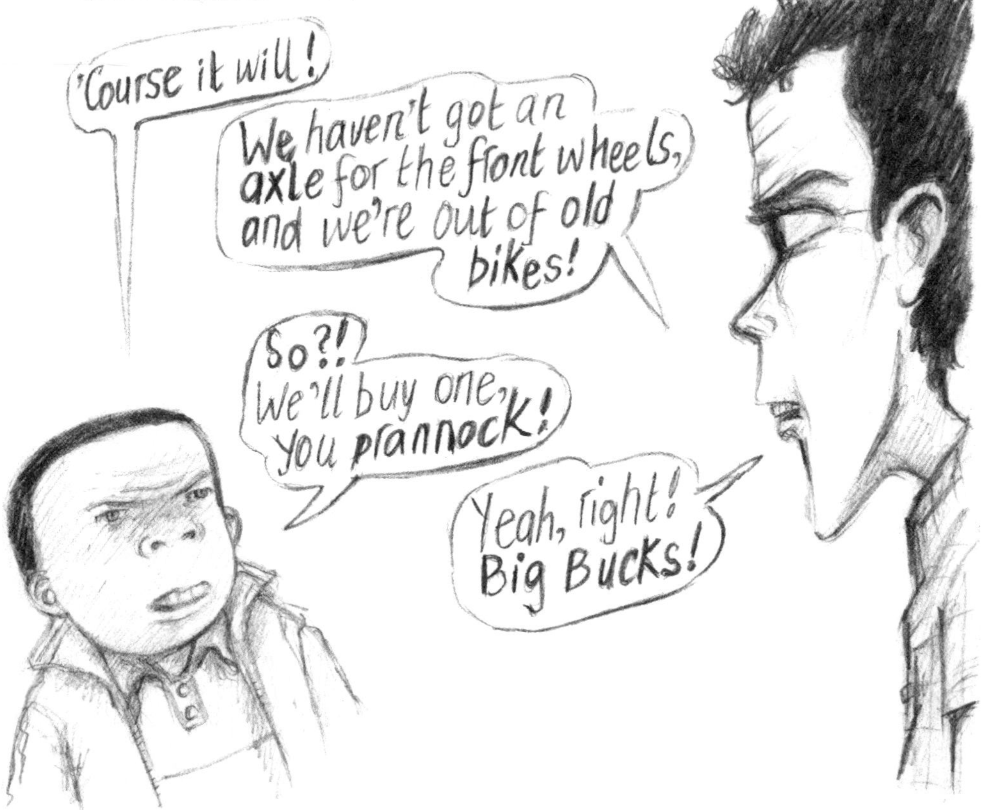
'Course it will!
We haven't got an axle for the front wheels, and we're out of old bikes!
So?! We'll buy one, you prannock!
Yeah, right! Big Bucks!

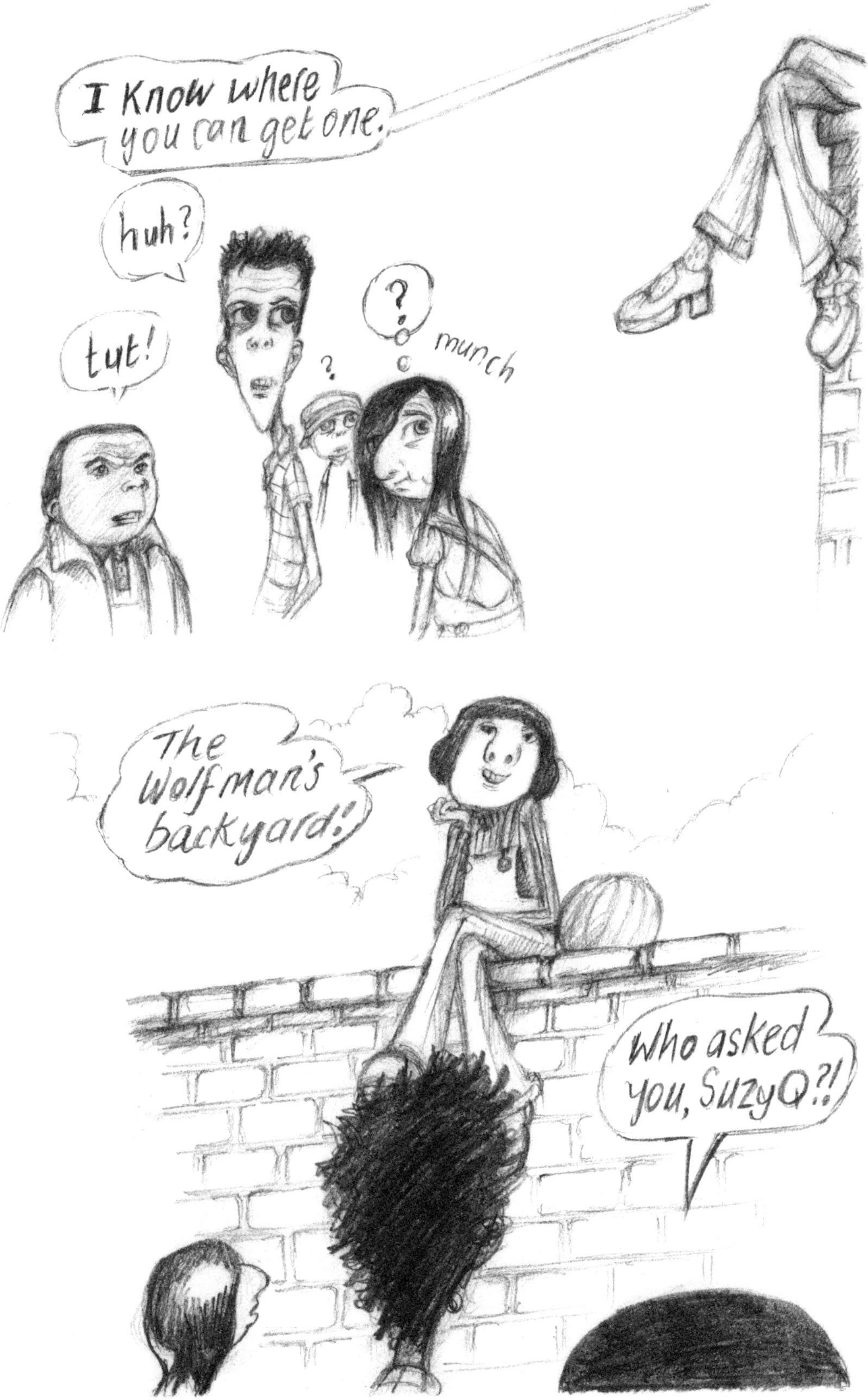
I Know where you can get one.
huh?
tut!
?
?
munch
The Wolfman's backyard!
Who asked you, SuzyQ?!

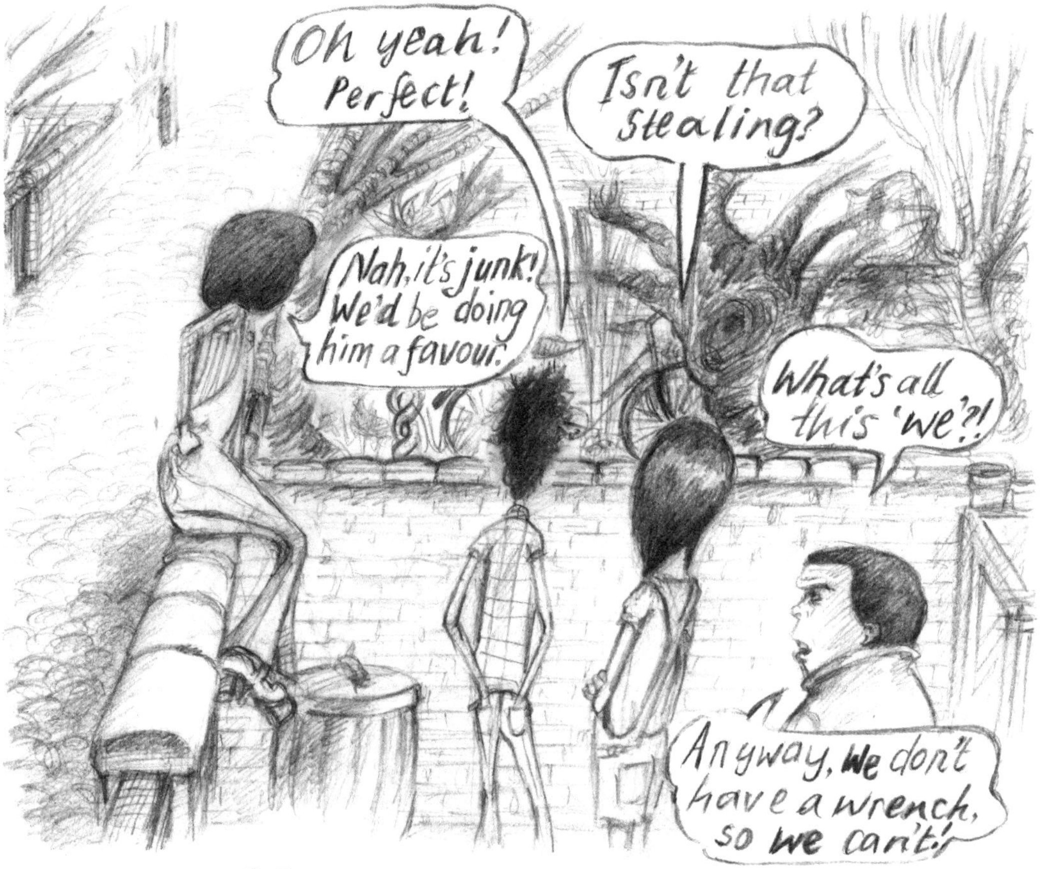
Oh yeah! Perfect!
Isn't that stealing?
Nah, it's junk! We'd be doing him a favour.
What's all this 'we'?!
Anyway, we don't have a wrench, so we can't!

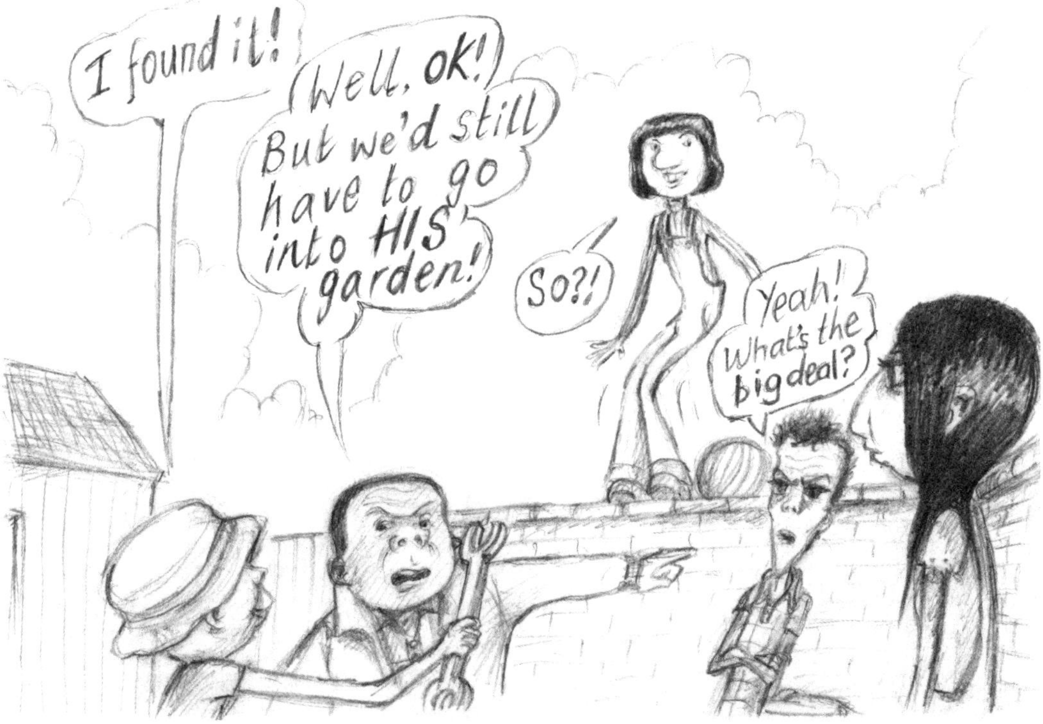
I found it!
Well, OK! But we'd still have to go into HIS garden!
So?!
Yeah! What's the big deal?

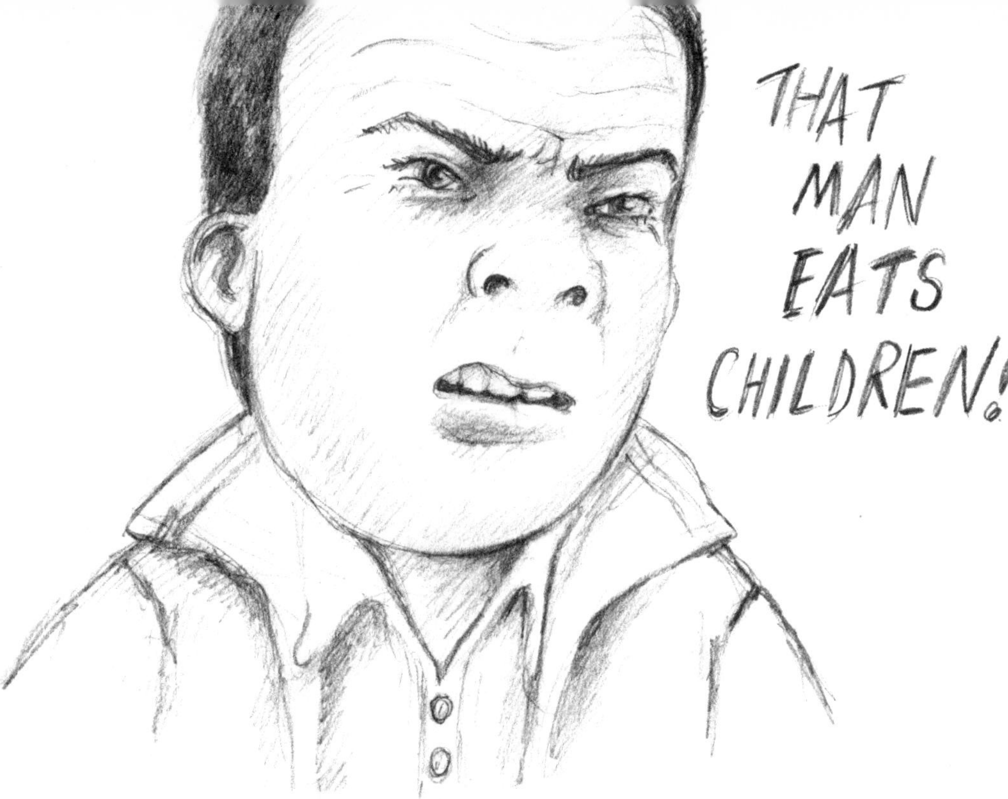
THAT MAN EATS CHILDREN!

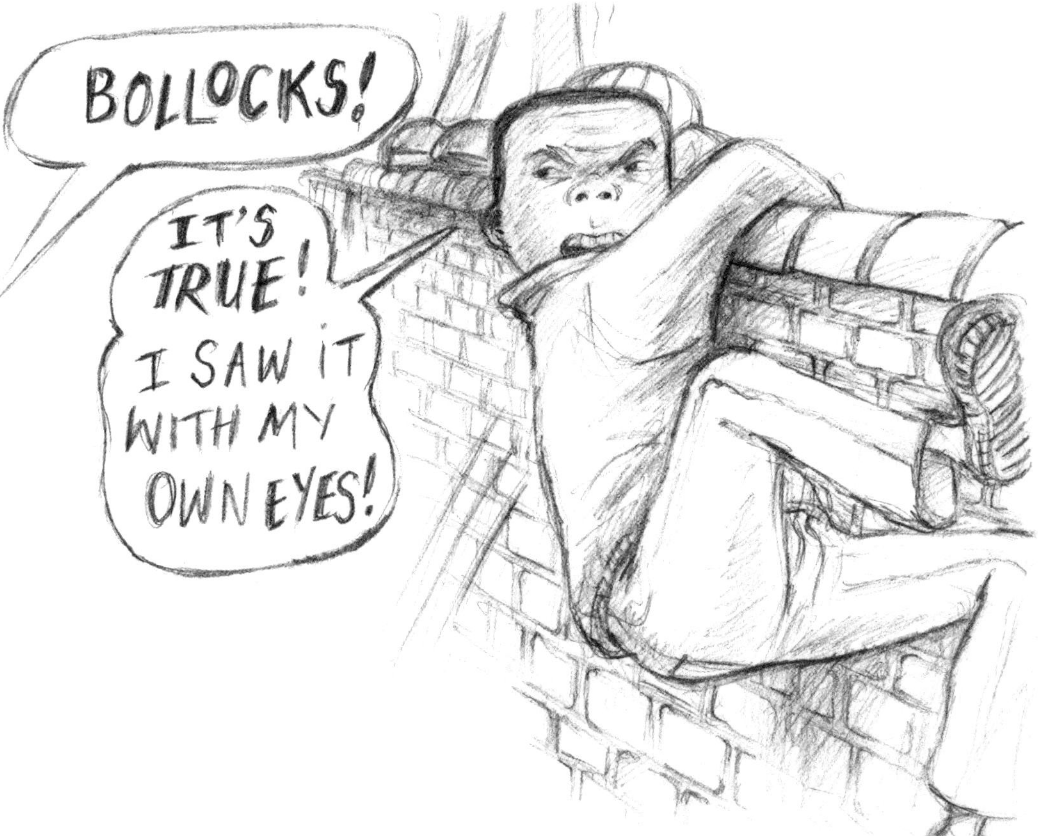
BOLLOCKS!
IT'S TRUE! I SAW IT WITH MY OWN EYES!

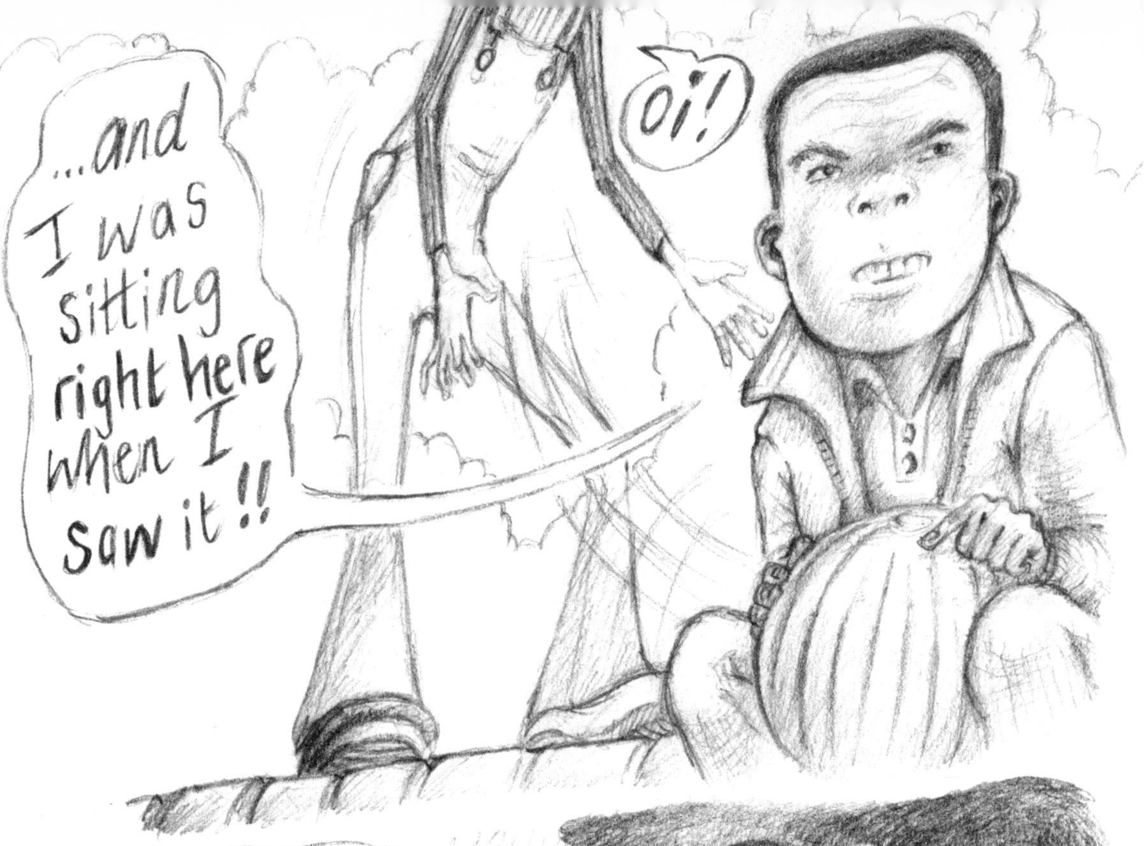
...and I was sitting right here when I saw it!!
Oi!

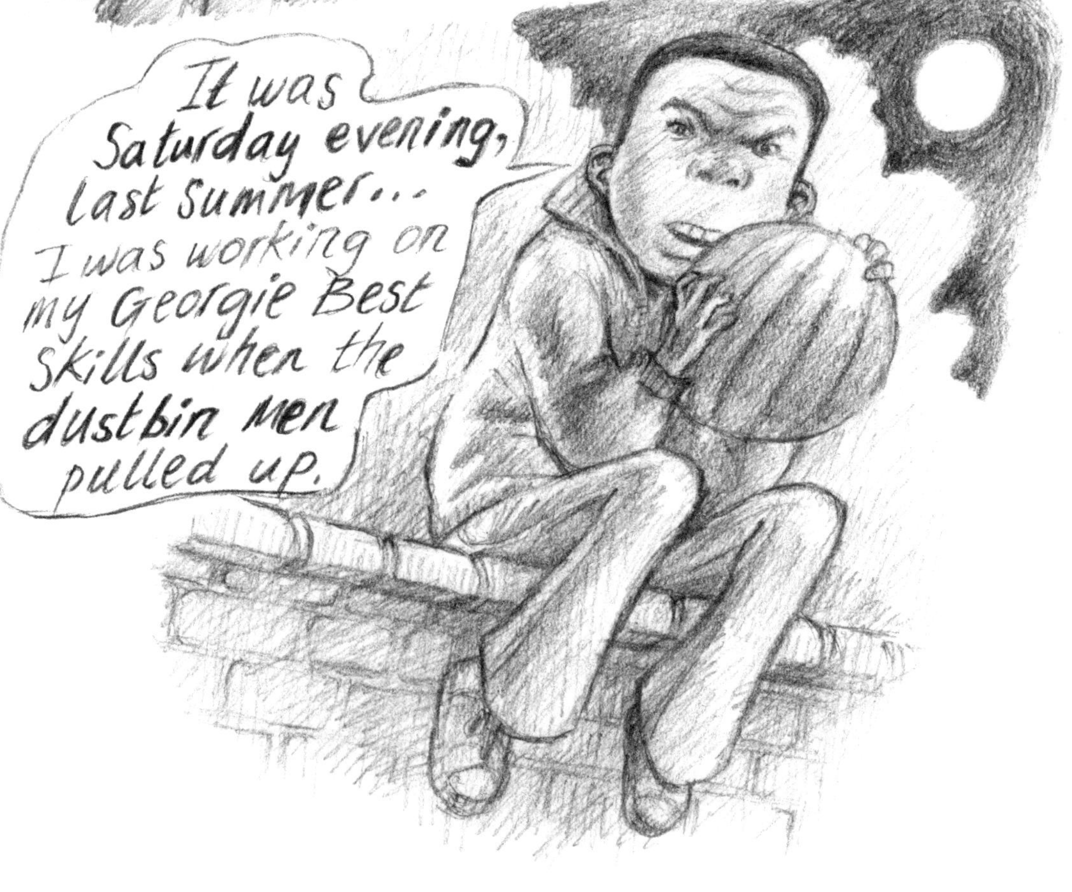
It was Saturday evening, last summer... I was working on my Georgie Best skills when the dustbin men pulled up.

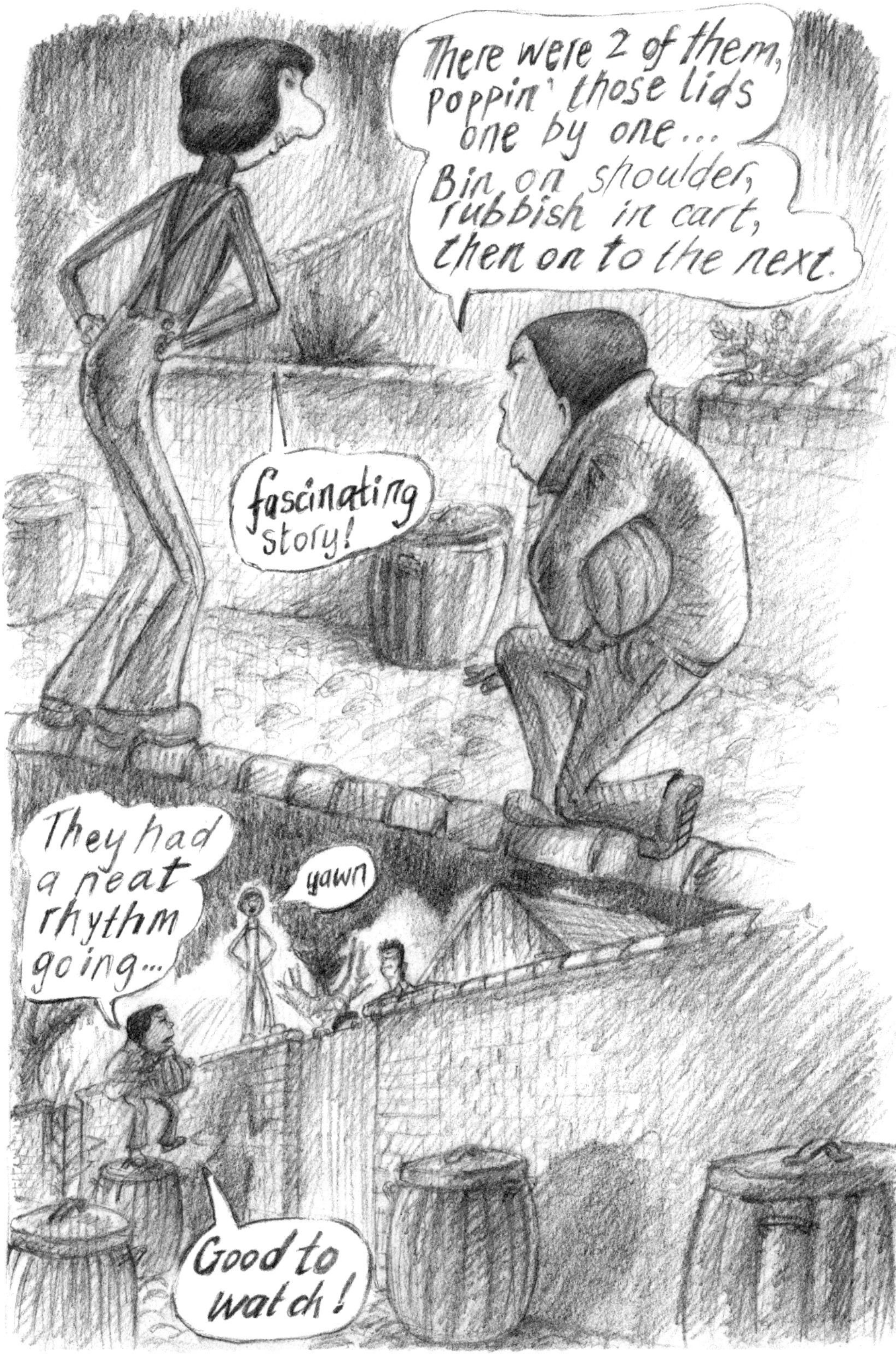
There were 2 of them, poppin' those lids one by one... Bin on shoulder, rubbish in cart, then on to the next.
fascinating story!
They had a neat rhythm going...
yawn
Good to watch!

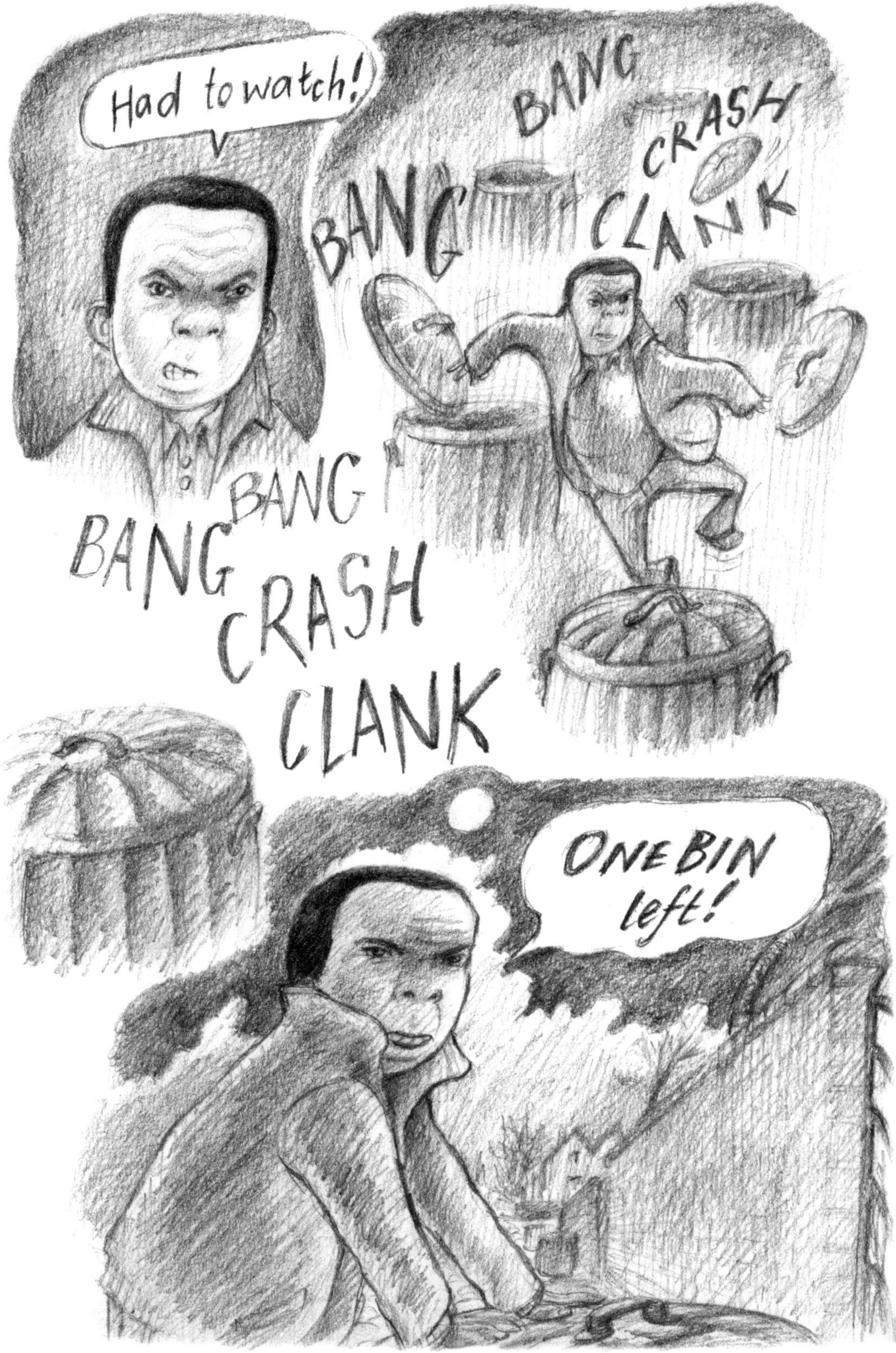
Had to watch!
BANG
BANG
CRASH
CLANK
BANG
BANG
CRASH
CLANK
ONE BIN left!

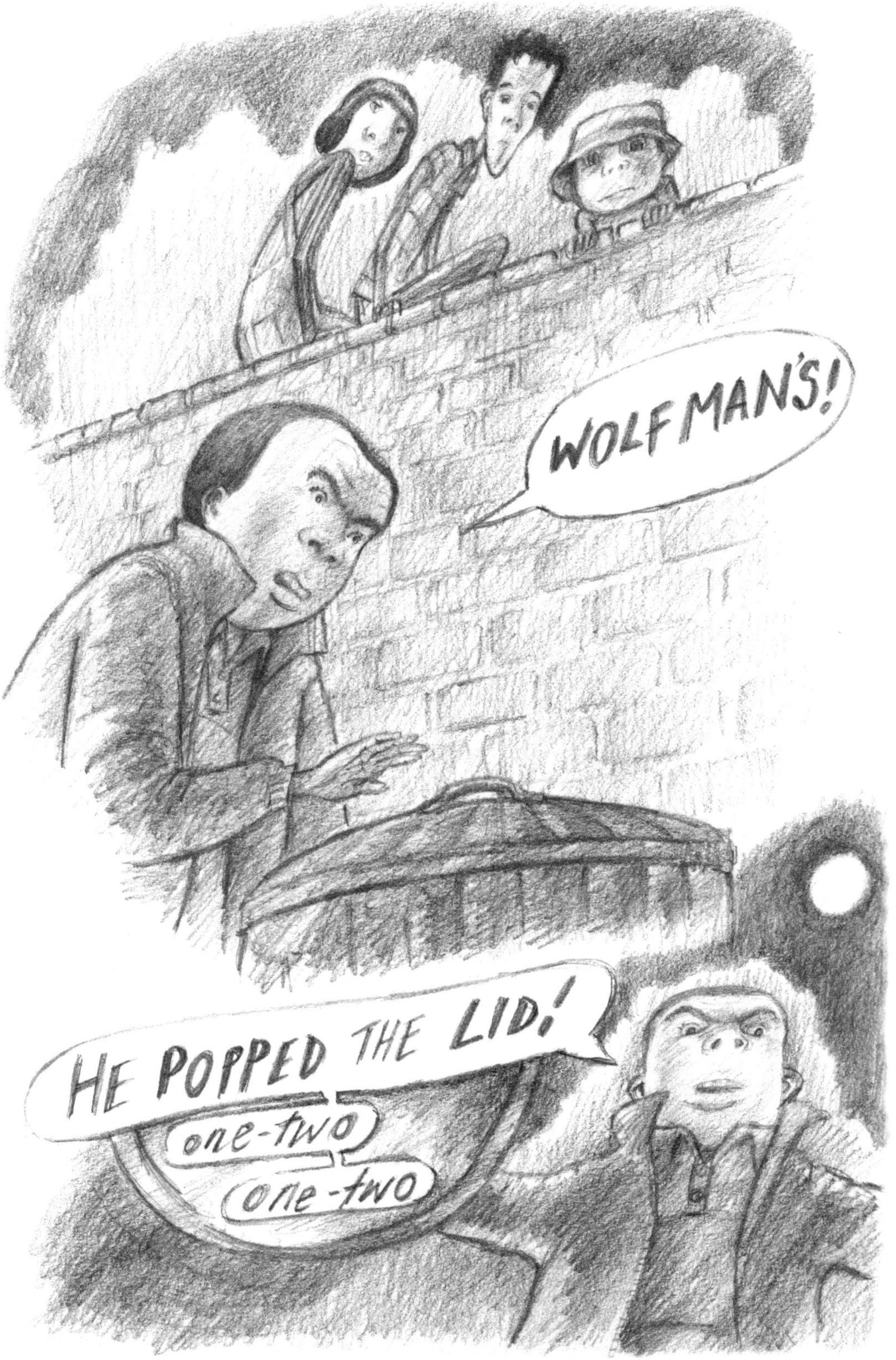
WOLFMAN'S!
HE POPPED THE LID!
one-two
one-two

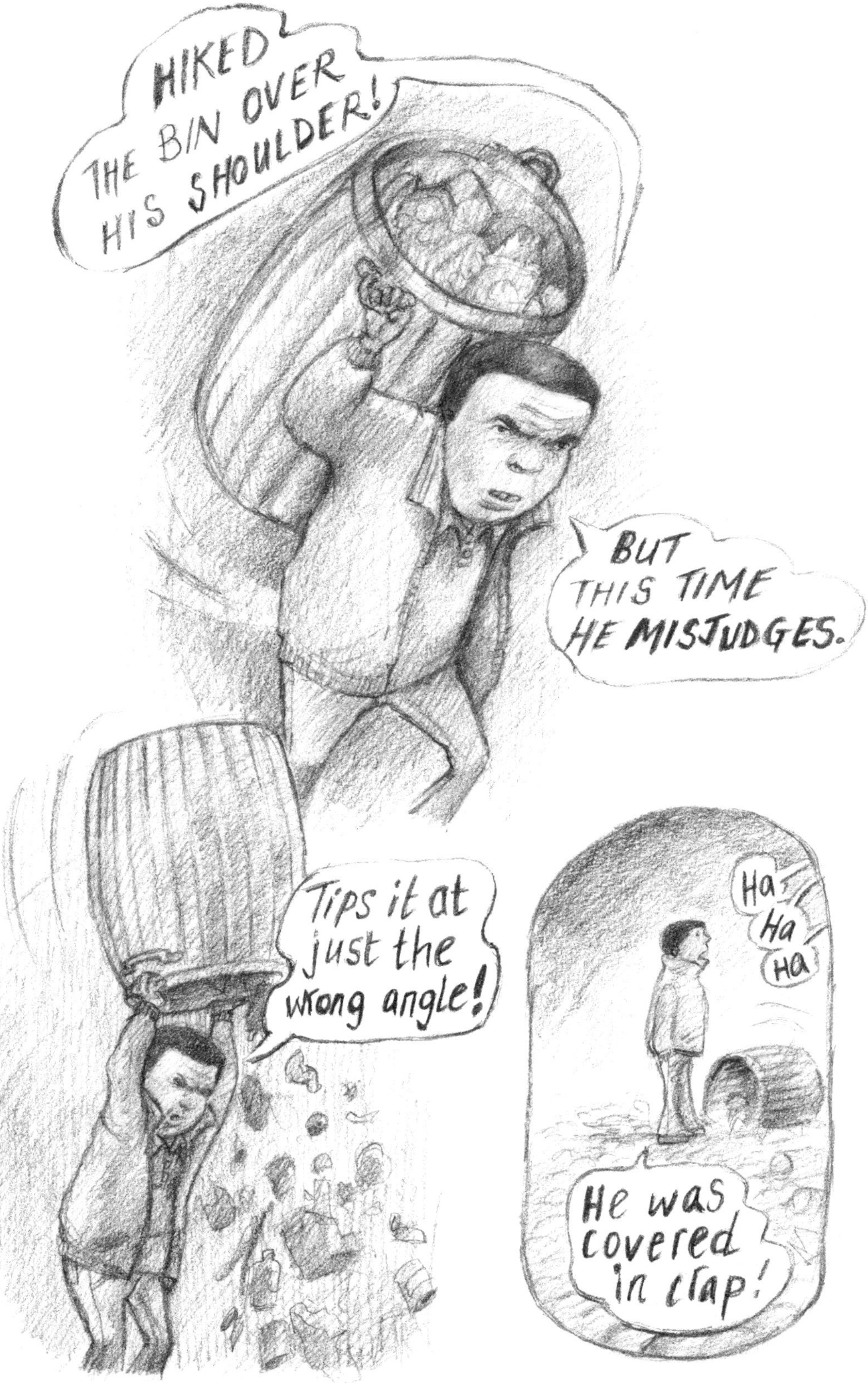

HIKED THE BIN OVER HIS SHOULDER!
BUT THIS TIME HE MISJUDGES.
Tips it at just the wrong angle!
Ha Ha Ha
He was covered in crap!

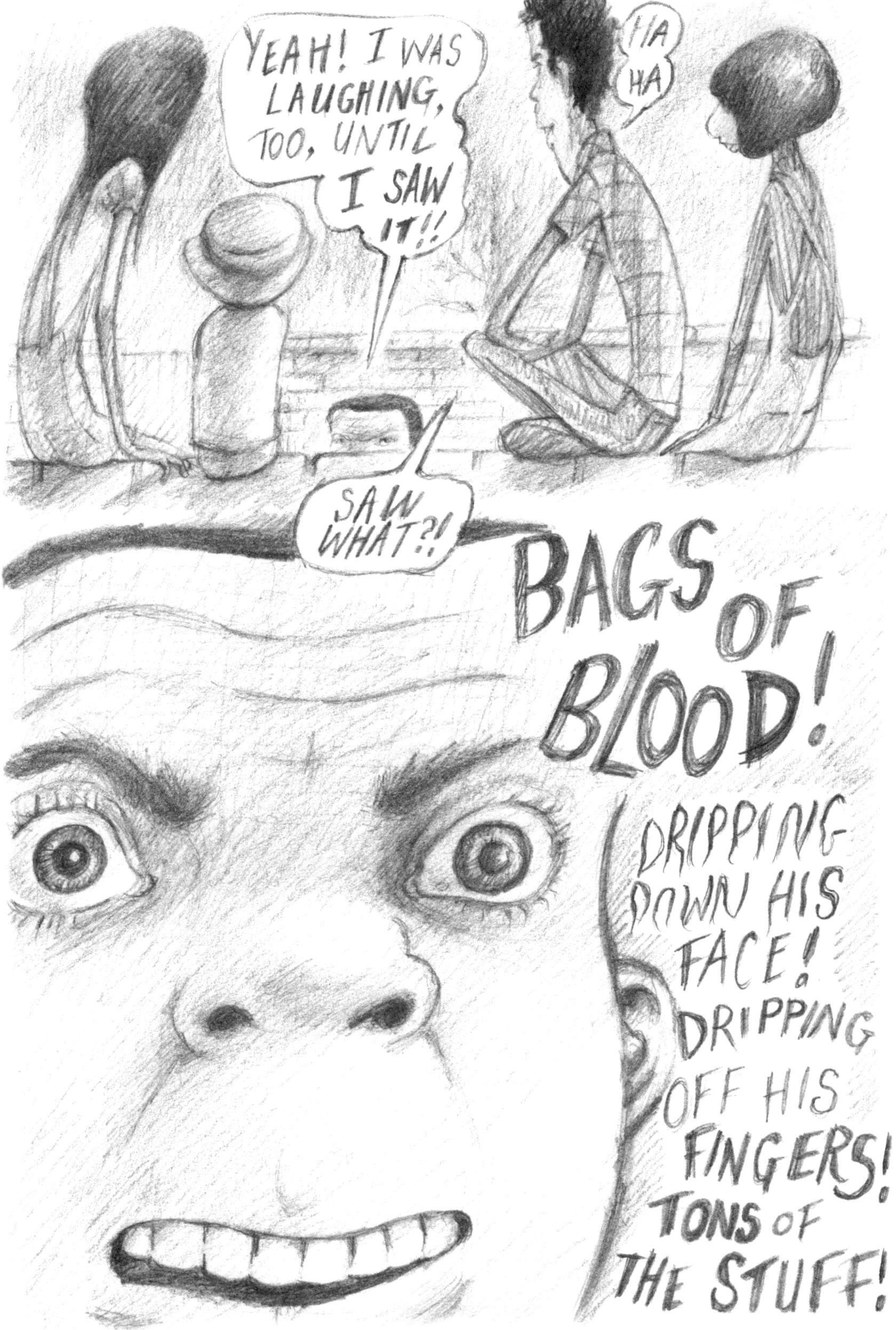
YEAH! I WAS LAUGHING, TOO, UNTIL I SAW IT!!
HA HA
SAW WHAT?!
BAGS OF BLOOD!
DRIPPING DOWN HIS FACE! DRIPPING OFF HIS FINGERS! TONS OF THE STUFF!

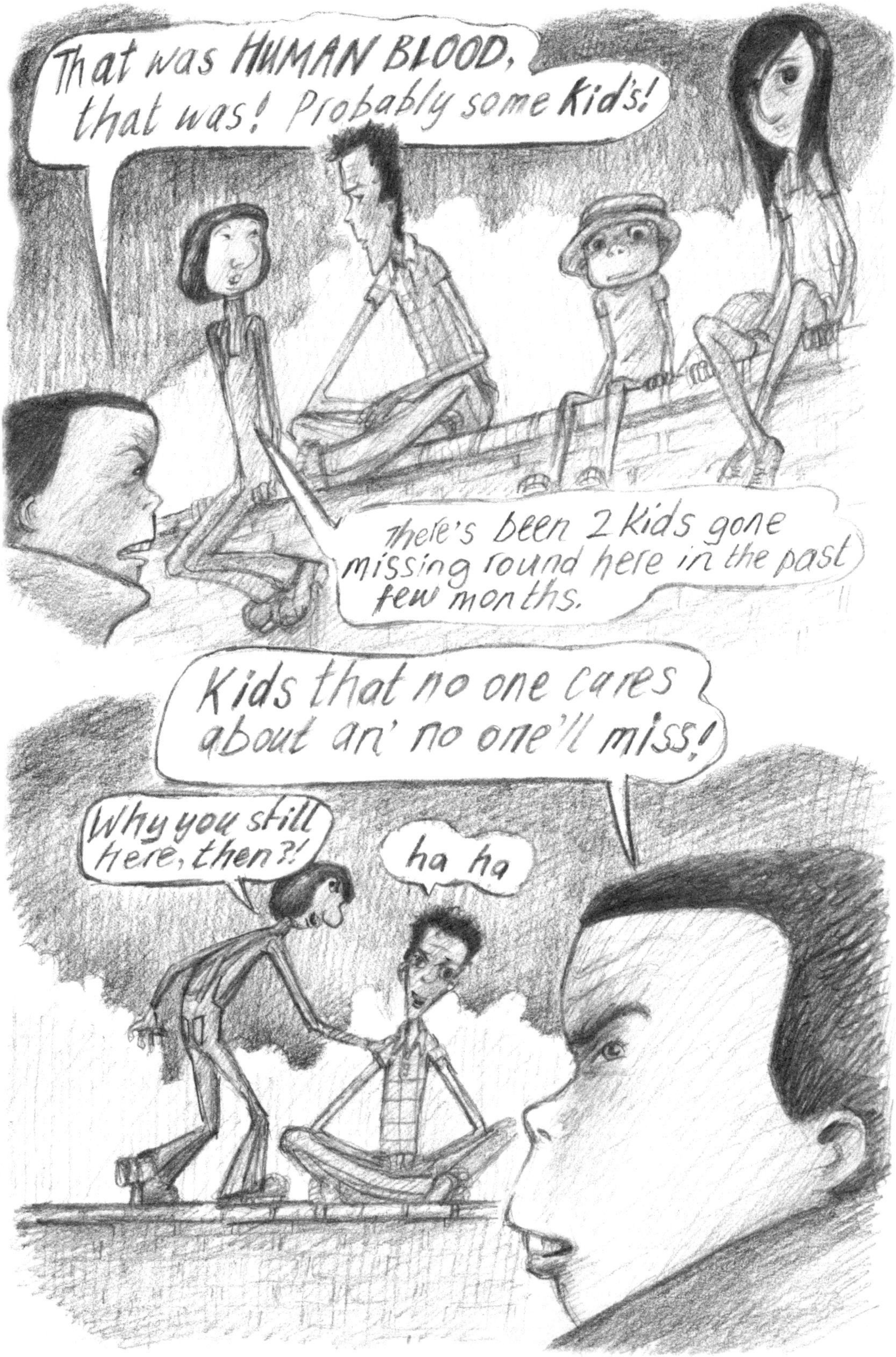
That was HUMAN BLOOD, that was! Probably some kid's!
There's been 2 kids gone missing round here in the past few months.
Kids that no one cares about an' no one'll miss!
Why you still here, then?!
ha ha

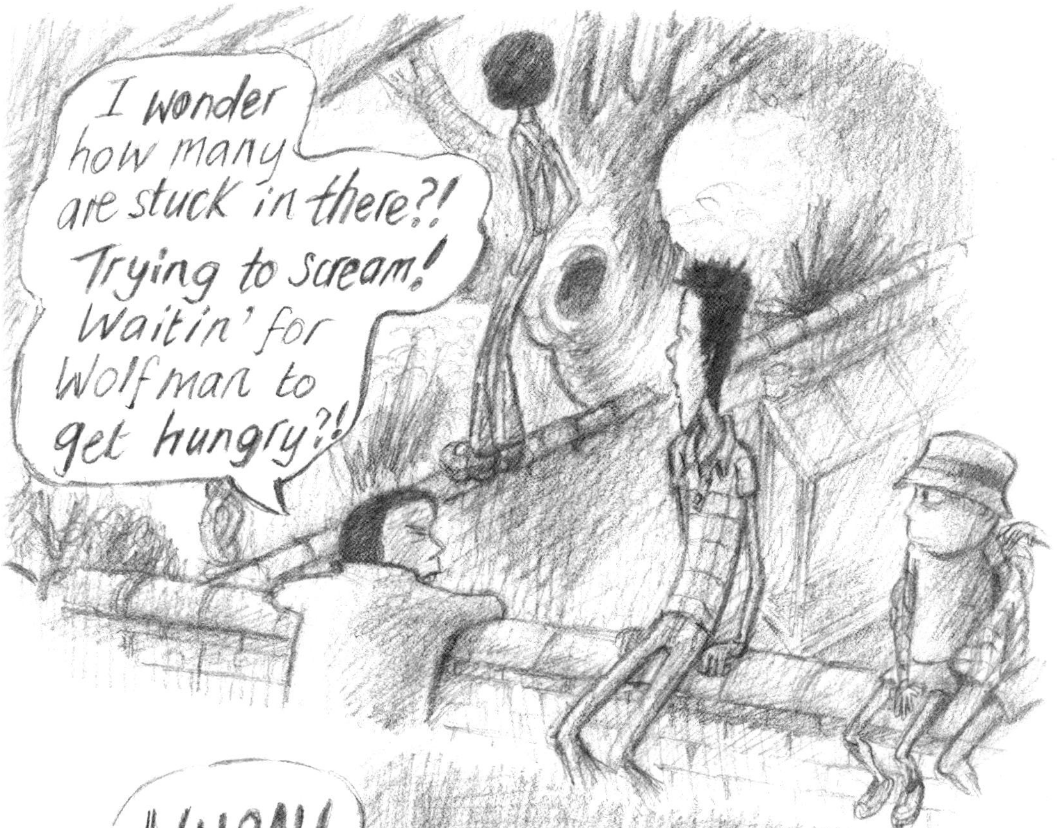
I wonder how many are stuck in there?! Trying to scream! Waitin' for Wolfman to get hungry?!

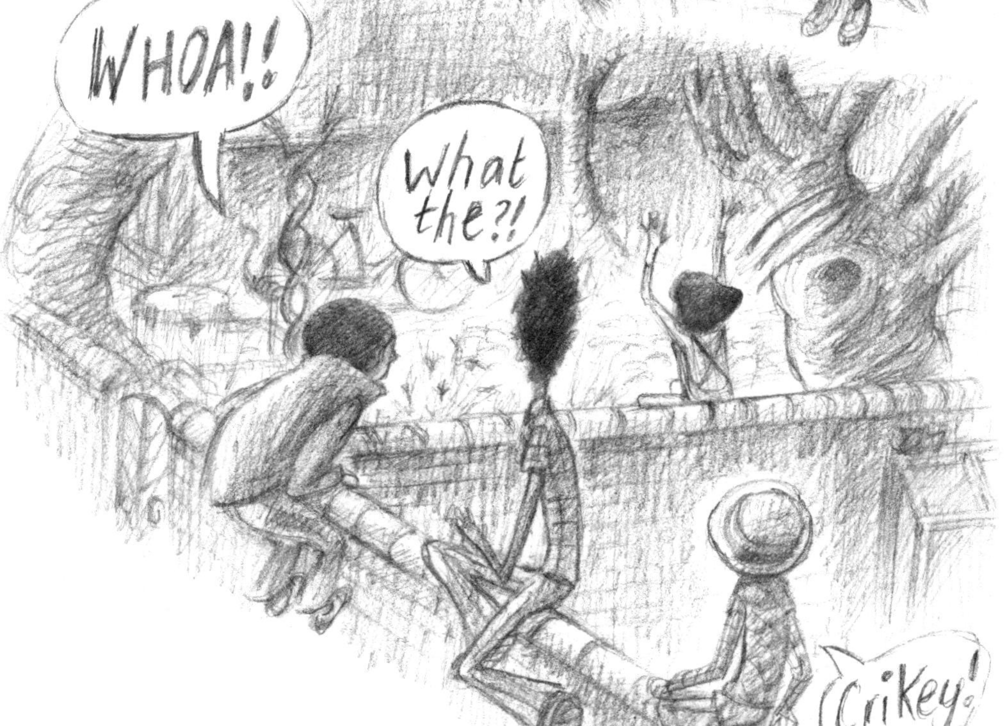
WHOA!!
What the?!
Crikey!

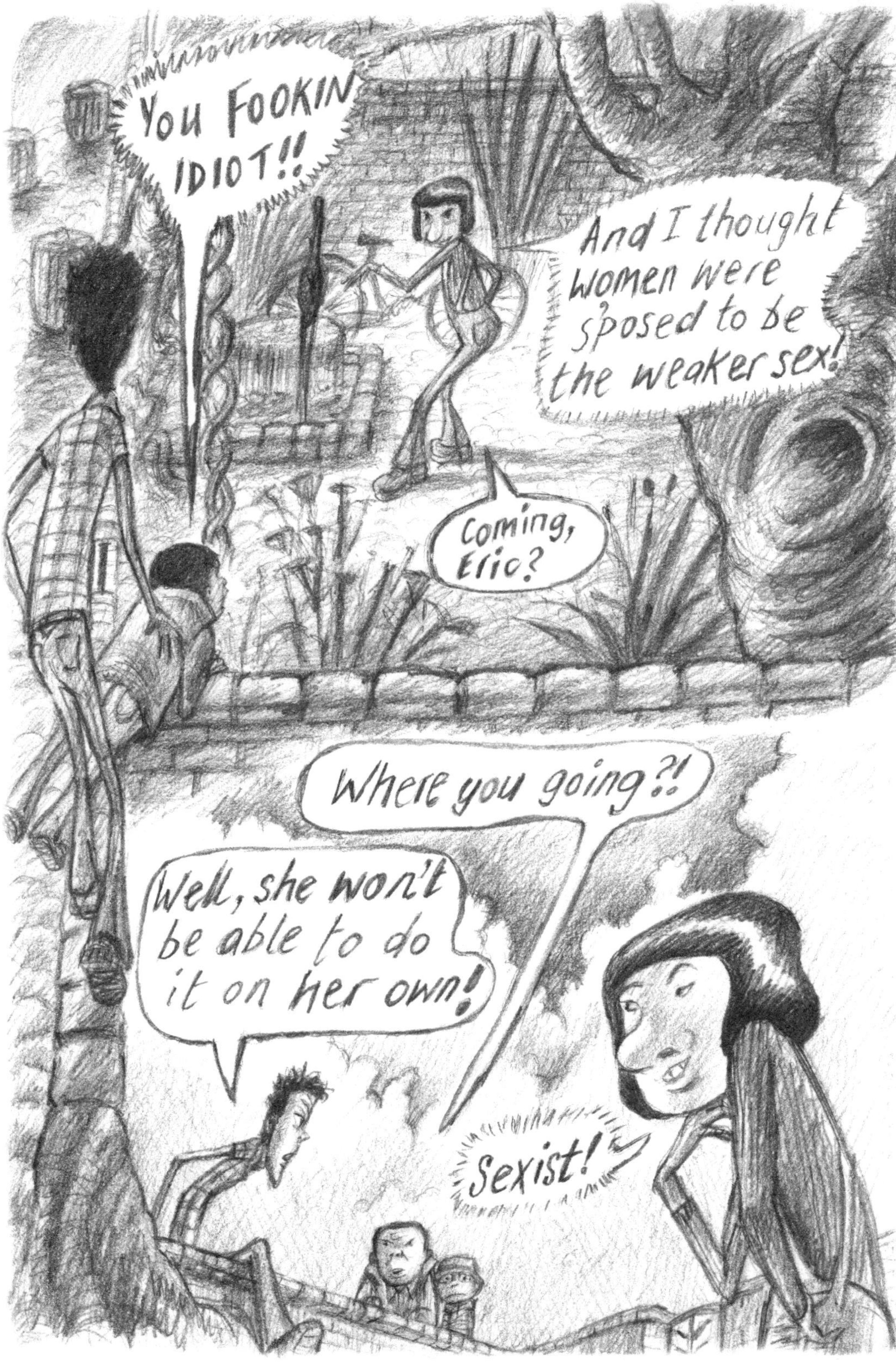
YOU FOOKIN IDIOT!!
And I thought women were s'posed to be the weaker sex!
Coming, Eric?
Where you going?!
Well, she won't be able to do it on her own!
Sexist!

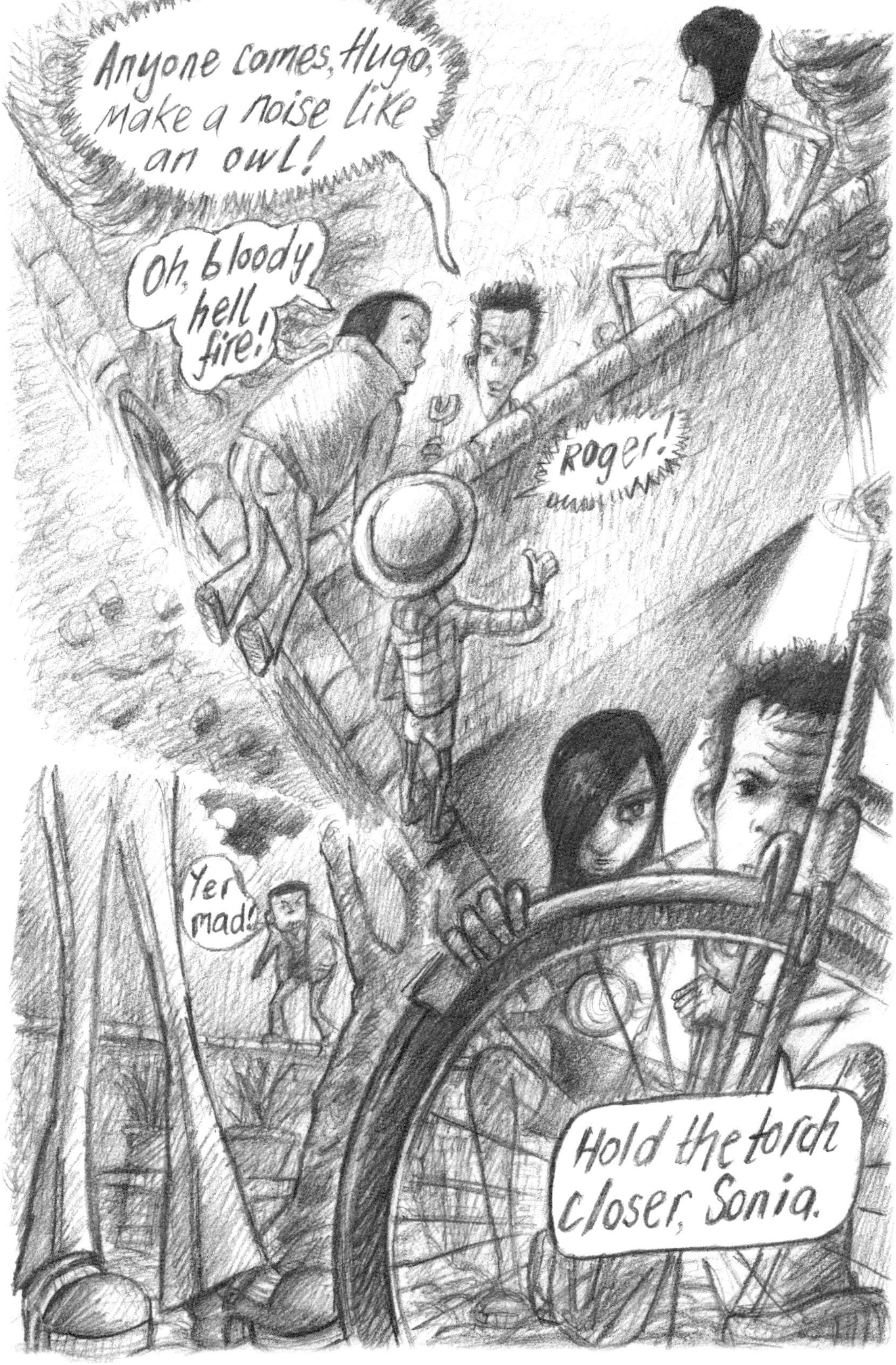
Anyone comes, Hugo, make a noise like an owl!
Oh, bloody hell fire!
Roger!
Yer mad!
Hold the torch closer, Sonia.

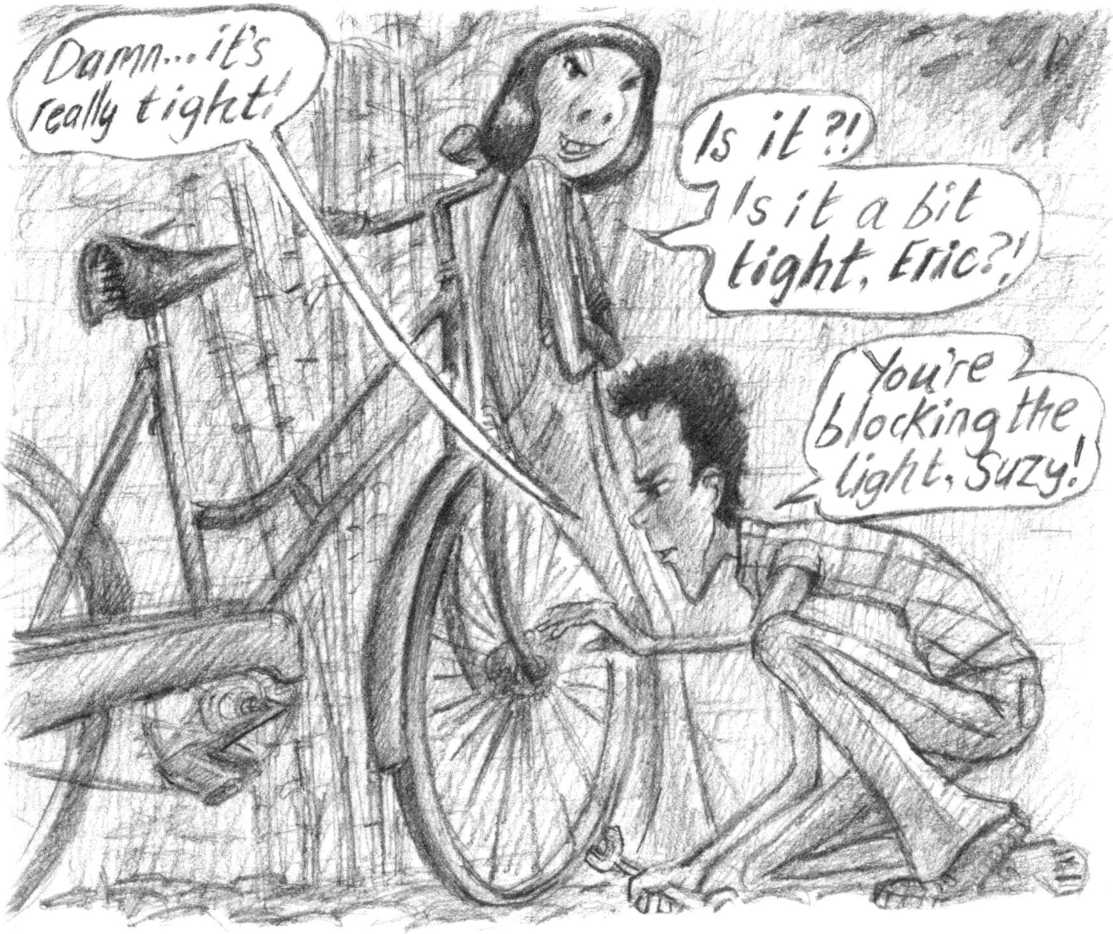
Damn... it's really tight!
Is it?! Is it a bit tight, Eric?!
You're blocking the light, Suzy!

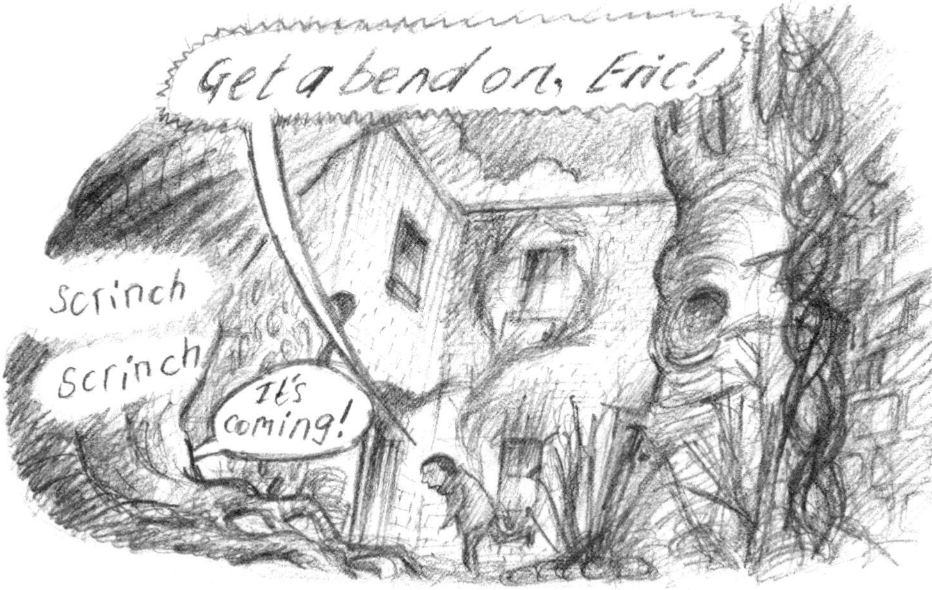
Get a bend on, Eric!
Scrinch
Scrinch
It's coming!

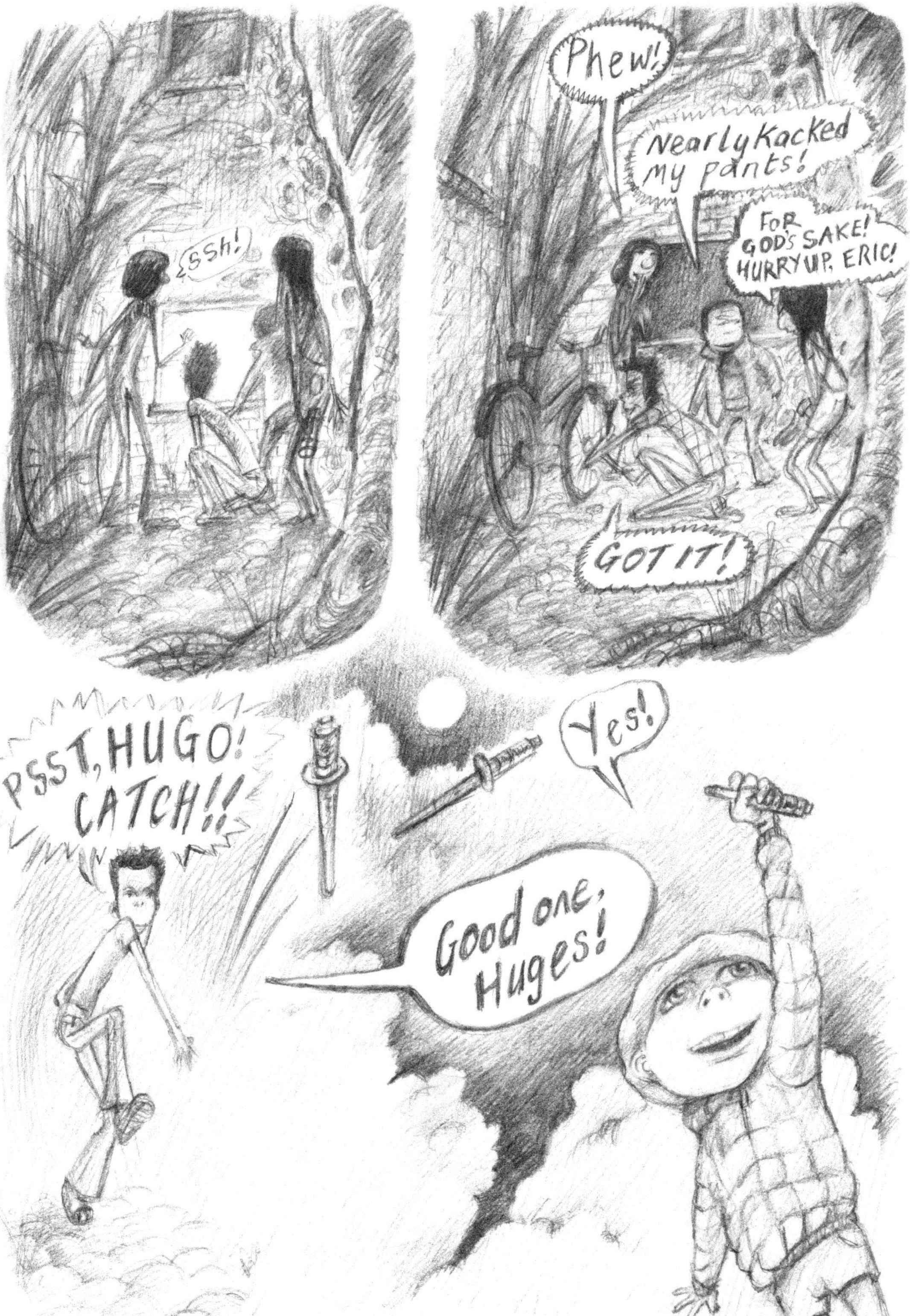
SSh!
Phew!
Nearly Kacked my pants!
FOR GOD'S SAKE! HURRY UP, ERIC!
GOT IT!
PSST, HUGO! CATCH!!
Yes!
Good one, Huges!

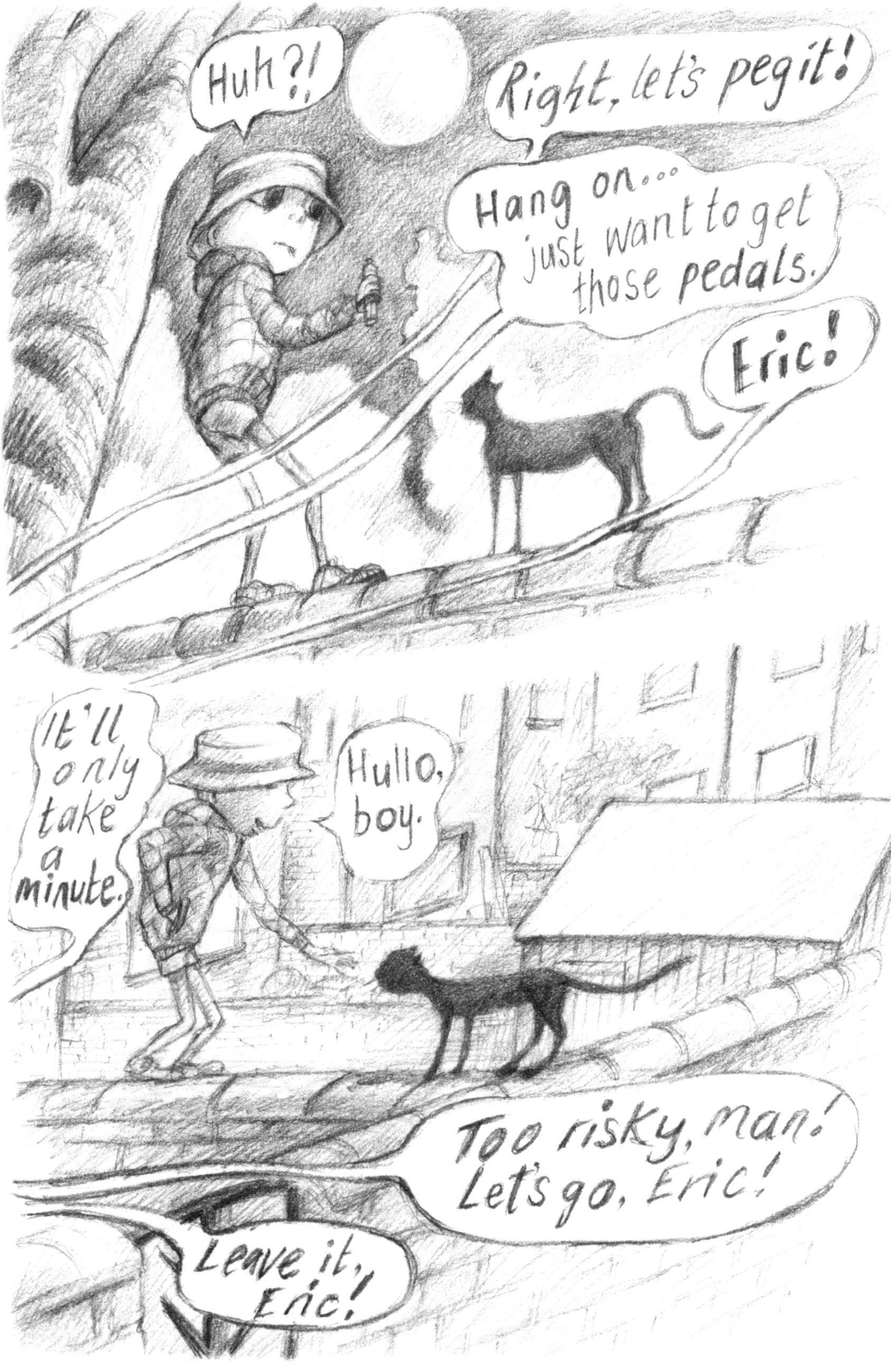
Huh?!
Right, let's pegit!
Hang on... just want to get those pedals.
Eric!
It'll only take a minute.
Hullo, boy.
Too risky, man! Let's go, Eric!
Leave it, Eric!

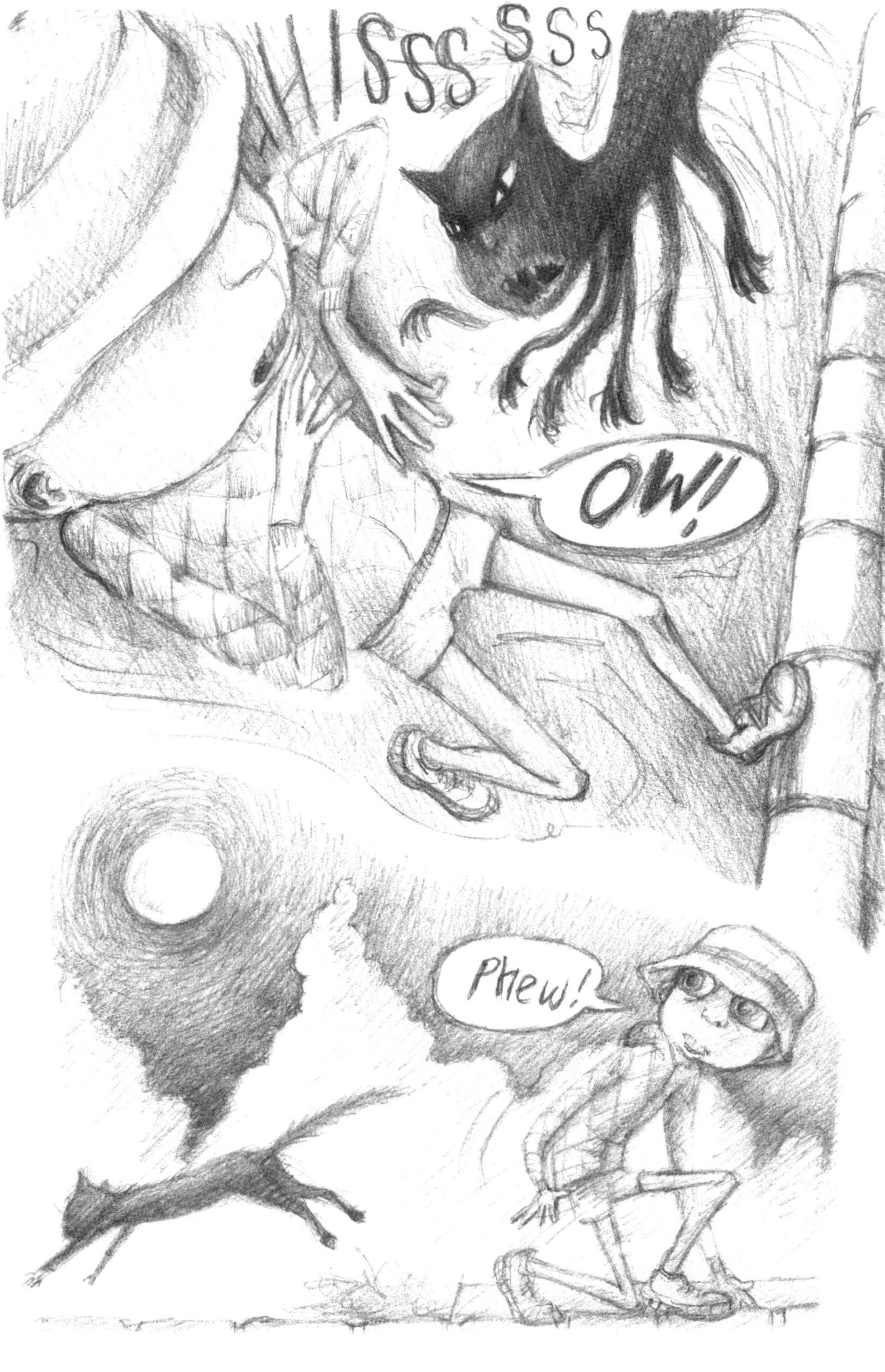
HISSS SSS
OW!
Phew!

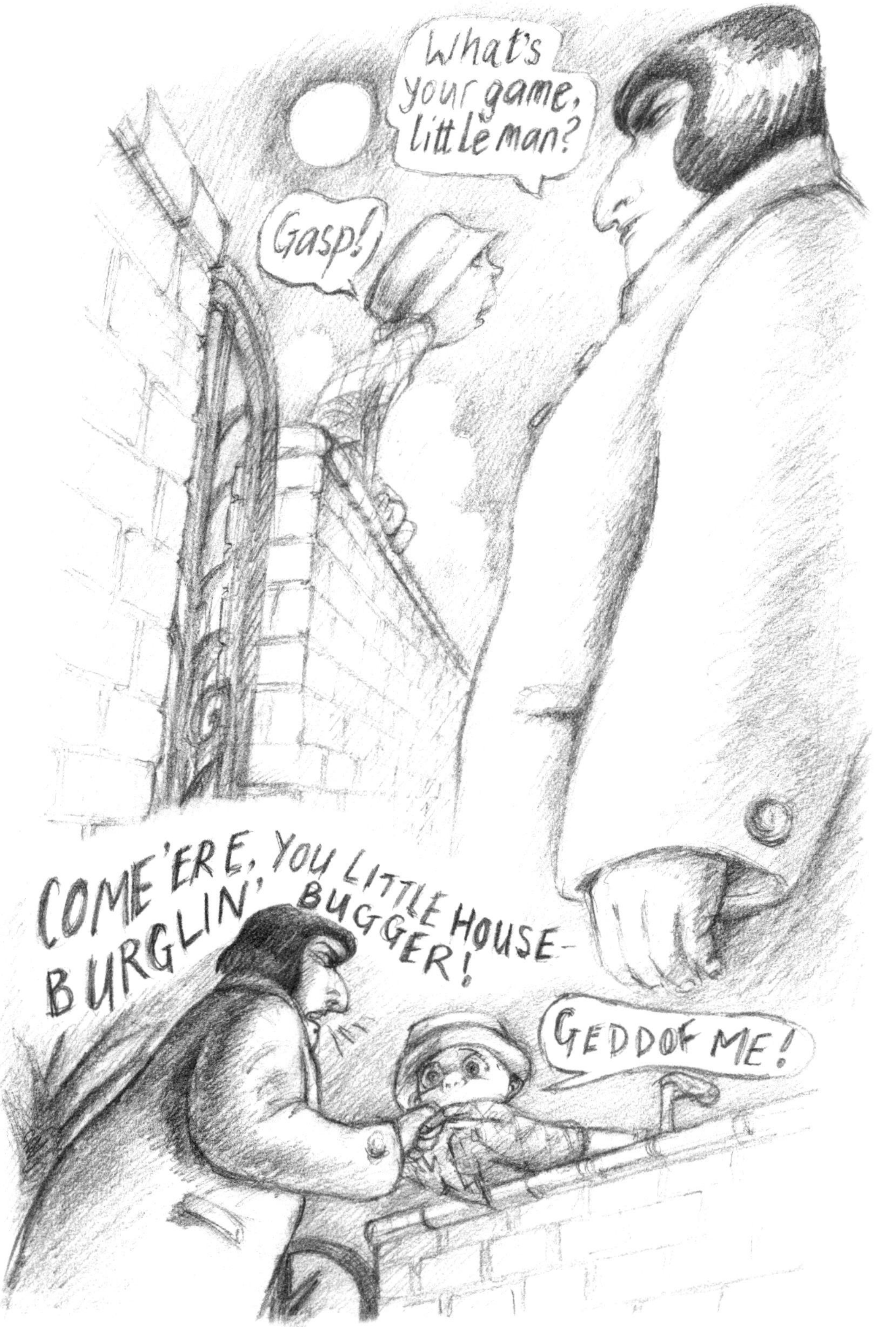
What's your game, little man?
Gasp!
COME 'ERE, YOU LITTLE HOUSE-BURGLIN' BUGGER!
GEDDOF ME!

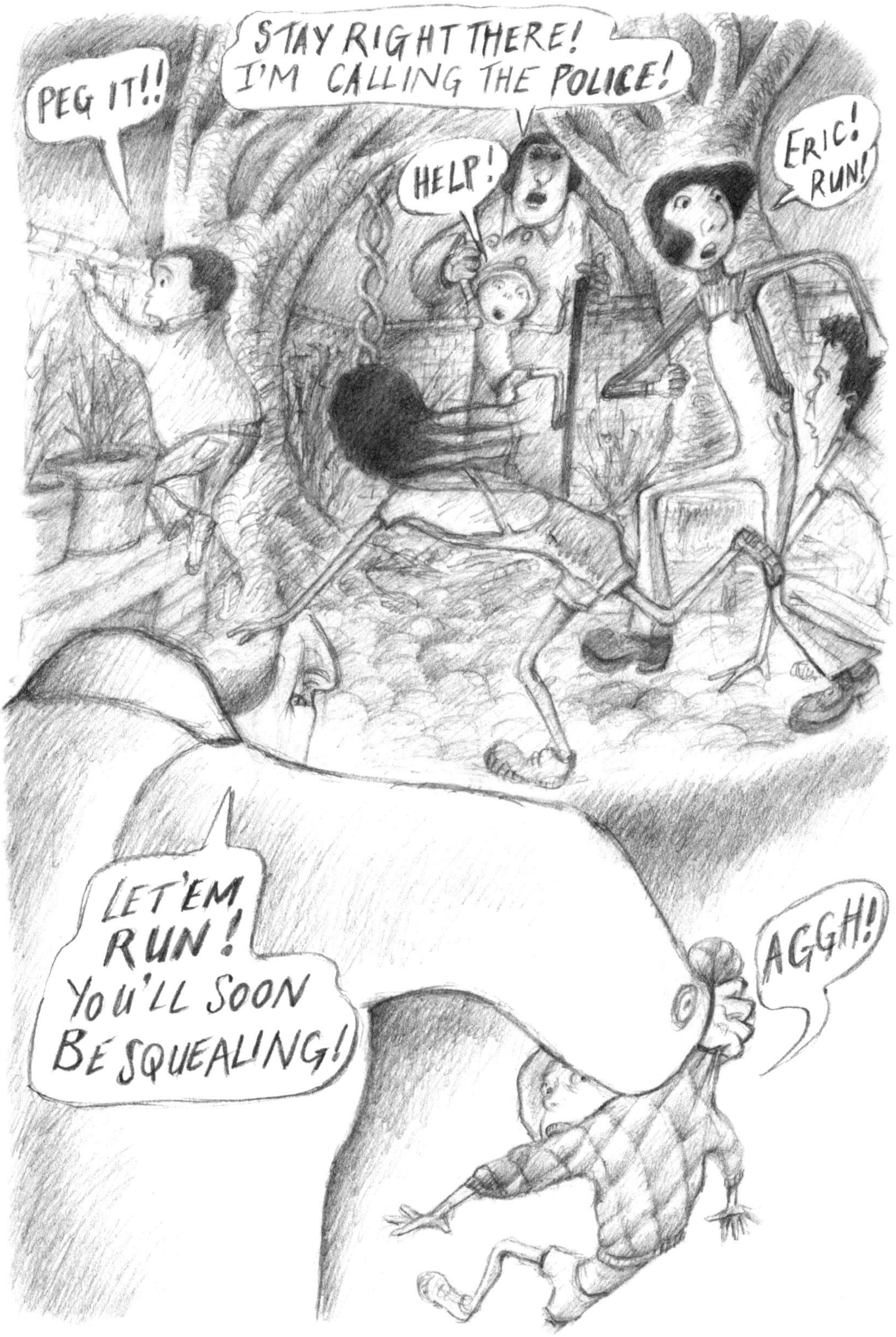
PEG IT!!
STAY RIGHT THERE! I'M CALLING THE POLICE!
HELP!
ERIC! RUN!
LET'EM RUN! YOU'LL SOON BE SQUEALING!
AGGH!

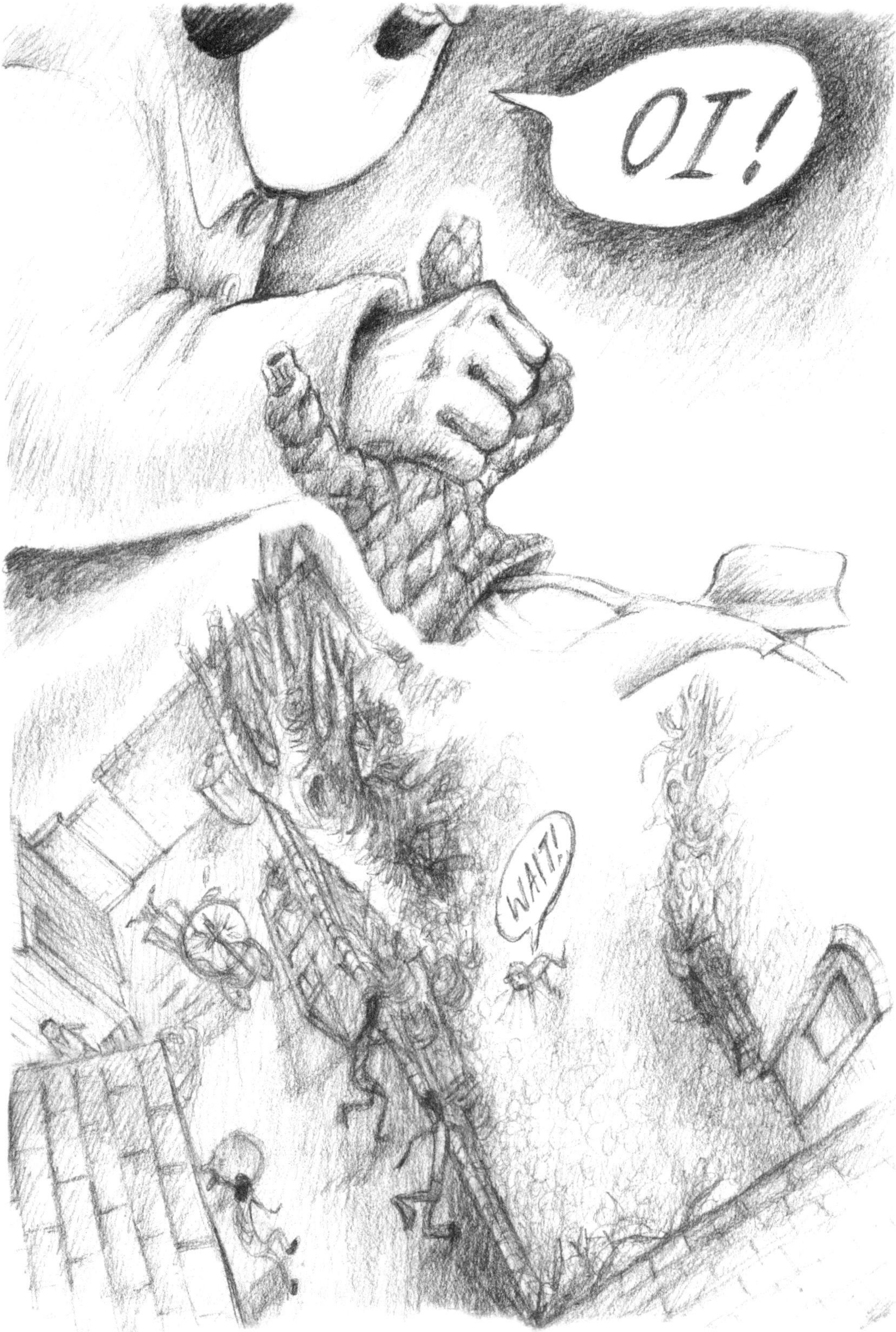
OI!
WAIT!

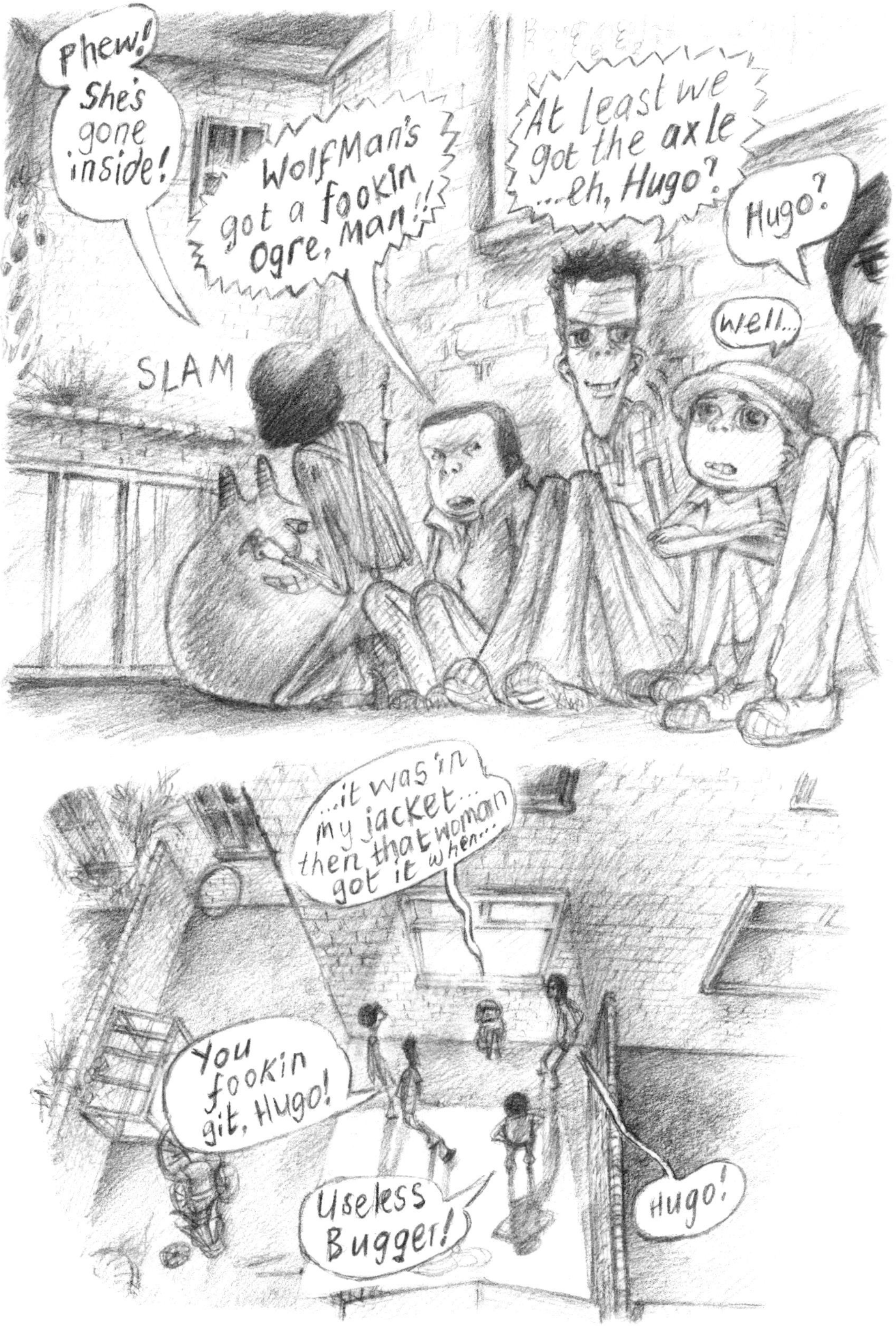
Phew! She's gone inside!
WolfMan's got a fookin Ogre, Man!!
At least we got the axle ...eh, Hugo?
Hugo?
Well...
SLAM
...it was in my jacket... then that woman got it when...
You fookin git, Hugo!
Useless Bugger!
Hugo!

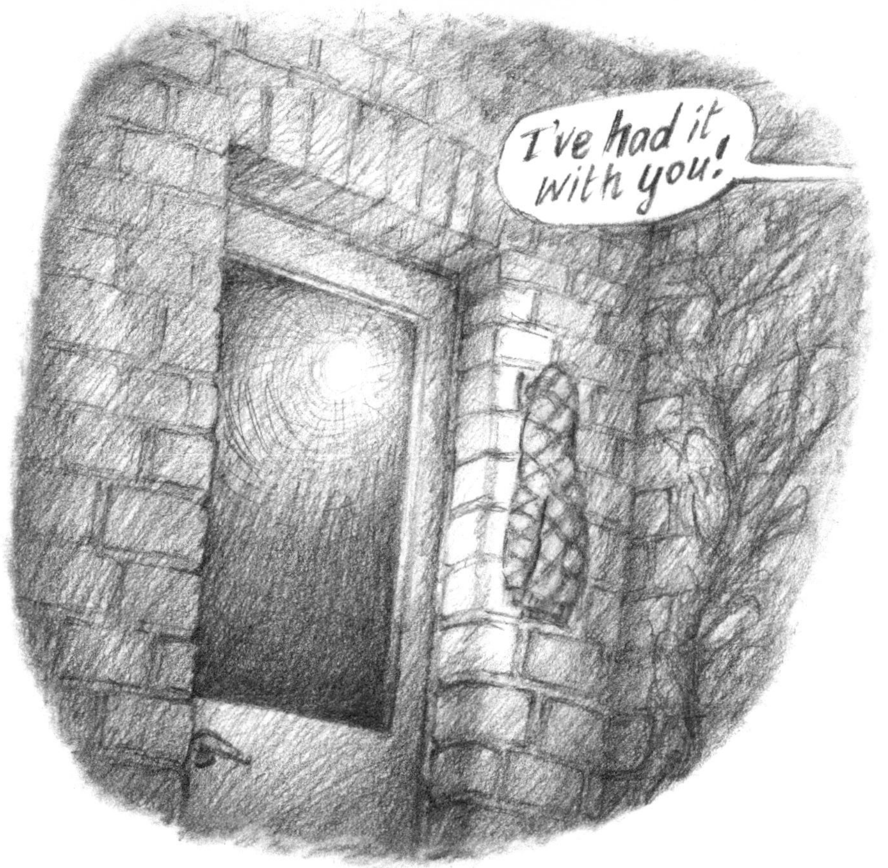
I've had it with you!

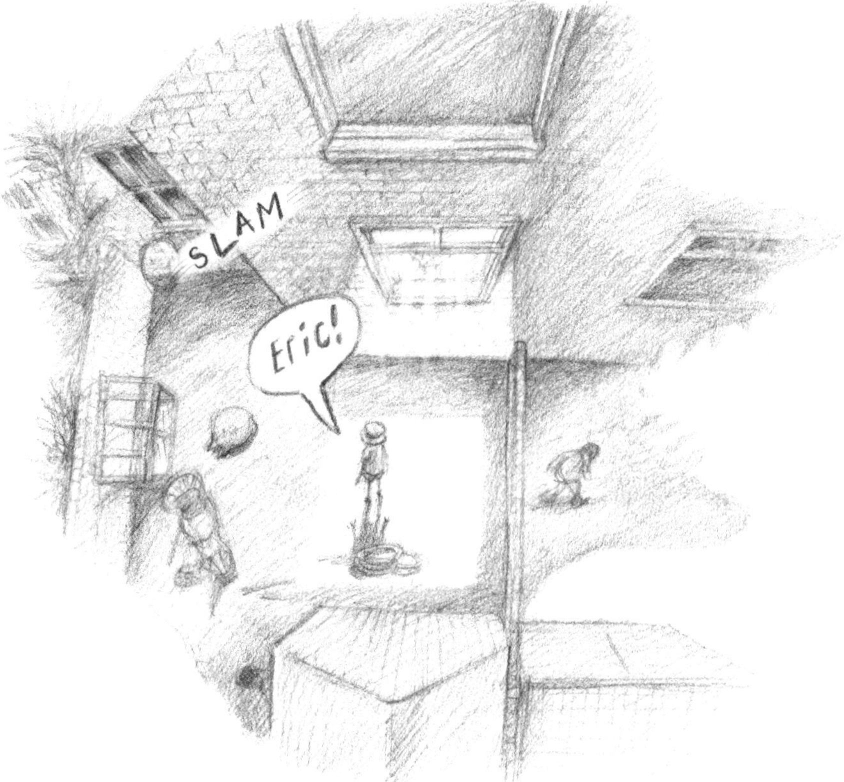
SLAM
Eric!

Chapter Six

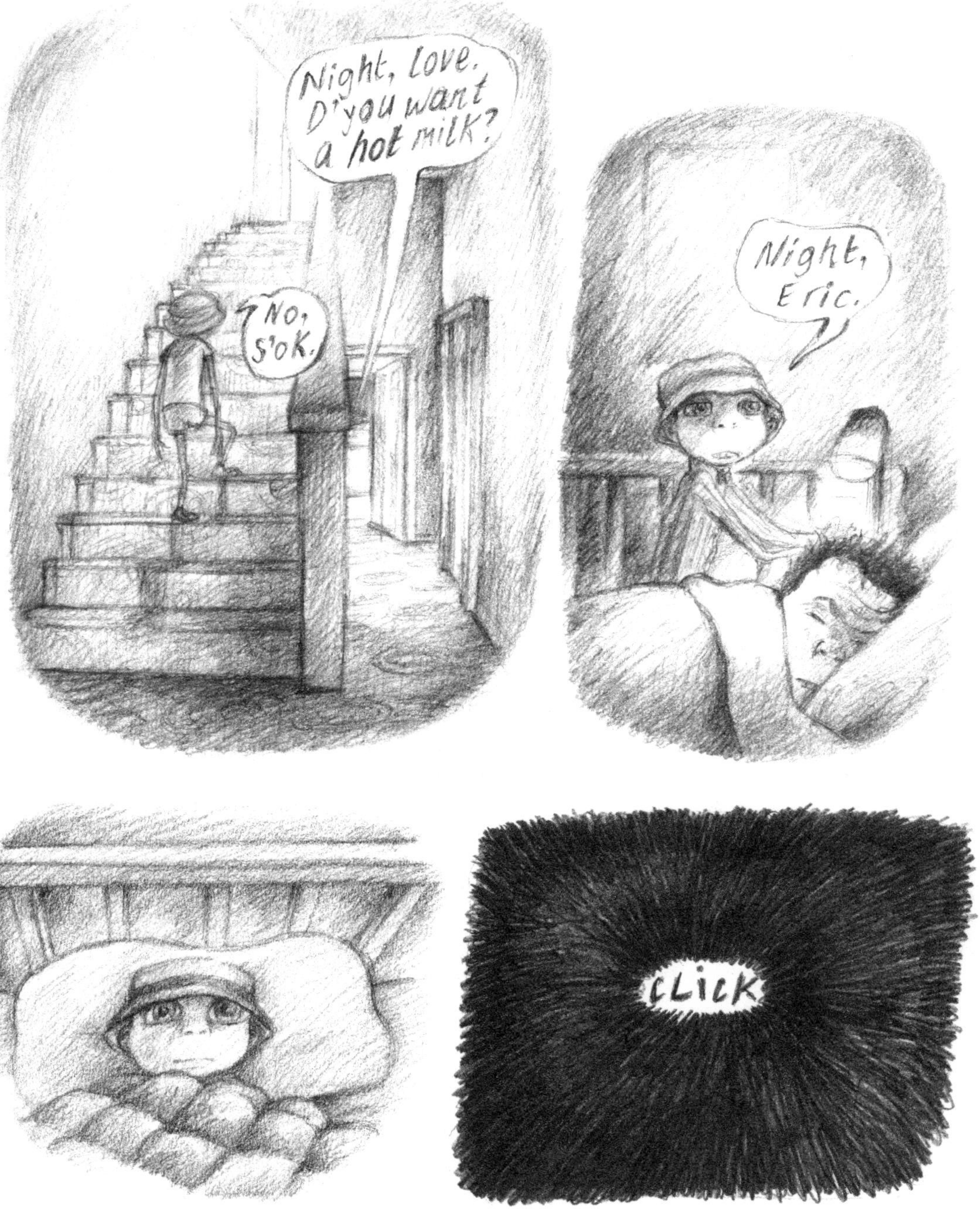
Night, love. D'you want a hot milk?
No, s'ok.
Night, Eric.
CLICK

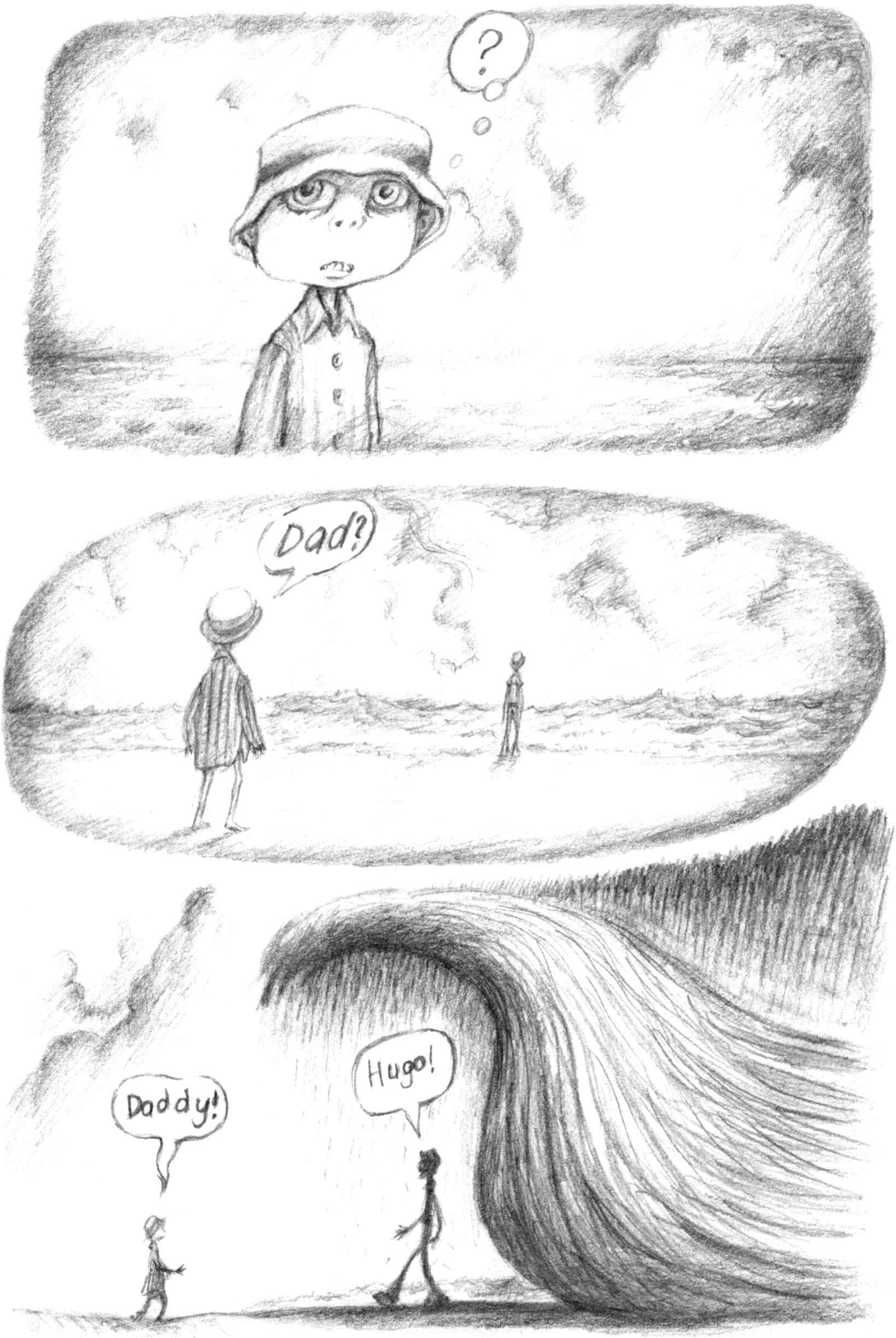
?
Dad?
Daddy!
Hugo!

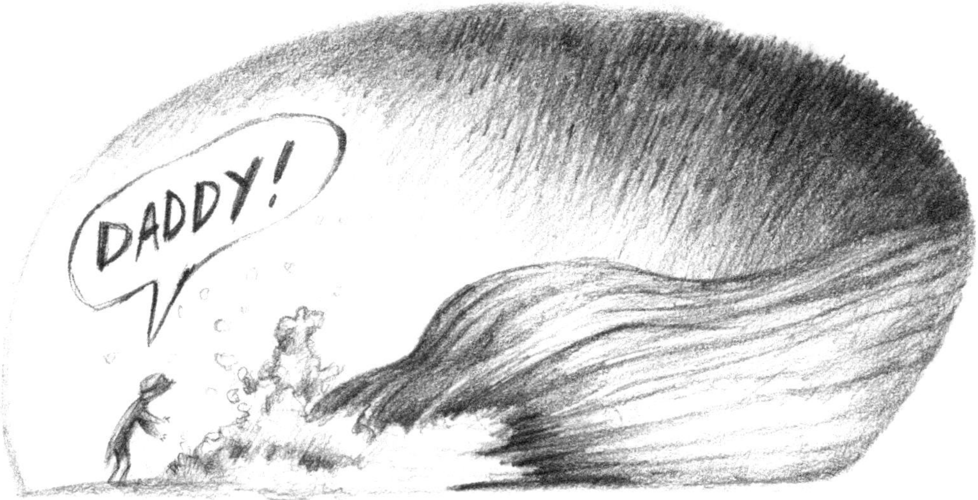
DADDY!

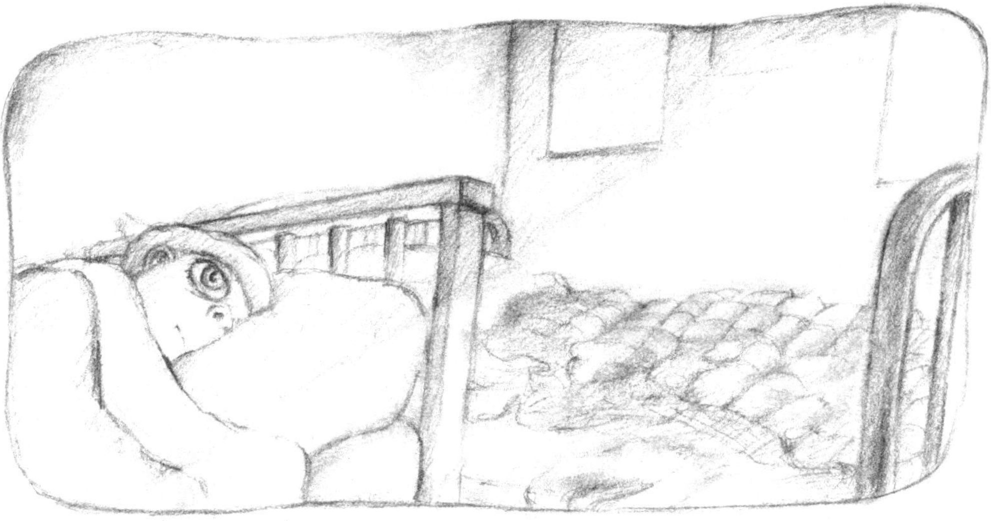

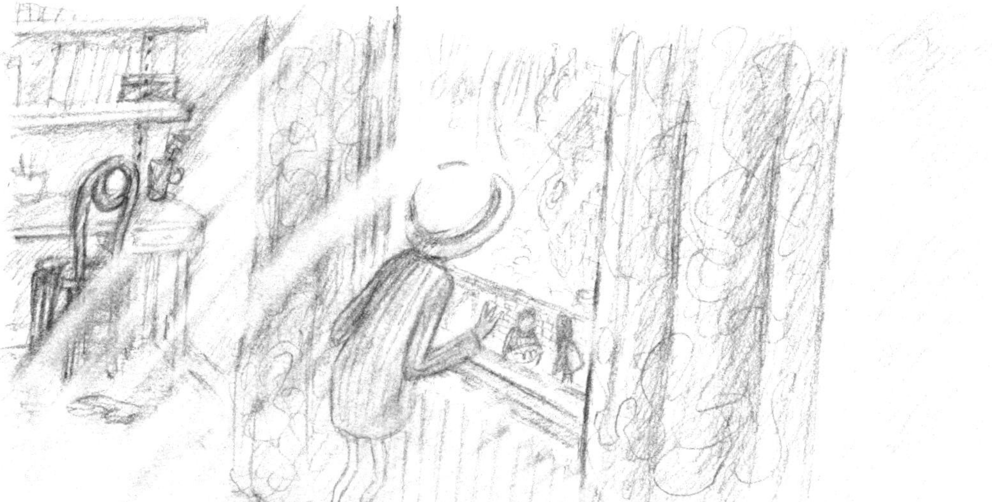

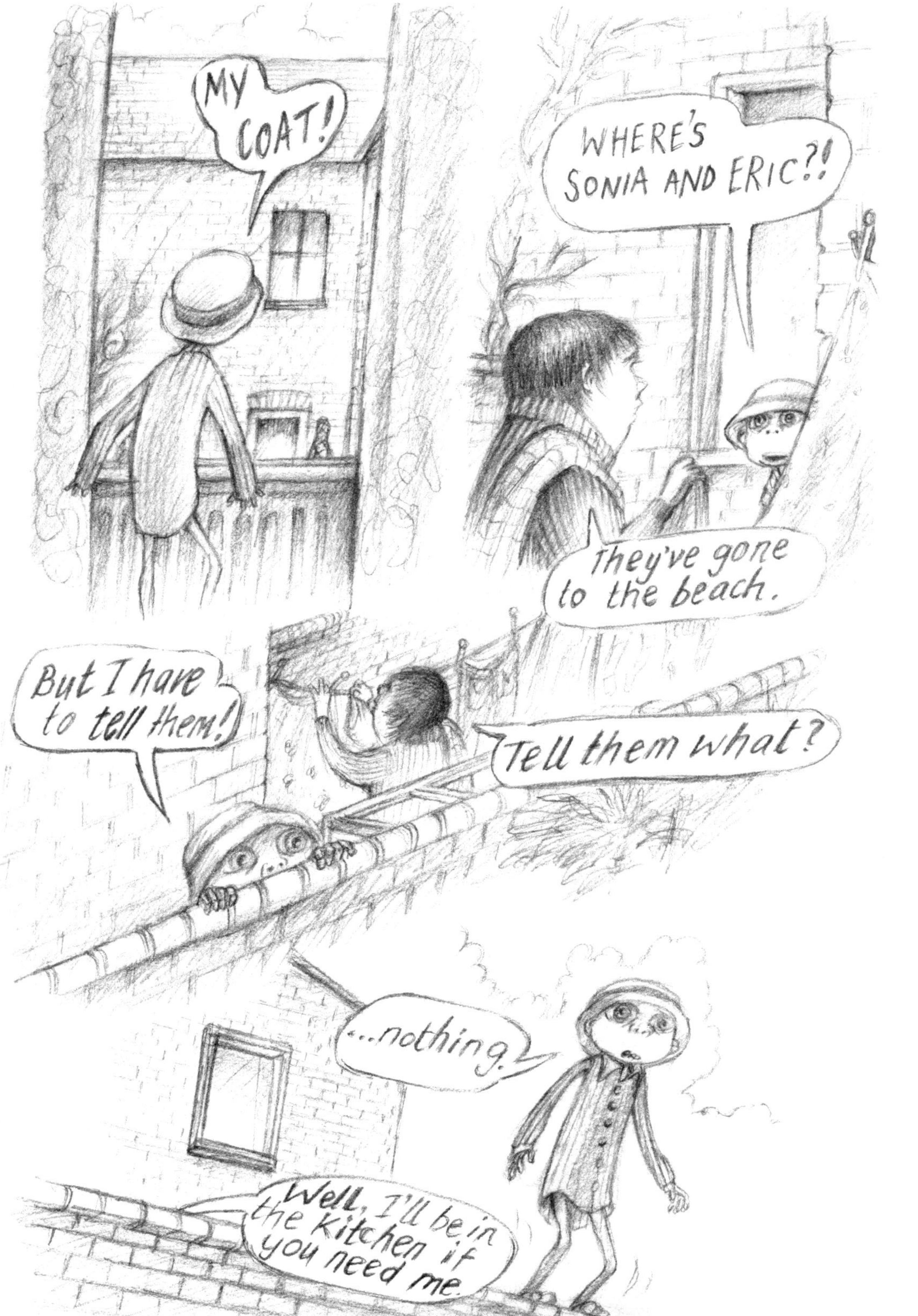
MY COAT!
WHERE'S SONIA AND ERIC?!
They've gone to the beach.
But I have to tell them!
Tell them what?
...nothing.
Well, I'll be in the kitchen if you need me.

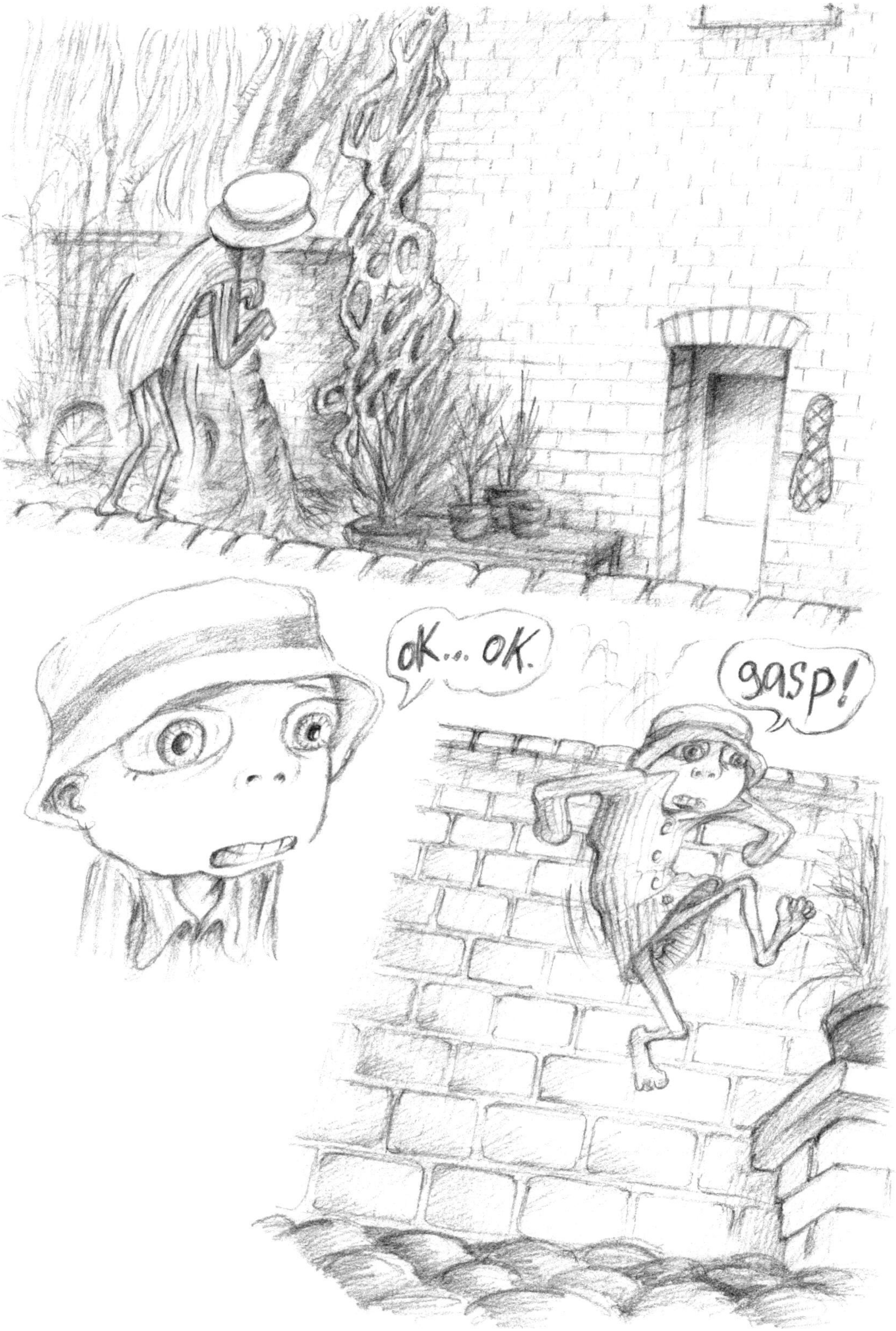
ok... ok.
gasp!

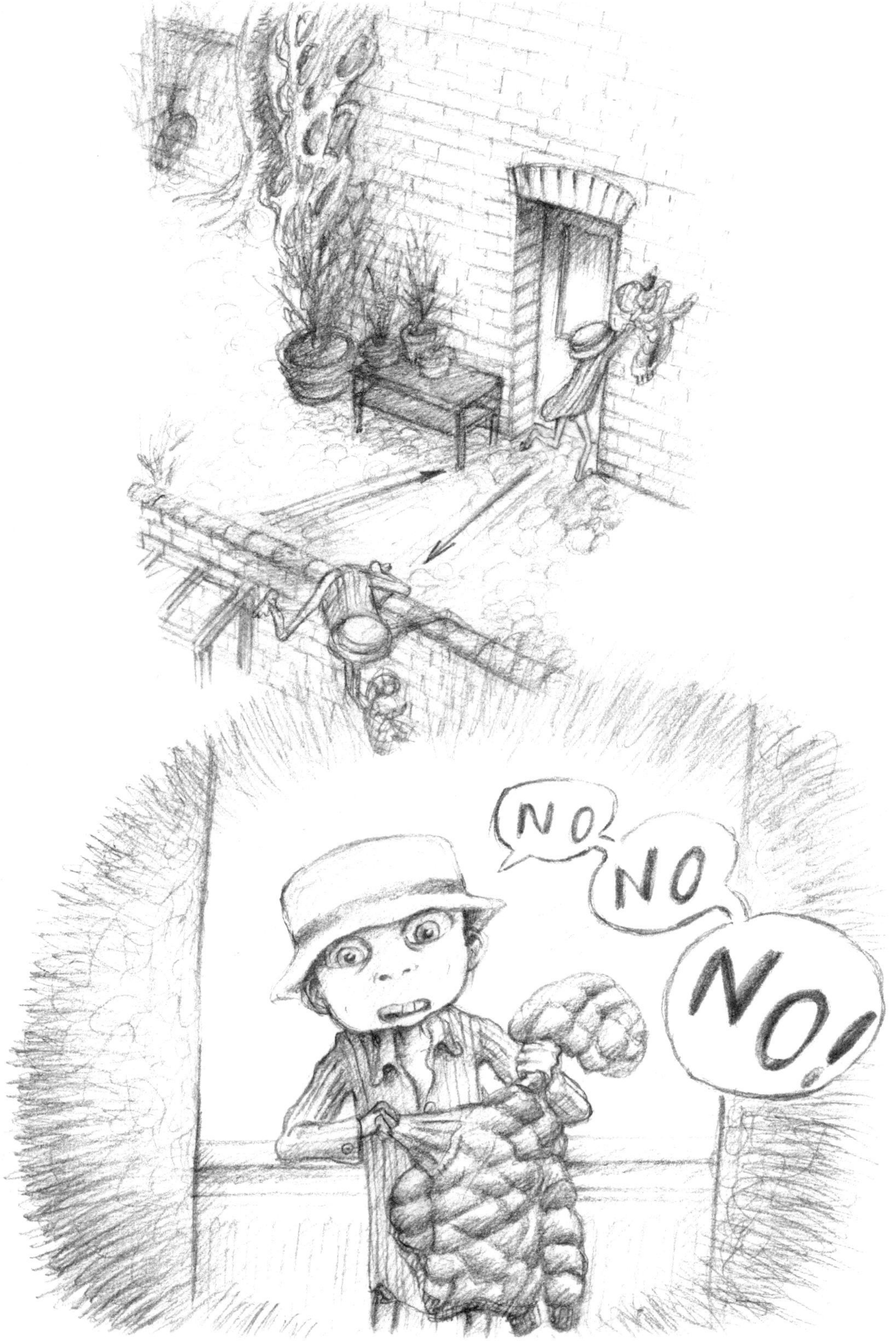
NO
NO
NO!

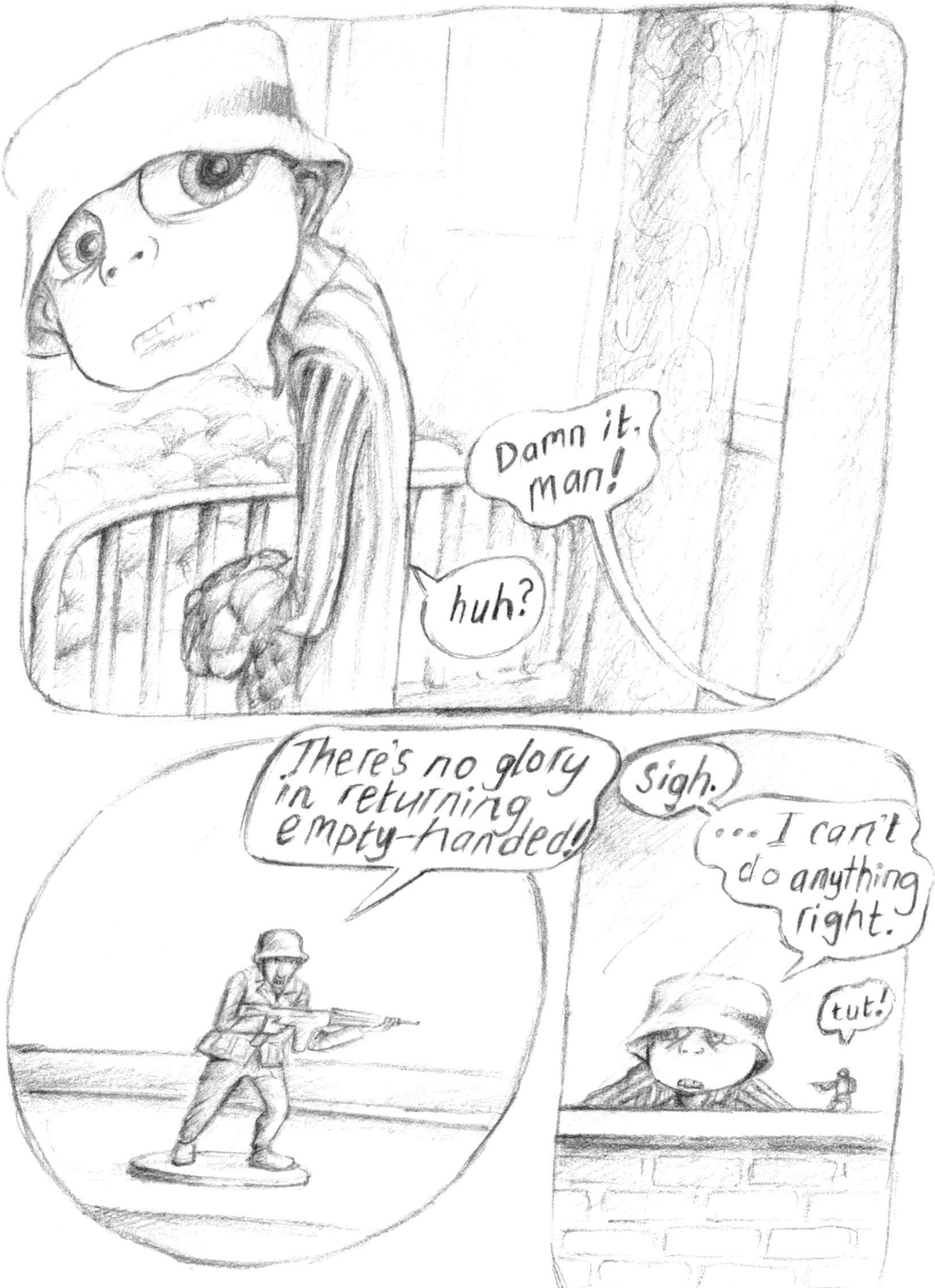
Damn it, man!
huh?
There's no glory in returning empty-handed!
Sigh.
...I can't do anything right.
tut!

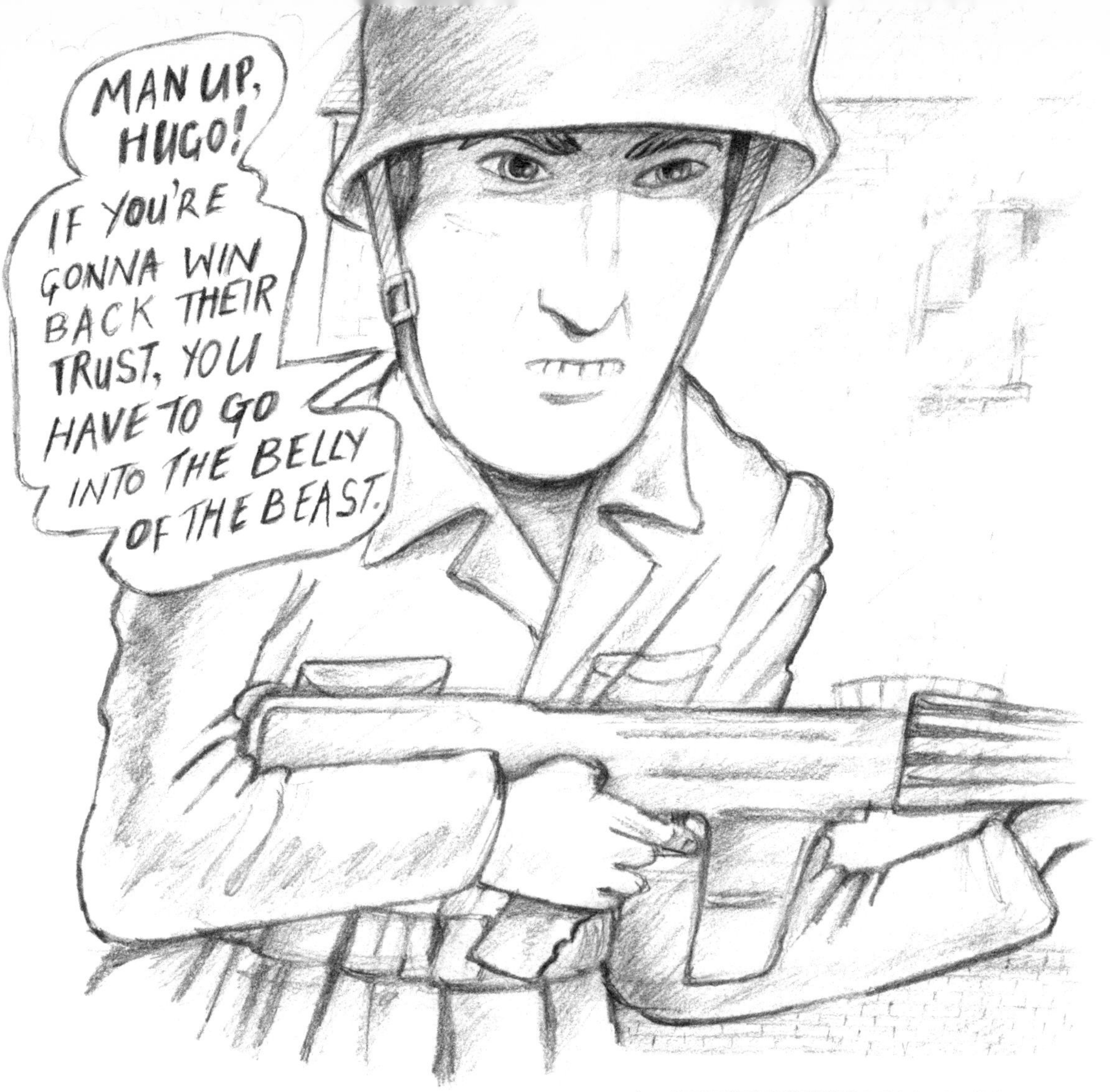
MAN UP, HUGO!
IF YOU'RE GONNA WIN BACK THEIR TRUST, YOU HAVE TO GO INTO THE BELLY OF THE BEAST.

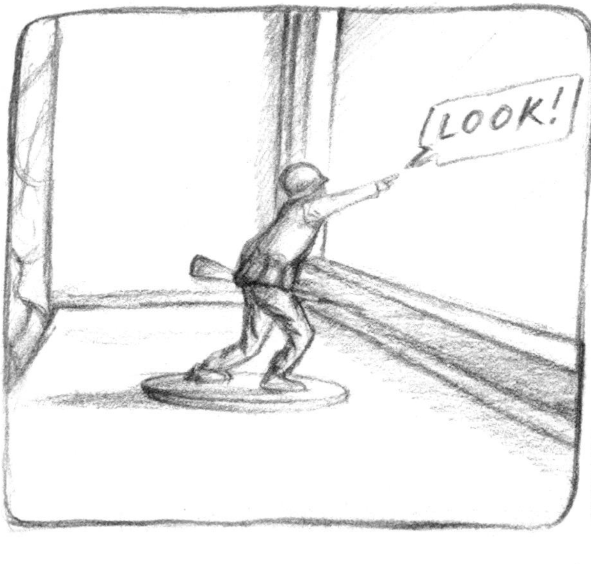
LOOK!

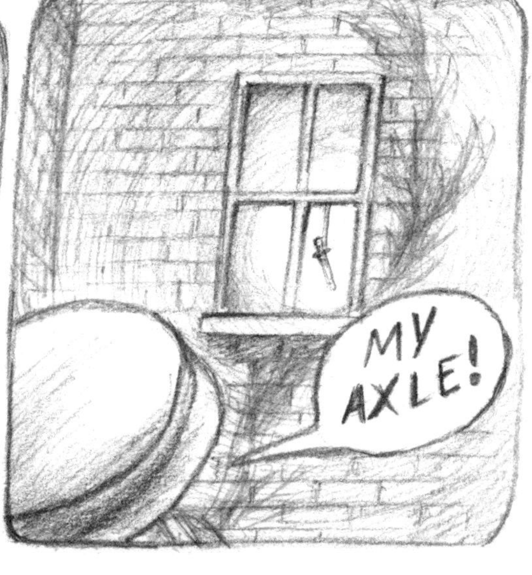
MY AXLE!

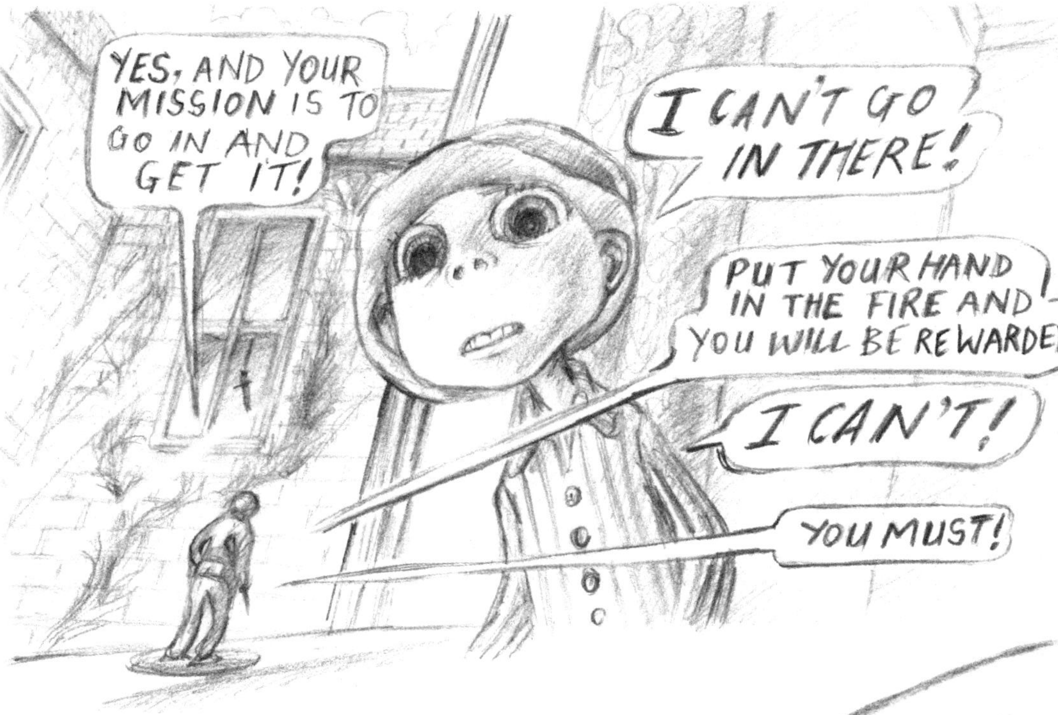
YES, AND YOUR MISSION IS TO GO IN AND GET IT!
I CAN'T GO IN THERE!
PUT YOUR HAND IN THE FIRE AND YOU WILL BE REWARDED!
I CAN'T!
YOU MUST!

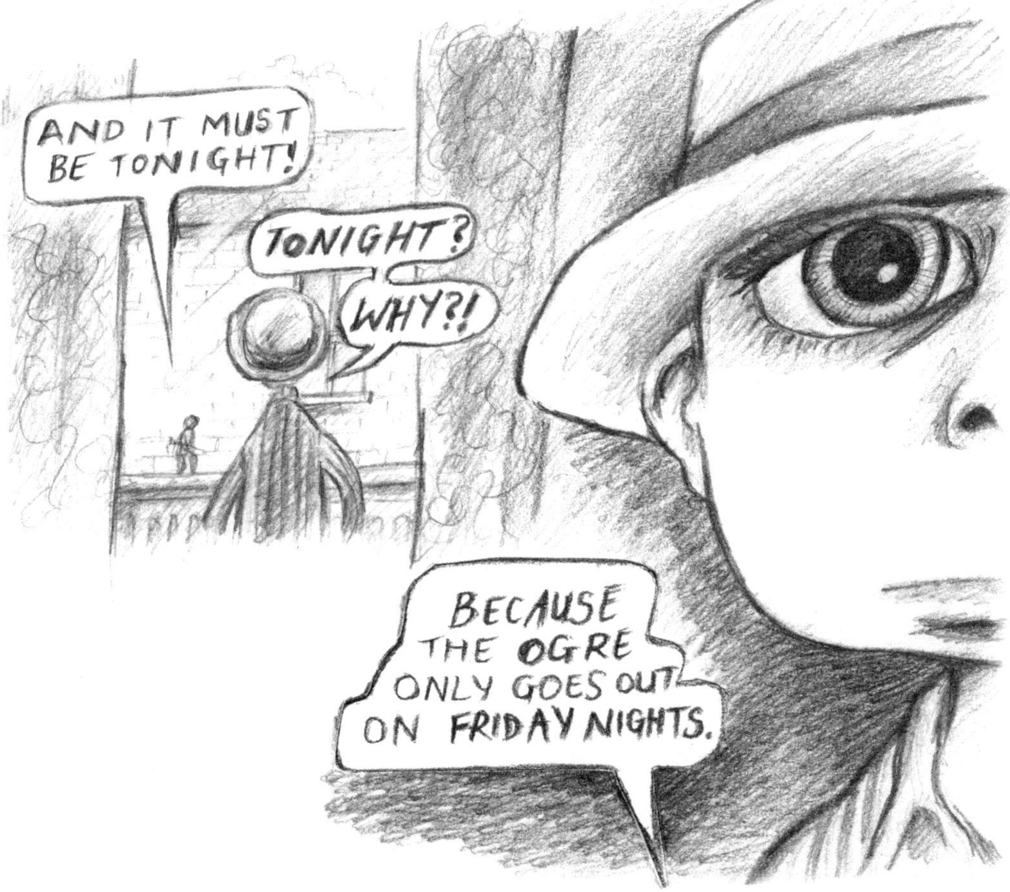
AND IT MUST BE TONIGHT!
TONIGHT?
WHY?!
BECAUSE THE OGRE ONLY GOES OUT ON FRIDAY NIGHTS.

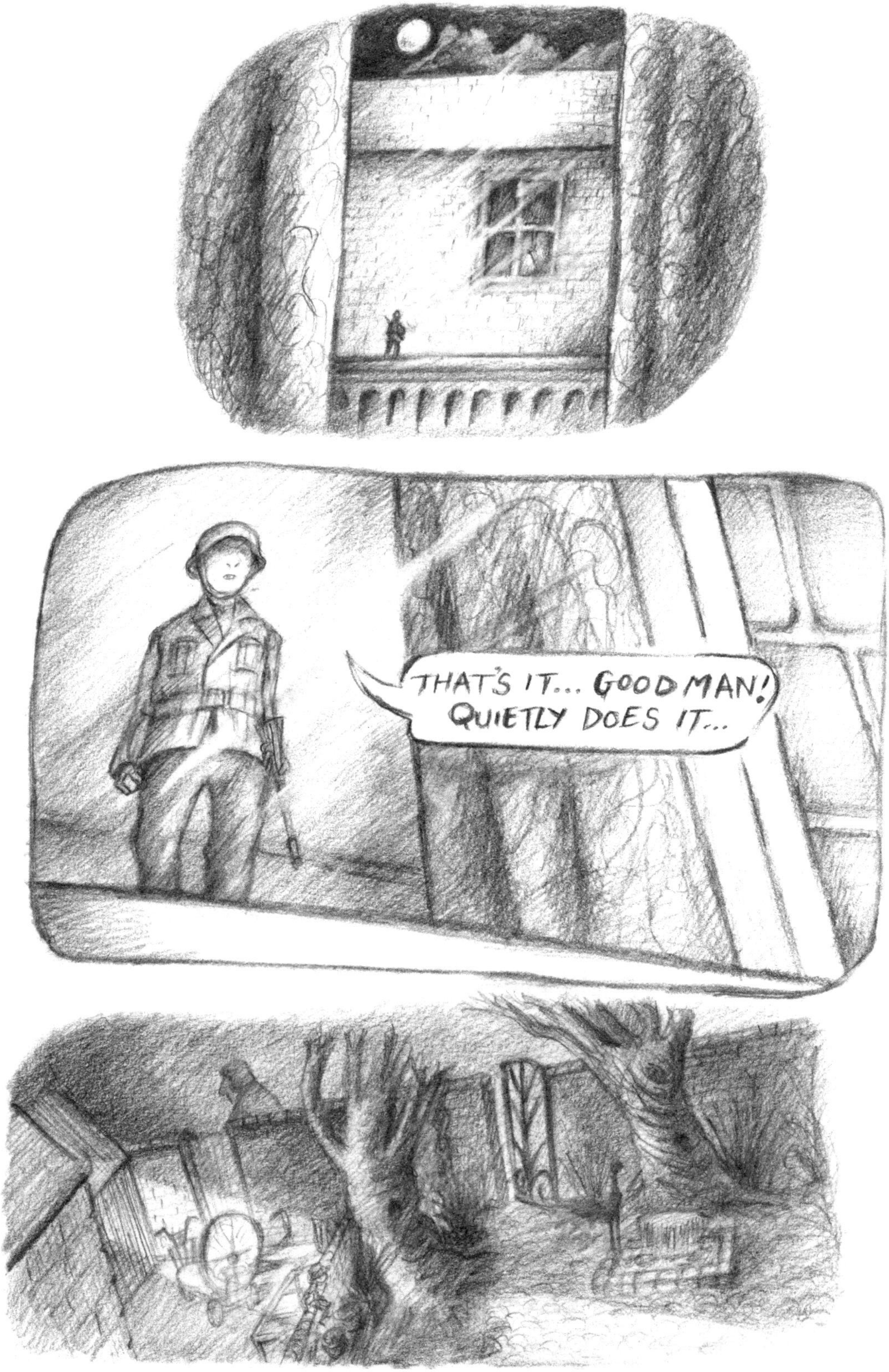
THAT'S IT... GOOD MAN! QUIETLY DOES IT...

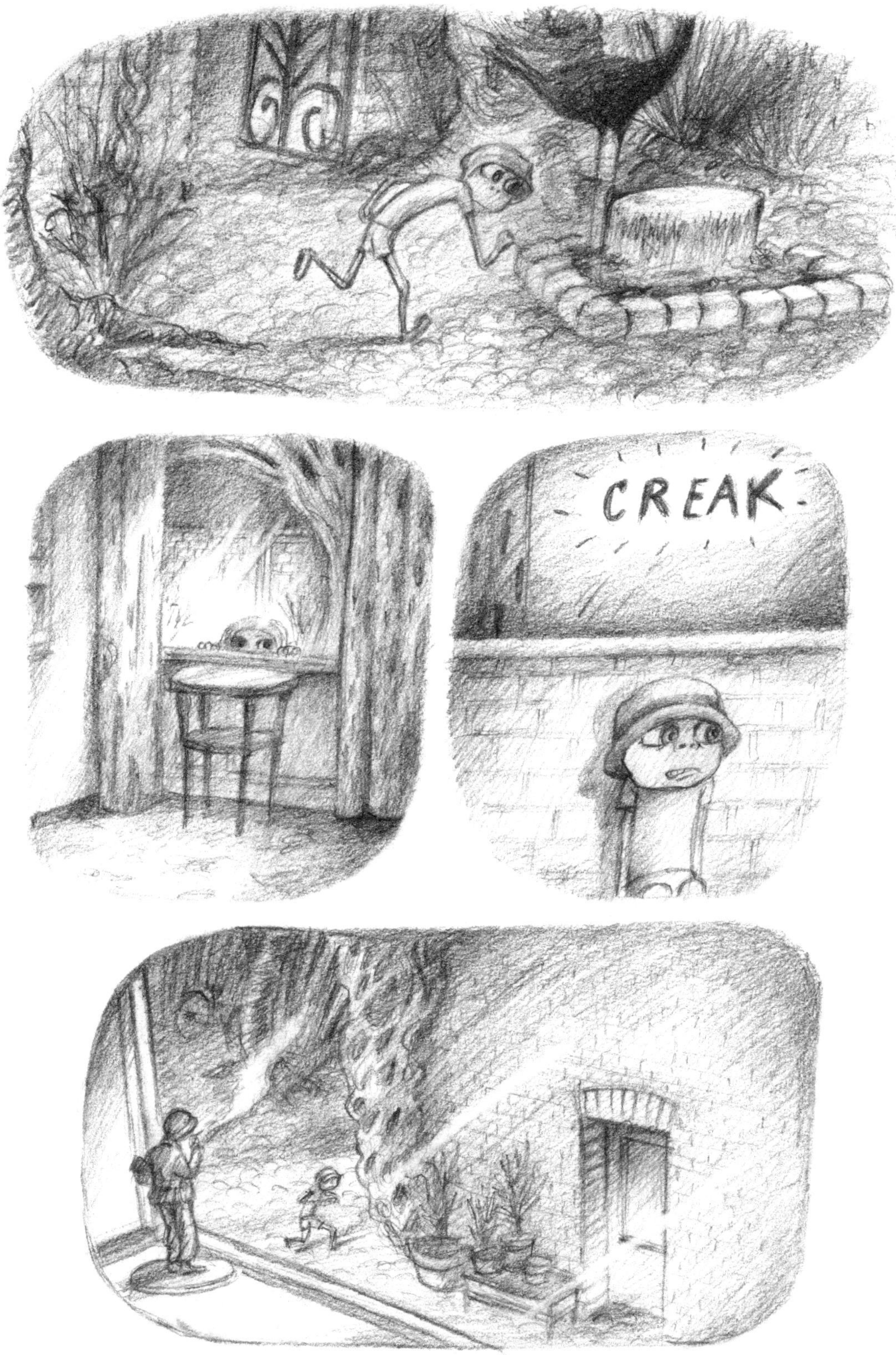
CREAK

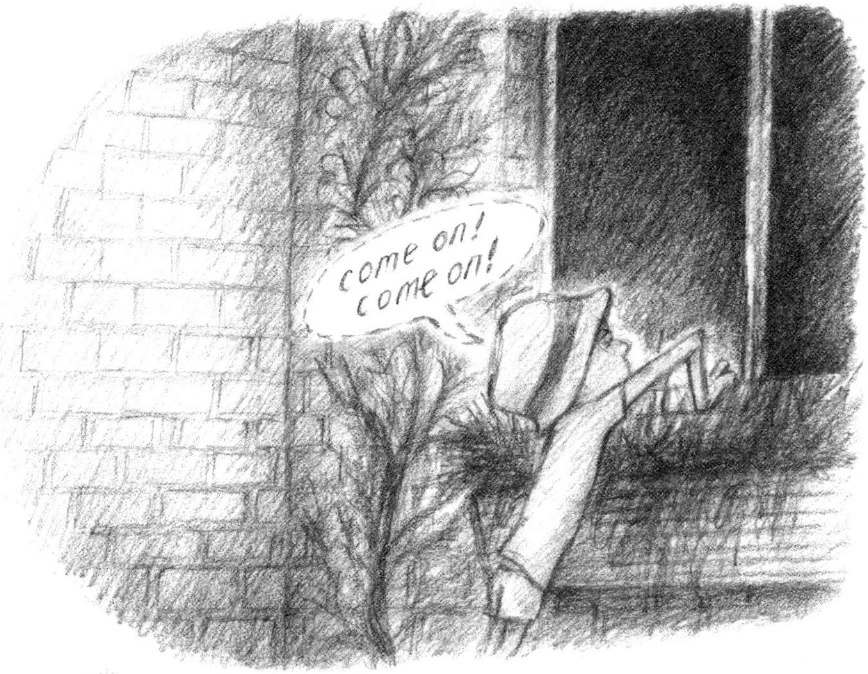
come on!
come on!

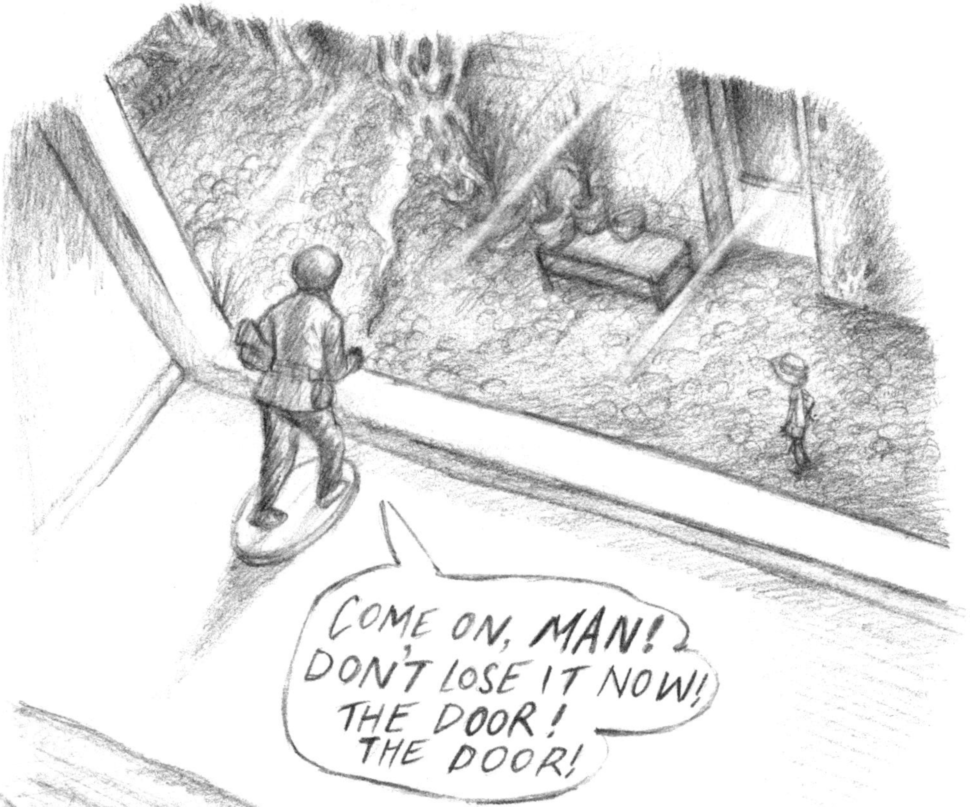
COME ON, MAN! DON'T LOSE IT NOW! THE DOOR! THE DOOR!

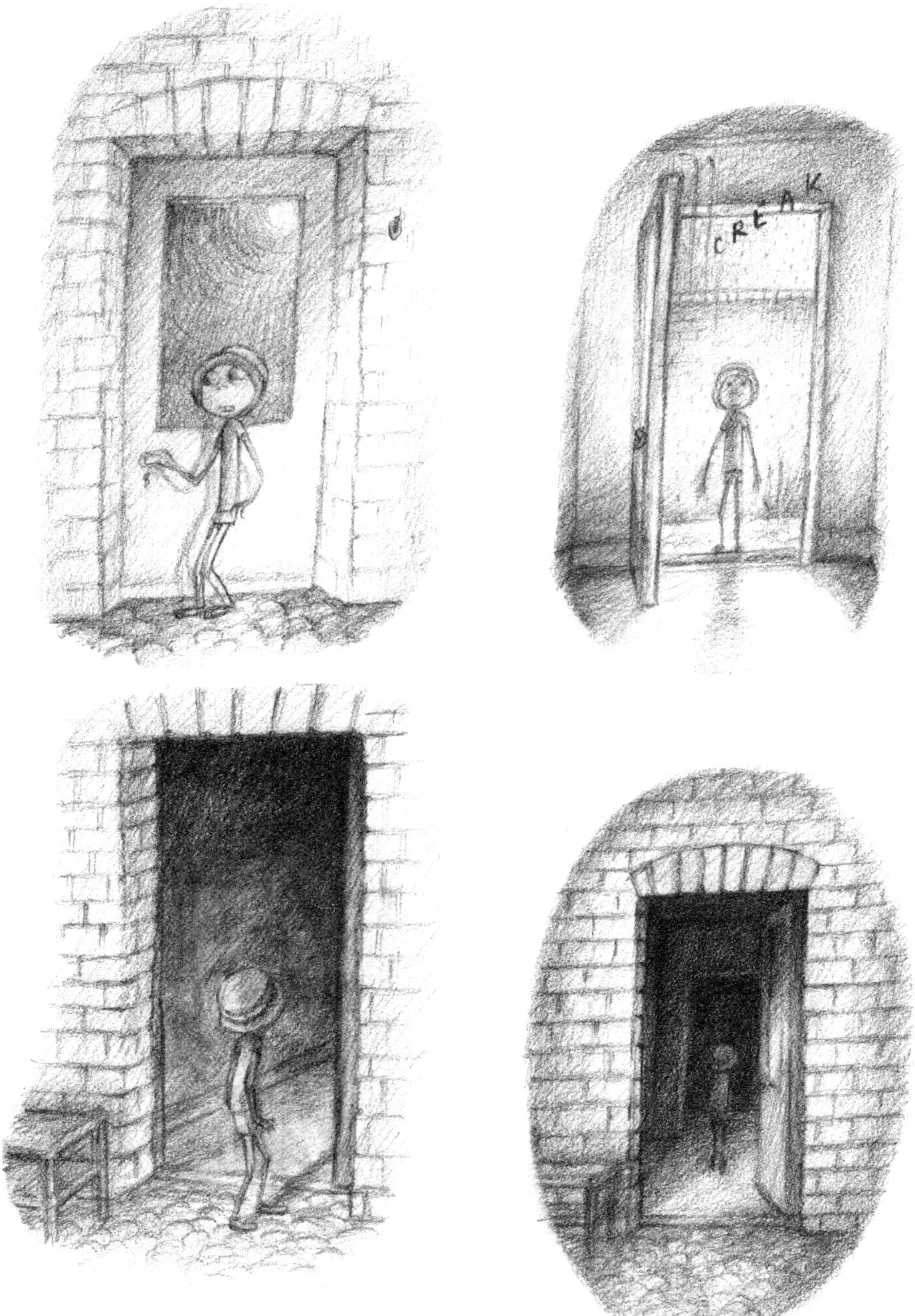
CREAK

Chapter Seven

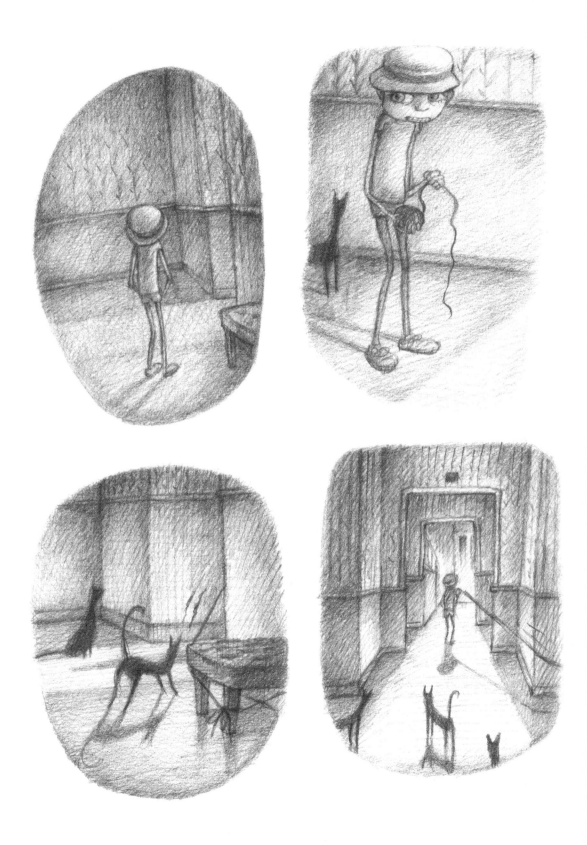

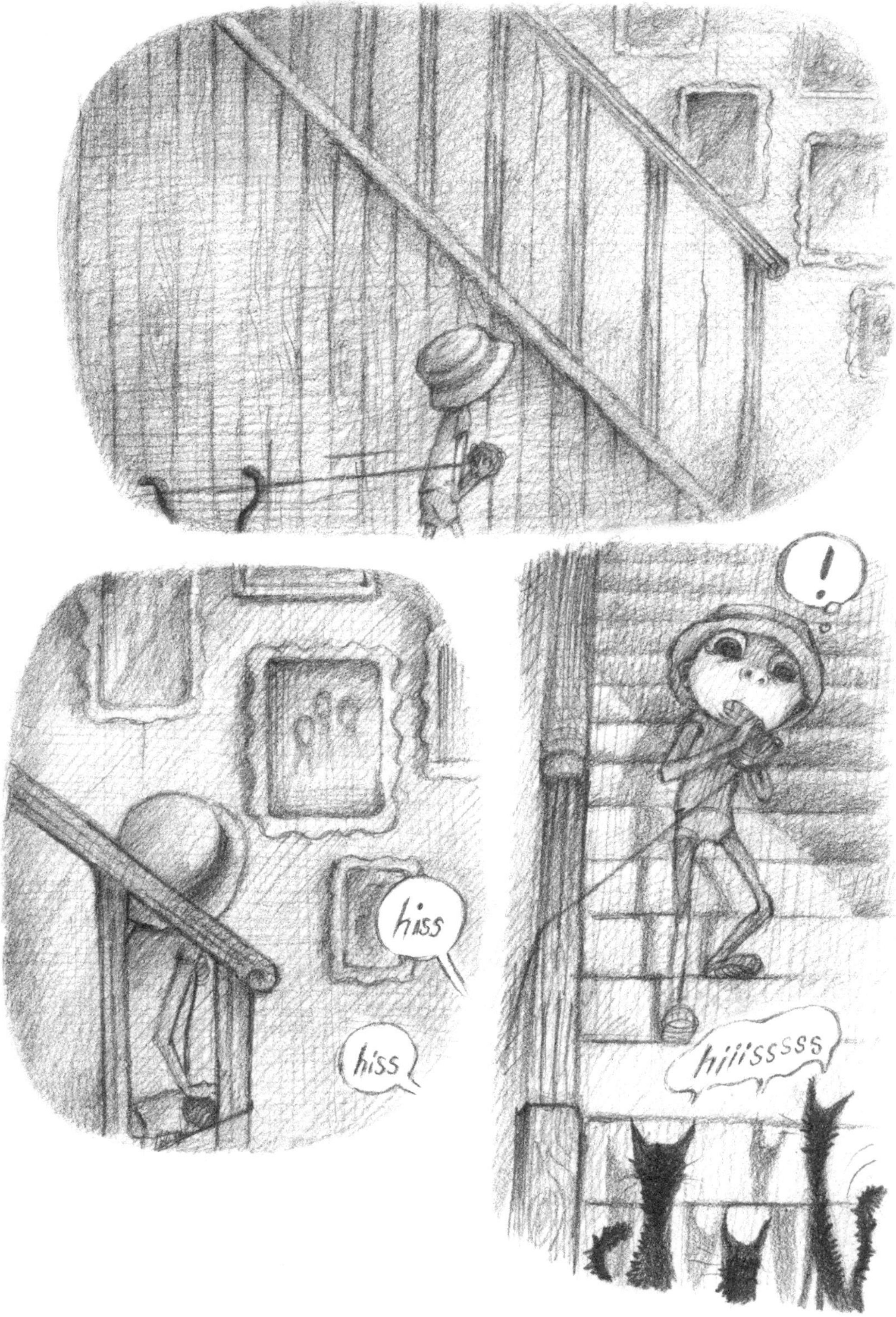
hiss
hiss
!
hiiissssss

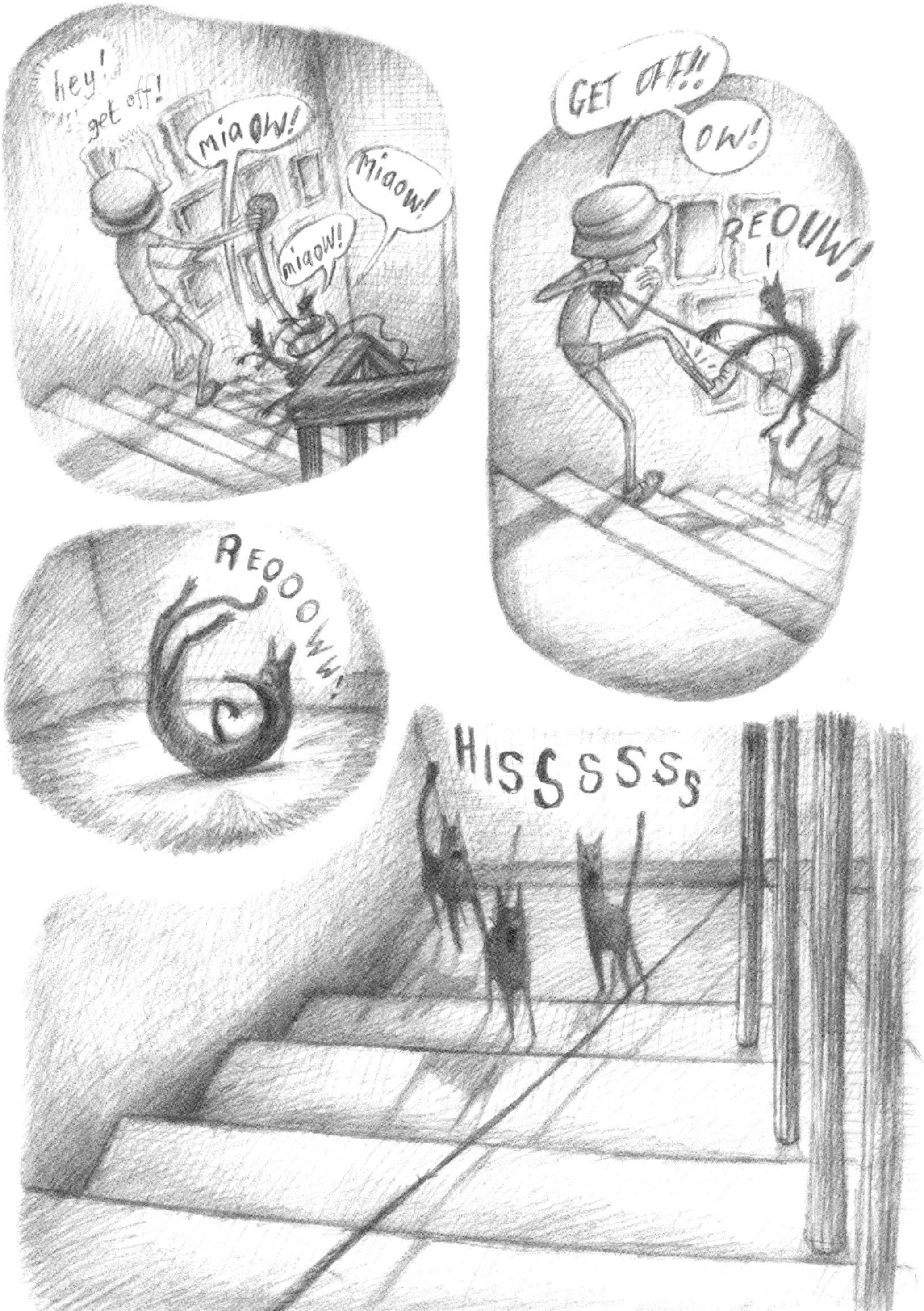
hey!
get off!
miaow!
miaow!
miaow!
GET OFF!!
OW!
REOUW!
REOOOOWW!
HISSSSSS

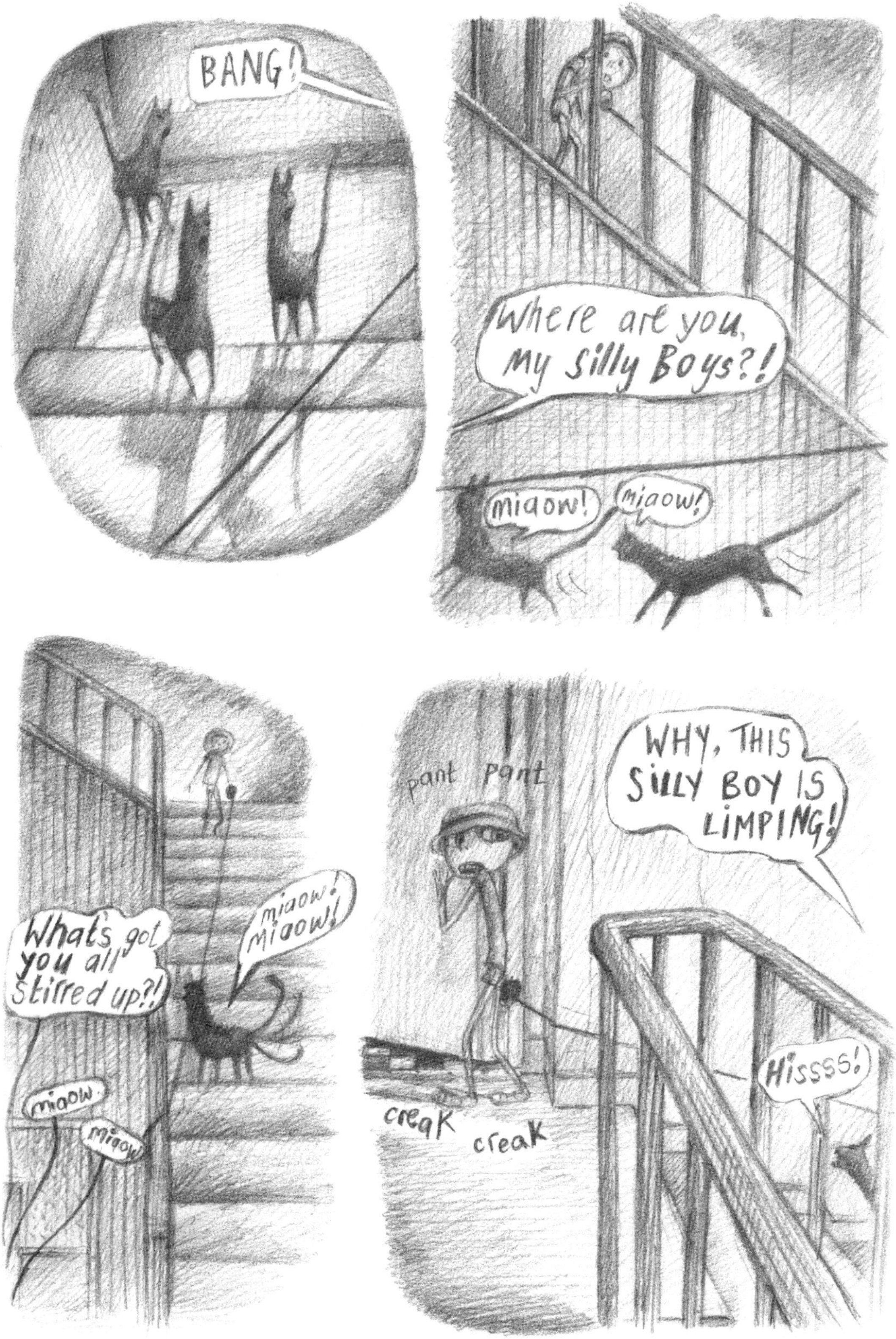
BANG!
Where are you, my silly Boys?!
miaow!
miaow!
What's got you all stirred up?!
miaow! miaow!
miaow.
miaow
pant pant
WHY, THIS SILLY BOY IS LIMPING!
creak
creak
Hissss!

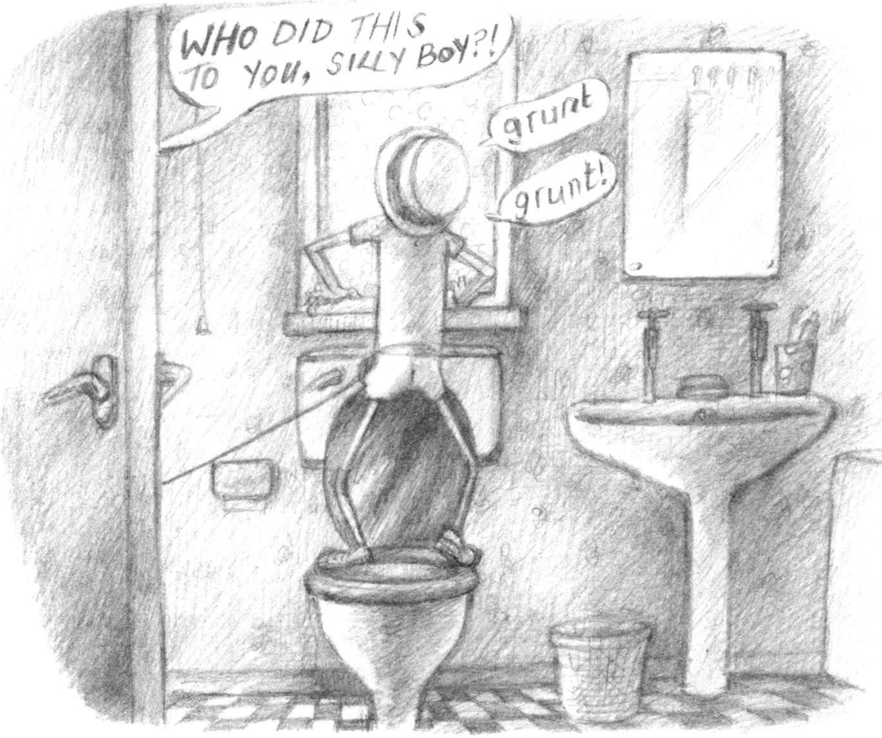
WHO DID THIS TO YOU, SILLY BOY?!
grunt
grunt!

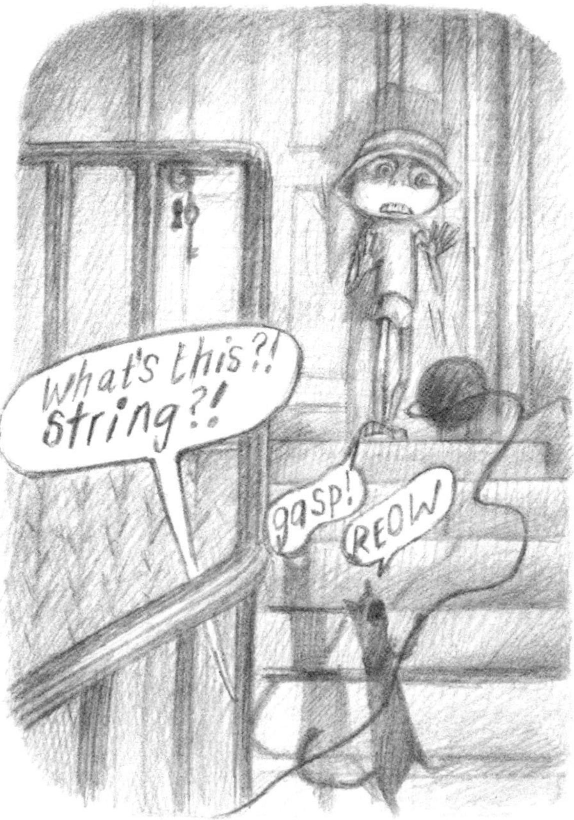
What's this?! String?!
gasp!
REOW

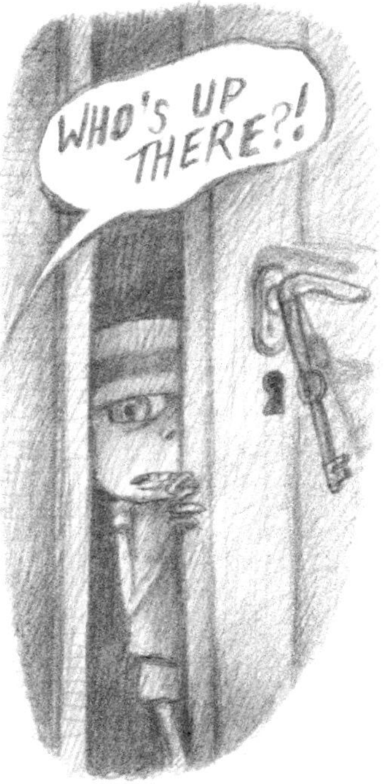
WHO'S UP THERE?!

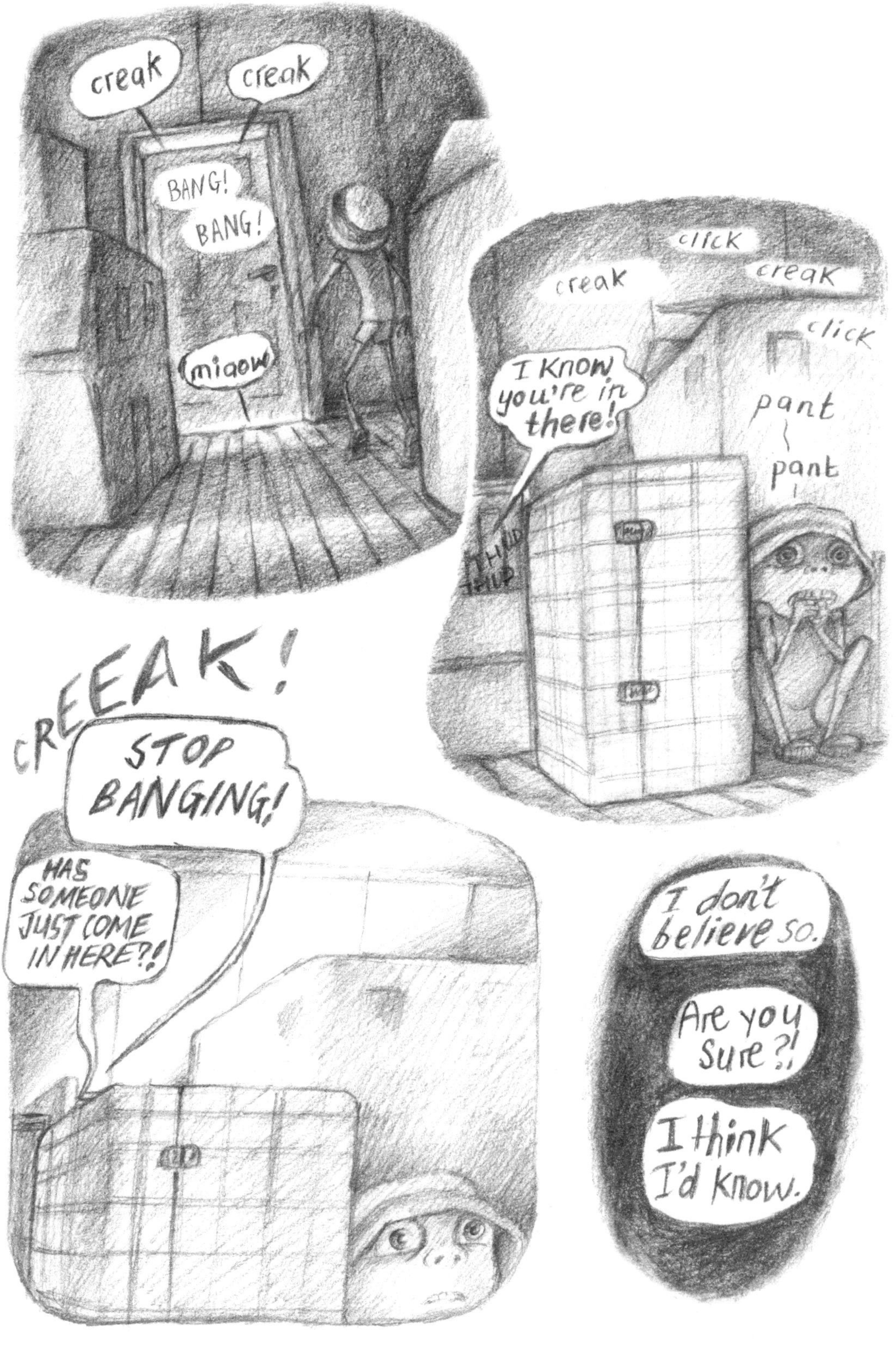
creak
creak
BANG!
BANG!
miaow
creak
click
creak
click
I know you're in there!
pant
pant
CREEEAK!
STOP BANGING!
HAS SOMEONE JUST COME IN HERE?!
I don't believe so.
Are you sure?!
I think I'd know.

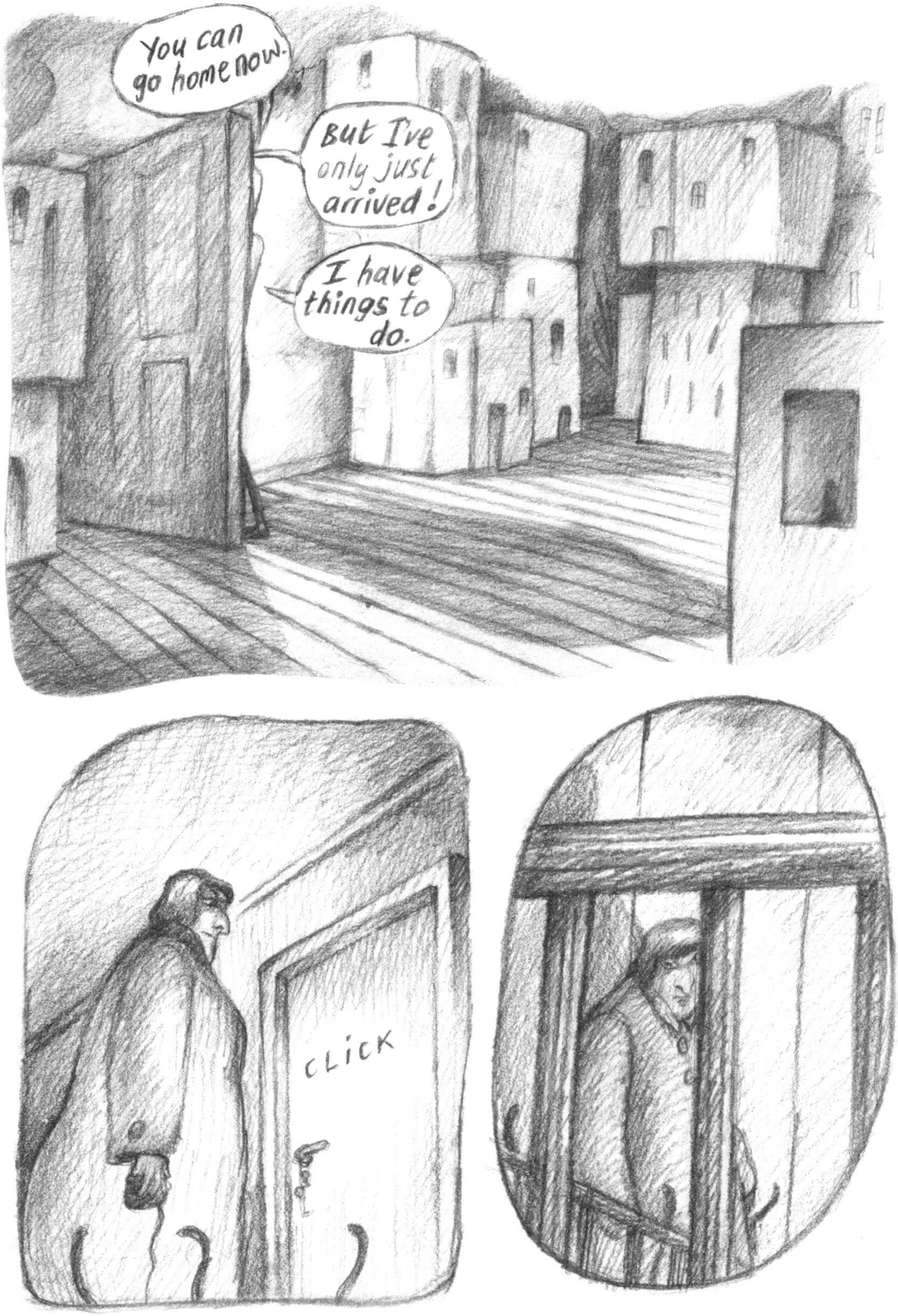
You can go home now.
But I've only just arrived!
I have things to do.
CLICK

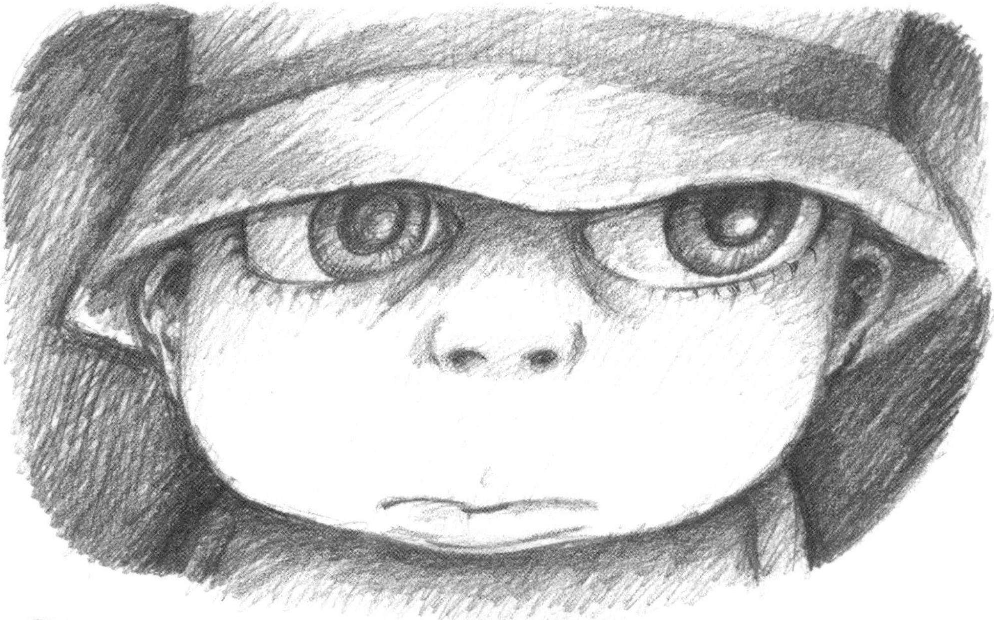

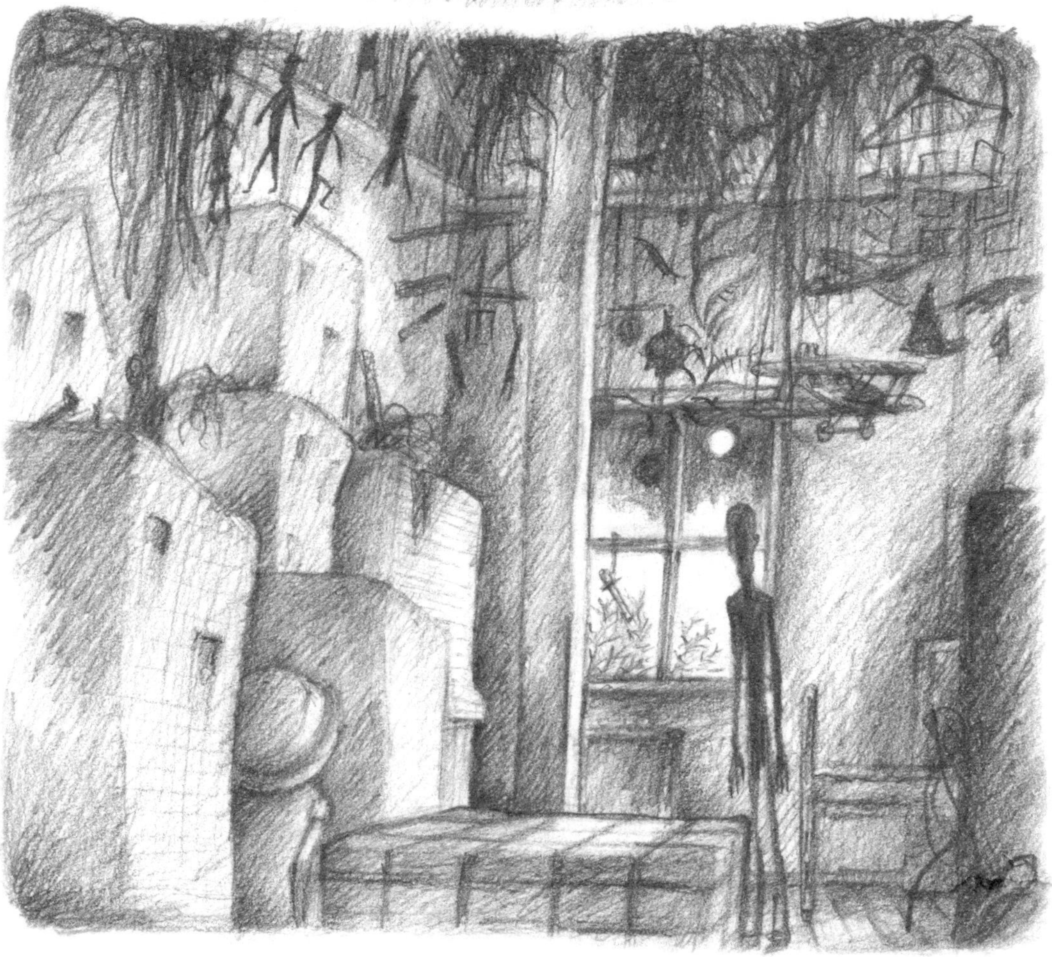

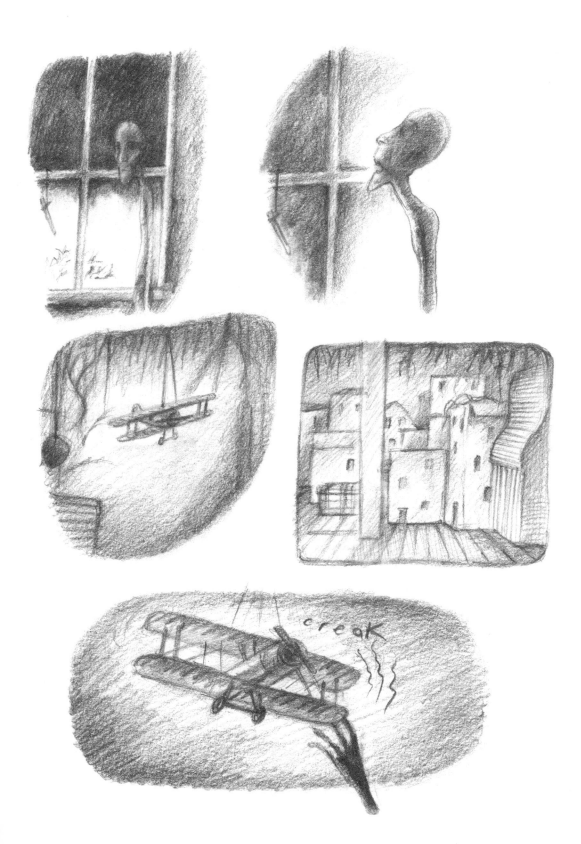

creak

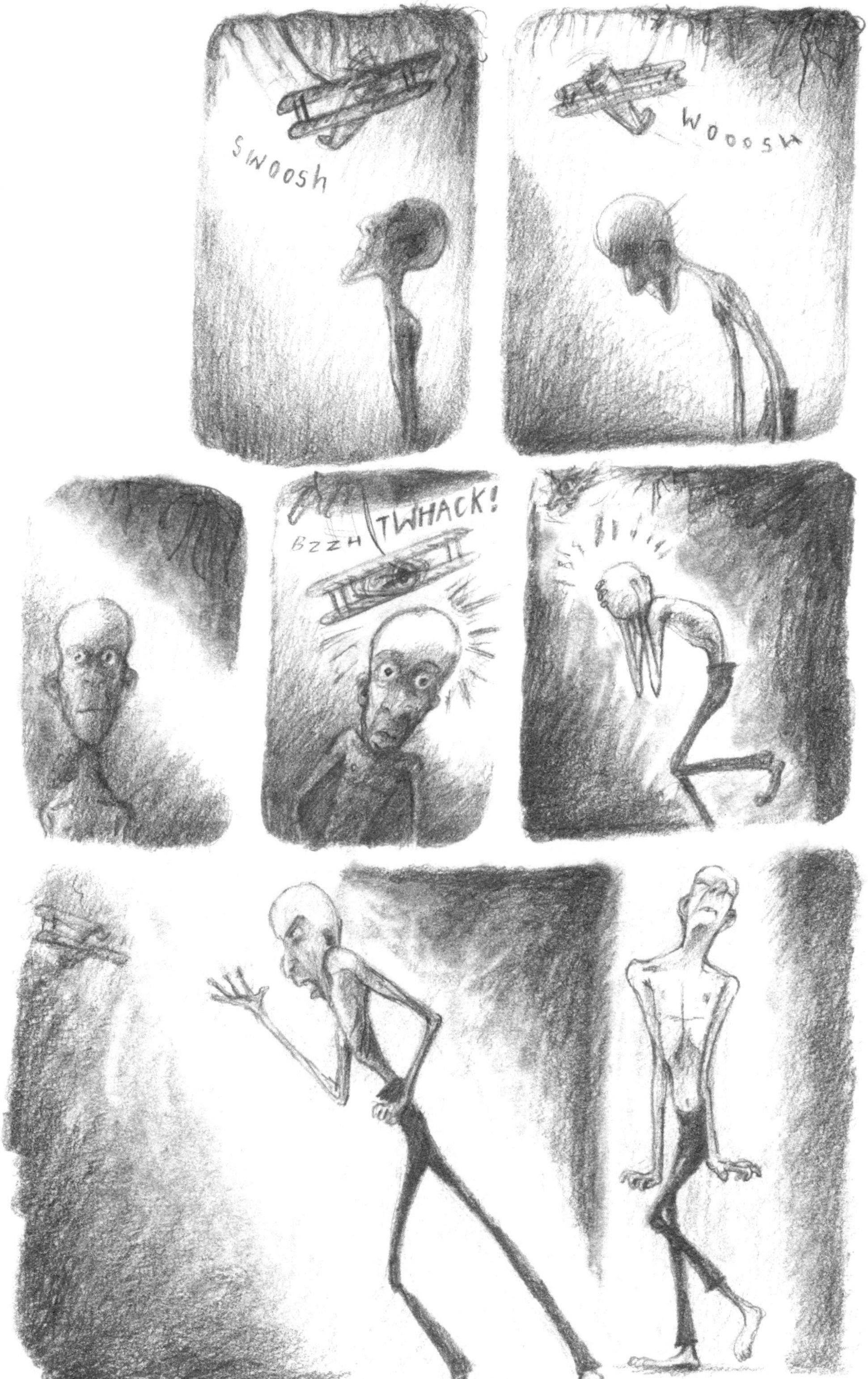
SWOOSH
WOOOSH
BZZH
TWHACK!

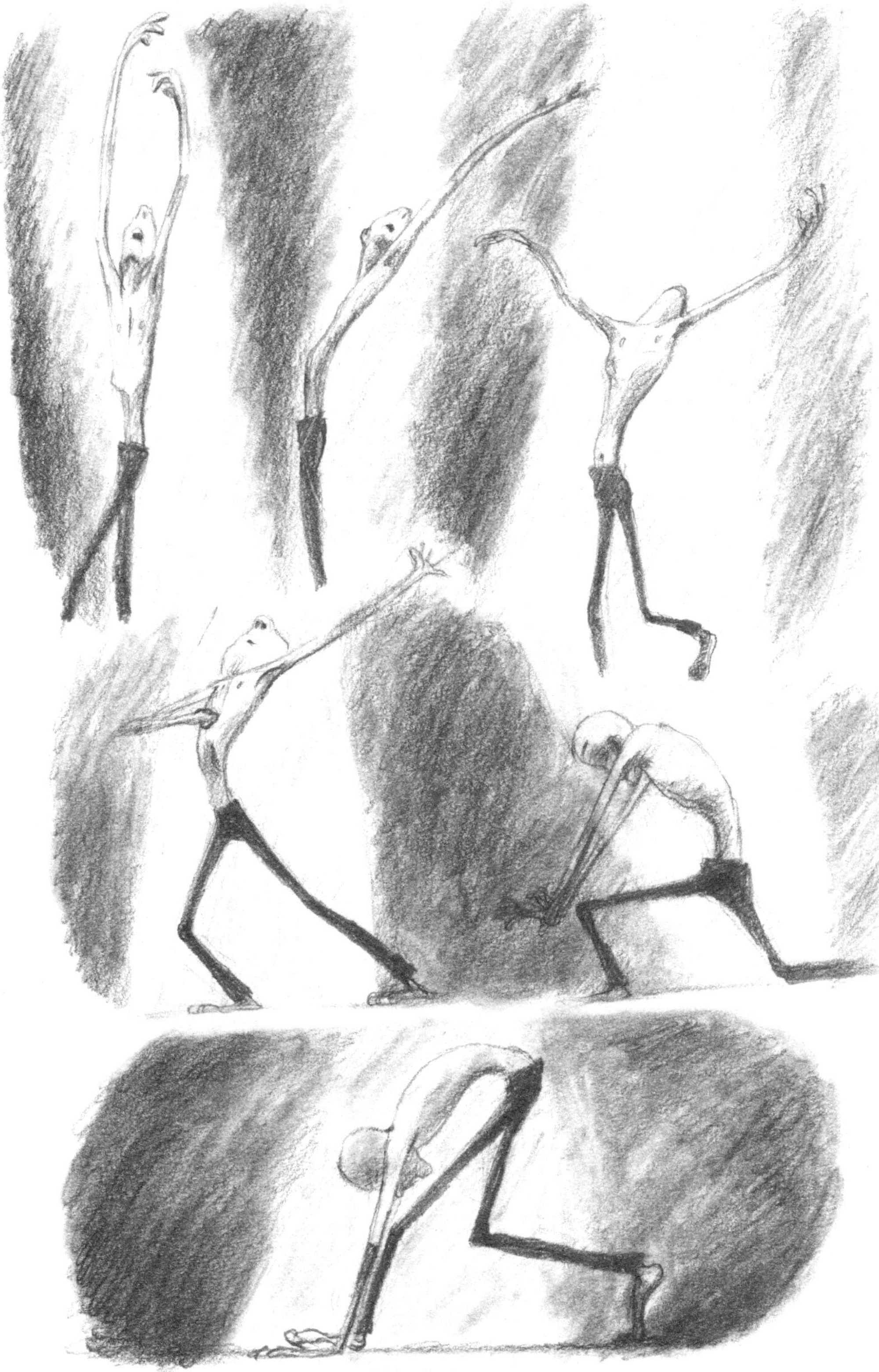

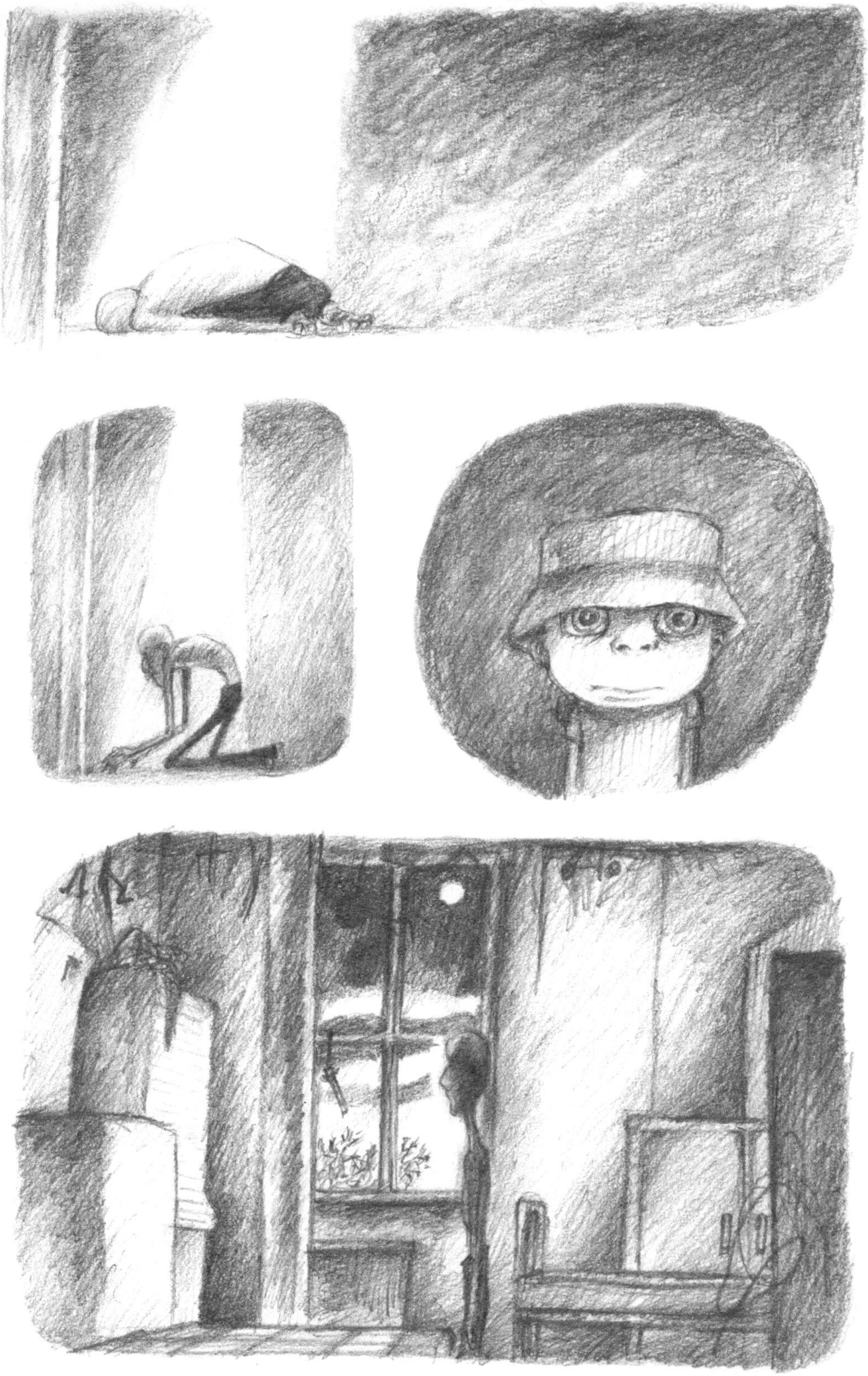

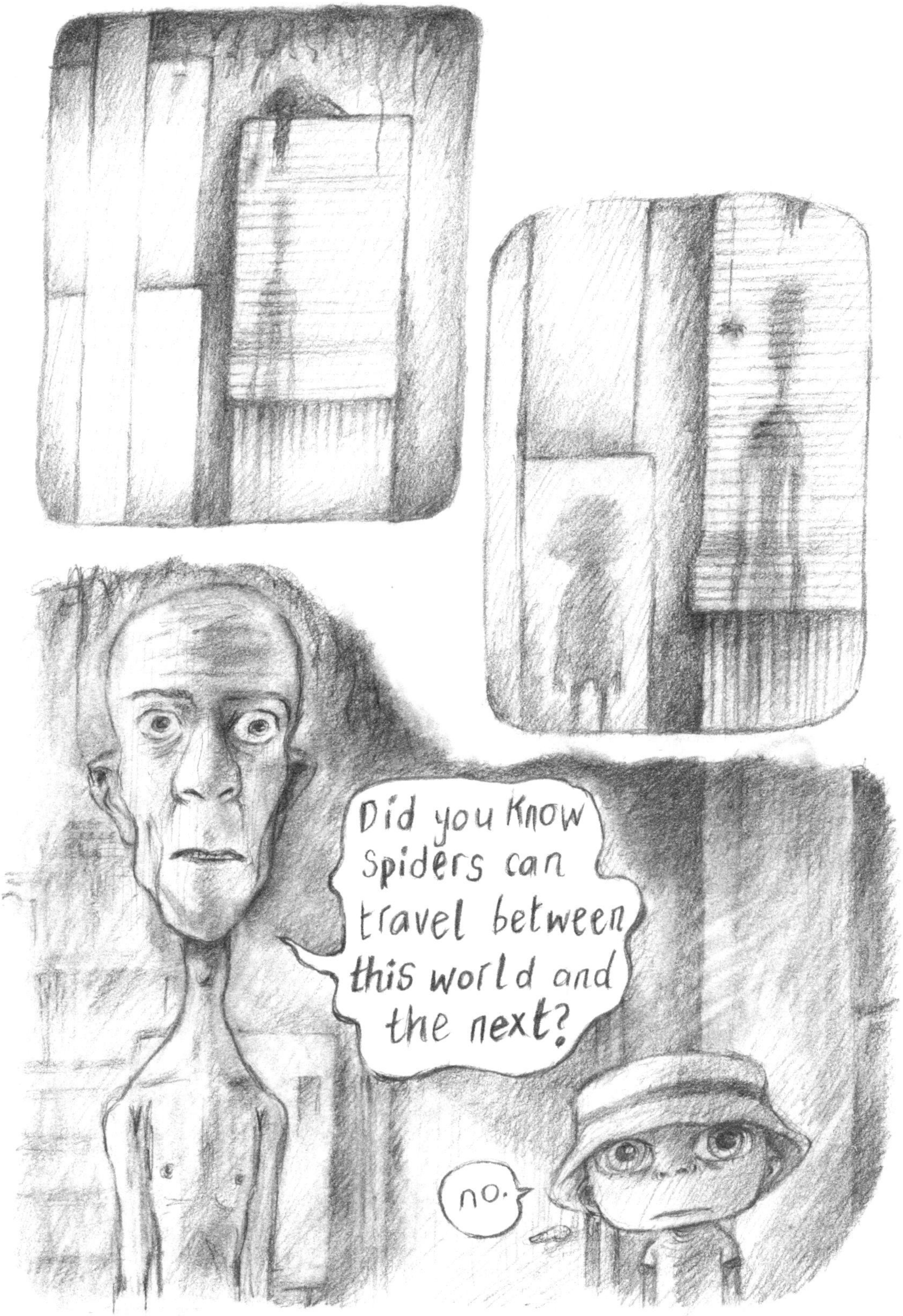
Did you know spiders can travel between this world and the next?
no.

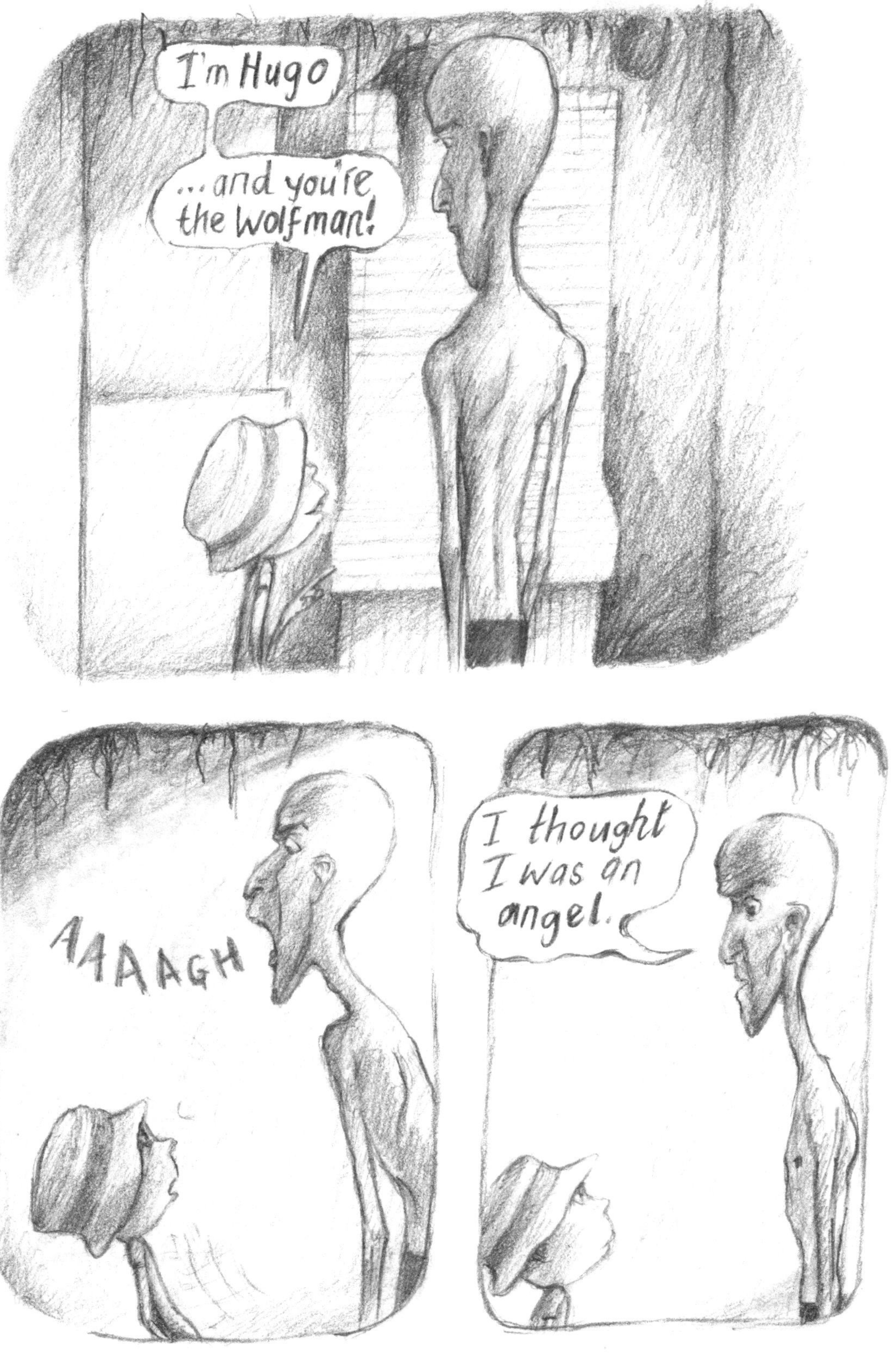
I'm Hugo
...and you're the Wolfman!
AAAAGH
I thought I was an angel.

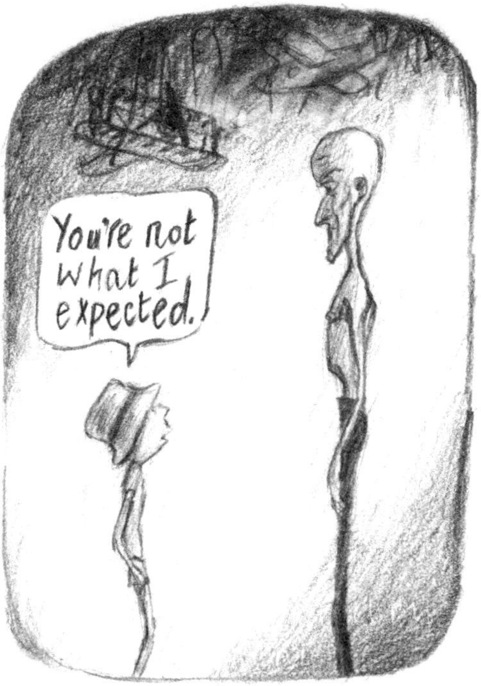
You're not what I expected.

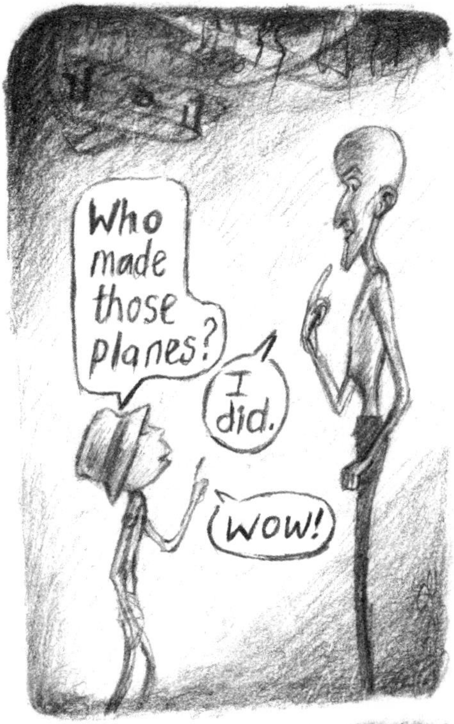
Who made those planes?
I did.
WOW!

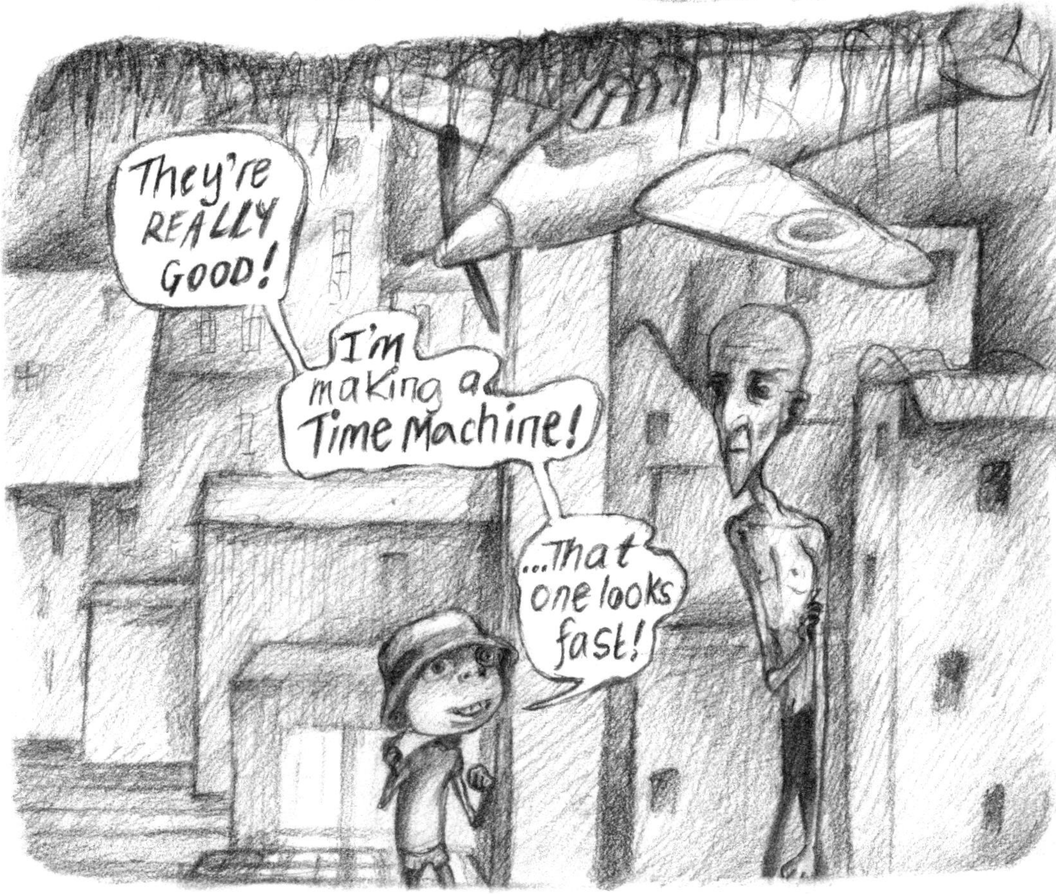
They're REALLY GOOD!
I'm making a Time Machine!
...That one looks fast!

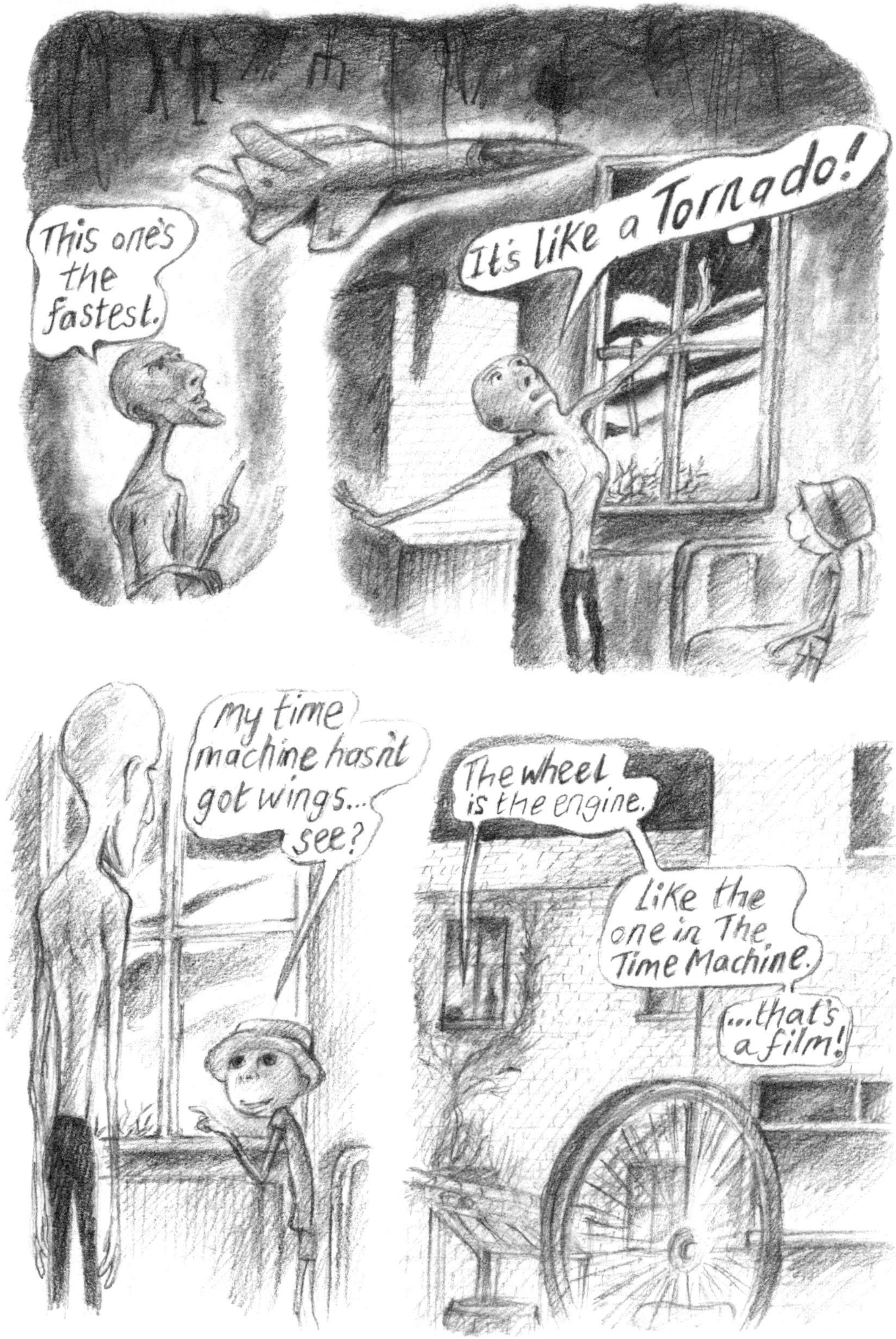
This one's the fastest.
It's like a Tornado!
my time machine hasn't got wings... see?
The wheel is the engine.
Like the one in The Time Machine.
...that's a film!

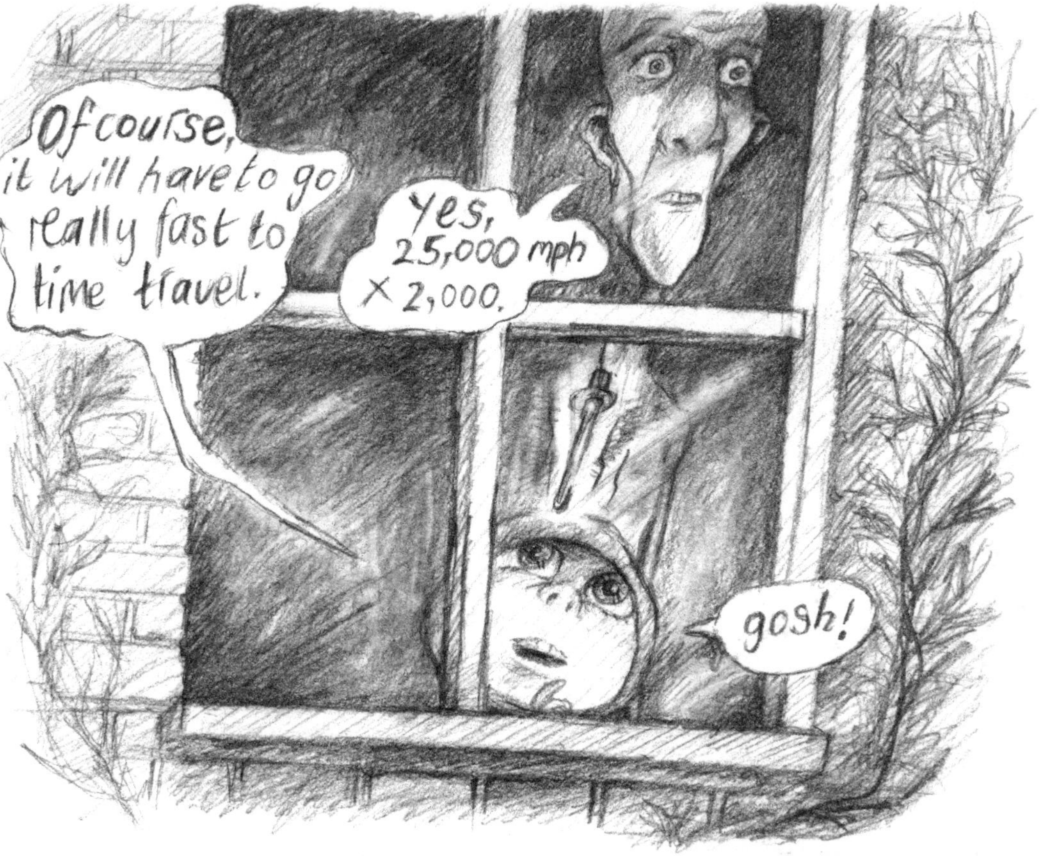
Of course, it will have to go really fast to time travel.
Yes, 25,000 mph × 2,000.
gosh!

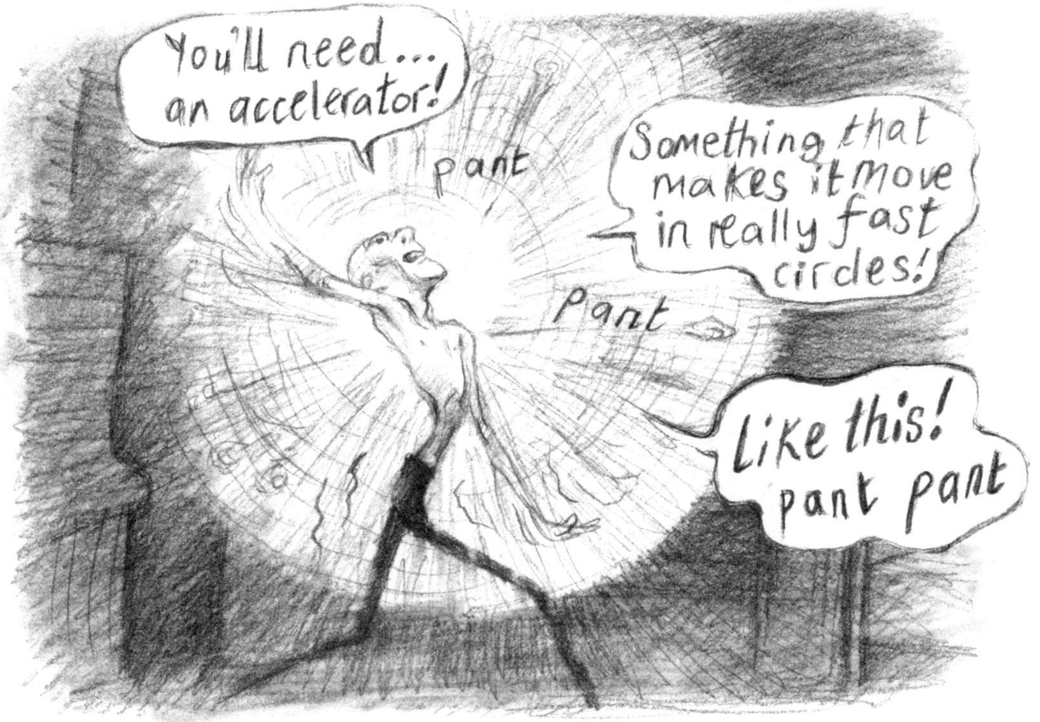
You'll need... an accelerator!
pant
Something that makes it move in really fast circles!
Pant
Like this! pant pant

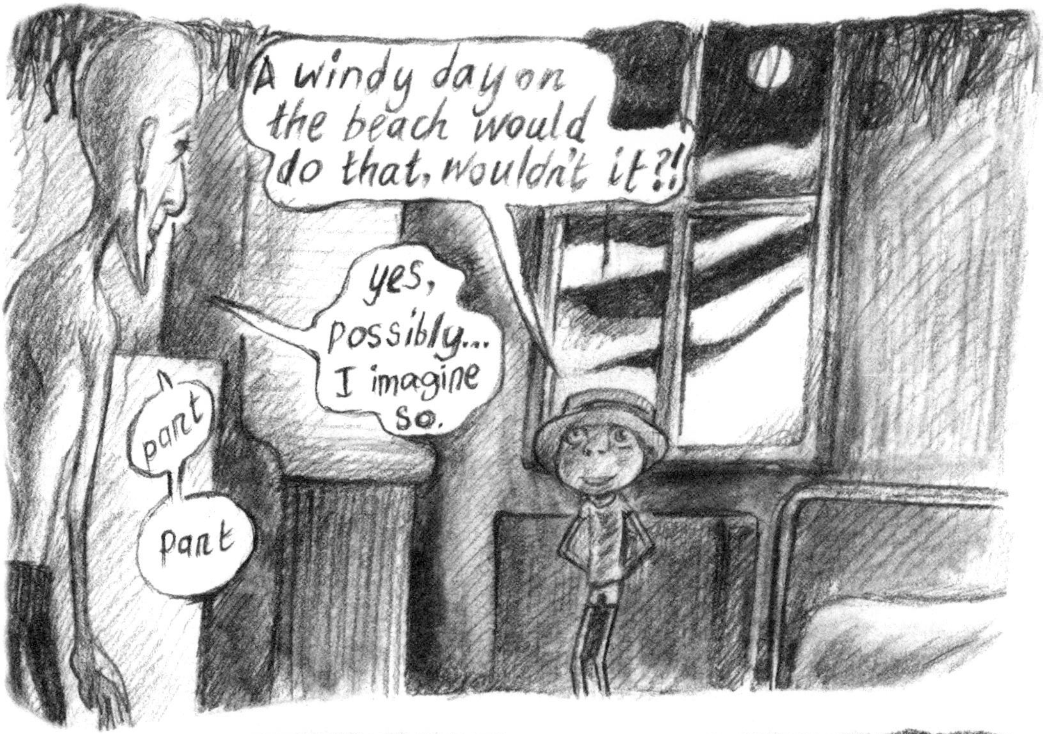
A windy day on the beach would do that, wouldn't it?!
yes, possibly... I imagine so.
pant
pant

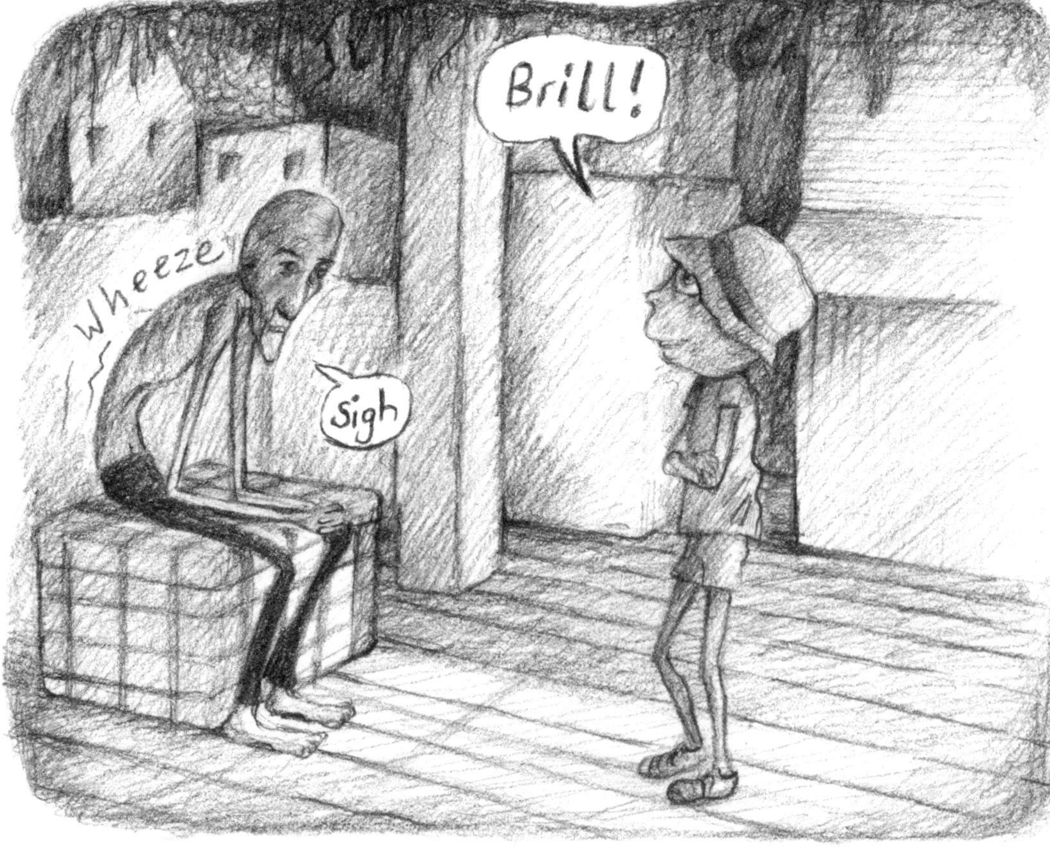
Brill!
Wheeze
Sigh

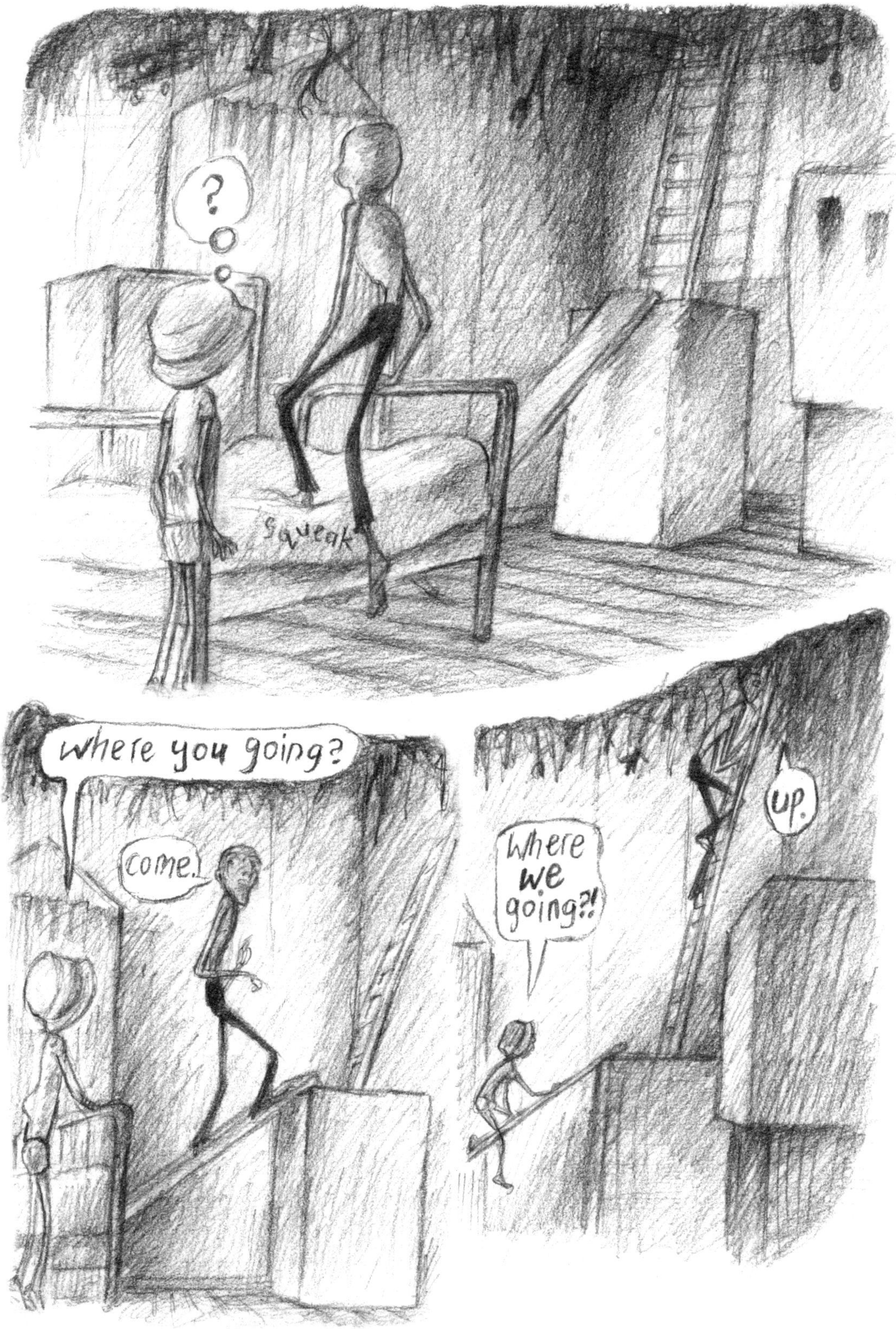
?
squeak
where you going?
come.
Where we going?!
up.

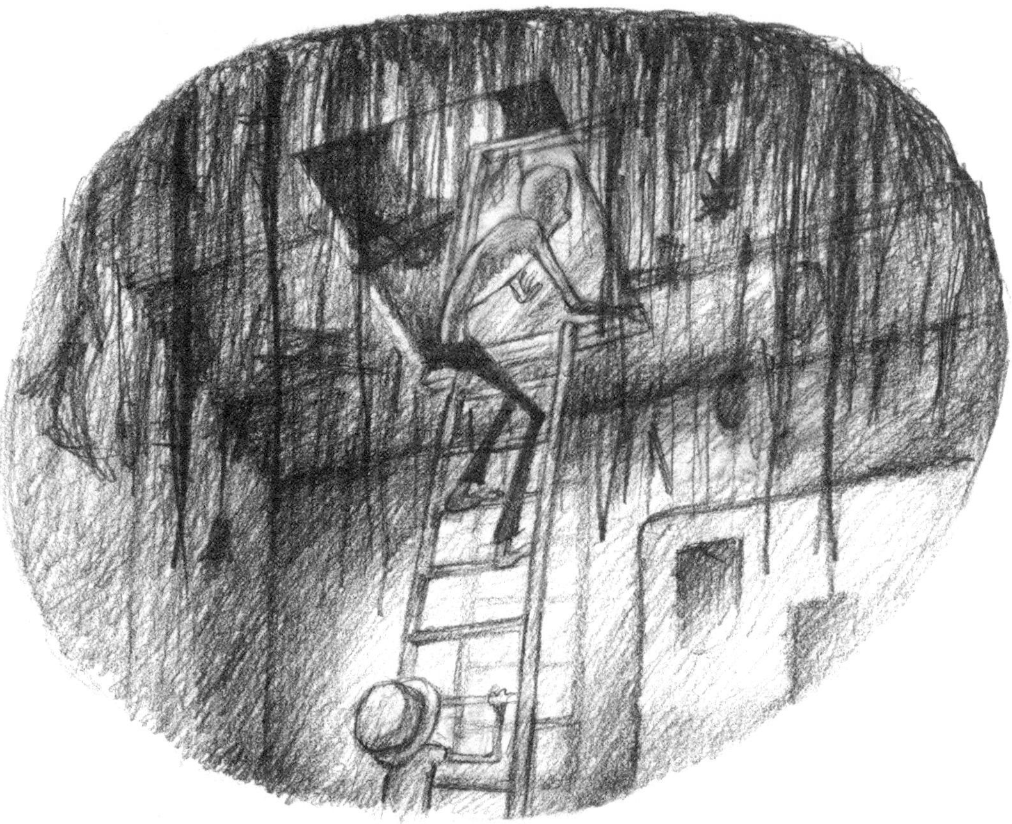

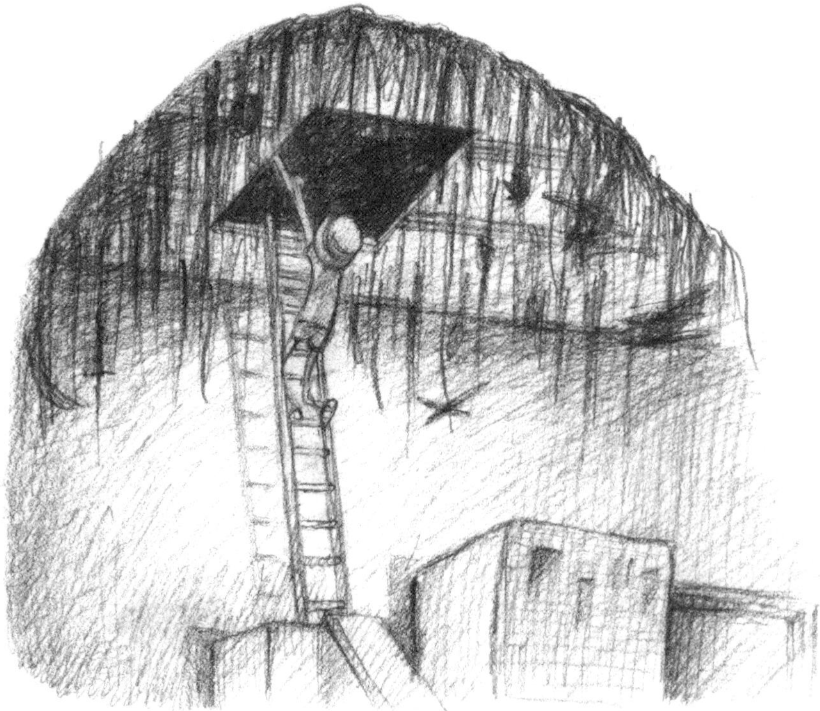

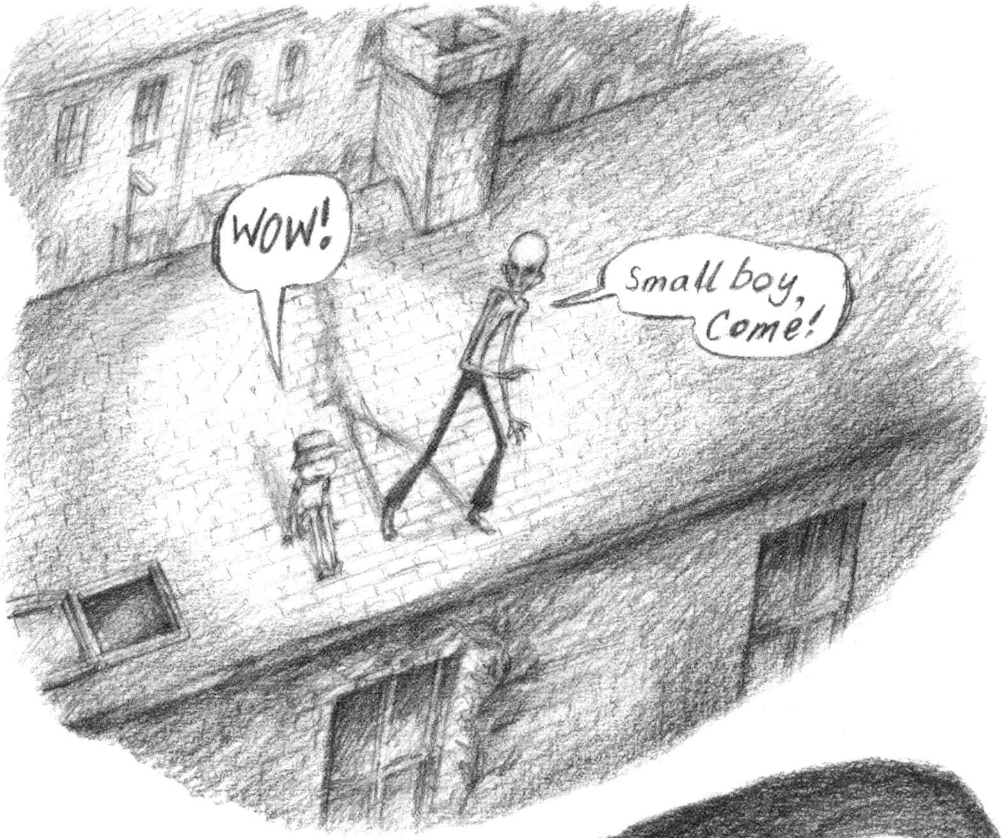
WOW!
Small boy, Come!

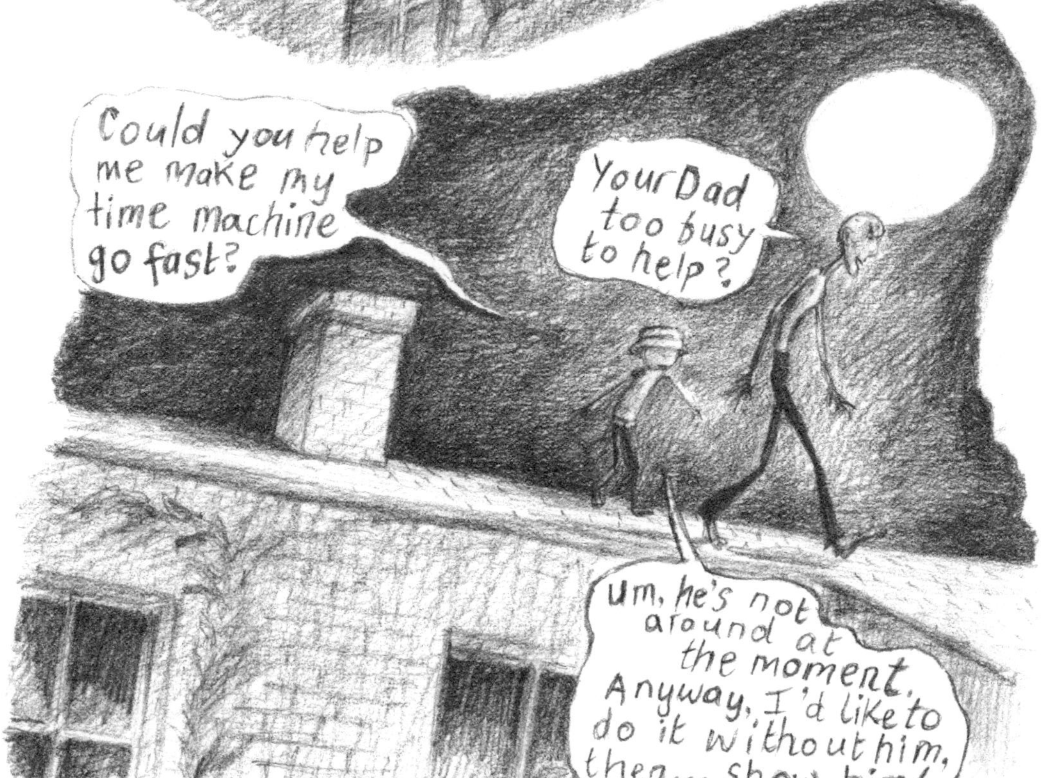
Could you help me make my time machine go fast?
Your Dad too busy to help?
Um, he's not around at the moment. Anyway, I'd like to do it without him, then... show him!

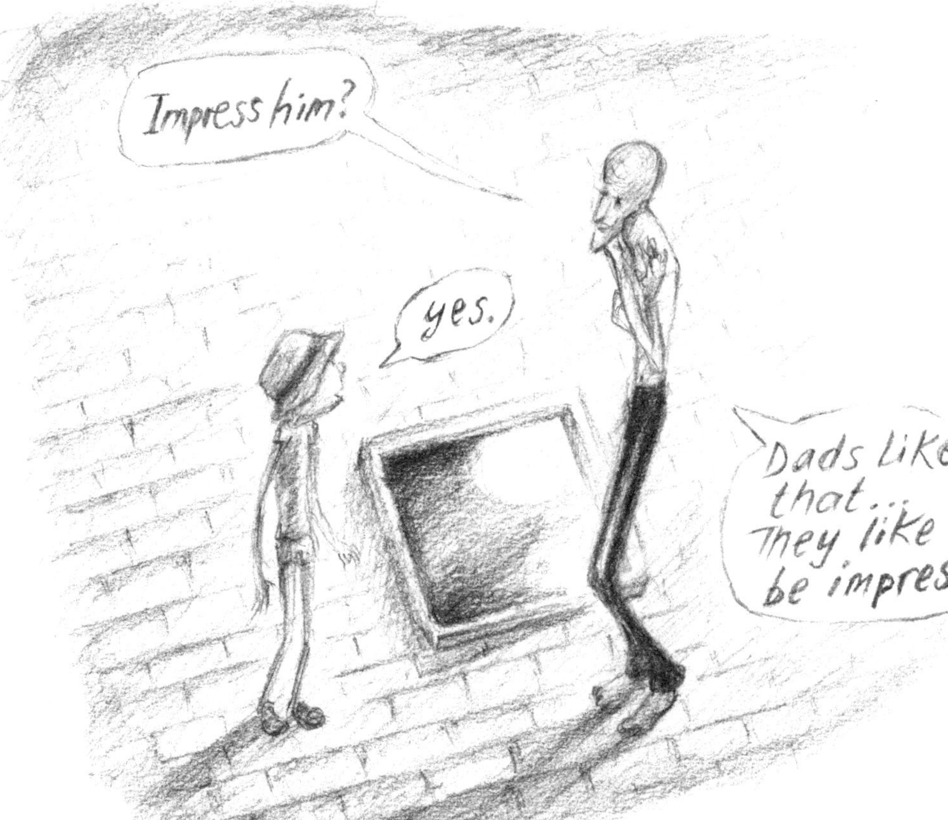
Impress him?
yes.
Dads like that... They like to be impressed.

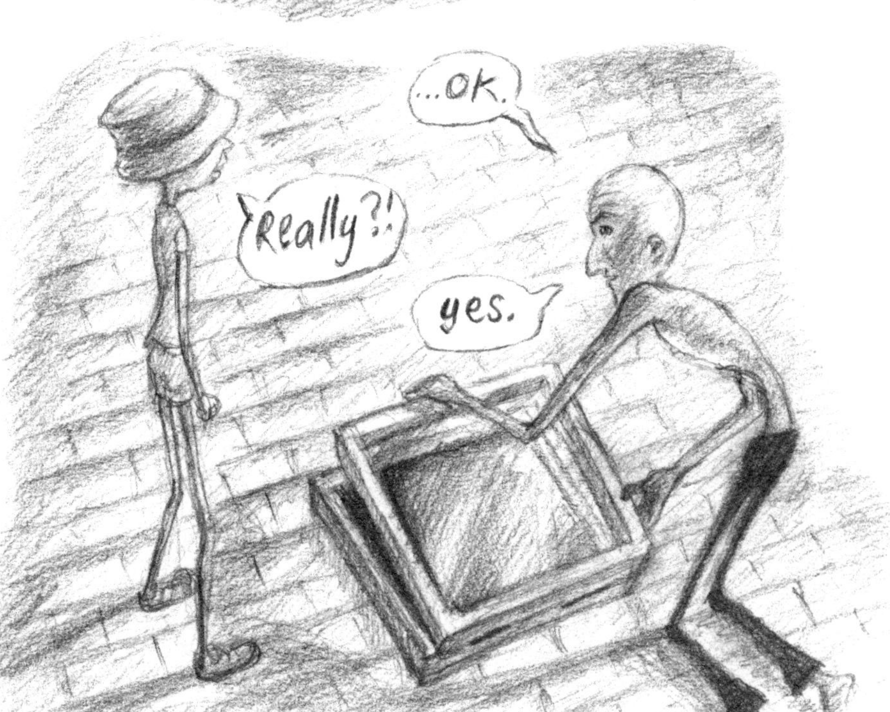
...ok.
Really?!
yes.

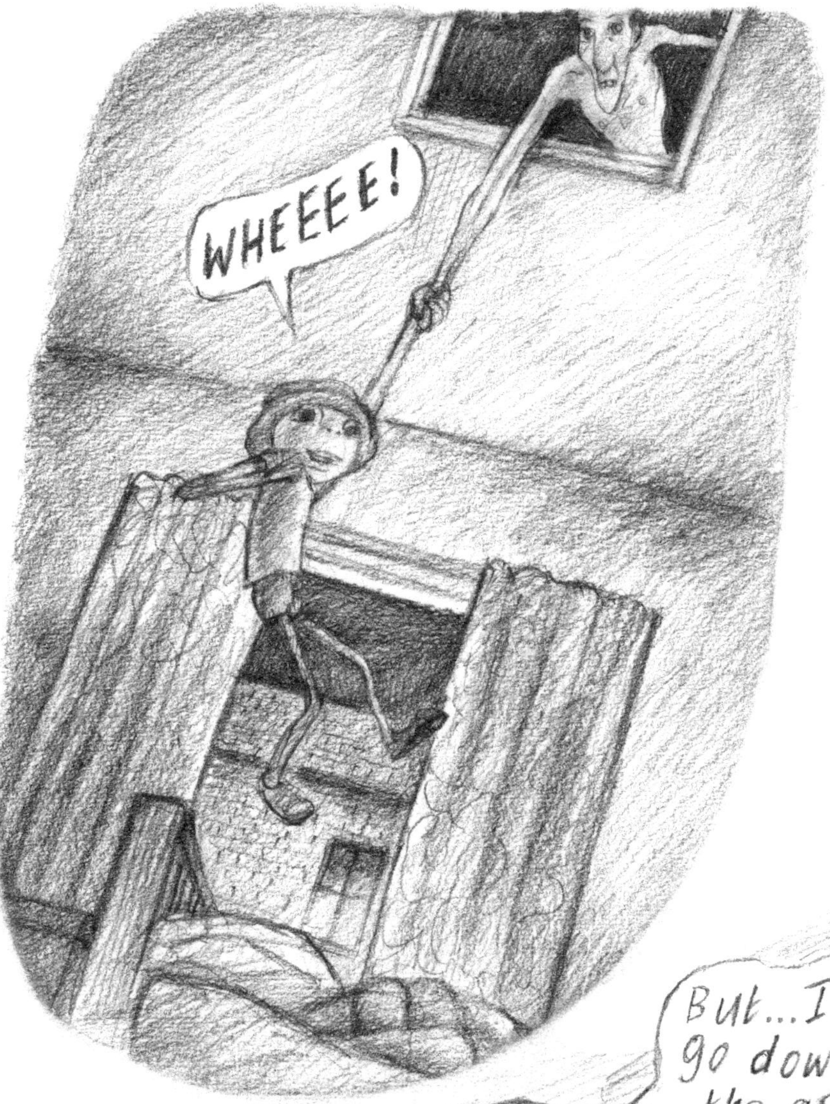
WHEEEE!

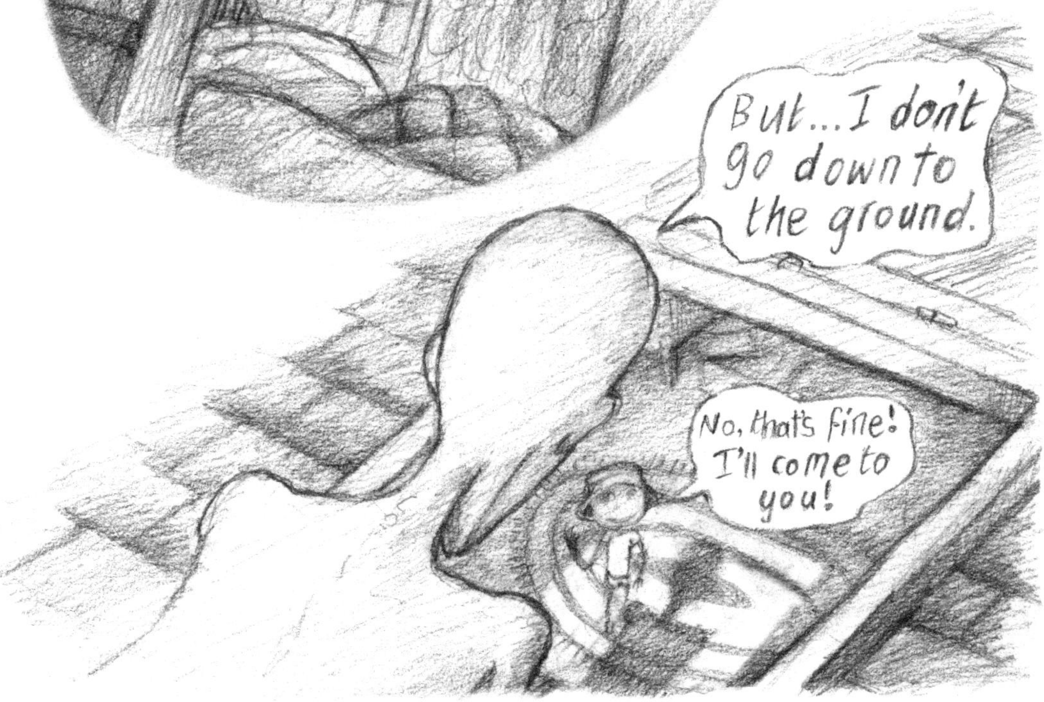
But... I don't go down to the ground.
No, that's fine! I'll come to you!

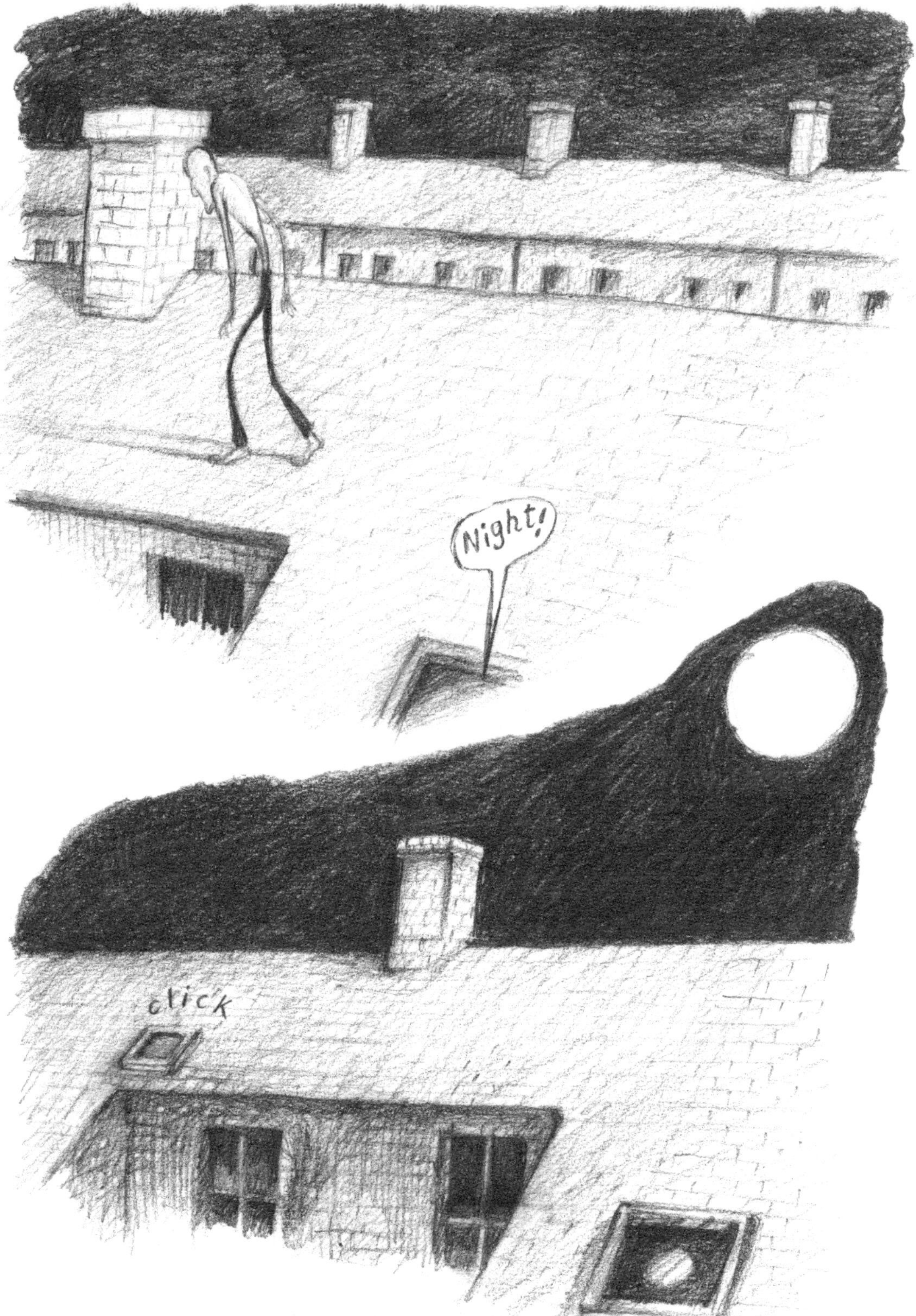
Night!
click

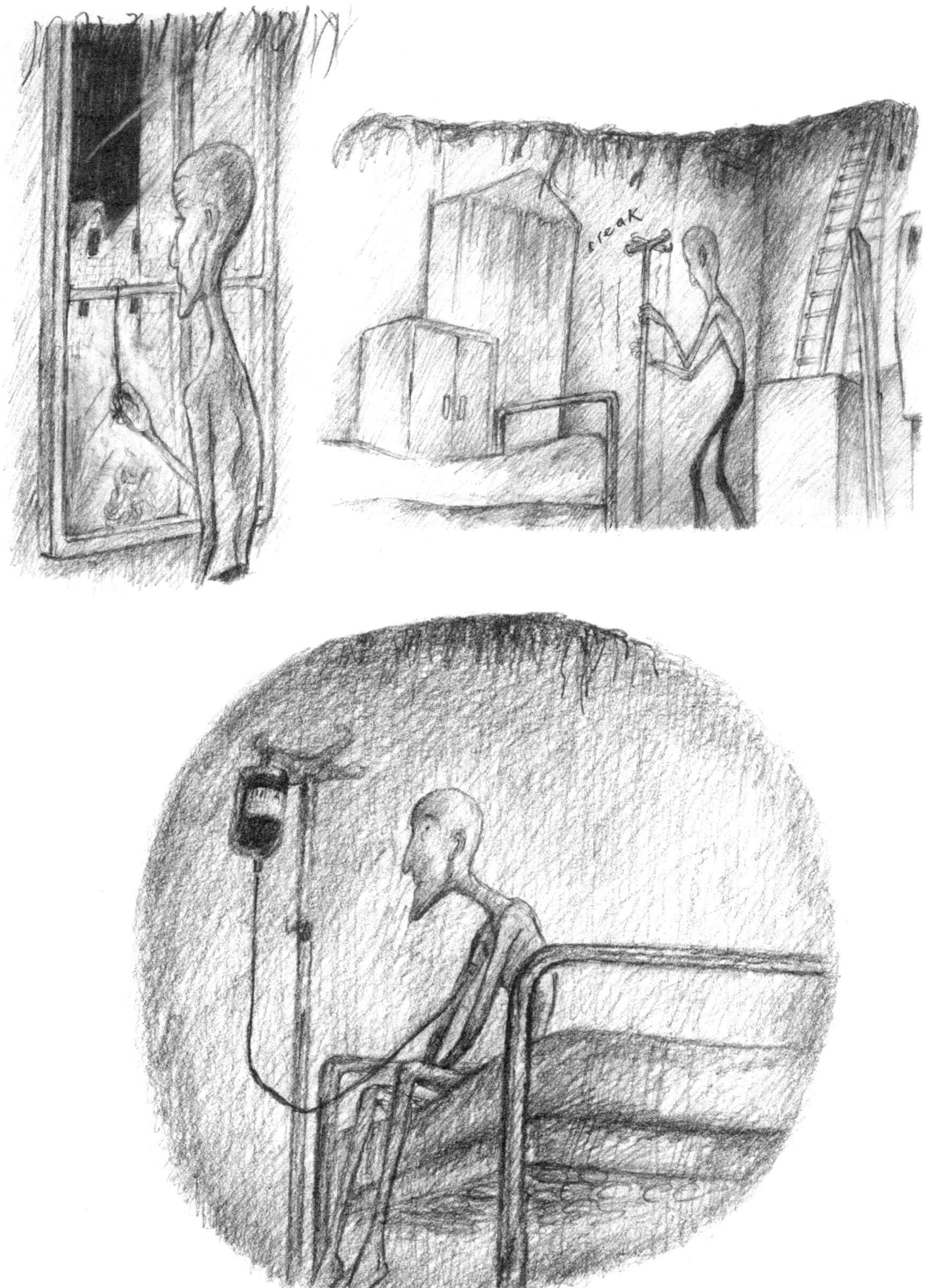
creak

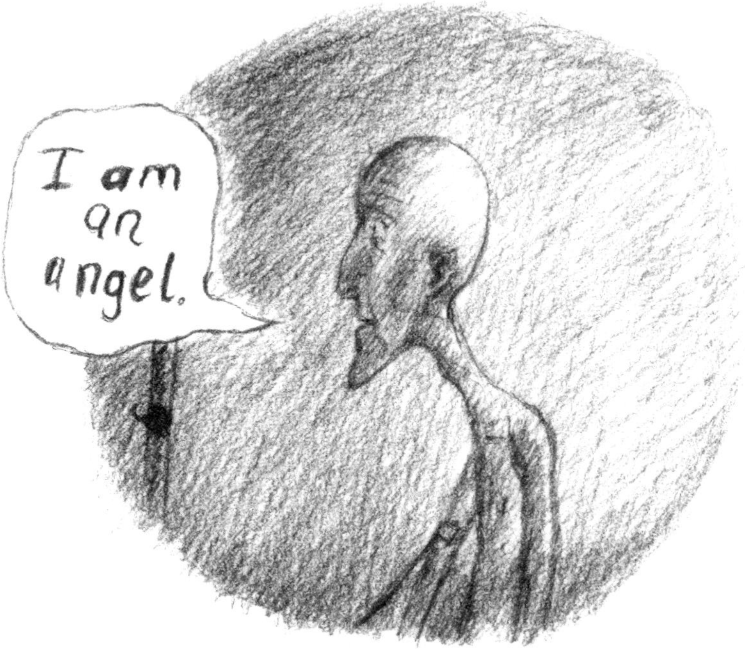
I am an angel.

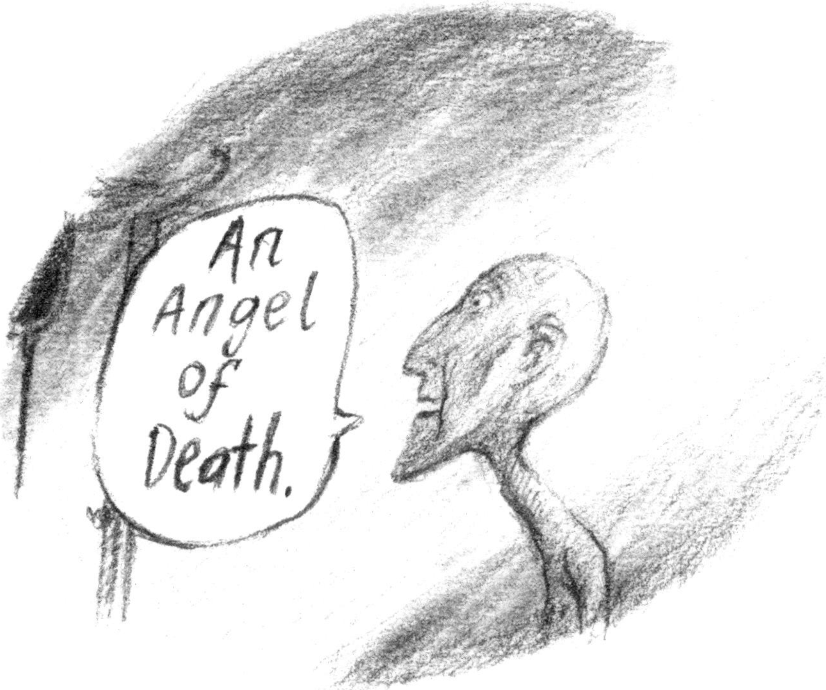
An Angel of Death.

Chapter Eight

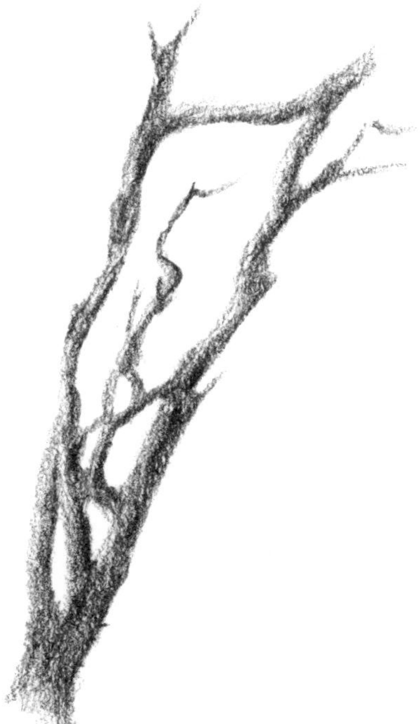

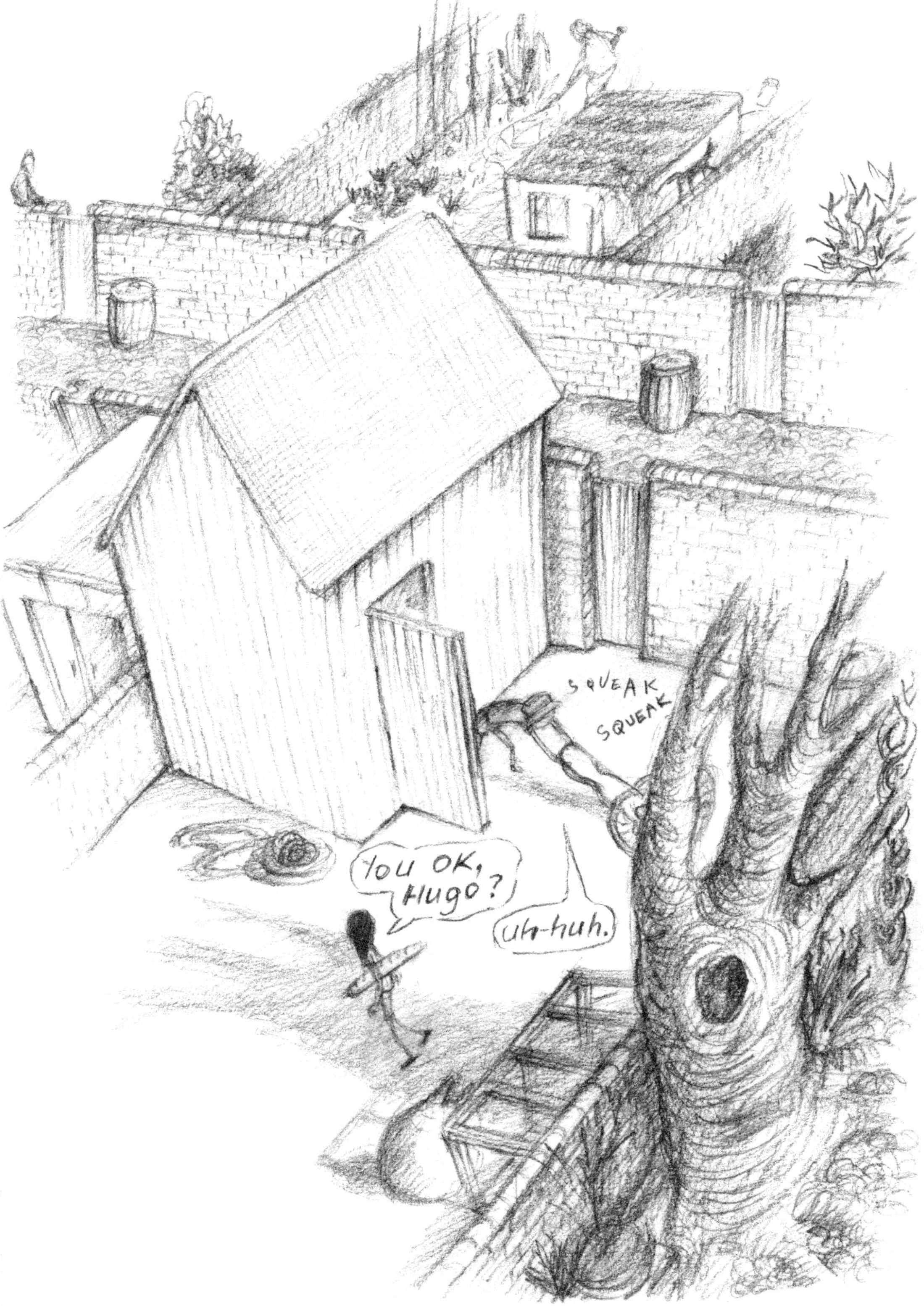
SQUEAK
SQUEAK
You OK, Hugo?
Uh-huh.

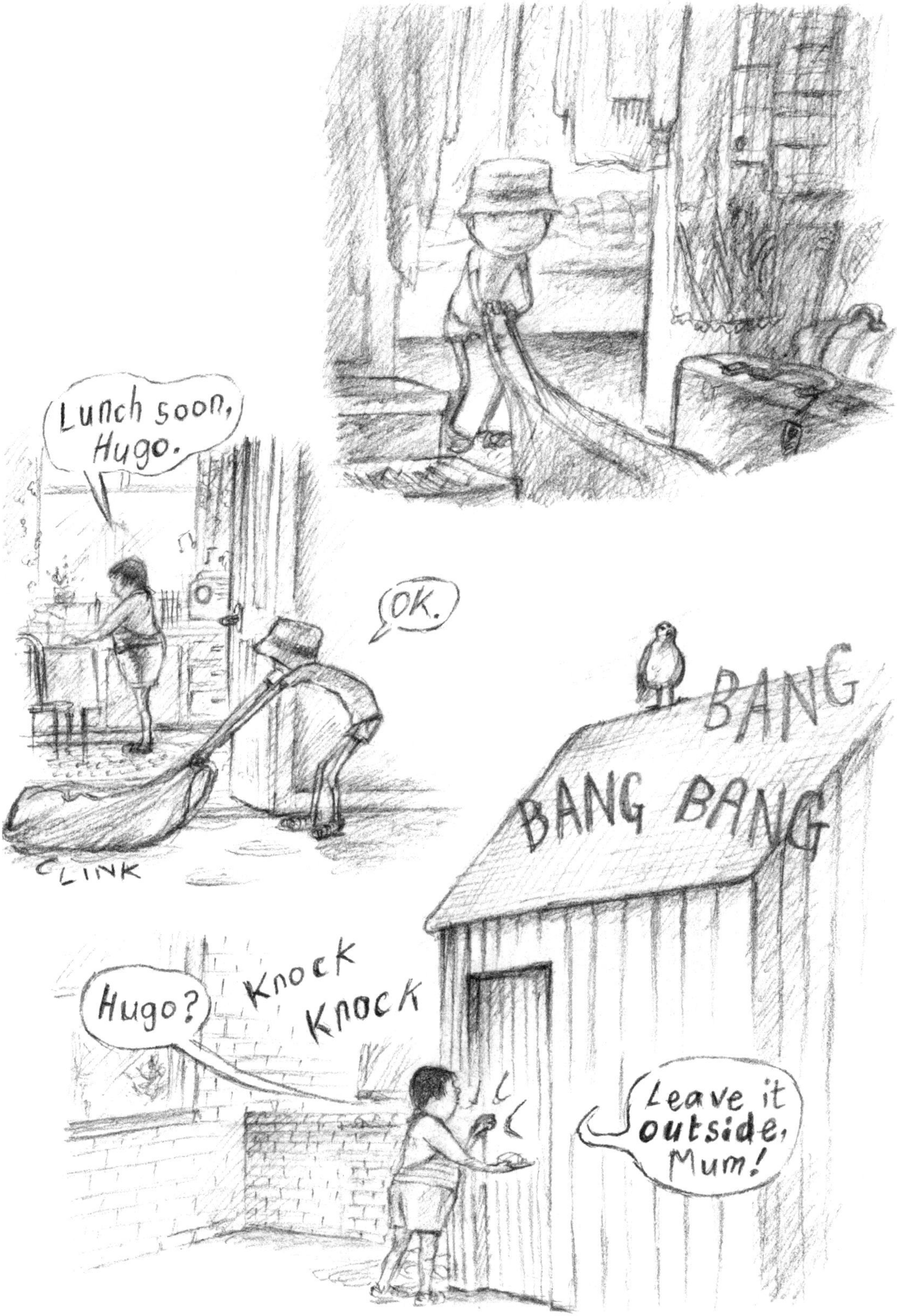
Lunch soon, Hugo.
OK.
CLINK
BANG
BANG BANG
Hugo?
Knock Knock
Leave it outside, Mum!

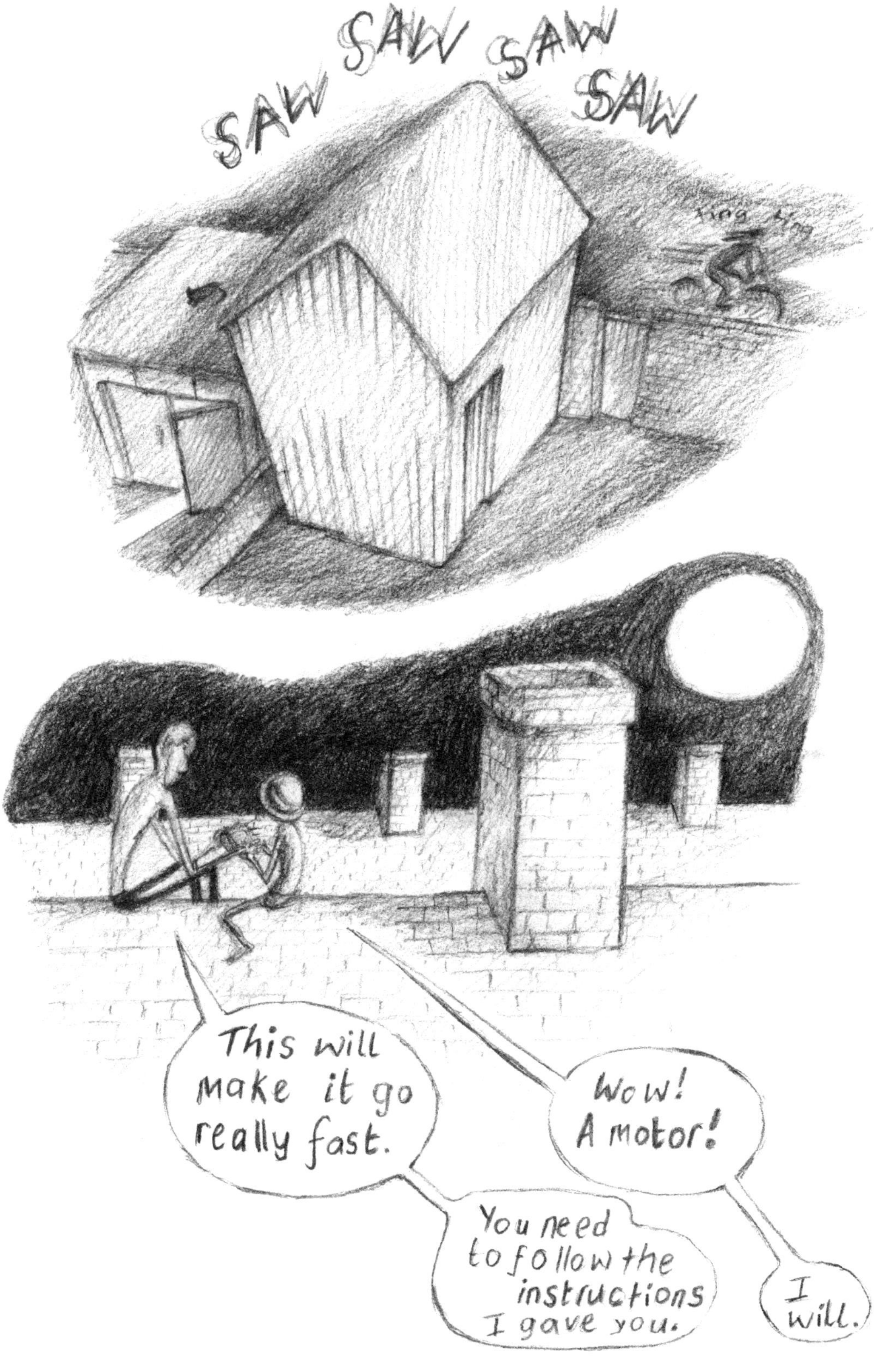
SAW SAW SAW SAW
ting ting
This will make it go really fast.
Wow! A motor!
You need to follow the instructions I gave you.
I will.

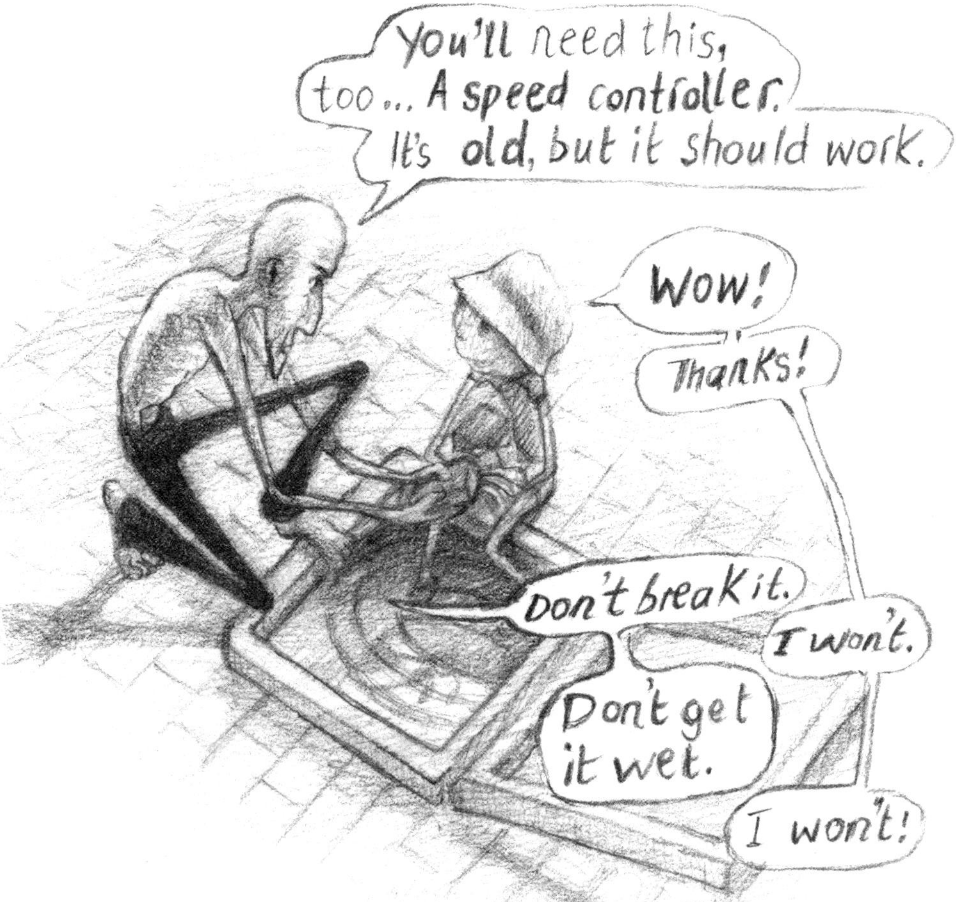
You'll need this, too... A speed controller. It's old, but it should work.
Wow!
Thanks!
Don't break it.
I won't.
Don't get it wet.
I won't!

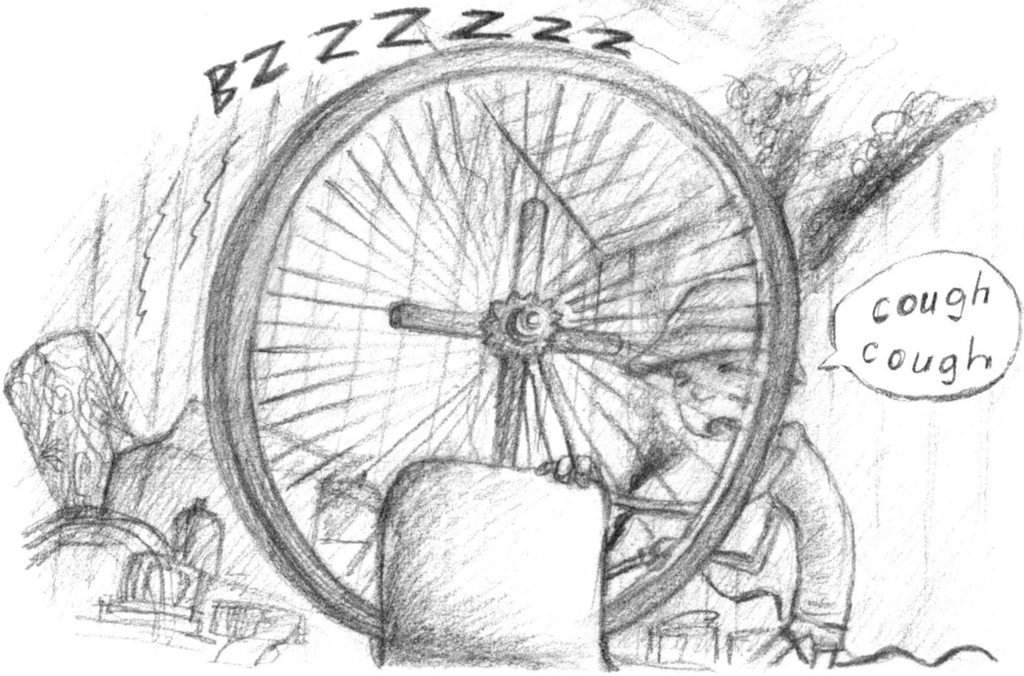
BZZZZZZZ
cough cough

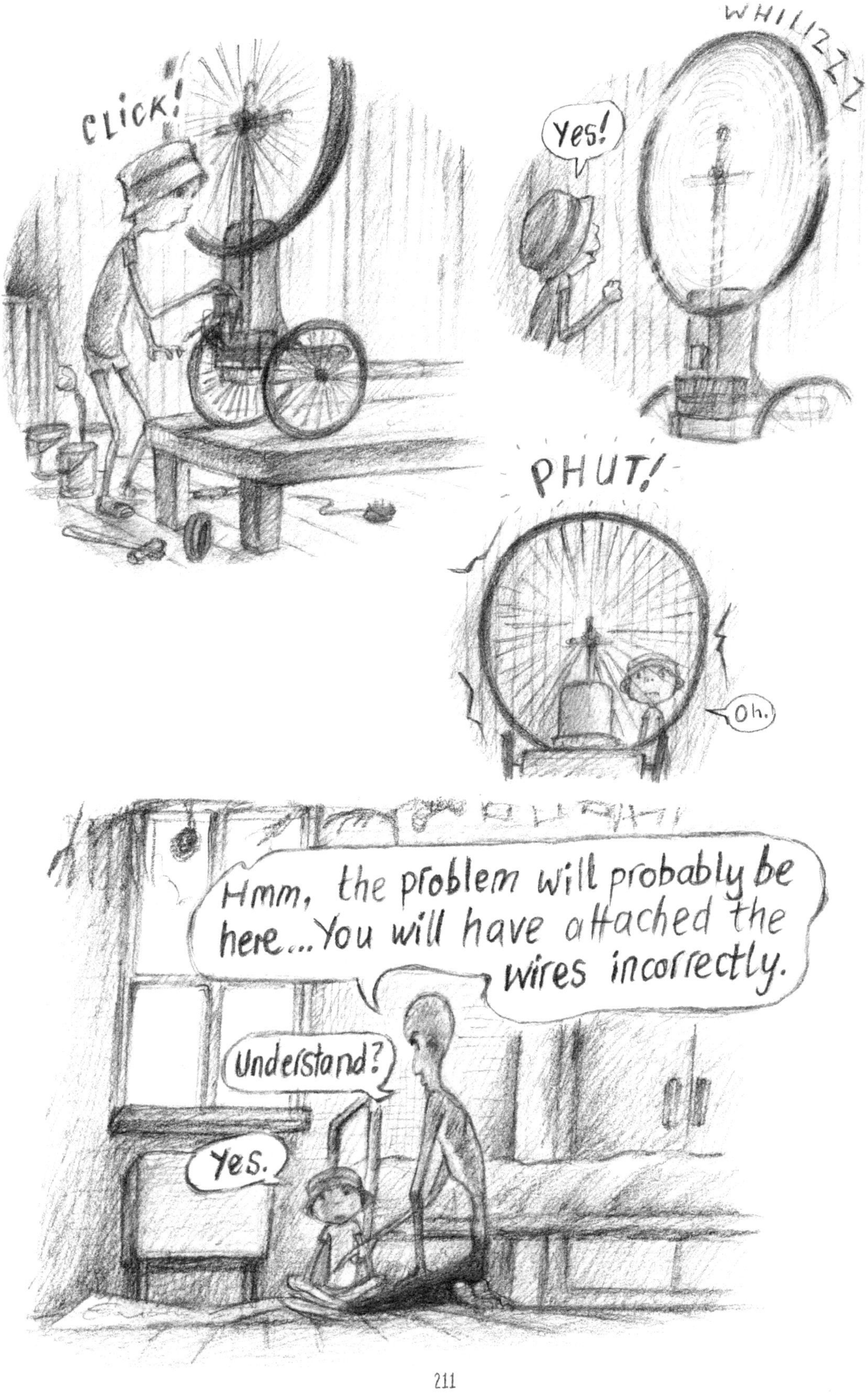
CLICK!
WHIIIZZZ
Yes!
PHUT!
Oh.
Hmm, the problem will probably be here... You will have attached the wires incorrectly.
Understand?
Yes.

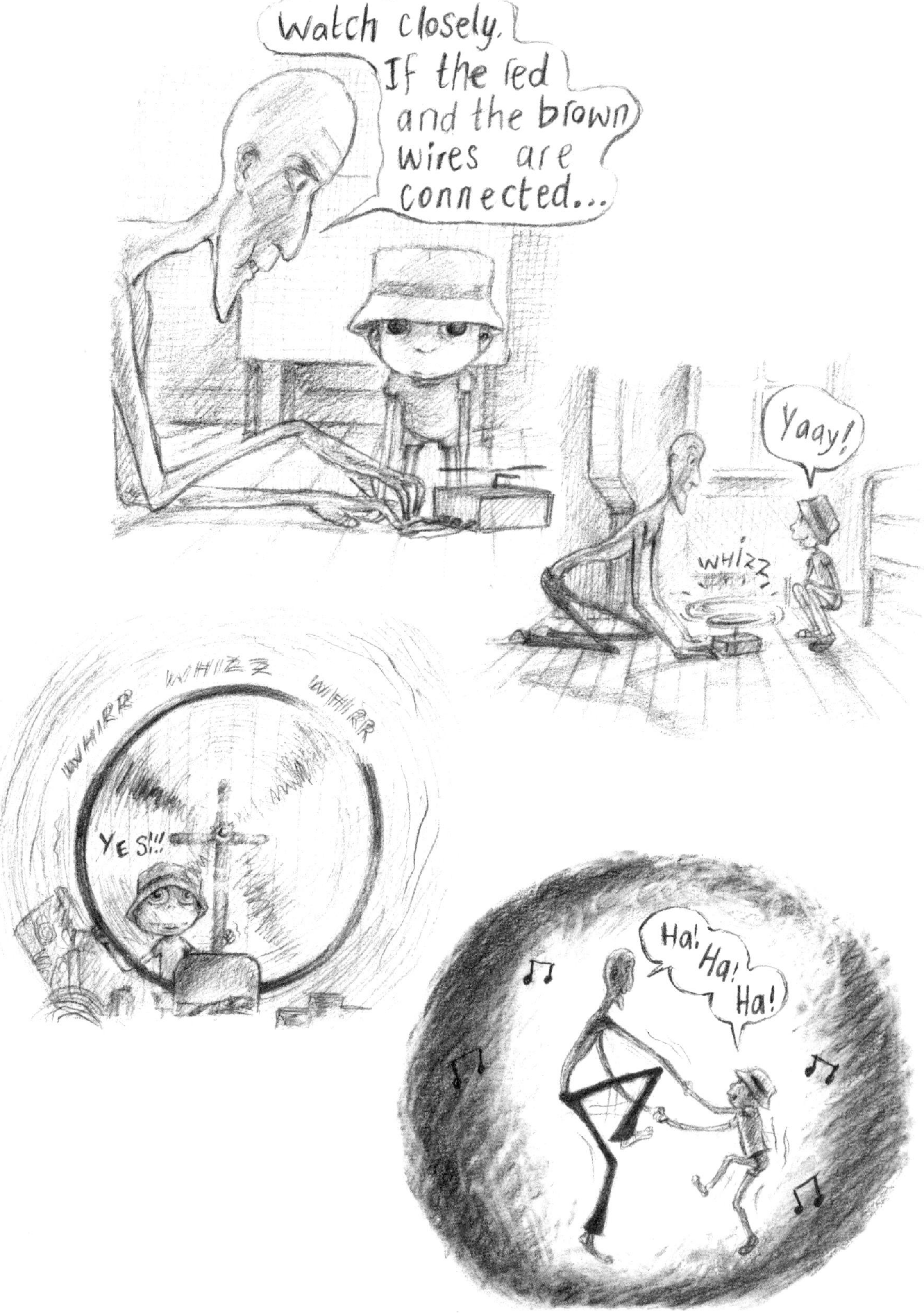
Watch closely. If the red and the brown wires are connected...
Yaay!
WHIZZ
WHIRR
WHIZZ
WHIRR
YES!!!
Ha! Ha! Ha!

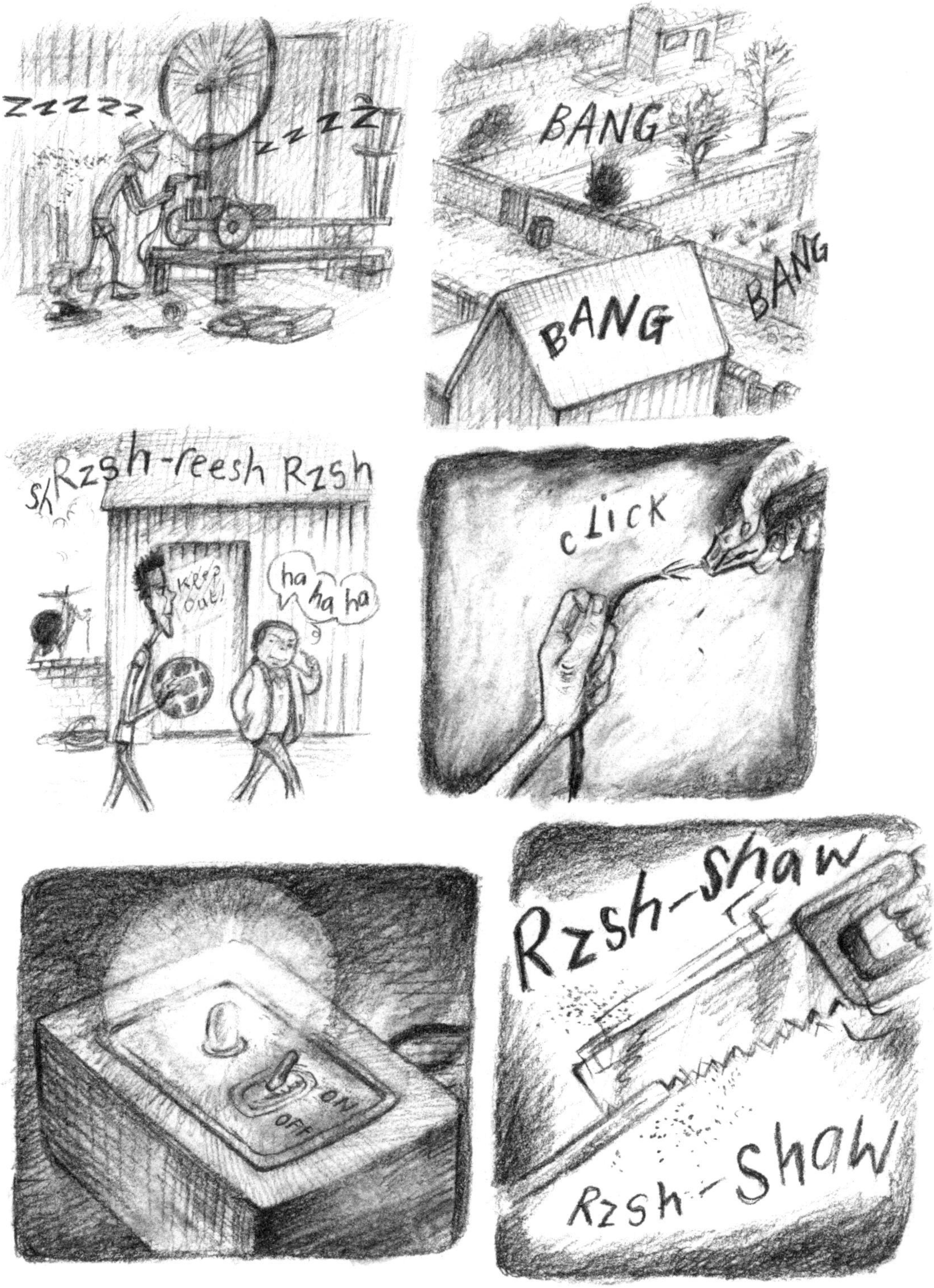
ZZZZZ
ZZZZZ
BANG
BANG
BANG
shRzsh-reesh Rzsh
KEEP OUT!
ha ha ha
CLICK
ON
OFF
Rzsh-shaw
Rzsh-shaw

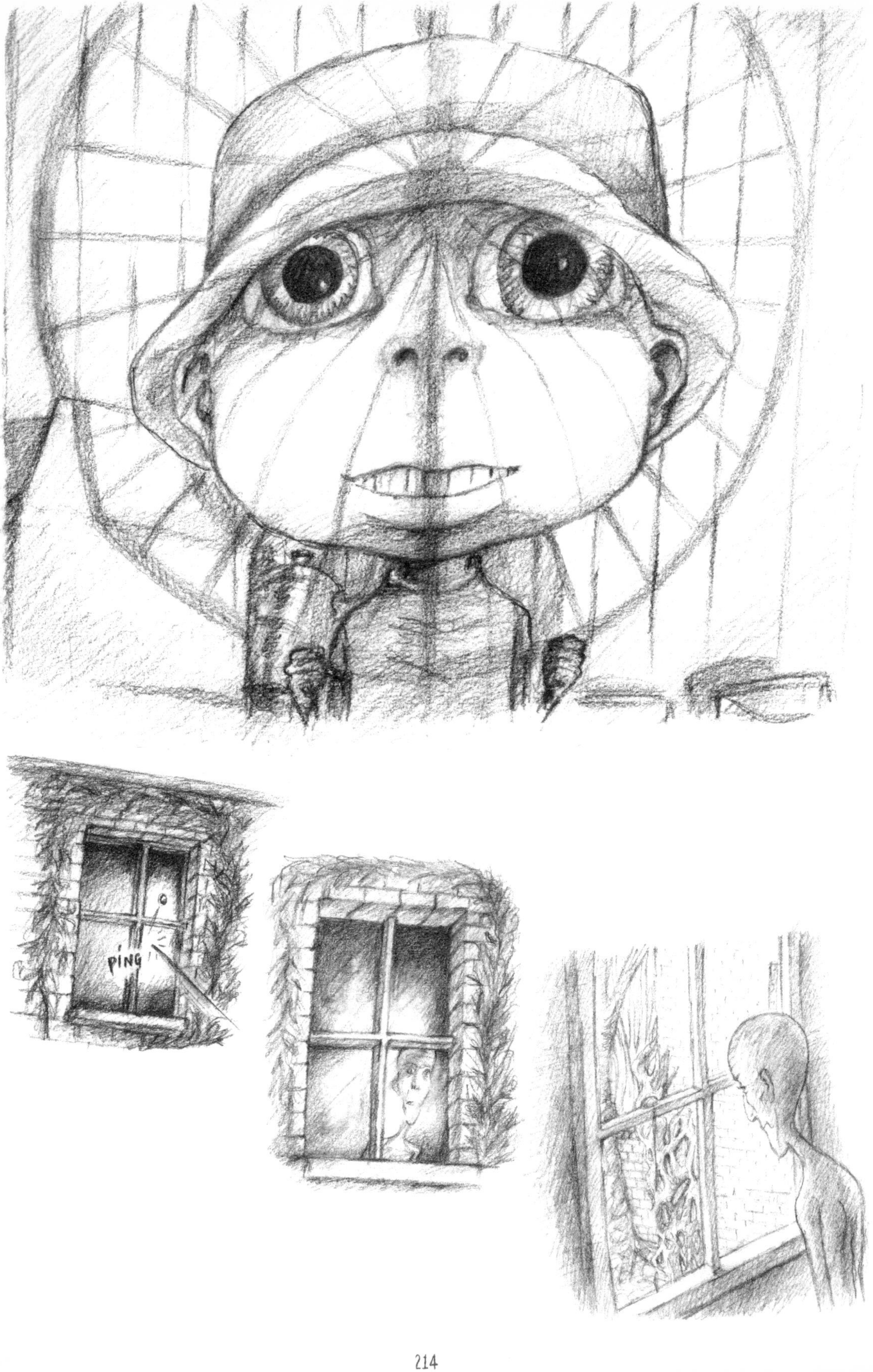
PING

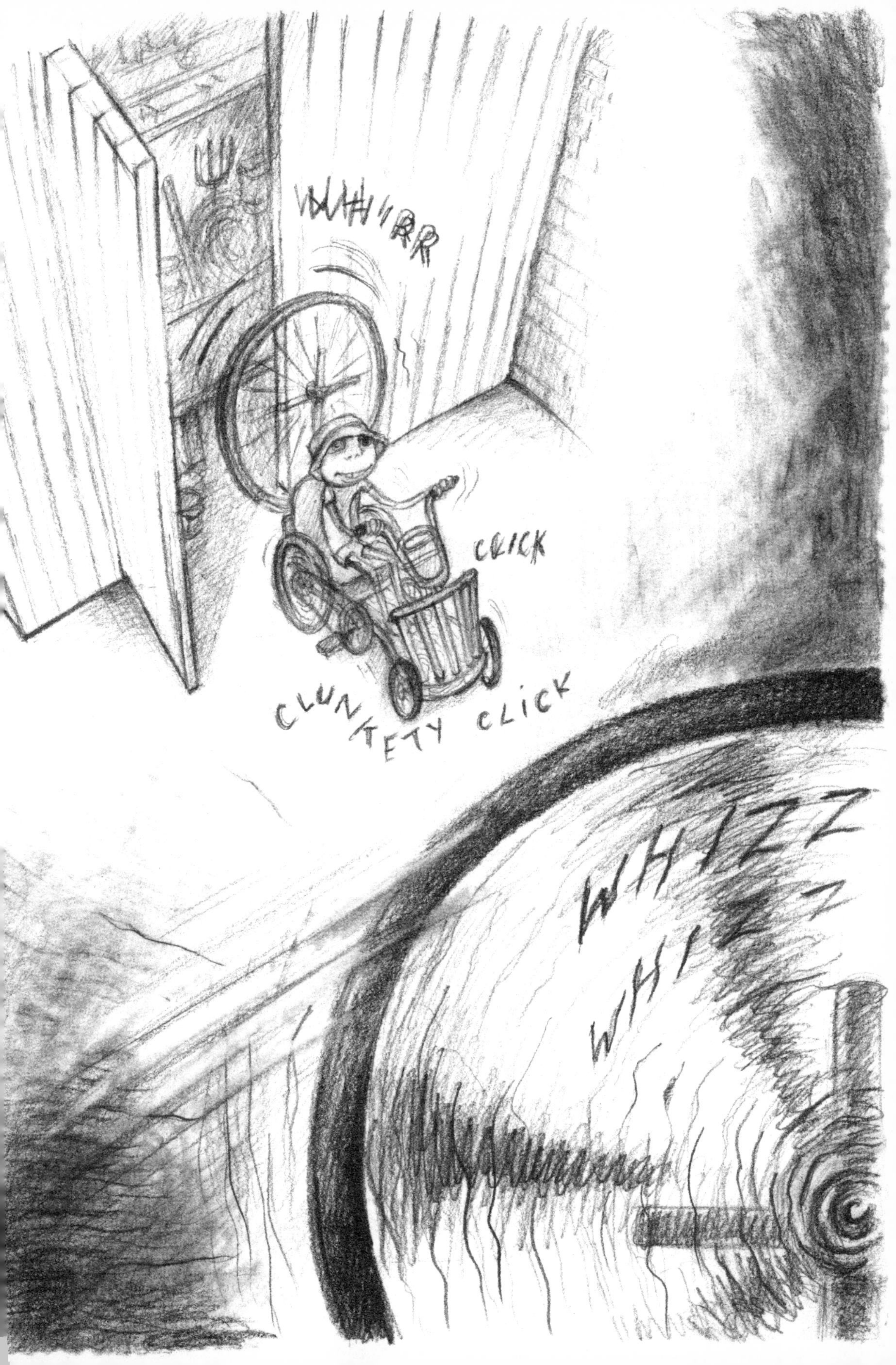
WHIRR
CRICK
CLUNKETY CLICK
WHIZZ
WHI

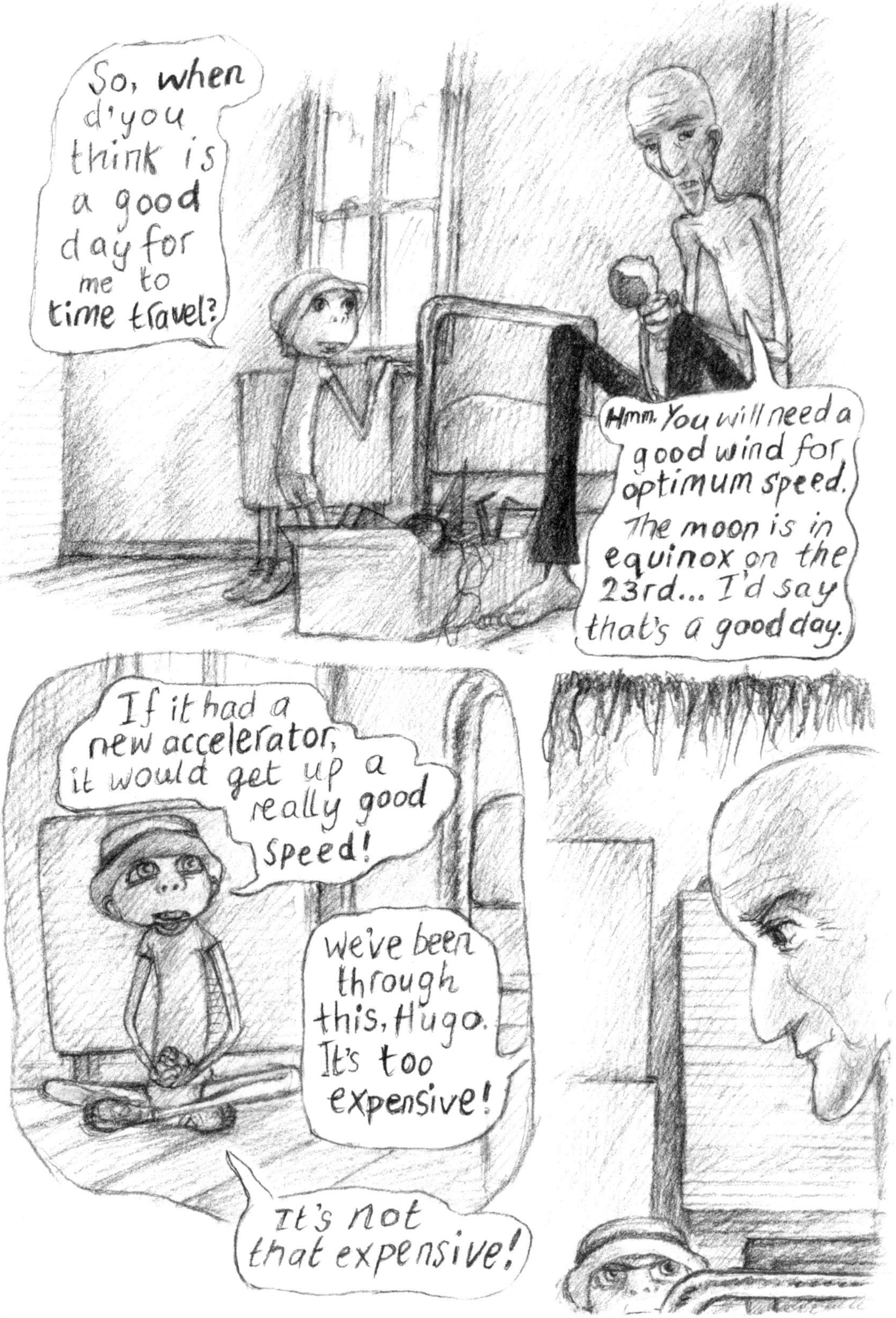
So, when d'you think is a good day for me to time travel?
Hmm. You will need a good wind for optimum speed. The moon is in equinox on the 23rd... I'd say that's a good day.
If it had a new accelerator, it would get up a really good speed!
We've been through this, Hugo. It's too expensive!
It's not that expensive!

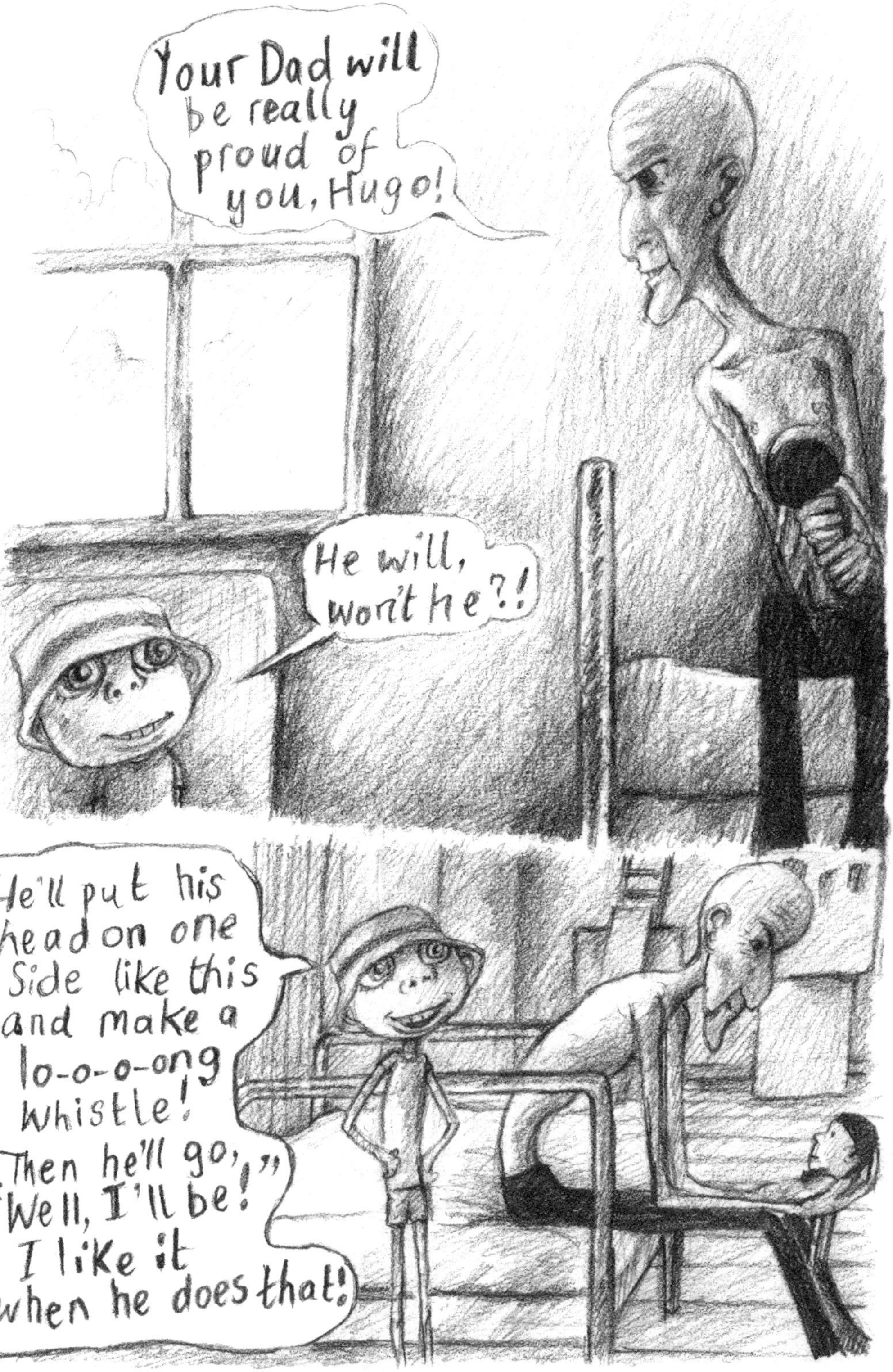
Your Dad will be really proud of you, Hugo!
He will, won't he?!
He'll put his head on one side like this and make a lo-o-o-ong whistle! Then he'll go, "Well, I'll be!" I like it when he does that!

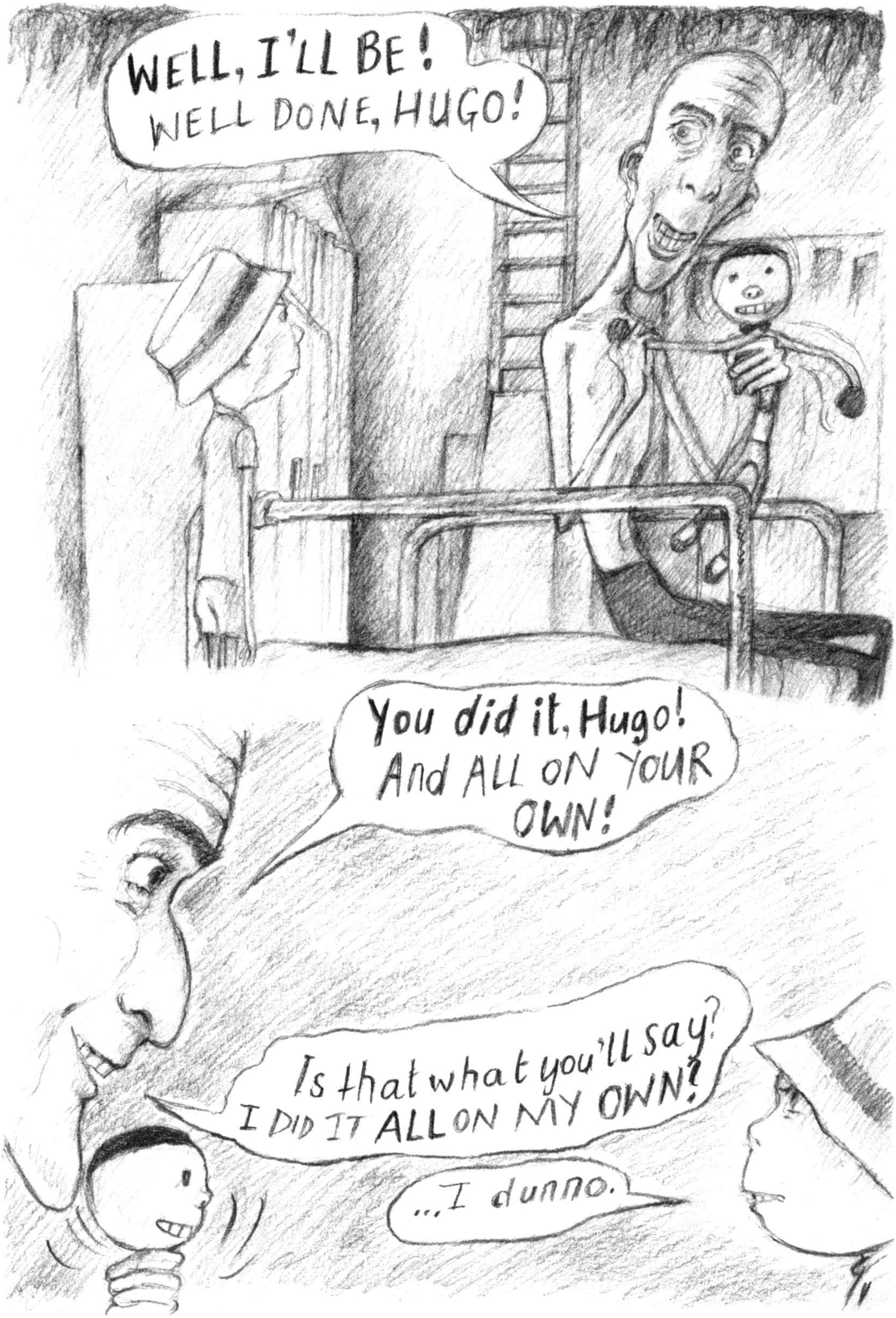
WELL, I'LL BE! WELL DONE, HUGO!
You did it, Hugo! And ALL ON YOUR OWN!
Is that what you'll say? I DID IT ALL ON MY OWN?
...I dunno.

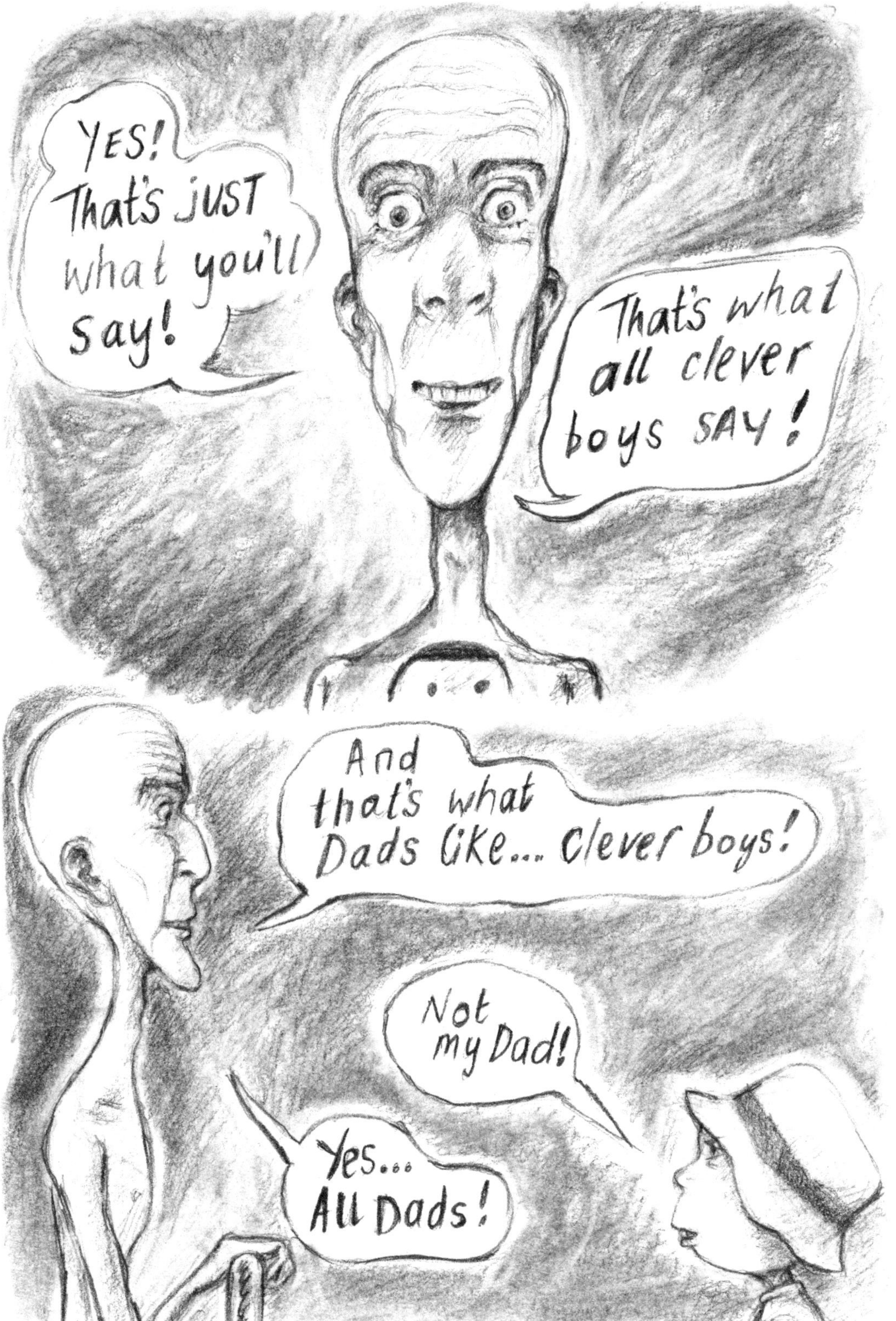
YES! That's JUST what you'll say!
That's what all clever boys SAY!
And that's what Dads like... Clever boys!
Not my Dad!
Yes... All Dads!

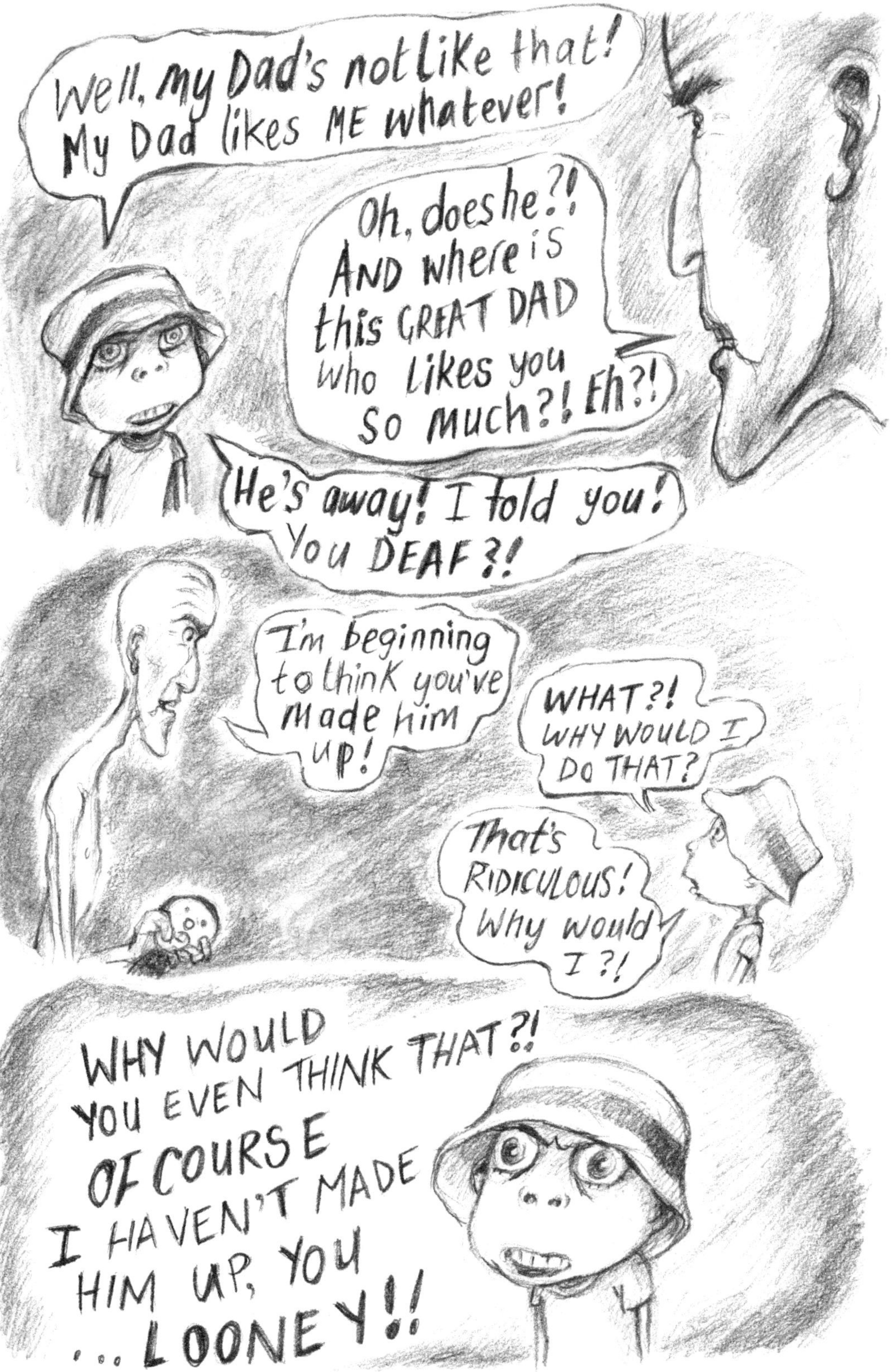
Well, my Dad's not like that! My Dad likes ME whatever!
Oh, does he?! AND where is this GREAT DAD who likes you so much?! Eh?!
He's away! I told you! You DEAF?!
I'm beginning to think you've made him up!
WHAT?! WHY WOULD I DO THAT?
That's RIDICULOUS! Why would I?!
WHY WOULD YOU EVEN THINK THAT?! OF COURSE I HAVEN'T MADE HIM UP, YOU ...LOONEY!!

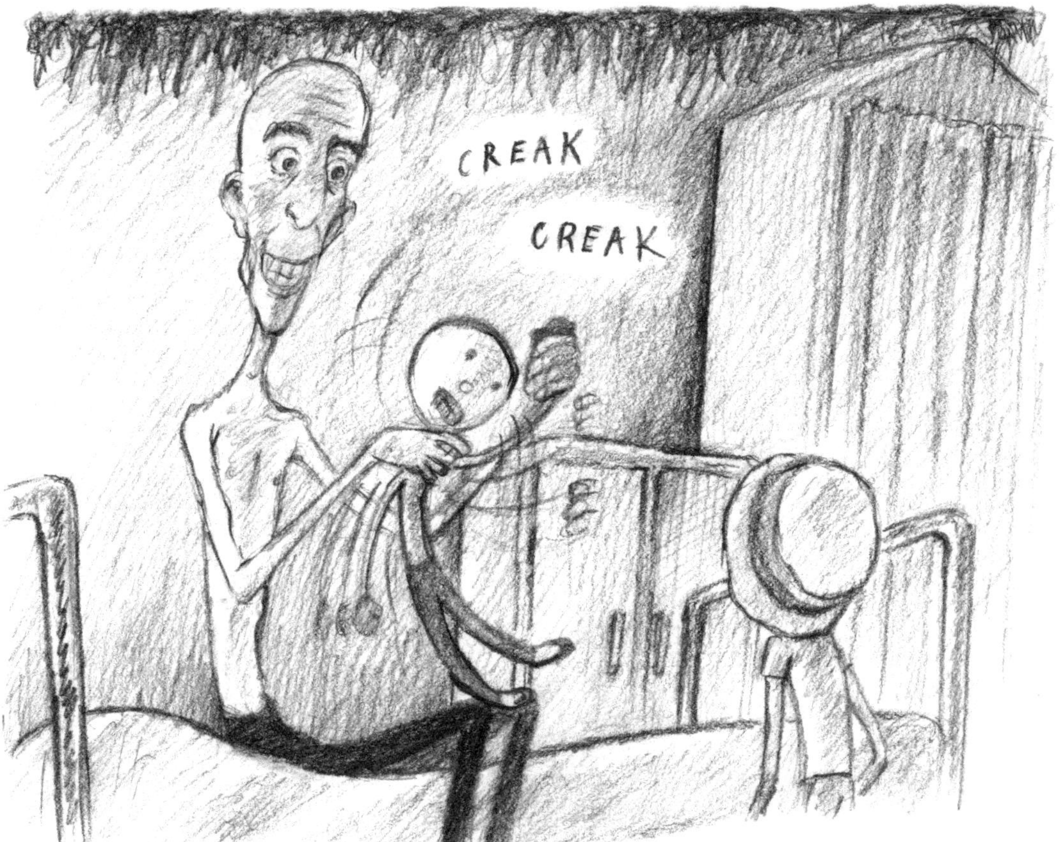
CREAK
CREAK

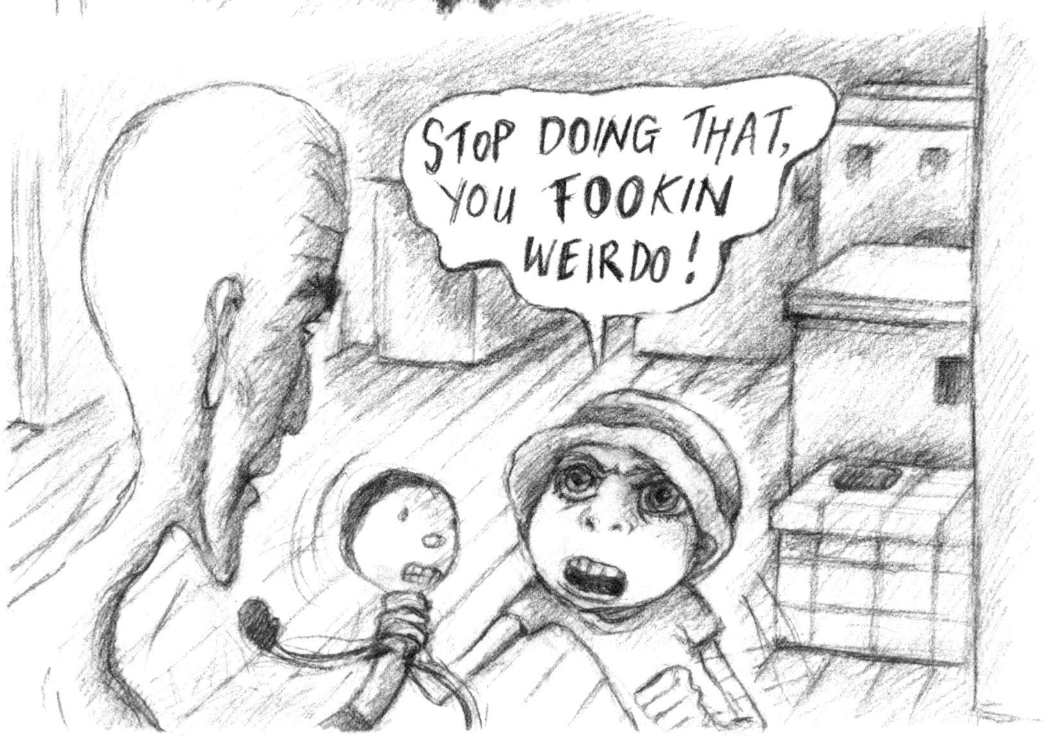
STOP DOING THAT, YOU FOOKIN WEIRDO!

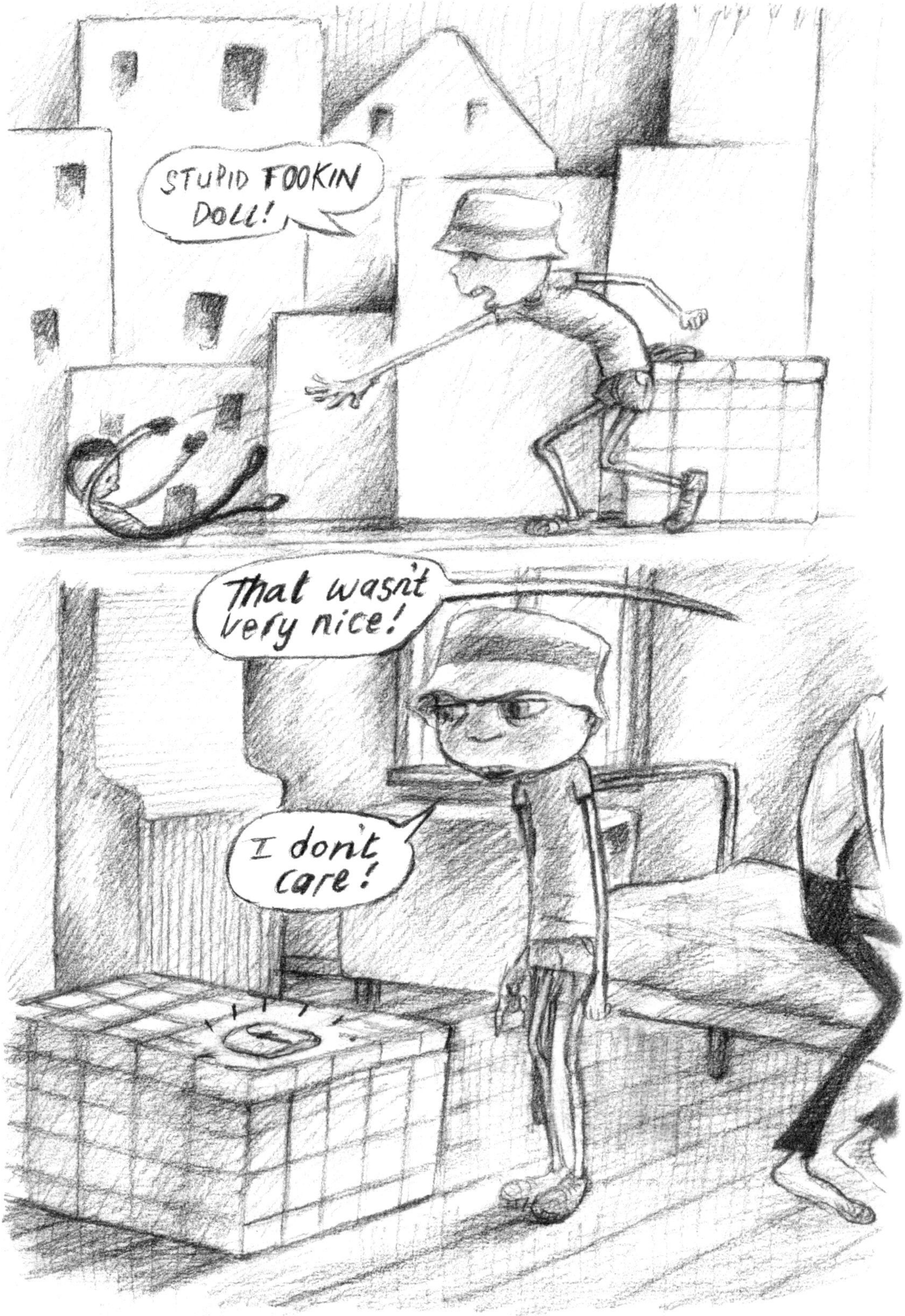
STUPID FOOKIN DOLL!
That wasn't very nice!
I don't care!

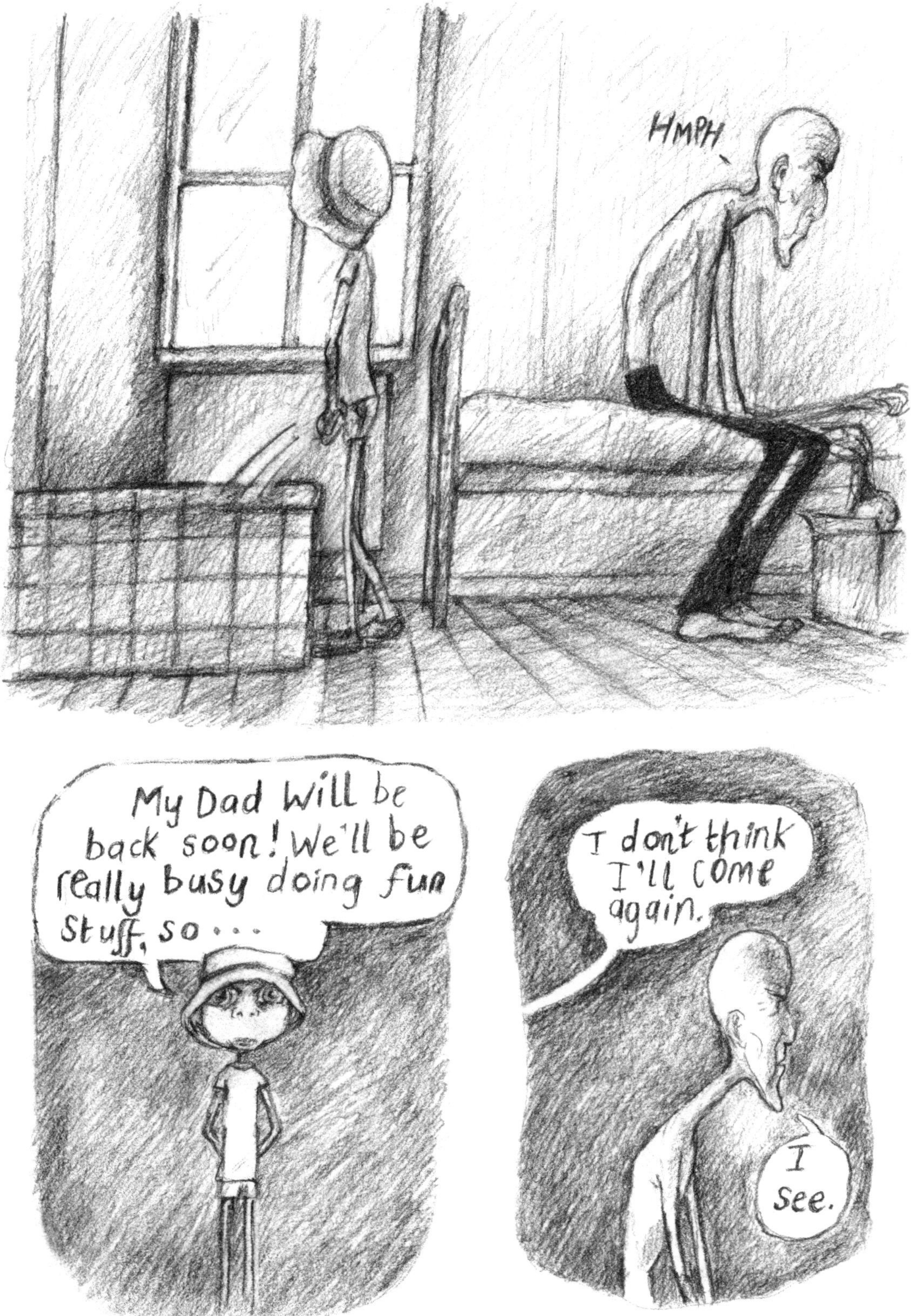
HMPH
My Dad Will be back soon! We'll be really busy doing fun stuff, so...
I don't think I'll come again.
I see.

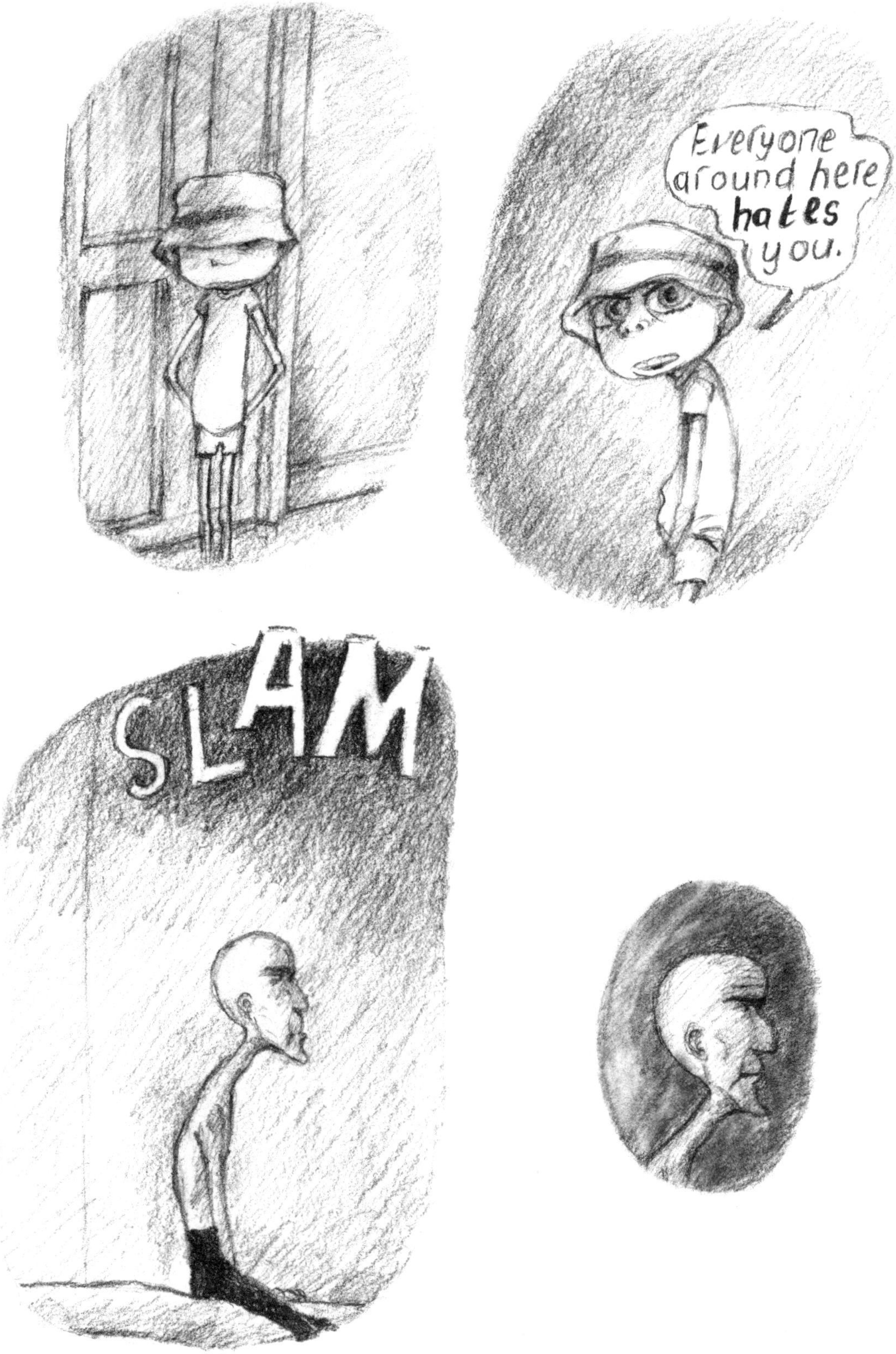
Everyone around here hates you.
SLAM

Chapter Nine

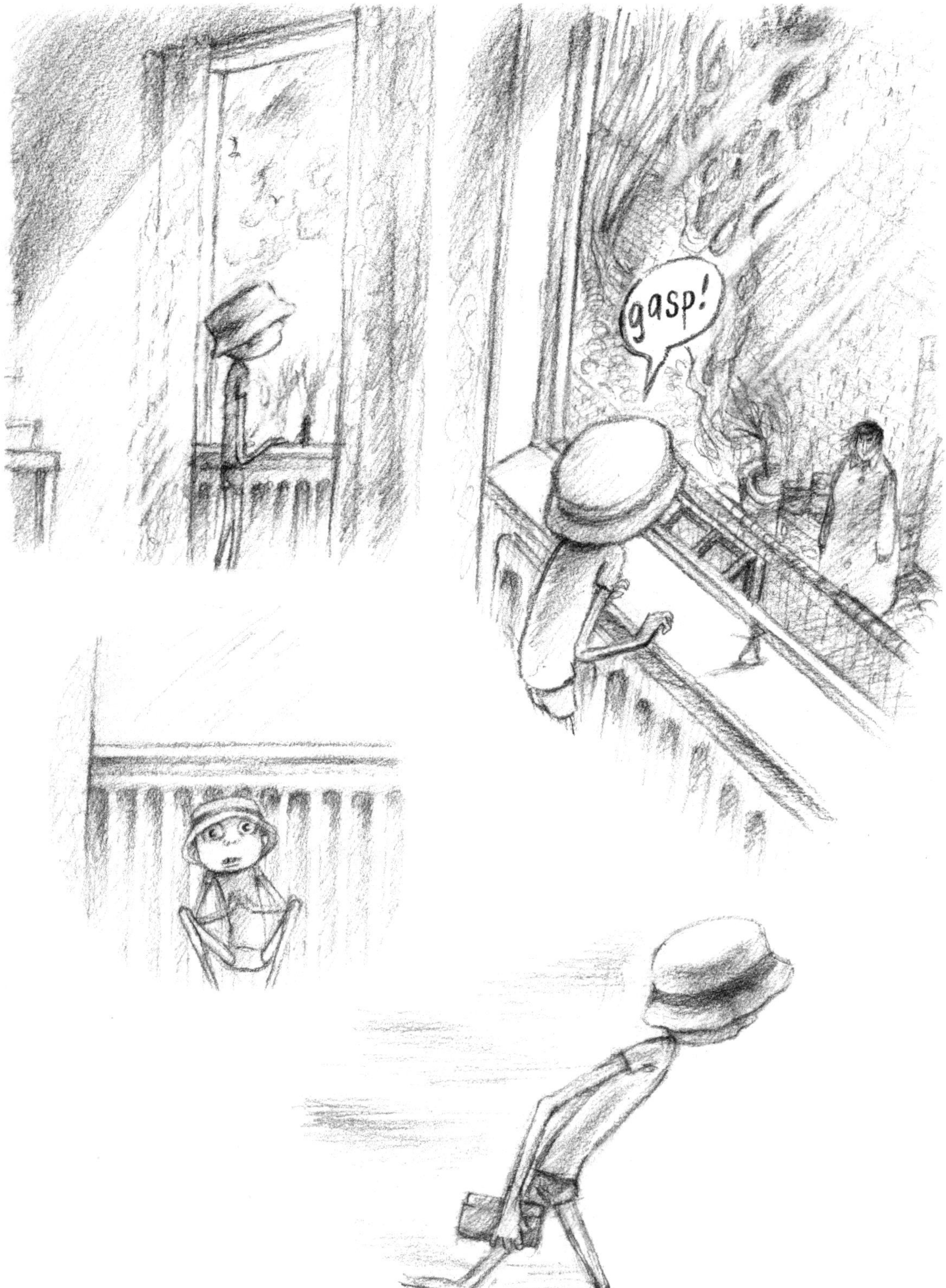
gasp!

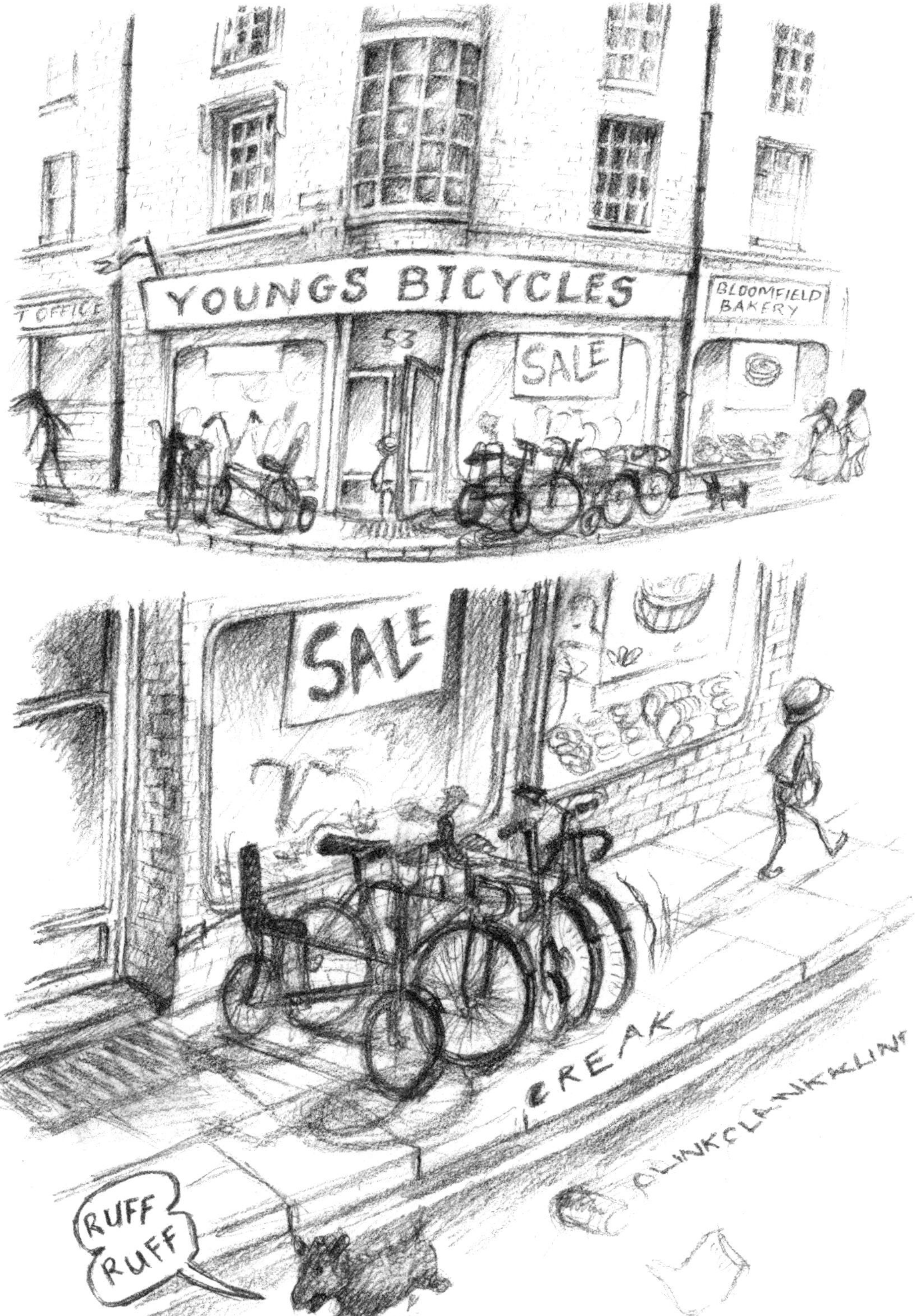
T OFFICE
YOUNGS BICYCLES
53
SALE
BLOOMFIELD BAKERY
SALE
CREAK
CLINKCLANKKLIN
RUFF RUFF

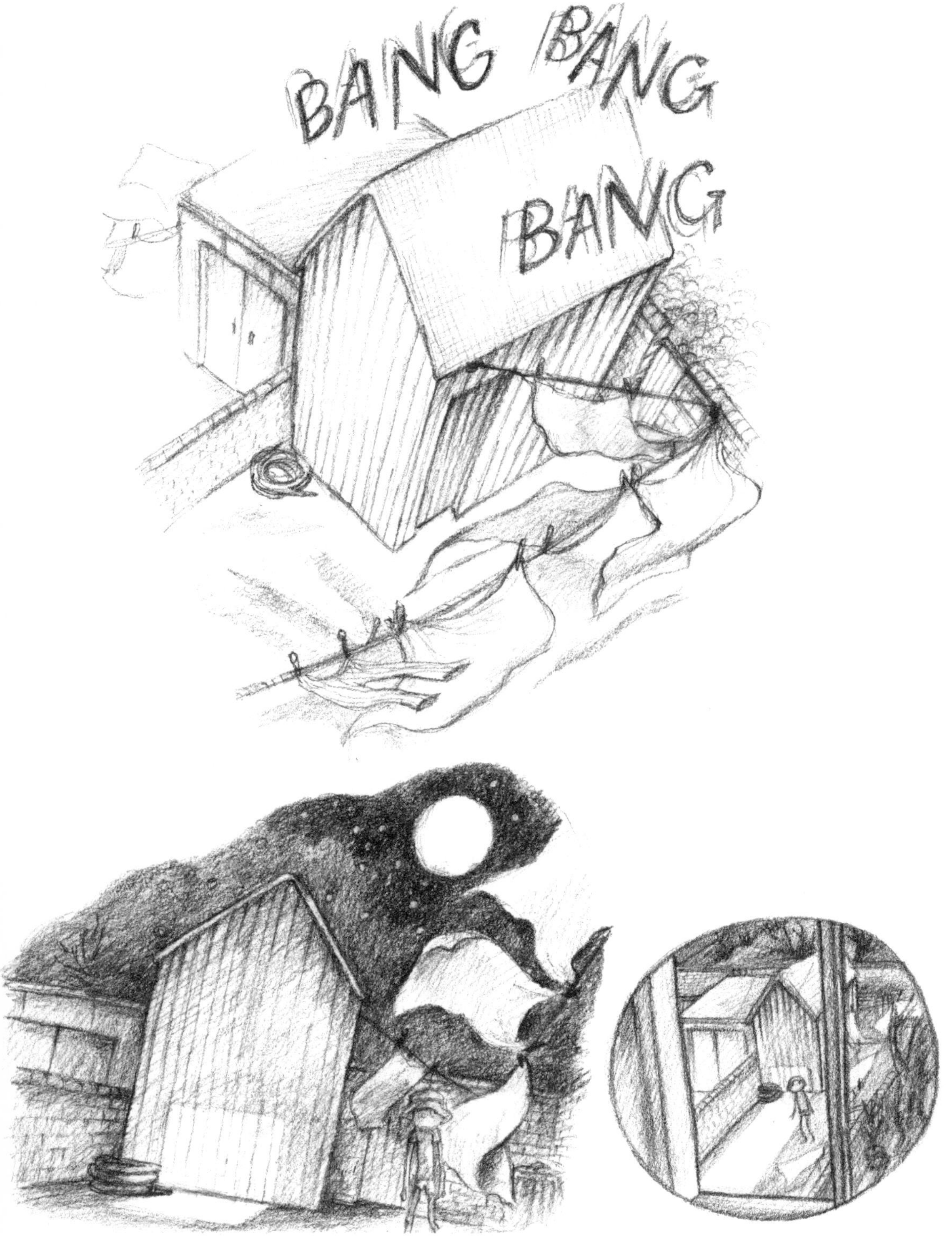
BANG BANG
BANG

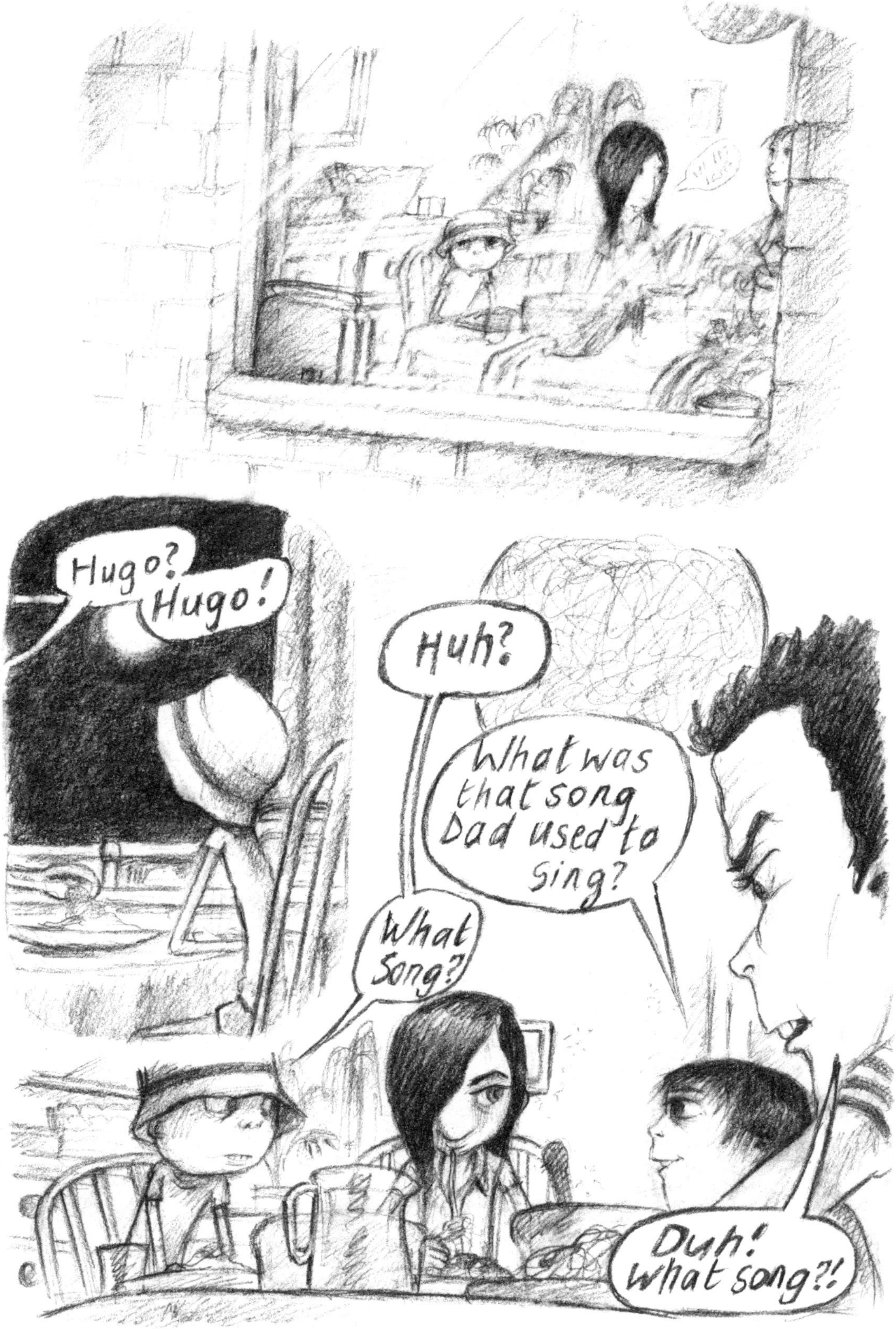
Hugo?
Hugo!
Huh?
What was that song Dad used to sing?
What song?
Duh! What song?!

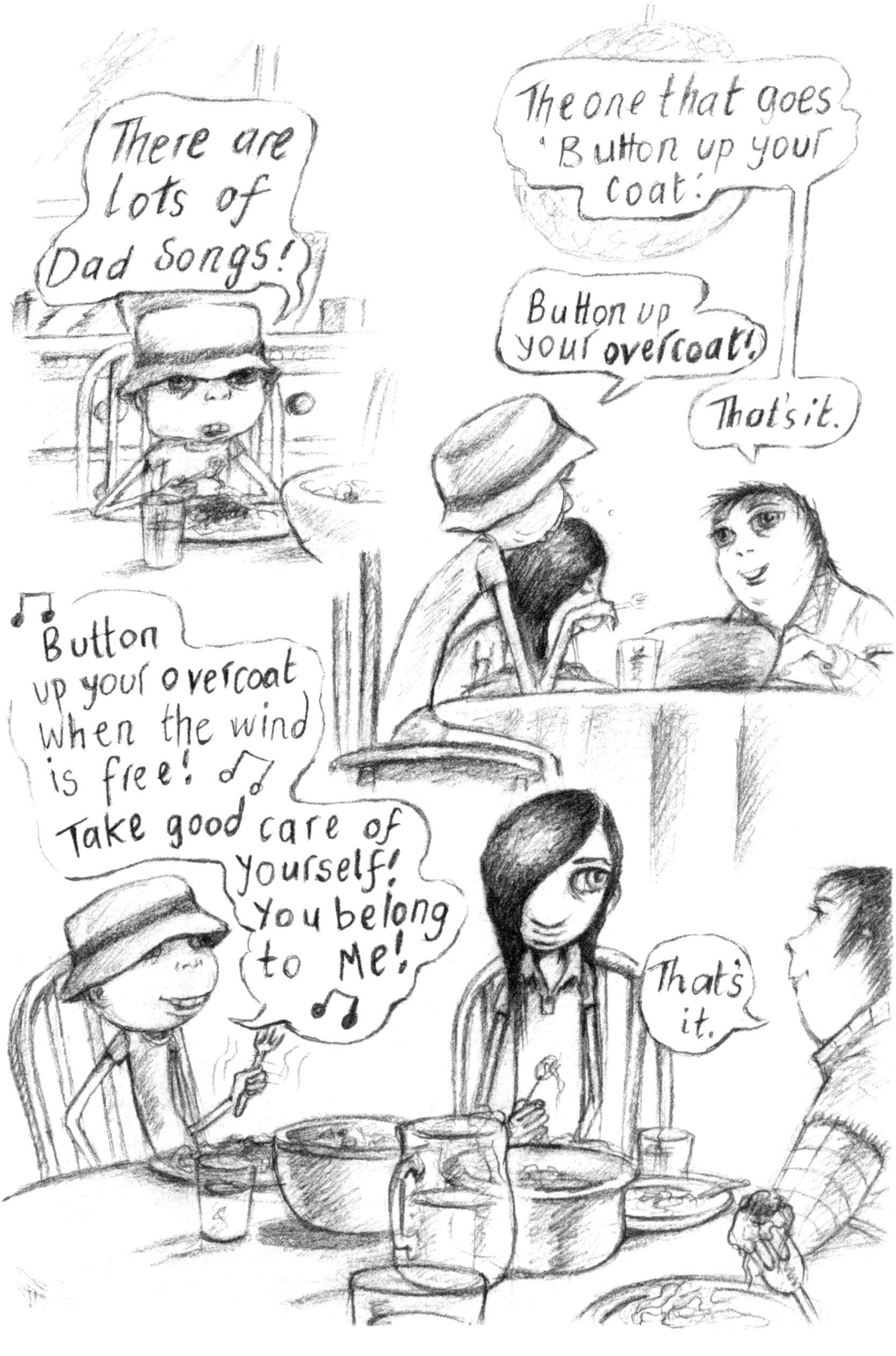
There are lots of Dad Songs!
The one that goes 'Button up your coat.'
Button up your overcoat!
That's it.
♫ Button up your overcoat when the wind is free! ♫ Take good care of yourself! You belong to Me! ♫
That's it.

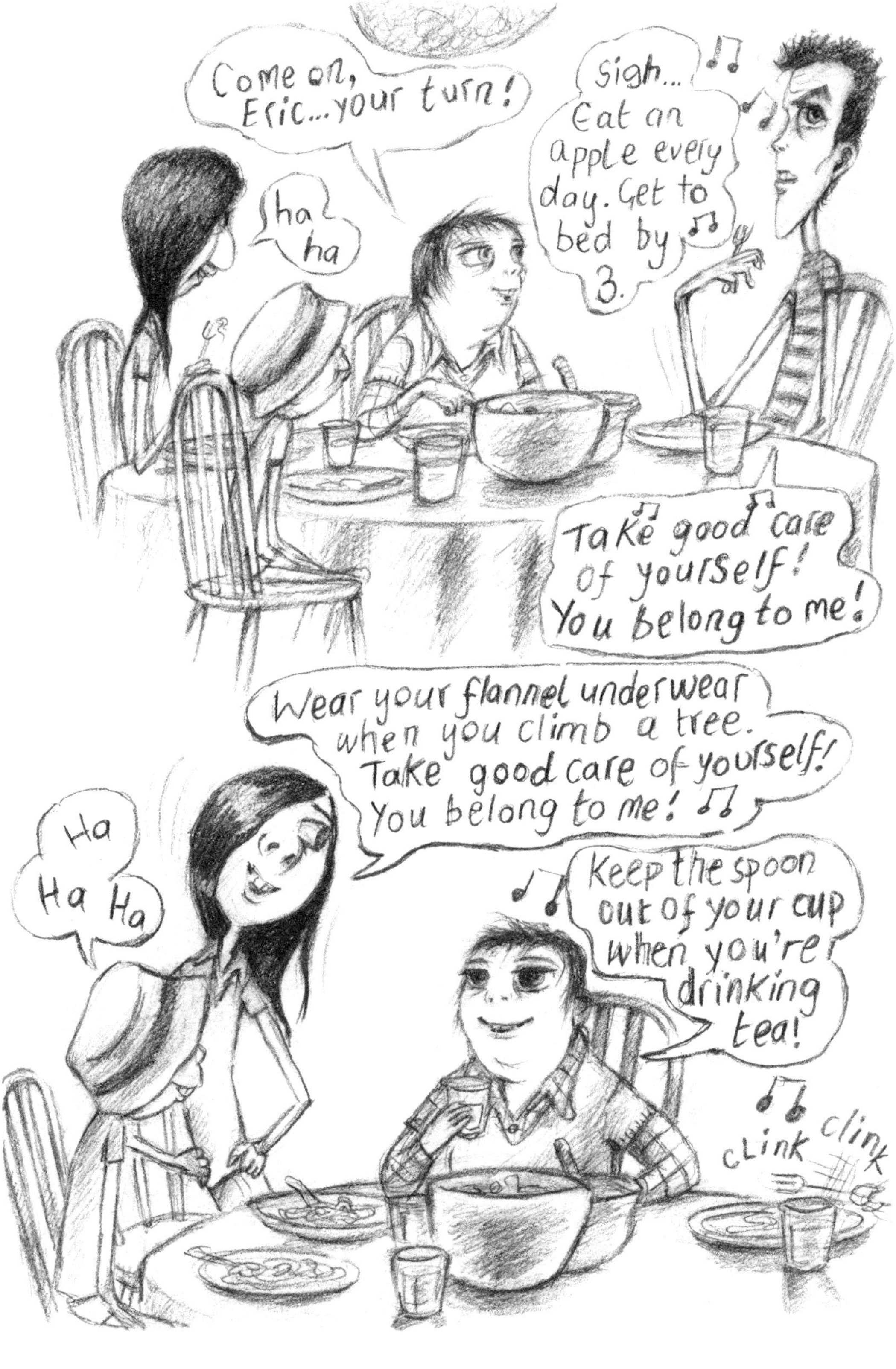
Come on, Eric... your turn!
Sigh... Eat an apple every day. Get to bed by 3.
ha ha
Take good care of yourself! You belong to me!
Wear your flannel underwear when you climb a tree. Take good care of yourself! You belong to me!
Ha Ha Ha
Keep the spoon out of your cup when you're drinking tea!
clink clink

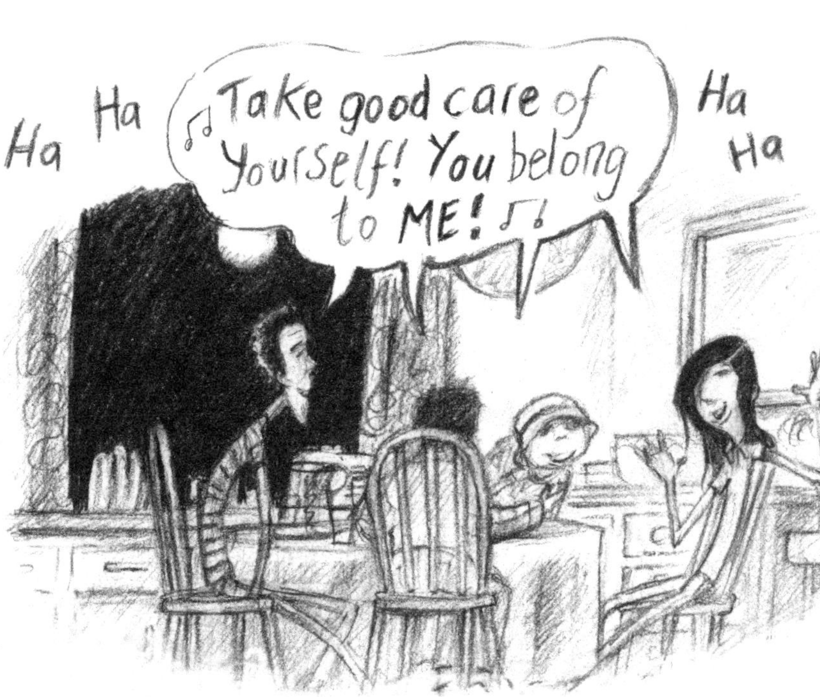
Ha
Ha
Take good care of Yourself! You belong to ME!
Ha
Ha

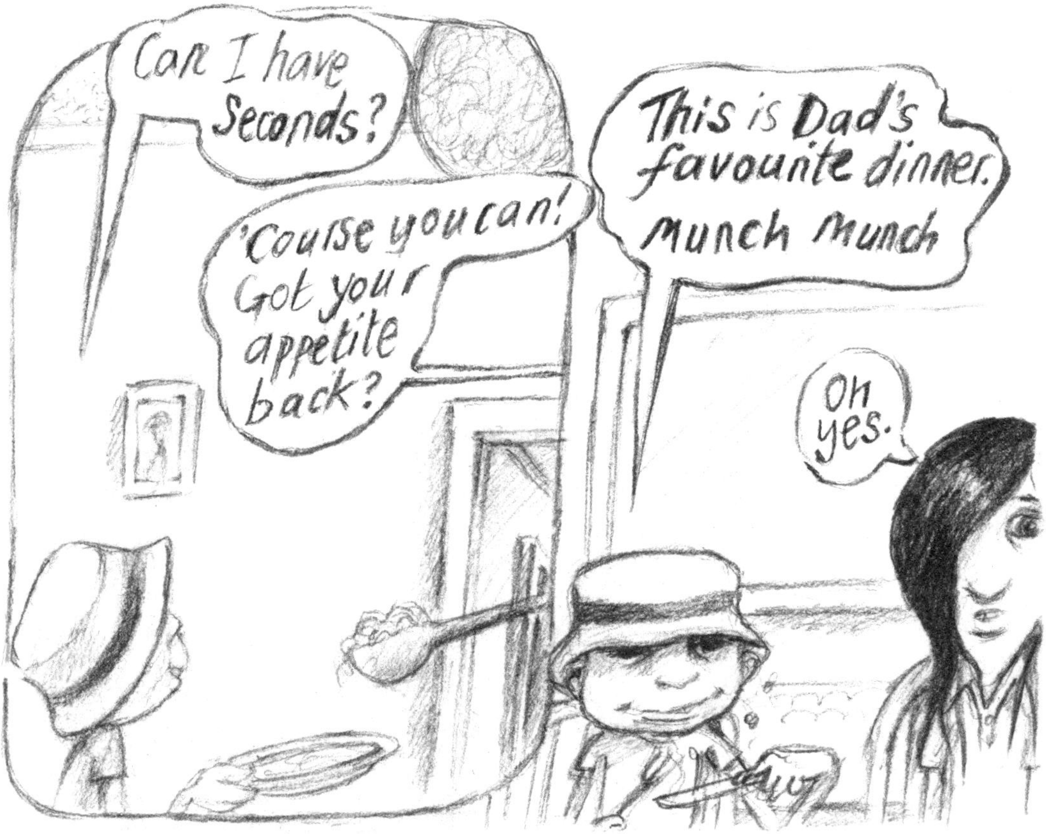
Can I have Seconds?
'Course you can! Got your appetite back?
This is Dad's favourite dinner.
munch munch
Oh yes.

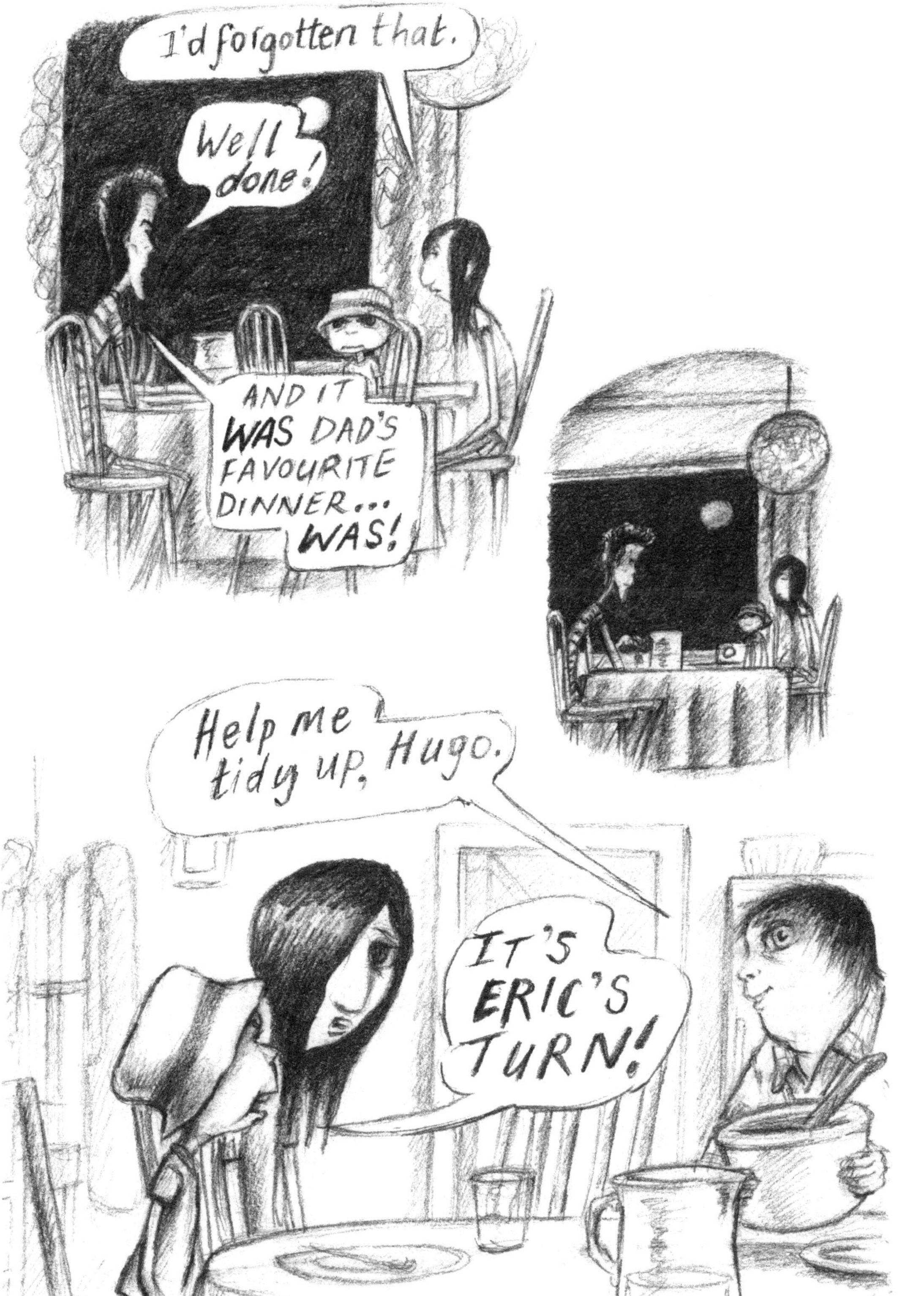
I'd forgotten that.
Well done!
AND IT WAS DAD'S FAVOURITE DINNER... WAS!
Help me tidy up, Hugo.
IT'S ERIC'S TURN!

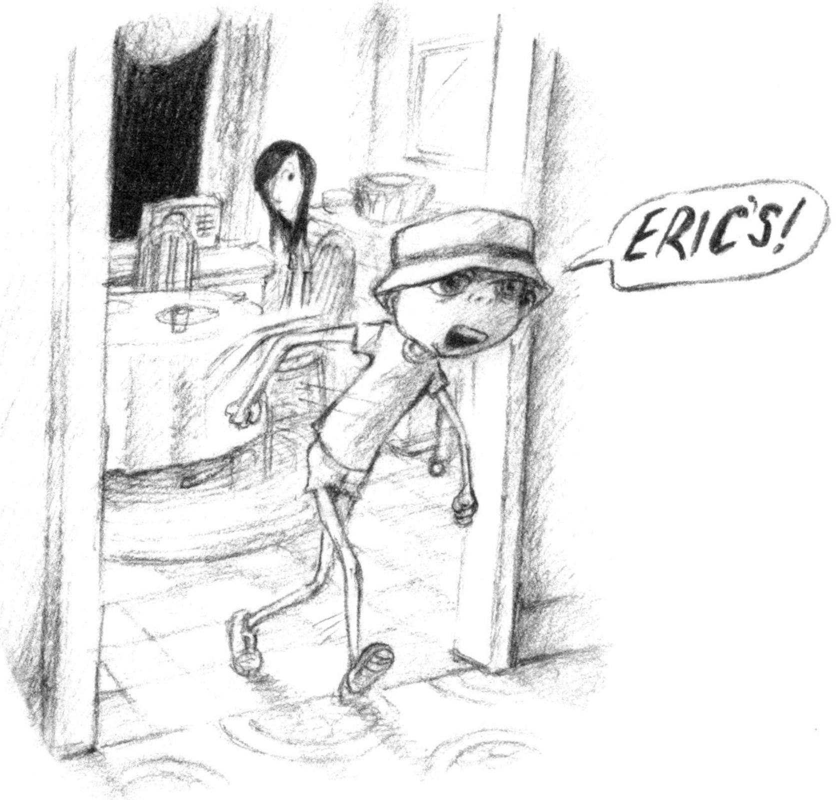
ERIC'S!

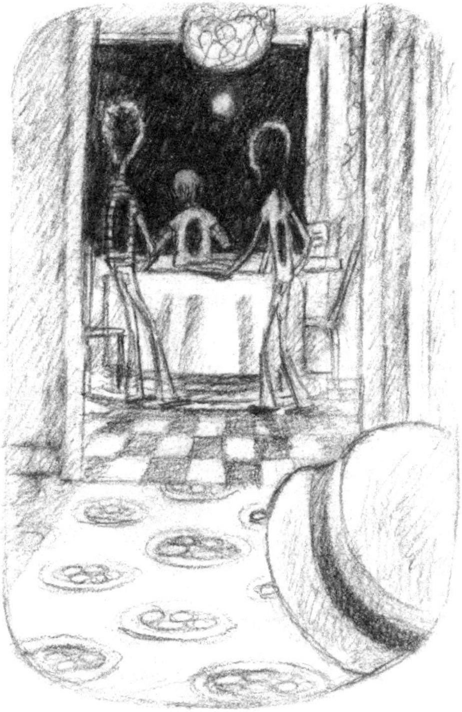

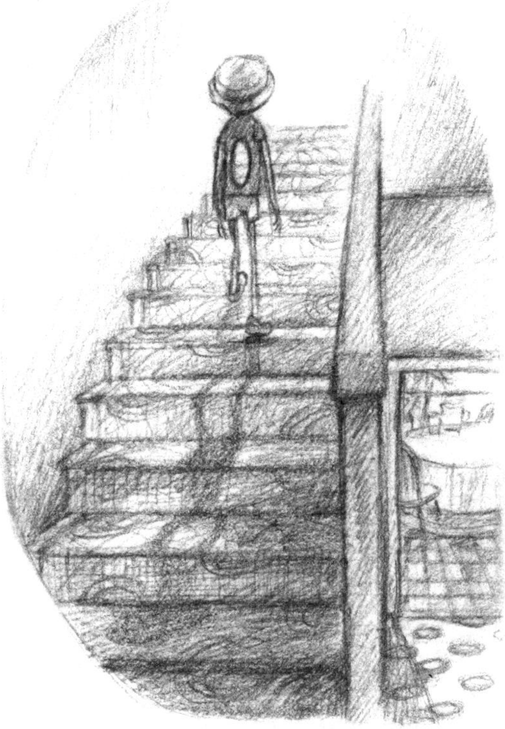

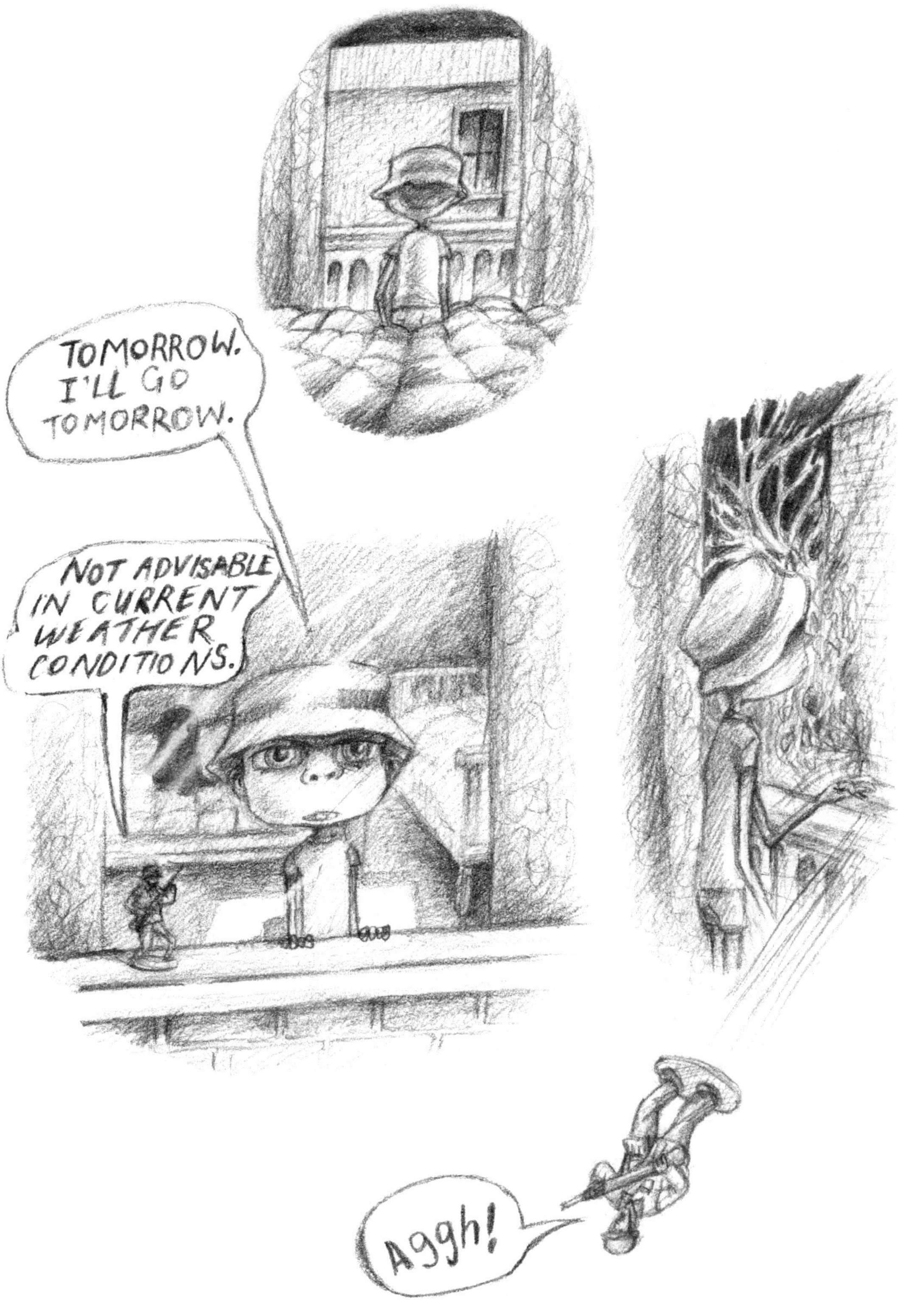
TOMORROW. I'LL GO TOMORROW.
NOT ADVISABLE IN CURRENT WEATHER CONDITIONS.
Aggh!

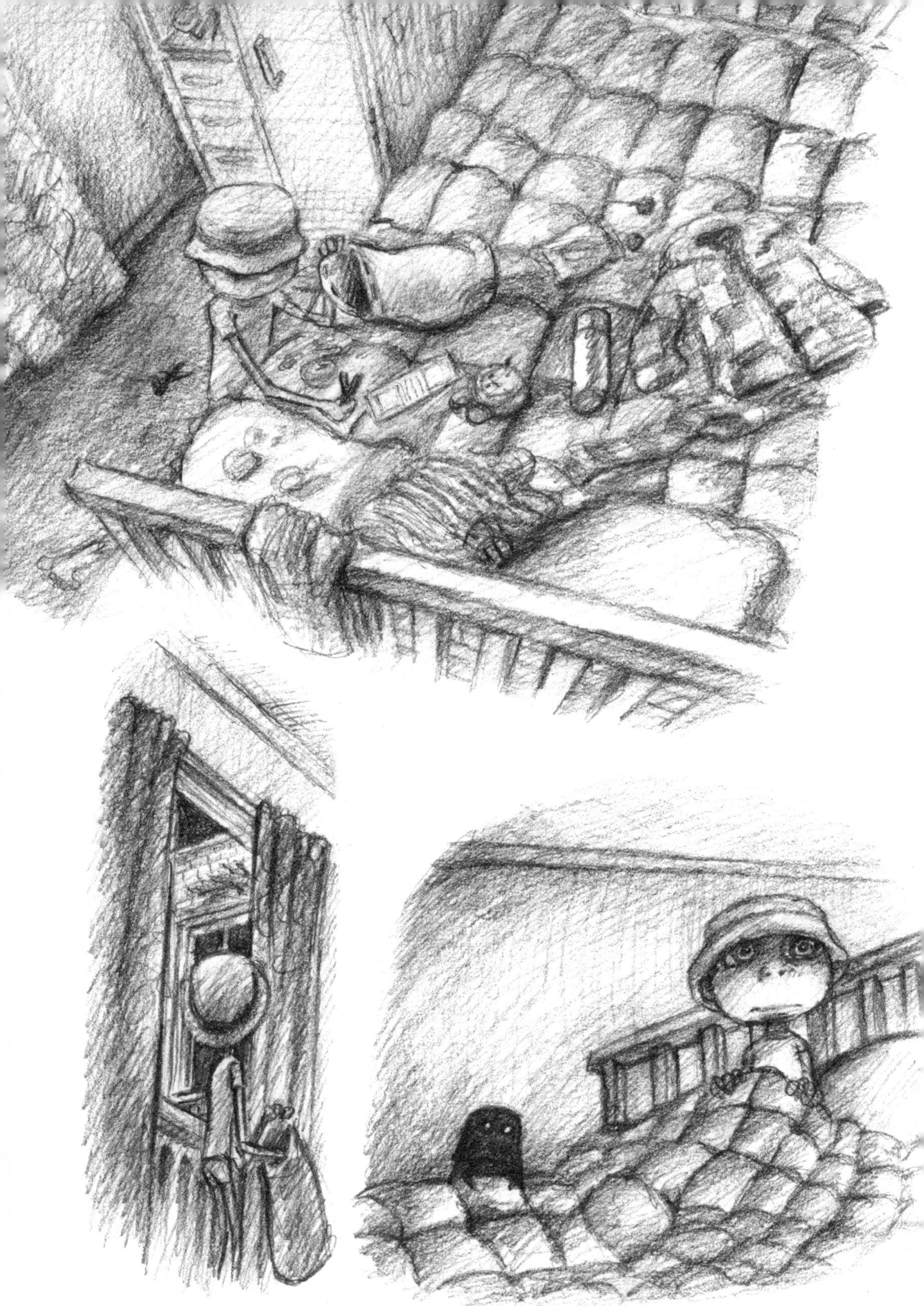

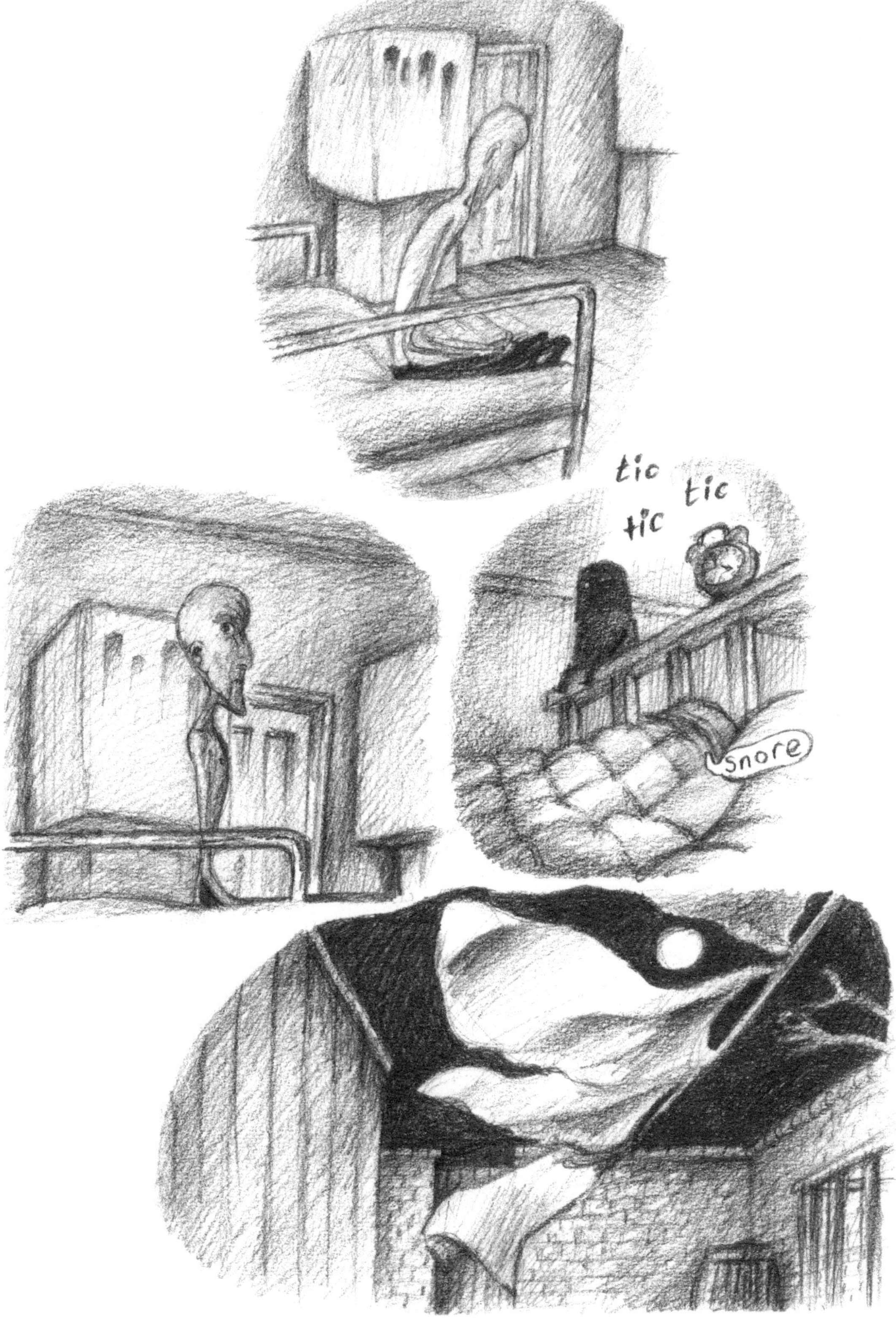
tic
tic
tic
snore

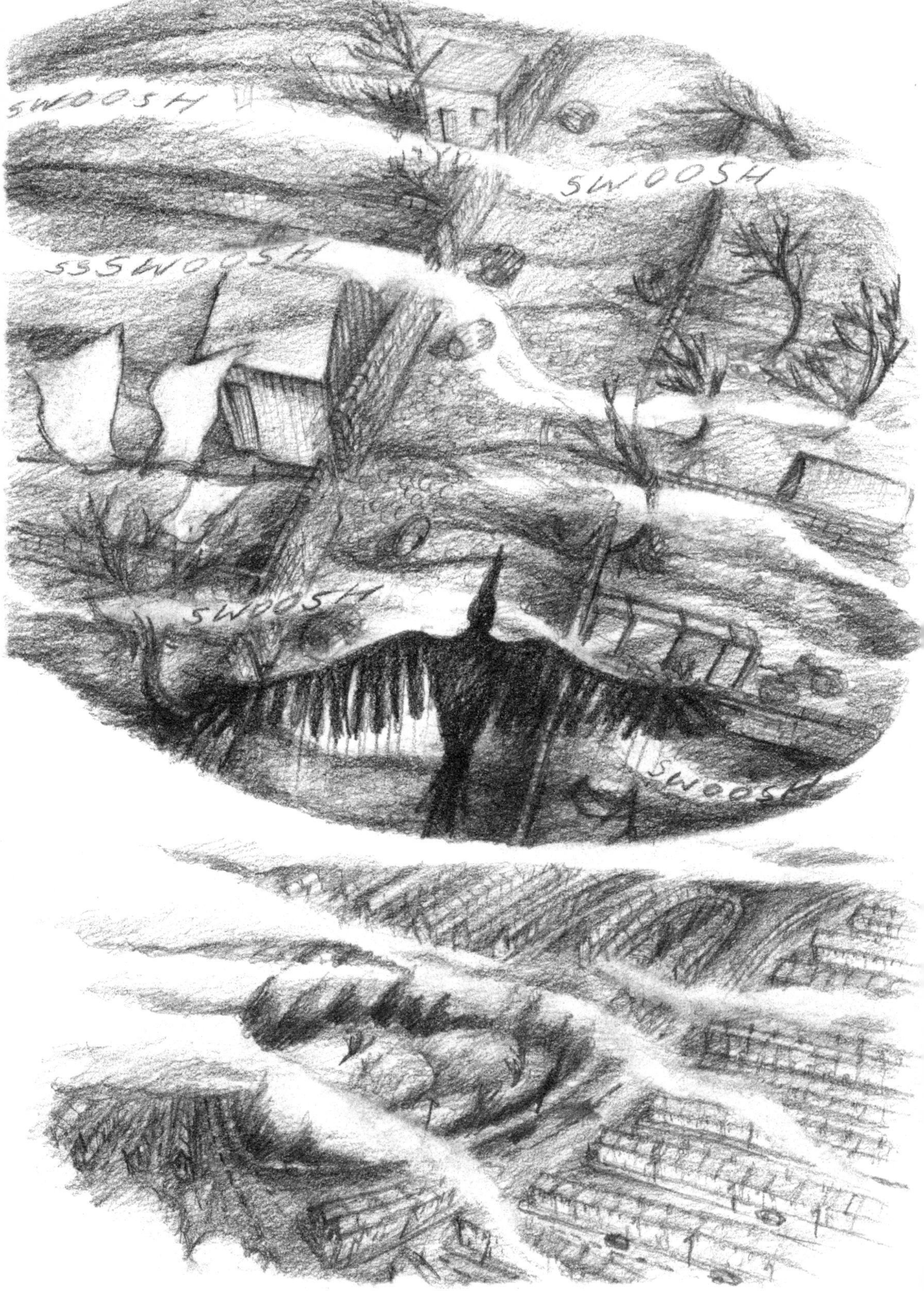
SWOOSH
SWOOSH
SSSWOOSH
SWOOSH
SWOOSH

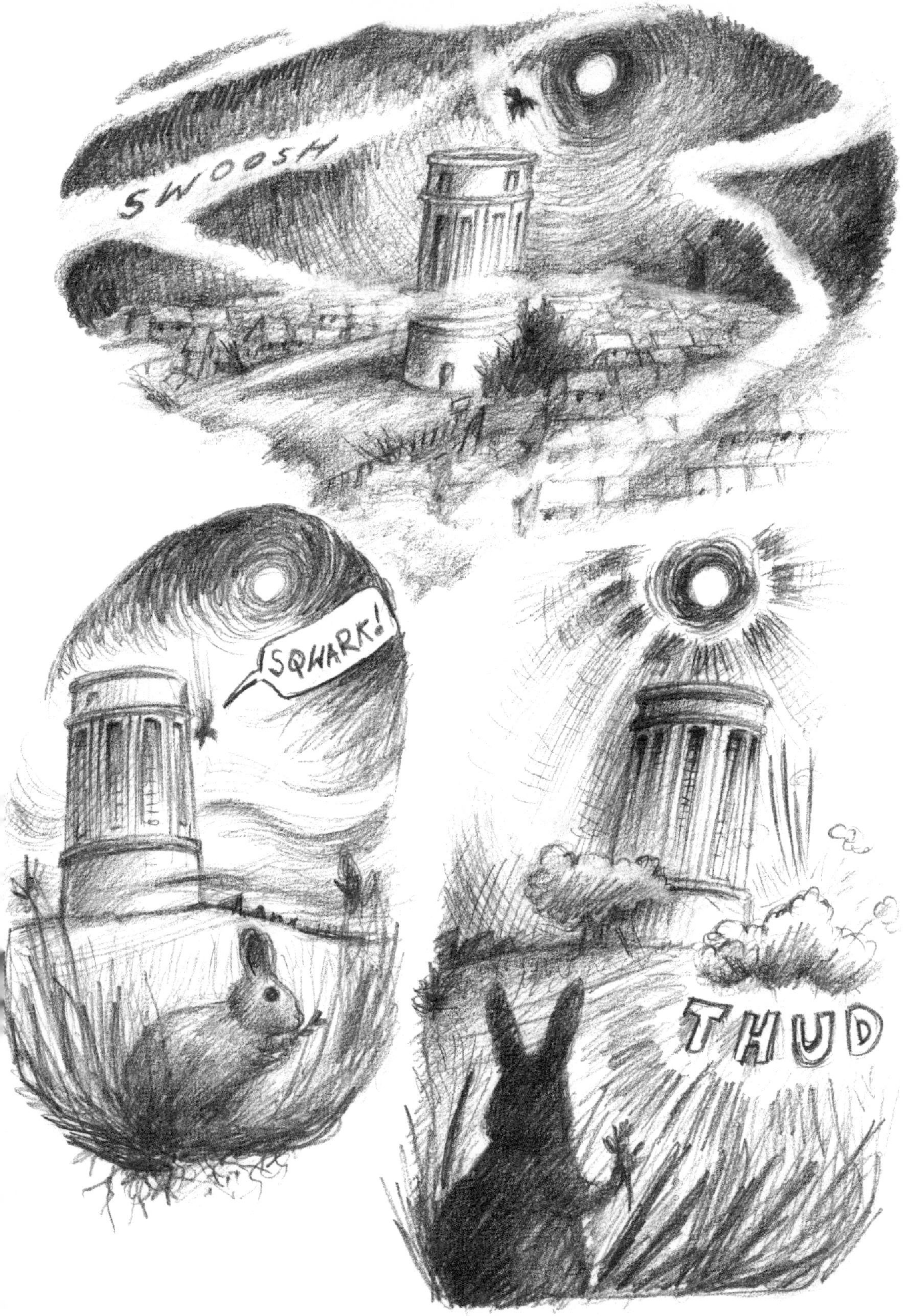
SWOOSH
SQWARK!
THUD

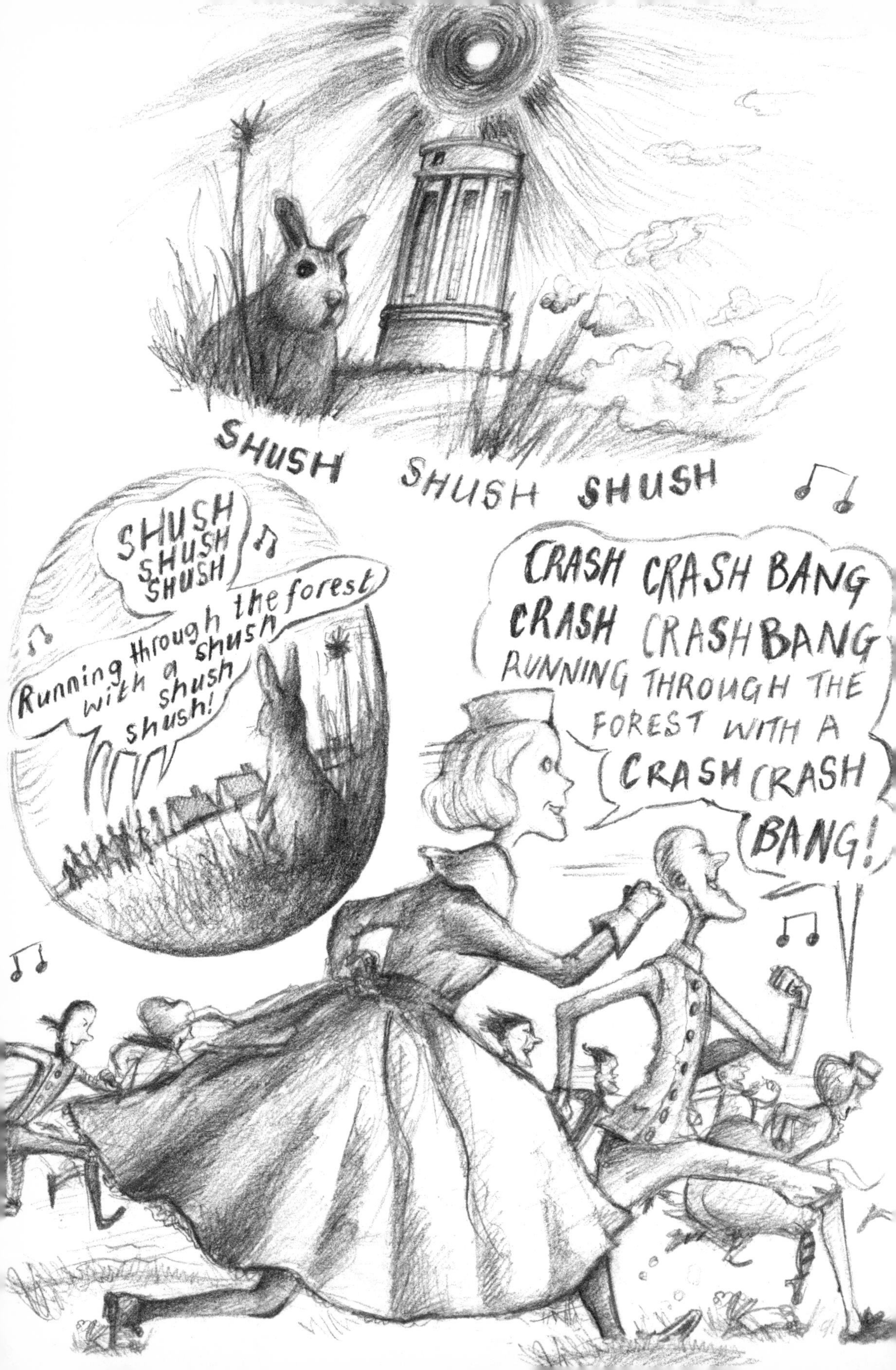
SHUSH SHUSH SHUSH
SHUSH SHUSH SHUSH
Running through the forest with a shush shush shush!
CRASH CRASH BANG CRASH CRASH BANG RUNNING THROUGH THE FOREST WITH A CRASH CRASH BANG!

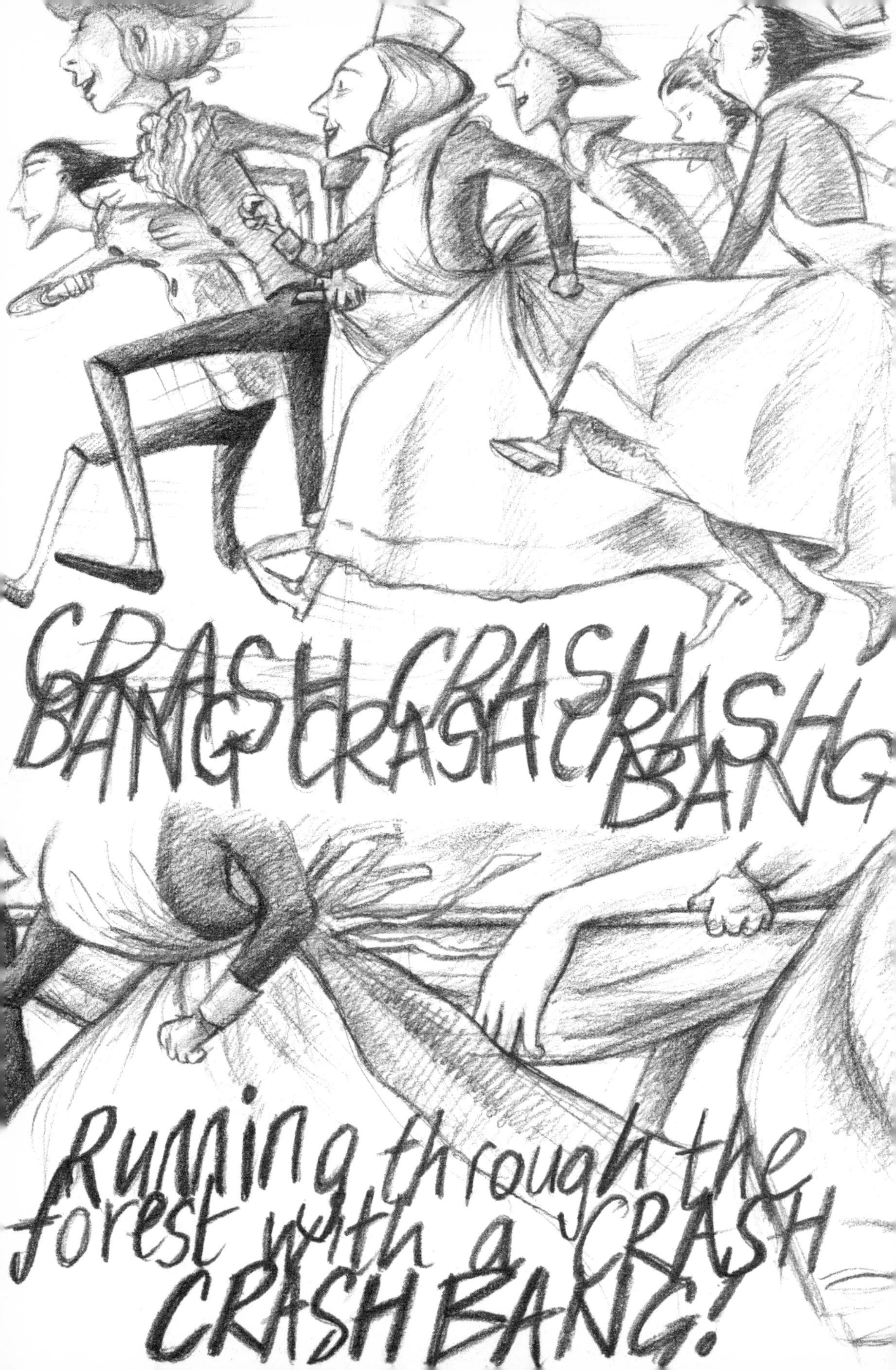
CRASH CRASH
BANG CRASH CRASH
BANG
Running through the forest with a CRASH CRASH BANG!

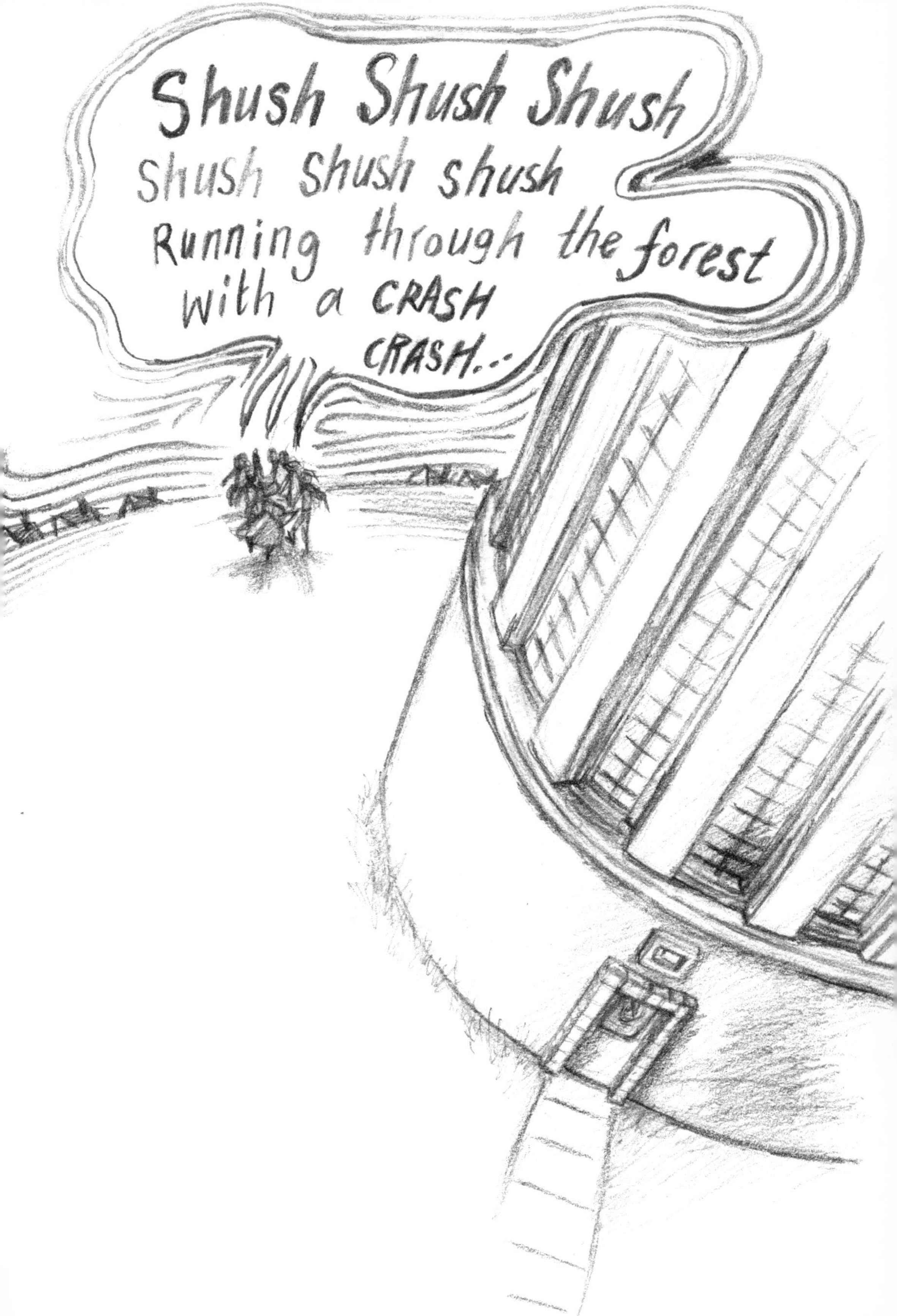
Shush Shush Shush
Shush Shush shush
Running through the forest
with a CRASH
CRASH...

BANG

Chapter Ten

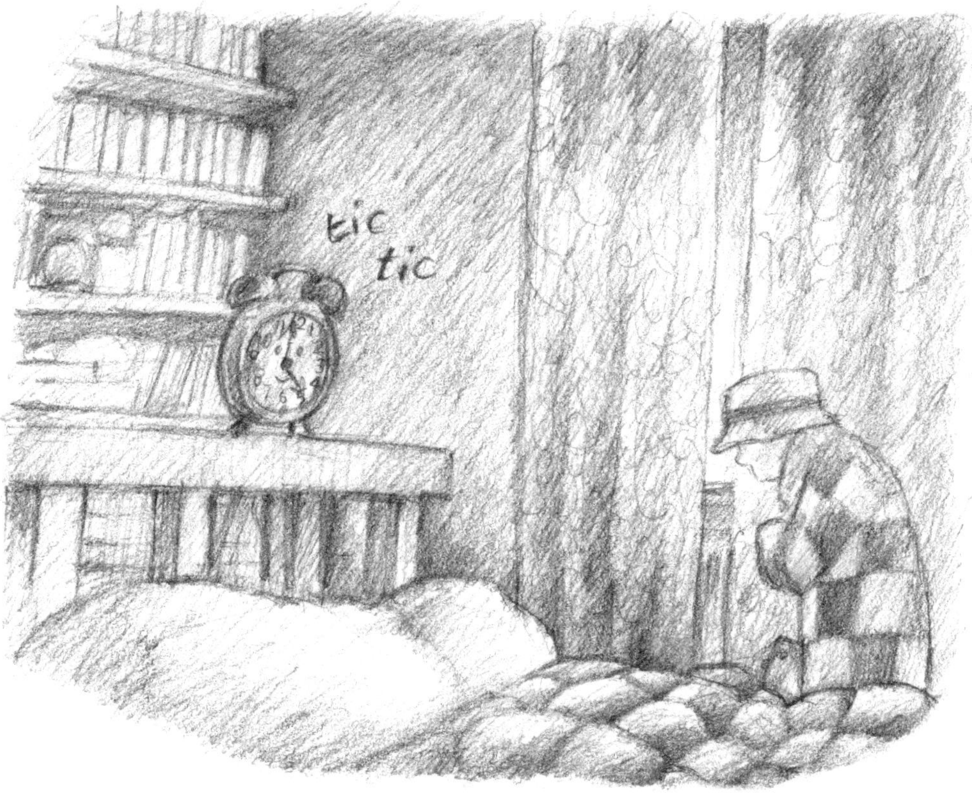
tic
tic

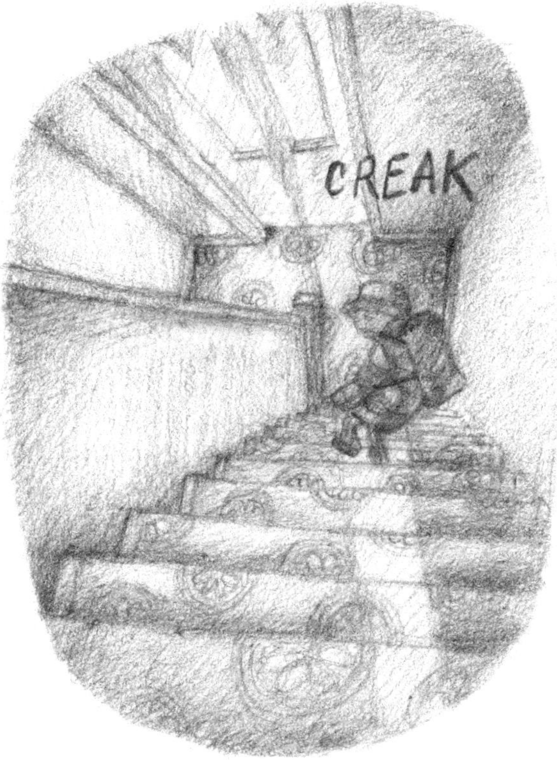
CREAK

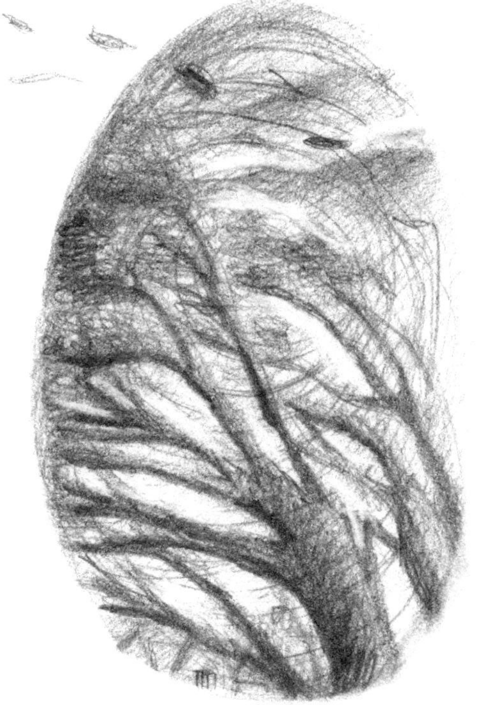

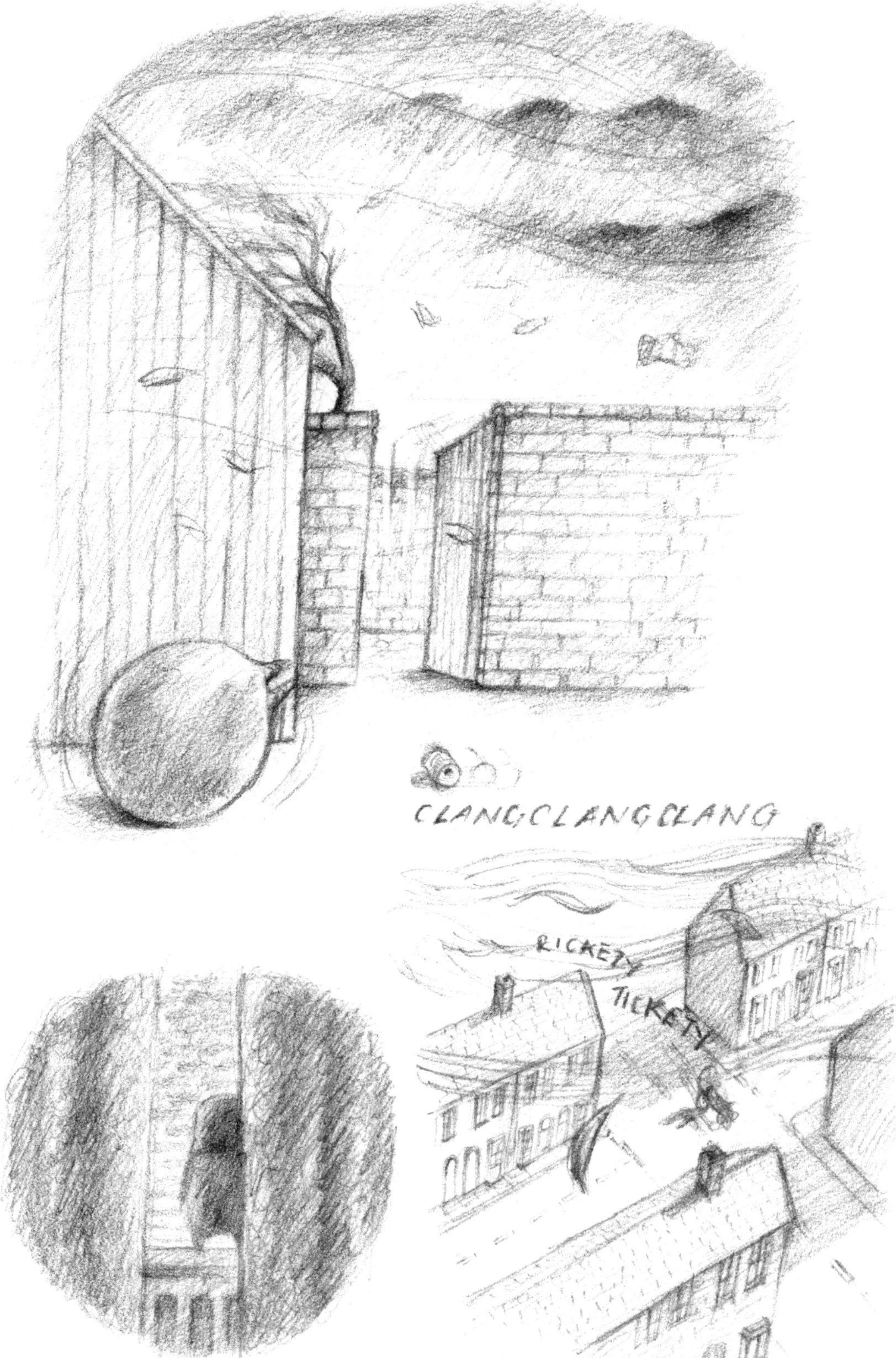
CLANGCLANGCLANG
RICKETY
TICKETY

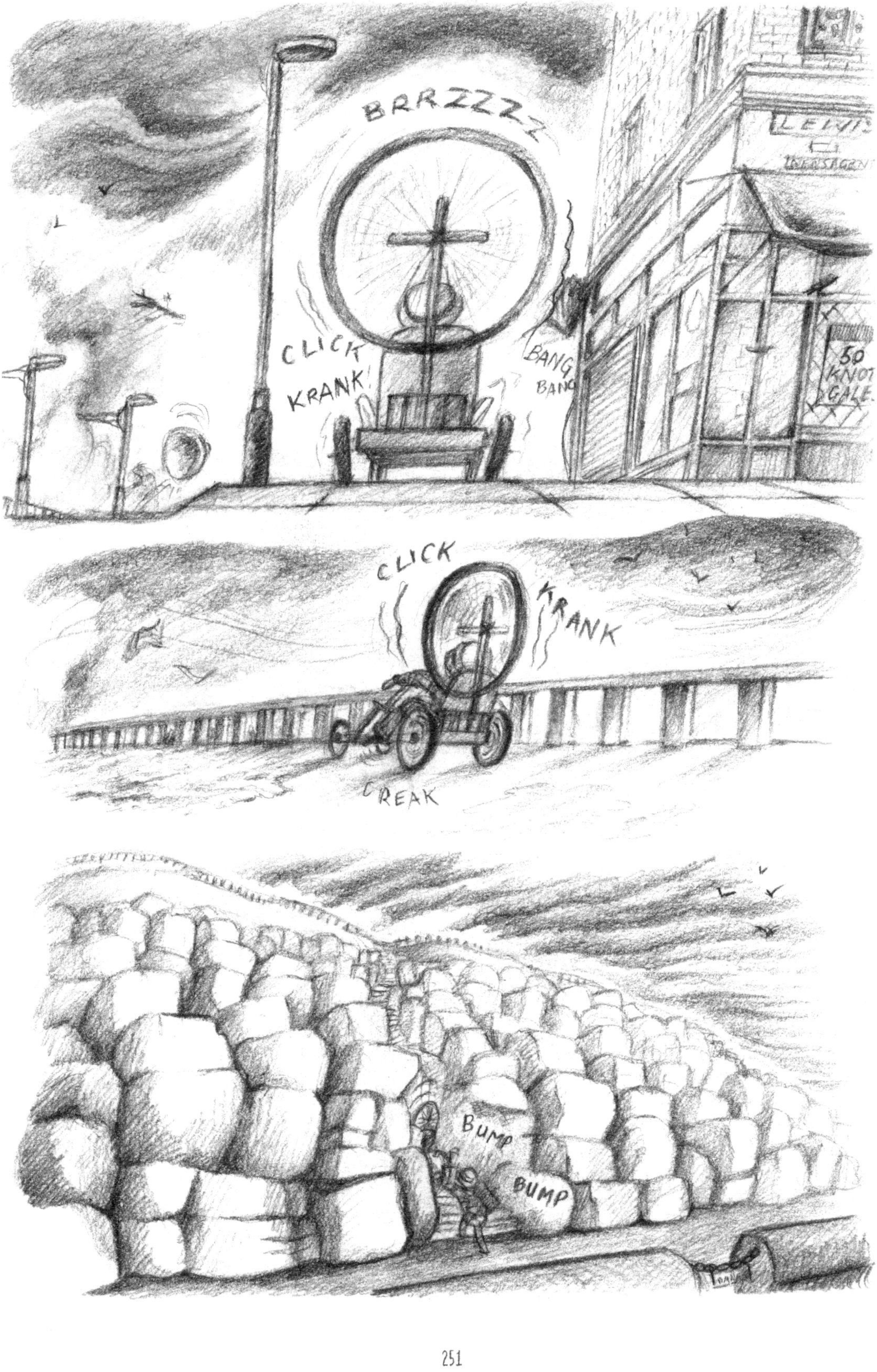
BRRZZZZZ
CLICK
KRANK!
BANG
BANG
50
KNOT
GALE
CLICK
KRANK
CREAK
BUMP
BUMP

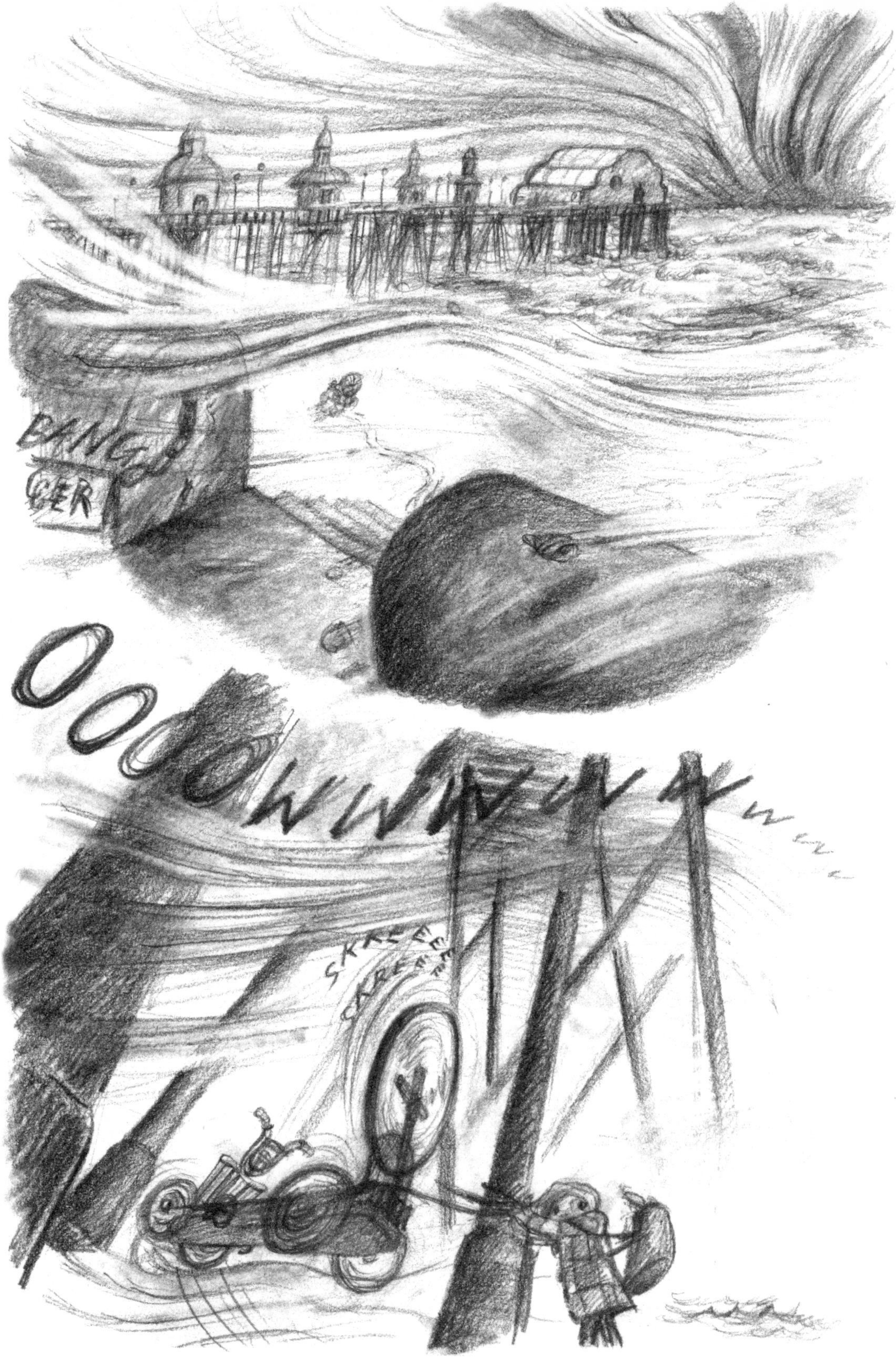
DANG
GER
OOOOWWWWWWW
SKREEE
SKREEE

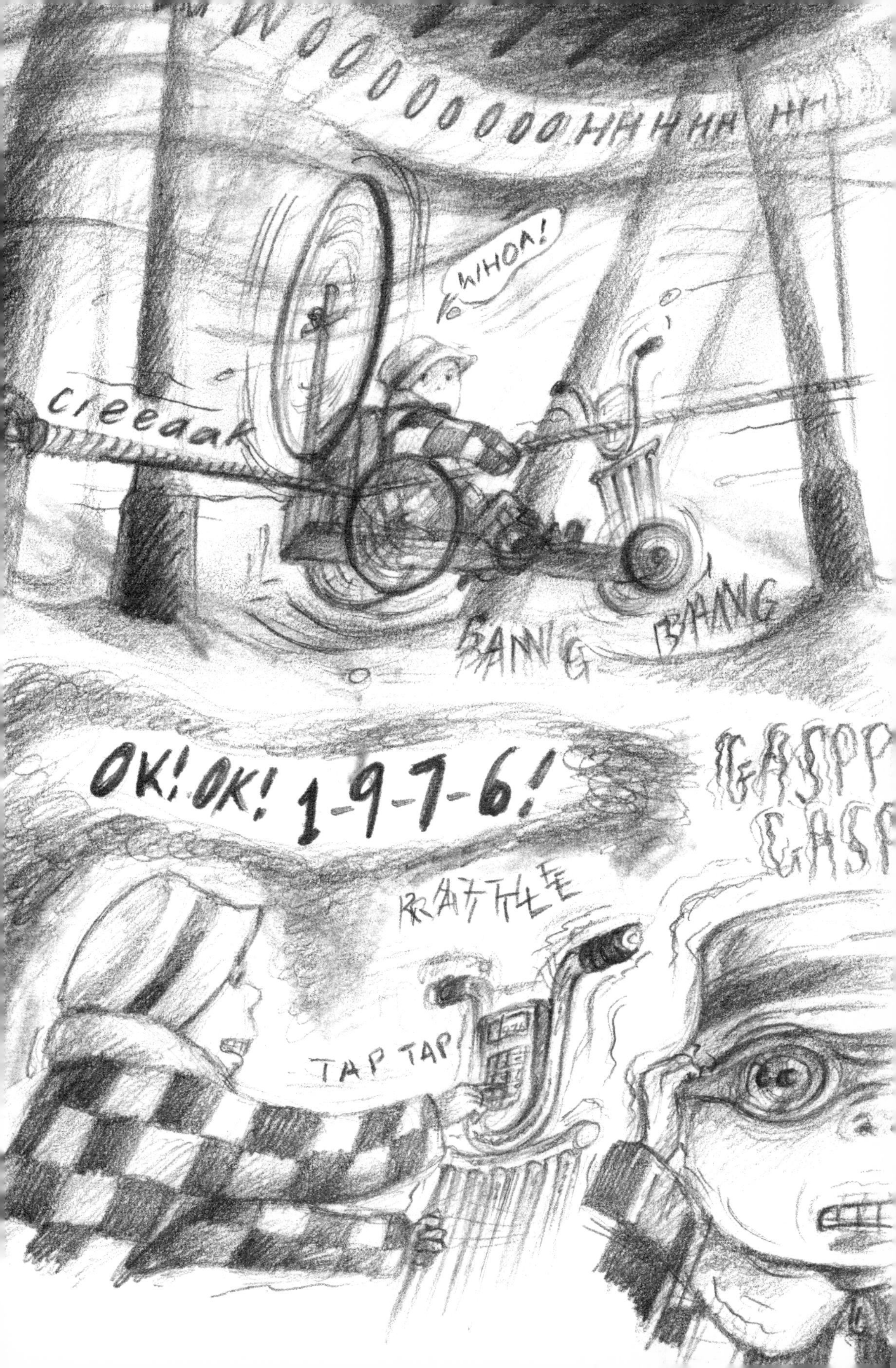

WOOOOOOOOOHHHHHH
WHOA!
creeaaak
BANNG
BANNG
OK! OK! 1-9-7-6!
GASPP
GASP
RATTLE
TAP TAP

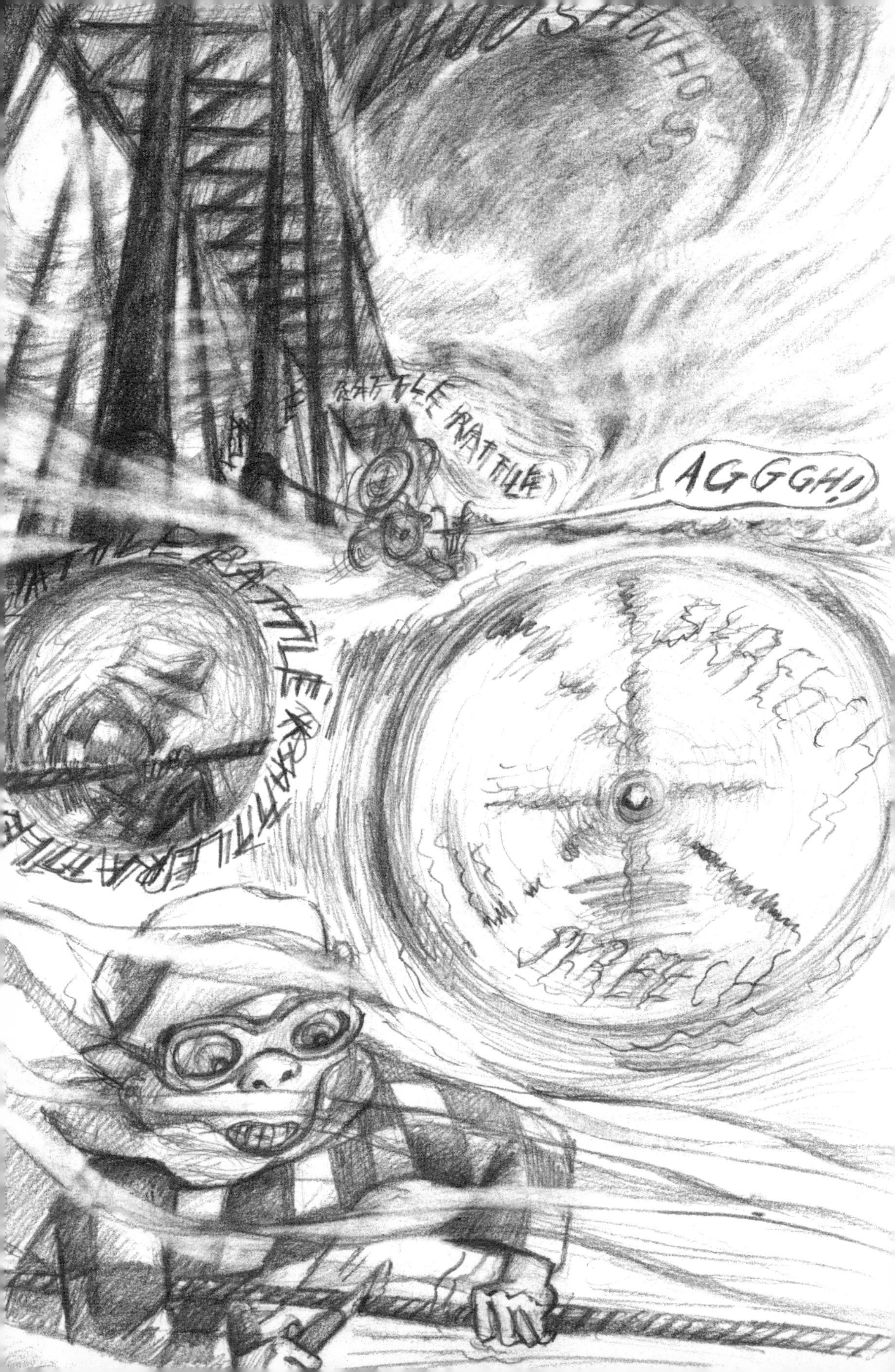
RATTLE RATTLE
AGGGH!
RATTLE RATTLE RATTLE RATTLE
SKREECH
SKREECH

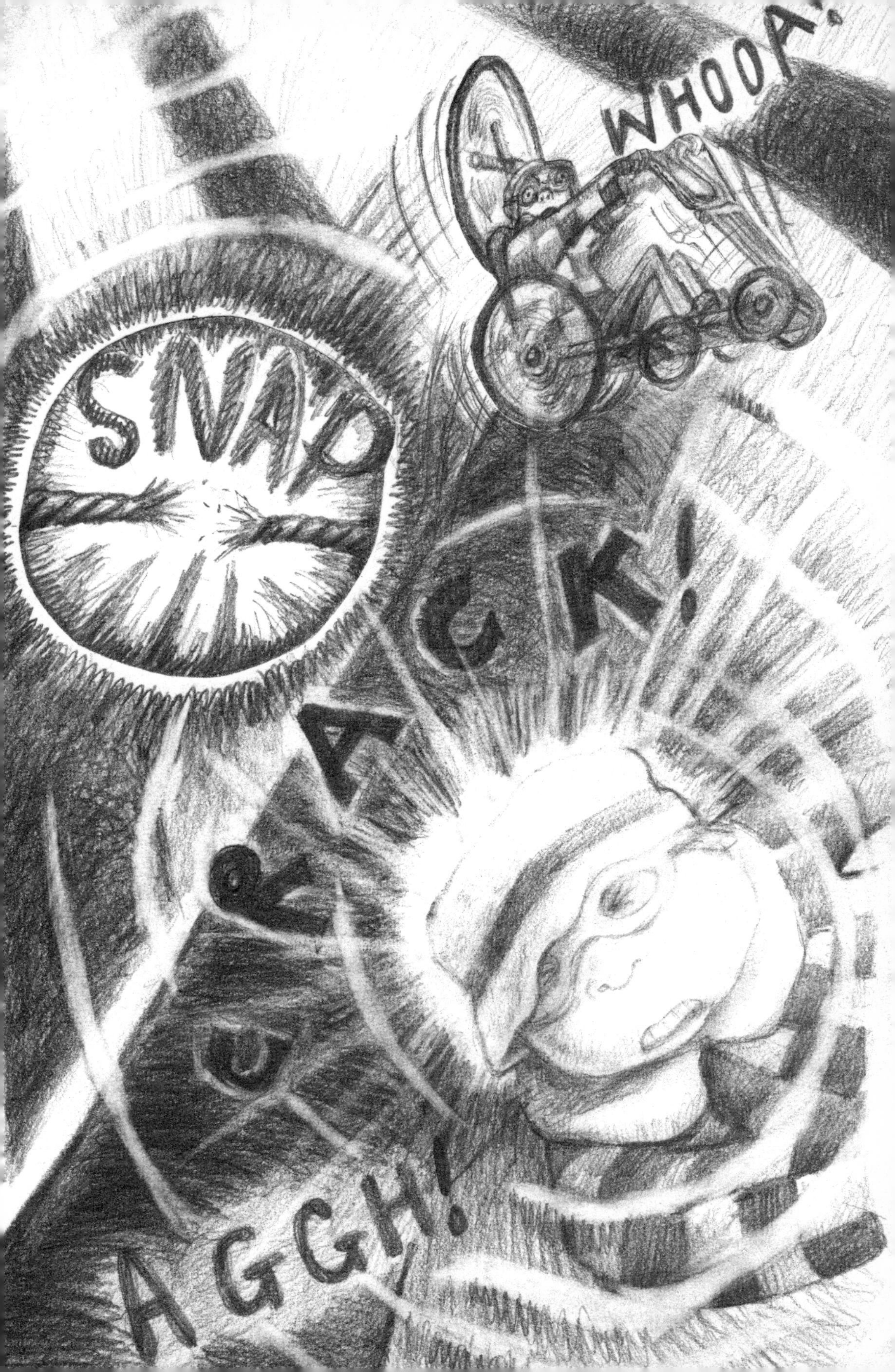

SNAP
WHOOA!
CRACK!
AGGH!

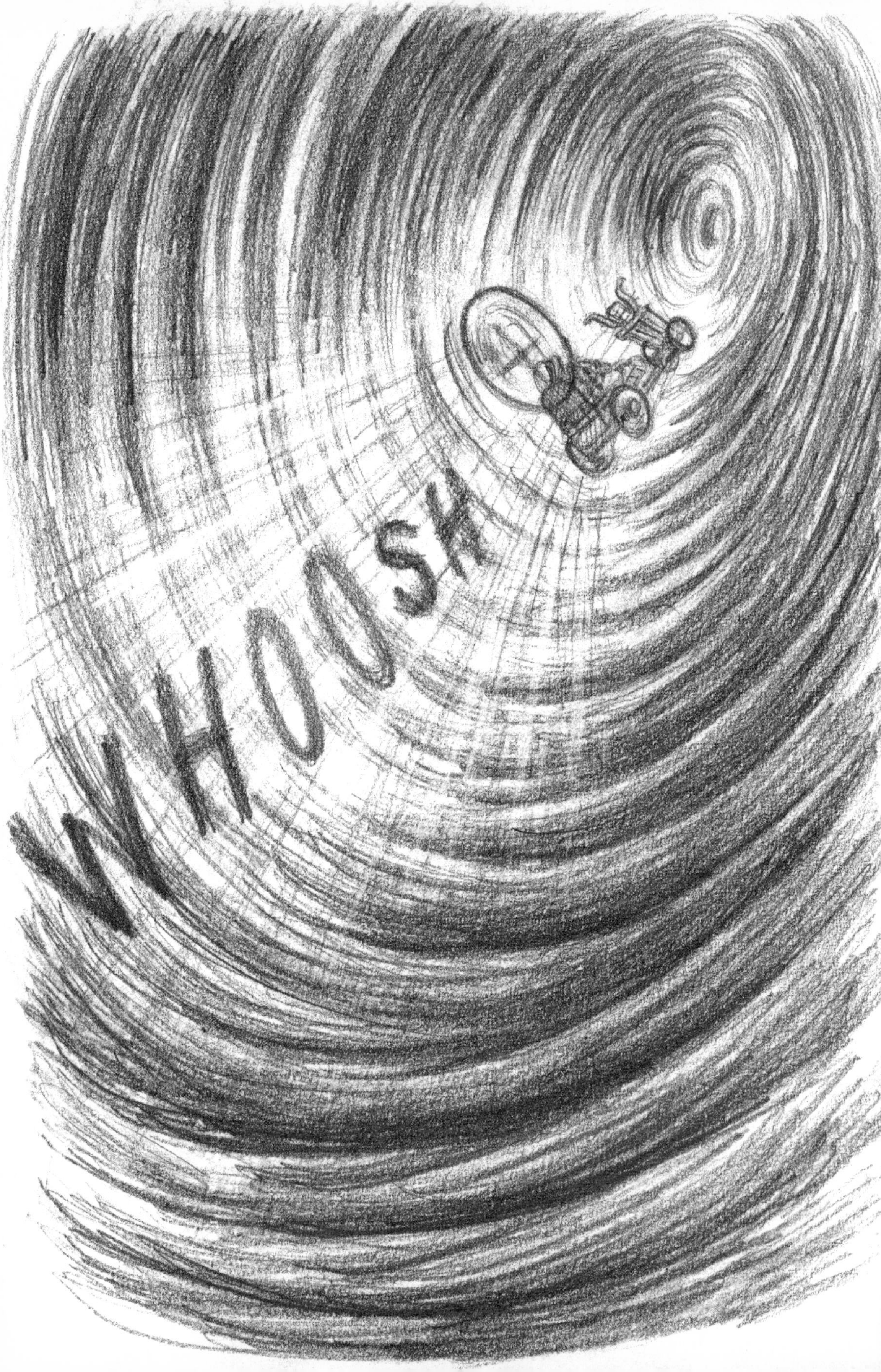
WHOOSH

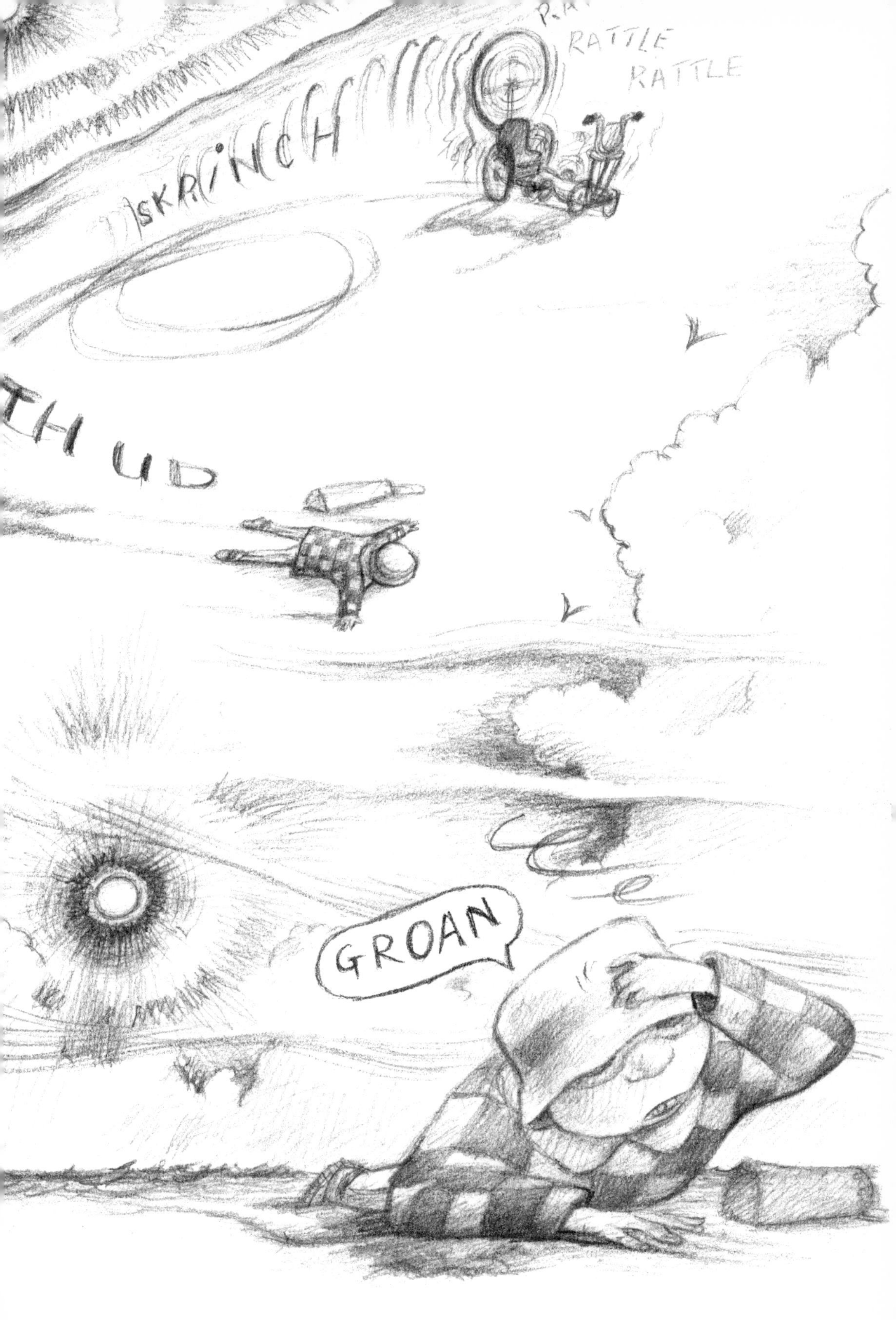
SKRINCH
RATTLE
RATTLE
THUD
GROAN

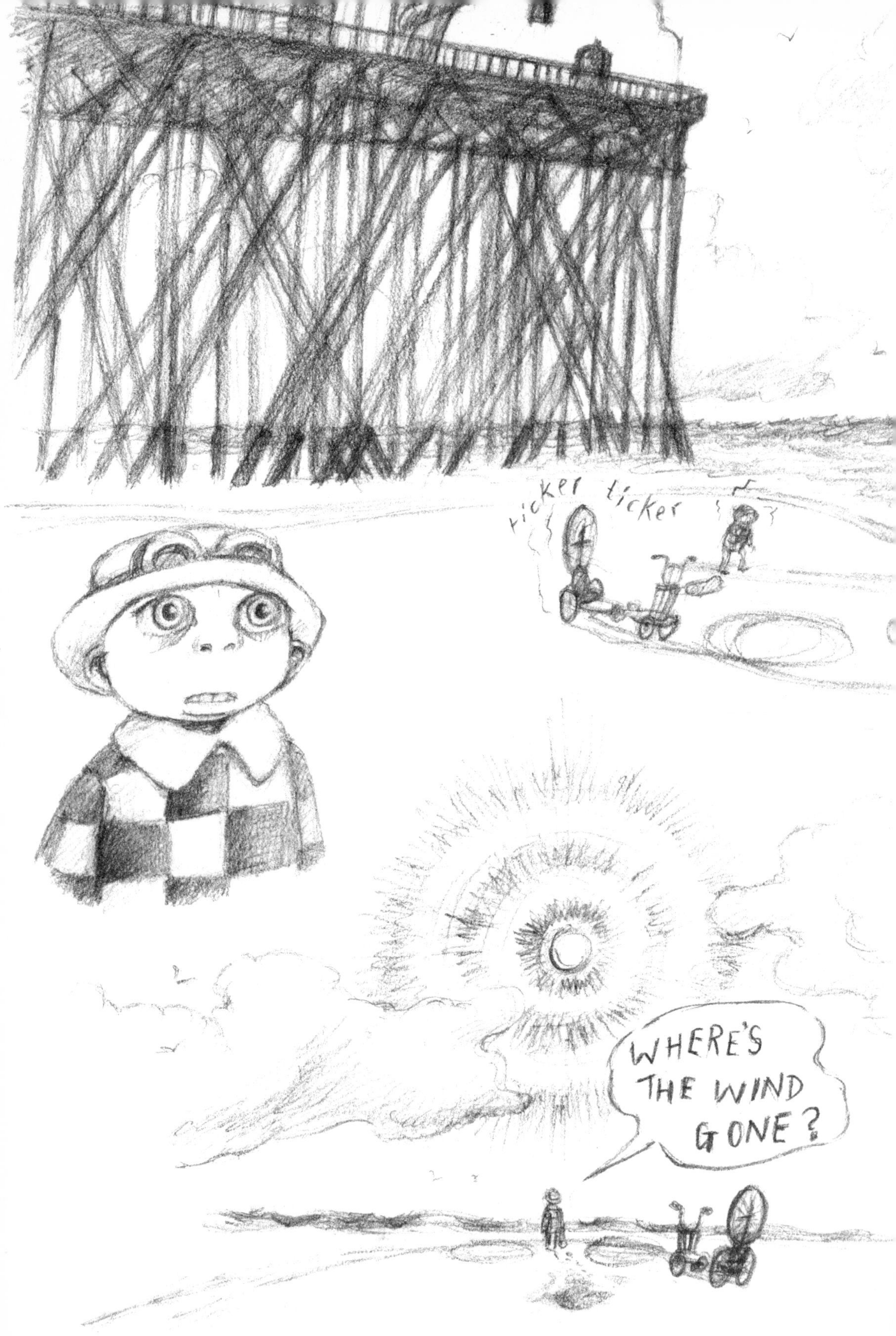
ticker ticker
WHERE'S THE WIND GONE?

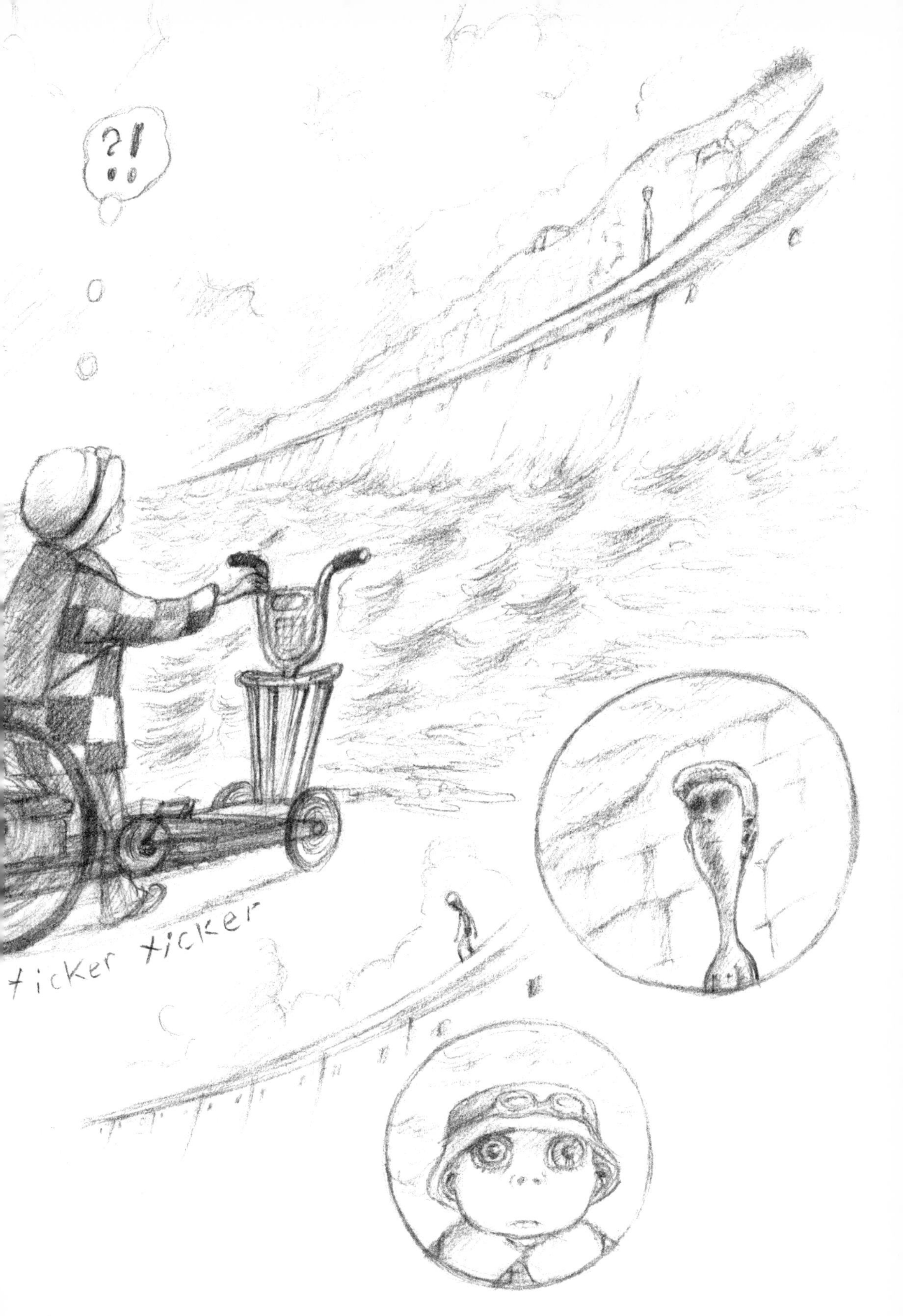
?!
ticker ticker

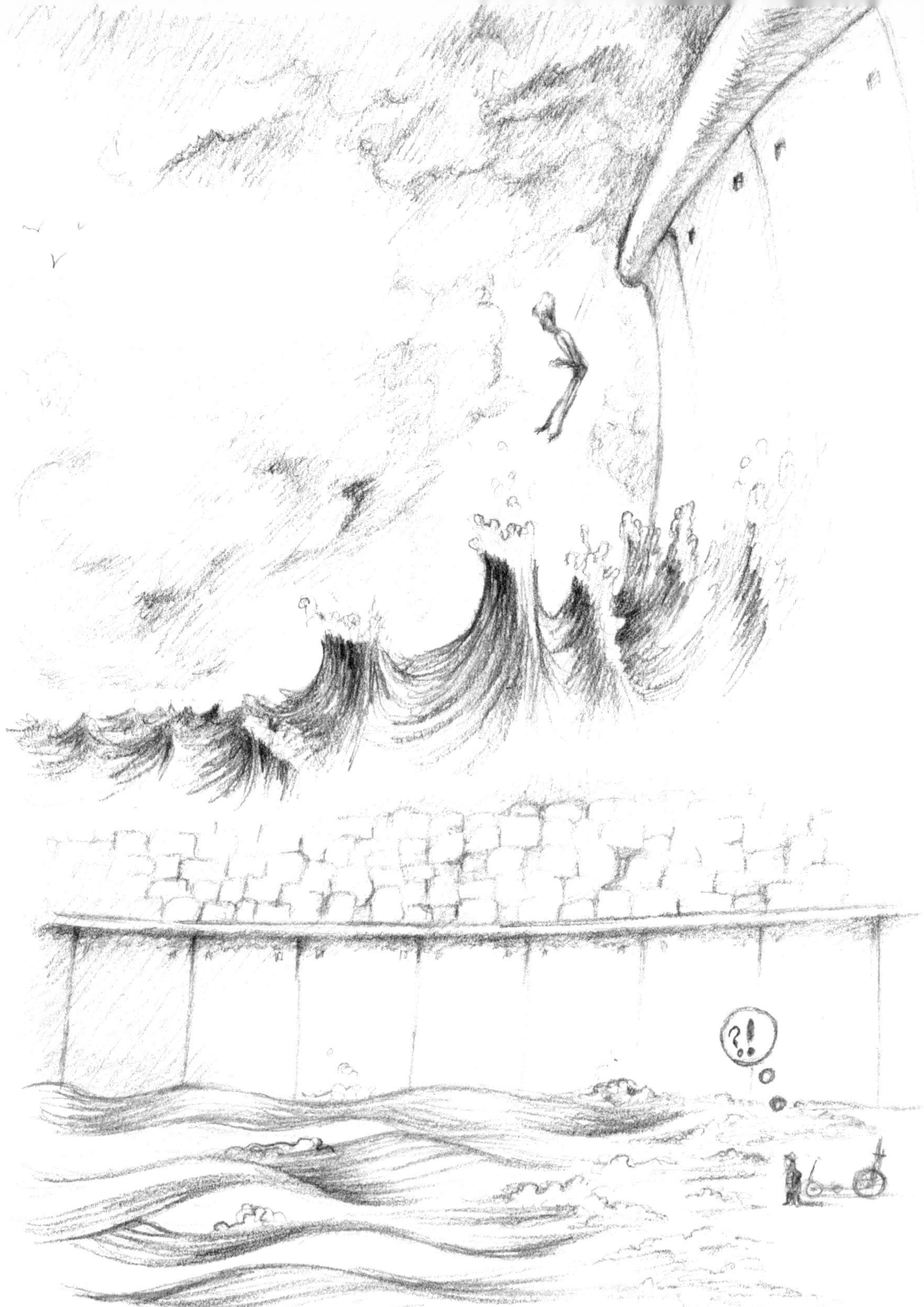
?!

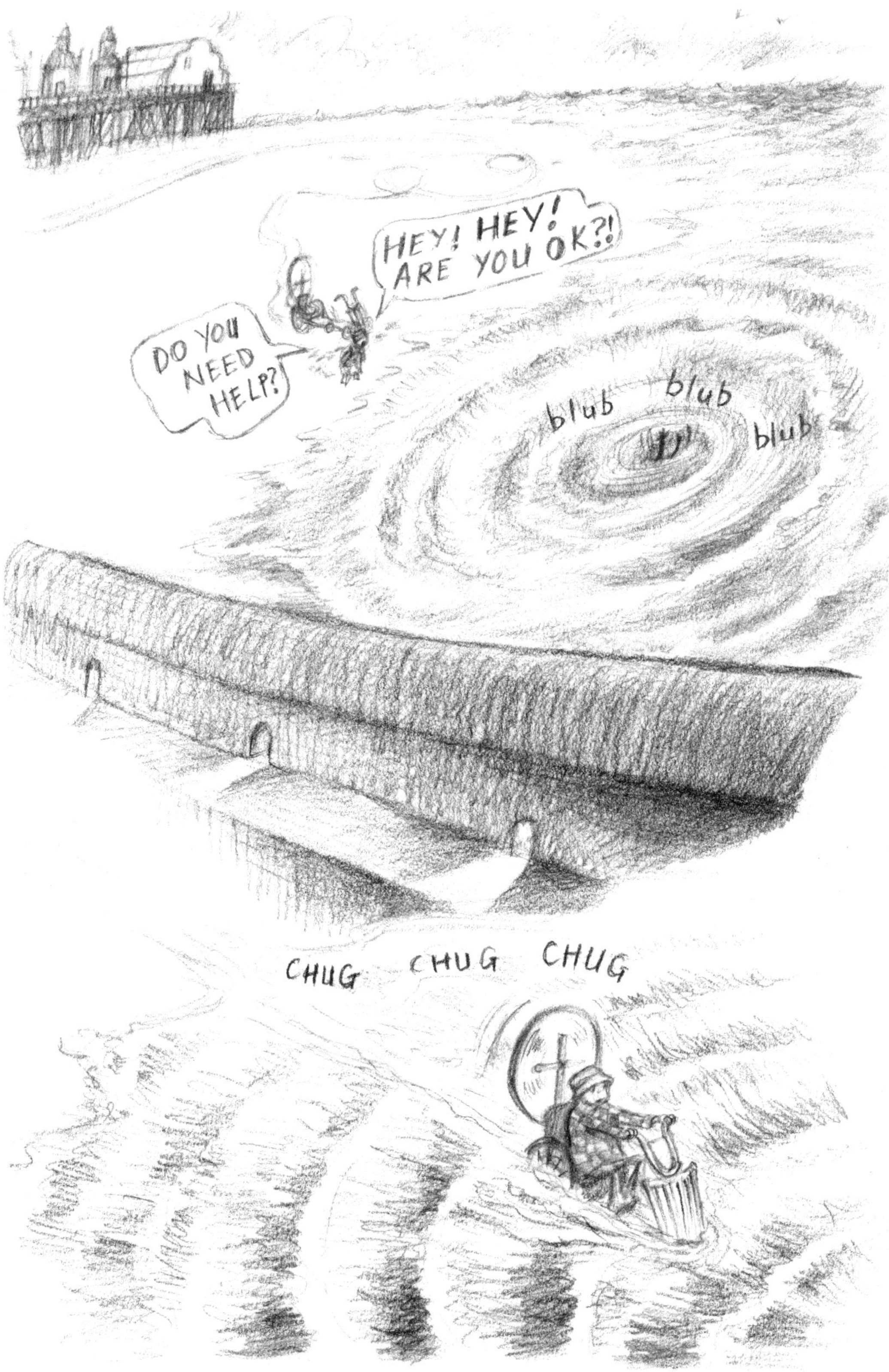
HEY! HEY! ARE YOU OK?!
DO YOU NEED HELP?
blub
blub
blub
CHUG CHUG CHUG

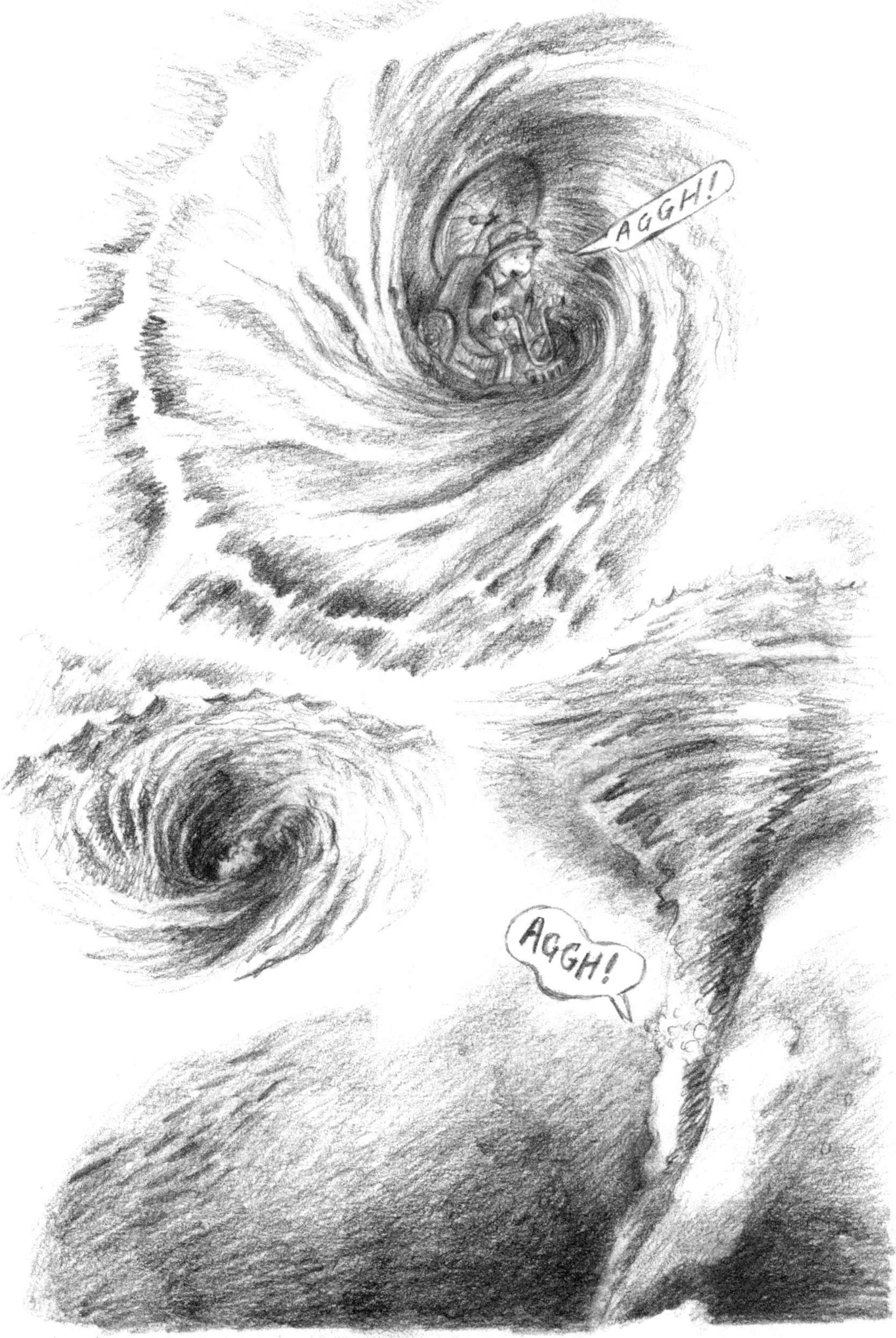
AGGH!
AGGH!

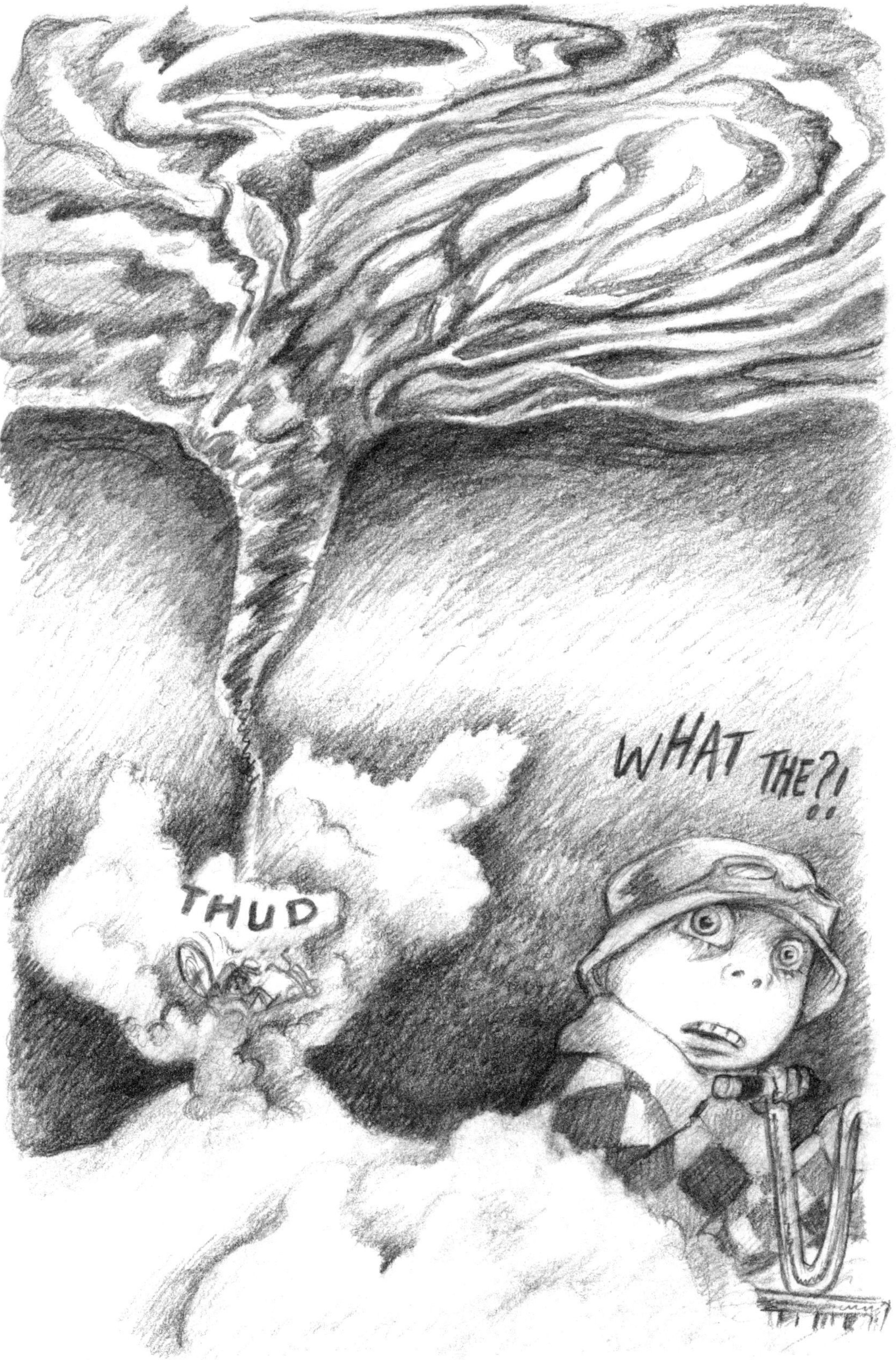
WHAT THE?!
THUD

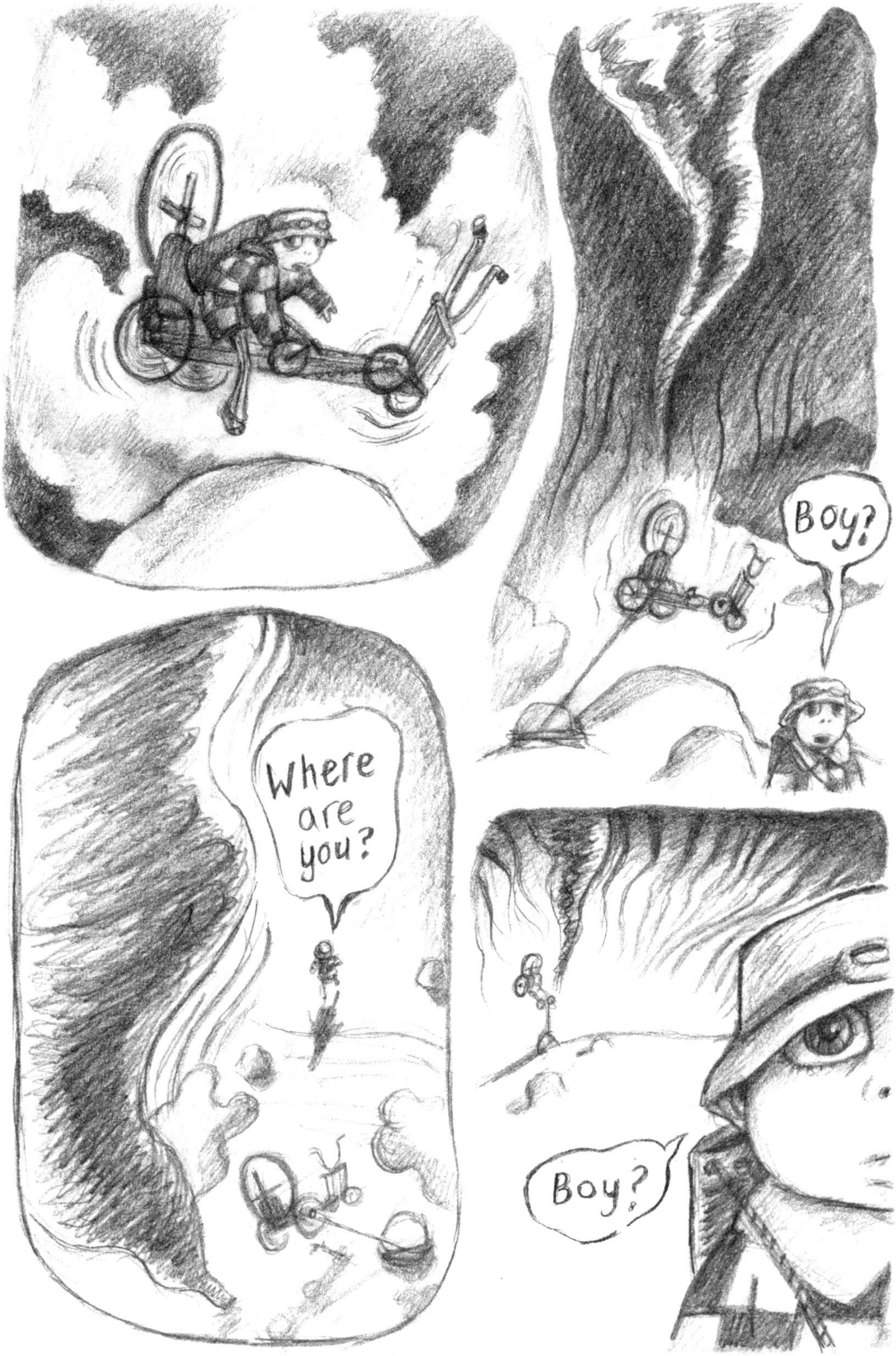
Boy?
Where are you?
Boy?

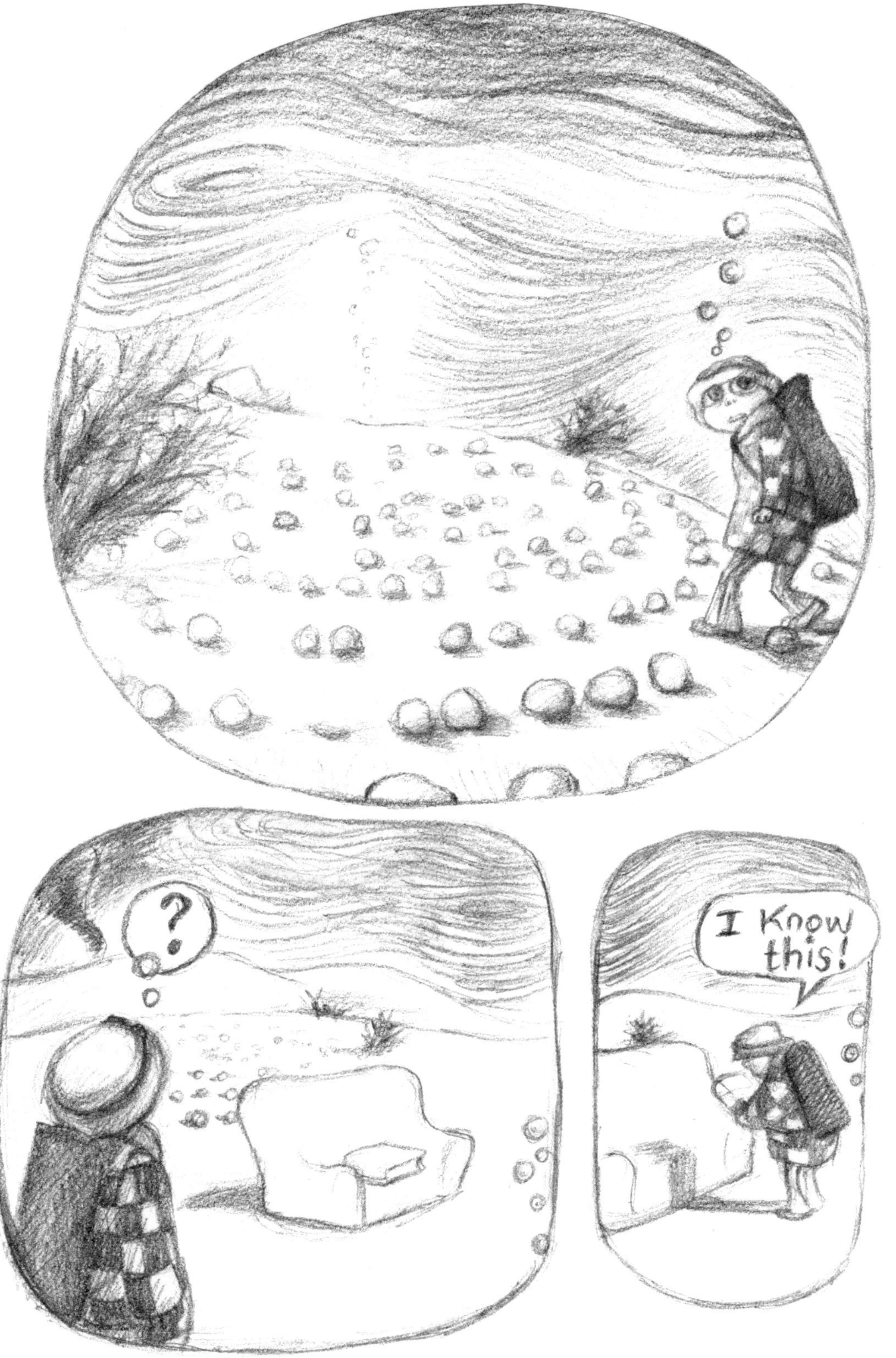
?
I Know this!

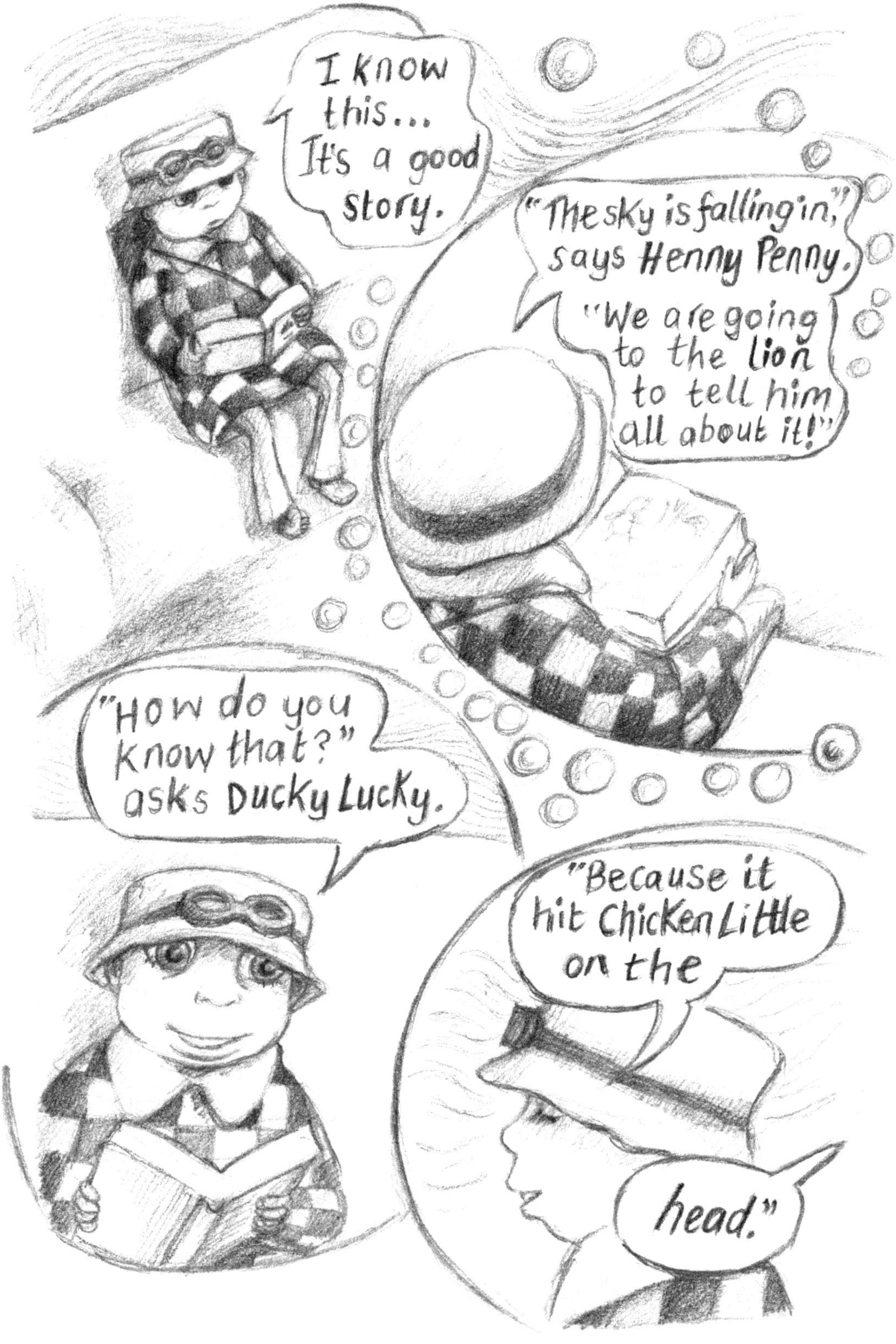
I know this... It's a good story.
"The sky is falling in," says Henny Penny.
"We are going to the lion to tell him all about it!"
"How do you know that?" asks Ducky Lucky.
"Because it hit Chicken Little on the
head."

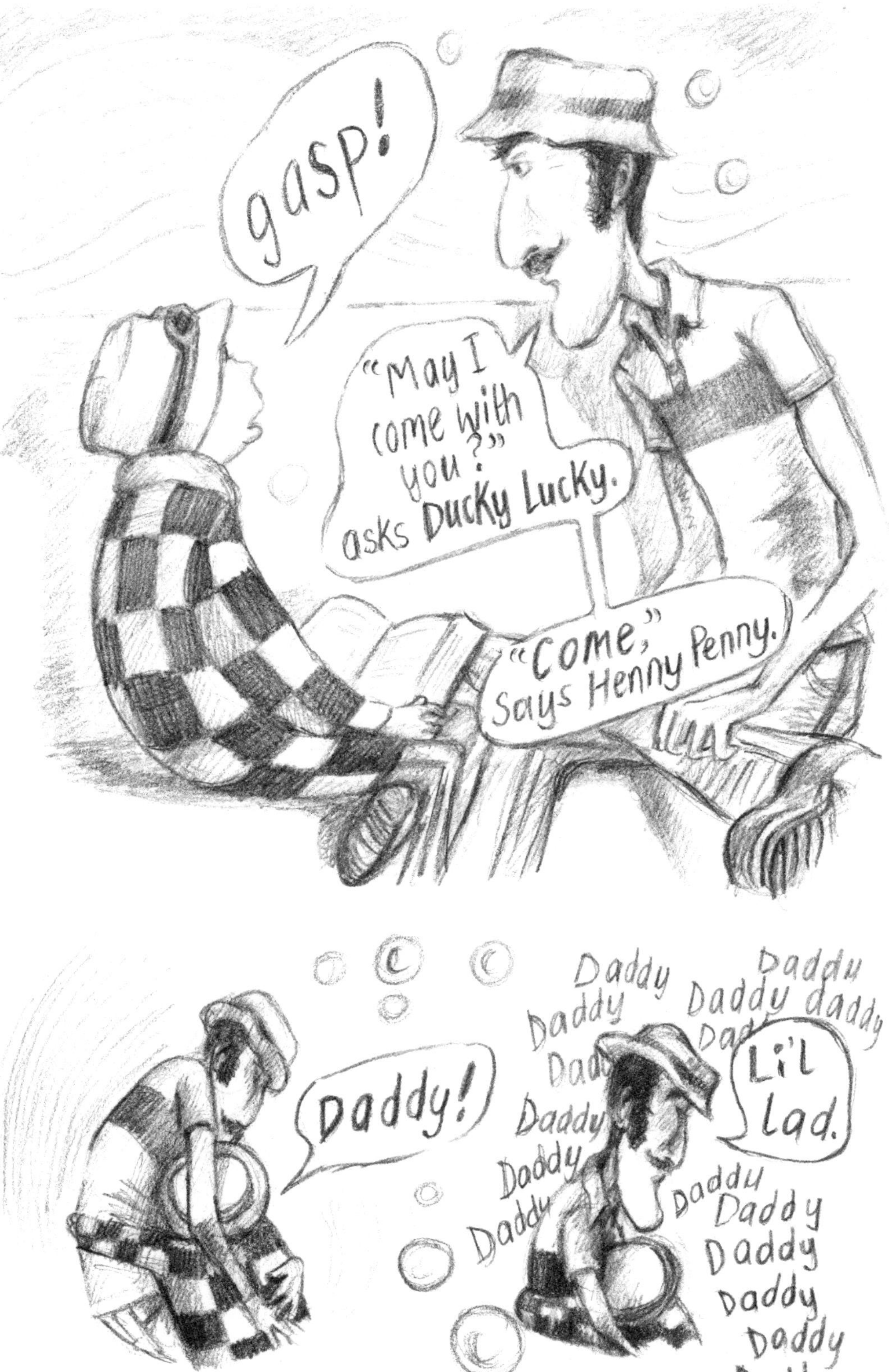
gasp!
"May I come with you?" asks Ducky Lucky.
"Come," Says Henny Penny.
Daddy!
Daddy Daddy Daddy Daddy daddy Daddy Daddy Daddy Daddy Daddy Daddy Daddy Daddy Daddy Daddy Daddy
Li'l Lad.

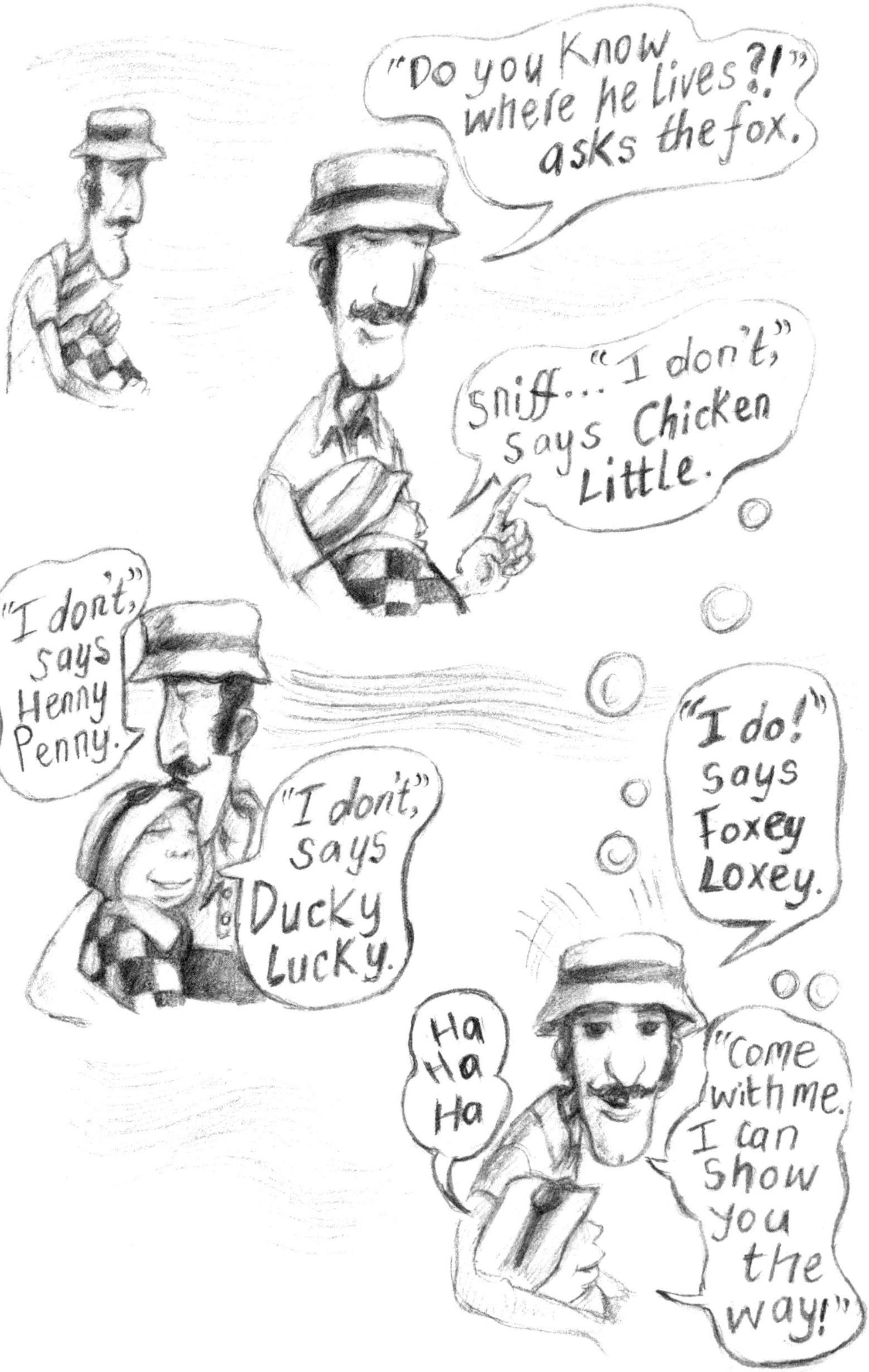
"Do you Know where he lives?!" asks the fox.
Sniff... "I don't," says Chicken Little.
"I don't," says Henny Penny.
"I don't," says Ducky Lucky.
"I do!" says Foxey Loxey.
Ha Ha Ha
"Come with me. I can show you the way!"

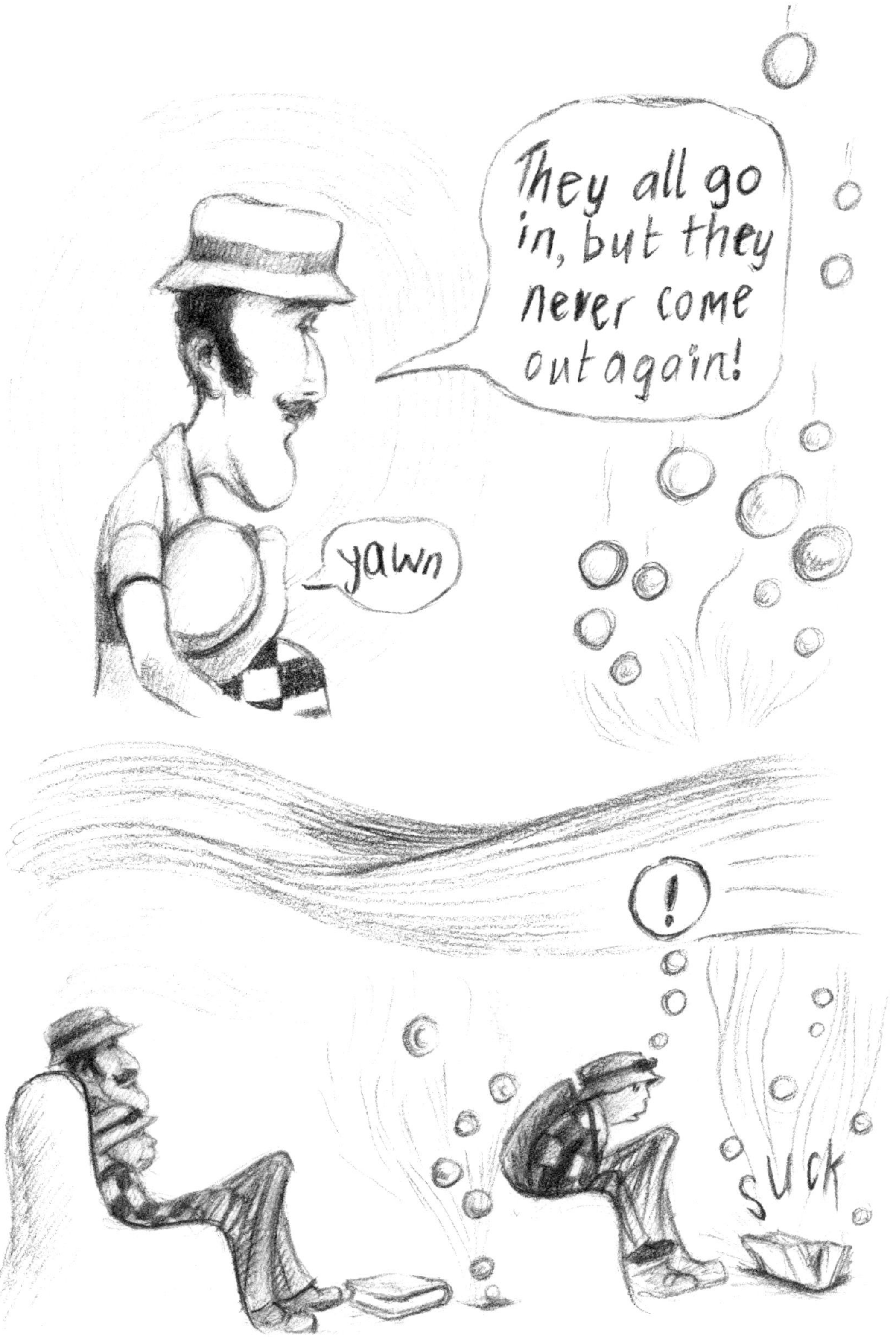
They all go in, but they never come out again!
yawn
!
SUCK

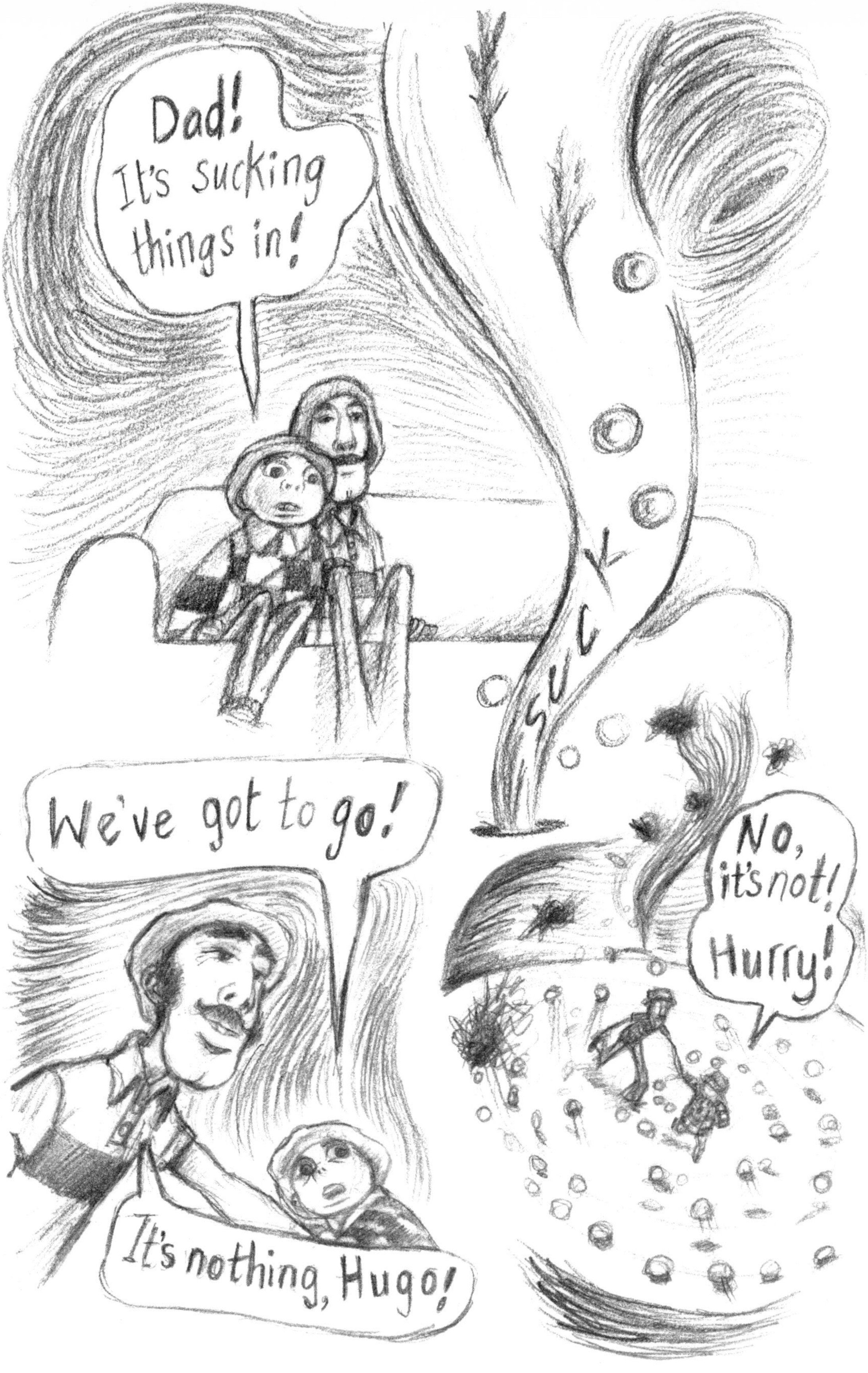
Dad! It's sucking things in!
SUCK
We've got to go!
It's nothing, Hugo!
No, it's not! Hurry!

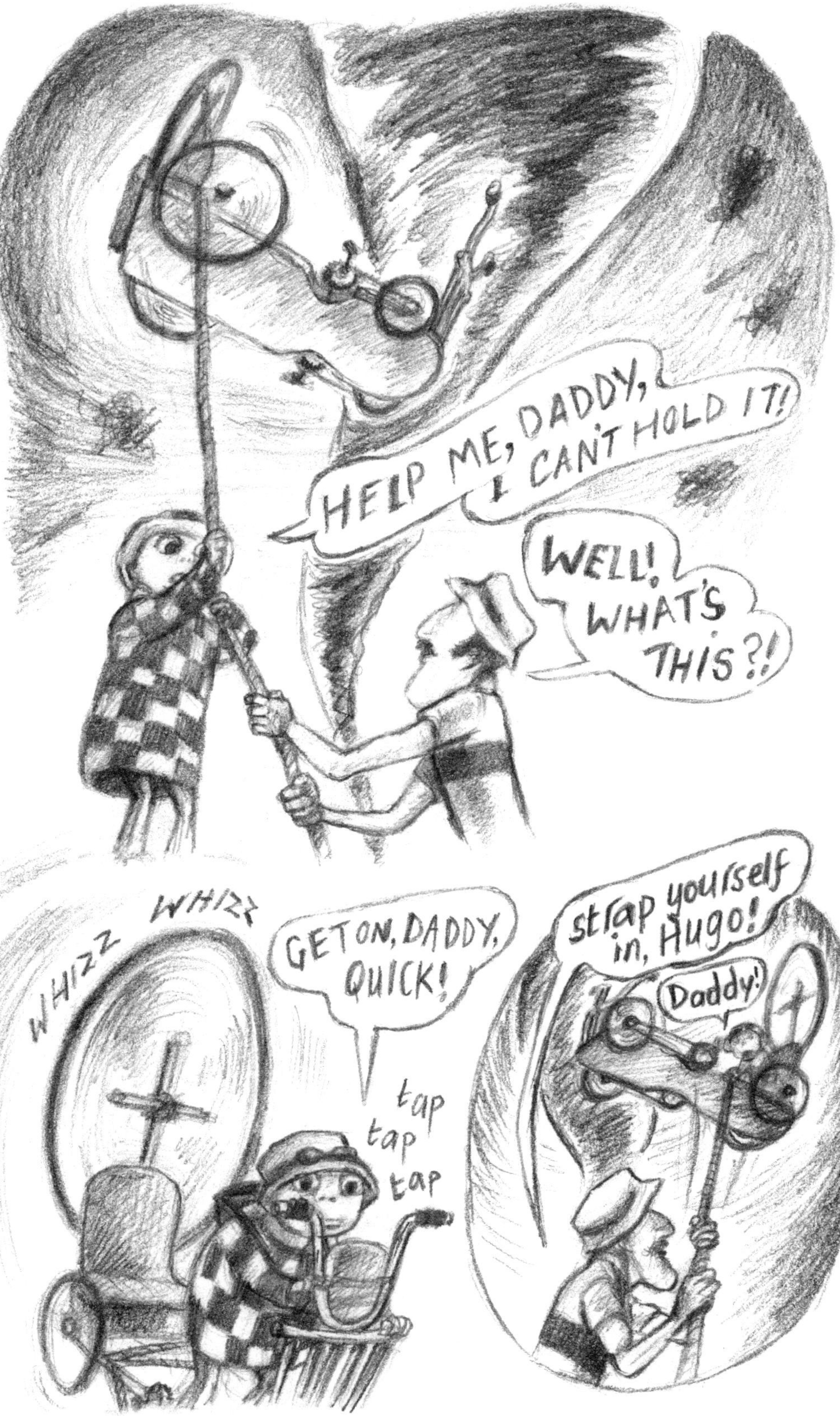
HELP ME, DADDY, I CAN'T HOLD IT!
WELL! WHAT'S THIS?!
WHIZZ
WHIZZ
GET ON, DADDY, QUICK!
tap
tap
tap
strap yourself in, Hugo!
Daddy!

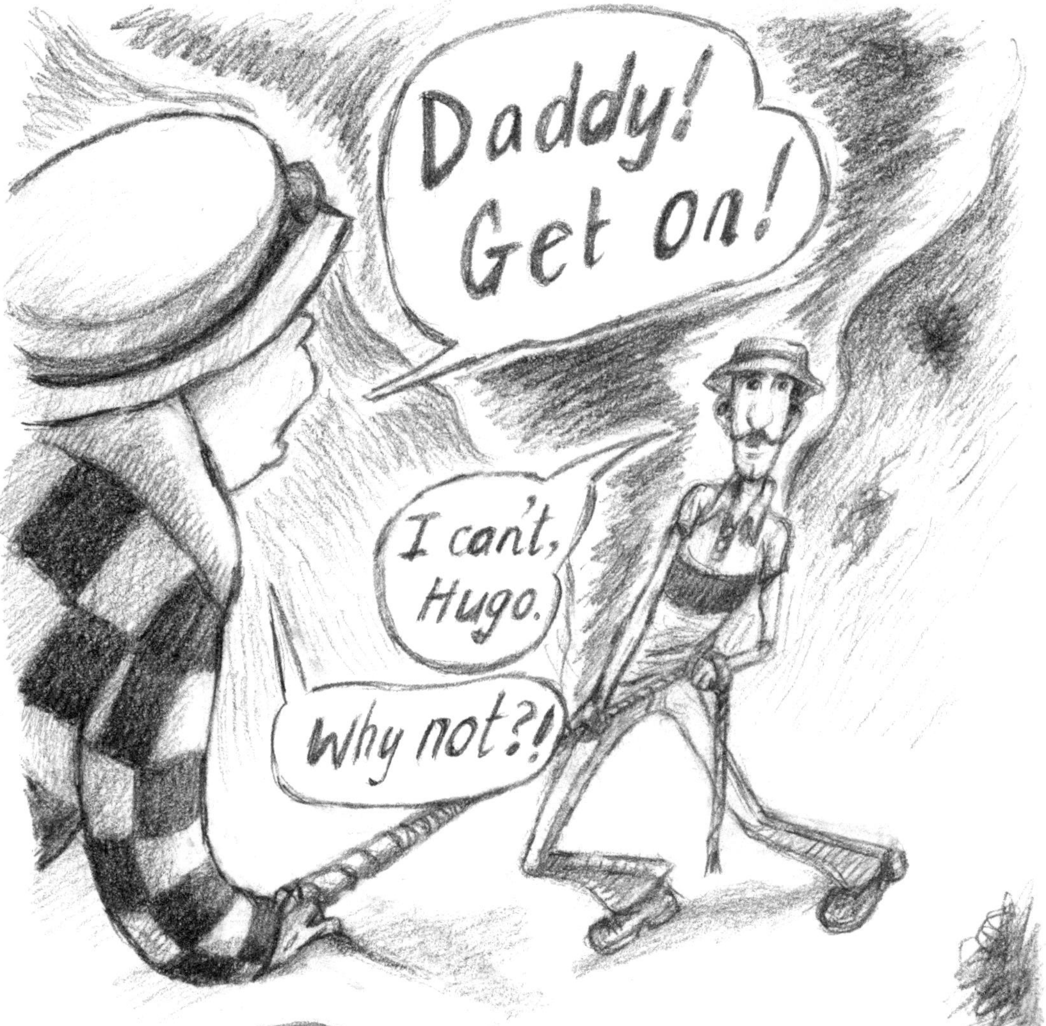
Daddy! Get on!
I can't, Hugo.
Why not?!

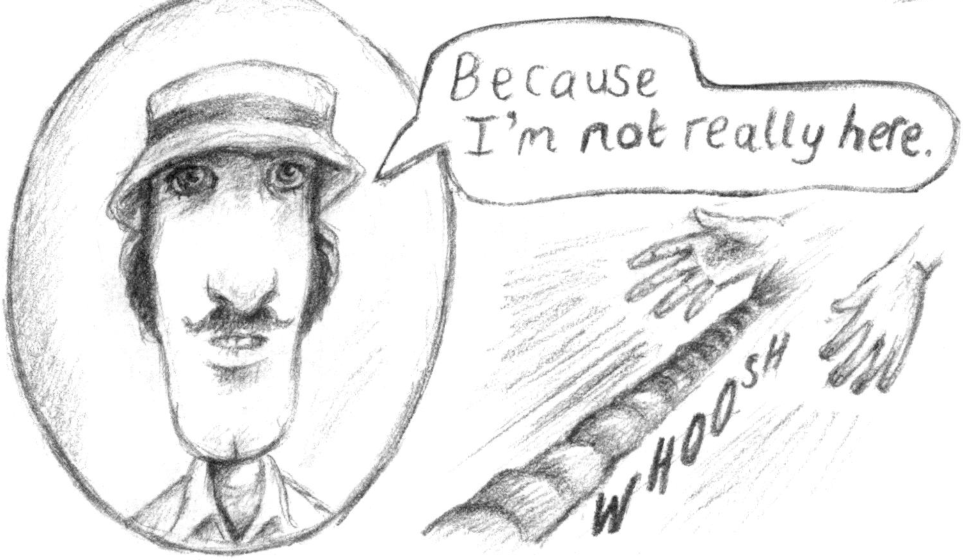
Because I'm not really here.
WHOOSH

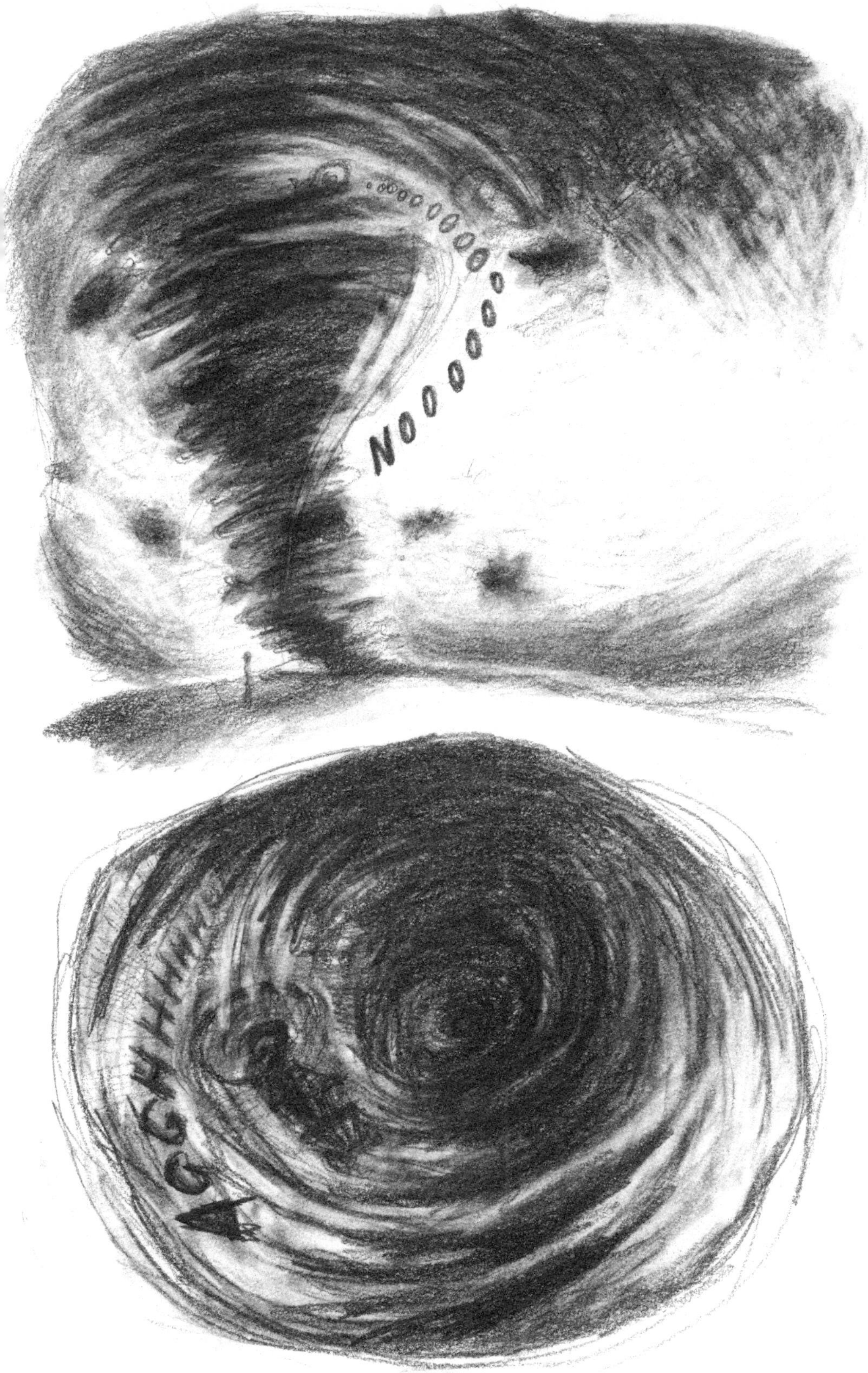
NOOOOOOOOOOOOOOO
AGGHHHHH

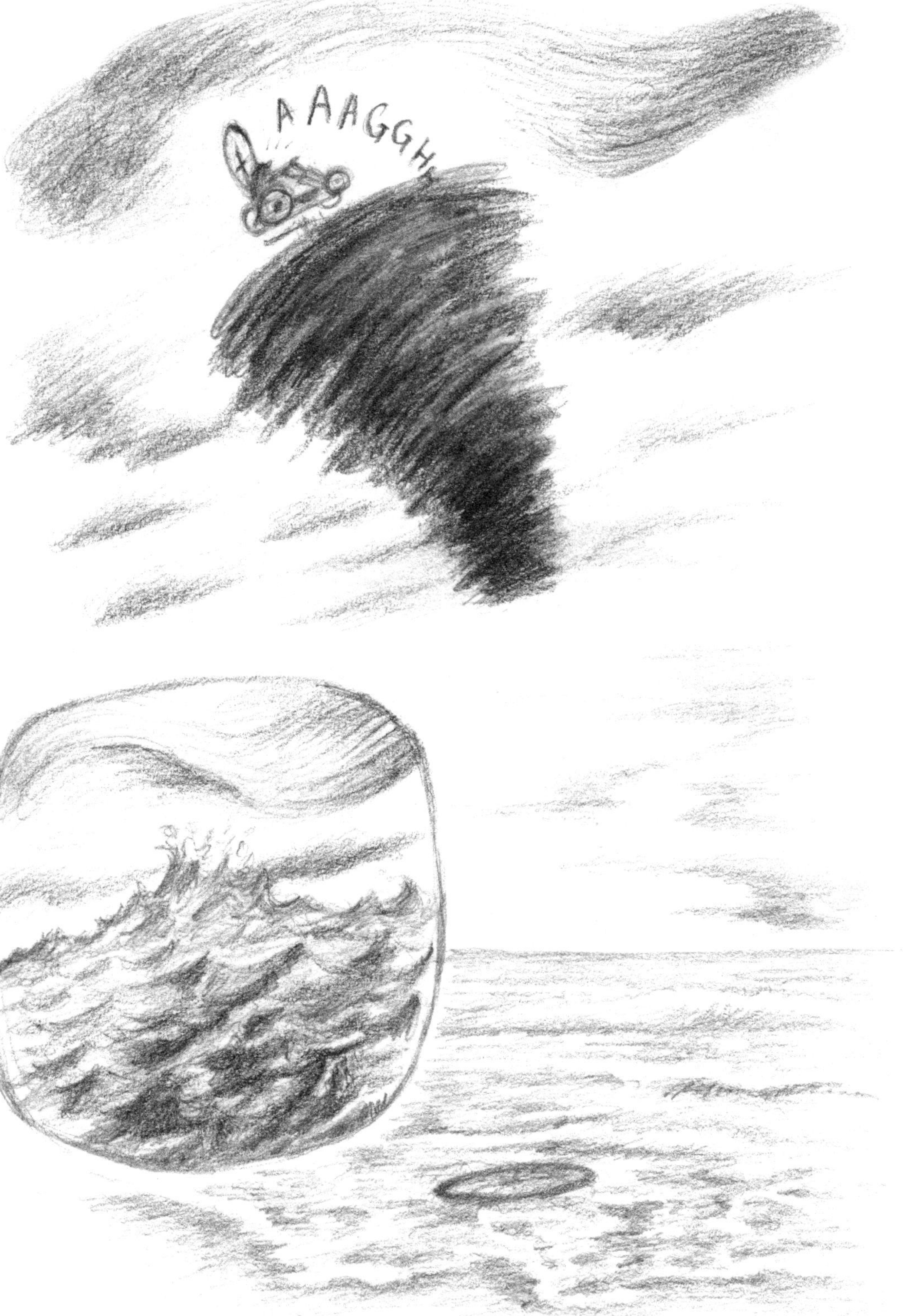
AAAGGH

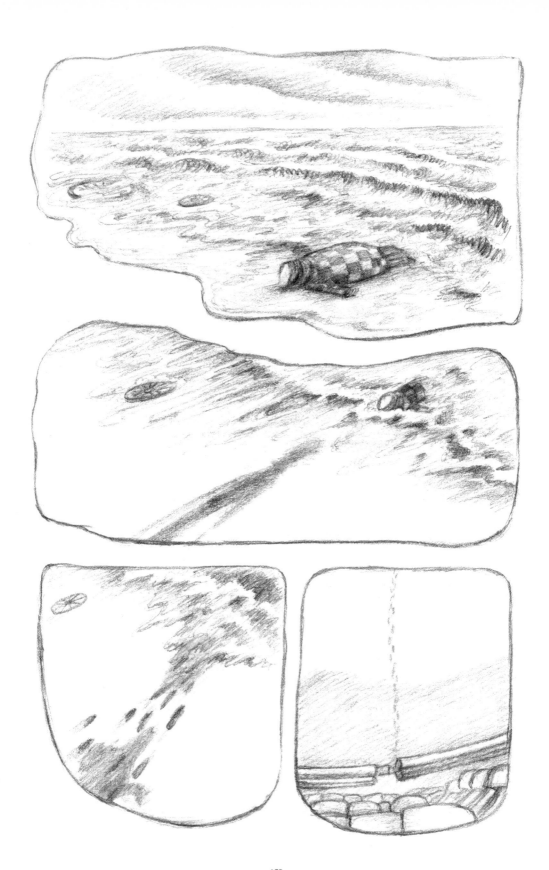

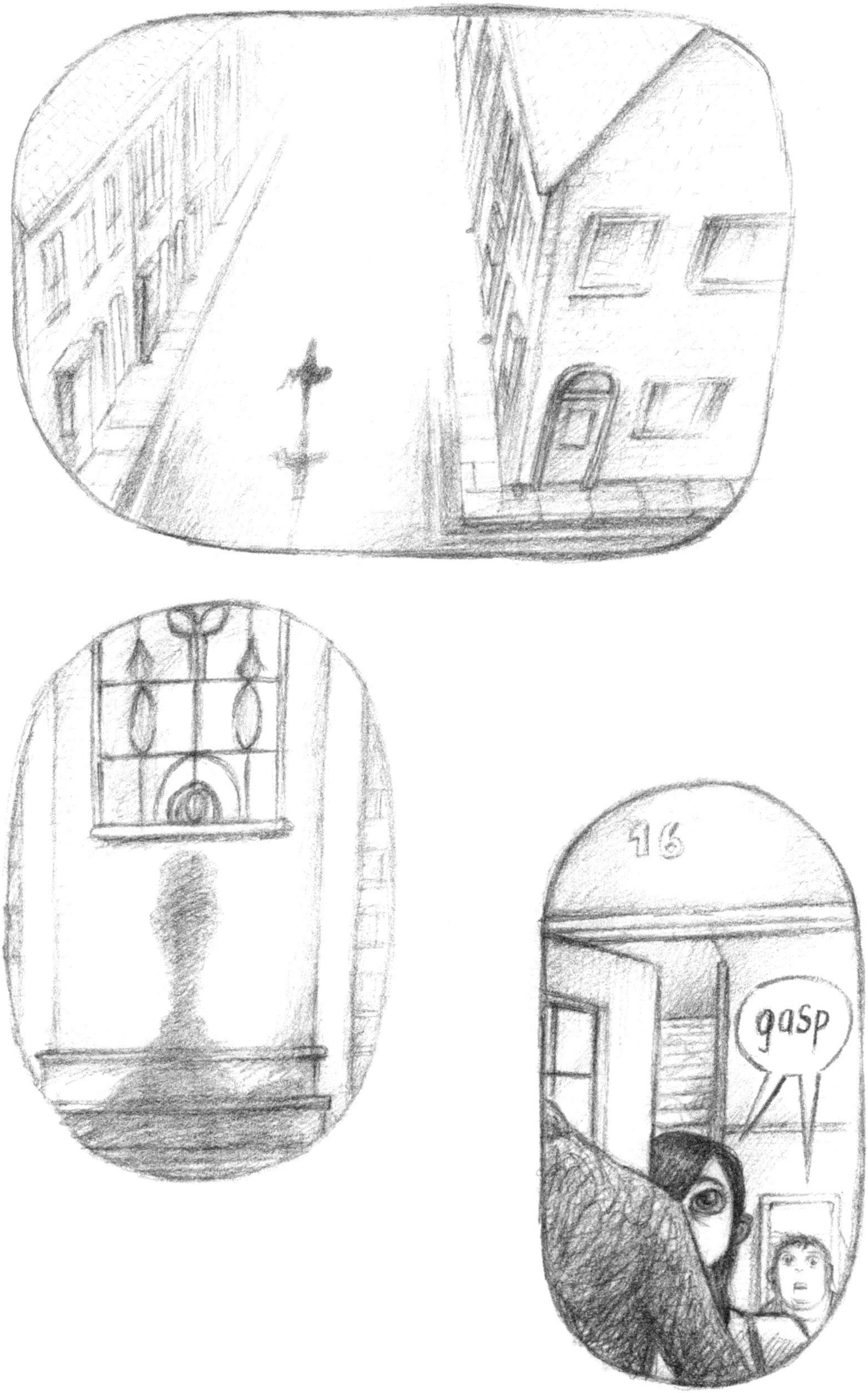
16
gasp

Chapter Eleven

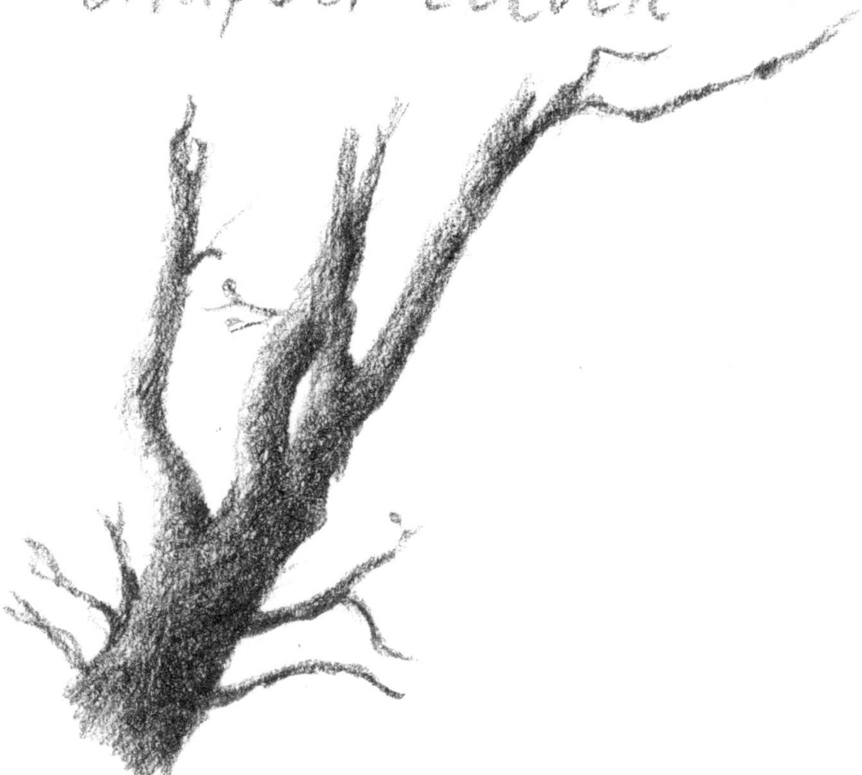

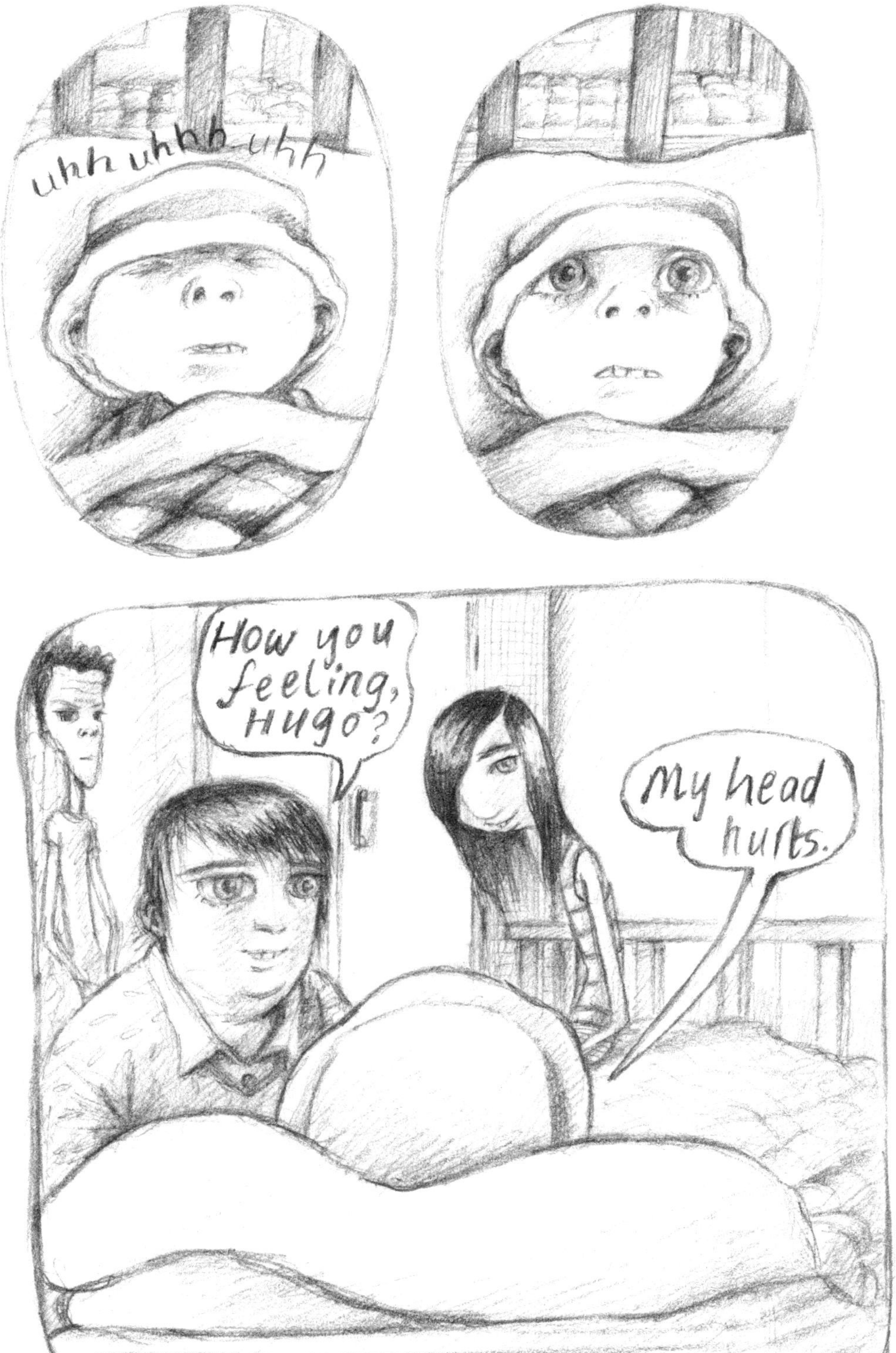
uhh uhhh uhh
How you feeling, Hugo?
My head hurts.

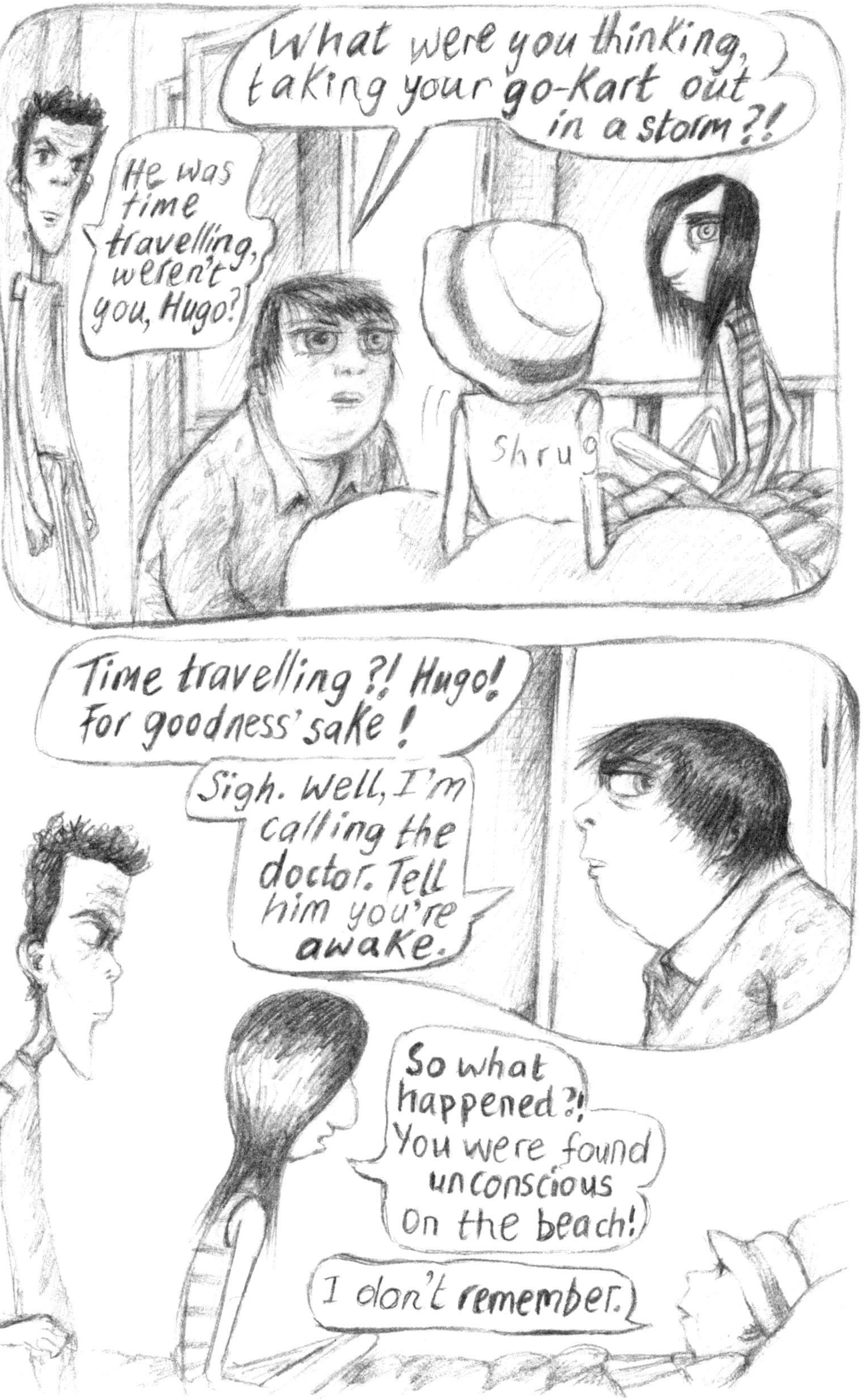
What were you thinking, taking your go-kart out in a storm?!
He was time travelling, weren't you, Hugo?
Shrug
Time travelling?! Hugo! For goodness' sake!
Sigh. Well, I'm calling the doctor. Tell him you're awake.
So what happened?! You were found unconscious on the beach!
I don't remember.

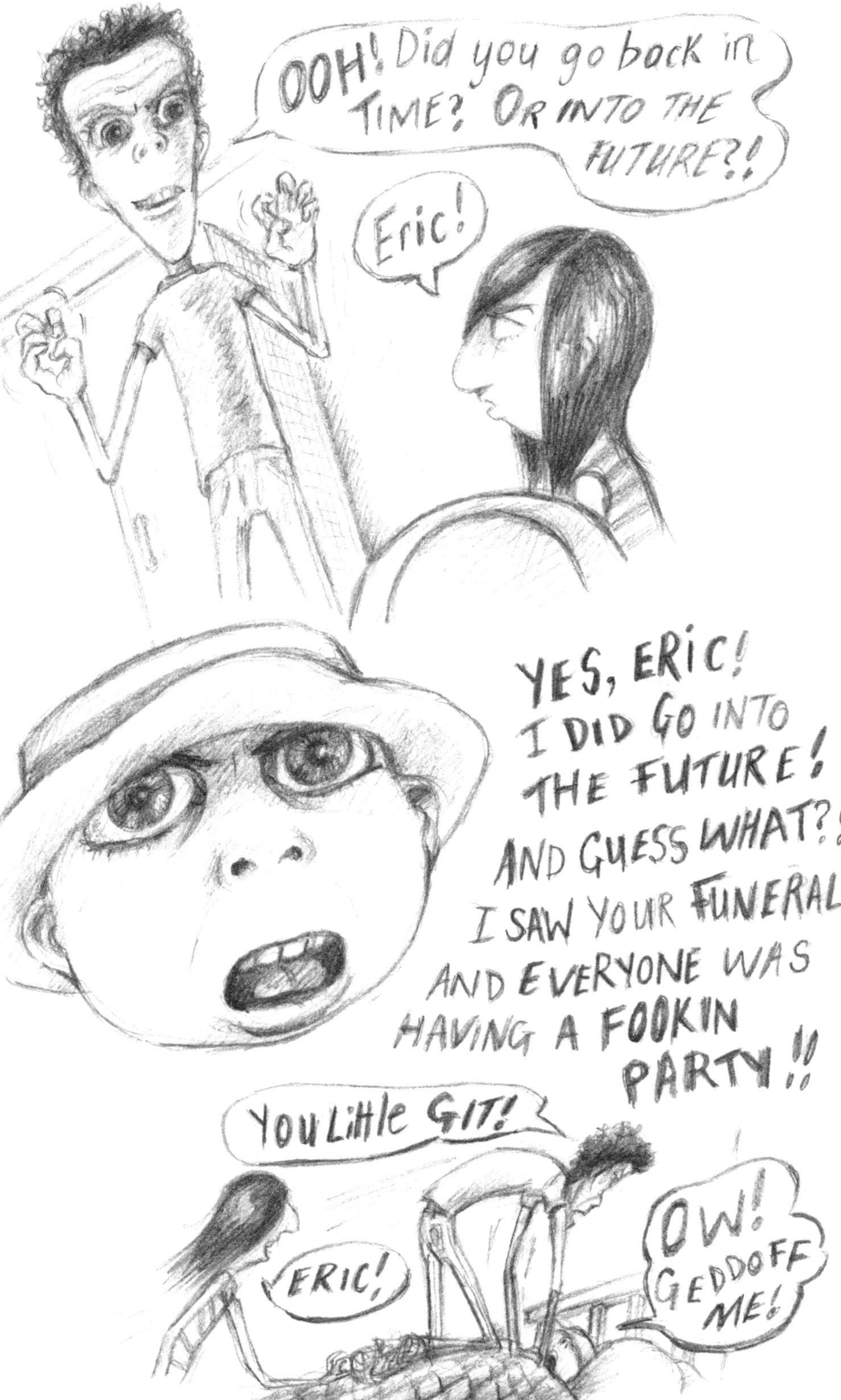
OOH! Did you go back in TIME? OR INTO THE FUTURE?!
Eric!
YES, ERIC! I DID GO INTO THE FUTURE! AND GUESS WHAT?! I SAW YOUR FUNERAL! AND EVERYONE WAS HAVING A FOOKIN PARTY!!
You Little GIT!
ERIC!
OW! GEDDOFF ME!

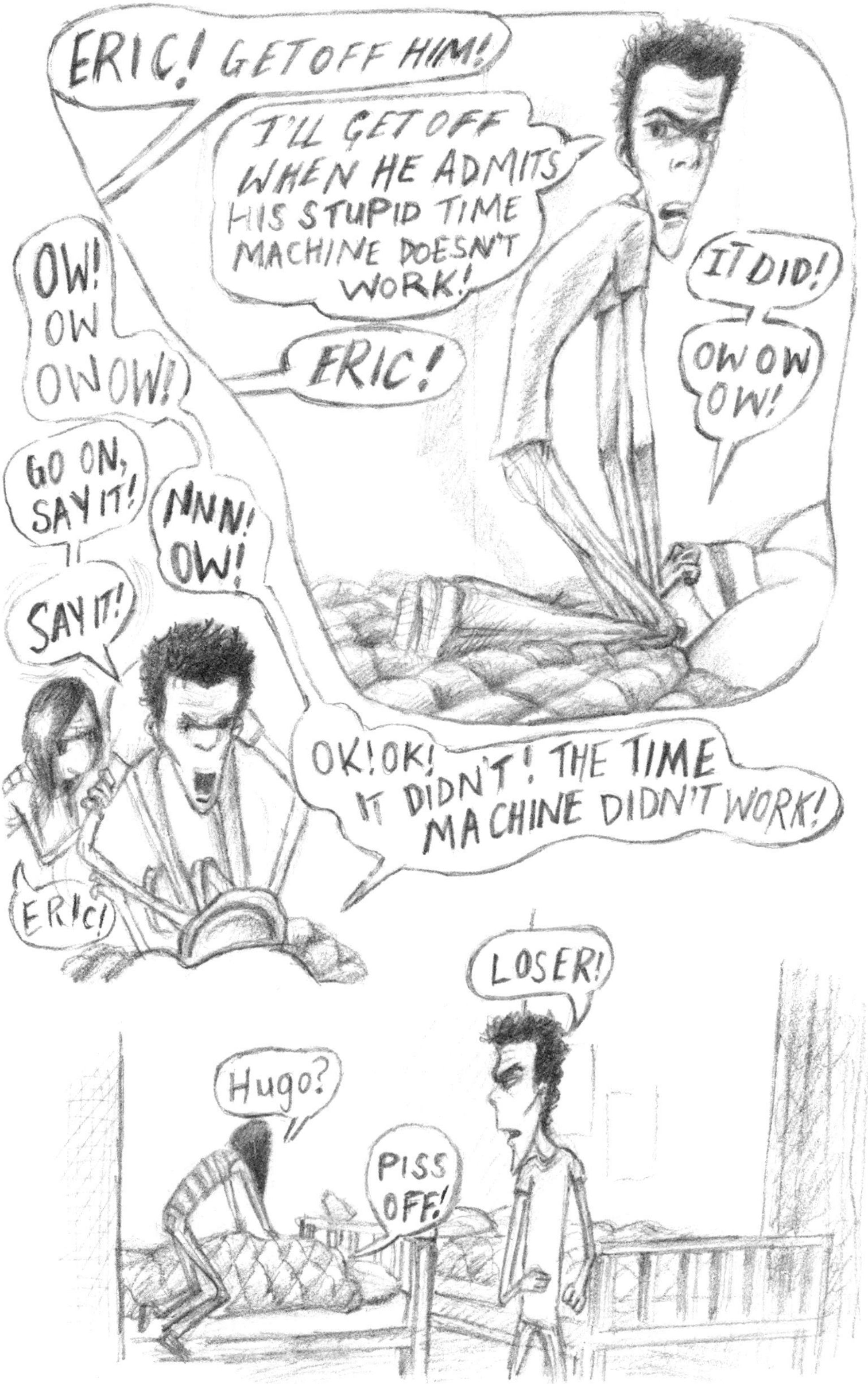
ERIC! GET OFF HIM!
I'LL GET OFF WHEN HE ADMITS HIS STUPID TIME MACHINE DOESN'T WORK!
IT DID!
OW OW OW!
OW! OW OWOW!
ERIC!
GO ON, SAY IT!
NNN! OW!
SAY IT!
OK! OK! IT DIDN'T! THE TIME MACHINE DIDN'T WORK!
ERIC!
LOSER!
Hugo?
PISS OFF!

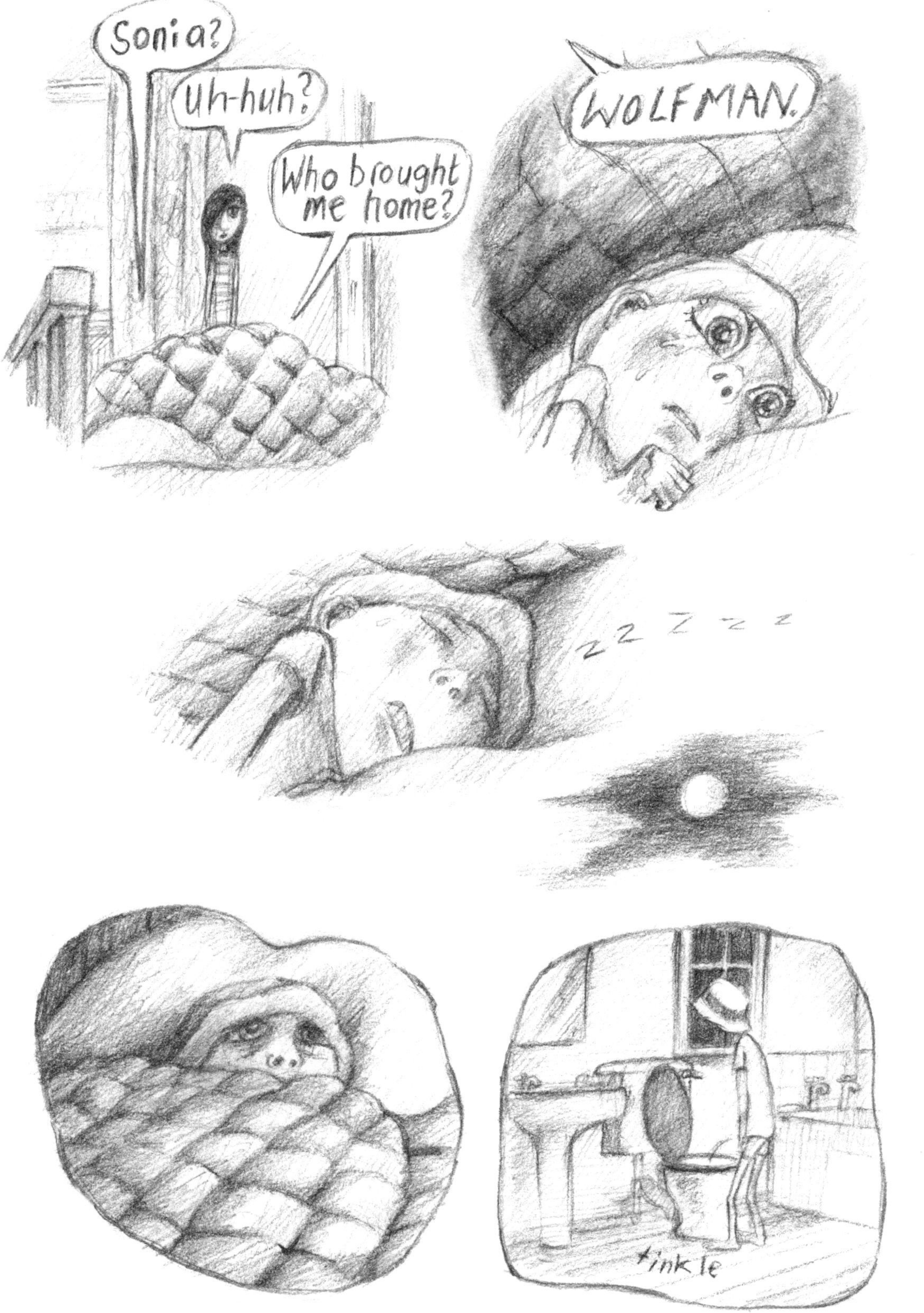
Sonia?
Uh-huh?
Who brought me home?
WOLFMAN.
z z Z z z
tinkle

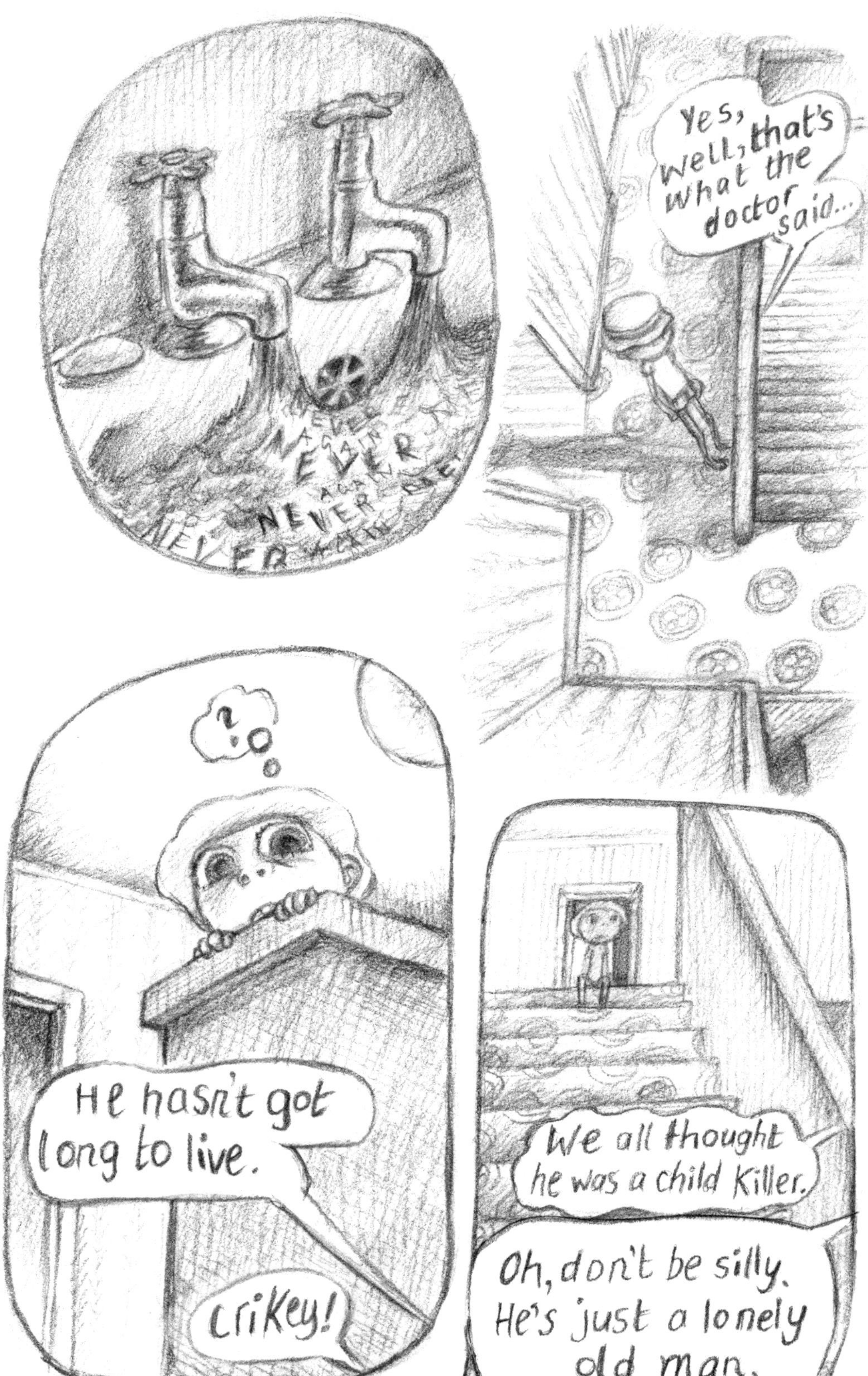
NEVER AGAIN NEVER AGAIN NEVER
Yes, well, that's what the doctor said...
He hasn't got long to live.
Crikey!
We all thought he was a child Killer.
Oh, don't be silly. He's just a lonely old man.

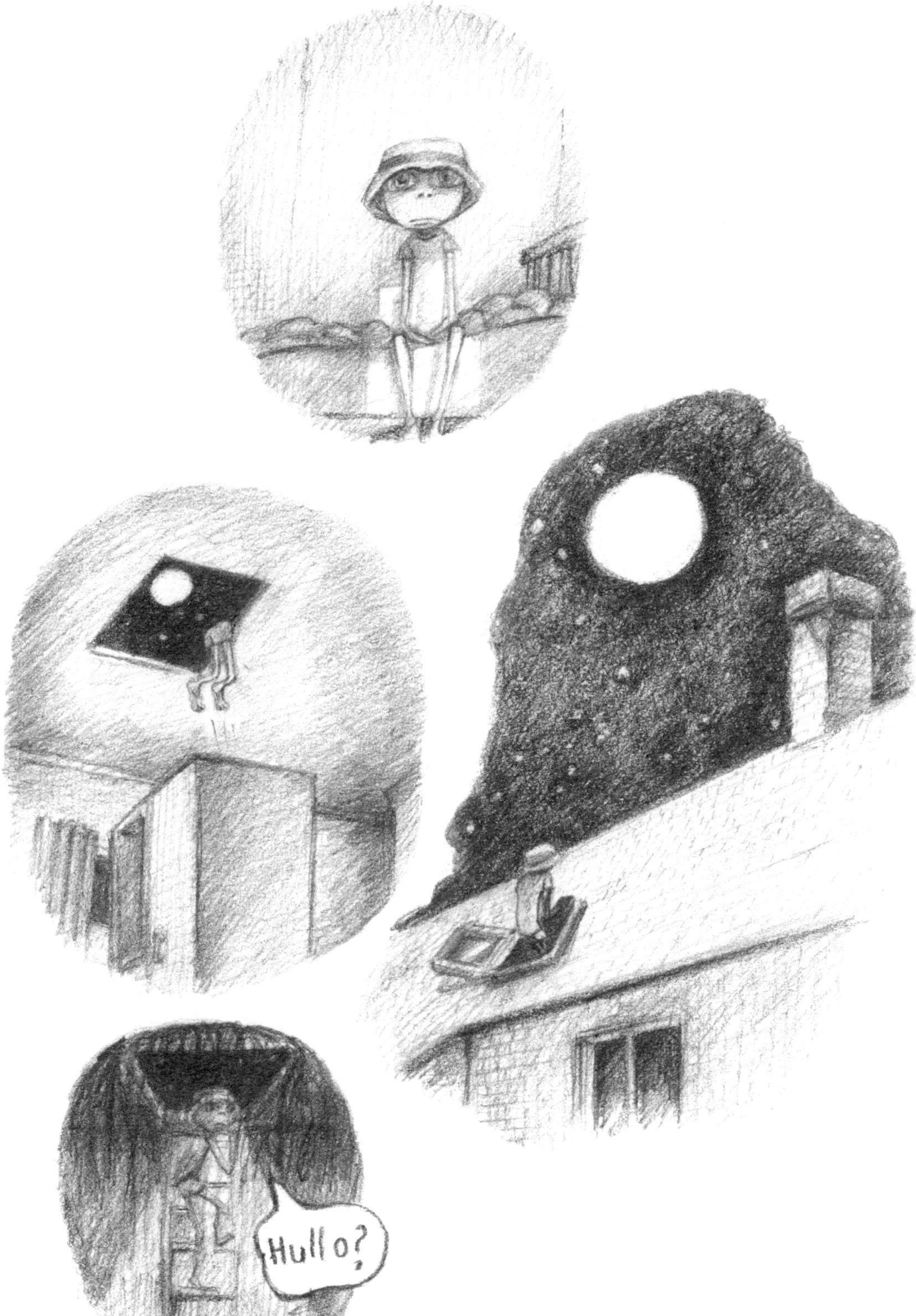
Hullo?

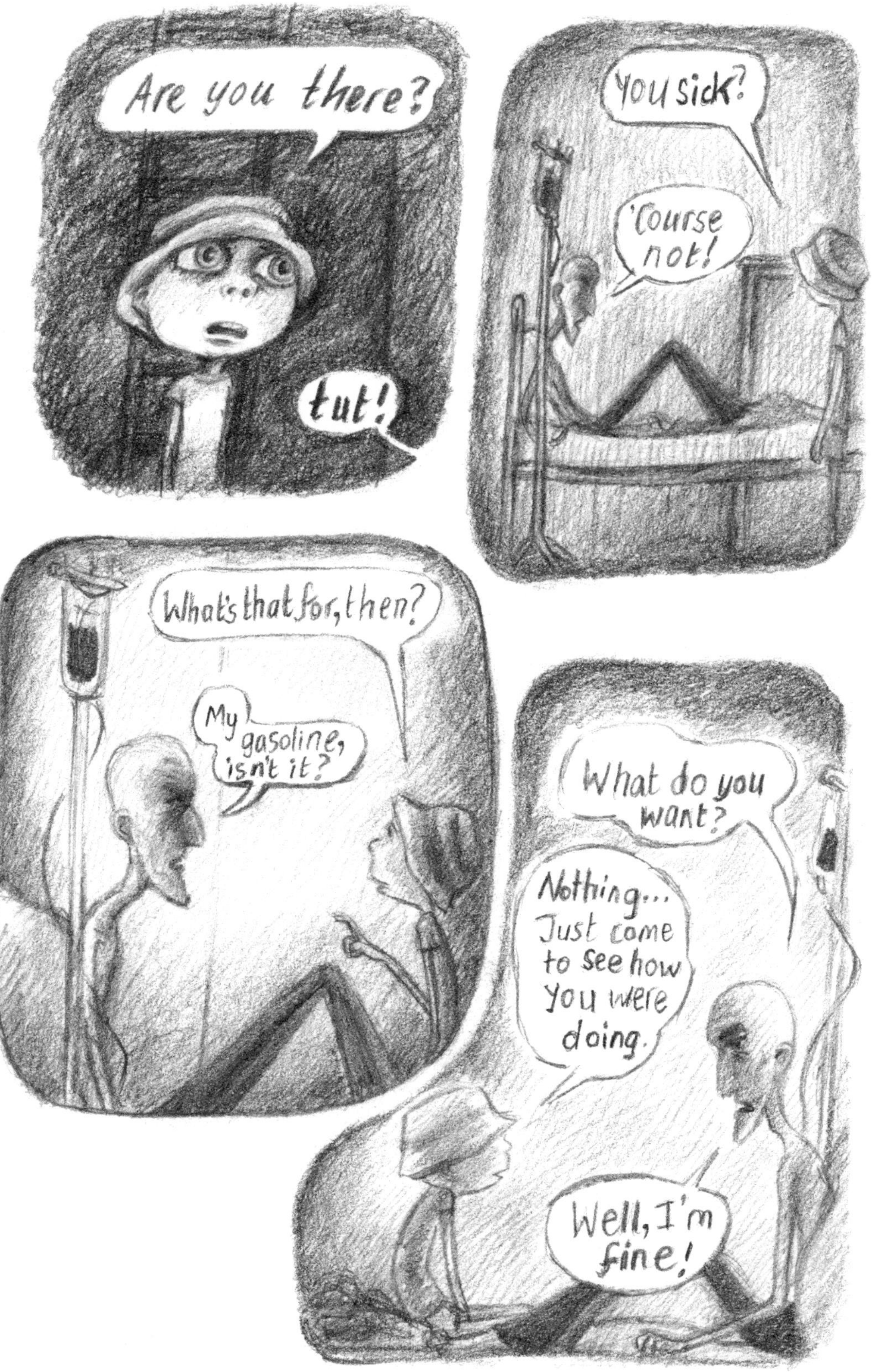
Are you there?
tut!
You sick?
'Course not!
What's that for, then?
My gasoline, isn't it?
What do you want?
Nothing... Just come to see how you were doing.
Well, I'm fine!

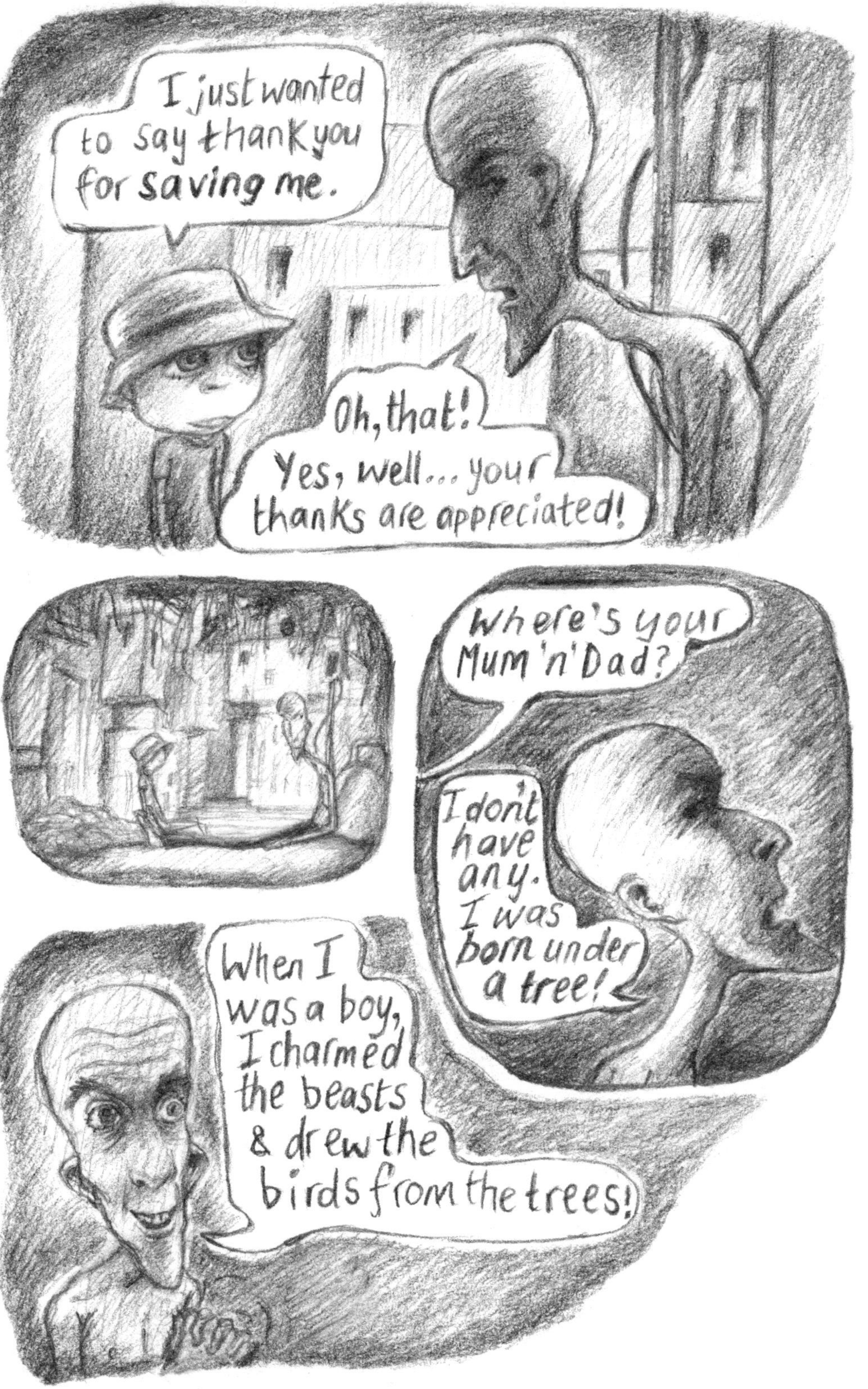
I just wanted to say thank you for saving me.
Oh, that! Yes, well... your thanks are appreciated!
Where's your Mum 'n' Dad?
I don't have any. I was born under a tree!
When I was a boy, I charmed the beasts & drew the birds from the trees!

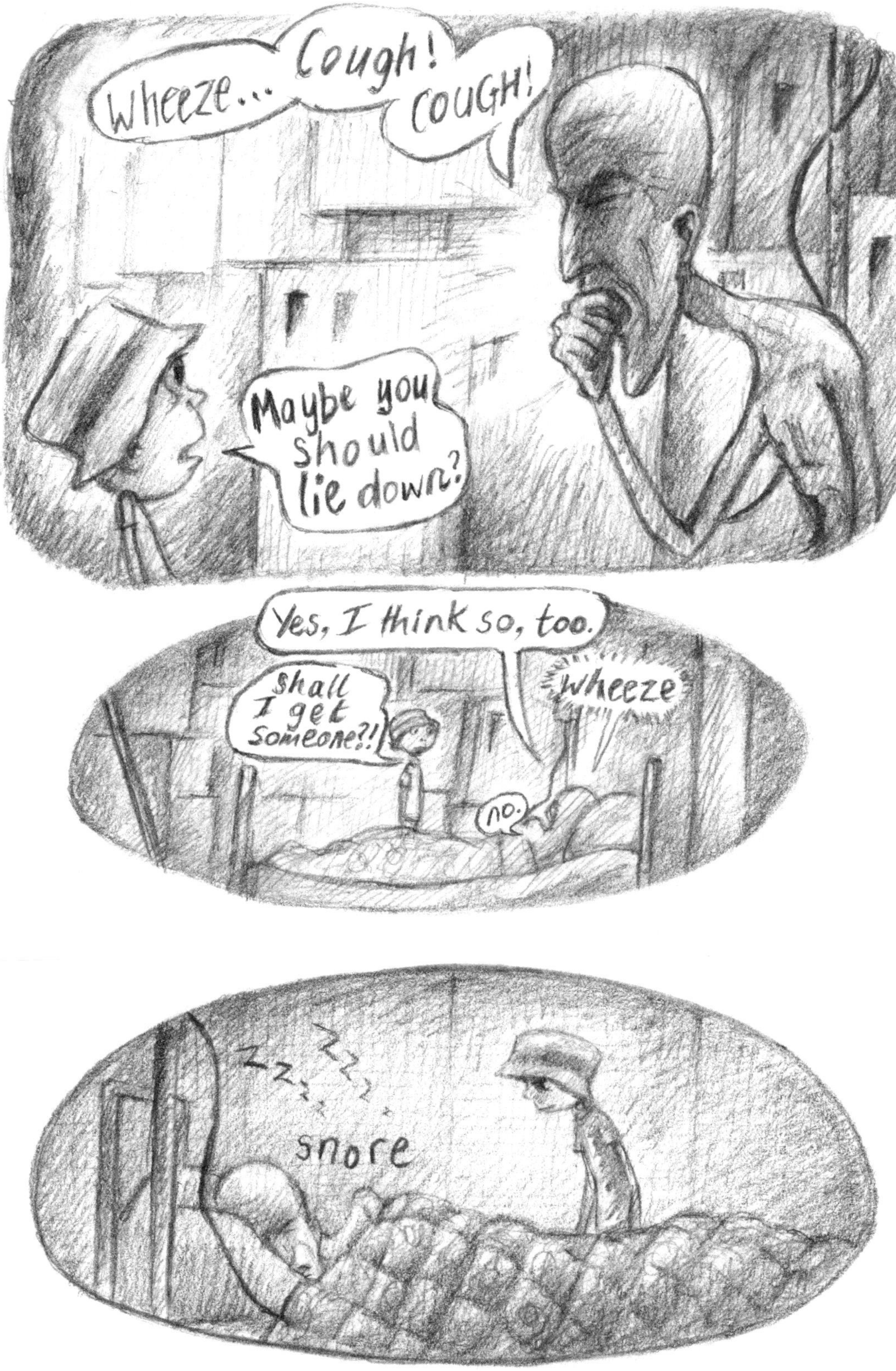
Wheeze...
Cough!
COUGH!
Maybe you should lie down?
Yes, I think so, too.
Shall I get someone?!
Wheeze
no.
Z z z
Z z z
snore

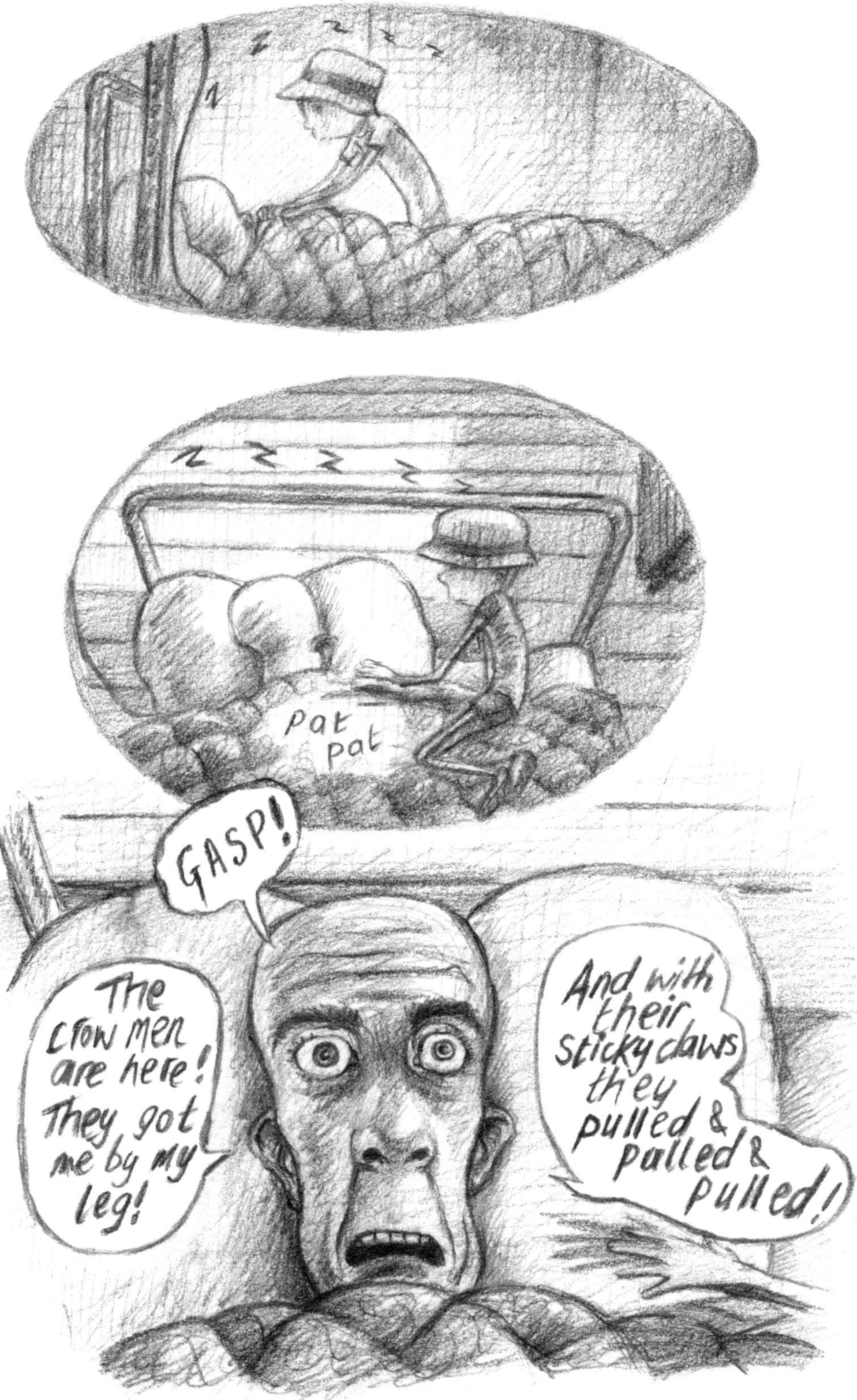
pat pat
GASP!
The crow men are here! They got me by my leg!
And with their sticky claws they pulled & pulled & pulled!

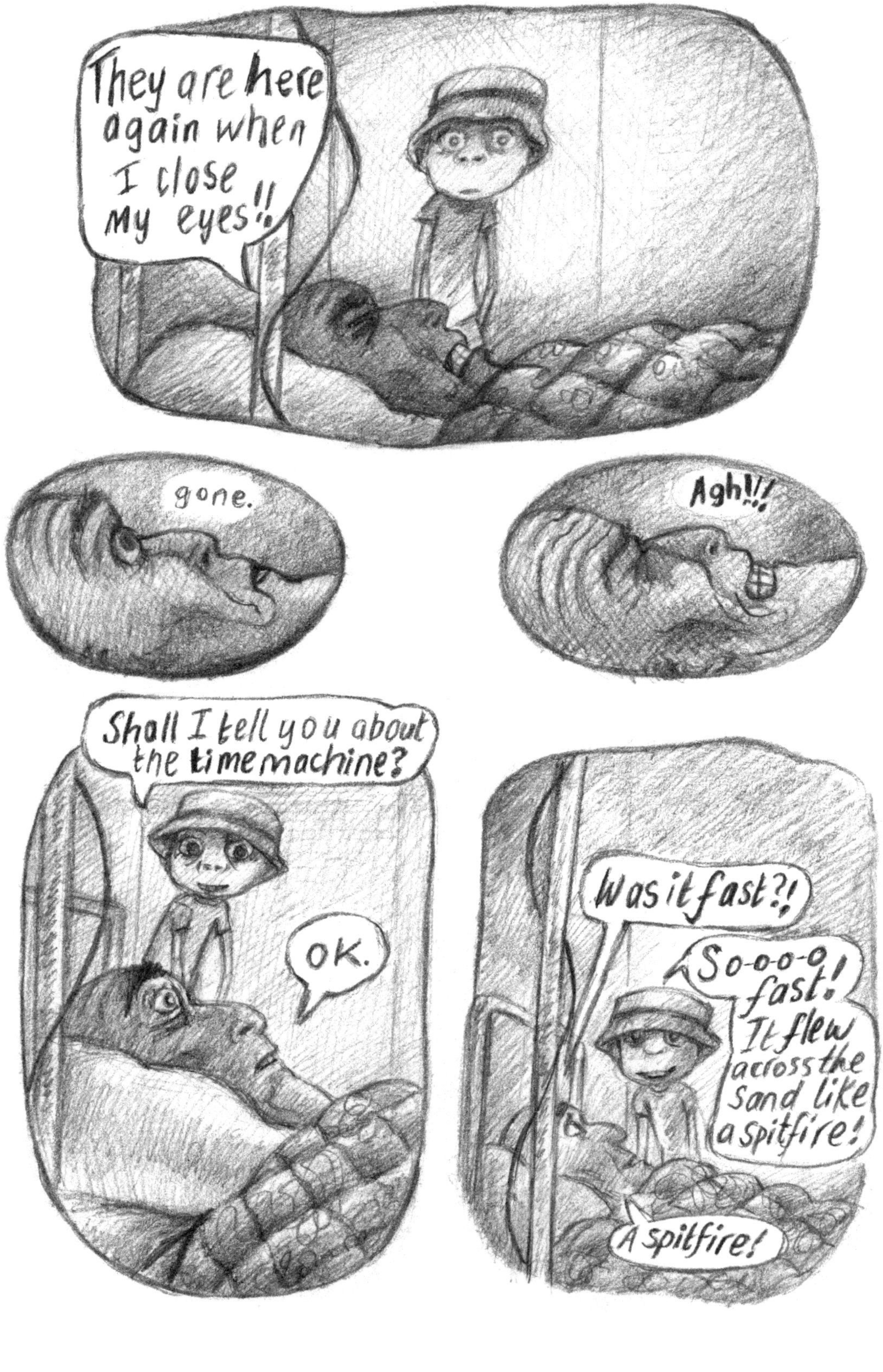
They are here again when I close my eyes!!
gone.
Agh!!!
Shall I tell you about the time machine?
OK.
Was it fast?!
So-o-o-o fast! It flew across the sand like a spitfire!
A spitfire!

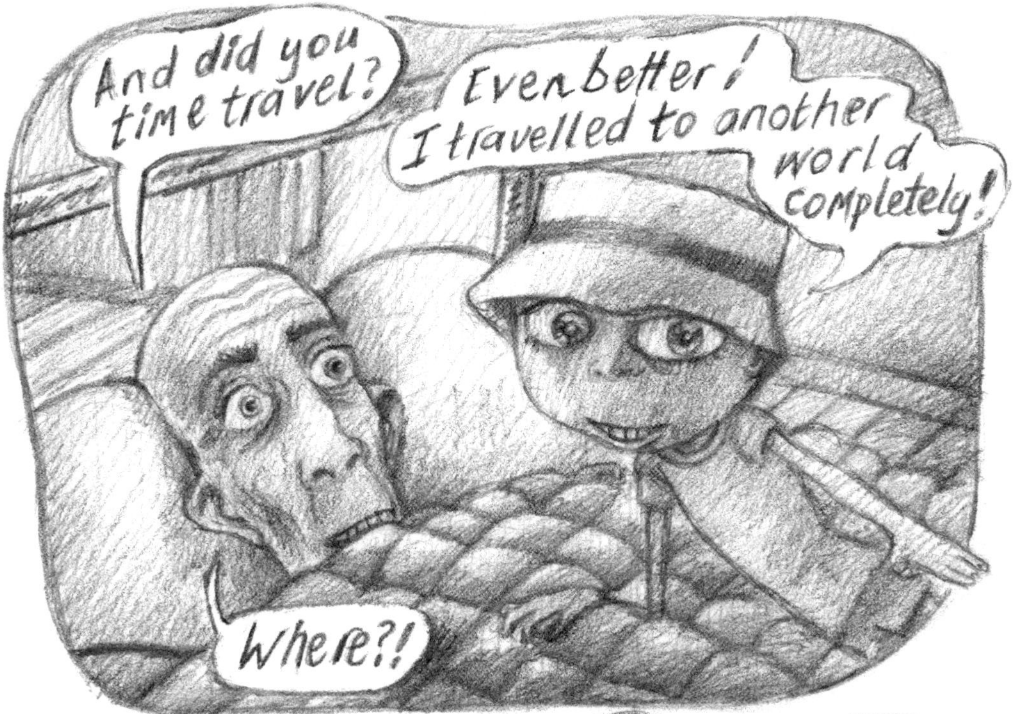
And did you time travel?
Even better! I travelled to another world completely!
Where?!

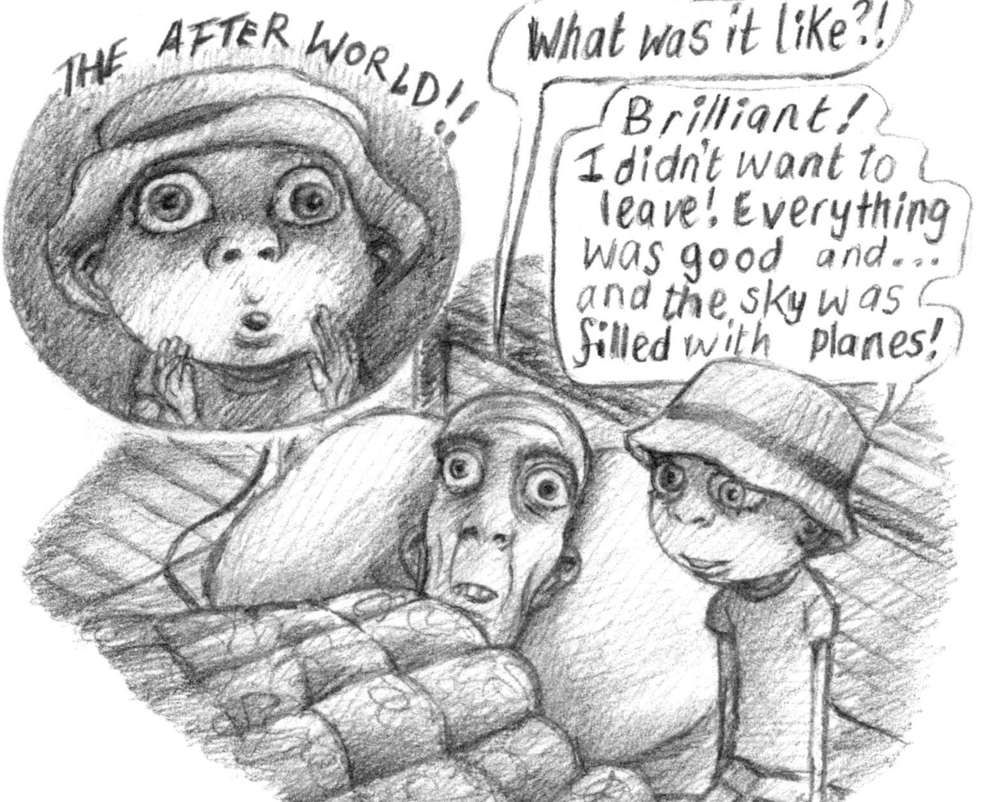
THE AFTER WORLD!!
What was it like?!
Brilliant! I didn't want to leave! Everything was good and... and the sky was filled with planes!

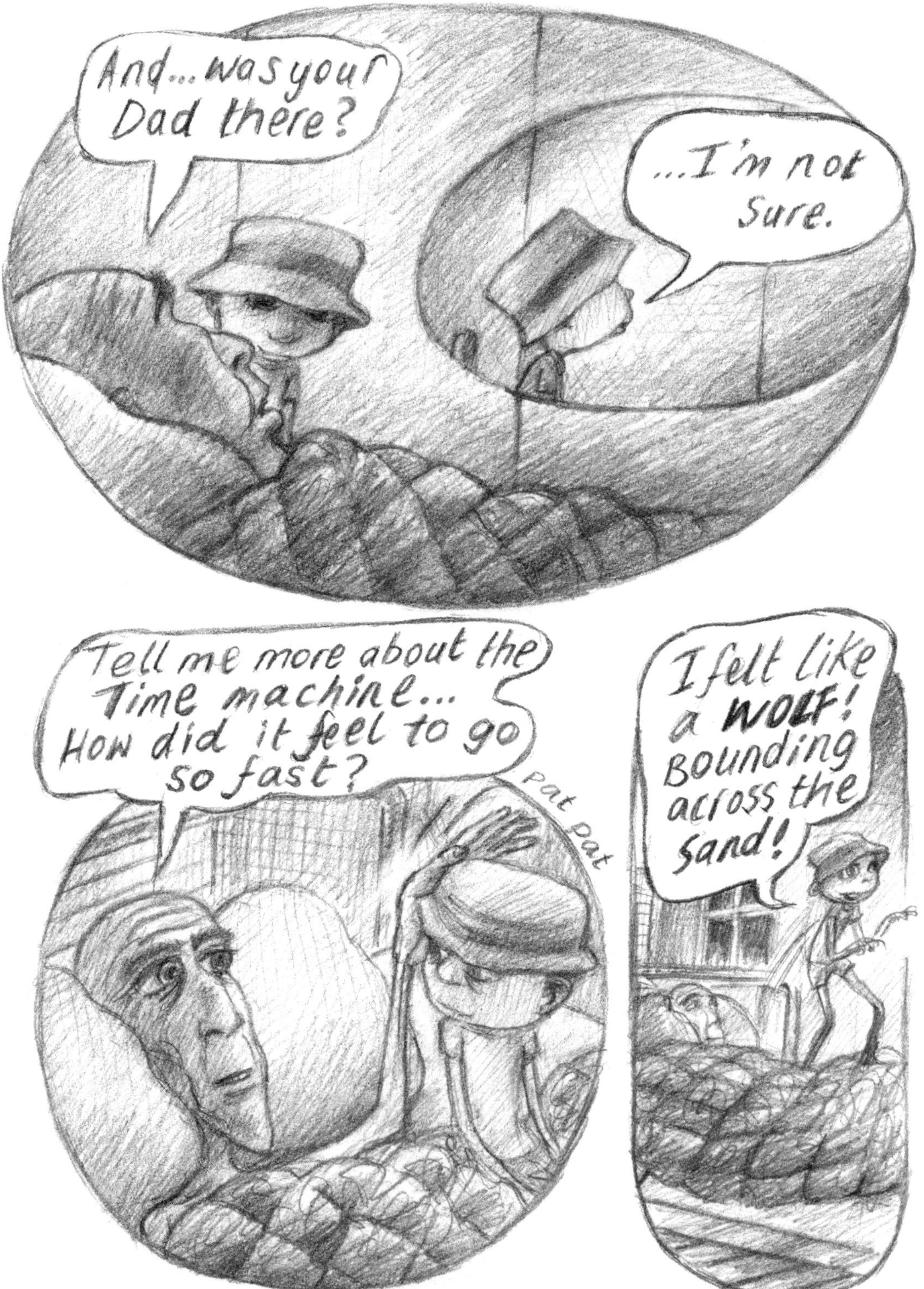
And... was your Dad there?
...I'm not sure.
Tell me more about the Time machine... How did it feel to go so fast?
pat pat
I felt like a WOLF! Bounding across the sand!

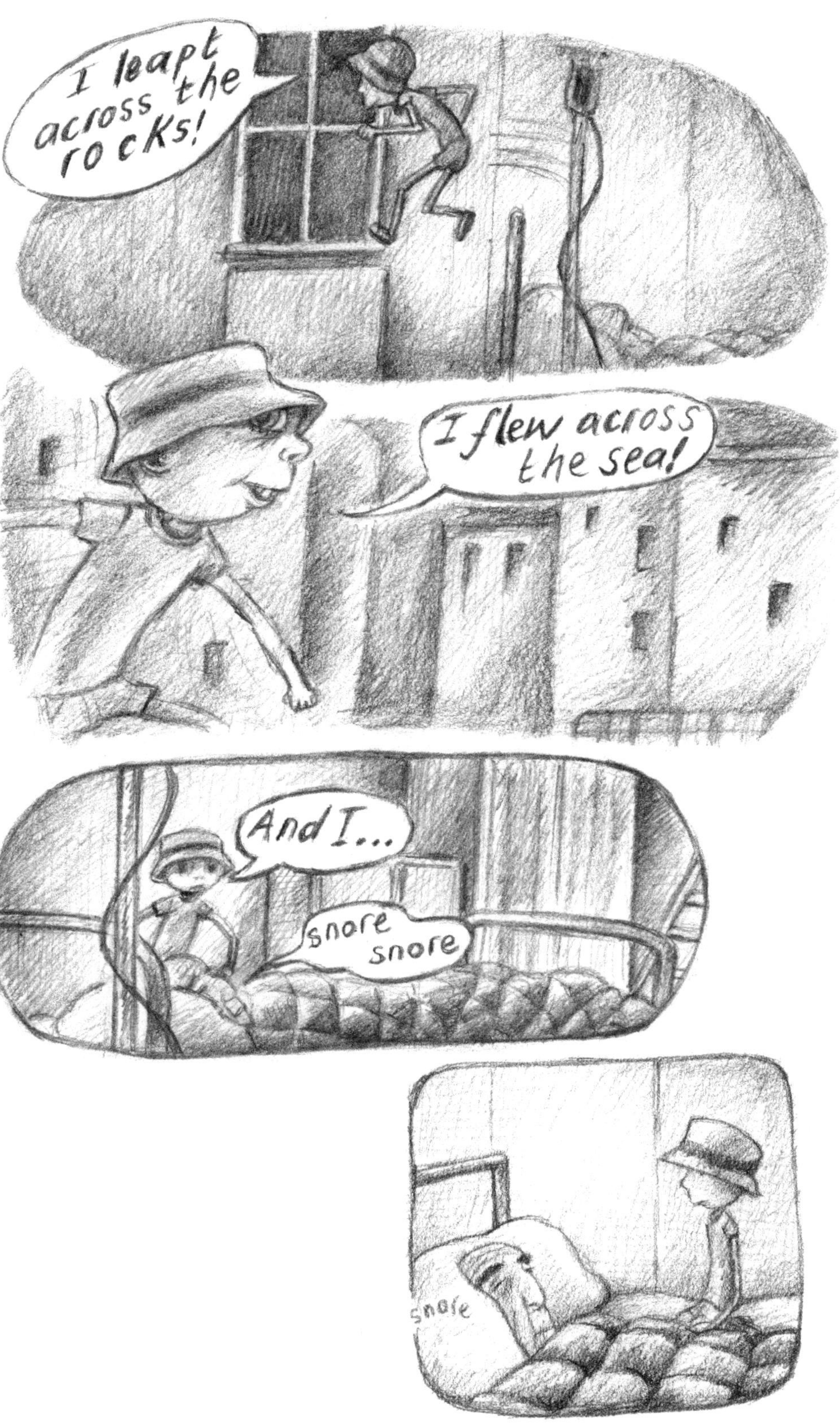
I leapt across the rocks!
I flew across the sea!
And I...
snore snore
snore

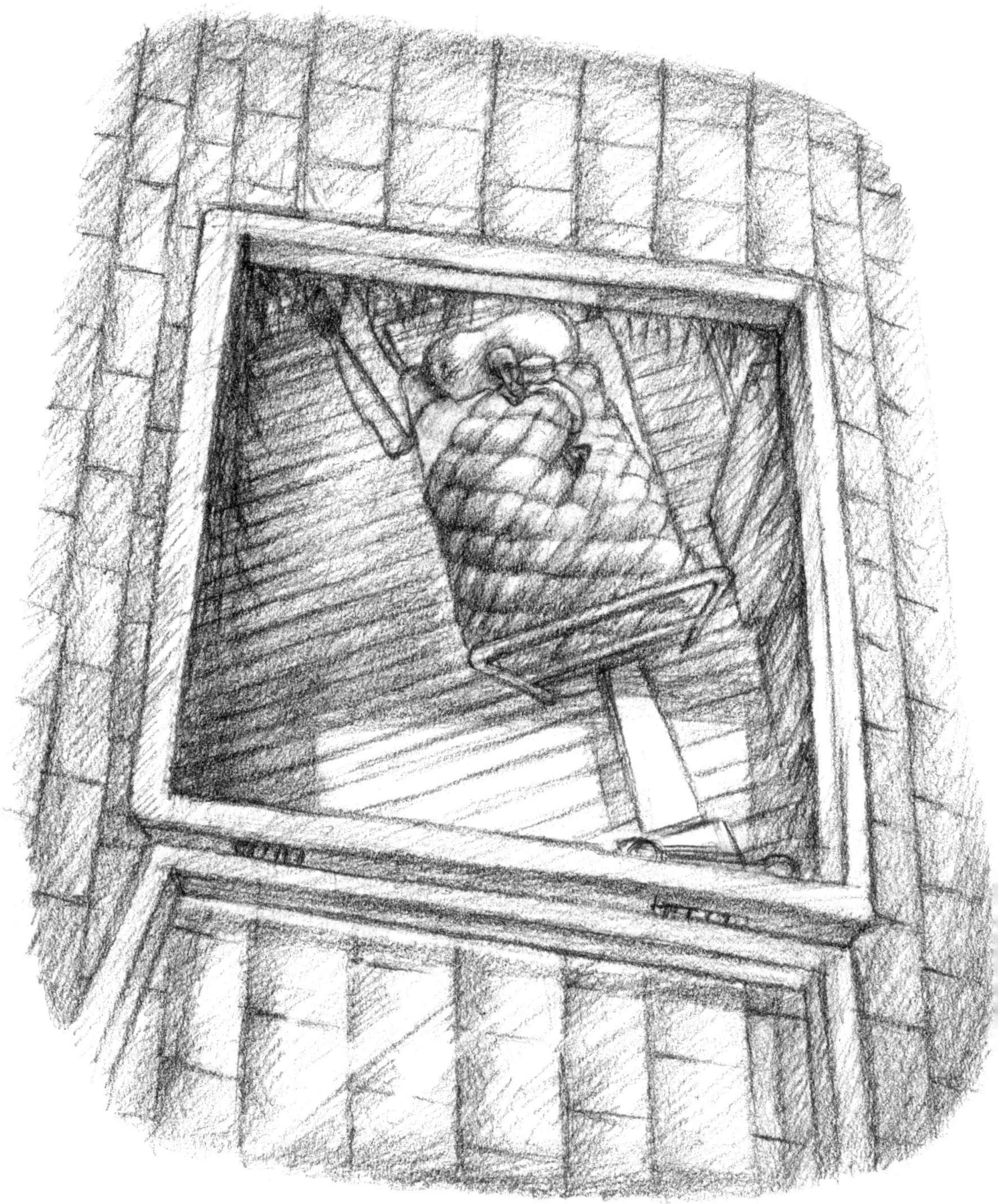

Epilogue

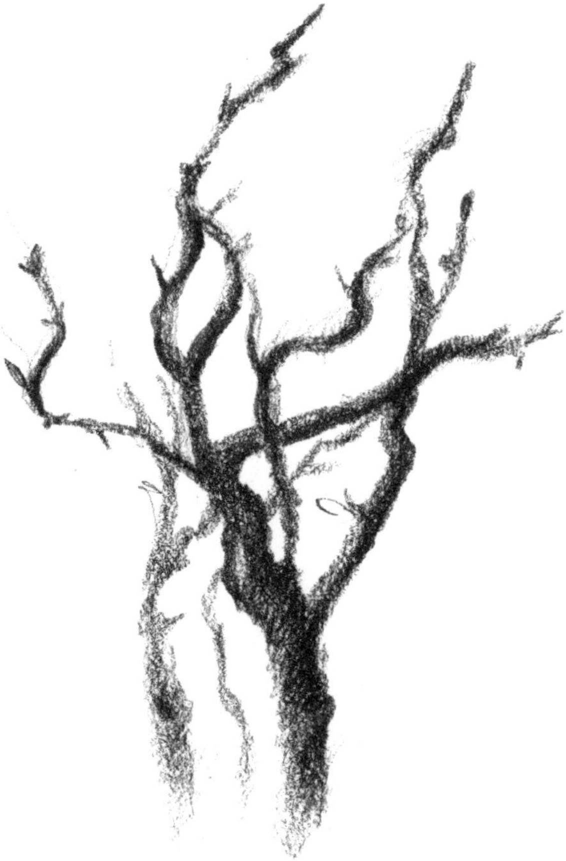

Two weeks later

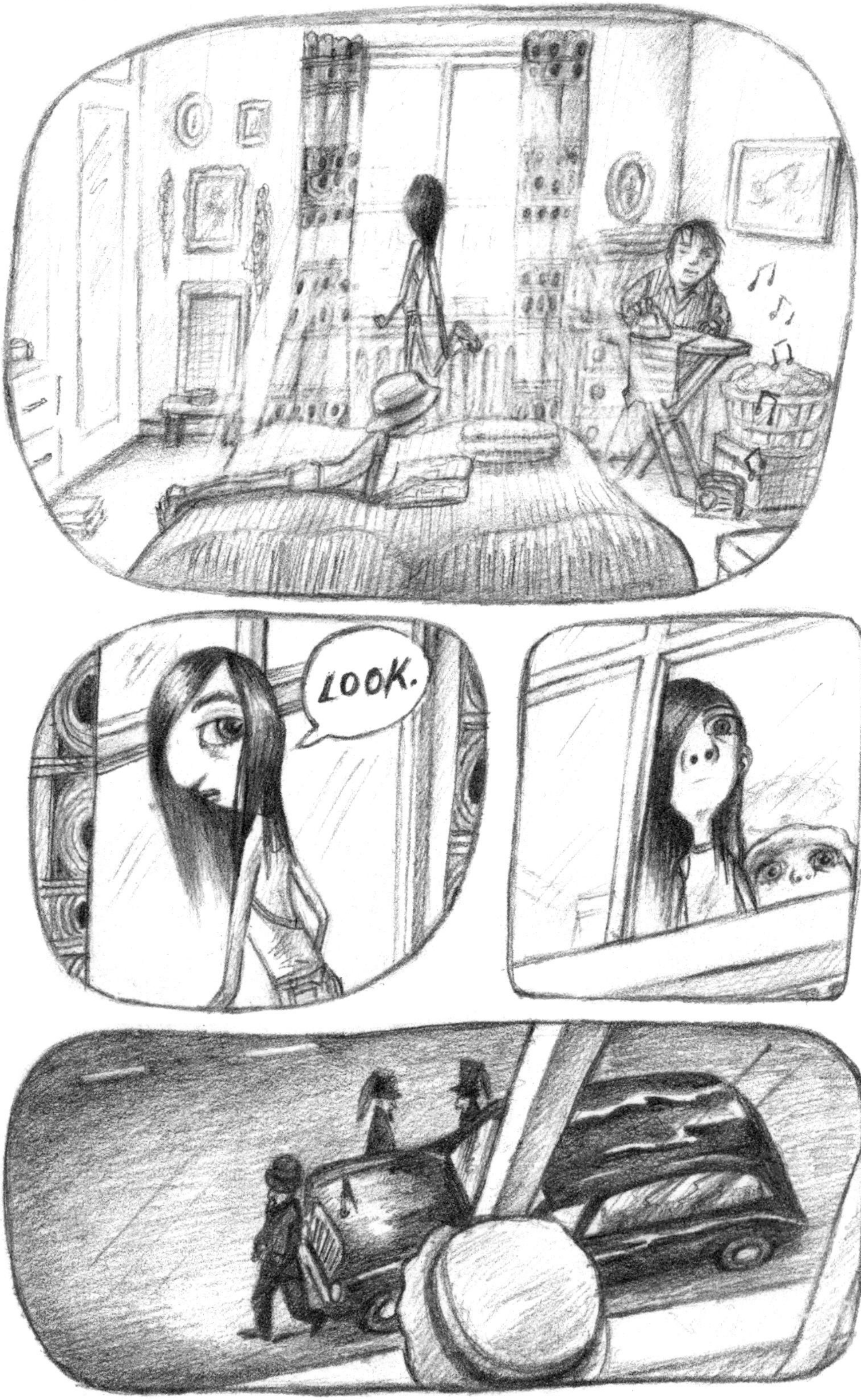
LOOK.

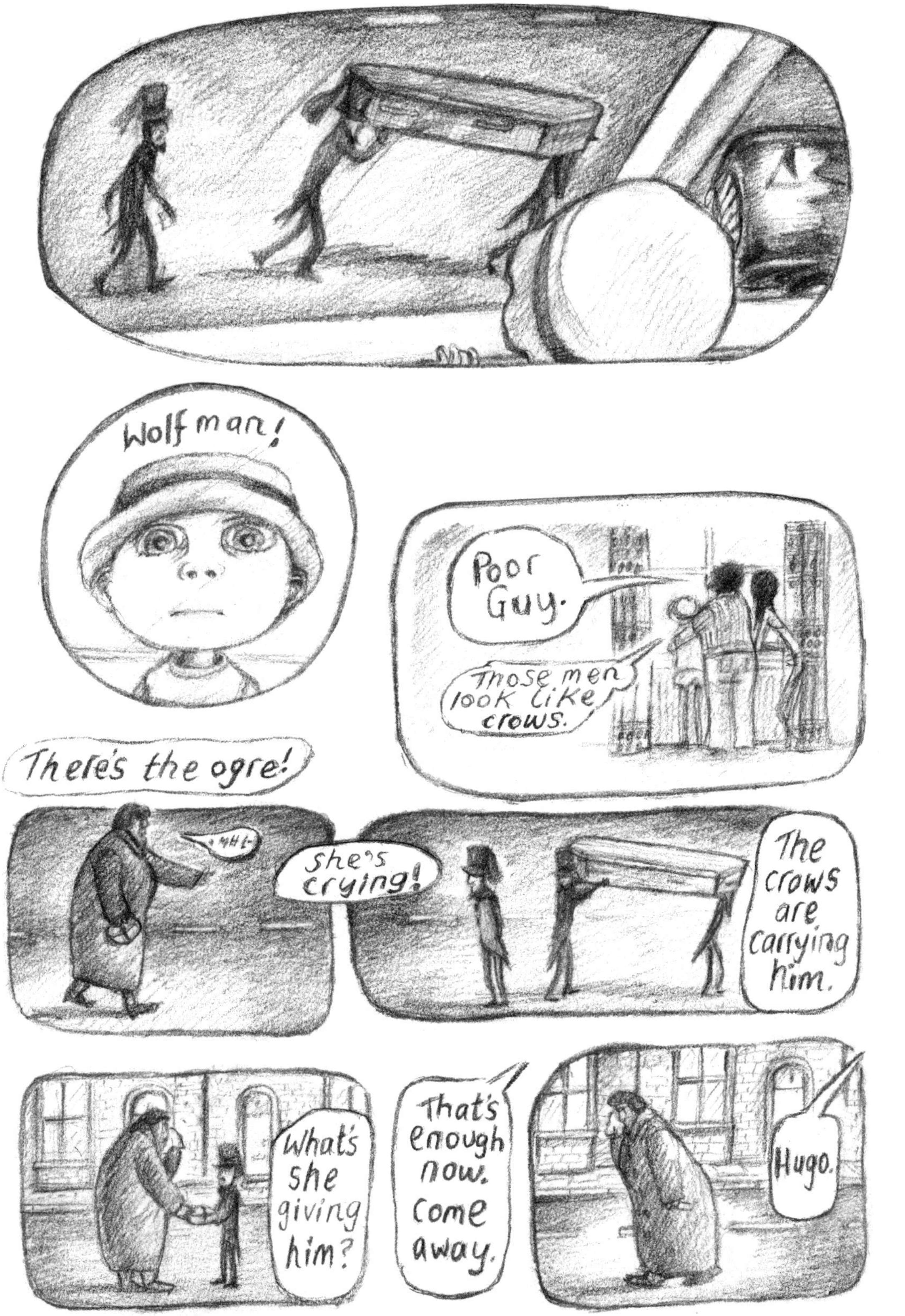
Wolf man!
Poor Guy.
Those men look like crows.
There's the ogre!
She's crying!
The crows are carrying him.
What's she giving him?
That's enough now. Come away.
Hugo.

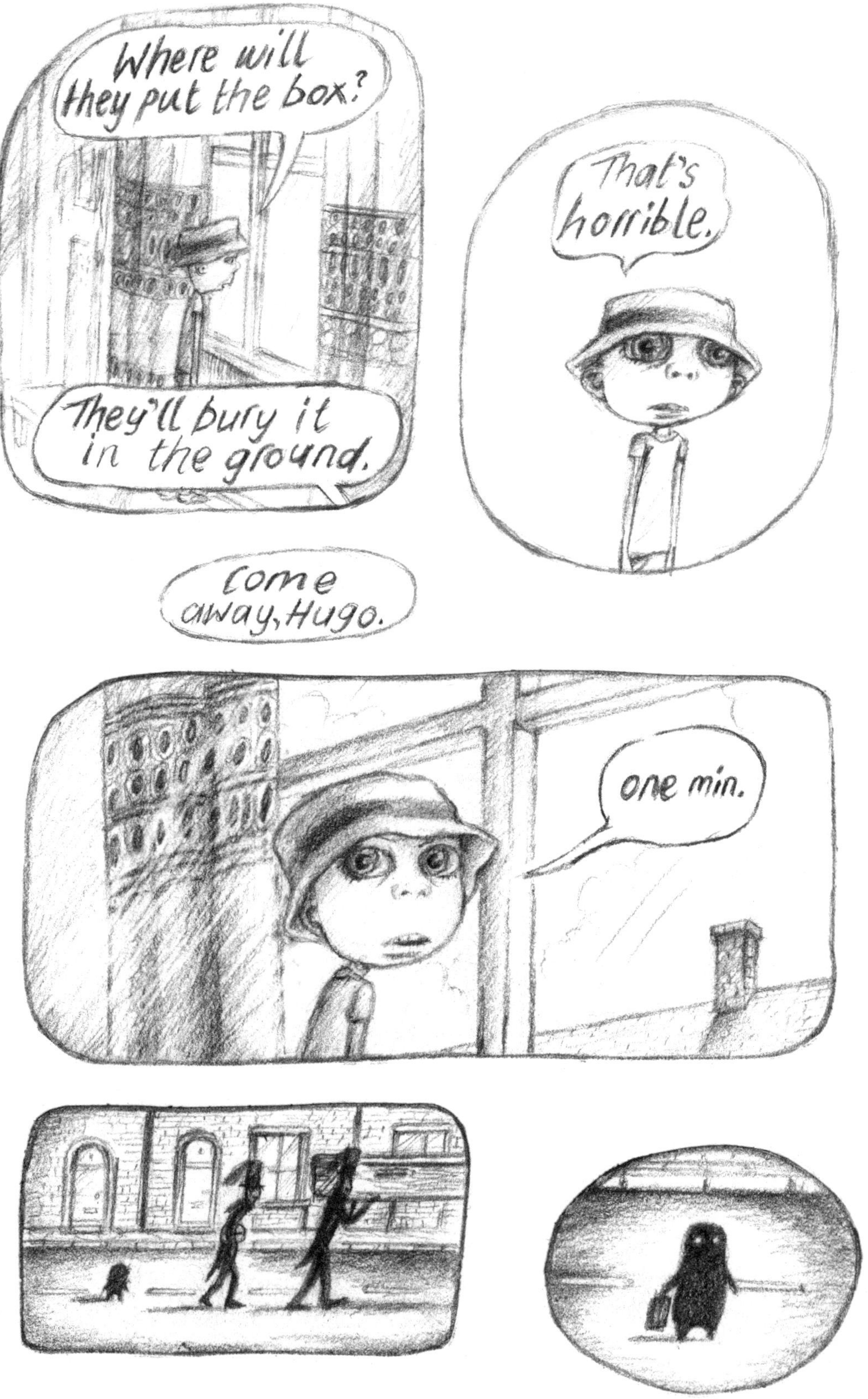
Where will they put the box?
They'll bury it in the ground.
That's horrible.
Come away, Hugo.
one min.

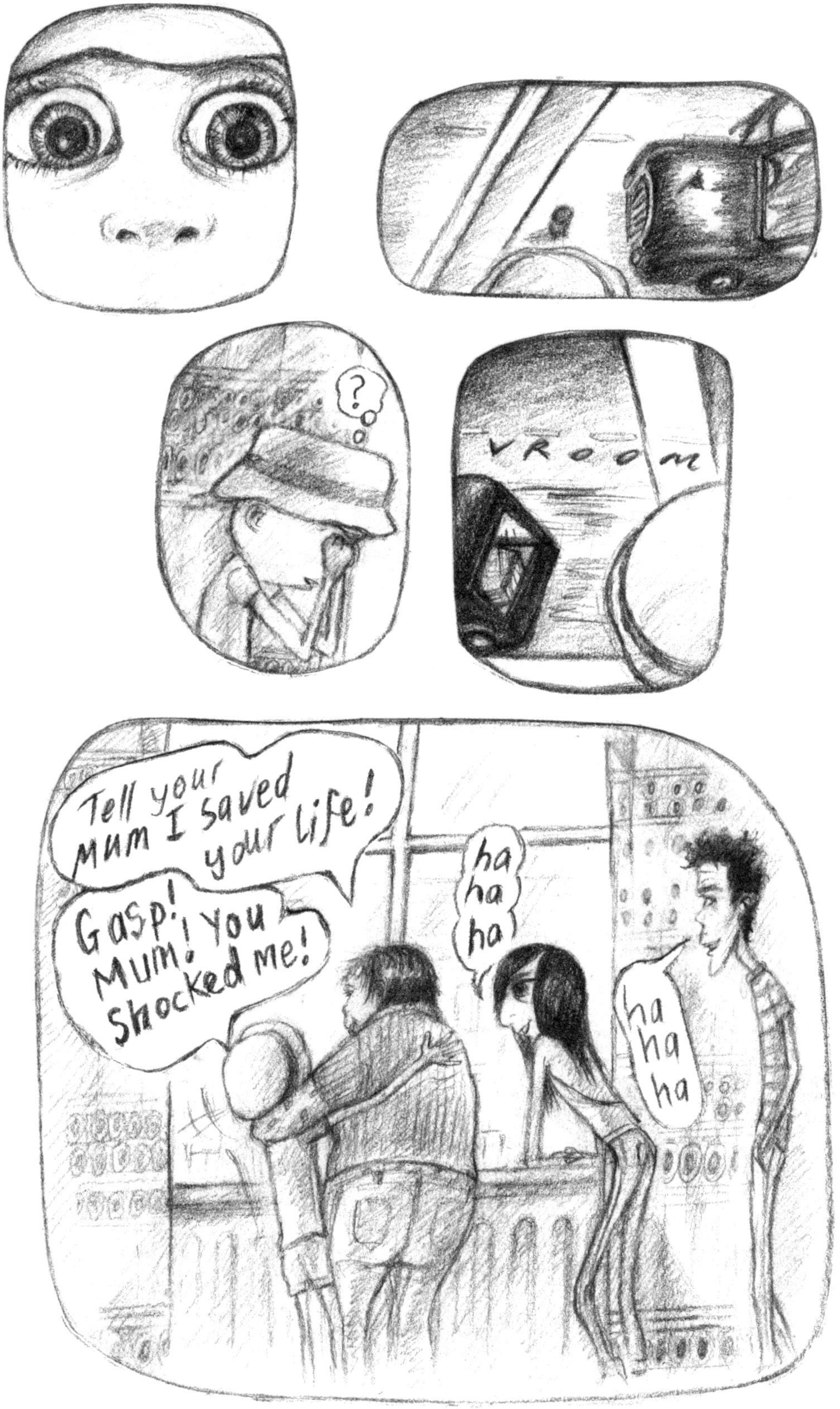
?
VROOM
Tell your Mum I saved your life!
Gasp! Mum! You Shocked me!
ha ha ha
ha ha ha

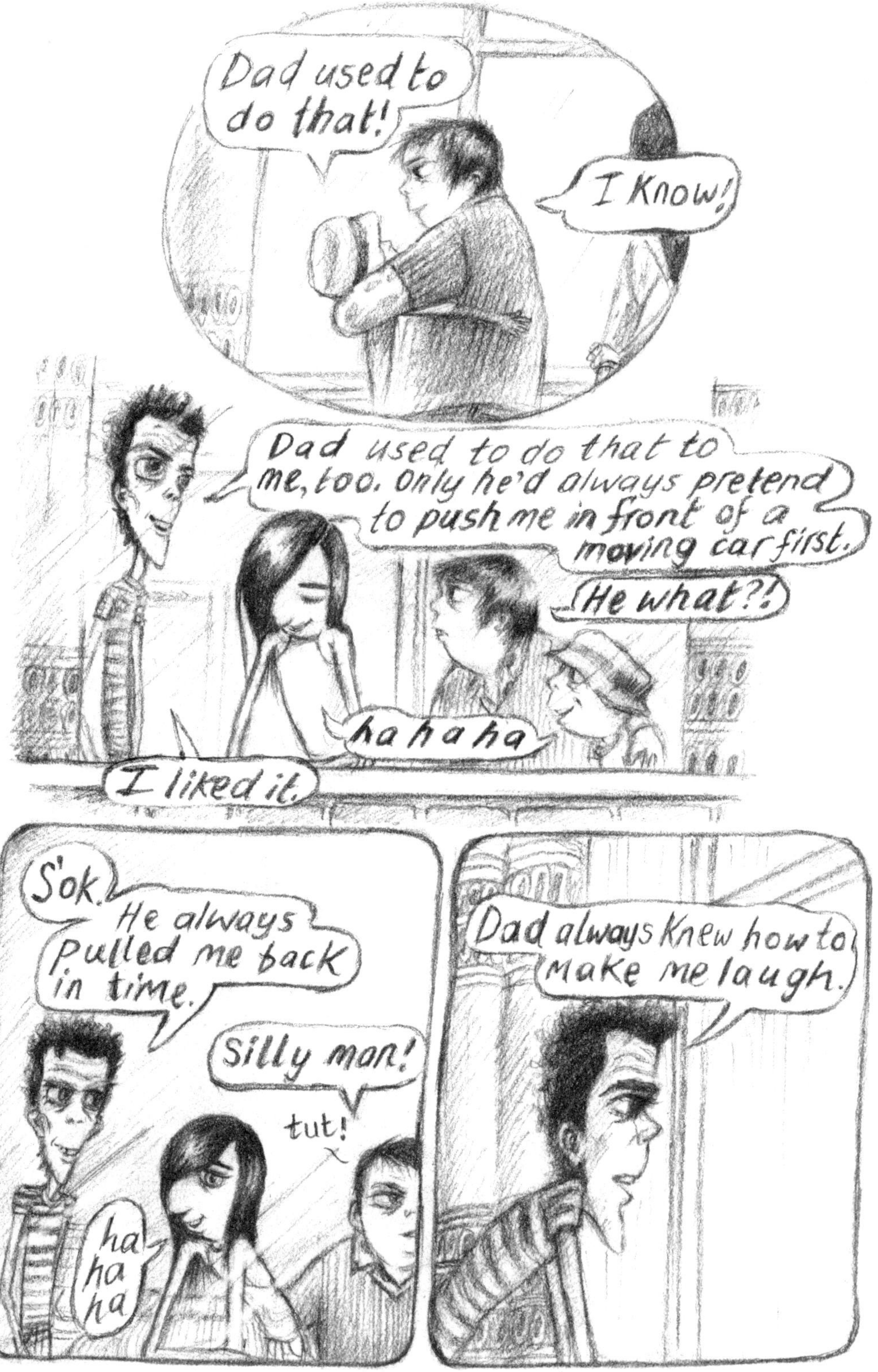
Dad used to do that!
I Know!
Dad used to do that to me, too. Only he'd always pretend to push me in front of a moving car first.
He what?!
haha ha
I liked it.
S'ok.
He always pulled me back in time.
Silly man!
tut!
ha ha ha
Dad always Knew how to make me laugh.

Thank you to the following wonderful people who helped *WOLF* come to life:

Emma Hayley for helping it find its way into print, Guillaume Rater for his creative and thoughtful editing skills, Txabi Jones for his Photoshop hands.

My agent Kirsty McLachlan.

The Arts Council for buying me the time off, Gemma Seltzer and Deborah Chinn for invaluable advice on my ACE application. Eve Warren for helping me make the break from school! Steve Marchant and Anita O'Brien for exhibiting *WOLF* at the Cartoon Museum. Margaret Paraskos and the Cyprus College of Art for hosting me in September 2017. *Art Review* for featuring an episode of *WOLF* (April 2018). Antony Esmond (*Awesome Podcasts*), Jessica Kemp (*Missed Deadline*) and Rees Finlay (*Declaration of Independents*) for great interviews. Paul Gravett for recommending me cool stuff! Joanna Quesnel, Bridge Williams and Wallis Eates for being great people who give great creative feedback! *Laydeez do Comics*, Nicola Streeten, Sarah Lightman, Wallis, Charlotte Bailey and Lou Crosby (love being part of such a talented and supportive team of grand folks!). Big thanks also to my very good friends: Sallie Bridgen, Nick, Jack and Maisie Hardiker, Lucy Fyson, Suzy Gillett, Paula Young, Caro Warboys, Lucie Marsh, Donna Lythgoe, Nicky Hewitt, Nick Abadzis, Maria Tavares, Alex Evans, Woz Ahmed and Anna Shannon, Hilary Anderson and Anne Bassi.

And to my family: my Mum always, Ruby Herrington, Andrew Ball, Simon and Nina Ball, Richard Parker, my compass Pema Chodron and to all my extended family across the world and to those that have left the world, too... Love you.

Rachael Ball is a cartoonist, a teacher and the author of *The Inflatable Woman*. Her illustrations and cartoons have appeared in *Deadline*, the *Times Educational Supplement*, the *Radio Times* and many other publications.